## THE DEFINITIVE COLLECTION OF
## CHILLING AMERICAN FICTION

Joyce Carol Oates has created the ultimate anthology of American literary tales of horror and suspense with more than forty of the best examples of the genre. Beginning with the nineteenth-century writers who established a particularly Yankee form of the gothic tale, Oates includes not only such obvious choices as Edgar Allan Poe and Nathaniel Hawthorne but works by Herman Melville, Mark Twain, and Charolette Perkins Gilman. From the early twentieth century come splendidly frightening tales by such influential figures as Ambrose Bierce, Edith Wharton, H. P. Lovecraft, and Gertrude Atherton.

Here, too, are exquisitely fashioned stories by a number of writers not traditionally associated with the gothic tale, including William Faulkner, Isaac Bashevis Singer, Shirley Jackson, E. B. White, Flannery O'Connor, and Paul Bowles. Contributions from contemporary masters include Ursula K. Le Guin, Robert Coover, Peter Straub, Anne Rice, and, of course, Stephen King.

Recognized herself as one of the leading modern gothic writers (she includes her story *The Temple*), Oates has chosen her stories expertly, with an eye not to the best-known examples but simply to those that are the best. *American Gothic Tales* delivers both literary discovery and the sheer frisson of superbly crafted fear.

JOYCE CAROL OATES is the editor of many popular anthologies, most recently *Haunted* and *The Sophisticated Cat* (both Dutton/Plume). Among the many literary awards she has won are the PEN/Faulkner Bernard Malamud Lifetime Achievement Award for the short story and the Bram Stoker Award for Lifetime Achievement given by the Horror Writers of America. Ms. Oates also won a 1996 Bram Stoker Award for her novel *Zombie*. Her latest novel, *We Were the Mulvaneys*, will be published by Dutton in September 1996. She lives in Princeton, New Jersey.

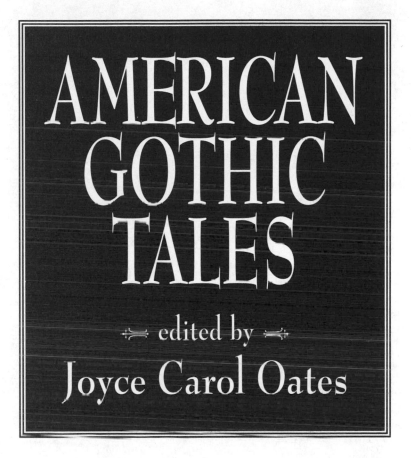

# AMERICAN GOTHIC TALES

edited by

## Joyce Carol Oates

A WILLIAM ABRAHAMS BOOK

PLUME

PLUME
Published by the Penguin Group
Penguin Books USA Inc., 375 Hudson Street, New York, New York 10014, U.S.A.
Penguin Books Ltd, 27 Wrights Lane, London W8 5TZ, England
Penguin Books Australia Ltd, Ringwood, Victoria, Australia
Penguin Books Canada Ltd, 10 Alcorn Avenue, Toronto, Ontario, Canada M4V 3B2
Penguin Books (N.Z.) Ltd, 182-190 Wairau Road, Auckland 10, New Zealand

Penguin Books Ltd, Registered Offices:
Harmondsworth, Middlesex, England

First published by Plume, an imprint of Dutton Signet,
a division of Penguin Books USA Inc.

ACKNOWLEDGMENTS

For permissions to reprint the stories within, please turn to page 545.

 REGISTERED TRADEMARK—MARCA REGISTRADA

ISBN 0-452-27489-3

Printed in the United States of America
Set in Bembo
Designed by Jesse Cohen

PUBLISHER'S NOTE
These are works of fiction. Names, characters, places, and incidents either are the products of the authors' imaginations or are used fictitiously, and any resemblance to actual persons, living or dead, events, or locales is entirely coincidental.

*Special thanks to Ellen Datlow,*
*Rosemary Ahern, and Robert Phillips*
*for their thoughtful advice*

# CONTENTS

# AMERICAN GOTHIC TALES

# INTRODUCTION

*Though in many of its aspects this visible world seems formed in love, the invisible spheres were formed in fright.*

—HERMAN MELVILLE, *MOBY DICK*

How uncanny, how mysterious, how unknowable and infinitely beyond their control must have seemed the vast wilderness of the New World, to the seventeenth-century Puritan settlers! The inscrutable silence of Nature—the muteness that, not heralding God, must be a dominion of Satan's; the tragic ambiguity of human nature with its predilection for what Christians call "original sin," inherited from our first parents, Adam and Eve. When Nature is so vast, man's need for control—for "settling" the wilderness—becomes obsessive. And how powerful the temptation to project mankind's divided self onto the very silence of Nature.

It was the intention of those English Protestants known as Puritans to "purify" the Church of England by eradicating everything in the Church that seemed to have no biblical justification. The most radical Puritans, "Separatists" and eventually "Pilgrims," settled Plymouth, Massachusetts, in the 1620s; others who followed, in subsequent years, were less zealous about defining themselves as "Separatists" (from the mother country England). Yet all were characterized by the intransigence of their faith; their fierce sense of moral rectitude and self-righteousness. The New England Puritans were an intolerant people whose theology could not have failed to breed paranoia, if not madness, in the sensitive among them. Consider, for instance, the curious Covenant of Grace, which taught that only those men and women upon whom God sheds His grace are saved, because this allows them to believe in Christ; those excluded from God's grace lack the power to believe in a Savior, thus are not only not saved, but damned. *We never had a chance!* those so excluded might cry out of the bowels of Hell. *We were doomed from the start.* The extreme gothic sensibility springs from such paradoxes: that the loving, paternal God and His son Jesus are nonetheless willful tyrants; "good" is inextricably bound up with the capacity to punish; one may wish to believe oneself free but in fact all human activities are determined, from the perspective of the deity, long before one's birth.

It comes as no surprise, then, that the very titles of celebrated Puritan works of the seventeenth and early eighteenth centuries strike a chord of anxiety. *The Spiritual Conflict, The Holy War, Day of Doom, Thirsty Sinner, Groans of the Damned, The Wonders of the Invisible World, Man Knows Not His Time, Repentant Sinners and Their Ministers, Memorable Providences Relating to Witchcraft and Possessions*—these might be the titles of lurid works of gothic fiction, not didactic sermons, prose pieces and poetry. The great Puritan poet Edward Taylor was also a minister; Taylor's subtle, intricately wrought metaphysical verse dwells upon God's love and terror almost exclusively, and man's insignificance in the face of God's omnipotence: "my Will is your Design." Taylor's poetry suggests a man of uncommon gifts, intelligence and sensitivity trapped in a fanatic religion as in a straitjacket; here is the gothic predilection for investing all things, even the most seemingly innocuous (weather, insects) with cosmological meaning. Is there nothing in the gothic imagination that can mean simply—"nothing"?

Our first American novelist of substance, Charles Brockden Brown, was born of a Philadelphia Quaker family; but his major novel *Wieland, or The Transformation* (1798) is suffused with the spirit of Puritan paranoia—"God is the object of my supreme passion," Wieland declares. Indeed, the very concept of rational self-determinism is challenged by this dark fantasy of domestic violence. Though Charles Brockden Brown provides a naturalistic explanation for Wieland's maniacal behavior, it is clearly not plausible; the novel is a nightmare expression of the fulfillment of repressed desire, anticipating Edgar Allan Poe's similarly claustrophobic tales of the grotesque. Wieland's deceased father was a Protestant religious fanatic who seems to have been literally immolated by guilt; Wieland Jr. is a disciple of the Enlightenment who is nonetheless driven mad by "voices" urging him to destruction.

> I was dazzled. My organs were bereaved of their
> activity. My eyelids were half-closed. . . . A name-
> less fear chilled my veins, and I stood motionless.

This irradiation did not retire or lessen. It seemed
as if some powerful effulgence covered me like a
mantle. . . . It was the element of heaven that flowed
around.

But the "element of heaven" demands that Wieland sacrifice those he
loves best—his wife and children.

Such assaults upon individual autonomy and identity characterize
the majority of the tales collected in this volume, by Washington
Irving, Nathaniel Hawthorne, Edgar Allan Poe, Charlotte Perkins
Gilman, H. P. Lovecraft and more recent twentieth-century writers for
whom the "supernatural" and the malevolent "unconscious" have
fused. Even in the more benign "enchanted region" of Washington
Irving's Sleepy Hollow (of *The Sketch Book*, 1820), an ordinary, decent
man like Ichabod Crane is subjected to an ordeal of psychic breakdown; Irving's imagination is essentially comic, but of that cruel, mor-
dant comedy tinctured by sadism.

Descendant of one of the judges of the notorious Salem witch
trials of 1692–93, Nathaniel Hawthorne became a historian-fantasist of
his own Puritan forbears in such symbolist romances as *The Scarlet Letter*
and *The House of the Seven Gables* and in the parable-like stories gathered in *Mosses from an Old Manse* (1846), of which "Young Goodman
Brown" is the most frequently reprinted and "The Man of Adamant,"
included here, is exemplary, though relatively little-known. Here is a
chilling tale of a developing psychosis in the guise of religious piety: a
radical Puritan preacher adopts "a plan of salvation . . . so narrow, that,
like a plank in a tempestuous sea, it could avail no sinner but himself."
In true gothic fashion, the man of adamant suffers a physical transformation commensurate with his spiritual condition: he becomes a calci-
fied, embalmed corpse. (The gothic-grotesque sensibility, graphically
expressed by such artists as Hieronymus Bosch, Goya, Francis Bacon,
insists upon the *physicality* of such spiritual transformations.) Unusual
for any gothic tale, Herman Melville's surreal, dream-like allegory
"The Tartarus of Maids" is informed by a political vision, the writer's
appalled sympathy with the fates of girls and women condemned to
factory work in New England mills—and condemned to being female
in a wholly patriarchal society. Usually paired with the cheery, jocose
"The Paradise of Bachelors," which is set in an affluent gentlemen-
lawyers' club in London, "The Tartarus of Maids" is a remarkable
work for its time (the 1850s) in its equation of sexual/biological and

social determinism: "At rows of blank-looking counters sat rows of blank-looking girls, with blank, white folders in their blank hands, all blankly folding blank paper." Yet somehow the paper-mill to which the girls are condemned to work like slaves is also the female body. The narrator is led through it by an affable guide named Cupid and learns that to be female, to be male chattel, to be condemned by impregnation by male seed, is for the virginal females their Tartarus, that region of Hades reserved for punishment of the wicked. Of what are these girls and women guilty except having been born of a debased female sex?—into a body "that is a mere machine, the essence of which is unvarying punctuality and precision."

"The Tartarus of Maids" is notable for exhibiting a rare feat of sexual identification, for virtually no male writers of Melville's era, or any other, have made the imaginative effort of trying to see from the perspective of the "other sex," let alone trying to see in a way highly critical of the advantages of masculinity. A more psychologically realistic portrayal of the trapped female, in this case a wife and mother of an economically comfortable class (her husband is a physician), is Charlotte Perkins Gilman's classic "The Yellow Wallpaper" whose inspired manic voice derives from Poe but whose vision of raging female despair is the author's own. In the work of our premier American gothicist, Edgar Allan Poe, from whose *Tales of the Grotesque and Arabesque* (1840), so much of twentieth-century horror and detective fiction springs, there are no fully realized female characters, indeed no fully realized characters at all; but the female is likely to be the obsessive object of desire, and her premature death, as in "The Fall of the House of Usher," "Ligeia," and the story anthologized here, "The Black Cat," is likely to be the precipitating factor.

"The Black Cat" demonstrates Poe at his most brilliant, presenting a madman's voice with such mounting plausibility that the reader almost—*almost*—identifies with his unmotivated and seemingly unresisted acts of insane violence against the affectionate black cat Pluto, and eventually his own wife. Like "The Tell-Tale Heart," with which it bears an obvious kinship, "The Black Cat" explores from within a burgeoning, blossoming evil; an evil exacerbated by alcohol, yet clearly a congenital evil unprovoked by the behavior of others. Ironically, the nameless narrator is one who has enjoyed since childhood the company of animals, and he and his wife live amid a Peaceable Kingdom of pets—"birds, a gold-fish, a dog, rabbits, a small monkey, and *a cat*." The narrator, drawn by degrees to escalating acts of cruelty, gouges out Pluto's eye with a pen-knife, and later hangs the mutilated creature: "And then came, as if to my final and irrevocable overthrow, the spirit of PERVERSENESS." In Poe's gothic cosmology, not the "I" but the "imp of the perverse" rules. With the logic of dream retribution, the murdered Pluto reappears in the guise of another one-eyed black cat who haunts the narrator in his own household and, after the narrator's murder of his wife, and his walling-up of her corpse in his cellar, brings about the murderer's arrest by police. The black cat trapped in the wall (or tomb) recalls not only the tell-tale heart of another brutally murdered victim but the prematurely entombed Madeline Usher of "The Fall of the House of Usher." Like Wieland, whose grotesque "confession" would have been known to Poe, this husband kills his wife for no apparent, or conscious, reason.

Perhaps the most artistically realized gothic tale in American literature is Henry James's enigmatic *The Turn of the Screw*. (It has certainly been the most analyzed.) James's ghost stories are masterpieces of style, irony, ambiguity; though distinguished by James's characteristic subtlety, in which "gothic" effects are subordinate to psychological drama, each of the tales—"The Romance of Certain Old Clothes," "The Friends of the Friends," "Maud-Evelyn," "Sir Edmund Orme" and "The Jolly Corner"—differs surprisingly from the others. ("Maud-Evelyn" is perhaps the most ingenious in conception; the very early, "The Romance of Certain Old Clothes," written when James was in his twenties, is the most conventional in gothic terms, presenting covert female sexual rivalry as the dynamic of the story and ending with an eruption of "real" ghostly revenge.) Like her one-time mentor James, Edith Wharton wrote a number of exquisitely crafted psychological ghost stories: "Pomegranate Seed," "The Eyes," "All Souls," and "Afterward," included here. Wharton's tales of the supernatural, genteel by gothic standards, ponder questions of individual conscience and destiny in a social context very different from that of the more sensational gothic writers, like Poe and Ambrose Bierce; often, they dramatize a distinctly female, perhaps feminist angle of vision, as in the not-quite-gothic story "A Journey," in which a young wife endures a nightmare train journey accompanied by the corpse of her husband. Edith Wharton and Henry James are virtually alone in their experimentation with gothic forms of fiction even as they forged distinguished literary careers as "realists" of the social and domestic American scene.

These canonical writers of the gothic-grotesque were all born, fittingly, in the nineteenth century. With the rise of realism in prose fiction in the late nineteenth century, and the more radical, more grindingly materialist school of naturalism derived from Flaubert and Zola, educated readers turned to the work of such writers as Stephen Crane, Frank Norris, Hamlin Garland and Theodore Dreiser. In the toughly Darwinian masculine-urban worlds of such writers, with their exposure of social and political corruption and their frank depiction of adult sexual relations, a subject largely taboo in gothic fiction, there would seem to have been no place, still less sympathy, for the idiosyncracies of the gothic imagination.

If there is a single gothic-grotesque writer of the American twentieth century to be compared with Poe, it is H. P. Lovecraft, born in 1890. The child of psychotic parents (his father died of tertiary syphilis when Lovecraft was three, his mother, a schizophrenic, died institutionalized), Lovecraft was a precocious, prolific talent who chose to live a reclusive life, producing a unique body of horror stories and novellas before his premature death, of cancer, at the age of forty-seven, in 1937. Long a revered cult figure to admirers of "weird fiction" (Lovecraft's own, somewhat deprecatory term for his art), Lovecraft is associated with crude, obsessive, rawly sensationalist and overwrought prose in the service of naming the unnameable. Like Poe, he may have been creating counter-worlds in which to speak his heart in frank, if codified terms: "Unhappy is he to whom the memories of childhood bring only fear and sadness. Wretched is he who looks back upon lone hours in vast and dismal chambers with . . . maddening rows of antique books," begins "The Outsider," an atypically compressed story. Lovecraft's compulsion is again and again to approach the horror that is a lurid twin of one's self, or that very self seen in an unsuspected mirror:

> I beheld in full, frightful vividness the inconceivable, indescribable, and unmentionable monstrosity . . . I cannot even hint what it was like, for it was a compound of all that is unclean, uncanny, unwelcome, abnormal, and detestable. It was the ghoulish shade of decay, antiquity, and dissolution; the putrid, dripping eidolon of unwelcome revelation, the awful baring of that which the merciful earth should always hide.

In short, the unloved monster-child sired by unknown parents, abandoned to a universe of infinite mystery in which he will always be an "outsider."

The accumulating horrors of "The Rats in the Walls," the lurid final epiphany of "The Dunwich Horror," the terrifying bizarrie of "The Shadow Out of Time," the prophetic reasonableness of "The Colour Out of Space"—Lovecraft's influence upon twentieth-century horror writers has been incalculable, and in certain quarters he is prized for the very traits (lurid excess, overstatement, fantastical and repetitive contrivance) for which, in more "literary" quarters, he is despised. The gothic imagination melds the sacred and the profane in startling and original ways, suggesting its close kinship with the religious imagination; Lovecraft's cosmology of demonic extraterrestrial beings (The Great Old Ones) whose intrusion into the human world brings disaster to human beings is readily recognizable as a mystic's vision in which God has become numerous Cronus gods bent upon devouring their unacknowledged offspring. There is a melancholy, operatic grandeur in Lovecraft's most passionate work; a curious elegiac poetry of loss, of adolescent despair and yearning; an existential loneliness so pervasive, so profound and convincing that it lingers in the reader's memory long after the rudiments of Lovecraftian plot have faded. Lovecraft is a hybrid of the traditional gothic and "science fiction" but his temperament is clearly gothic. His "science" is never future-oriented but a mystic's minute, compulsive scrutinizing of the inner self or soul. Some tragic, prehistoric conjunction of the "human" and the "inhuman" has blighted what should have been a natural life; and nature itself is consequently contaminated. ("The Colour Out of Space" with its meticulous, poetic descriptions of a once-fertile and now blighted New England landscape seems uncannily to be prophesizing ecological devastation.) Here is the wholly obverse vision of American destiny; the repudiation of American-Transcendentalist optimism, in which the individual is somehow divine, or shares in nature's divinity. In the gothic imagination, there has been a profound and irrevocable split between mankind and nature in the romantic sense, and a tragic division between what we wish to know and what may be staring us in the face. So "The Colour Out of Space" concludes elegiacally: "It was just a colour out of space—a frightful messenger from unformed realms of infinity beyond all Nature as we know it . . ."

Beyond H. P. Lovecraft, with such notable exceptions as August Derleth, Shirley Jackson, Peter Straub, Stephen King and Anne Rice, many of the writers in this volume are not "gothic" writers but simply—writers. Their inclusion here is meant to suggest the richness and magnitude of the gothic-grotesque vision and the inadequacy of genre labels if by "genre" is meant mere formula. William Faulkner has long been recognized as *sui generis*, beyond taxonomy: is Faulkner a realist? a naturalist? a symbolist? a fantasist? There is no mistaking the influence of Poe in Faulkner's most famous short story, "A Rose for Emily"; but one might argue that the gothic influence is ubiquitous in Faulkner's work, frequently transmogrified as a wild, lurid, demonic humor. Similarly, the work of Issac Bashevis Singer, John Cheever, Sylvia Plath, William Goyen, E. L. Doctorow, and Paul Bowles belongs to a rich, imaginative gothic tradition, though these writers are rarely included in such anthologies. Paul Bowles, in particular, has written numerous macabre and disturbing stories; the problem for the anthologist is which to select among "The Delicate Prey," "A Distant Episode," "Call at Corazón," "Papers from Cold Point," "The Circular Valley," and the hallucinatory tale here included, "Allal." Appropriately, Bowles dedicated his first story collection, *The Delicate Prey* (1950), "to my mother, who first read me the stories of Poe."

My original intention in assembling *American Gothic Tales* was to provide an historic overview of "gothicism" in our literature and, of course, to bring together favorite, distinctive stories. As the months passed and I immersed myself in reading, particularly in the burgeoning contemporary field, I discovered that frank eroticism and female-male relations are no longer taboo in gothic tales (see Lisa Tuttle's ominous "Replacements" and Kathe Koja's and Barry N. Malzberg's lyrically sadomasochistic "Ursus Triad, Later"); and that an older classic like Ray Bradbury's "The Veldt" has acquired, in our age of children's and adolescents' video games, a terrifying prescience. And there is a degree of psychological realism, a quality one might call an unexpected tenderness of subjectivity, in such stories as Melissa Pritchard's "Spirit Seizures" and the chillingly heartrending "The Girl Who Loved Animals" by Bruce McAllister. I was challenged by the hope of introducing newly emerging or too narrowly classified writers whose excellent work merits a wider audience; and there was the intention, too, of broadening "gothic" to include seemingly mainstream writers like Raymond Carver, E. L. Doctorow, Don DeLillo, and Charles Johnson, whose highly idiosyncratic work constitutes, among other things, brooding commentary upon America from the perspective of the working class (Raymond Carver), history (Doctorow, DeLillo) and race (Johnson). (I would have liked to include more stories by African-Americans and other American ethnic writers, but the "gothic" has not been a popular mode among such writers, for the obvious reason that the "real"—the America of social, political, and moral immediacy—is irresistibly compelling at this stage of their history.) The surreal, raised to the level of poetry, is the very essence of "gothic": that which displays the range, depth, audacity and fantastical extravagance of the human imagination.

Spatial limitations made it impossible for me to include as many contemporaries as I'd wished, so I direct the interested reader to the invaluable annual *The Year's Best Fantasy and Horror*, edited by Ellen Datlow and Terri Windling (St. Martin's Press). I should note that, if popular names are missing in this volume, it may be because prominent horror writers have shrewdly specialized in the novel and not the short story; and there were, unfortunately, excellent stories simply too long for inclusion.

—Joyce Carol Oates
February 1996

# CHARLES BROCKDEN BROWN
## From *Wieland, or The Transformation*

## CHAPTER XIX

"Theodore Wieland, the prisoner at the bar, was now called upon for his defence. He looked around him for some time in silence, and with a mild countenance. At length he spoke:

"It is strange; I am known to my judges and my auditors. Who is there present a stranger to the character of Wieland? who knows him not as a husband—as a father—as a friend? yet here am I arraigned as a criminal. I am charged with diabolical malice; I am accused of the murder of my wife and my children!

"It is true, they were slain by me; they all perished by my hand. The task of vindication is ignoble. What is it that I am called to vindicate? and before whom?

"You know that they are dead, and that they were killed by me. What more would you have? Would you extort from me a statement of my motives? Have you failed to discover them already? You charge me with malice; but your eyes are not shut; your reason is still vigorous; your memory has not forsaken you. You know whom it is that you thus charge. The habits of his life are known to you; his treatment of his wife and his offspring is known to you; the soundness of his integrity, and the unchangeableness of his principles, are familiar to your apprehension; yet you persist in this charge! You lead me hither manacled as a felon; you deem me worthy of a vile and tormenting death!

"Who are they whom I have devoted to death? My wife—the little ones, that drew their being from me—that creature who, as she surpassed them in excellence, claimed a larger affection than those whom natural affinities bound to my heart. Think ye that malice could have urged me to this deed? Hide your audacious fronts from the scrutiny of heaven. Take refuge in some cavern unvisited by human eyes. Ye may deplore your wickedness or folly, but ye cannot expiate it.

"Think not that I speak for your sakes. Hug to your hearts this detestable infatuation. Deem me still a murderer, and drag me to untimely death. I make not an effort to dispel your illusion: I utter not a word to cure you of your sanguinary folly: but there are probably some in this assembly who have come from far: for their sakes, whose distance has disabled them from knowing me, I will tell what I have done, and why.

"It is needless to say that God is the object of my supreme passion. I have cherished, in his presence, a single and upright heart. I have thirsted for the knowledge of his will. I have burnt with ardour to approve my faith and my obedience.

"My days have been spent in searching for the revelation of that will; but my days have been mournful, because my search failed. I solicited direction: I turned on every side where glimmerings of light could be discovered. I have not been wholly uninformed; but my knowledge has always stopped short of certainty. Dissatisfaction has insinuated itself into all my thoughts. My purposes have been pure; my wishes indefatigable; but not till lately were these purposes thoroughly accomplished, and these wishes fully gratified.

"I thank thee, my father, for thy bounty; that thou didst not ask a less sacrifice than this; that thou placedst me in a condition to testify my submission to thy will! What have I withheld which it was thy pleasure to exact? Now may I, with dauntless and erect eye, claim my reward, since I have given thee the treasure of my soul.

"I was at my own house: it was late in the evening: my sister had gone to the city, but proposed to return. It was in expectation of her return that my wife and I delayed going to bed beyond the usual hour; the rest of the family, however, were retired.

"My mind was contemplative and calm; not wholly devoid of apprehension on account of my sister's safety. Recent events, not easily explained, had suggested the existence of some danger; but this danger was without a distinct form in our imagination, and scarcely ruffled our tranquillity.

"Time passed, and my sister did not arrive; her house is at some distance from mine, and though her arrangements had been made with a view to residing with us, it was possible that, through forgetfulness, or the occurrence of unforeseen emergencies, she had returned to her own dwelling.

"Hence it was conceived proper that I should ascertain the truth by going thither. I went. On my way my mind was full of these ideas which related to my intellectual condition. In the torrent of fervid conceptions, I lost sight of my purpose. Some times I stood still; some times I wandered from my path, and experienced some difficulty, on recovering from my fit of musing, to regain it.

"The series of my thoughts is easily traced. At first every vein beat with raptures known only to the man whose parental and conjugal love is without limits, and the cup of whose desires, immense as it is, overflows with gratification. I know not why emotions that were perpetual visitants should now have recurred with unusual energy. The transition was not new from sensations of joy to a consciousness of gratitude. The author of my being was likewise the dispenser of every gift with which that being was embellished. The service to which a benefactor like this was entitled, could not be circumscribed. My social sentiments were indebted to their alliance with devotion for all their value. All passions are base, all joys feeble, all energies malignant, which are not drawn from this source.

"For a time, my contemplations soared above earth and its inhabitants. I stretched forth my hands; I lifted my eyes, and exclaimed, O! that I might be admitted to thy presence; that mine were the supreme delight of knowing thy will, and of performing it! The blissful privilege of direct communication with thee, and of listening to the audible enunciation of thy pleasure!

"What task would I not undertake, what privation would I not cheerfully endure, to testify my love of thee? Alas! thou hidest thyself from my view: glimpses only of thy excellence and beauty are afforded me. Would that a momentary emanation from thy glory would visit me! that some unambiguous token of thy presence would salute my senses!

"In this mood, I entered the house of my sister. It was vacant. Scarcely had I regained recollection of the purpose that brought me hither. Thoughts of a different tendency had such absolute possession of my mind, that the relations of time and space were almost obliterated from my understanding. These wanderings, however, were restrained, and I ascended to her chamber.

"I had no light, and might have known by external observation, that the house was without any inhabitant. With this, however, I was not satisfied. I entered the room, and the object of my search not appearing, I prepared to return.

"The darkness required some caution in descending the stair. I stretched my hand to seize the balustrade by which I might regulate my steps. How shall I describe the lustre, which, at that moment, burst upon my vision!

"I was dazzled. My organs were bereaved of their activity. My eye-lids were half-closed, and my hands withdrawn from the balustrade. A nameless fear chilled my veins, and I stood motionless. This irradiation did not retire or lessen. It seemed as if some powerful effulgence covered me like a mantle.

"I opened my eyes and found all about me luminous and glowing. It was the element of heaven that flowed around. Nothing but a fiery stream was at first visible; but, anon, a shrill voice from behind called upon me to attend.

"I turned: It is forbidden to describe what I saw: Words, indeed, would be wanting to the task. The lineaments of that being, whose veil was now lifted, and whose visage beamed upon my sight, no hues of pencil or of language can pourtray.

"As it spoke, the accents thrilled to my heart. 'Thy prayers are heard. In proof of thy faith, render me thy wife. This is the victim I chuse. Call her hither, and here let her fall.'—The sound, and visage, and light vanished at once.

"What demand was this? The blood of Catharine was to be shed! My wife was to perish by my hand! I sought opportunity to attest my virtue. Little did I expect that a proof like this would have been demanded.

"My wife! I exclaimed: O God! substitute some other victim. Make me not the butcher of my wife. My own blood is cheap. This will I pour out before thee with a willing heart; but spare, I beseech thee, this precious life, or commission some other than her husband to perform the bloody deed.

"In vain. The conditions were prescribed; the decree had gone forth, and nothing remained but to execute it. I rushed out of the house and across the intermediate fields, and stopped not till I entered my own parlour.

"My wife had remained here during my absence, in anxious expectation of my return with some tidings of her sister. I had none to communicate. For a time, I was breathless with my speed: This, and the tremors that shook my frame, and the wildness of my looks, alarmed her. She immediately suspected some disaster to have happened to her friend, and her own speech was as much overpowered by emotion as mine.

"She was silent, but her looks manifested her impatience to hear what I had to communicate. I spoke, but with so much precipitation as scarcely to be understood; catching her, at the same time, by the arm, and forcibly pulling her from her seat.

" 'Come along with me: fly: waste not a moment: time will be lost, and the deed will be omitted. Tarry not; question not; but fly with me!'

"This deportment added afresh to her alarms. Her eyes pursued mine, and she said, 'What is the matter? For God's sake what is the matter? Where would you have me go?'

"My eyes were fixed upon her countenance while she spoke. I thought upon her virtues; I viewed her as the mother of my babes; as my wife: I recalled the purpose for which I thus urged her attendance. My heart faltered, and I saw that I must rouse to this work all my faculties. The danger of the least delay was imminent.

"I looked away from her, and again exerting my force, drew her towards the door—'You must go with me—indeed you must.'

"In her fright she half-resisted my efforts, and again exclaimed, 'Good heaven! what is it you mean? Where go? What has happened? Have you found Clara?'

" 'Follow me, and you will see,' I answered, still urging her reluctant steps forward.

" 'What phrenzy has seized you? Something must needs have happened. Is she sick? Have you found her?'

" 'Come and see. Follow me, and know for yourself.'

"Still she expostulated and besought me to explain this mysterious behaviour. I could not trust myself to answer her; to look at her; but grasping her arm, I drew her after me. She hesitated, rather through confusion of mind than from unwillingness to accompany me. This confusion gradually abated, and she moved forward, but with irresolute footsteps, and continual exclamations of wonder and terror. Her interrogations of 'what was the matter?' and 'whither was I going?' were ceaseless and vehement.

"It was the scope of my efforts not to think; to keep up a conflict and uproar in my mind in which all order and distinctness should be lost; to escape from the sensations produced by her voice. I was, therefore, silent. I strove to abridge this interval by my haste, and to waste all my attention in furious gesticulations.

"In this state of mind we reached my sister's door. She looked at the windows and saw that all was desolate—'Why come we here? There is no body here. I will not go in.'

"Still I was dumb; but opening the door, I drew her into the entry. This was the allotted scene: here she was to fall. I let go her hand, and pressing my palms against my forehead, made one mighty effort to work up my soul to the deed.

"In vain; it would not be; my courage was appalled; my arms nerveless: I muttered prayers that my strength might be aided from above. They availed nothing.

"Horror diffused itself over me. This conviction of my cowardice, my rebellion, fastened upon me, and I stood rigid and cold as marble. From this state I was somewhat relieved by my wife's voice, who renewed her supplications to be told why we came hither, and what was the fate of my sister.

"What could I answer? My words were broken and inarticulate. Her fears naturally acquired force from the observation of these symptoms; but these fears were misplaced. The only inference she deduced from my conduct was, that some terrible mishap had befallen Clara.

"She wrung her hands, and exclaimed in an agony, 'O tell me, where is she? What has become of her? Is she sick? Dead? Is she in her chamber? O let me go thither and know the worst!'

"This proposal set my thoughts once more in motion. Perhaps what my rebellious heart refused to perform here, I might obtain strength enough to execute elsewhere.

" 'Come then,' said I, 'let us go.'

" 'I will, but not in the dark. We must first procure a light.'

" 'Fly then and procure it; but I charge you, linger not. I will await for your return.'

"While she was gone, I strode along the entry. The fellness of a gloomy hurricane but faintly resembled the discord that reigned in my mind. To omit this sacrifice must not be; yet my sinews had refused to perform it. No alternative was offered. To rebel against the mandate was impossible; but obedience would render me the executioner of my wife. My will was strong, but my limbs refused their office.

"She returned with a light; I led the way to the chamber; she looked round her; she lifted the curtain of the bed; she saw nothing.

"At length, she fixed inquiring eyes upon me. The light now enabled her to discover in my visage what darkness had hitherto concealed. Her cares were now transferred from my sister to myself, and she said in a tremulous voice, 'Wieland! you are not well: What ails you? Can I do nothing for you?'

"That accents and looks so winning should disarm me of my resolution, was to be expected. My thoughts were thrown anew into anarchy. I spread my hand before my eyes that I might not see her, and answered only by groans. She took my other hand between hers, and pressing it to her heart, spoke with that voice which had ever swayed my will, and wafted away sorrow.

" 'My friend! my soul's friend! tell me thy cause of grief. Do I not merit to partake with thee in thy cares? Am I not thy wife?'

"This was too much. I broke from her embrace, and retired to a corner of the room. In this pause, courage was once more infused into me. I resolved to execute my duty. She followed me, and renewed her passionate entreaties to know the cause of my distress.

"I raised my head and regarded her with steadfast looks. I muttered something about death, and the injunctions of my duty. At these words she shrunk back, and looked at me with a new expression of anguish. After a pause, she clasped her hands, and exclaimed—

" 'O Wieland! Wieland! God grant that I am mistaken; but surely something is wrong. I see it: it is too plain: thou art undone—lost to me and to thyself.' At the same time she gazed on my features with intensest anxiety, in hope that different symptoms would take place. I replied to her with vehemence—

" 'Undone! No; my duty is known, and I thank my God that my cowardice is now vanquished, and I have power to fulfil it. Catharine! I pity the weakness of thy nature: I pity thee, but must not spare. Thy life is claimed from my hands: thou must die!'

"Fear was now added to her grief. 'What mean you? Why talk you of death? Bethink yourself, Wieland: bethink yourself, and this fit will pass. O why came I hither! Why did you drag me hither?'

" 'I brought thee hither to fulfil a divine command. I am appointed thy destroyer, and destroy thee I must.' Saying this I seized her wrists. She shrieked aloud, and endeavoured to free herself from my grasp; but her efforts were vain.

" 'Surely, surely Wieland, thou dost not mean it. Am I not thy wife? and wouldst thou kill me? Thou wilt not; and yet—I see—thou

art Wieland no longer! A fury resistless and horrible possesses thee—
Spare me—spare—help—help——'

"Till her breath was stopped she shrieked for help—for mercy.
When she could speak no longer, her gestures, her looks appealed to
my compassion. My accursed hand was irresolute and tremulous. I
meant thy death to be sudden, thy struggles to be brief. Alas! my heart
was infirm; my resolves mutable. Thrice I slackened my grasp, and life
kept its hold, though in the midst of pangs. Her eye-balls started from
their sockets. Grimness and distortion took place of all that used to
bewitch me into transport, and subdue me into reverence.

"I was commissioned to kill thee, but not to torment thee with
the foresight of thy death; not to multiply thy fears, and prolong thy
agonies. Haggard, and pale, and lifeless, at length thou ceasedst to contend with thy destiny.

"This was a moment of triumph. Thus had I successfully subdued
the stubbornness of human passions: the victim which had been
demanded was given: the deed was done past recall.

"I lifted the corpse in my arms and laid it on the bed. I gazed
upon it with delight. Such was the elation of my thoughts, that I even
broke into laughter. I clapped my hands and exclaimed, 'It is done! My
sacred duty is fulfilled! To that I have sacrificed, O my God! thy last
and best gift, my wife!'

"For a while I thus soared above frailty. I imagined I had set
myself forever beyond the reach of selfishness; but my imaginations
were false. This rapture quickly subsided. I looked again at my wife.
My joyous ebullitions vanished, and I asked myself who it was whom I
saw. Methought it could not be Catharine. It could not be the woman
who had lodged for years in my heart; who had slept, nightly, in my
bosom; who had borne in her womb, who had fostered at her breast,
the beings who called me father; whom I had watched with delight,
and cherished with a fondness ever new and perpetually growing: it
could not be the same.

"Where was her bloom! These deadly and blood-suffused orbs
but ill resemble the azure and exstatic tenderness of her eyes. The lucid
stream that meandered over that bosom, the glow of love that was
wont to sit upon that cheek, are much unlike these livid stains and this
hideous deformity. Alas! these were the traces of agony; the gripe of the
assassin had been here!

"I will not dwell upon my lapse into desperate and outrageous
sorrow. The breath of heaven that sustained me was withdrawn, and I

sunk into *mere man*. I leaped from the floor: I dashed my head against the wall: I uttered screams of horror: I panted after torment and pain. Eternal fire, and the bickerings of hell, compared with what I felt, were music and a bed of roses.

"I thank my God that this degeneracy was transient, that he designed once more to raise me aloft. I thought upon what I had done as a sacrifice to duty, and *was calm*. My wife was dead; but I reflected, that though this source of human consolation was closed, yet others were still open. If the transports of an husband were no more, the feelings of a father had still scope for exercise. When remembrance of their mother should excite too keen a pang, I would look upon them, and *be comforted*.

"While I revolved these ideas, new warmth flowed in upon my heart—I was wrong. These feelings were the growth of selfishness. Of this I was not aware, and to dispel the mist that obscured my perceptions, a new effulgence and a new mandate were necessary.

"From these thoughts I was recalled by a ray that was shot into the room. A voice spake like that which I had before heard—'Thou hast done well; but all is not done—the sacrifice is incomplete—thy children must be offered—they must perish with their mother!—'

# WASHINGTON IRVING
## The Legend of Sleepy Hollow

FOUND AMONG THE PAPERS OF THE LATE
DIEDRICH KNICKERBOCKER

*A pleasing land of drowsy head it was,*
*Of dreams that wave before the half-shut eye,*
*And of gay castles in the clouds that pass,*
*For ever flushing round a summer sky.*
CASTLE OF INDOLENCE

In the bosom of one of those spacious coves which indent the eastern shore of the Hudson, at that broad expansion of the river denominated by the ancient Dutch navigators the Tappan Zee, and where they always prudently shortened sail, and implored the protection of St. Nicholas when they crossed, there lies a small market-town or rural port, which by some is called Greensburgh, but which is more generally and properly known by the name of Tarry Town. This name was given, we are told, in former days, by the good housewives of the adjacent country, from the inveterate propensity of their husbands to linger about the village tavern on market days. Be that as it may, I do not vouch for the fact, but merely advert to it, for the sake of being precise and authentic. Not far from this village, perhaps about two miles, there is a little valley, or rather lap of land, among high hills, which is one of the quietest places in the whole world. A small brook glides through it, with just murmur enough to lull one to repose; and the occasional whistle of a quail, or tapping of a woodpecker, is almost the only sound that ever breaks in upon the uniform tranquillity.

I recollect that, when a stripling, my first exploit in squirrel-shooting was in a grove of tall walnut-trees that shades one side of the valley. I had wandered into it at noon time, when all nature is peculiarly quiet, and was startled by the roar of my own gun, as it broke the Sabbath stillness around, and was prolonged and reverberated by the angry echoes. If ever I should wish for a retreat, whither I might steal from the world and its distractions, and dream quietly away the remnant of a troubled life, I know of none more promising than this little valley.

From the listless repose of the place, and the peculiar character of its inhabitants, who are descendants from the original Dutch settlers, this sequestered glen has long been known by the name of SLEEPY HOLLOW, and its rustic lads are called the Sleepy Hollow Boys throughout all the neighboring country. A drowsy, dreamy influence seems to hang over the land, and to pervade the very atmosphere. Some say that the place was bewitched by a high German doctor, during the early days of the settlement; others, that an old Indian chief, the prophet or wizard of his tribe, held his powwows there before the country was discovered by Master Hendrick Hudson. Certain it is, the place still continues under the sway of some witching power, that holds a spell over the minds of the good people, causing them to walk in a continual reverie. They are given to all kinds of marvellous beliefs; are subject to trances and visions; and frequently see strange sights, and hear music and voices in the air. The whole neighborhood abounds with local tales, haunted spots, and twilight superstitions; stars shoot and meteors glare oftener across the valley than in any part of the country, and the nightmare, with her whole nine fold, seems to make it the favorite scene of her gambols.

The dominant spirit, however, that haunts this enchanted region, and seems to be commander-in-chief of all the powers of the air, is the apparition of a figure on horseback without a head. It is said by some to be the ghost of a Hessian trooper, whose head had been carried away by a cannon-ball, in some nameless battle during the revolutionary war; and who is ever and anon seen by the country folk, hurrying along in the gloom of night, as if on the wings of the wind. His haunts are not confined to the valley, but extend at times to the adjacent roads, and especially to the vicinity of a church at no great distance. Indeed, certain of the most authentic historians of those parts, who have been careful in collecting and collating the floating facts concerning this spectre, allege that the body of the trooper, having been buried in the church-yard, the ghost rides forth to the scene of battle in nightly quest of his head; and that the rushing speed with which he sometimes passes along the Hollow, like a midnight blast, is owing to his being belated, and in a hurry to get back to the church-yard before daybreak.

Such is the general purport of this legendary superstition, which has furnished materials for many a wild story in that region of shadows;

and the spectre is known, at all the country firesides, by the name of the Headless Horseman of Sleepy Hollow.

It is remarkable that the visionary propensity I have mentioned is not confined to the native inhabitants of the valley, but is unconsciously imbibed by every one who resides there for a time. However wide awake they may have been before they entered that sleepy region, they are sure, in a little time, to inhale the witching influence of the air, and begin to grow imaginative—to dream dreams, and see apparitions.

I mention this peaceful spot with all possible laud; for it is in such little retired Dutch valleys, found here and there embosomed in the great State of New York, that population, manners, and customs, remain fixed; while the great torrent of migration and improvement, which is making such incessant changes in other parts of this restless country, sweeps by them unobserved. They are like those little nooks of still water which border a rapid stream; where we may see the straw and bubble riding quietly at anchor, or slowly revolving in their mimic harbor, undisturbed by the rush of the passing current. Though many years have elapsed since I trod the drowsy shades of Sleepy Hollow, yet I question whether I should not still find the same trees and the same families vegetating in its sheltered bosom.

In this by-place of nature, there abode, in a remote period of American history, that is to say, some thirty years since, a worthy wight of the name of Ichabod Crane; who sojourned, or, as he expressed it, "tarried," in Sleepy Hollow, for the purpose of instructing the children of the vicinity. He was a native of Connecticut; a State which supplies the Union with pioneers for the mind as well as for the forest, and sends forth yearly its legions of frontier woodsmen and country schoolmasters. The cognomen of Crane was not inapplicable to his person. He was tall, but exceedingly lank, with narrow shoulders, long arms and legs, hands that dangled a mile out of his sleeves, feet that might have served for shovels, and his whole frame most loosely hung together. His head was small, and flat at top, with huge ears, large green glassy eyes, and a long snipe nose, so that it looked like a weather-cock, perched upon his spindle neck, to tell which way the wind blew. To see him striding along the profile of a hill on a windy day, with his clothes bagging and fluttering about him, one might have mistaken him for the genius of famine descending upon the earth, or some scarecrow eloped from a cornfield.

His school-house was a low building of one large room, rudely constructed of logs; the windows partly glazed, and partly patched with leaves of old copy-books. It was most ingeniously secured at vacant hours, by a withe twisted in the handle of the door, and stakes set against the window shutters; so that, though a thief might get in with perfect ease, he would find some embarrassment in getting out; an idea most probably borrowed by the architect, Yost Van Houten, from the mystery of an eel-pot. The school-house stood in a rather lonely but pleasant situation, just at the foot of a woody hill, with a brook running close by, and a formidable birch tree growing at one end of it. From hence the low murmur of his pupils' voices, conning over their lessons, might be heard in a drowsy summer's day, like the hum of a bee-hive; interrupted now and then by the authoritative voice of the master, in the tone of menace or command; or, peradventure, by the appalling sound of the birch, as he urged some tardy loiterer along the flowery path of knowledge. Truth to say, he was a conscientious man, and ever bore in mind the golden maxim, "Spare the rod and spoil the child."— Ichabod Crane's scholars certainly were not spoiled.

I would not have it imagined, however, that he was one of those cruel potentates of the school, who joy in the smart of their subjects; on the contrary, he administered justice with discrimination rather than severity; taking the burthen off the backs of the weak, and laying it on those of the strong. Your mere puny stripling, that winced at the least flourish of the rod, was passed by with indulgence; but the claims of justice were satisfied by inflicting a double portion on some little, tough, wrong-headed, broad-skirted Dutch urchin, who sulked and swelled and grew dogged and sullen beneath the birch. All this he called "doing his duty by their parents"; and he never inflicted a chastisement without following it by the assurance, so consolatory to the smarting urchin, that "he would remember it, and thank him for it the longest day he had to live."

When school hours were over, he was even the companion and playmate of the larger boys; and on holiday afternoons would convoy some of the smaller ones home, who happened to have pretty sisters, or good housewives for mothers, noted for the comforts of the cupboard. Indeed it behooved him to keep on good terms with his pupils. The revenue arising from his school was small, and would have been scarcely sufficient to furnish him with daily bread, for he was a huge feeder, and though lank, had the dilating powers of an anaconda; but to help out his maintenance, he was, according to country custom in those parts, boarded and lodged at the houses of the farmers, whose children he instructed. With these he lived successively a week at a time; thus going the rounds of the neighborhood, with all his worldly effects tied up in a cotton handkerchief.

That all this might not be too onerous on the purses of his rustic patrons, who are apt to consider the costs of schooling a grievous burden, and schoolmasters as mere drones, he had various ways of rendering himself both useful and agreeable. He assisted the farmers occasionally in the lighter labors of their farms; helped to make hay; mended the fences; took the horses to water; drove the cows from pasture; and cut wood for the winter fire. He laid aside, too, all the dominant dignity and absolute sway with which he lorded it in his little empire, the school, and became wonderfully gentle and ingratiating. He found favor in the eyes of the mothers, by petting the children, particularly the youngest; and like the lion bold, which whilom so magnanimously the lamb did hold, he would sit with a child on one knee, and rock a cradle with his foot for whole hours together.

In addition to his other vocations, he was the singing-master of the neighborhood, and picked up many bright shillings by instructing the young folks in psalmody. It was a matter of no little vanity to him, on Sundays, to take his station in front of the church gallery, with a band of chosen singers; where, in his own mind, he completely carried away the psalm from the parson. Certain it is, his voice resounded far above all the rest of the congregation; and there are peculiar quavers still to be heard in that church, and which may even be heard half a mile off, quite to the opposite side of the mill-pond, on a still Sunday morning, which are said to be legitimately descended from the nose of Ichabod Crane. Thus, by divers little makeshifts in that ingenious way which is commonly denominated "by hook and by crook," the worthy pedagogue got on tolerably enough, and was thought, by all who understood nothing of the labor of headwork, to have a wonderfully easy life of it.

The schoolmaster is generally a man of some importance in the female circle of a rural neighborhood; being considered a kind of idle gentlemanlike personage, of vastly superior taste and accomplishments to the rough country swains, and, indeed, inferior in learning only to the parson. His appearance, therefore, is apt to occasion some little stir at the tea-table of a farmhouse, and the addition of a supernumerary dish of cakes or sweetmeats, or peradventure, the parade of a silver teapot. Our man of letters, therefore, was peculiarly happy in the smiles of all the country damsels. How he would figure among them in the church-yard, between services on Sundays! gathering grapes for them from the wild vines that overrun the surrounding trees; reciting for their amusement all the epitaphs on the tombstones; or sauntering, with a whole bevy of them, along the banks of the adjacent mill-pond; while the more bashful country bumpkins hung sheepishly back, envying his superior elegance and address.

From his half itinerant life, also, he was a kind of travelling gazette, carrying the whole budget of local gossip from house to house; so that his appearance was always greeted with satisfaction. He was, moreover, esteemed by the women as a man of great erudition, for he had read several books quite through, and was a perfect master of Cotton Mather's History of New England Witchcraft, in which, by the way, he most firmly and potently believed.

He was, in fact, an odd mixture of small shrewdness and simple credulity. His appetite for the marvellous, and his powers of digesting it, were equally extraordinary; and both had been increased by his residence in this spellbound region. No tale was too gross or monstrous for his capacious swallow. It was often his delight, after his school was dismissed in the afternoon, to stretch himself on the rich bed of clover, bordering the little brook that whimpered by his school-house, and there con over old Mather's direful tales, until the gathering dusk of the evening made the printed page a mere mist before his eyes. Then, as he wended his way, by swamp and stream and awful woodland, to the farmhouse where he happened to be quartered, every sound of nature, at that witching hour, fluttered his excited imagination: the moan of the whip-poor-will from the hillside; the boding cry of the tree-toad, that harbinger of storm; the dreary hooting of the screech-owl, or the sudden rustling in the thicket of birds frightened from their roost. The fire-flies, too, which sparkled most vividly in the darkest places, now and then startled him, as one of uncommon brightness would stream across his path; and if, by chance, a huge blockhead of a beetle came winging his blundering flight against him, the poor varlet was ready to give up the ghost, with the idea that he was struck with a witch's token. His only resource on such occasions, either to drown thought, or drive away evil spirits, was to sing psalm tunes;—and the good people of Sleepy Hollow, as they sat by their doors of an evening, were often filled with awe, at hearing his nasal melody, "in linked sweetness long drawn out," floating from the distant hill, or along the dusky road.

Another of his sources of fearful pleasure was, to pass long winter evenings with the old Dutch wives, as they sat spinning by the fire, with a row of apples roasting and spluttering along the hearth, and listen to their marvellous tales of ghosts and goblins, and haunted fields, and haunted brooks, and haunted bridges, and haunted houses, and particularly of the headless horseman, or galloping Hessian of the Hollow, as they sometimes called him. He would delight them equally by his anecdotes of witchcraft, and of the direful omens and portentous sights and sounds in the air, which prevailed in the earlier times of Connecticut; and would frighten them woefully with speculations upon comets and shooting stars; and with the alarming fact that the world did absolutely turn round, and that they were half the time topsyturvy!

But if there was a pleasure in all this, while snugly cuddling in the chimney corner of a chamber that was all of a ruddy glow from the crackling wood fire, and where, of course, no spectre dared to show his face, it was dearly purchased by the terrors of his subsequent walk homewards. What fearful shapes and shadows beset his path amidst the dim and ghastly glare of a snowy night!—With what wistful look did he eye every trembling ray of light streaming across the waste fields from some distant window!—How often was he appalled by some shrub covered with snow, which, like a sheeted spectre, beset his very path!—How often did he shrink with curdling awe at the sound of his own steps on the frosty crust beneath his feet; and dread to look over his shoulder, lest he should behold some uncouth being tramping close behind him!—and how often was he thrown into complete dismay by some rushing blast, howling among the trees, in the idea that it was the Galloping Hessian on one of his nightly scourings!

All these, however, were mere terrors of the night, phantoms of the mind that walk in darkness; and though he had seen many spectres in his time, and been more than once beset by Satan in divers shapes, in his lonely perambulations, yet daylight put an end to all these evils; and he would have passed a pleasant life of it, in despite of the devil and all his works, if his path had not been crossed by a being that causes more perplexity to mortal man than ghosts, goblins, and the whole race of witches put together, and that was—a woman.

Among the musical disciples who assembled, one evening in each week, to receive his instructions in psalmody, was Katrina Van Tassel, the daughter and only child of a substantial Dutch farmer. She was a blooming lass of fresh eighteen; plump as a partridge; ripe and melting and rosy cheeked as one of her father's peaches, and universally famed, not merely for her beauty, but her vast expectations. She was withal a little of a coquette, as might be perceived even in her dress, which was a mixture of ancient and modern fashions, as most suited to set off her charms. She wore the ornaments of pure yellow gold, which her great-great-grandmother had brought over from Saardam; the tempting stomacher of the older time; and withal a provokingly short petticoat, to display the prettiest foot and ankle in the country round.

Ichabod Crane had a soft and foolish heart towards the sex; and it is not to be wondered at, that so tempting a morsel soon found favor in his eyes; more especially after he had visited her in her paternal mansion. Old Baltus Van Tassel was a perfect picture of a thriving, contented, liberal-hearted farmer. He seldom, it is true, sent either his eyes or his thoughts beyond the boundaries of his own farm; but within those every thing was snug, happy, and well-conditioned. He was satisfied with his wealth, but not proud of it; and piqued himself upon the hearty abundance, rather than the style in which he lived. His stronghold was situated on the banks of the Hudson, in one of those green sheltered, fertile nooks, in which the Dutch farmers are so fond of nestling. A great elm-tree spread its broad branches over it; at the foot of which bubbled up a spring of the softest and sweetest water, in a little well, formed of a barrel; and then stole sparkling away through the grass, to a neighboring brook, that bubbled along among alders and dwarf willows. Hard by the farmhouse was a vast barn, that might have served for a church; every window and crevice of which seemed bursting forth with the treasures of the farm; the flail was busily resounding within it from morning to night; swallows and martins skimmed twittering about the eaves; and rows of pigeons, some with one eye turned up, as if watching the weather, some with their heads under their wings, or buried in their bosoms, and others swelling, and cooing, and bowing about their dames, were enjoying the sunshine on the roof. Sleek unwieldy porkers were grunting in the repose and abundance of their pens; whence sallied forth, now and then, troops of sucking pigs, as if to snuff the air. A stately squadron of snowy geese were riding in an adjoining pond, convoying whole fleets of ducks; regiments of turkeys were gobbling through the farmyard, and guinea fowls fretting about it, like ill-tempered housewives, with their peevish discontented cry. Before the barn door strutted the gallant cock, that pattern of a husband, a warrior, and a fine gentleman, clapping his burnished wings, and crowing in the pride and gladness of his heart— sometimes tearing up the earth with his feet, and then generously calling his ever-hungry family of wives and children to enjoy the rich morsel which he had discovered.

The pedagogue's mouth watered, as he looked upon this sumptuous promise of luxurious winter fare. In his devouring mind's eye, he pictured to himself every roasting-pig running about with a pudding in his belly, and an apple in his mouth; the pigeons were snugly put to bed in a comfortable pie, and tucked in with a coverlet of crust; the geese were swimming in their own gravy; and the ducks pairing cosily in dishes, like snug married couples, with a decent competency of onion sauce. In the porkers he saw carved out the future sleek side of bacon, and juicy relishing ham; not a turkey but he beheld daintily trussed up, with its gizzard under its wing, and, peradventure, a necklace of savory sausages; and even bright chanticleer himself lay sprawling on his back, in a side dish with uplifted claws, as if craving that quarter which his chivalrous spirit disdained to ask while living.

As the enraptured Ichabod fancied all this, and as he rolled his great green eyes over the fat meadowlands, the rich fields of wheat, of rye, of buckwheat, and Indian corn, and the orchards burthened with ruddy fruit, which surrounded the warm tenement of Van Tassel, his heart yearned after the damsel who was to inherit these domains, and his imagination expanded with the idea, how they might be readily turned into cash, and the money invested in immense tracts of wild land, and shingle palaces in the wilderness. Nay, his busy fancy already realized his hopes, and presented to him the blooming Katrina, with a whole family of children, mounted on the top of a wagon loaded with household trumpery, with pots and kettles dangling beneath; and he beheld himself bestriding a pacing mare, with a colt at her heels, setting out for Kentucky, Tennessee, or the Lord knows where.

When he entered the house the conquest of his heart was complete. It was one of those spacious farmhouses, with high-ridged, but lowly-sloping roofs, built in the style handed down from the first Dutch settlers; the low projecting eaves forming a piazza along the front, capable of being closed up in bad weather. Under this were hung flails, harness, various utensils of husbandry, and nets for fishing in the neighboring river. Benches were built along the sides for summer use; and a great spinning-wheel at one end, and a churn at the other, showed the various uses to which this important porch might be devoted. From this piazza the wondering Ichabod entered the hall, which formed the centre of the mansion and the place of usual residence. Here, rows of resplendent pewter, ranged on a long dresser, dazzled his eyes. In one corner stood a huge bag of wool ready to be spun; in another a quantity of linsey-woolsey just from the loom; ears of Indian corn, and strings of dried apples and peaches, hung in gay festoons along the walls, mingled with the gaud of red peppers; and a door left ajar gave him a peep into the best parlor, where the claw-footed chairs, and dark mahogany tables, shone like mirrors; andirons, with their accompanying shovel and tongs, glistened from their covert of asparagus tops; mock-oranges and conch-shells decorated the mantelpiece; strings of various colored birds' eggs were suspended above it: a great ostrich egg was hung from the centre of the room, and a corner cupboard, knowingly left open, displayed immense treasures of old silver and well-mended china.

From the moment Ichabod laid his eyes upon these regions of delight, the peace of his mind was at an end, and his only study was how to gain the affections of the peerless daughter of Van Tassel. In this enterprise, however, he had more real difficulties than generally fell to the lot of a knight-errant of yore, who seldom had any thing but giants, enchanters, fiery dragons, and such like easily-conquered adversaries, to contend with; and had to make his way merely through gates of iron and brass, and walls of adamant, to the castle keep, where the lady of his heart was confined; all which he achieved as easily as a man would carve his way to the centre of a Christmas pie; and then the lady gave him her hand as a matter of course. Ichabod, on the contrary, had to win his way to the heart of a country coquette, beset with a labyrinth of whims and caprices, which were for ever presenting new difficulties and impediments; and he had to encounter a host of fearful adversaries of real flesh and blood, and numerous rustic admirers, who beset every portal to her heart; keeping a watchful and angry eye upon each other, but ready to fly out in the common cause against any new competitor.

Among these the most formidable was a burly, roaring, roystering blade, of the name of Abraham, or, according to the Dutch abbreviation, Brom Van Brunt, the hero of the country round, which rang with his feats of strength and hardihood. He was broad-shouldered and double-jointed, with short curly black hair, and a bluff, but not unpleasant countenance, having a mingled air of fun and arrogance. From his Herculean frame and great powers of limb, he had received the nickname of BROM BONES, by which he was universally known. He was famed for great knowledge and skill in horsemanship, being as dexterous on horseback as a Tartar. He was foremost at all races and cock-fights; and, with the ascendency which bodily strength acquires in rustic life, was the umpire in all disputes, setting his hat on one side, and giving his decisions with an air and tone admitting of no gainsay or appeal. He was always ready for either a fight or a frolic; but had more mischief than ill-will in his composition; and, with all his over-bearing roughness, there was a strong dash of waggish good humor at bottom. He had three or four boon companions, who regarded him as their model, and at the head of whom he scoured the country, attending every scene of feud or merriment for miles round. In cold weather he was distinguished by a fur cap, surmounted with a flaunting fox's tail; and when folks at a country gathering described this well-known crest at a distance, whisking about among a squad of hard riders, they always stood by for a squall. Sometimes his crew would be heard dashing along past the farmhouses at midnight, with whoop and halloo, like a troop of Don Cossacks; and the old dames, startled out of their sleep, would listen for a moment till the hurry-scurry had clattered by, and then exclaim, "Ay, there goes Brom Bones and his gang!" The neighbors looked upon him with a mixture of awe, admiration, and good will; and when any madcap prank, or rustic brawl, occurred in the vicinity, always shook their heads, and warranted Brom Bones was at the bottom of it.

This rantipole hero had for some time singled out the blooming Katrina for the object of his uncouth gallantries, and though his amorous toyings were something like the gentle caresses and endearments of a bear, yet it was whispered that she did not altogether discourage his hopes. Certain it is, his advances were signals for rival candidates to retire, who felt no inclination to cross a lion in his amours; insomuch, that when his horse was seen tied to Van Tassel's paling, on a Sunday night, a sure sign that his master was courting, or, as it is termed, "sparking," within, all other suitors passed by in despair, and carried the war into other quarters.

Such was the formidable rival with whom Ichabod Crane had to contend, and, considering all things, a stouter man than he would have shrunk from the competition, and a wiser man would have despaired. He had, however, a happy mixture of pliability and perseverance in his nature; he was in form and spirit like a supple-jack—yielding, but tough; though he bent, he never broke; and though he bowed beneath the slightest pressure, yet, the moment it was away—jerk! he was as erect, and carried his head as high as ever.

To have taken the field openly against his rival would have been madness; for he was not a man to be thwarted in his amours, any more than the stormy lover, Achilles. Ichabod, therefore, made his advances in a quiet and gently-insinuating manner. Under cover of his character of singing-master, he made frequent visits at the farmhouse; not that he had any thing to apprehend from the meddlesome interference of parents, which is so often a stumbling-block in the path of lovers. Balt Van Tassel was an easy indulgent soul; he loved his daughter better even than his pipe, and like a reasonable man and an excellent father, let her have her way in every thing. His notable little wife, too, had enough to do to attend to her housekeeping and manage her poultry; for, as she sagely observed, ducks and geese are foolish things, and must be looked after, but girls can take care of themselves. Thus while the busy dame bustled about the house, or plied her spinning-wheel at one end of the piazza, honest Balt would sit smoking his evening pipe at the other, watching the achievements of a little wooden warrior, who, armed with a sword in each hand, was most valiantly fighting the wind on the pinnacle of the barn. In the mean time, Ichabod would carry on his suit with the daughter by the side of the spring under the great elm, or sauntering along in the twilight, that hour so favorable to the lover's eloquence.

I profess not to know how women's hearts are wooed and won. To me they have always been matters of riddle and admiration. Some seem to have but one vulnerable point, or door of access; while others have a thousand avenues, and may be captured in a thousand different ways. It is a great triumph of skill to gain the former, but a still greater proof of generalship to maintain possession of the latter, for the man must battle for his fortress at every door and window. He who wins a thousand common hearts is therefore entitled to some renown; but he who keeps undisputed sway over the heart of a coquette, is indeed a hero. Certain it is, that this was not the case with the redoubtable Brom Bones; and from the moment Ichabod Crane made his advances, the interests of the former evidently declined; his horse was no longer seen tied at the palings on Sunday nights, and a deadly feud gradually arose between him and the preceptor of Sleepy Hollow.

Brom, who had a degree of rough chivalry in his nature, would fain have carried matters to open warfare, and have settled their pretensions to the lady, according to the mode of those most concise and simple reasoners, the knights-errant of yore—by single combat; but Ichabod was too conscious of the superior might of his adversary to enter the lists against him: he had overheard a boast of Bones, that he would "double the schoolmaster up, and lay him on a shelf of his own school-house"; and he was too wary to give him an opportunity. There was something extremely provoking in this obstinately pacific system; it left Brom no alternative but to draw upon the funds of rustic waggery in his disposition, and to play off boorish practical jokes upon his rival: Ichabod became the object of whimsical persecution to Bones, and his gang of rough riders. They harried his hitherto peaceful domains; smoked out his singing school, by stopping up the chimney; broke into the school-house at night, in spite of its formidable fastenings of withe and window stakes, and turned every thing topsy-turvy: so that the poor schoolmaster began to think all the witches in the country held their meetings there. But what was still more annoying, Brom took all opportunities of turning him into ridicule in presence of his mistress, and had a scoundrel dog whom he taught to whine in the most ludicrous manner, and introduced as a rival of Ichabod's to instruct her in psalmody.

In this way matters went on for some time, without producing any material effect on the relative situation of the contending powers. On a fine autumnal afternoon, Ichabod, in pensive mood, sat enthroned on the lofty stool whence he usually watched all the concerns of his little literary realm. In his hand he swayed a ferule, that sceptre of despotic power; the birch of justice reposed on three nails, behind the throne, a constant terror to evil doers; while on the desk before him might be seen sundry contraband articles, and prohibited weapons, detected upon the persons of idle urchins; such as half-munched apples, popguns, whirligigs, fly-cages, and whole legions of rampant little paper game-cocks. Apparently there had been some appalling act of justice recently inflicted, for his scholars were all busily intent upon their books, or slyly whispering behind them with one eye kept upon the master; and a kind of buzzing stillness reigned throughout the schoolroom. It was suddenly interrupted by the appearance of a negro, in tow-cloth jacket and trowsers, a round-crowned fragment of a hat, like the cap of Mercury, and mounted on the back of a ragged, wild, half-broken colt, which he managed with a rope by way of halter. He came clattering up to the school door with an invitation to Ichabod to attend a merry-making or "quilting frolic," to be held that evening at Mynheer Van Tassel's; and having delivered his message with that air of importance, and effort at fine language, which a negro is apt to display on petty embassies of the kind, he dashed over the brook, and was seen scampering away up the hollow, full of the importance and hurry of his mission.

All was now bustle and hubbub in the late quiet schoolroom. The scholars were hurried through their lessons, without stopping at trifles; those who were nimble skipped over half with impunity, and those who were tardy, had a smart application now and then in the rear, to quicken their speed, or help them over a tall word. Books were flung aside without being put away on the shelves, inkstands were overturned, benches thrown down, and the whole school was turned loose an hour before the usual time, bursting forth like a legion of young imps, yelping and racketing about the green, in joy at their early emancipation.

The gallant Ichabod now spent at least an extra hour at his toilet, brushing and furbishing up his best, and indeed only suit of rusty black, and arranging his looks by a bit of broken looking-glass, that hung up in the school-house. That he might make his appearance before his mistress in the true style of a cavalier, he borrowed a horse from the farmer with whom he was domiciliated, a choleric old Dutchman, of the name of Hans Van Ripper, and, thus gallantly mounted, issued forth, like a knight-errant in quest of adventures. But it is meet I should, in the true spirit of romantic story, give some account of the looks and equipments of my hero and his steed. The animal he bestrode was a broken-down plough-horse, that had out-lived almost every thing but his viciousness. He was gaunt and shagged, with a ewe neck and a head like a hammer; his rusty mane and tail was tangled and knotted with burrs; one eye had lost its pupil, and was glaring and spectral; but the other had the gleam of a genuine devil in it. Still he must have had fire and mettle in his day, if we may judge from the name he bore of Gunpowder. He had, in fact, been a favorite steed of his master's, the choleric Van Ripper, who was a furious rider, and had infused, very probably, some of his own spirit into the animal; for, old and broken-down as he looked, there was more of the lurking devil in him than in any young filly in the country.

Ichabod was a suitable figure for such a steed. He rode with short stirrups, which brought his knees nearly up to the pommel of the saddle; his sharp elbows stuck out like grasshoppers'; he carried his whip perpendicularly in his hand, like a sceptre, and, as his horse jogged on, the motion of his arms was not unlike the flapping of a pair of wings. A small wool hat rested on the top of his nose, for so his scanty strip of forehead might be called; and the skirts of his black coat fluttered out almost to the horse's tail. Such was the appearance of

Ichabod and his steed, as they shambled out of the gate of Hans Van Ripper, and it was altogether such an apparition as is seldom to be met with in broad daylight.

It was, as I have said, a fine autumnal day, the sky was clear and serene, and nature wore that rich and golden livery which we always associate with the idea of abundance. The forests had put on their sober brown and yellow, while some trees of the tenderer kind had been nipped by the frosts into brilliant dyes of orange, purple, and scarlet. Streaming files of wild ducks began to make their appearance high in the air; the bark of the squirrel might be heard from the groves of beech and hickory nuts, and the pensive whistle of the quail at intervals from the neighboring stubble-field.

The small birds were taking their farewell banquets. In the fulness of their revelry, they fluttered, chirping and frolicking, from bush to bush, and tree to tree, capricious from the very profusion and variety around them. There was the honest cock-robin, the favorite game of stripling sportsmen, with its loud querulous note; and the twittering blackbirds flying in sable clouds; and the golden-winged woodpecker, with his crimson crest, his broad black gorget, and splendid plumage; and the cedar bird, with its red-tipt wings and yellow-tipt tail, and its little monteiro cap of feathers; and the blue jay, that noisy coxcomb, in his gay light-blue coat and white underclothes; screaming and chattering, nodding and bobbing and bowing, and pretending to be on good terms with every songster of the grove.

As Ichabod jogged slowly on his way, his eye, ever open to every symptom of culinary abundance, ranged with delight over the treasures of jolly autumn. On all sides he beheld vast store of apples; some hanging in oppressive opulence on the trees; some gathered into baskets and barrels for the market; others heaped up in rich piles for the cider-press. Farther on he beheld great fields of Indian corn, with its golden ears peeping from their leafy coverts, and holding out the promise of cakes and hasty pudding; and the yellow pumpkins lying beneath them, turning up their fair round bellies to the sun, and giving ample prospects of the most luxurious of pies; and anon he passed the fragrant buckwheat fields, breathing the odor of the bee-hive, and as he beheld them, soft anticipations stole over his mind of dainty slapjacks, well buttered, and garnished with honey or treacle, by the delicate little dimpled hand of Katrina Van Tassel.

Thus feeding his mind with many sweet thoughts and "sugared suppositions," he journeyed along the sides of a range of hills which look out upon some of the goodliest scenes of the mighty Hudson. The sun gradually wheeled his broad disk down into the west. The wide bosom of the Tappan Zee lay motionless and glassy, excepting that here and there a gentle undulation waved and prolonged the blue shadow of the distant mountain. A few amber clouds floated in the sky, without a breath of air to move them. The horizon was of a fine golden tint, changing gradually into a pure apple green, and from that into the deep blue of the mid-heaven. A slanting ray lingered on the woody crests of the precipices that overhung some parts of the river, giving greater depth to the dark-gray and purple of their rocky sides. A sloop was loitering in the distance, dropping slowly down with the tide, her sail hanging uselessly against the mast; and as the reflection of the sky gleamed along the still water, it seemed as if the vessel was suspended in the air.

It was toward evening that Ichabod arrived at the castle of the Heer Van Tassel, which he found thronged with the pride and flower of the adjacent country. Old farmers, a spare leathern-faced race, in homespun coats and breeches, blue stockings, huge shoes, and magnificent pewter buckles. Their brisk withered little dames, in close crimped caps, long-waisted shortgowns, homespun petticoats, with scissors and pin-cushions, and gay calico pockets hanging on the outside. Buxom lasses, almost as antiquated as their mothers, excepting where a straw hat, a fine ribbon, or perhaps a white frock, gave symptoms of city innovation. The sons, in short square-skirted coats with rows of stupendous brass buttons, and their hair generally queued in the fashion of the times, especially if they could procure an eel-skin for the purpose, it being esteemed throughout the country, as a potent nourisher and strengthener of the hair.

Brom Bones, however, was the hero of the scene, having come to the gathering on his favorite steed Daredevil, a creature, like himself, full of mettle and mischief, and which no one but himself could manage. He was, in fact, noted for preferring vicious animals, given to all kinds of tricks, which kept the rider in constant risk of his neck, for he held a tractable well-broken horse as unworthy of a lad of spirit.

Fain would I pause to dwell upon the world of charms that burst upon the enraptured gaze of my hero, as he entered the state parlor of Van Tassel's mansion. Not those of the bevy of buxom lasses, with their luxurious display of red and white; but the ample charms of a genuine Dutch country tea-table, in the sumptuous time of autumn. Such heaped-up platters of cakes of various and almost indescribable kinds, known only to experienced Dutch housewives! There was the doughty dough-nut, the tenderer oly koek, and the crisp and crumbling cruller; sweet cakes and short cakes, ginger cakes and honey cakes, and the whole family of cakes. And then there were apple pies and peach pies and pumpkin pies; besides slices of ham and smoked beef; and moreover delectable dishes of preserved plums, and peaches, and pears, and quinces; not to mention broiled shad and roasted chicken; together with bowls of milk and cream, all mingled higgledy-piggledy, pretty much as I have enumerated them, with the motherly tea-pot sending up its clouds of vapor from the midst—Heaven bless the mark! I want breath and time to discuss this banquet as it deserves, and am too eager to get on with my story. Happily, Ichabod Crane was not in so great a hurry as his historian, but did ample justice to every dainty.

He was a kind and thankful creature, whose heart dilated in proportion as his skin was filled with good cheer; and whose spirits rose with eating as some men's do with drink. He could not help, too, rolling his large eyes round him as he ate, and chuckling with the possibility that he might one day be lord of all this scene of almost unimaginable luxury and splendor. Then, he thought, how soon he'd turn his back upon the old school-house; snap his fingers in the face of Hans Van Ripper, and every other niggardly patron, and kick any itinerant pedagogue out of doors that should dare to call him comrade!

Old Baltus Van Tassel moved about among his guests with a face dilated with content and good humor, round and jolly as the harvest moon. His hospitable attentions were brief, but expressive, being confined to a shake of a hand, a slap on the shoulder, a loud laugh, and a pressing invitation to "fall to, and help themselves."

And now the sound of the music from the common room, or hall, summoned to the dance. The musician was an old grayheaded negro, who had been the itinerant orchestra of the neighborhood for more than half a century. His instrument was as old and battered as himself. The greater part of the time he scraped on two or three strings, accompanying every movement of the bow with a motion of the head; bowing almost to the ground, and stamping with his foot whenever a fresh couple were to start.

Ichabod prided himself upon his dancing as much as upon his vocal powers. Not a limb, not a fibre about him was idle; and to have seen his loosely hung frame in full motion, and clattering about the room, you would have thought Saint Vitus himself, that blessed patron of the dance, was figuring before you in person. He was the admiration of all the negroes; who, having gathered, of all ages and sizes, from the farm and the neighborhood, stood forming a pyramid of shining black faces at every door and window, gazing with delight at the scene, rolling their white eye-balls, and showing grinning rows of ivory from ear to ear. How could the flogger of urchins be otherwise than animated and joyous? the lady of his heart was his partner in the dance, and smiling graciously in reply to all his amorous oglings; while Brom Bones, sorely smitten with love and jealousy, sat brooding by himself in one corner.

When the dance was at an end, Ichabod was attracted to a knot of the sager folks, who, with old Van Tassel, sat smoking at one end of the piazza, gossiping over former times, and drawing out long stories about the war.

This neighborhood, at the time of which I am speaking, was one of those highly-favored places which abound with chronicle and great men. The British and American line had run near it during the war; it had, therefore, been the scene of marauding, and infested with refugees, cow-boys, and all kinds of border chivalry. Just sufficient time had elapsed to enable each story-teller to dress up his tale with a little becoming fiction, and, in the indistinctness of his recollection, to make himself the hero of every exploit.

There was the story of Doffue Martling, a large blue-bearded Dutchman, who had nearly taken a British frigate with an old iron nine-pounder from a mud breastwork, only that his gun burst at the sixth discharge. And there was an old gentleman who shall be nameless, being too rich a mynheer to be lightly mentioned, who, in the battle of Whiteplains, being an excellent master of defence, parried a musket ball with a small sword, insomuch that he absolutely felt it whiz round the blade, and glance off at the hilt: in proof of which he was ready at any time to show the sword, with the hilt a little bent. There were several more that had been equally great in the field, not one of whom but was persuaded that he had a considerable hand in bringing the war to a happy termination.

But all these were nothing to the tales of ghosts and apparitions that succeeded. The neighborhood is rich in legendary treasures of the kind. Local tales and superstitions thrive best in these sheltered long-settled retreats; but are trampled under foot by the shifting throng that forms the population of most of our country places. Besides, there is no encouragement for ghosts in most of our villages, for they have scarcely had time to finish their first nap, and turn themselves in their graves, before their surviving friends have travelled away from the neighborhood; so that when they turn out at night to walk their rounds, they have no acquaintance left to call upon. This is perhaps the reason why we so seldom hear of ghosts except in our long-established Dutch communities.

The immediate cause, however, of the prevalence of supernatural stories in these parts, was doubtless owing to the vicinity of Sleepy Hollow. There was a contagion in the very air that blew from that haunted region; it breathed forth an atmosphere of dreams and fancies infecting all the land. Several of the Sleepy Hollow people were present at Van Tassel's, and, as usual, were doling out their wild and wonderful legends. Many dismal tales were told about funeral trains, and mourning cries and wailings heard and seen about the great tree where the unfortunate Major André was taken, and which stood in the neighborhood. Some mention was made also of the woman in white, that haunted the dark glen at Raven Rock, and was often heard to shriek on winter nights before a storm, having perished there in the snow. The chief part of the stories, however, turned upon the favorite spectre of Sleepy Hollow, the headless horseman, who had been heard several times of late, patrolling the country; and, it was said, tethered his horse nightly among the graves in the church-yard.

The sequestered situation of this church seems always to have made it a favorite haunt of troubled spirits. It stands on a knoll, surrounded by locust-trees and lofty elms, from among which its decent whitewashed walls shine modestly forth, like Christian purity beaming through the shades of retirement. A gentle slope descends from it to a silver sheet of water, bordered by high trees, between which, peeps may be caught at the blue hills of the Hudson. To look upon its grass-grown yard, where the sunbeams seem to sleep so quietly, one would think that there at least the dead might rest in peace. On one side of the church extends a wide woody dell, along which raves a large brook among broken rocks and trunks of fallen trees. Over a deep black part of the stream, not far from the church, was formerly thrown a wooden bridge; the road that led to it, and the bridge itself, were thickly shaded by overhanging trees, which cast a gloom about it, even in the daytime; but occasioned a fearful darkness at night. This was one of the favorite haunts of the headless horseman; and the place where he was most frequently encountered. The tale was told of old Brouwer, a most heretical disbeliever in ghosts, how he met the horseman returning from his foray into Sleepy Hollow, and was obliged to get up behind him; how they galloped over bush and brake, over hill and swamp, until they reached the bridge; when the horseman suddenly turned into a skeleton, threw old Brouwer into the brook, and sprang away over the tree-tops with a clap of thunder.

This story was immediately matched by a thrice marvellous adventure of Brom Bones, who made light of the galloping Hessian as an arrant jockey. He affirmed that, on returning one night from the neighboring village of Sing Sing, he had been overtaken by this midnight trooper; that he had offered to race with him for a bowl of punch, and should have won it too, for Daredevil beat the goblin-horse all hollow, but, just as they came to the church-bridge, the Hessian bolted, and vanished in a flash of fire.

All these tales, told in that drowsy undertone with which men talk in the dark, the countenances of the listeners only now and then receiving a casual gleam from the glare of a pipe, sank deep in the mind of Ichabod. He repaid them in kind with large extracts from his invaluable author, Cotton Mather, and added many marvellous events that had taken place in his native State of Connecticut, and fearful sights which he had seen in his nightly walks about Sleepy Hollow.

The revel now gradually broke up. The old farmers gathered together their families in their wagons, and were heard for some time rattling along the hollow roads, and over the distant hills. Some of the damsels mounted on pillions behind their favorite swains, and their light-hearted laughter, mingling with the clatter of hoofs, echoed along the silent woodlands, sounding fainter and fainter until they gradually died away—and the late scene of noise and frolic was all silent and deserted. Ichabod only lingered behind, according to the custom of country lovers to have tête-à-tête with the heiress, fully convinced that he was now on the high road to success. What passed at this interview I will not pretend to say, for in fact I do not know. Something, however, I fear me, must have gone wrong, for he certainly sallied forth, after no very great interval, with an air quite desolate and chop-fallen.—Oh these women! these women! Could that girl have been playing off any of her coquettish tricks?— Was her encouragement of the poor pedagogue all a mere sham to secure her conquest of his rival?—Heaven only knows, not I!—Let it suffice to say, Ichabod stole forth with the air of one who had been sacking a hen-roost, rather than a fair lady's heart. Without looking to the right or left to notice the scene of rural wealth, on which he had so often gloated, he went straight to the stable, and with several hearty cuffs and kicks, roused his steed most uncourteously from the comfortable quarters in which he was soundly sleeping, dreaming of mountains of corn and oats, and whole valleys of timothy and clover.

It was the very witching time of night that Ichabod, heavy-hearted and crest-fallen, pursued his travel homewards, along the sides of the lofty hills which rise about Tarry Town, and which he had traversed so cheerily in the afternoon. The hour was as dismal as himself. Far below him, the Tappan Zee spread its dusky and indistinct waste of waters, with here and there the tall mast of a sloop, riding quietly at anchor under the land. In the dead hush of midnight, he could even hear the barking of a watchdog from the opposite shore of the Hudson; but it was so vague and faint as only to give an idea of his distance from this faithful companion of man. Now and then, too, the long-drawn crowing of a cock, accidentally awakened, would sound far, far off, from some farmhouse away among the hills—but it was like a dreaming sound in his ear. No signs of life occurred near him, but occasionally the melancholy chirp of a cricket, or perhaps the guttural twang of a bullfrog, from a neighboring marsh, as if sleeping uncomfortably, and turning suddenly in his bed.

All the stories of ghosts and goblins that he had heard in the afternoon, now came crowding upon his recollection. The night grew darker and darker; the stars seemed to sink deeper in the sky, and driving clouds occasionally hid them from his sight. He had never felt so lonely and dismal. He was, moreover, approaching the very place where many of the scenes of the ghost stories had been laid. In the centre of the road stood an enormous tulip-tree, which towered like a giant above all the other trees of the neighborhood, and formed a kind of landmark. Its limbs were gnarled, and fantastic, large enough to form trunks for ordinary trees, twisting down almost to the earth, and rising again into the air. It was connected with the tragical story of the unfortunate André, who had been taken prisoner hard by; and was universally known by the name of Major André's tree. The common people regarded it with a mixture of respect and superstition, partly out of sympathy for the fate of its ill-starred namesake, and partly from the tales of strange sights and doleful lamentations told concerning it.

As Ichabod approached this fearful tree, he began to whistle:

he thought his whistle was answered—it was but a blast sweeping sharply through the dry branches. As he approached a little nearer, he thought he saw something white, hanging in the midst of the tree—he paused and ceased whistling; but on looking more narrowly, perceived that it was a place where the tree had been scathed by lightning, and the white wood laid bare. Suddenly he heard a groan—his teeth chattered and his knees smote against the saddle: it was but the rippling of one huge bough upon another, as they were swayed about by the breeze. He passed the tree in safety, but new perils lay before him.

About two hundred yards from the tree a small brook crossed the road, and ran into a marshy and thickly-wooded glen, known by the name of Wiley's swamp. A few rough logs, laid side by side, served for a bridge over this stream. On that side of the road where the brook entered the wood, a group of oaks and chestnuts, matted thick with wild grapevines, threw a cavernous gloom over it. To pass this bridge was the severest trial. It was at this identical spot that the unfortunate André was captured, and under the covert of those chestnuts and vines were the sturdy yeomen concealed who surprised him. This has ever since been considered a haunted stream, and fearful are the feelings of the schoolboy who has to pass it alone after dark.

As he approached the stream his heart began to thump; he summoned up, however, all his resolution, gave his horse half a score of kicks in the ribs, and attempted to dash briskly across the bridge; but instead of starting forward, the perverse old animal made a lateral movement, and ran broadside against the fence. Ichabod, whose fears increased with the delay, jerked the reins on the other side, and kicked lustily with the contrary foot: it was all in vain; his steed started, it is true, but it was only to plunge to the opposite side of the road into a thicket of brambles and alder bushes. The schoolmaster now bestowed both whip and heel upon the starveling ribs of old Gunpowder, who dashed forward, snuffling and snorting, but came to a stand just by the bridge, with a suddenness that had nearly sent his rider sprawling over his head. Just at this moment a plashy tramp by the side of the bridge caught the sensitive ear of Ichabod. In the dark shadow of the grove, on the margin of the brook, he beheld something huge, misshapen, black and towering. It stirred not, but seemed gathered up in the gloom, like some gigantic monster ready to spring upon the traveller.

The hair of the affrighted pedagogue rose upon his head with terror. What was to be done? To turn and fly was now too late; and besides, what chance was there of escaping ghost or goblin, if such it was, which could ride upon the wings of the wind? Summoning up, therefore, a show of courage, he demanded in stammering accents— "Who are you?" He received no reply. He repeated his demand in a still more agitated voice. Still there was no answer. Once more he cud gelled the sides of the inflexible Gunpowder, and, shutting his eyes, broke forth with involuntary fervor into a psalm tune. Just then the shadowy object of alarm put itself in motion, and, with a scramble and a bound, stood at once in the middle of the road. Though the night was dark and dismal, yet the form of the unknown might now in some degree be ascertained. He appeared to be a horseman of large dimensions, and mounted on a black horse of powerful frame. He made no offer of molestation or sociability, but kept aloof on one side of the road, jogging along on the blind side of old Gunpowder, who had now got over his fright and waywardness.

Ichabod, who had no relish for this strange midnight companion, and bethought himself of the adventure of Brom Bones with the Galloping Hessian, now quickened his steed, in hopes of leaving him behind. The stranger, however, quickened his horse to an equal pace. Ichabod pulled up, and fell into a walk, thinking to lag behind—the other did the same. His heart began to sink within him; he endeavored to resume his psalm tune, but his parched tongue clove to the roof of his mouth, and he could not utter a stave. There was something in the moody and dogged silence of his pertinacious companion, that was mysterious and appalling. It was soon fearfully accounted for. On mounting a rising ground, which brought the figure of his fellow-traveller in relief against the sky, gigantic in height, and muffled in a cloak, Ichabod was horror-struck, on perceiving that he was headless!—but his horror was still more increased, on observing that the head, which should have rested on his shoulders, was carried before him on the pommel of the saddle; his terror rose to desperation; he rained a shower of kicks and blows upon Gunpowder, hoping, by a sudden movement, to give his companion the slip—but the spectre started full jump with him. Away then they dashed, through thick and thin; stones flying, and sparks flashing at every bound. Ichabod's flimsy garments fluttered in the air, as he stretched his long lank body away over his horse's head, in the eagerness of his flight.

They had now reached the road which turns off to Sleepy Hollow, but Gunpowder, who seemed possessed with a demon, instead of keeping up it, made an opposite turn, and plunged headlong down hill to the left. This road leads through a sandy hollow, shaded by trees for about a quarter of a mile, where it crosses the bridge famous in goblin story, and just beyond swells the green knoll on which stands the whitewashed church.

As yet the panic of the steed had given his unskilful rider an apparent advantage in the chase; but just as he had got halfway through the hollow, the girths of the saddle gave way, and he felt it slipping from under him. He seized it by the pommel, and endeavored to hold it firm, but in vain; and had just time to save himself by clasping old Gunpowder round the neck, when the saddle fell to the earth, and he heard it trampled under foot by his pursuer. For a moment the terror of Hans Van Ripper's wrath passed across his mind—for it was his Sunday saddle; but this was no time for petty fears; the goblin was hard on his haunches; and (unskilful rider that he was!) he had much ado to maintain his seat; sometimes slipping on one side, sometimes on another, and sometimes jolted on the high ridge of his horse's backbone, with a violence that he verily feared would cleave him asunder.

An opening in the trees now cheered him with the hopes that the church bridge was at hand. The wavering reflection of a silver star in the bosom of the brook told him that he was not mistaken. He saw the walls of the church dimly glaring under the trees beyond. He recollected the place where Brom Bones' ghostly competitor had disappeared. "If I can but reach the bridge," thought Ichabod, "I am safe." Just then he heard the black steed panting and blowing close behind him; he even fancied that he felt his hot breath. Another convulsive kick in the ribs and old Gunpowder sprang upon the bridge; he thundered over the resounding planks; he gained the opposite side; and now Ichabod cast a look behind to see if his pursuer should vanish, according to rule, in a flash of fire and brimstone. Just then he saw the goblin rising in his stirrups, and in the very act of hurling his head at him. Ichabod endeavored to dodge the horrible missile, but too late. It encountered his cranium with a tremendous crash—he was tumbled headlong into the dust, and Gunpowder, the black steed, and the goblin rider, passed by like a whirlwind.

The next morning the old horse was found without his saddle, and with the bridle under his feet, soberly cropping the grass at his master's gate. Ichabod did not make his appearance at breakfast—dinner-hour came, but no Ichabod. The boys assembled at the school-house, and strolled idly about the banks of the brook; but no school-master. Hans Van Ripper now began to feel some uneasiness about the fate of poor Ichabod, and his saddle. An inquiry was set on foot, and after diligent investigation they came upon his traces. In one part of the road leading to the church was found the saddle trampled in the dirt; the tracks of horses' hoofs deeply dented in the road, and evidently at furious speed, were traced to the bridge, beyond which, on the bank of a broad part of the brook, where the water ran deep and black, was found the hat of the unfortunate Ichabod, and close beside it a shattered pumpkin.

The brook was searched, but the body of the schoolmaster was not to be discovered. Hans Van Ripper, as executor of his estate, examined the bundle which contained all his worldly effects. They consisted of two shirts and a half; two stocks for the neck; a pair or two of worsted stockings; an old pair of corduroy small-clothes; a rusty razor; a book of psalm tunes, full of dogs' ears; and a broken pitch-pipe. As to the books and furniture of the schoolhouse, they belonged to the community, excepting Cotton Mather's History of Witchcraft, a New England Almanac, and a book of dreams and fortune-telling; in which last was a sheet of foolscap much scribbled and blotted in several fruit-less attempts to make a copy of verses in honor of the heiress of Van Tassel. These magic books and the poetic scrawl were forthwith con-signed to the flames by Hans Van Ripper; who from that time forward determined to send his children no more to school; observing, that he never knew any good come of this same reading and writing. What-ever money the schoolmaster possessed, and he had received his quarter's pay but a day or two before, he must have had about his person at the time of his disappearance.

The mysterious event caused much speculation at the church on the following Sunday. Knots of gazers and gossips were collected in the church-yard, at the bridge, and at the spot where the hat and pumpkin had been found. The stories of Brouwer, of Bones, and a whole budget of others, were called to mind; and when they had diligently consid-ered them all, and compared them with the symptoms of the present case, they shook their heads, and came to the conclusion that Ichabod had been carried off by the Galloping Hessian. As he was a bachelor, and in nobody's debt, nobody troubled his head any more about him. The school was removed to a different quarter of the hollow, and another pedagogue reigned in his stead.

It is true, an old farmer, who had been down to New York on a visit several years after, and from whom this account of the ghostly adventure was received, brought home the intelligence that Ichabod Crane was still alive; that he had left the neighborhood, partly through fear of the goblin and Hans Van Ripper, and partly in mortification at having been suddenly dismissed by the heiress; that he had changed his quarters to a distant part of the country; had kept school and studied law at the same time, had been admitted to the bar, turned politician, electioneered, written for the newspapers, and finally had been made a justice of the Ten Pound Court. Brom Bones too, who, shortly after his rival's disappearance, conducted the blooming Katrina in triumph to the altar, was observed to look exceedingly knowing whenever the story of Ichabod was related, and always burst into a hearty laugh at the mention of the pumpkin; which led some to suspect that he knew more about the matter than he chose to tell.

The old country wives, however, who are the best judges of these matters, maintain to this day that Ichabod was spirited away by supernatural means; and it is a favorite story often told about the neighborhood round the winter evening fire. The bridge became more than ever an object of superstitious awe, and that may be the reason why the road has been altered of late years, so as to approach the church by the border of the mill-pond. The schoolhouse being deserted, soon fell to decay, and was reported to be haunted by the ghost of the unfortunate pedagogue; and the plough boy, loitering homeward of a still summer evening, has often fancied his voice at a distance, chanting a melancholy psalm tune among the tranquil solitudes of Sleepy Hollow.

# NATHANIEL HAWTHORNE
## The Man of Adamant

AN APOLOGUE

In the old times of religious gloom and intolerance, lived Richard Digby, the gloomiest and most intolerant of a stern brotherhood. His plan of salvation was so narrow, that, like a plank in a tempestuous sea, it could avail no sinner but himself, who bestrode it triumphantly, and hurled anathemas against the wretches whom he saw struggling with the billows of eternal death. In his view of the matter, it was a most abominable crime—as, indeed, it is a great folly—for men to trust to their own strength, or even to grapple to any other fragment of the wreck, save this narrow plank, which, moreover, he took special care to keep out of their reach. In other words, as his creed was like no man's else, and being well pleased that Providence had intrusted him alone, of mortals, with the treasure of a true faith, Richard Digby determined to seclude himself to the sole and constant enjoyment of his happy fortune.

"And verily," thought he, "I deem it a chief condition of Heaven's mercy to myself, that I hold no communion with those abominable myriads which it hath cast off to perish. Peradventure, were I to tarry longer in the tents of Kedar, the gracious boon would be revoked, and I also be swallowed up in the deluge of wrath, or consumed in the storm of fire and brimstone, or involved in whatever new kind of ruin is ordained for the horrible perversity of this generation."

So Richard Digby took an axe, to hew space enough for a tabernacle in the wilderness, and some few other necessaries, especially a sword and gun, to smite and slay any intruder upon his hallowed seclusion; and plunged into the dreariest depths of the forest. On its verge, however, he paused a moment, to shake off the dust of his feet against the village where he had dwelt, and to invoke a curse on the meeting-house, which he regarded as a temple of heathen idolatry. He felt a curiosity, also, to see whether the fire and brimstone would not rush down from Heaven at once, now that the one righteous man had provided for his own safety. But, as the sunshine continued to fall peacefully on the cottages and fields, and the husbandmen labored and children played, and as there were many tokens of present happiness, and nothing ominous of a speedy judgment, he turned away, somewhat disappointed. The further he went, however, and the lonelier he felt himself, and the thicker the trees stood along his path, and the darker the shadow overhead, so much the more did Richard Digby exult. He talked to himself, as he strode onward; he read his Bible to himself, as he sat beneath the trees; and, as the gloom of the forest hid the blessed sky, I had almost added, that, at morning, noon, and eventide, he prayed to himself. So congenial was this mode of life to his disposition, that he often laughed to himself, but was displeased when an echo tossed him back the long, loud roar.

In this manner, he journeyed onward three days and two nights, and came, on the third evening, to the mouth of a cave, which, at first sight, reminded him of Elijah's cave at Horeb, though perhaps it more resembled Abraham's sepulchral cave, at Machpelah. It entered into the heart of a rocky hill. There was so dense a veil of tangled foliage about it, that none but a sworn lover of gloomy recesses would have discovered the low arch of its entrance, or have dared to step within its vaulted chamber, where the burning eyes of a panther might encounter him. If Nature meant this remote and dismal cavern for the use of man, it could only be to bury in its gloom the victims of a pestilence, and then to block up its mouth with stones, and avoid the spot forever after. There was nothing bright nor cheerful near it, except a bubbling fountain, some twenty paces off, at which Richard Digby hardly threw away a glance. But he thrust his head into the cave, shivered, and congratulated himself.

"The finger of Providence hath pointed my way!" cried he, aloud, while the tomb-like den returned a strange echo, as if some one within were mocking him. "Here my soul will be at peace; for the wicked will not find me. Here I can read the Scriptures and be no more provoked with lying interpretations. Here I can offer up acceptable prayers because my voice will not be mingled with the sinful supplications of the multitude. Of a truth, the only way to heaven leadeth through the narrow entrance of this cave,—and I alone have found it!"

In regard to this cave, it was observable that the roof, so far as the imperfect light permitted it to be seen, was hung with substances resembling opaque icicles; for the damps of unknown centuries, dripping down continually, had become as hard as adamant; and wherever that moisture fell, it seemed to possess the power of converting what it bathed to stone. The fallen leaves and sprigs of foliage, which the wind had swept into the cave, and the little feathery shrubs, rooted near the threshold, were not wet with a natural dew, but had been embalmed by this wondrous process. And here I am put in mind that Richard Digby, before he withdrew himself from the world, was supposed by skilful physicians to have contracted a disease for which no remedy was written in their medical books. It was a deposition of calculous particles within his heart, caused by an obstructed circulation of the blood; and, unless a miracle should be wrought for him, there was danger that the malady might act on the entire substance of the organ, and change his fleshy heart to stone. Many, indeed, affirmed that the process was already near its consummation. Richard Digby, however, could never be convinced that any such direful work was going on within him; nor when he saw the sprigs of marble foliage, did his heart even throb the quicker, at the similitude suggested by these once tender herbs. It may be that this same insensibility was a symptom of the disease.

Be that as it might, Richard Digby was well contented with his sepulchral cave. So dearly did he love this congenial spot, that, instead of going a few paces to the bubbling spring for water, he allayed his thirst with now and then a drop of moisture from the roof, which, had it fallen anywhere but on his tongue, would have been congealed into a pebble. For a man predisposed to stoniness of the heart, this surely was unwholesome liquor. But there he dwelt, for three days more, eating herbs and roots, drinking his own destruction, sleeping, as it were, in a tomb, and awaking to the solitude of death, yet esteeming this horrible mode of life as hardly inferior to celestial bliss. Perhaps superior; for, above the sky, there would be angels to disturb him. At the close of the third day he sat in the portal of his mansion, reading the Bible aloud, because no other ear could profit by it, and reading it amiss, because the rays of the setting sun did not penetrate the dismal depth of shadow round about him, nor fall upon the sacred page. Suddenly, however, a faint gleam of light was thrown over the volume, and, raising his eyes, Richard Digby saw that a young woman stood before the mouth of the cave, and that the sunbeams bathed her white garment, which thus seemed to possess a radiance of its own.

"Good-evening, Richard," said the girl; "I have come from afar to find thee."

The slender grace and gentle loveliness of this young woman were at once recognized by Richard Digby. Her name was Mary Goffe. She had been a convert to his preaching of the word in England, before he yielded himself to that exclusive bigotry which now enfolded him with such an iron grasp that no other sentiment could reach his bosom. When he came a pilgrim to America, she had remained in her father's hall; but now, as it appeared, had crossed the ocean after him, impelled by the same faith that led other exiles hither, and perhaps by love almost as holy. What else but faith and love united could have sustained so delicate a creature, wandering thus far into the forest, with her golden hair dishevelled by the boughs, and her feet wounded by the thorns? Yet, weary and faint though she must have been, and affrighted at the dreariness of the cave, she looked on the lonely man with a mild and pitying expression, such as might beam from an angel's eyes, towards an afflicted mortal. But the recluse, frowning sternly upon her, and keeping his finger between the leaves of his half-closed Bible, motioned her away with his hand.

"Off!" cried he. "I am sanctified, and thou art sinful. Away!"

"O, Richard," said she, earnestly, "I have come this weary way because I heard that a grievous distemper had seized upon thy heart; and a great Physician hath given me the skill to cure it. There is no other remedy than this which I have brought thee. Turn me not away, therefore, nor refuse my medicine; for then must this dismal cave be thy sepulchre."

"Away!" replied Richard Digby, still with a dark frown. "My heart is in better condition than thine own. Leave me, earthly one; for the sun is almost set; and when no light reaches the door of the cave, then is my prayer-time."

Now, great as was her need, Mary Goffe did not plead with this stony-hearted man for shelter and protection, nor ask anything whatever for her own sake. All her zeal was for his welfare.

"Come back with me!" she exclaimed, clasping her hands,— "come back to thy fellow-men; for they need thee, Richard, and thou hast ten-fold need of them. Stay not in this evil den; for the air is chill, and the damps are fatal; nor will any that perish within it ever find the path to heaven. Hasten hence, I entreat thee, for thine own soul's sake;

for either the roof will fall upon thy head, or some other speedy destruction is at hand."

"Perverse woman!" answered Richard Digby, laughing aloud,— for he was moved to bitter mirth by her foolish vehemence,—"I tell thee that the path to heaven leadeth straight through this narrow portal where I sit. And, moreover, the destruction thou speakest of is ordained, not for this blessed cave, but for all other habitations of mankind, throughout the earth. Get thee hence speedily, that thou mayst have thy share!"

So saying, he opened his Bible again, and fixed his eyes intently on the page, being resolved to withdraw his thoughts from this child of sin and wrath, and to waste no more of his holy breath upon her. The shadow had now grown so deep, where he was sitting, that he made continual mistakes in what he read, converting all that was gracious and merciful to denunciations of vengeance and unutterable woe on every created being but himself. Mary Goffe, meanwhile, was leaning against a tree, beside the sepulchral cave, very sad, yet with something heavenly and ethereal in her unselfish sorrow. The light from the setting sun still glorified her form and was reflected a little way within the darksome den, discovering so terrible a gloom that the maiden shuddered for its self-doomed inhabitant. Espying the bright fountain near at hand, she hastened thither, and scooped up a portion of its water in a cup of birchen bark. A few tears mingled with the draught, and perhaps gave it all its efficacy. She then returned to the mouth of the cave, and knelt down at Richard Digby's feet.

"Richard," she said, with passionate fervor, yet a gentleness in all her passion, "I pray thee, by thy hope of heaven, and as thou wouldst not dwell in this tomb forever, drink of this hallowed water, be it but a single drop! Then, make room for me by thy side, and let us read together one page of that blessed volume,—and, lastly, kneel down with me and pray! Do this, and thy stony heart shall become softer than a babe's, and all be well."

But Richard Digby, in utter abhorrence of the proposal, cast the Bible at his feet, and eyed her with such a fixed and evil frown, that he looked less like a living man than a marble statue, wrought by some dark-imagined sculptor to express the most repulsive mood that human features could assume. And, as his look grew even devilish, so, with an equal change, did Mary Goffe become more sad, more mild, more pitiful, more like a sorrowing angel. But, the more heavenly she was, the more hateful did she seem to Richard Digby, who at length raised his hand, and smote down the cup of hallowed water upon the threshold of the cave, thus rejecting the only medicine that could have cured his stony heart. A sweet perfume lingered in the air for a moment, and then was gone.

"Tempt me no more, accursed woman," exclaimed he, still with his marble frown, "lest I smite thee down also! What hast thou to do with my prayers?—what with my heaven?"

No sooner had he spoken these dreadful words, than Richard Digby's heart ceased to beat; while—so the legend says—the form of Mary Goffe melted into the last sunbeams, and returned from the sepulchral cave to heaven. For Mary Goffe had been buried in an English church-yard, months before; and either it was her ghost that haunted the wild forest, or else a dreamlike spirit, typifying pure Religion.

Above a century afterwards, when the trackless forest of Richard Digby's day had long been interspersed with settlements, the children of a neighboring farmer were playing at the foot of a hill. The trees, on account of the rude and broken surface of this acclivity, had never been felled, and were crowded so densely together as to hide all but a few rocky prominences, wherever their roots could grapple with the soil. A little boy and girl, to conceal themselves from their playmates, had crept into the deepest shade, where not only the darksome pines, but a thick veil of creeping plants suspended from an overhanging rock, combined to make a twilight at noonday, and almost a midnight at all other seasons. There the children hid themselves, and shouted, repeating the cry at intervals, till the whole party of pursuers were drawn thither, and pulling aside the matted foliage, let in a doubtful glimpse of daylight. But scarcely was this accomplished, when the little group uttered a simultaneous shriek, and tumbled headlong down the hill, making the best of their way homeward, without a second glance into the gloomy recess. Their father, unable to comprehend what had so startled them, took his axe, and, by felling one or two trees, and tearing away the creeping plants, laid the mystery open to the day. He had discovered the entrance of a cave, closely resembling the mouth of a sepulchre, within which sat the figure of a man, whose gesture and attitude warned the father and children to stand back, while his visage wore a most forbidding frown. This repulsive personage seemed to have been carved in the same gray stone that formed the walls and portal of the cave. On minuter inspection, indeed, such blemishes were observed, as made it doubtful whether the figure were really a statue, chiselled by human art, and somewhat worn and defaced by the lapse of ages, or a freak of Nature, who might have chosen to imitate, in stone, her usual handiwork of flesh. Perhaps it was the least unreasonable idea, suggested by this strange spectacle, that the moisture of the cave possessed a petrifying quality, which had thus awfully embalmed a human corpse.

There was something so frightful in the aspect of this Man of Adamant, that the farmer, the moment that he recovered from the fascination of his first gaze, began to heap stones into the mouth of the cavern. His wife, who had followed him to the hill, assisted her husband's efforts. The children, also, approached as near as they durst, with their little hands full of pebbles, and cast them on the pile. Earth was then thrown into the crevices, and the whole fabric overlaid with sods. Thus all traces of the discovery were obliterated, leaving only a marvellous legend, which grew wilder from one generation to another, as the children told it to their grandchildren, and they to their posterity, till few believed that there had ever been a cavern or a statue, where now they saw but a grassy path on the shadowy hill-side. Yet, grown people avoid the spot, nor do children play there. Friendship, and Love, and Piety, all human and celestial sympathies, should keep aloof from that hidden cave; for there still sits, and, unless an earthquake crumble down the roof upon his head, shall sit forever, the shape of Richard Digby, in the attitude of repelling the whole race of mortals—not from heaven—but from the horrible loneliness of his dark, cold sepulchre!

# NATHANIEL HAWTHORNE
## Young Goodman Brown

Young Goodman Brown came forth at sunset into the street at Salem village; but put his head back, after crossing the threshold, to exchange a parting kiss with his young wife. And Faith, as the wife was aptly named, thrust her own pretty head into the street, letting the wind play with the pink ribbons of her cap while she called to Goodman Brown.

"Dearest heart," whispered she, softly and rather sadly, when her lips were close to his ear, "prithee put off your journey until sunrise and sleep in your own bed tonight. A lone woman is troubled with such dreams and such thoughts that she's afeard of herself sometimes. Pray tarry with me this night, dear husband, of all nights in the year."

"My love and my Faith," replied young Goodman Brown, "of all nights in the year, this one night must I tarry away from thee. My journey, as thou callest it, forth and back again, must needs be done 'twixt now and sunrise. What, my sweet, pretty wife, dost thou doubt me already, and we but three months married?"

"Then God bless you!" said Faith, with the pink ribbons, "and may you find all well when you come back."

"Amen!" cried Goodman Brown. "Say thy prayers, dear Faith, and go to bed at dusk, and no harm will come to thee."

So they parted; and the young man pursued his way until, being about to turn the corner by the meetinghouse, he looked back and saw the head of Faith still peeping after him with a melancholy air, in spite of her pink ribbons.

"Poor little Faith!" thought he, for his heart smote him. "What a wretch am I to leave her on such an errand! She talks of dreams, too. Methought as she spoke there was trouble in her face, as if a dream had warned her what work is to be done tonight. But no, no; 'twould kill her to think it. Well, she's a blessed angel on earth; and after this one night I'll cling to her skirts and follow her to heaven."

With this excellent resolve for the future, Goodman Brown felt himself justified in making more haste on his present evil purpose. He had taken a dreary road, darkened by all the gloomiest trees of the forest, which barely stood aside to let the narrow path creep through, and closed immediately behind. It was all as lonely as could be; and there is this peculiarity in such a solitude, that the traveler knows not who may be concealed by the innumerable trunks and the thick boughs overhead; so that with lonely footsteps he may yet be passing through an unseen multitude.

"There may be a devilish Indian behind every tree," said Goodman Brown to himself; and he glanced fearfully behind him as he added, "What if the devil himself should be at my very elbow!"

His head being turned back, he passed a crook of the road, and, looking forward again, beheld the figure of a man, in grave and decent attire, seated at the foot of an old tree. He arose at Goodman Brown's approach and walked onward side by side with him.

"You are late, Goodman Brown," said he. "The clock of the Old South was striking as I came through Boston, and that is full fifteen minutes agone."

"Faith kept me back awhile," replied the young man, with a tremor in his voice, caused by the sudden appearance of his companion, though not wholly unexpected.

It was now deep dusk in the forest, and deepest in that part of it where these two were journeying. As nearly as could be discerned, the second traveler was about fifty years old, apparently in the same rank of life as Goodman Brown, and bearing a considerable resemblance to him, though perhaps more in expression than features. Still they might have been taken for father and son. And yet, though the elder person was as simply clad as the younger, and as simple in manner, too, he had an indescribable air of one who knew the world, and who would not have felt abashed at the Governor's dinner table or in King William's court, were it possible that his affairs should call him thither. But the only thing about him that could be fixed upon as remarkable was his staff, which bore the likeness of a great black snake, so curiously wrought that it might almost be seen to twist and wriggle itself like a living serpent. This, of course, must have been an ocular deception, assisted by the uncertain light.

"Come, Goodman Brown," cried his fellow traveler, "this is a dull pace for the beginning of a journey. Take my staff, if you are so soon weary."

"Friend," said the other, exchanging his slow pace for a full stop, "having kept covenant by meeting thee here, it is my purpose now to return whence I came. I have scruples touching the matter thou wot'st of."

"Sayest thou so?" replied he of the serpent, smiling apart. "Let us walk on, nevertheless, reasoning as we go; and if I convince thee not, thou shalt turn back. We are but a little way in the forest yet."

"Too far! too far!" exclaimed the goodman, unconsciously resuming his walk. "My father never went into the woods on such an errand, nor his father before him. We have been a race of honest men and good Christians since the days of the martyrs; and shall I be the first of the name of Brown that ever took this path and kept—"

"Such company, thou wouldst say," observed the elder person, interpreting his pause. "Well said, Goodman Brown! I have been as well acquainted with your family as with ever a one among the Puritans; and that's no trifle to say. I helped your grandfather, the constable, when he lashed the Quaker woman so smartly through the streets of Salem; and it was I that brought your father a pitch-pine knot, kindled at my own hearth, to set fire to an Indian village, in King Philip's war. They were my good friends, both; and many a pleasant walk have we had along this path, and returned merrily after midnight. I would fain be friends with you for their sake."

"If it be as thou sayest," replied Goodman Brown, "I marvel they never spoke of these matters; or, verily, I marvel not, seeing that the least rumor of the sort would have driven them from New England. We are a people of prayer, and good works to boot, and abide no such wickedness."

"Wickedness or not," said the traveler with the twisted staff, "I have a very general acquaintance here in New England. The deacons of many a church have drunk the communion wine with me; the selectmen of divers towns make me their chairman; and a majority of the Great and General Court are firm supporters of my interest. The Governor and I, too— But these are state secrets."

"Can this be so?" cried Goodman Brown, with a stare of amazement at his undisturbed companion. "Howbeit, I have nothing to do with the Governor and council; they have their own ways, and are no rule for a simple husbandman like me. But, were I to go on with thee, how should I meet the eye of that good old man, our minister, at Salem village? Oh, his voice would make me tremble both Sabbath day and lecture day."

Thus far the elder traveler had listened with due gravity; but now burst into a fit of irrepressible mirth, shaking himself so violently that his snakelike staff actually seemed to wriggle in sympathy.

"Ha! ha! ha!" shouted he again and again; then composing himself, "Well, go on, Goodman Brown, go on; but, prithee, don't kill me with laughing."

"Well, then, to end the matter at once," said Goodman Brown, considerably nettled, "there is my wife, Faith. It would break her dear little heart; and I'd rather break my own."

"Nay, if that be the case," answered the other, "e'en go thy ways, Goodman Brown. I would not for twenty old women like the one hobbling before us that Faith should come to any harm."

As he spoke, he pointed his staff at a female figure on the path, in whom Goodman Brown recognized a very pious and exemplary dame, who had taught him his catechism in youth, and was still his moral and spiritual adviser, jointly with the minister and Deacon Gookin.

"A marvel, truly, that Goody Cloyse should be so far in the wilderness at nightfall," said he. "But with your leave, friend, I shall take a cut through the woods until we have left this Christian woman behind. Being a stranger to you, she might ask whom I was consorting with and whither I was going."

"Be it so," said his fellow traveler. "Betake you to the woods, and let me keep the path."

Accordingly the young man turned aside, but took care to watch his companion, who advanced softly along the road until he had come within a staff's length of the old dame. She, meanwhile, was making the best of her way, with singular speed for so aged a woman, and mumbling some indistinct words—a prayer, doubtless—as she went. The traveler put forth his staff and touched her withered neck with what seemed the serpent's tail.

"The devil!" screamed the pious old lady.

"Then Goody Cloyse knows her old friend?" observed the traveler, confronting her and leaning on his writhing stick.

"Ah, forsooth, and is it your worship indeed?" cried the good dame. "Yea, truly is it, and in the very image of my old gossip Goodman Brown, the grandfather of the silly fellow that now is. But— would your worship believe it?—my broomstick hath strangely disappeared, stolen, as I suspect, by that unhanged witch, Goody Cory, and that, too, when I was all anointed with the juice of smallage, and cinquefoil, and wolfsbane—"

"Mingled with fine wheat and the fat of a newborn babe," said the shape of old Goodman Brown.

"Ah, your worship knows the recipe," cried the old lady, cackling aloud. "So, as I was saying, being all ready for the meeting, and no horse to ride on, I made up my mind to foot it; for they tell me there is a nice young man to be taken into communion tonight. But now your good worship will lend me your arm, and we shall be there in a twinkling."

"That can hardly be," answered her friend. "I may not spare you my arm, Goody Cloyse; but here is my staff, if you will."

So saying, he threw it down at her feet, where, perhaps, it assumed life, being one of the rods which its owner had formerly lent to the Egyptian magi. Of this fact, however, Goodman Brown could not take cognizance. He had cast up his eyes in astonishment, and, looking down again, beheld neither Goody Cloyse nor the serpentine staff, but his fellow traveler alone, who waited for him as calmly as if nothing had happened.

"That old woman taught me my catechism," said the young man; and there was a world of meaning in this simple comment.

They continued to walk onward, while the elder traveler exhorted his companion to make good speed and persevere in the path, discoursing so aptly that his arguments seemed rather to spring up in the bosom of his auditor than to be suggested by himself. As they went, he plucked a branch of maple to serve for a walking stick, and began to strip it of the twigs and little boughs, which were wet with evening dew. The moment his fingers touched them, they became strangely withered and dried up as with a week's sunshine. Thus the pair proceeded, at a good free pace, until suddenly, in a gloomy hollow of the road, Goodman Brown sat himself down on the stump of a tree and refused to go any farther.

"Friend," said he, stubbornly, "my mind is made up. Not another step will I budge on this errand. What if a wretched old woman do choose to go to the devil when I thought she was going to heaven: is that any reason why I should quit my dear Faith and go after her?"

"You will think better of this by and by," said his acquaintance, composedly. "Sit here and rest yourself awhile; and when you feel like moving again, there is my staff to help you along."

Without more words, he threw his companion the maple stick, and was as speedily out of sight as if he had vanished into the deepening gloom. The young man sat a few moments by the roadside, applauding himself greatly, and thinking with how clear a conscience he should meet the minister in his morning walk, nor shrink from the eye of good old Deacon Gookin. And what calm sleep would be his that very night, which was to have been spent so wickedly, but so purely and sweetly now, in the arms of Faith! Amidst these pleasant and praise-worthy meditations, Goodman Brown heard the tramp of horses along the road, and deemed it advisable to conceal himself within the verge of the forest, conscious of the guilty purpose that had brought him thither, though now so happily turned from it.

On came the hoof tramps and the voices of the riders, two grave old voices, conversing soberly as they drew near. These mingled sounds appeared to pass along the road, within a few yards of the young man's hiding place; but, owing doubtless to the depth of the gloom at that particular spot, neither the travelers nor their steeds were visible. Though their figures brushed the small boughs by the wayside, it could not be seen that they intercepted, even for a moment, the faint gleam from the strip of bright sky athwart which they must have passed. Goodman Brown alternately crouched and stood on tiptoe, pulling aside the branches and thrusting forth his head as far as he durst without discerning so much as a shadow. It vexed him the more, because he could have sworn, were such a thing possible, that he recognized the voices of the minister and Deacon Gookin, jogging along quietly, as they were wont to do, when bound to some ordination or ecclesiastical council. While yet within hearing, one of the riders stopped to pluck a switch.

"Of the two, reverend sir," said the voice like the deacon's, "I had rather miss an ordination dinner than tonight's meeting. They tell me that some of our community are to be here from Falmouth and beyond, and others from Connecticut and Rhode Island, besides several of the Indian powwows, who, after their fashion, know almost as much deviltry as the best of us. Moreover, there is a goodly young woman to be taken into communion."

"Mighty well, Deacon Gookin!" replied the solemn old tones of the minister. "Spur up, or we shall be late. Nothing can be done, you know, until I get on the ground."

The hoofs clattered again; and the voices, talking so strangely in the empty air, passed on through the forest, where no church had ever been gathered or solitary Christian prayed. Whither, then, could these holy men be journeying so deep into the heathen wilderness? Young Goodman Brown caught hold of a tree for support, being ready to sink down on the ground, faint and overburdened with the heavy sickness of his heart. He looked up to the sky, doubting whether there really was a heaven above him. Yet there was the blue arch, and the stars brightening in it.

"With heaven above and Faith below, I will yet stand firm against the devil!" cried Goodman Brown.

While he still gazed upward into the deep arch of the firmament and had lifted his hands to pray, a cloud, though no wind was stirring, hurried across the zenith and hid the brightening stars. The blue sky was still visible, except directly overhead, where this black mass of cloud was sweeping swiftly northward. Aloft in the air, as if from the depths of the cloud, came a confused and doubtful sound of voices. Once the listener fancied that he could distinguish the accents of townspeople of his own, men and women, both pious and ungodly, many of whom he had met at the communion table, and had seen others rioting at the tavern. The next moment, so indistinct were the sounds, he doubted whether he had heard aught but the murmur of the old forest, whispering without a wind. Then came a stronger swell of those familiar tones, heard daily in the sunshine at Salem village, but never until now from a cloud of night. There was one voice, of a young woman, uttering lamentations, yet with an uncertain sorrow, and entreating for some favor, which, perhaps, it would grieve her to obtain; and all the unseen multitude, both saints and sinners, seemed to encourage her onward.

"Faith!" shouted Goodman Brown, in a voice of agony and desperation; and the echoes of the forest mocked him, crying, "Faith! Faith!" as if bewildered wretches were seeking her all through the wilderness.

The cry of grief, rage, and terror was yet piercing the night, when the unhappy husband held his breath for a response. There was a scream, drowned immediately in a louder murmur of voices, fading into far-off laughter, as the dark cloud swept away, leaving the clear and silent sky above Goodman Brown. But something fluttered lightly down through the air and caught on the branch of a tree. The young man seized it, and beheld a pink ribbon.

"My Faith is gone!" cried he, after one stupefied moment. "There is no good on earth; and sin is but a name. Come, devil; for to thee is this world given."

And, maddened with despair, so that he laughed loud and long, did Goodman Brown grasp his staff and set forth again, at such a rate that he seemed to fly along the forest path rather than to walk or run. The road grew wilder and drearier and more faintly traced, and vanished at length, leaving him in the heart of the dark wilderness, still rushing onward with the instinct that guides mortal man to evil. The whole forest was peopled with frightful sounds the creaking of the trees, the howling of wild beasts, and the yell of Indians; while sometimes the wind tolled like a distant church bell, and sometimes gave a broad roar around the traveler, as if all Nature were laughing him to scorn. But he was himself the chief horror of the scene, and shrank not from its other horrors.

"Ha! ha! ha!" roared Goodman Brown when the wind laughed at him. "Let us hear which will laugh loudest. Think not to frighten me with your deviltry. Come witch, come wizard, come Indian powwow, come devil himself, and here comes Goodman Brown. You may as well fear him as he fear you."

In truth, all through the haunted forest there could be nothing more frightful than the figure of Goodman Brown. On he flew among the black pines, brandishing his staff with frenzied gestures, now giving vent to an inspiration of horrid blasphemy, and now shouting forth such laughter as set all the echoes of the forest laughing like demons around him. The fiend in his own shape is less hideous than when he rages in the breast of man. Thus sped the demoniac on his course, until, quivering among the trees, he saw a red light before him, as when the felled trunks and branches of a clearing have been set on fire, and throw up their lurid blaze against the sky, at the hour of midnight. He paused, in a lull of the tempest that had driven him onward, and heard the swell of what seemed a hymn, rolling solemnly from a distance with the weight of many voices. He knew the tune; it was a familiar one in the choir of the village meetinghouse. The verse died heavily away, and was lengthened by a chorus, not of human voices, but of all the sounds of the benighted wilderness pealing in awful harmony together. Goodman Brown cried out, and his cry was lost to his own ear by its unison with the cry of the desert.

In the interval of silence, he stole forward until the light glared full upon his eyes. At one extremity of an open space, hemmed in by the dark wall of the forest, arose a rock, bearing some rude, natural resemblance either to an altar or a pulpit, and surrounded by four blazing pines, their tops aflame, their stems untouched, like candles at an evening meeting. The mass of foliage that had overgrown the summit of the rock was all on fire, blazing high into the night and fitfully illuminating the whole field. Each pendent twig and leafy festoon was in a blaze. As the red light arose and fell, a numerous congregation alternately shone forth, then disappeared in shadow, and again grew, as it were, out of the darkness, peopling the heart of the solitary woods at once.

"A grave and dark-clad company," quoth Goodman Brown.

In truth they were such. Among them, quivering to and fro between gloom and splendor, appeared faces that would be seen next day at the council board of the province, and others which, Sabbath after Sabbath, looked devoutly heavenward, and benignantly over the crowded pews, from the holiest pulpits in the land. Some affirm that the lady of the Governor was there. At least, there were high dames well known to her, and wives of honored husbands, and widows, a great multitude, and ancient maidens, all of excellent repute, and fair young girls, who trembled lest their mothers should espy them. Either the sudden gleams of light flashing over the obscure field bedazzled Goodman Brown, or he recognized a score of the church members of Salem village famous for their especial sanctity. Good old Deacon Gookin had arrived, and waited at the skirts of that venerable saint, his revered pastor. But, irreverently consorting with these grave, reputable, and pious people, these elders of the church, these chaste dames and dewy virgins, there were men of dissolute lives and women of spotted fame, wretches given over to all mean and filthy vice, and suspected even of horrid crimes. It was strange to see that the good shrank not from the wicked, nor were the sinners abashed by the saints. Scattered also among their pale-faced enemies were the Indian priests, or pow-wows, who had often scared their native forest with more hideous incantations than any known to English witchcraft.

"But where is Faith?" thought Goodman Brown; and, as hope came into his heart, he trembled.

Another verse of the hymn arose, a slow and mournful strain, such as the pious love, but joined to words which expressed all that our nature can conceive of sin, and darkly hinted at far more. Unfathomable to mere mortals is the lore of fiends. Verse after verse was sung; and still the chorus of the desert swelled between like the deepest tone of a mighty organ; and with the final peal of that dreadful anthem there came a sound, as if the roaring wind, the rushing streams, the howling beasts, and every other voice of the unconcerted wilderness were mingling and according with the voice of guilty man in homage to the prince of all. The four blazing pines threw up a loftier flame, and obscurely discovered shapes and visages of horror on the smoke wreaths above the impious assembly. At the same moment, the fire on the rock shot redly forth and formed a glowing arch above its base, where now appeared a figure. With reverence be it spoken, the figure bore no slight similitude, both in garb and manner, to some grave divine of the New England churches.

"Bring forth the converts!" cried a voice that echoed through the field and rolled into the forest.

At the word, Goodman Brown stepped forth from the shadow of the trees and approached the congregation, with whom he felt a loathful brotherhood by the sympathy of all that was wicked in his heart. He could have well-nigh sworn that the shape of his own dead father beckoned him to advance, looking downward from a smoke wreath, while a woman, with dim features of despair, threw out her hand to warn him back. Was it his mother? But he had no power to retreat one step, nor to resist, even in thought, when the minister and good old Deacon Gookin seized his arms and led him to the blazing rock. Thither came also the slender form of a veiled female, led between Goody Cloyse, that pious teacher of the catechism, and Martha Carrier, who had received the devil's promise to be queen of hell. A rampant hag was she. And there stood the proselytes beneath the canopy of fire.

"Welcome, my children," said the dark figure, "to the communion of your race. Ye have found thus young your nature and your destiny. My children, look behind you!"

They turned; and flashing forth, as it were, in a sheet of flame, the fiend-worshipers were seen; the smile of welcome gleamed darkly on every visage.

"There," resumed the sable form, "are all whom ye have reverenced from youth. Ye deemed them holier than yourselves, and shrank from your own sin, contrasting it with their lives of righteousness and prayerful aspirations heavenward. Yet here are they all in my worshiping assembly. This night it shall be granted you to know their secret deeds: how hoary-bearded elders of the church have whispered wanton words to the young maids of their households; how many a woman, eager for widows' weeds, has given her husband a drink at bedtime and let him sleep his last sleep in her bosom; how beardless youths have made haste to inherit their fathers' wealth; and how fair damsels—blush not, sweet ones—have dug little graves in the garden, and bidden me, the sole guest, to an infant's funeral. By the sympathy of your human hearts for sin ye shall scent out all the places—whether in church, bedchamber, street, field, or forest—where crime has been committed, and shall exult to behold the whole earth one stain of guilt, one mighty blood spot. Far more than this. It shall be yours to penetrate, in every bosom, the deep mystery of sin, the fountain of all wicked arts, and which inexhaustibly supplies more evil impulses than human power—than my power at its utmost—can make manifest in deeds. And now, my children, look upon each other."

They did so; and, by the blaze of the hell-kindled torches, the wretched man beheld his Faith, and the wife her husband, trembling before that unhallowed altar.

"Lo, there ye stand, my children," said the figure, in a deep and solemn tone, almost sad with its despairing awfulness, as if his once angelic nature could yet mourn for our miserable race. "Depending upon one another's hearts, ye had still hoped that virtue were not all a dream. Now are ye undeceived. Evil is the nature of mankind. Evil must be your only happiness. Welcome again, my children, to the communion of your race."

"Welcome," repeated the fiend-worshipers, in one cry of despair and triumph.

And there they stood, the only pair, as it seemed, who were yet hesitating on the verge of wickedness in this dark world. A basin was hollowed, naturally, in the rock. Did it contain water, reddened by the lurid light? or was it blood? or, perchance, a liquid flame? Herein did the shape of evil dip his hand and prepare to lay the mark of baptism upon their foreheads, that they might be partakers of the mystery of sin, more conscious of the secret guilt of others, both in deed and thought, than they could now be of their own. The husband cast one look at his pale wife, and Faith at him. What polluted wretches would the next glance show them to each other, shuddering alike at what they disclosed and what they saw!

"Faith! Faith!" cried the husband, "look up to heaven, and resist the wicked one."

Whether Faith obeyed he knew not. Hardly had he spoken when he found himself amid calm night and solitude, listening to a roar of the wind which died heavily away through the forest. He staggered against the rock, and felt it chill and damp; while a hanging twig, that had been all on fire, besprinkled his cheek with the coldest dew.

The next morning, young Goodman Brown came slowly into the street of Salem village, staring around him like a bewildered man. The good old minister was taking a walk along the graveyard to get an appetite for breakfast and meditate his sermon, and bestowed a blessing, as he passed, on Goodman Brown. He shrank from the venerable saint as if to avoid an anathema. Old Deacon Gookin was at domestic worship, and the holy words of his prayer were heard through the open window. "What God doth the wizard pray to?" quoth Goodman Brown. Goody Cloyse, that excellent old Christian, stood in the early sunshine at her own lattice, catechizing a little girl who had brought her a pint of morning's milk. Goodman Brown snatched away the child as from the grasp of the fiend himself. Turning the corner by the meetinghouse, he spied the head of Faith, with the pink ribbons, gazing anxiously forth, and bursting into such joy at sight of him that she skipped along the street and almost kissed her husband before the whole village. But Goodman Brown looked sternly and sadly into her face, and passed on without a greeting.

Had Goodman Brown fallen asleep in the forest and only dreamed a wild dream of a witch meeting?

Be it so if you will; but, alas! it was a dream of evil omen for young Goodman Brown. A stern, a sad, a darkly meditative, a distrustful, if not a desperate man did he become from the night of that fearful dream. On the Sabbath day, when the congregation were singing a holy psalm, he could not listen because an anthem of sin rushed loudly upon his ear and drowned all the blessed strain. When the minister spoke from the pulpit with power and fervid eloquence, and, with his hand on the open Bible, of the sacred truths of our religion, and of saintlike lives and triumphant deaths, and of future bliss or misery unutterable, then did Goodman Brown turn pale, dreading lest the roof should thunder down upon the gray blasphemer and his hearers. Often, awaking suddenly at midnight, he shrank from the bosom of Faith; and at morning or eventide, when the family knelt down at prayer, he scowled and muttered to himself, and gazed sternly at his wife, and turned away. And when he had lived long, and was borne to his grave a hoary corpse, followed by Faith, an aged woman, and children and grandchildren, a goodly procession, besides neighbors not a few, they carved no hopeful verse upon his tombstone, for his dying hour was gloom.

# HERMAN MELVILLE
## The Tartarus of Maids

It lies not far from Woedolor Mountain in New England. Turning to the east, right out from among bright farms and sunny meadows, nodding in early June with odorous grasses, you enter ascendingly among bleak hills. These gradually close in upon a dusky pass, which, from the violent Gulf Stream of air unceasingly diving between its cloven walls of haggard rock, as well as from the tradition of a crazy spinster's hut having long ago stood somewhere here-abouts, is called the Mad Maid's Bellows'-pipe.

Winding along at the bottom of the gorge is a dangerously narrow wheel-road, occupying the bed of a former torrent. Following this road to its highest point, you stand as within a Dantean gateway. From the steepness of the walls here, their strangely ebon hue, and the sudden contraction of the gorge, this particular point is called the Black Notch. The ravine now expandingly descends into a great, purple, hopper-shapped hollow, far sunk among many Plutonian, shaggy-wooded mountains. By the country people this hollow is called the Devil's Dungeon. Sounds of torrents fall on all sides upon the ear. These rapid waters unite at last in one turbid brick-colored stream, boiling through a flume among enormous boulders. They call this strange-colored torrent Blood River. Gaining a dark precipice it wheels suddenly to the west, and makes one maniac spring of sixty feet into the arms of a stunted wood of gray-haired pines, between which it thence eddies on its further way down to the invisible lowlands.

Conspicuously crowning a rocky bluff high to one side, at the cataract's verge, is the ruin of an old saw-mill, built in those primitive times when vast pines and hemlocks superabounded throughout the neighboring region. The black-mossed bulk of those immense, rough-hewn, and spike-knotted logs, here and there tumbled all together, in long abandonment and decay, or left in solitary, perilous projection over the cataract's gloomy brink, impart to this rude wooden ruin not only much of the aspect of one of rough-quarried stone, but also a sort of feudal, Rhineland, and Thurmberg look, derived from the pinnacled wildness of the neighboring scenery.

Not far from the bottom of the Dungeon stands a large white-washed building, relieved, like some great whited sepulchre, against the sullen background of mountain-side firs, and other hardy evergreens, inaccessibly rising in grim terraces for some two thousand feet.

The building is a paper-mill.

Having embarked on a large scale in the seedsman's business (so extensively and broadcast, indeed, that at length my seeds were distributed through all the Eastern and Northern States, and even fell into the far soil of Missouri and the Carolinas), the demand for paper at my place became so great, that the expenditure soon amounted to a most important item in the general account. It need hardly be hinted how paper comes into use with seedsmen, as envelopes. These are mostly made of yellowish paper, folded square; and when filled, are all but flat, and being stamped, and superscribed with the nature of the seeds contained, assume not a little the appearance of business-letters ready for the mail. Of these small envelopes I used an incredible quantity— several hundreds of thousands in a year. For a time I had purchased my paper from the whole-sale dealers in a neighboring town. For economy's sake, and partly for the adventure of the trip, I now resolved to cross the mountains, some sixty miles, and order my future paper at the Devil's Dungeon paper-mill.

The sleighing being uncommonly fine toward the end of January, and promising to hold so for no small period, in spite of the bitter cold I started one gray Friday noon in my pung, well fitted with buffalo and wolf robes; and, spending one night on the road, next noon came in sight of Woedolor Mountain.

The far summit fairly smoked with frost; white vapors curled up from its white-wooded top, as from a chimney. The intense congelation made the whole country look like one petrifaction. The steel shoes of my pung craunched and gritted over the vitreous, chippy snow, as if it had been broken glass. The forests here and there skirting the route, feeling the same all-stiffening influence, their inmost fibres penetrated with the cold, strangely groaned—not in the swaying branches merely, but likewise in the vertical trunk—as the fitful gusts remorselessly swept through them. Brittle with excessive frost, many colossal tough-grained maples, snapped in twain like pipe-stems, cumbered the unfeeling earth.

Flaked all over with frozen sweat, white as a milky ram, his nostrils at each breath sending forth two horn-shaped shoots of heated respiration, Black, my good horse, but six years old, started at a sudden turn, where, right across the track—not ten minutes fallen—an old distorted hemlock lay, darkly undulatory as an anaconda.

Gaining the Bellows'-pipe, the violent blast, dead from behind, all but shoved my high-backed pung up-hill. The gust shrieked through the shivered pass, as if laden with lost spirits bound to the unhappy world. Ere gaining the summit, Black, my horse, as if exasperated by the cutting wind, slung out with his strong hind legs, tore the light pung straight up-hill, and sweeping grazingly through the narrow notch, sped downward madly past the ruined saw-mill. Into the Devil's Dungeon horse and cataract rushed together.

With might and main, quitting my seat and robes, and standing backward, with one foot braced against the dash-board, I rasped and churned the bit, and stopped him just in time to avoid collision, at a turn, with the bleak nozzle of a rock, couchant like a lion in the way—a road-side rock.

At first I could not discover the paper-mill.

The whole hollow gleamed with the white, except, here and there, where a pinnacle of granite showed one wind-swept angle bare. The mountains stood pinned in shrouds—a pass of Alpine corpses. Where stands the mill? Suddenly a whirling, humming sound broke upon my ear. I looked, and there, like an arrested avalanche, lay the large whitewashed factory. It was subordinately surrounded by a cluster of other and smaller buildings, some of which, from their cheap, blank air, great length, gregarious windows, and comfortless expression, no doubt were boarding-houses of the operatives. A snow-white hamlet amidst the snows. Various rude, irregular squares and courts resulted from the somewhat picturesque clusterings of these buildings, owing to the broken, rocky nature of the ground, which forbade all method in their relative arrangement. Several narrow lanes and alleys, too, partly blocked with snow fallen from the roof, cut up the hamlet in all directions.

When, turning from the traveled highway, jingling with bells of numerous farmers—who, availing themselves of the fine sleighing, were dragging their wood to market—and frequently diversified with swift cutters dashing from inn to inn of the scattered villages—when, I say, turning from that bustling main-road, I by degrees wound into the Mad Maid's Bellows'-pipe, and saw the grim Black Notch beyond, then something latent, as well as something obvious in the time and scene, strangely brought back to my mind my first sight of dark and grimy Temple-Bar. And when Black, my horse, went darting through the Notch, perilously grazing its rocky wall, I remembered being in a runaway London omnibus, which in much the same sort of style, though by no means at an equal rate, dashed through the ancient arch of Wren. Though the two objects did by no means completely correspond, yet this partial inadequacy but served to tinge the similitude not less with the vividness than the disorder of a dream. So that, when upon reining up at the protruding rock I at last caught sight of the quaint groupings of the factory-buildings, and with the traveled highway and the Notch behind, found myself all alone, silently and privily stealing through deep-cloven passages into this sequestered spot, and saw the long, high-gabled main factory edifice, with a rude tower—for hoisting heavy boxes—at one end, standing among its crowded outbuildings and boarding-houses, as the Temple Church amidst the surrounding offices and dormitories, and when the marvelous retirement of this mysterious mountain nook fastened its whole spell upon me, then, what memory lacked, all tributary imagination furnished, and I said to myself, "This is the very counterpart of the Paradise of Bachelors, but snowed upon, and frost-painted to a sepulchre."

Dismounting, and warily picking my way down the dangerous declivity—horse and man both sliding now and then upon the icy ledges—at length I drove, or the blast drove me, into the largest square, before one side of the main edifice. Piercingly and shrilly the shotted blast blew by the corner; and redly and demoniacally boiled Blood River at one side. A long woodpile, of many scores of cords, all glittering in mail of crusted ice, stood crosswise in the square. A row of horse-posts, their north sides plastered with adhesive snow, flanked the factory wall. The bleak frost packed and paved the square as with some ringing metal.

The inverted similitude recurred—"The sweet, tranquil Temple-garden, with the Thames bordering its green beds," strangely meditated I.

But where are the gay bachelors?

Then, as I and my horse stood shivering in the wind-spray, a girl ran from a neighboring dormitory door, and throwing her thin apron over her bare head, made for the opposite building.

"One moment, my girl; is there no shed here-abouts which I may drive into?"

Pausing, she turned upon me a face pale with work, and blue with cold; an eye supernatural with unrelated misery.

"Nay," faltered I, "I mistook you. Go on; I want nothing."

Leading my horse close to the door from which she had come, I knocked. Another pale, blue girl appeared, shivering in the doorway as, to prevent the blast, she jealously held the door ajar.

"Nay, I mistake again. In God's name shut the door. But hold, is there no man about?"

That moment a dark-complexioned well-wrapped personage passed, making for the factory door, and spying him coming, the girl rapidly closed the other one.

"Is there no horse-shed here, Sir?"

"Yonder, to the wood-shed," he replied, and disappeared inside the factory.

With much ado I managed to wedge in horse and pung between the scattered piles of wood all sawn and split. Then, blanketing my horse, and piling my buffalo on the blanket's top, tucking in its edges well around the breast-band and breeching, so that the wind might not strip him bare, I tied him fast, and ran lamely for the factory door, stiff with frost, and cumbered with my driver's dread-naught.

Immediately I found myself standing in a spacious place, intolerably lighted by long rows of windows, focusing inward the snowy scene without.

At rows of blank-looking counters sat rows of blank-looking girls, with blank, white folders in the blank hands, all blankly folding blank paper.

In one corner stood some huge frame of ponderous iron, with a vertical thing like a piston periodically rising and falling upon a heavy wooden block. Before it—its tame minister—stood a tall girl, feeding the iron animal with half-quires of rose-hued note paper, which, at every downward dab of the piston-like machine, received in the corner the impress of a wreath of roses. I looked from the rosy paper to the pallid cheek, but said nothing.

Seated before a long apparatus, strung with long, slender strings like any harp, another girl was feeding it with foolscap sheets, which, so soon as they curiously traveled from her on the cords, were withdrawn at the opposite end of the machine by a second girl. They came to the first girl blank; they went to the second girl ruled.

I looked upon the first girl's brow, and saw it was young and fair; I looked upon the second girl's brow, and saw it was ruled and wrinkled. Then, as I still looked, the two—for some small variety to the monotony—changed places; and where had stood the young, fair brow, now stood the ruled and wrinkled one.

Perched high upon a narrow platform, and still higher upon a high stool crowning it, sat another figure serving some other iron animal; while below the platform sat her mate in some sort of reciprocal attendance.

Not a syllable was breathed. Nothing was heard but the low, steady, overruling hum of the iron animals. The human voice was banished from the spot. Machinery—that vaunted slave of humanity—here stood menially served by human beings, who served mutely and cringingly as the slave serves the Sultan. The girls did not so much seem accessory wheels to the general machinery as mere cogs to the wheels.

All this scene around me was instantaneously taken in at one sweeping glance—even before I had proceeded to unwind the heavy fur tippet from around my neck. But as soon as this fell from me the dark-complexioned man, standing close by, raised a sudden cry, and seizing my arm, dragged me out into the open air, and without pausing for a word instantly caught up some congealed snow and began rubbing both my cheeks.

"Two white spots like the whites of your eyes," he said; "man, your cheeks are frozen."

"That may well be," muttered I, " 'tis some wonder the frost of the Devil's Dungeon strikes in no deeper. Rub away."

Soon a horrible, tearing pain caught at my reviving cheeks. Two gaunt blood-hounds, one on each side, seemed mumbling them. I seemed Actæon.

Presently, when all was over, I re-entered the factory, made known my business, concluded it satisfactorily, and then begged to be conducted throughout the place to view it.

"Cupid is the boy for that," said the dark-complexioned man. "Cupid!" and by this odd fancy-name calling a dimpled, red-cheeked, spirited-looking, forward little fellow, who was rather impudently, I thought, gliding about among the passive-looking girls—like a gold fish through hueless waves—yet doing nothing in particular that I could see, the man bade him lead the stranger through the edifice.

"Come first and see the water-wheel," said this lively lad, with the air of boyishly-brisk importance.

Quitting the folding-room, we crossed some damp, cold boards, and stood beneath a great wet shed, incessantly showering with foam, like the green barnacled bow of some East India-man in a gale. Round and round here went the enormous revolutions of the dark colossal water-wheel, grim with its one immutable purpose.

"This sets our whole machinery a-going, Sir; in every part of all these buildings; where the girls work and all."

I looked, and saw that the turbid waters of Blood River had not changed their hue by coming under the use of man.

"You make only blank paper; no printing of any sort, I suppose? All blank paper, don't you?"

"Certainly; what else should a paper-factory make?"

The lad here looked at me as if suspicious of my common-sense.

"Oh, to be sure!" said I, confused and stammering; "it only struck me as so strange that red waters should turn out pale chee—paper, I mean."

He took me up a wet and rickety stair to a great light room, furnished with no visible thing but rude, manger-like receptacles running all round its side; and up to these mangers, like so many mares haltered to the rack, stood rows of girls. Before each was vertically thrust up a long, glittering scythe, immovably fixed at bottom to the manger-edge. The curve of the scythe, and its having no snath to it, made it look exactly like a sword. To and fro, across the sharp edge, the girls forever dragged long strips of rags, washed white, picked from baskets at one side; thus ripping asunder every seam and converting the tatters almost into lint. The air swam with the fine, poisonous particles, which from all sides darted, subtilely, as motes in sunbeams, into the lungs.

"This is the rag-room," coughed the boy.

"You find it rather stifling here," coughed I, in answer; "but the girls don't cough."

"Oh, they are used to it."

"Where do you get such hosts of rags?" picking up a handful from a basket.

"Some from the country round about; some from far over sea— Leghorn and London."

" 'Tis not unlikely, then," murmured I, "that among these heaps of rags there may be some old shirts, gathered from the dormitories of the Paradise of Bachelors. But the buttons are all dropped off. Pray, my lad, do you ever find any bachelor's buttons here-abouts?"

"None grow in this part of the country. The Devil's Dungeon is no place for flowers."

"Oh! you mean the *flowers* so called—the Bachelor's Buttons?"

"And was not that what you asked about? Or did you mean the gold bosom-buttons of our boss, Old Bach, as our whispering girls all call him?"

"The man, then, I saw below is a bachelor, is he?"

"Oh, yes, he's a Bach."

"The edges of those swords, they are turned outward from the girls, if I see right; but their rags and fingers fly so, I can not distinctly see."

"Turned outward."

Yes, murmured I to myself; I see it now, turned outward; and each erected sword is so borne, edge-outward, before each girl. If my reading fails me not, just so, of old, condemned state-prisoners went from the hall of judgment to their doom: an officer before, bearing a sword, its edge turned outward, in significance of their fatal sentence. So, through consumptive pallors of this blank, raggy life, go these white girls to death.

"Those scythes look very sharp," again turning toward the boy.

"Yes; they have to keep them so. Look!"

That moment two of the girls, dropping their rags, plied each a whet-stone up and down the sword-blade. My unaccustomed blood curdled at the sharp shriek of the tormented steel.

Their own executioners; themselves whetting the very swords that slay them; meditated I.

"What makes those girls so sheet-white, my lad?"

"Why"—with a roguish twinkle, pure ignorant drollery, not knowing heartlessness—"I suppose the handling of such white bits of sheets all the time makes them so sheety."

"Let us leave the rag-room now, my lad."

More tragical and more inscrutably mysterious than any mystic sight, human or machine, throughout the factory, was the strange innocence of cruel-heartedness in this usage-hardened boy.

"And now," said he, cheerily, "I suppose you want to see our great machine, which cost us twelve thousand dollars only last autumn. That's the machine that makes the paper, too. This way, Sir."

Following him, I crossed a large, bespattered place, with two great round vats in it, full of a white, wet, woolly-looking stuff, not unlike the albuminous part of an egg, soft-boiled.

"There," said Cupid, tapping the vats carelessly, "these are the first beginnings of the paper, this white pulp you see. Look how it swims bubbling round and round, moved by the paddle here. From hence it pours from both vats into that one common channel yonder; and so goes, mixed up and leisurely, to the great machine. And now for that."

He led me into a room, stifling with a strange, blood-like, abdominal heat, as if here, true enough, were being finally developed the germinous particles lately seen.

Before me, rolled out like some long Eastern manuscript, lay stretched one continuous length of iron frame-work—multitudinous and mystical, with all sorts of rollers, wheels, and cylinders, in slowly-measured and unceasing motion.

"Here first comes the pulp now," said Cupid, pointing to the nighest end of the machine. "See; first it pours out and spreads itself upon this wide, sloping board; and then—look—slides, thin and quivering, beneath the first roller there. Follow on now, and see it as it slides from under that to the next cylinder. There; see how it has become just a very little less pulpy now. One step more, and it grows still more to some slight consistence. Still another cylinder, and it is so knitted—though as yet mere dragon-fly wing—that it forms an air-bridge here, like a suspended cobweb, between two more separated rollers; and flowing over the last one, and under again, and doubling about there out of sight for a minute among all those mixed cylinders you indistinctly see, it reappears here, looking now at last a little less like pulp and more like paper, but still quite delicate and defective yet awhile. But—a little further onward, Sir, if you please—here now, at this further point, it puts on something of a real look, as if it might turn out to be something you might possibly handle in the end. But it's not yet done, Sir. Good way to travel yet, and plenty more cylinders must roll it."

"Bless my soul!" said I, amazed at the elongation, interminable convolutions, and deliberate slowness of the machine; "it must take a long time for the pulp to pass from end to end, and come out paper."

"Oh! not so long," smiled the precocious lad, with a superior and patronizing air; "only nine minutes. But look; you may try it for yourself. Have you a bit of paper? Ah! here's a bit on the floor. Now mark that with any word you please, and let me dab it on here, and we'll see how long before it comes out at the other end."

"Well, let me see," said I, taking out my pencil; "come, I'll mark it with your name."

Bidding me take out my watch, Cupid adroitly dropped the inscribed slip on an exposed part of the incipient mass.

Instantly my eye marked the second-hand on my dial-plate.

Slowly I followed the slip, inch by inch; sometimes pausing for full half a minute as it disappeared beneath inscrutable groups of the lower cylinders, but only gradually to emerge again; and so, on, and on, and on—inch by inch; now in open sight, sliding along like a freckle on the quivering sheet; and then again wholly vanished; and so, on, and on, and on—inch by inch; all the time the main sheet growing more and more to final firmness—when, suddenly, I saw a sort of paper-fall, not wholly unlike a water-fall; a scissory sound smote my ear, as of some cord being snapped: and down dropped an unfolded sheet of perfect foolscap, with my "Cupid" half faded out of it, and still moist and warm.

My travels were at an end, for here was the end of the machine.

"Well, how long was it?" said Cupid.

"Nine minutes to a second," replied I, watch in hand.

"I told you so."

For a moment a curious emotion filled me, not wholly unlike that which one might experience at the fulfillment of some mysterious prophecy. But how absurd, thought I again; the thing is a mere machine, the essence of which is unvarying punctuality and precision.

Previously absorbed by the wheels and cylinders, my attention was now directed to a sad-looking woman standing by.

"That is rather an elderly person so silently tending the machine-end here. She would not seem wholly used to it either."

"Oh," knowingly whispered Cupid, through the din, "she only came last week. She was a nurse formerly. But the business is poor in these parts, and she's left it. But look at the paper she is piling there."

"Ay, foolscap," handling the piles of moist, warm sheets, which continually were being delivered into the woman's waiting hands. "Don't you turn out any thing but foolscap at this machine?"

"Oh, sometimes, but not often, we turn out finer work—cream-laid and royal sheets, we call them. But foolscap being in chief demand, we turn out foolscap most."

It was very curious. Looking at that blank paper continually dropping, dropping, dropping, my mind ran on in wonderings of those strange uses to which those thousand sheets eventually would be put. All sorts of writings would be writ on those now vacant things— sermons, lawyers' briefs, physicians' prescriptions, love-letters, marriage certificates, bills of divorce, registers of births, death-warrants, and so on, without end. Then, recurring back to them as they here lay all blank, I could not but bethink me of that celebrated comparison of John Locke, who, in demonstration of his theory that man had no innate ideas, compared the human mind at birth to a sheet of blank paper; something destined to be scribbled on, but what sort of characters no soul might tell.

Pacing slowly to and fro along the involved machine, still humming with its play, I was struck as well by the inevitability as the evolvement-power in all its motions.

"Does that thin cobweb there," said I, pointing to the sheet in its more imperfect stage, "does that never tear or break? It is marvelous fragile, and yet this machine it passes through is so mighty."

"It never is known to tear a hair's point."

"Does it never stop—get clogged?"

"No. It *must* go. The machinery makes it go just *so*; just that very way, and at that very pace you there plainly *see* it go. The pulp can't help going."

Something of awe now stole over me, as I gazed upon this inflexible iron animal. Always, more or less, machinery of this ponderous, elaborate sort strikes, in some moods, strange dread into the human heart, as some living, panting Behemoth might. But what made the thing I saw so specially terrible to me was the metallic necessity, the unbudging fatality which governed it. Though, here and there, I could not follow the thin, gauzy vail of pulp in the course of its more mysterious or entirely invisible advance, yet it was indubitable that, at those points where it eluded me, it still marched on in unvarying docility to the autocratic cunning of the machine. A fascination fastened on me. I stood spellbound and wandering in my soul. Before my eyes—there, passing in slow procession along the wheeling cylinders, I seemed to see, glued to the pallid incipience of the pulp, the yet more pallid faces of all the pallid girls I had eyed that heavy day. Slowly, mournfully, beseechingly, yet unresistingly, they gleamed along, their agony dimly outlined on the imperfect paper, like the print of the tormented face on the handkerchief of Saint Veronica.

"Halloa! the heat of the room is too much for you," cried Cupid, staring at me.

"No—I am rather chill, if any thing."

"Come out, Sir—out—out," and, with the protecting air of a careful father, the precocious lad hurried me outside.

In a few moments, feeling revived a little, I went into the folding-room—the first room I had entered, and where the desk for transacting business stood, surrounded by the blank counters and blank girls engaged at them.

"Cupid here has led me a strange tour," said I to the dark-complexioned man before mentioned, whom I had ere this discovered not only to be an old bachelor, but also the principal proprietor. "Yours is a most wonderful factory. Your great machine is a miracle of inscrutable intricacy."

"Yes, all our visitors think it so. But we don't have many. We are in a very out-of-the-way corner here. Few inhabitants, too. Most of our girls come from far-off villages."

"The girls," echoed I, glancing round at their silent forms. "Why is it, Sir, that in most factories, female operatives, of whatever age, are indiscriminately called girls, never women?"

"Oh! as to that—why, I suppose, the fact of their being generally unmarried—that's the reason, I should think. But it never struck me before. For our factory here, we will not have married women; they are apt to be off-and-on too much. We want none but steady workers: twelve hours to the day, day after day, through the three hundred and sixty-five days, excepting Sundays, Thanksgiving, and Fastdays. That's our rule. And so, having no married women, what females we have are rightly enough called girls."

"Then these are all maids," said I, while some pained homage to their pale virginity made me involuntarily bow.

"All maids."

Again the strange emotion filled me.

"Your cheeks look whitish yet, Sir," said the man, gazing at me narrowly. "You must be careful going home. Do they pain you at all now? It's a bad sign, if they do."

"No doubt, Sir," answered I, "when once I have got out of the Devil's Dungeon, I shall feel them mending."

"Ah, yes; the winter air in valleys, or gorges, or any sunken place, is far colder and more bitter than elsewhere. You would hardly believe it now, but it is colder here than at the top of Woedolor Mountain."

"I dare say it is, Sir. But time presses me; I must depart."

With that, remuffling myself in dread-naught and tippet, thrusting my hands into my huge seal-skin mittens, I sallied out into the nipping air, and found poor Black, my horse, all cringing and doubled up with the cold.

Soon, wrapped in furs and meditations, I ascended from the Devil's Dungeon.

At the Black Notch I paused, and once more bethought me of Temple-Bar. Then, shooting through the pass, all alone with inscrutable nature, I exclaimed—Oh! Paradise of Bachelors! and oh! Tartarus of Maids!

# EDGAR ALLAN POE
## The Black Cat

For the most wild, yet most homely narrative which I am about to pen, I neither expect nor solicit belief. Mad indeed would I be to expect it, in a case where my very senses reject their own evidence. Yet, mad am I not—and very surely do I not dream. But to-morrow I die, and to-day I would unburthen my soul. My immediate purpose is to place before the world, plainly, succinctly, and without comments, a series of mere household events. In their consequences, these events have terri-fied—have tortured—have destroyed me. Yet I will attempt to expound them. To me, they have presented little but Horror—to many they will seem less terrible than *barroques*. Hereafter, perhaps, some intellect may be found which will reduce my phantasm to the common-place—some intellect more calm, more logical, and far less excitable than my own, which will perceive, in the circumstances I detail with awe, nothing more than an ordinary succession of very natural causes and effects.

From my infancy I was noted for the docility and humanity of my disposition. My tenderness of heart was even so conspicuous as to make me the jest of my companions. I was especially fond of animals, and was indulged by my parents with a great variety of pets. With these I spent most of my time, and never was so happy as when feeding and caressing them. This peculiarity of character grew with my growth, and, in my manhood, I derived from it one of my principal sources of pleasure. To those who have cherished an affection for a faithful and sagacious dog, I need hardly be at the trouble of explaining the nature or the intensity of the gratification thus derivable. There is something in the unselfish and self-sacrificing love of a brute, which goes directly to the heart of him who has had frequent occasion to test the paltry friendship and gossamer fidelity of mere *Man*.

I married early, and was happy to find in my wife a disposition not uncongenial with my own. Observing my partiality for domestic pets, she lost no opportunity of procuring those of the most agreeable kind. We had birds, gold-fish, a fine dog, rabbits, a small monkey, and *a cat*.

This latter was a remarkably large and beautiful animal, entirely black, and sagacious to an astonishing degree. In speaking of his intelligence, my wife, who at heart was not a little tinctured with superstition, made frequent allusion to the ancient popular notion, which regarded all black cats as witches in disguise. Not that she was ever *serious* upon this point—and I mention the matter at all for no better reason than that it happens, just now, to be remembered.

Pluto—this was the cat's name—was my favorite pet and playmate. I alone fed him, and he attended me wherever I went about the house. It was even with difficulty that I could prevent him from following me through the streets.

Our friendship lasted, in this manner, for several years, during which my general temperament and character—through the instrumentality of the Fiend Intemperance—had (I blush to confess it) experienced a radical alteration for the worse. I grew, day by day, more moody, more irritable, more regardless of the feelings of others. I suffered myself to use intemperate language to my wife. At length, I even offered her personal violence. My pets, of course, were made to feel the change in my disposition. I not only neglected, but ill-used them. For Pluto, however, I still retained sufficient regard to restrain me from maltreating him, as I made no scruple of maltreating the rabbits, the monkey, or even the dog, when by accident, or through affection, they came in my way. But my disease grew upon me—for what disease is like Alcohol!—and at length even Pluto, who was now becoming old, and consequently somewhat peevish—even Pluto began to experience the effects of my ill temper.

One night, returning home, much intoxicated, from one of my haunts about town, I fancied that the cat avoided my presence. I seized him; when, in his fright at my violence, he inflicted a slight wound upon my hand with his teeth. The fury of a demon instantly possessed me. I knew myself no longer. My original soul seemed, at once, to take its flight from my body; and a more than fiendish malevolence, gin-nurtured, thrilled every fibre of my frame. I took from my waistcoat-pocket a pen-knife, opened it, grasped the poor beast by the throat, and deliberately cut one of its eyes from the socket! I blush, I burn, I shudder, while I pen the damnable atrocity.

When reason returned with the morning—when I had slept off the fumes of the night's debauch—I experienced a sentiment half of horror, half of remorse, for the crime of which I had been guilty; but it was, at best, a feeble and equivocal feeling, and the soul remained untouched. I again plunged into excess, and soon drowned in wine all memory of the deed.

In the meantime the cat slowly recovered. The socket of the lost eye presented, it is true, a frightful appearance, but he no longer appeared to suffer any pain. He went about the house as usual, but, as might be expected, fled in extreme terror at my approach. I had so much of my old heart left, as to be at first grieved by this evident dislike on the part of a creature which had once so loved me. But this feeling soon gave place to irritation. And then came, as if to my final and ir-revocable overthrow, the spirit of PERVERSENESS. Of this spirit philosophy takes no account. Yet I am not more sure that my soul lives, than I am that perverseness is one of the primitive impulses of the human heart—one of the indivisible primary faculties, or sentiments, which give direction to the character of Man. Who has not, a hundred times, found himself committing a vile or a silly action, for no other reason than because he knows he should *not*? Have we not a perpetual inclination, in the teeth of our best judgment, to violate that which is *Law*, merely because we understand it to be such? This spirit of per-verseness, I say, came to my final overthrow. It was this unfathomable longing of the soul *to vex itself*—to offer violence to its own nature—to do wrong for the wrong's sake only—that urged me to continue and finally to consummate the injury I had inflicted upon the unoffending brute. One morning, in cool blood, I slipped a noose about its neck and hung it to the limb of a tree;—hung it with the tears streaming from my eyes, and with the bitterest remorse at my heart;—hung it *because* I knew that it had loved me, and *because* I felt it had given me no reason of offence;—hung it *because* I knew that in so doing I was com-mitting a sin—a deadly sin that would so jeopardize my immortal soul as to place it—if such a thing were possible—even beyond the reach of the infinite mercy of the Most Merciful and Most Terrible God.

On the night of the day on which this cruel deed was done, I was aroused from sleep by the cry of fire. The curtains of my bed were in flames. The whole house was blazing. It was with great difficulty that my wife, a servant, and myself, made our escape from the conflagration. The destruction was complete. My entire worldly wealth was swallowed up, and I resigned myself thenceforward to despair.

I am above the weakness of seeking to establish a sequence of cause and effect, between the disaster and the atrocity. But I am detailing a chain of facts—and wish not to leave even a possible link imperfect. On the day succeeding the fire, I visited the ruins. The walls, with one exception, had fallen in. This exception was found in a compartment wall, not very thick, which stood about the middle of the house, and against which had rested the head of my bed. The plastering had here, in great measure, resisted the action of the fire—a fact which I attributed to its having been recently spread. About this wall a dense crowd were collected, and many persons seemed to be examining a particular portion of it with very minute and eager attention. The words "strange!" "singular!" and other similar expressions, excited my curiosity. I approached and saw, as if graven in *bas relief* upon the white surface, the figure of a gigantic *cat*. The impression was given with an accuracy truly marvellous. There was a rope about the animal's neck.

When I first beheld this apparition—for I could scarcely regard it as less—my wonder and my terror were extreme. But at length reflection came to my aid. The cat, I remembered, had been hung in a garden adjacent to the house. Upon the alarm of fire, this garden had been immediately filled by the crowd—by some one of whom the animal must have been cut from the tree and thrown, through an open window, into my chamber. This had probably been done with the view of arousing me from sleep. The falling of other walls had compressed the victim of my cruelty into the substance of the freshly-spread plaster; the lime of which, with the flames, and the *ammonia* from the carcass, had then accomplished the portraiture as I saw it.

Although I thus readily accounted to my reason, if not altogether to my conscience, for the startling fact just detailed, it did not the less fail to make a deep impression upon my fancy. For months I could not rid myself of the phantasm of the cat; and, during this period, there came back into my spirit a half-sentiment that seemed, but was not, remorse. I went so far as to regret the loss of the animal, and to look about me, among the vile haunts which I now habitually frequented, for another pet of the same species, and of somewhat similar appearance, with which to supply its place.

One night as I sat, half stupefied, in a den of more than infamy, my attention was suddenly drawn to some black object, reposing upon the head of one of the immense hogsheads of Gin, or of Rum, which constituted the chief furniture of the apartment. I had been looking steadily at the top of this hogshead for some minutes, and what now caused me surprise was the fact that I had not sooner perceived the object thereupon. I approached it, and touched it with my hand. It was a black cat—a very large one—fully as large as Pluto, and closely resembling him in every respect but one. Pluto had not a white hair upon any portion of his body; but this cat had a large, although indefinite splotch of white, covering nearly the whole region of the breast.

Upon my touching him, he immediately arose, purred loudly, rubbed against my hand, and appeared delighted with my notice. This, then, was the very creature of which I was in search. I at once offered to purchase it of the landlord; but this person made no claim to it— knew nothing of it—had never seen it before.

I continued my caresses, and, when I prepared to go home, the animal evinced a disposition to accompany me. I permitted it to do so; occasionally stooping and patting it as I proceeded. When it reached the house it domesticated itself at once, and became immediately a great favorite with my wife.

For my own part, I soon found a dislike to it arising within me. This was just the reverse of what I had anticipated; but—I know not how or why it was—its evident fondness for myself rather disgusted and annoyed. By slow degrees, these feelings of disgust and annoyance rose into the bitterness of hatred. I avoided the creature; a certain sense of shame, and the remembrance of my former deed of cruelty, preventing me from physically abusing it. I did not, for some weeks, strike, or otherwise violently ill use it; but gradually—very gradually—I came to look upon it with unutterable loathing, and to flee silently from its odious presence, as from the breath of a pestilence.

What added, no doubt, to my hatred of the beast, was the discovery, on the morning after I brought it home, that, like Pluto, it also had been deprived of one of its eyes. This circumstance, however, only endeared it to my wife, who, as I have already said, possessed, in a high degree, that humanity of feeling which had once been my distinguishing trait, and the source of many of my simplest and purest pleasures.

With my aversion to this cat, however, its partiality for myself seemed to increase. It followed my footsteps with a pertinacity which it would be difficult to make the reader comprehend. Whenever I sat, it would crouch beneath my chair, or spring upon my knees, covering me with its loathsome caresses. If I arose to walk it would get between my feet and thus nearly throw me down, or, fastening its long and sharp claws in my dress, clamber, in this manner, to my breast. At such times, although I longed to destroy it with a blow, I was yet withheld from so doing, partly by a memory of my former crime, but chiefly—let me confess it at once—by absolute *dread* of the beast.

This dread was not exactly a dread of physical evil—and yet I should be at a loss how otherwise to define it. I am almost ashamed to own—yes, even in this felon's cell, I am almost ashamed to own—that the terror and horror with which the animal inspired me, had been heightened by one of the merest chimaeras it would be possible to conceive. My wife had called my attention, more than once, to the character of the mark of white hair, of which I have spoken, and which constituted the sole visible difference between the strange beast and the one I had destroyed. The reader will remember that this mark, although large, had been originally very indefinite; but, by slow degrees—degrees nearly imperceptible, and which for a long time my Reason struggled to reject as fanciful—it had, at length, assumed a rigorous distinctness of outline. It was now the representation of an object that I shudder to name—and for this, above all, I loathed, and dreaded, and would have rid myself of the monster *had I dared*—it was now, I say, the image of a hideous—of a ghastly thing—of the GALLOWS!—oh, mournful and terrible engine of Horror and of Crime—of Agony and of Death!

And now was I indeed wretched beyond the wretchedness of mere Humanity. And *a brute beast*—whose fellow I had contemptuously destroyed—*a brute beast* to work out for *me*—for me a man, fashioned in the image of the High God—so much of insufferable woe! Alas! neither by day nor by night knew I the blessing of Rest any more! During the former the creature left me no moment alone; and, in the latter, I started, hourly, from dreams of unutterable fear, to find the hot breath of *the thing* upon my face, and its vast weight—an incarnate Night-Mare that I had no power to shake off—incumbent eternally upon my *heart!*

Beneath the pressure of torments such as these, the feeble remnant of the good within me succumbed. Evil thoughts became my sole intimates—the darkest and most evil of thoughts. The moodiness of my usual temper increased to hatred of all things and of all mankind; while, from the sudden, frequent, and ungovernable outbursts of a fury to which I now blindly abandoned myself, my uncomplaining wife, alas! was the most usual and the most patient of sufferers.

One day she accompanied me, upon some household errand, into the cellar of the old building which our poverty compelled us to inhabit. The cat followed me down the steep stairs, and, nearly throwing me headlong, exasperated me to madness. Uplifting an axe, and forgetting, in my wrath, the childish dread which had hitherto stayed my hand, I aimed a blow at the animal which, of course, would have proved instantly fatal had it descended as I wished. But this blow was arrested by the hand of my wife. Goaded, by the interference, into a rage more than demoniacal, I withdrew my arm from her grasp and buried the axe in her brain. She fell dead upon the spot, without a groan.

This hideous murder accomplished, I set myself forthwith, and with entire deliberation, to the task of concealing the body. I knew that I could not remove it from the house, either by day or by night, without the risk of being observed by the neighbors. Many projects entered my mind. At one period I thought of cutting the corpse into minute fragments, and destroying them by fire. At another, I resolved to dig a grave for it in the floor of the cellar. Again, I deliberated about casting it in the well in the yard—about packing it in a box, as if merchandize, with the usual arrangements, and so getting a porter to take it from the house. Finally I hit upon what I considered a far better expedient than either of these. I determined to wall it up in the cellar—as the monks of the middle ages are recorded to have walled up their victims.

For a purpose such as this the cellar was well adapted. Its walls were loosely constructed, and had lately been plastered throughout with a rough plaster, which the dampness of the atmosphere had prevented from hardening. Moreover, in one of the walls was a projection, caused by a false chimney, or fireplace, that had been filled up, and made to resemble the rest of the cellar. I made no doubt that I could readily displace the bricks at this point, insert the corpse, and wall the whole up as before, so that no eye could detect anything suspicious.

And in this calculation I was not deceived. By means of a crowbar I easily dislodged the bricks, and, having carefully deposited the body against the inner wall, I propped it in that position, while, with little trouble, I re-laid the whole structure as it originally stood. Having procured mortar, sand, and hair, with every possible precaution, I prepared a plaster which could not be distinguished from the old, and with this I very carefully went over the new brick-work. When I had finished, I felt satisfied that all was right. The wall did not present the slightest appearance of having been disturbed. The rubbish on the floor was picked up with the minutest care. I looked around triumphantly, and said to myself—"Here at least, then, my labor has not been in vain."

My next step was to look for the beast which had been the cause of so much wretchedness; for I had, at length, firmly resolved to put it to death. Had I been able to meet with it, at the moment, there could have been no doubt of its fate; but it appeared that the crafty animal had been alarmed at the violence of my previous anger, and forebore to present itself in my present mood. It is impossible to describe, or to imagine, the deep, the blissful sense of relief which the absence of the detested creature occasioned in my bosom. It did not make its appearance during the night—and thus for one night at least, since its introduction into the house, I soundly and tranquilly slept; aye, *slept* even with the burden of murder upon my soul!

The second and the third day passed, and still my tormentor came not. Once again I breathed as a freeman. The monster, in terror, had fled the premises forever! I should behold it no more! My happiness was supreme! The guilt of my dark deed disturbed me but little. Some few inquiries had been made, but these had been readily answered. Even a search had been instituted—but of course nothing was to be discovered. I looked upon my future felicity as secured.

Upon the fourth day of the assassination, a party of the police came, very unexpectedly, into the house, and proceeded again to make rigorous investigation of the premises. Secure, however, in the inscrutability of my place of concealment, I felt no embarrassment whatever. The officers bade me accompany them in their search. They left no nook or corner unexplored. At length, for the third or fourth time, they descended into the cellar. I quivered not in a muscle. My heart beat calmly as that of one who slumbers in innocence. I walked the cellar from end to end. I folded my arms upon my bosom, and roamed easily to and fro. The police were thoroughly satisfied and prepared to depart. The glee at my heart was too strong to be restrained. I burned to say if but one word, by the way of triumph, and to render doubly sure their assurance of my guiltlessness.

"Gentlemen," I said at last, as the party ascended the steps, "I delight to have allayed your suspicions. I wish you all health, and a little more courtesy. By the bye, gentlemen, this—this is a very well constructed house." [In the rabid desire to say something easily, I scarcely knew what I uttered at all.]—"I may say an *excellently* well constructed house. These walls—are you going, gentlemen?—these walls are solidly put together;" and here, through the mere phrenzy of bravado, I rapped heavily, with a cane which I held in my hand, upon that very portion of the brick-work behind which stood the corpse of the wife of my bosom.

But may God shield and deliver me from the fangs of the Arch-Fiend! No sooner had the reverberation of my blows sunk into silence, than I was answered by a voice from within the tomb!—by a cry, at first muffled and broken, like the sobbing of a child, and then quickly swelling into one long, loud, and continuous scream, utterly anomalous and inhuman—a howl—a wailing shriek, half of horror and half of triumph, such as might have arisen only out of hell, conjointly from the throats of the damned in their agony and of the demons that exult in the damnation.

Of my own thoughts it is folly to speak. Swooning, I staggered to the opposite wall. For one instant the party upon the stairs remained motionless, through extremity of terror and of awe. In the next, a dozen stout arms were toiling at the wall. It fell bodily. The corpse, already greatly decayed and clotted with gore, stood erect before the eyes of the spectators. Upon its head, with red extended mouth and solitary eye of fire, sat the hideous beast whose craft had seduced me into murder, and whose informing voice had consigned me to the hangman. I had walled the monster up within the tomb!

# CHARLOTTE PERKINS GILMAN
## The Yellow Wallpaper

It is very seldom that mere ordinary people like John and myself secure ancestral halls for the summer.

A colonial mansion, a hereditary estate, I would say a haunted house, and reach the height of romantic felicity—but that would be asking too much of fate!

Still I will proudly declare that there is something queer about it.

Else, why should it be let so cheaply? And why have stood so long untenanted?

John laughs at me, of course, but one expects that in man. John is practical in the extreme. He has no patience with faith, an intense horror of superstition, and he scoffs openly at any talk of things not to be felt and seen and put down in figures.

John is a physician, and *perhaps*—(I would not say it to a living soul, of course, but this is dead paper and a great relief to my mind)—*perhaps* that is one reason I do not get well faster.

You see he does not believe I am sick! And what can one do?

If a physician of high standing, and one's own husband, assures friends and relatives that there is really nothing the matter with one but temporary nervous depression—a slight hysterical tendency—what is one to do?

My brother is also a physician, and also of high standing, and he says the same thing.

So I take phosphates or phosphites—whichever it is—and tonics, and journeys, and air, and exercise, and am absolutely forbidden to "work" until I am well again.

Personally, I disagree with their ideas.

Personally, I believe that congenial work, with excitement and change, would do me good.

But what is one to do?

I did write for a while in spite of them; but it *does* exhaust me a good deal—having to be so sly about it, or else meet with heavy opposition.

I sometimes fancy that in my condition if I had less opposition and more society and stimulus—but John says the very worst thing I can do is to think about my condition, and I confess it always makes me feel bad.

So I will let it alone and talk about the house.

The most beautiful place! It is quite alone, standing well back from the road, quite three miles from the village. It makes me think of English places that you read about, for there are hedges and walls and gates that lock, and lots of separate little houses for the gardeners and people.

There is a *delicious* garden! I never saw such a garden—large and shady, full of box-bordered paths, and lined with long grape-covered arbors with seats under them.

There were greenhouses, too, but they are all broken now.

There was some legal trouble, I believe, something about the heirs and co-heirs; anyhow, the place has been empty for years.

That spoils my ghostliness, I am afraid, but I don't care—there is something strange about the house—I can feel it.

I even said so to John one moonlight evening, but he said what I felt was a draught, and shut the window.

I get unreasonably angry with John sometimes. I'm sure I never used to be so sensitive. I think it is due to this nervous condition.

But John says if I feel so I shall neglect proper self-control; so I take pains to control myself—before him, at least, and that makes me very tired.

I don't like our room a bit. I wanted one downstairs that opened on the piazza and had roses all over the window, and such pretty old-fashioned chintz hangings! But John would not hear of it.

He said there was only one window and not room for two beds, and no near room for him if he took another.

He is very careful and loving, and hardly lets me stir without special direction.

I have a schedule prescription for each hour in the day; he takes all care from me, and so I feel basely ungrateful not to value it more.

He said we came here solely on my account; that I was to have perfect rest and all the air I could get. "Your exercise depends on your strength, my dear," said he, "and your food somewhat on your appetite; but air you can absorb all the time." So we took the nursery at the top of the house.

It is a big, airy room, the whole floor nearly, with windows that look all ways, and air and sunshine galore. It was nursery first and then playroom and gymnasium, I should judge; for the windows are barred for little children, and there are rings and things in the walls.

The paint and paper look as if a boys' school had used it. It is stripped off—the paper—in great patches all around the head of my bed, about as far as I can reach, and in a great place on the other side of the room low down. I never saw a worse paper in my life.

One of those sprawling flamboyant patterns committing every artistic sin.

It is dull enough to confuse the eye in following, pronounced enough constantly to irritate and provoke study, and when you follow the lame uncertain curves for a little distance they suddenly commit suicide—plunge off at outrageous angles, destroy themselves in unheard of contradictions.

The color is repellant, almost revolting; a smouldering unclean yellow, strangely faded by the slow-turning sunlight.

It is a dull yet lurid orange in some places, a sickly sulphur tint in others.

No wonder the children hated it! I should hate it myself if I had to live in this room long.

There comes John, and I must put this away—he hates to have me write a word.

We have been here two weeks, and I haven't felt like writing before, since that first day.

I am sitting by the window now, up in this atrocious nursery, and there is nothing to hinder my writing as much as I please, save lack of strength.

John is away all day, and even some nights when his cases are serious.

I am glad my case is not serious!

But these nervous troubles are dreadfully depressing.

John does not know how much I really suffer. He knows there is no *reason* to suffer, and that satisfies him.

Of course it is only nervousness. It does weigh on me so not to do my duty in any way!

I meant to be such a help to John, such a real rest and comfort, and here I am a comparative burden already!

Nobody would believe what an effort it is to do what little I am able—to dress and entertain, and order things.

It is fortunate Mary is so good with the baby. Such a dear baby!

And yet I *cannot* be with him, it makes me so nervous.

I suppose John never was nervous in his life. He laughs at me so about this wallpaper!

At first he meant to repaper the room, but afterwards he said that I was letting it get the better of me, and that nothing was worse for a nervous patient than to give way to such fancies.

He said that after the wallpaper was changed it would be the heavy bedstead, and then the barred windows, and then that gate at the head of the stairs, and so on.

"You know the place is doing you good," he said, "and really, dear, I don't care to renovate the house just for a three months' rental."

"Then do let us go downstairs," I said, "there are such pretty rooms there."

Then he took me in his arms and called me a blessed little goose, and said he would go down cellar, if I wished, and have it whitewashed into the bargain.

But he is right enough about the beds and windows and things.

It is an airy and comfortable room as any one need wish, and, of course, I would not be so silly as to make him uncomfortable just for a whim.

I'm really getting quite fond of the big room, all but that horrid paper.

Out of one window I can see the garden, those mysterious deep-shaded arbors, the riotous old-fashioned flowers, and bushes and gnarly trees.

Out of another I get a lovely view of the bay and a little private wharf belonging to the estate. There is a beautiful shaded lane that runs down there from the house. I always fancy I see people walking in these numerous paths and arbors, but John has cautioned me not to give way to fancy in the least. He says that with my imaginative power and habit of story-making, a nervous weakness like mine is sure to lead to all manner of excited fancies, and that I ought to use my will and good sense to check the tendency. So I try.

I think sometimes that if I were only well enough to write a little it would relieve the press of ideas and rest me.

But I find I get pretty tired when I try.

It is so discouraging not to have any advice and companionship about my work. When I get really well, John says we will ask Cousin Henry and Julia down for a long visit; but he says he would as soon put fireworks in my pillowcase as to let me have those stimulating people about now.

I wish I could get well faster.

But I must not think about that. This paper looks to me as if it *knew* what a vicious influence it had!

There is a recurrent spot where the pattern lolls like a broken neck and two bulbous eyes stare at you upside down.

I get positively angry with the impertinence of it and the everlast-ingness. Up and down and sideways they crawl, and those absurd, unblinking eyes are everywhere. There is one place where two breadths didn't match, and the eyes go all up and down the line, one a little higher than the other.

I never saw so much expression in an inanimate thing before, and we all know how much expression they have! I used to lie awake as a child and get more entertainment and terror out of blank walls and plain furniture than most children could find in a toy-store.

I remember what a kindly wink the knobs of our big, old bureau used to have, and there was one chair that always seemed like a strong friend.

I used to feel that if any of the other things looked too fierce I could always hop into that chair and be safe.

The furniture in this room is no worse than inharmonious, how-ever, for we had to bring it all from downstairs. I suppose when this was used as a playroom they had to take the nursery things out, and no wonder! I never saw such ravages as the children have made here.

The wallpaper, as I said before, is torn off in spots, and it sticketh closer than a brother—they must have had perseverance as well as hatred.

Then the floor is scratched and gouged and splintered, the plaster itself is dug out here and there, and this great heavy bed which is all we found in the room, looks as if it had been through the wars.

But I don't mind it a bit—only the paper.

There comes John's sister. Such a dear girl as she is, and so careful of me! I must not let her find me writing.

She is a perfect and enthusiastic housekeeper, and hopes for no better profession. I verily believe she thinks it is the writing which made me sick!

But I can write when she is out, and see her a long way off from these windows.

There is one that commands the road, a lovely shaded winding road, and one that just looks off over the country. A lovely country, too, full of great elms and velvet meadows.

This wallpaper has a kind of sub-pattern in a different shade, a particularly irritating one, for you can only see it in certain lights, and not clearly then.

But in the places where it isn't faded and where the sun is just so—I can see a strange, provoking, formless sort of figure, that seems to skulk about behind that silly and conspicuous front design.

There's sister on the stairs!

Well, the Fourth of July is over! The people are all gone and I am tired out. John thought it might do me good to see a little company, so we just had mother and Nellie and the children down for a week.

Of course I didn't do a thing. Jennie sees to everything now.

But it tired me all the same.

John says if I don't pick up faster he shall send me to Weir Mitchell in the fall.

But I don't want to go there at all. I had a friend who was in his hands once, and she says he is just like John and my brother, only more so!

Besides, it is such an undertaking to go so far.

I don't feel as if it was worth while to turn my hand over for anything, and I'm getting dreadfully fretful and querulous.

I cry at nothing, and cry most of the time.

Of course I don't when John is here, or anybody else, but when I am alone.

And I am alone a good deal just now. John is kept in town very often by serious cases, and Jennie is good and lets me alone when I want her to.

So I walk a little in the garden or down that lovely lane, sit on the porch under the roses, and lie down up here a good deal.

I'm getting really fond of the room in spite of the wallpaper. Perhaps *because* of the wallpaper.

It dwells in my mind so!

I lie here on this great immovable bed—it is nailed down, I believe—and follow that pattern about by the hour. It is as good as gymnastics, I assure you. I start, we'll say, at the bottom, down in the corner over there where it has not been touched, and I determine for the thousandth time that I *will* follow that pointless pattern to some sort of a conclusion.

I know a little of the principle of design, and I know this thing was not arranged on any laws of radiation, or alternation, or repetition, or symmetry, or anything else that I ever heard of.

It is repeated, of course, by the breadths, but not otherwise.

Looked at in one way each breadth stands alone, the bloated curves and flourishes—a kind of "debased Romanesque" with delirium tremens—go waddling up and down in isolated columns of fatuity.

But, on the other hand, they connect diagonally, and the sprawling outlines run off in great slanting waves of optic horror, like a lot of wallowing sea-weeds in full chase.

The whole thing goes horizontally, too, at least it seems so, and I exhaust myself trying to distinguish the order of its going in that direction.

They have used a horizontal breadth for a frieze, and that adds wonderfully to the confusion.

There is one end of the room where it is almost intact, and there, when the crosslights fade and the low sun shines directly upon it, I can almost fancy radiation after all,—the interminable grotesques seem to form around a common centre and rush off in headlong plunges of equal distraction.

It makes me tired to follow it. I will take a nap I guess.

I don't know why I should write this.

I don't want to.

I don't feel able.

And I know John would think it absurd. But I *must* say what I feel and think in some way—it is such a relief!

But the effort is getting to be greater than the relief.

Half the time now I am awfully lazy, and lie down ever so much.

John says I mustn't lose my strength, and has me take cod liver oil and lots of tonics and things, to say nothing of ale and wine and rare meat.

Dear John! He loves me very dearly, and hates to have me sick. I tried to have a real earnest reasonable talk with him the other day, and tell him how I wish he would let me go and make a visit to Cousin Henry and Julia.

But he said I wasn't able to go, nor able to stand it after I got there; and I did not make out a very good case for myself, for I was crying before I had finished.

It is getting to be a great effort for me to think straight. Just this nervous weakness I suppose.

And dear John gathered me up in his arms, and just carried me upstairs and laid me on the bed, and sat by me and read to me till it tired my head.

He said I was his darling and his comfort and all he had, and that I must take care of myself for his sake, and keep well.

He says no one but myself can help me out of it, that I must use my will and self-control and not let my silly fancies run away with me.

There's one comfort, the baby is well and happy, and does not have to occupy this nursery with the horrid wallpaper.

If we had not used it, that blessed child would have! What a fortunate escape! Why, I wouldn't have a child of mine, an impressionable little thing, live in such a room for worlds.

I never thought of it before, but it is lucky that John kept me here after all, I can stand it so much easier than a baby, you see.

Of course I never mention it to them any more—I am too wise—but I keep watch for it all the same.

There are things in that paper that nobody knows but me, or ever will.

Behind that outside pattern the dim shapes get clearer every day.

It is always the same shape, only very numerous.

And it is like a woman stooping down and creeping about behind that pattern. I don't like it a bit. I wonder—I begin to think—I wish John would take me away from here!

It is so hard to talk with John about my case, because he is so wise, and because he loves me so.

But I tried it last night.

It was moonlight. The moon shines in all around just as the sun does.

I hate to see it sometimes, it creeps so slowly, and always comes in by one window or another.

John was asleep and I hated to waken him, so I kept still and watched the moonlight on that undulating wallpaper till I felt creepy.

The faint figure behind seemed to shake the pattern, just as if she wanted to get out.

I got up softly and went to feel and see if the paper *did* move, and when I came back John was awake.

"What is it, little girl?" he said. "Don't go walking about like that—you'll get cold."

I thought it was a good time to talk so I told him that I really was not gaining here, and that I wished he would take me away.

"Why darling!" said he, "our lease will be up in three weeks, and I can't see how to leave before.

"The repairs are not done at home, and I cannot possibly leave town just now. Of course if you were in any danger, I could and would, but you really are better, dear, whether you can see it or not. I am a doctor, dear, and I know. You are gaining flesh and color, your appetite is better, I feel really much easier about you."

"I don't weigh a bit more," said I, "nor as much; and my appetite may be better in the evening when you are here, but it is worse in the morning when you are away!"

"Bless her little heart!" said he with a big hug, "she shall be as sick as she pleases! But now let's improve the shining hours by going to sleep, and talk about it in the morning!"

"And you won't go away?" I asked gloomily.

"Why, how can I, dear? It is only three weeks more and then we will take a nice little trip of a few days while Jennie is getting the house ready. Really, dear, you are better!"

"Better in body perhaps—" I began, and stopped short, for he sat up straight and looked at me with such a stern, reproachful look that I could not say another word.

"My darling," said he, "I beg of you, for my sake and for our child's sake, as well as for your own, that you will never for one instant let that idea enter your mind! There is nothing so dangerous, so fascinating, to a temperament like yours. It is a false and foolish fancy. Can you not trust me as a physician when I tell you so?"

So of course I said no more on that score, and we went to sleep before long. He thought I was asleep first, but I wasn't, and lay there for hours trying to decide whether that front pattern and the back pattern really did move together or separately.

On a pattern like this, by daylight, there is a lack of sequence, a defiance of law, that is a constant irritant to a normal mind.

The color is hideous enough, and unreliable enough, and infuriating enough, but the pattern is torturing.

You think you have mastered it, but just as you get well underway in following, it turns a back-somersault and there you are. It slaps you in the face, knocks you down, and tramples upon you. It is like a bad dream.

The outside pattern is a florid arabesque, reminding one of a fungus. If you can imagine a toadstool in joints, an interminable string of toadstools, budding and sprouting in endless convolutions—why, that is something like it.

That is, sometimes!

There is one marked peculiarity about this paper, a thing nobody seems to notice but myself, and that is that it changes as the light changes.

When the sun shoots in through the east window—I always watch for that first, long, straight ray—it changes so quickly that I never can quite believe it.

That is why I watch it always.

By moonlight—the moon shines in all night when there is a moon—I wouldn't know it was the same paper.

At night in any kind of light, in twilight, candlelight, lamplight, and worst of all by moonlight, it becomes bars! The outside pattern I mean, and the woman behind it is as plain as can be.

I didn't realize for a long time what the thing was that showed behind, that dim sub-pattern, but now I am quite sure it is a woman.

By daylight she is subdued, quiet. I fancy it is the pattern that keeps her so still. It is so puzzling. It keeps me quiet by the hour.

I lie down ever so much now. John says it is good for me, and to sleep all I can.

Indeed he started the habit by making me lie down for an hour after each meal.

It is a very bad habit I am convinced, for you see I don't sleep.

And that cultivates deceit, for I don't tell them I'm awake—O, no!

The fact is I am getting a little afraid of John.

He seems very queer sometimes, and even Jennie has an inexplicable look.

It strikes me occasionally, just as a scientific hypothesis, that perhaps it is the paper!

I have watched John when he did not know I was looking, and come into the room suddenly on the most innocent excuses, and I've caught him several times *looking at the paper!* And Jennie too. I caught Jennie with her hand on it once.

She didn't know I was in the room, and when I asked her in a quiet, a very quiet voice, with the most restrained manner possible, what she was doing with the paper—she turned around as if she had been caught stealing, and looked quite angry—asked me why I should frighten her so!

Then she said that the paper stained everything it touched, that she had found yellow smooches on all my clothes and John's, and she wished we would be more careful!

Did not that sound innocent? But I know she was studying that pattern, and I am determined that nobody shall find it out but myself!

Life is very much more exciting now than it used to be. You see I have something more to expect, to look forward to, to watch. I really do eat better, and am more quiet than I was.

John is so pleased to see me improve! He laughed a little the other day, and said I seemed to be flourishing in spite of my wallpaper.

I turned it off with a laugh. I had no intention of telling him it was *because* of the wallpaper—he would make fun of me. He might even want to take me away.

I don't want to leave now until I have found it out. There is a week more, and I think that will be enough.

I'm feeling ever so much better! I don't sleep much at night, for it is so interesting to watch developments, but I sleep a good deal in the daytime.

In the daytime it is tiresome and perplexing.

There are always new shoots on the fungus, and new shades of yellow all over it. I cannot keep count of them, though I have tried conscientiously.

It is the strangest yellow, that wallpaper! It makes me think of all the yellow things I ever saw—not beautiful ones like buttercups, but old foul, bad yellow things.

But there is something else about that paper—the smell! I noticed it the moment we came into the room, but with so much air and sun it was not bad. Now we have had a week of fog and rain, and whether the windows are open or not, the smell is here.

It creeps all over the house.

I find it hovering in the dining-room, skulking in the parlor, hiding in the hall, lying in wait for me on the stairs.

It gets into my hair.

Even when I go to ride, if I turn my head suddenly and surprise it—there is that smell!

Such a peculiar odor, too! I have spent hours in trying to analyze it, to find what it smelled like.

It is not bad—at first, and very gentle, but quite the subtlest, most enduring odor I ever met.

In this damp weather it is awful, I wake up in the night and find it hanging over me.

It used to disturb me at first. I thought seriously of burning the house—to reach the smell.

But now I am used to it. The only thing I can think of that it is like is the *color* of the paper! A yellow smell.

There is a very funny mark on this wall, low down, near the mopboard. A streak that runs around the room. It goes behind every piece of furniture, except the bed, a long, straight, even *smooch*, as if it had been rubbed over and over.

I wonder how it was done and who did it, and what they did it for. Round and round and round—round and round and round—it makes me dizzy!

I really have discovered something at last.

Through watching so much at night, when it changes so, I have finally found out.

The front pattern *does* move—and no wonder! The woman behind shakes it!

Sometimes I think there are a great many women behind, and sometimes only one, and she crawls around fast, and her crawling shakes it all over.

Then in the very bright spots she keeps still, and in the very shady spots she just takes hold of the bars and shakes them hard.

And she is all the time trying to climb through. But nobody could climb through that pattern—it strangles so; I think that is why it has so many heads.

They get through, and then the pattern strangles them off and turns them upside down, and makes their eyes white!

If those heads were covered or taken off it would not be half so bad.

I think that woman gets out in the daytime!

And I'll tell you why—privately—I've seen her!

I can see her out of every one of my windows!

It is the same woman, I know, for she is always creeping, and most women do not creep by daylight.

I see her in that long shaded lane, creeping up and down. I see her in those dark grape arbors, creeping all around the garden.

I see her on that long road under the trees, creeping along, and when a carriage comes she hides under the blackberry vines.

I don't blame her a bit. It must be very humiliating to be caught creeping by daylight!

I always lock the door when I creep by daylight. I can't do it at night, for I know John would suspect something at once.

And John is so queer now, that I don't want to irritate him. I wish he would take another room! Besides, I don't want anybody to get that woman out at night but myself.

I often wonder if I could see her out of all the windows at once.

But, turn as fast as I can, I can only see out of one at one time.

And though I always see her, she *may* be able to creep faster than I can turn!

I have watched her sometimes away off in the open country, creeping as fast as a cloud shadow in a high wind.

If only that top pattern could be gotten off from the under one! I mean to try it, little by little.

I have found out another funny thing, but I shan't tell it this time! It does not do to trust people too much.

There are only two more days to get this paper off, and I believe John is beginning to notice. I don't like the look in his eyes.

And I heard him ask Jennie a lot of professional questions about me. She had a very good report to give.

She said I slept a good deal in the daytime.

John knows I don't sleep very well at night, for all I'm so quiet!

He asked me all sorts of questions, too, and pretended to be very loving and kind.

As if I couldn't see through him!

Still, I don't wonder he acts so, sleeping under this paper for three months.

It only interests me, but I feel sure John and Jennie are secretly affected by it.

Hurrah! This is the last day, but it is enough. John is to stay in town over night, and won't be out until this evening.

Jennie wanted to sleep with me—the sly thing! but I told her I should undoubtedly rest better for a night all alone.

That was clever, for really I wasn't alone a bit! As soon as it was moonlight and that poor thing began to crawl and shake the pattern, I got up and ran to help her.

I pulled and she shook, I shook and she pulled, and before morning we had peeled off yards of that paper.

A strip about as high as my head and half around the room.

And then when the sun came and that awful pattern began to laugh at me, I declared I would finish it to-day!

We go away to-morrow, and they are moving all my furniture down again to leave things as they were before.

Jennie looked at the wall in amazement, but I told her merrily that I did it out of pure spite at the vicious thing.

She laughed and said she wouldn't mind doing it herself, but I must not get tired.

How she betrayed herself that time!

But I am here, and no person touches this paper but Me—not *alive*!

She tried to get me out of the room—it was too patent! But I said it was so quiet and empty and clean now that I believed I would lie down again and sleep all I could; and not to wake me even for dinner—I would call when I woke.

So now she is gone, and the servants are gone, and the things are gone, and there is nothing left but that great bedstead nailed down, with the canvas mattress we found on it.

We shall sleep downstairs to-night, and take the boat home to-morrow.

I quite enjoy the room, now it is bare again.

How those children did tear about here!

This bedstead is fairly gnawed!

But I must get to work.

I have locked the door and thrown the key down into the front path.

I don't want to go out, and I don't want to have anybody come in, till John comes.

I want to astonish him.

I've got a rope up here that even Jennie did not find. If that woman does get out, and tries to get away, I can tie her!

But I forgot I could not reach far without anything to stand on! This bed will *not* move!

I tried to lift and push it until I was lame, and then I got so angry I bit off a little piece at one corner—but it hurt my teeth.

Then I peeled off all the paper I could reach standing on the floor. It sticks horribly and the pattern just enjoys it! All those strangled heads and bulbous eyes and waddling fungus growths just shriek with derision!

I am getting angry enough to do something desperate. To jump out of the window would be admirable exercise, but the bars are too strong even to try.

Besides I wouldn't do it. Of course not. I know well enough that a step like that is improper and might be misconstrued.

I don't like to *look* out of the windows even—there are so many of those creeping women, and they creep so fast.

I wonder if they all come out of that wallpaper as I did?

But I am securely fastened now by my well-hidden rope—you don't get *me* out in the road there!

I suppose I shall have to get back behind the pattern when it comes night, and that is hard!

It is so pleasant to be out in this great room and creep around as I please!

I don't want to go outside. I won't, even if Jennie asks me to.

For outside you have to creep on the ground, and everything is green instead of yellow.

But here I can creep smoothly on the floor, and my shoulder just fits that long smooch around the wall, so I cannot lose my way.

Why there's John at the door!

It is no use, young man, you can't open it!

How he does call and pound!

Now he's crying for an axe.

It would be a shame to break down that beautiful door!

"John dear!" said I in the gentlest voice, "the key is down by the front steps, under a plantain leaf!"

That silenced him for a few moments.

Then he said, very quietly indeed, "Open the door, my darling!"

"I can't," said I. "The key is down by the front door under a plantain leaf!"

And then I said it again, several times, very gently and slowly, and said it so often that he had to go and see, and he got it of course, and came in. He stopped short by the door.

"What is the matter?" he cried. "For God's sake, what are you doing!"

I kept on creeping just the same, but I looked at him over my shoulder.

"I've got out at last," said I, "in spite of you and Jane. And I've pulled off most of the paper, so you can't put me back!"

Now why should that man have fainted? But he did, and right across my path by the wall, so that I had to creep over him every time!

# HENRY JAMES
## The Romance of Certain Old Clothes

Toward the middle of the eighteenth century there lived in the Province of Massachusetts a widowed gentlewoman, the mother of three children. Her name is of little account: I shall take the liberty of calling her Mrs Willoughby,—a name, like her own, of a highly respectable sound. She had been left a widow after some six years of marriage, and had devoted herself to the care of her progeny. These young persons grew up in a manner to reward her zeal and to gratify her fondest hopes. The first-born was a son, whom she had called Bernard, after his father. The others were daughters,—born at an interval of three years apart. Good looks were traditional in the family, and this youthful trio were not likely to allow the tradition to perish. The boy was of that fair and ruddy complexion and of that athletic mould which in those days (as in these) were the sign of genuine English blood,—a frank, affectionate young fellow, a deferential son, a patronizing brother, and a steadfast friend. Clever, however, he was not; the wit of the family had been apportioned chiefly to his sisters. Mr Willoughby had been a great reader of Shakespeare, at a time when this pursuit implied more liberality of taste than at the present day, and in a community where it required much courage to patronize the drama even in the closet; and he had wished to record his admiration of the great poet by calling his daughters out of his favorite plays. Upon the elder he had bestowed the romantic name of Viola; and upon the younger, the more serious one of Perdita, in memory of a little girl born between them, who had lived but a few weeks.

When Bernard Willoughby came to his sixteenth year, his mother put a brave face upon it, and prepared to execute her husband's last request. This had been an earnest entreaty that, at the proper age, his son should be sent out to England, to complete his education at the University of Oxford, which had been the seat of his own studies. Mrs Willoughby fancied that the lad's equal was not to be found in the two hemispheres, but she had the antique wifely submissiveness. She swallowed her sobs, and made up her boy's trunk and his simple provincial outfit, and sent him on his way across the seas. Bernard was entered at his father's college, and spent five years in England, without great honor, indeed, but with a vast deal of pleasure and no discredit. On leaving the University he made the journey to France. In his twenty-third year he took ship for home, prepared to find poor little New England (New England was very small in those days) an utterly intolerable place of abode. But there had been changes at home, as well as in Mr Bernard's opinions. He found his mother's house quite habitable, and his sisters grown into two very charming young ladies, with all the accomplishments and graces of the young women of Britain, and a certain native-grown gentle *brusquerie* and wildness, which, if it was not an accomplishment, was certainly a grace the more. Bernard privately assured his mother that his sisters were fully a match for the most genteel young women in England; whereupon poor Mrs Willoughby you may be sure, bade them hold up their heads. Such was Bernard's opinion, and such, in a tenfold higher degree, was the opinion of Mr Arthur Lloyd. This gentleman, I hasten to add, was a college-mate of Mr Bernard, a young man of reputable family, of a good person and a handsome inheritance, which latter appurtenance he proposed to invest in trade in this country. He and Bernard were warm friends; they had crossed the ocean together, and the young American had lost no time in presenting him at his mother's house, where he had made quite as good an impression as that which he had received, and of which I have just given a hint.

The two sisters were at this time in all the freshness of their youthful bloom; each wearing, of course, this natural brilliancy in the manner that became her best. They were equally dissimilar in appearance and character. Viola, the elder,—now in her twenty-second year,—was tall and fair, with calm gray eyes and auburn tresses; a very faint likeness to the Viola of Shakespeare's comedy, whom I imagine as a brunette (if you will), but a slender, airy creature, full of the softest and finest emotions. Miss Willoughby, with her candid complexion, her fine arms, her majestic height, and her slow utterance, was not cut out for adventures. She would never have put on a man's jacket and hose; and, indeed, being a very plump beauty, it is perhaps as well that she would not. Perdita, too, might very well have exchanged the sweet melancholy of her name against something more in consonance with her aspect and disposition. She was a positive brunette, short of stature, light of foot, with a vivid dark brown eye. She had been from her childhood a creature of smiles and gayety; and so far from making you wait for an answer to your speech, as her handsome sister was wont to do (while she gazed at you with her somewhat cold gray eyes), she had given you the choice of half a dozen, suggested by the successive clauses of your proposition, before you had got to the end of it.

The young girls were very glad to see their brother once more; but they found themselves quite able to maintain a reserve of good-will for their brother's friend. Among the young men their friends and neighbors, the *belle jeunesse* of the Colony, there were many excellent fellows, several devoted swains, and some two or three who enjoyed the reputation of universal charmers and conquerors. But the home-bred arts and the somewhat boisterous gallantry of those honest young colonists were completely eclipsed by the good looks, the fine clothes, the punctilious courtesy, the perfect elegance, the immense information, of Mr Arthur Lloyd. He was in reality no paragon; he was an honest, resolute, intelligent young man rich in pounds sterling, in his health and comfortable hopes, and his little capital of uninvested affections. But he was a gentleman; he had a handsome face; he had studied and travelled; he spoke French, he played on the flute, and he read verses aloud with very great taste. There were a dozen reasons why Miss Willoughby and her sister should forthwith have been rendered fastidious in the choice of their male acquaintance. The imagination of woman is especially adapted to the various small conventions and mysteries of polite society. Mr Lloyd's talk told our little New England maidens a vast deal more of the ways and means of people of fashion in European capitals than he had any idea of doing. It was delightful to sit by and hear him and Bernard discourse upon the fine people and fine things they had seen. They would all gather round the fire after tea, in the little wainscoted parlor,—quite innocent then of any intention of being picturesque or of being anything else, indeed, than economical, and saving an outlay in stamped papers and tapestries,—and the two young men would remind each other, across the rug, of this, that, and the other adventure. Viola and Perdita would often have given their ears to know exactly what adventure it was, and where it happened, and who was there, and what the ladies had on; but in those days a well-bred young woman was not expected to break into the conversation of her own movement or to ask too many questions; and the poor girls used therefore to sit fluttering behind the more languid—or more discreet—curiosity of their mother.

That they were both very fine girls Arthur Lloyd was not slow to discover; but it took him some time to satisfy himself as to the apportionment of their charms. He had a strong presentiment—an emotion of a nature entirely too cheerful to be called a foreboding—that he was destined to marry one of them; yet he was unable to arrive at a preference, and for such a consummation a preference was certainly indispensable, inasmuch as Lloyd was quite too gallant a fellow to make a choice by lot and be cheated of the heavenly delight of falling in love. He resolved to take things easily, and to let his heart speak. Meanwhile, he was on a very pleasant footing. Mrs Willoughby showed a dignified indifference to his "intentions," equally remote from a carelessness of her daughters' honor and from that odious alacrity to make him commit himself, which, in his quality of a young man of property, he had but too often encountered in the venerable dames of his native islands. As for Bernard, all that he asked was that his friend should take his sisters as his own; and as for the poor girls themselves, however each may have secretly longed for the monopoly of Mr Lloyd's attentions, they observed a very decent and modest and contented demeanor.

Towards each other, however, they were somewhat more on the offensive. They were good sisterly friends, betwixt whom it would take more than a day for the seeds of jealousy to sprout and bear fruit; but the young girls felt that the seeds had been sown on the day that Mr Lloyd came into the house. Each made up her mind that, if she should be slighted, she would bear her grief in silence, and that no one should be any the wiser; for if they had a great deal of love, they had also a great deal of pride. But each prayed in secret, nevertheless, that upon *her* the glory might fall. They had need of a vast deal of patience, of self-control, and of dissimulation. In those days a young girl of decent breeding could make no advances whatever, and barely respond, indeed, to those that were made. She was expected to sit still in her chair with her eyes on the carpet, watching the spot where the mystic handkerchief should fall. Poor Arthur Lloyd was obliged to undertake his wooing in the little wainscoted parlor, before the eyes of Mrs Willoughby, her son, and his prospective sister-in-law. But youth and love are so cunning that a hundred signs and tokens might travel to and fro, and not one of these three pair of eyes detect them in their passage. The young girls had but one chamber and one bed between them, and for long hours together they were under each other's direct inspection. That each knew that she was being watched, however, made not a grain of difference in those little offices which they mutually rendered, or in the various household tasks which they performed in common. Neither flinched nor fluttered beneath the silent batteries of her sister's eyes. The only apparent change in their habits was that they had less to say to each other. It was impossible to talk about Mr Lloyd, and it was ridiculous to talk about anything else. By tacit agreement they began to wear all their choice finery, and to devise such little implements of coquetry, in the way of ribbons and top knots and furbelows as were sanctioned by indubitable modesty. They executed in the same inarticulate fashion an agreement of sincerity on these delicate matters. "Is it better so?" Viola would ask, tying a bunch of ribbons on her bosom, and turning about from her glass to her sister. Perdita would look up gravely from her work and examine the decoration. "I think you had better give it another loop," she would say, with great solemnity, looking hard at her sister with eyes that added, "upon my honor!" So they were forever stitching and trimming their petticoats, and pressing out their muslins, and contriving washes and ointments and cosmetics, like the ladies in the household of the Vicar of Wakefield. Some three or four months went by; it grew to be mid-winter, and as yet Viola knew that if Perdita had nothing more to boast of than she, there was not much to be feared from her rivalry. But Perdita by this time, the charming Perdita, felt that her secret had grown to be tenfold more precious than her sister's.

One afternoon Miss Willoughby sat alone before her toilet-glass combing out her long hair. It was getting too dark to see; she lit the two candles in their sockets on the frame of her mirror, and then went to the window to draw her curtains. It was a gray December evening; the landscape was bare and bleak, and the sky heavy with snow-clouds. At the end of the long garden into which her window looked was a wall with a little postern door, opening into a lane. The door stood ajar, as she could vaguely see in the gathering darkness, and moved slowly to and fro, as if someone were swaying it from the lane without. It was doubtless a servant-maid. But as she was about to drop her curtain, Viola saw her sister step within the garden and hurry along the path toward the house. She dropped the curtain, all save a little crevice for her eyes. As Perdita came up the path, she seemed to be examining something in her hand, holding it close to her eyes. When she reached the house she stopped a moment, looked intently at the object, and pressed it to her lips.

Poor Viola slowly came back to her chair, and sat down before her glass, where, if she had looked at it less abstractedly, she would have seen her handsome features sadly disfigured by jealousy. A moment afterwards the door opened behind her, and her sister came into the room, out of breath, and her cheeks aglow with the chilly air.

Perdita started. "Ah," said she, "I thought you were with our mother." The ladies were to go to a tea-party, and on such occasions it was the habit of one of the young girls to help their mother to dress. Instead of coming in Perdita lingered at the door.

"Come in, come in," said Viola. "We've more than an hour yet. I should like you very much to give a few strokes to my hair." She knew her sister wished to retreat, and that she could see in the glass all her movements in the room. "Nay, just help me with my hair," she said, "and I'll go to mamma."

Perdita came reluctantly, and took the brush. She saw her sister's eyes, in the glass, fastened hard upon her hands. She had not made three passes, when Viola clapped her own right hand upon her sister's left, and started out of her chair. "Whose ring is that?" she cried passionately, drawing her towards the light.

On the young girl's third finger glistened a little gold ring, adorned with a couple of small rubies. Perdita felt that she need no longer keep her secret, yet that she must put a bold face on her avowal. "It's mine," she said proudly.

"Who gave it to you?" cried the other.

Perdita hesitated a moment. "Mr Lloyd."

"Mr Lloyd is generous, all of a sudden."

"Ah no," cried Perdita, with spirit, "not all of a sudden. He offered it to me a month ago."

"And you needed a month's begging to take it?" said Viola, looking at the little trinket; which indeed was not especially elegant, although it was the best that the jeweller of the Province could furnish. "I shouldn't have taken it in less than two."

"It isn't the ring," said Perdita, "it's what it means!"

"It means that you're not a modest girl," cried Viola. "Pray does your mother know of your conduct? does Bernard?"

"My mother has approved my 'conduct,' as you call it. Mr Lloyd has asked my hand, and mamma has given it. Would you have had him apply to you, sister?"

Viola gave her sister a long look, full of passionate envy and sorrow. Then she dropped her lashes on her pale cheeks and turned away. Perdita felt that it had not been a pretty scene; but it was her sister's fault. But the elder girl rapidly called back her pride, and turned herself about again. "You have my very best wishes," she said, with a low curtsey. "I wish you every happiness, and a very long life."

Perdita gave a bitter laugh. "Don't speak in that tone," she cried. "I'd rather you cursed me outright. Come, sister," she added, "he couldn't marry both of us."

"I wish you very great joy," Viola repeated mechanically, sitting down to her glass again, "and a very long life, and plenty of children."

There was something in the sound of these words not at all to Perdita's taste. "Will you give me a year, at least?" she said. "In a year I can have one little boy,—or one little girl at least. If you'll give me your brush again I'll do your hair."

"Thank you," said Viola. "You had better go to mamma. It isn't becoming that a young lady with a promised husband should wait on a girl with none."

"Nay," said Perdita, good-humoredly, "I have Arthur to wait upon me. You need my service more than I need yours."

But her sister motioned her away, and she left the room. When she had gone poor Viola fell on her knees before her dressing-table, buried her head in her arms, and poured out a flood of tears and sobs. She felt very much better for this effusion of sorrow. When her sister came back, she insisted upon helping her to dress, and upon her wearing her prettiest things. She forced upon her acceptance a bit of lace of her own, and declared that now that she was to be married she should do her best to appear worthy of her lover's choice. She discharged these offices in stern silence; but, such as they were, they had to do duty as an apology and an atonement; she never made any other.

Now that Lloyd was received by the family as an accepted suitor, nothing remained but to fix the wedding-day. It was appointed for the following April, and in the interval preparations were diligently made for the marriage. Lloyd, on his side, was busy with his commercial arrangements, and with establishing a correspondence with the great mercantile house to which he had attached himself in England. He was therefore not so frequent a visitor at Mrs Willoughby's as during the months of his diffidence and irresolution, and poor Viola had less to suffer than she had feared from the sight of the mutual endearments of the young lovers. Touching his future sister-in-law, Lloyd had a perfectly clear conscience. There had not been a particle of sentiment uttered between them, and he had not the slightest suspicion that she coveted anything more than his fraternal regard. He was quite at his ease; life promised so well, both domestically and financially. The lurid clouds of revolution were as yet twenty years beneath the horizon, and that his connubial felicity should take a tragic turn it was absurd, it was blasphemous, to apprehend. Meanwhile at Mrs Willoughby's there was a greater rustling of silks, a more rapid clicking of scissors and flying of needles, than ever. Mrs Willoughby had determined that her daughter should carry from home the most elegant outfit that her money could buy, or that the country could furnish. All the sage women in the county were convened, and their united taste was brought to bear on Perdita's wardrobe. Viola's situation, at this moment, was assuredly not to be envied. The poor girl had an inordinate love of dress, and the very best taste in the world, as her sister perfectly well knew. Viola was tall, she was stately and sweeping, she was made to carry stiff brocade and masses of heavy lace, such as belong to the toilet of a rich man's wife. But Viola sat aloof, with her beautiful arms folded and her head averted, while her mother and sister and the venerable women aforesaid worried and wondered over their materials, oppressed by the multitude of their resources. One day there came in a beautiful piece of white silk, brocaded with celestial blue and silver, sent by the bridegroom himself,—it not being thought amiss in those days that the husband-elect should contribute to the bride's trousseau. Perdita was quite at a loss to imagine a fashion which should do sufficient honor to the splendor of the material.

"Blue's your color, sister, more than mine," she said, with appealing eyes. "It's a pity it's not for you. You'd know what to do with it."

Viola got up from her place and looked at the great shining fabric as it lay spread over the back of a chair. Then she took it up in her hands and felt it,—lovingly, as Perdita could see,—and turned about toward the mirror with it. She let it roll down to her feet, and flung the other end over her shoulder, gathering it in about her waist with her white arm bare to the elbow. She threw back her head, and looked at her image, and a hanging tress of her auburn hair fell upon the gorgeous surface of the silk. It made a dazzling picture. The women standing about uttered a little "Ah!" of admiration. "Yes, indeed," said

Viola, quietly, "blue is my color." But Perdita could see that her fancy had been stirred, and that she would now fall to work and solve all their silken riddles. And indeed she behaved very well, as Perdita, knowing her insatiable love of millinery, was quite ready to declare. Innumerable yards of lustrous silk and satin, of muslin, velvet, and lace, passed through her cunning hands, without a word of envy coming from her lips. Thanks to her industry, when the wedding-day came Perdita was prepared to espouse more of the vanities of life than any fluttering young bride who had yet challenged the sacramental blessing of a New England divine.

It had been arranged that the young couple should go out and spend the first days of their wedded life at the country house of an English gentleman,—a man of rank and a very kind friend to Lloyd. He was an unmarried man; he professed himself delighted to withdraw and leave them for a week to their billing and cooing. After the ceremony at church,—it had been performed by an English parson,—young Mrs Lloyd hastened back to her mother's house to change her wedding gear for a riding-dress. Viola helped her to effect the change, in the little old room in which they had been fond sisters together. Perdita then hurried off to bid farewell to her mother, leaving Viola to follow. The parting was short; the horses were at the door and Arthur impatient to start. But Viola had not followed, and Perdita hastened back to her room, opening the door abruptly. Viola, as usual, was before the glass, but in a position which caused the other to stand still, amazed. She had dressed herself in Perdita's cast-off wedding veil and wreath, and on her neck she had hung the heavy string of pearls which the young girl had received from her husband as a wedding gift. These things had been hastily laid aside, to await their possessor's disposal on her return from the country. Bedizened in this unnatural garb, Viola stood at the mirror, plunging a long look into its depths, and reading Heaven knows what audacious visions. Perdita was horrified. It was a hideous image of their old rivalry come to life again. She made a step toward her sister, as if to pull off the veil and the flowers. But catching her eyes in the glass, she stopped.

"Farewell, Viola," she said. "You might at least have waited till I had got out of the house." And she hurried away from the room.

Mr Lloyd had purchased in Boston a house which, in the taste of those days, was considered a marvel of elegance and comfort; and here he very soon established himself with his young wife. He was thus separated by a distance of twenty miles from the residence of his mother-in-law. Twenty miles, in that primitive era of roads and conveyances, were as serious a matter as a hundred at the present day, and Mrs Willoughby saw but little of her daughter during the first twelvemonth of her marriage. She suffered in no small degree from her absence; and her affliction was not diminished by the fact that Viola had fallen into terribly low spirits and was not to be roused or cheered but by change of air and circumstances. The real cause of the young girl's dejection the reader will not be slow to suspect. Mrs Willoughby and her gossips, however, deemed her complaint a purely physical one, and doubted not that she would obtain relief from the remedy just mentioned. Her mother accordingly proposed on her behalf a visit to certain relatives on the paternal side, established in New York, who had long complained that they were able to see so little of their New England cousins. Viola was despatched to these good people, under a suitable escort, and remained with them for several months. In the interval her brother Bernard, who had begun the practice of the law, made up his mind to take a wife. Viola came home to the wedding, apparently cured of her heartache, with honest roses and lilies in her face, and a proud smile on her lips. Arthur Lloyd came over from Boston to see his brother-in-law married, but without his wife, who was expecting shortly to present him with an heir. It was nearly a year since Viola had seen him. She was glad—she hardly knew why—that Perdita had stayed at home. Arthur looked happy, but he was more grave and solemn than before his marriage. She thought he looked "interesting,"—for although the word in its modern sense was not then invented, we may be sure that the idea was. The truth is, he was simply preoccupied with his wife's condition. Nevertheless, he by no means failed to observe Viola's beauty and splendor, and how she quite effaced the poor little bride. The allowance that Perdita had enjoyed for her dress had now been transferred to her sister, who turned it to prodigious account. On the morning after the wedding, he had a lady's saddle put on the horse of the servant who had come with him from town, and went out with the young girl for a ride. It was a keen, clear morning in January; the ground was bare and hard, and the horses in good condition,—to say nothing of Viola, who was charming in her hat and plume, and her dark blue riding-coat, trimmed with fur. They rode all the morning, they lost their way, and were obliged to stop for dinner at a farm-house. The early winter dusk had fallen when they got home. Mrs Willoughby met them with a long face. A messenger had arrived at noon from Mrs Lloyd; she was beginning to be ill, and desired her husband's immediate return. The young man, at the thought that he had lost several hours, and that by hard riding he might already have been with his wife, uttered a passionate oath. He barely consented to stop for a mouthful of supper, but mounted the messenger's horse and started off at a gallop.

He reached home at midnight. His wife had been delivered of a little girl. "Ah, why weren't you with me?" she said, as he came to her bedside.

"I was out of the house when the man came. I was with Viola," said Lloyd, innocently.

Mrs Lloyd made a little moan, and turned about. But she continued to do very well, and for a week her improvement was uninterrupted. Finally, however, through some indiscretion in the way of diet or of exposure, it was checked, and the poor lady grew rapidly worse. Lloyd was in despair. It very soon became evident that she was breathing her last. Mrs Lloyd came to a sense of her approaching end, and declared that she was reconciled with death. On the third evening after the change took place she told her husband that she felt she would not outlast the night. She dismissed her servants, and also requested her mother to withdraw,—Mrs Willoughby having arrived on the preceding day. She had had her infant placed on the bed beside her, and she lay on her side, with the child against her breast, holding her husband's hands. The night-lamp was hidden behind the heavy curtain of the bed, but the room was illumined with a red glow from the immense fire of logs on the hearth.

"It seems strange to die by such a fire as that," the young woman said, feebly trying to smile. "If I had but a little of such fire in my veins! But I've given it all to this little spark of mortality." And she dropped her eyes on her child. Then raising them she looked at her husband with a long penetrating gaze. The last feeling which lingered in her heart was one of mistrust. She had not recovered from the shock which Arthur had given her by telling her that in the hour of her agony he had been with Viola. She trusted her husband very nearly as well as she loved him; but now that she was called away forever, she felt a cold horror of her sister. She felt in her soul that Viola had never ceased to envy her good fortune; and a year of happy security had not effaced the young girl's image, dressed in her wedding garments, and smiling with coveted triumph. Now that Arthur was to be alone, what might not Viola do? She was beautiful, she was engaging; what arts might she not use, what impression might she not make upon the young man's melancholy heart? Mrs Lloyd looked at her husband in silence. It seemed hard, after all, to doubt of his constancy. His fine eyes were filled with tears; his face was convulsed with weeping; the clasp of his hands was warm and passionate. How noble he looked, how tender, how faithful and devoted! "Nay," thought Perdita, "he's not for such as Viola. He'll never forget me. Nor does Viola truly care for him; she cares only for vanities and finery and jewels." And she dropped her eyes on her white hands, which her husband's liberality had covered with rings, and on the lace ruffles which trimmed the edge of her nightdress. "She covets my rings and my laces more than she covets my husband."

At this moment the thought of her sister's rapacity seemed to cast a dark shadow between her and the helpless figure of her little girl. "Arthur," she said, "you must take off my rings. I shall not be buried in them. One of these days my daughter shall wear them,—my rings and my laces and silks. I had them all brought out and shown me to-day. It's a great wardrobe,—there's not such another in the Province; I can say it without vanity now that I've done with it. It will be a great inheritance for my daughter, when she grows into a young woman. There are things there that a man never buys twice, and if they're lost you'll never again see the like. So you'll watch them well. Some dozen things I've left to Viola; I've named them to my mother. I've given her that blue and silver; it was meant for her; I wore it only once, I looked ill in it. But the rest are to be sacredly kept for this little innocent. It's such a providence that she should be my color; she can wear my gowns; she has her mother's eyes. You know the same fashions come back every twenty years. She can wear my gowns as they are. They'll lie there quietly waiting till she grows into them,—wrapped in camphor and rose-leaves, and keeping their colors in the sweet-scented darkness. She shall have black hair, she shall wear my carnation satin. Do you promise me, Arthur?"

"Promise you what, dearest?"

"Promise me to keep your poor little wife's old gowns."

"Are you afraid I'll sell them?"

"No, but that they may get scattered. My mother will have them properly wrapped up, and you shall lay them away under a double-lock. Do you know the great chest in the attic, with the iron bands? There's no end to what it will hold. You can lay them all there. My mother and the housekeeper will do it, and give you the key. And you'll keep the key in your secretary, and never give it to any one but your child. Do you promise me?"

"Ah, yes, I promise you," said Lloyd, puzzled at the intensity with which his wife appeared to cling to this idea.

"Will you swear?" repeated Perdita.

"Yes, I swear."

"Well—I trust you—I trust you," said the poor lady, looking into his eyes with eyes in which, if he had suspected her vague apprehensions, he might have read an appeal quite as much as an assurance.

Lloyd bore his bereavement soberly and manfully. A month after his wife's death, in the course of commerce, circumstances arose which offered him an opportunity of going to England. He embraced it as a diversion from gloomy thoughts. He was absent nearly a year, during which his little girl was tenderly nursed and cherished by her grandmother. On his return he had his house again thrown open, and announced his intention of keeping the same state as during his wife's lifetime. It very soon came to be predicted that he would marry again, and there were at least a dozen young women of whom one may say that it was by no fault of theirs that, for six months after his return, the prediction did not come true. During this interval he still left his little daughter in Mrs Willoughby's hands, the latter assuring him that a change of residence at so tender an age was perilous to her health. Finally, however, he declared that his heart longed for his daughter's presence, and that she must be brought up to town. He sent his coach and his housekeeper to fetch her home. Mrs Willoughby was in terror lest something should befall her on the road; and, in accordance with this feeling, Viola offered to ride along with her. She could return the next day. So she went up to town with her little niece, and Mr Lloyd met her on the threshold of his house, overcome with her kindness and with gratitude. Instead of returning the next day, Viola stayed out the week; and when at last she reappeared, she had only come for her clothes. Arthur would not hear of her coming home, nor would the baby. She cried and moaned if Viola left her; and at the sight of her grief Arthur lost his wits, and swore that she was going to die. In fine, nothing would suit them but that Viola should remain until the poor child had grown used to strange faces.

It took two months to bring this consummation about; for it was not until this period had elapsed that Viola took leave of her brother-in-law. Mrs Willoughby had shaken her head over her daughter's absence; she declared it was not becoming, and that it was the talk of the town. She had reconciled herself to it only because, during the young girl's visit, the household enjoyed an unwonted term of peace. Bernard Willoughby had brought his wife home to live, between whom and her sister-in-law there existed a bitter hostility. Viola was perhaps no angel; but in the daily practice of life she was a sufficiently good-natured girl, and if she quarrelled with Mrs Bernard, it was not without provocation. Quarrel, however, she did, to the great annoyance not only of her antagonist, but of the two spectators of these constant altercations. Her stay in the household of her brother-in-law, therefore, would have been delightful, if only because it removed her from contact with the object of her antipathy at home. It was doubly—it was ten times—delightful, in that it kept her near the object of her old passion. Mrs Lloyd's poignant mistrust had fallen very far short of the truth. Viola's sentiment had been a passion at first, and a passion it remained,—a passion of whose radiant heat, tempered to the delicate state of his feelings, Mr Lloyd very soon felt the influence. Lloyd, as I have hinted, was not a modern Petrarch; it was not in his nature to practise an ideal constancy. He had not been many days in the house with his sister-in-law before he began to assure himself that she was, in the language of that day, a devilish fine woman. Whether Viola really practised those insidious arts that her sister had been tempted to impute to her it is needless to inquire. It is enough to say that she found means to appear to the very best advantage. She used to seat herself every morning before the great fireplace in the dining-room, at work upon a piece of tapestry, with her little niece disporting herself on the carpet at her feet, or on the train of her dress, and playing with her woollens balls. Lloyd would have been a very stupid fellow if he had remained insensible to the rich suggestions of this charming picture. He was prodigiously fond of his little girl, and was never weary of taking her in his arms and tossing her up and down, and making her crow with delight. Very often, however, he would venture upon greater liberties than the young lady was yet prepared to allow, and she would suddenly vociferate her displeasure. Viola would then drop her tapestry, and put out her handsome hands with the serious smile of the young girl whose virgin fancy has revealed to her all a mother's healing arts. Lloyd would give up the child, their eyes would meet, their hands would touch, and Viola would extinguish the little girl's sobs upon the snowy folds of her kerchief that crossed her bosom. Her dignity was perfect, and nothing could be more discreet than the manner in which she accepted her brother-in-law's hospitality. It may be almost said, perhaps, that there was something harsh in her reserve. Lloyd had a provoking feeling that she was in the house, and yet that she was unapproachable. Half an hour after supper, at the very outset of the long winter evenings, she would light her candle, and make the young man a most respectful curtsey, and march off to bed. If these were arts, Viola was a great artist. But their effect was so gentle, so gradual, they were calculated to work upon the young widower's fancy with such a finely shaded *crescendo*, that, as the reader has seen, several weeks elapsed before Viola began to feel sure that her return would cover her outlay. When this became morally certain, she packed up her trunk, and returned to her mother's house. For three days she waited; on the fourth Mr Lloyd made his appearance, a respectful but ardent suitor. Viola heard him out with great humility, and accepted him with infinite modesty. It is hard to imagine that Mrs Lloyd should have forgiven her husband; but if anything might have disarmed her resentment, it would have been the ceremonious continence of this interview. Viola imposed upon her lover but a short probation. They were married, as was becoming, with great privacy,—almost with secrecy,—in the hope perhaps, as was waggishly remarked at the time, that the late Mrs Lloyd wouldn't hear of it.

The marriage was to all appearance a happy one, and each party obtained what each had desired—Lloyd "a devilish fine woman," and Viola—but Viola's desires, as the reader will have observed, have remained a good deal of a mystery. There were, indeed, two blots upon their felicity; but time would, perhaps, efface them. During the first three years of her marriage Mrs Lloyd failed to become a mother, and her husband on his side suffered heavy losses of money. This latter circumstance compelled a material retrenchment in his expenditure, and Viola was perforce less of a great lady than her sister had been. She contrived, however, to sustain with unbroken consistency the part of an elegant woman, although it must be confessed that it required the exercise of more ingenuity than belongs to your real aristocratic repose. She had long since ascertained that her sister's immense wardrobe had been sequestrated for the benefit of her daughter, and that it lay languishing in thankless gloom in the dusty attic. It was a revolting thought that these exquisite fabrics should await the commands of a little girl who sat in a high chair and ate bread-and-milk with a wooden spoon. Viola had the good taste, however, to say nothing about the matter until several months had expired. Then, at last, she timidly broached it to her husband. Was it not a pity that so much finery should be lost?—for lost it would be, what with colors fading, and moths eating it up, and the change of fashions. But Lloyd gave so abrupt and peremptory a negative to her inquiry, that she saw that for the present her attempt was vain. Six months went by, however, and brought with them new needs and new fancies. Viola's thoughts hovered lovingly about her sister's relics. She went up and looked at the chest in which they lay imprisoned. There was a sullen defiance in its three great padlocks and its iron bands, which only quickened her desires. There was something exasperating in its incorruptible immobility. It was like a grim and grizzled old household servant, who locks his jaws over a family secret. And then there was a look of capacity in its vast extent, and a sound as of dense fulness, when Viola knocked its side with the toe of her little slipper, which caused her to flush with baffled longing. "It's absurd," she cried; "it's improper, it's wicked"; and she forthwith resolved upon another attack upon her husband. On the following day, after dinner, when he had had his wine, she bravely began it. But he cut her short with great sternness.

"Once and for all, Viola," said he, "it's out of the question. I shall be gravely displeased if you return to the matter."

"Very good," said Viola. "I'm glad to learn the value at which I'm held. Great Heaven!" she cried, "I'm a happy woman. It's an agreeable thing to feel one's self sacrificed to a caprice!" And her eyes filled with tears of anger and disappointment.

Lloyd had a good-natured man's horror of a woman's sobs, and he attempted—I may say he condescended—to explain. "It's not a caprice, dear, it's a promise," he said,—"an oath."

"An oath? It's a pretty matter for oaths! and to whom, pray?"

"To Perdita," said the young man, raising his eyes for an instant, but immediately dropping them.

"Perdita,—ah, Perdita!" and Viola's tears broke forth. Her bosom heaved with stormy sobs,—sobs which were the long-deferred counterpart of the violent fit of weeping in which she had indulged herself on the night when she discovered her sister's betrothal. She had hoped, in her better moments, that she had done with her jealousy; but her temper, on that occasion, had taken an ineffaceable fold. "And pray, what right," she cried, "had Perdita to dispose of my future? What right had she to bind you to meanness and cruelty? Ah, I occupy a dignified place, and I make a very fine figure! I'm welcome to what Perdita has left! And what has she left? I never knew till now how little! Nothing, nothing, nothing."

This was very poor logic, but it was very good passion. Lloyd put his arm around his wife's waist and tried to kiss her, but she shook him off with magnificent scorn. Poor fellow! he had coveted a "devilish fine woman," and he had got one. Her scorn was intolerable. He walked away with his ears tingling,—irresolute, distracted. Before him was his secretary, and in it the sacred key which with his own hand he had turned in the triple lock. He marched up and opened it, and took the key from a secret drawer, wrapped in a little packet which he had sealed with his own honest bit of blazonry. *Teneo*, said the motto,—"I hold." But he was ashamed to put it back. He flung it upon the table beside his wife.

"Keep it!" she cried. " I want it not. I hate it!"

"I wash my hands of it," cried her husband. "God forgive me!"

Mrs Lloyd gave an indignant shrug of her shoulders, and swept out of the room, while the young man retreated by another door. Ten minutes later Mrs Lloyd returned, and found the room occupied by her little step-daughter and the nursery-maid. The key was not on the table. She glanced at the child. The child was perched on a chair with the packet in her hands. She had broken the seal with her own little fingers. Mrs Lloyd hastily took possession of the key.

At the habitual supper-hour Arthur Lloyd came back from his counting-room. It was the month of June, and supper was served by daylight. The meal was placed on the table, but Mrs Lloyd failed to make her appearance. The servant whom his master sent to call her came back with the assurance that her room was empty, and that the women informed him that she had not been seen since dinner. They had in truth observed her to have been in tears, and, supposing her to be shut up in her chamber, had not disturbed her. Her husband called her name in various parts of the house, but without response. At last it occurred to him that he might find her by taking the way to the attic. The thought gave him a strange feeling of discomfort, and he bade his servants remain behind, wishing no witness in his quest. He reached the foot of the staircase leading to the topmost flat, and stood with his hand on the banisters, pronouncing his wife's name. His voice trembled. He called again, louder and more firmly. The only sound which disturbed the absolute silence was a faint echo of his own tones, repeating his question under the great eaves. He nevertheless felt irresistibly moved to ascend the staircase. It opened upon a wide hall, lined with wooden closets, and terminating in a window which looked westward, and admitted the last rays of the sun. Before the window stood the great chest. Before the chest, on her knees, the young man saw with amazement and horror the figure of his wife. In an instant he crossed the interval between them, bereft of utterance. The lid of the chest stood open, exposing, amid their perfumed napkins, its treasure of stuffs and jewels. Viola had fallen backward from a kneeling posture, with one hand supporting her on the floor and the other pressed to her heart. On her limbs was the stiffness of death, and on her face, in the fading light of the sun, the terror of something more than death. Her lips were parted in entreaty, in dismay, in agony; and on her bloodless brow and cheeks there glowed the marks of ten hideous wounds from two vengeful ghostly hands.

AMBROSE BIERCE
The Damned Thing

# I

## ONE DOES NOT ALWAYS EAT WHAT IS ON THE TABLE

By the light of a tallow candle which had been placed on one end of a rough table a man was reading something written in a book. It was an old account book, greatly worn; and the writing was not, apparently, very legible, for the man sometimes held the page close to the flame of the candle to get a stronger light on it. The shadow of the book would then throw into obscurity a half of the moon, darkening a number of faces and figures; for besides the reader, eight other men were present. Seven of them sat against the rough log walls, silent, motionless, and the room being small, not very far from the table. By extending an arm any one of them could have touched the eighth man, who lay on the table, face upward, partly covered by a sheet, his arms at his sides. He was dead.

The man with the book was not reading aloud, and no one spoke; all seemed to be waiting for something to occur; the dead man only was without expectation. From the blank darkness outside came in, through the aperture that served for a window, all the ever unfamiliar noises of night in the wilderness—the long nameless note of a distant coyote; the stilly pulsing thrill of tireless insects in trees; strange cries of night birds, so different from those of the birds of day; the drone of great blundering beetles, and all that mysterious chorus of small sounds that seem always to have been but half heard when they have suddenly ceased, as if conscious of an indiscretion. But nothing of all this was noted in that company; its members were not overmuch addicted to idle interest in matters of no practical importance; that was obvious in every line of their rugged faces—obvious even in the dim light of the single candle. They were evidently men of the vicinity—farmers and woodsmen.

The person reading was a trifle different; one would have said of him that he was of the world, worldly, albeit there was that in his attire which attested a certain fellowship with the organisms of his environment. His coat would hardly have passed muster in San Francisco; his foot-gear was not of urban origin, and the hat that lay by him on the floor (he was the only one uncovered) was such that if one had considered it as an article of mere personal adornment he would have missed its meaning. In countenance the man was rather prepossessing, with just a hint of sternness; though that he may have assumed or cultivated, as appropriate to one in authority. For he was a coroner. It was by virtue of his office that he had possession of the book in which he was reading; it had been found among the dead man's effects—in his cabin, where the inquest was now taking place.

When the coroner had finished reading he put the book into his breast pocket. At that moment the door was pushed open and a young man entered. He, clearly, was not of mountain birth and breeding: he was clad as those who dwell in cities. His clothing was dusty, however, as from travel. He had, in fact, been riding hard to attend the inquest.

The coroner nodded; no one else greeted him.

"We have waited for you," said the coroner. "It is necessary to have done with this business to-night."

The young man smiled. "I am sorry to have kept you," he said. "I went away, not to evade your summons, but to post to my newspaper an account of what I suppose I am called back to relate."

The coroner smiled.

"The account that you posted to your newspaper," he said, "differs, probably, from that which you will give here under oath."

"That," replied the other, rather hotly and with a visible flush, "is as you please. I used manifold paper and have a copy of what I sent. It was not written as news, for it is incredible, but as fiction. It may go as a part of my testimony under oath."

"But you say it is incredible."

"That is nothing to you, sir, if I also swear that it is true."

The coroner was silent for a time, his eyes upon the floor. The men about the sides of the cabin talked in whispers, but seldom withdrew their gaze from the face of the corpse. Presently the coroner lifted his eyes and said: "We will resume the inquest."

The men removed their hats. The witness was sworn.

"What is your name?" the coroner asked.

"William Harker."

"Age?"

"Twenty-seven."

"You knew the deceased, Hugh Morgan?"

"Yes."

"You were with him when he died?"

"Near him."

"How did that happen—your presence, I mean?"

"I was visiting him at this place to shoot and fish. A part of my purpose, however, was to study him and his odd, solitary way of life. He seemed a good model for a character in fiction. I sometimes write stories."

"I sometimes read them."

"Thank you."

"Stories in general—not yours."

Some of the jurors laughed. Against a sombre background humor shows high lights. Soldiers in the intervals of battle laugh easily, and a jest in the death chamber conquers by surprise.

"Relate the circumstances of this man's death," said the coroner. "You may use any notes or memoranda that you please."

The witness understood. Pulling a manuscript from his breast pocket he held it near the candle and turning the leaves until he found the passage that he wanted began to read.

## II

### WHAT MAY HAPPEN IN A FIELD OF WILD OATS

" . . . The sun had hardly risen when we left the house. We were looking for quail, each with a shotgun, but we had only one dog. Morgan said that our best ground was beyond a certain ridge that he pointed out, and we crossed it by a trail through the *chaparral*. On the other side was comparatively level ground, thickly covered with wild oats. As we emerged from the *chaparral* Morgan was but a few yards in advance. Suddenly we heard, at a little distance to our right and partly in front, a noise as of some animal thrashing about in the bushes, which we could see were violently agitated.

" 'We've started a deer,' I said. 'I wish we had brought a rifle.'

"Morgan, who had stopped and was intently watching the agitated *chaparral*, said nothing, but had cocked both barrels of his gun and was holding it in readiness to aim. I thought him a trifle excited, which surprised me, for he had a reputation for exceptional coolness, even in moments of sudden and imminent peril.

" 'O, come,' I said. 'You are not going to fill up a deer with quail-shot, are you?'

"Still he did not reply; but catching a sight of his face as he turned it slightly toward me I was struck by the intensity of his look. Then I understood that we had serious business in hand and my first conjecture was that we had 'jumped' a grizzly. I advanced to Morgan's side, cocking my piece as I moved.

"The bushes were now quiet and the sounds had ceased, but Morgan was as attentive to the place as before.

" 'What is it? What the devil is it?' I asked.

" 'That Damned Thing!' he replied, without turning his head. His voice was husky and unnatural. He trembled visibly.

"I was about to speak further, when I observed the wild oats near the place of the disturbance moving in the most inexplicable way. I can hardly describe it. It seemed as if stirred by a streak of wind, which not only bent it, but pressed it down—crushed it so that it did not rise; and this movement was slowly prolonging itself directly toward us.

"Nothing that I had ever seen had affected me so strangely as this unfamiliar and unaccountable phenomenon, yet I am unable to recall any sense of fear. I remember—and tell it here because, singularly enough, I recollected it then—that once in looking carelessly out of an open window I momentarily mistook a small tree close at hand for one of a group of larger trees at a little distance away. It looked the same size as the others, but being more distinctly and sharply defined in mass and detail seemed out of harmony with them. It was a mere falsification of the law of aërial perspective, but it startled, almost terrified me. We so rely upon the orderly operation of familiar natural laws that any seeming suspension of them is noted as a menace to our safety, a warning of unthinkable calamity. So now the apparently causeless movement of the herbage and the slow, undeviating approach of the line of disturbance were distinctly disquieting. My companion appeared actually frightened, and I could hardly credit my senses when I saw him suddenly throw his gun to his shoulder and fire both barrels at the agitated grain! Before the smoke of the discharge had cleared away I heard a loud savage cry—a scream like that of a wild animal—and flinging his gun upon the ground Morgan sprang away and ran swiftly from the spot. At the same instant I was thrown violently to the ground by the impact of something unseen in the smoke—some soft, heavy substance that seemed thrown against me with great force.

"Before I could get upon my feet and recover my gun, which seemed to have been struck from my hands, I heard Morgan crying out as if in mortal agony, and mingling with his cries were such hoarse, savage sounds as one hears from fighting dogs. Inexpressibly terrified, I struggled to my feet and looked in the direction of Morgan's retreat; and may Heaven in mercy spare me from another sight like that! At a distance of less than thirty yards was my friend, down upon one knee, his head thrown back at a frightful angle, hatless, his long hair in disorder and his whole body in violent movement from side to side, backward and forward. His right arm was lifted and seemed to lack the hand—at least, I could see none. The other arm was invisible. At times, as my memory now reports this extraordinary scene, I could discern but a part of his body; it was as if he had been partly blotted out—I cannot otherwise express it—then a shifting of his position would bring it all into view again.

"All this must have occurred within a few seconds, yet in that time Morgan assumed all the postures of a determined wrestler vanquished by superior weight and strength. I saw nothing but him, and him not always distinctly. During the entire incident his shouts and curses were heard, as if through an enveloping uproar of such sounds of rage and fury as I had never heard from the throat of man or brute!

"For a moment only I stood irresolute, then throwing down my gun I ran forward to my friend's assistance. I had a vague belief that he was suffering from a fit, or some form of convulsion. Before I could reach his side he was down and quiet. All sounds had ceased, but with a feeling of such terror as even these awful events had not inspired I now saw again the mysterious movement of the wild oats, prolonging itself from the trampled area about the prostrate man toward the edge of a wood. It was only when it had reached the wood that I was able to withdraw my eyes and look at my companion. He was dead."

III

A MAN THOUGH NAKED MAY BE IN RAGS

The coroner rose from his seat and stood beside the dead man. Lifting an edge of the sheet he pulled it away, exposing the entire body, altogether naked and showing in the candle-light a claylike yellow. It had, however, broad maculations of bluish black, obviously caused by extravasated blood from contusions. The chest and sides looked as if they had been beaten with a bludgeon. There were dreadful lacerations; the skin was torn in strips and shreds.

The coroner moved round to the end of the table and undid a silk handkerchief which had been passed under the chin and knotted on the top of the head. When the handkerchief was drawn away it exposed what had been the throat. Some of the jurors who had risen to get a better view repented their curiosity and turned away their faces. Witness Harker went to the open window and leaned out across the sill, faint and sick. Dropping the handkerchief upon the dead man's neck the coroner stepped to an angle of the room and from a pile of clothing produced one garment after another, each of which he held up a moment for inspection. All were torn, and stiff with blood. The jurors did not make a closer inspection. They seemed rather uninterested. They had, in truth, seen all this before; the only thing that was new to them being Harker's testimony.

"Gentlemen," the coroner said, "we have no more evidence, I think. Your duty has been already explained to you; if there is nothing you wish to ask you may go outside and consider your verdict."

The foreman rose—a tall, bearded man of sixty, coarsely clad.

"I should like to ask one question, Mr. Coroner," he said. "What asylum did this yer last witness escape from?"

"Mr. Harker," said the coroner, gravely and tranquilly, "from what asylum did you last escape?"

Harker flushed crimson again, but said nothing, and the seven jurors rose and solemnly filed out of the cabin.

"If you have done insulting me, sir," said Harker, as soon as he and the officer were left alone with the dead man, "I suppose I am at liberty to go?"

"Yes."

Harker started to leave, but paused, with his hand on the door latch. The habit of his profession was strong in him—stronger than his sense of personal dignity. He turned about and said:

"The book that you have there—I recognize it as Morgan's diary. You seemed greatly interested in it; you read in it while I was testifying. May I see it? The public would like——"

"The book will cut no figure in this matter," replied the official, slipping it into his coat pocket; "all the entries in it were made before the writer's death."

As Harker passed out of the house the jury reëntered and stood about the table, on which the now covered corpse showed under the sheet with sharp definition. The foreman seated himself near the candle, produced from his breast pocket a pencil and scrap of paper and wrote rather laboriously the following verdict, which with various degrees of effort all signed:

"We, the jury, do find that the remains come to their death at the hands of a mountain lion, but some of us thinks, all the same, they had fits."

## IV

### AN EXPLANATION FROM THE TOMB

In the diary of the late Hugh Morgan are certain interesting entries having, possibly, a scientific value as suggestions. At the inquest upon his body the book was not put in evidence; possibly the coroner thought it not worth while to confuse the jury. The date of the first of the entries mentioned cannot be ascertained; the upper part of the leaf is torn away; the part of the entry remaining follows:

" . . . would run in a half-circle, keeping his head turned always toward the centre, and again he would stand still, barking furiously. At last he ran away into the brush as fast as he could go. I thought at first that he had gone mad, but on returning to the house found no other alteration in his manner than what was obviously due to fear of punishment.

"Can a dog see with his nose? Do odors impress some cerebral centre with images of the thing that emitted them? . . .

"Sept. 2.—Looking at the stars last night as they rose above the crest of the ridge east of the house, I observed them successively disappear—from left to right. Each was eclipsed but an instant, and only a few at the same time, but along the entire length of the ridge all that were within a degree or two of the crest were blotted out. It was as if something had passed along between me and them; but I could not see it, and the stars were not thick enough to define its outline. Ugh! I don't like this." . . .

Several weeks' entries are missing, three leaves being torn from the book.

"Sept. 27.—It has been about here again—I find evidences of its presence every day. I watched again all last night in the same cover, gun in hand, double-charged with buckshot. In the morning the fresh footprints were there, as before. Yet I would have sworn that I did not sleep—indeed, I hardly sleep at all. It is terrible, insupportable! If these amazing experiences are real I shall go mad; if they are fanciful I am mad already.

"Oct. 3.—I shall not go—it shall not drive me away. No, this is *my* house, *my* land. God hates a coward. . . .

"Oct. 5.—I can stand it no longer; I have invited Harker to pass a few weeks with me—he has a level head. I can judge from his manner if he thinks me mad.

"Oct. 7.—I have the solution of the mystery; it came to me last night—suddenly, as by revelation. How simple—how terribly simple!

"There are sounds that we cannot hear. At either end of the scale are notes that stir no chord of that imperfect instrument, the human ear. They are too high or too grave. I have observed a flock of black-birds occupying an entire tree-top—the tops of several trees—and all in full song. Suddenly—in a moment—at absolutely the same instant—all spring into the air and fly away. How? They could not all see one another—whole tree-tops intervened. At no point could a leader have been visible to all. There must have been a signal of warning or command, high and shrill above the din, but by me unheard. I have observed, too, the same simultaneous flight when all were silent, among not only blackbirds, but other birds—quail, for example, widely separated by bushes—even on opposite sides of a hill.

"It is known to seamen that a school of whales basking or sporting on the surface of the ocean, miles apart, with the convexity of the earth between, will sometimes dive at the same instant—all gone out of sight in a moment. The signal has been sounded—too grave for the ear of the sailor at the masthead and his comrades on the deck—who never-theless feel its vibrations in the ship as the stones of a cathedral are stirred by the bass of the organ.

"As with sounds, so with colors. At each end of the solar spectrum the chemist can detect the presence of what are known as 'actinic' rays. They represent colors—integral colors in the composition of light—which we are unable to discern. The human eye is an imperfect instru-ment; its range is but a few octaves of the real 'chromatic scale.' I am not mad; there are colors that we cannot see.

"And, God help me! the Damned Thing is of such a color!"

"Oh, there *is* one, of course, but you'll never know it."

The assertion, laughingly flung out six months earlier in a bright June garden, came back to Mary Boyne with a new perception of its significance as she stood, in the December dusk, waiting for the lamps to be brought into the library.

The words had been spoken by their friend Alida Stair, as they sat at tea on her lawn at Pangbourne, in reference to the very house of which the library in question was the central, the pivotal "feature." Mary Boyne and her husband, in quest of a country place in one of the southern or southwestern counties, had, on their arrival in England, carried their problem straight to Alida Stair, who had successfully solved it in her own case; but it was not until they had rejected, almost capriciously, several practical and judicious suggestions that she threw out: "Well, there's Lyng, in Dorsetshire. It belongs to Hugo's cousins, and you can get it for a song."

The reason she gave for its being obtainable on these terms—its remoteness from a station, its lack of electric light, hot water pipes, and other vulgar necessities—were exactly those pleading in its favor with two romantic Americans perversely in search of the economic draw-backs which were associated, in their tradition, with unusual architec-tural felicities.

"I should never believe I was living in an old house unless I was thoroughly uncomfortable," Ned Boyne, the more extravagant of the two, had jocosely insisted; "the least hint of convenience would make me think it had been bought out of an exhibition, with the pieces numbered, and set up again." And they had proceeded to enumerate, with humorous precision, their various doubts and demands, refusing to believe that the house their cousin recommended was *really* Tudor till they learned it had no heating system, or that the village church was literally in the grounds, till she assured them of the deplorable uncertainty of the water supply.

"It's too uncomfortable to be true!" Edward Boyne had continued to exult as the avowal of each disadvantage was successively wrung from her; but he had cut short his rhapsody to ask, with a relapse to distrust: "And the ghost? You've been concealing from us the fact that there is no ghost!"

Mary, at the moment, had laughed with him, yet almost with her laugh, being possessed of several sets of independent perceptions, had been struck by a note of flatness in Alida's answering hilarity.

"Oh, Dorsetshire's full of ghosts, you know."

"Yes, yes; but that won't do. I don't want to have to drive ten miles to see somebody else's ghost. I want one of my own on the premises. *Is* there a ghost at Lyng?"

His rejoinder had made Alida laugh again, and it was then that she had flung back tantalizingly: "Oh, there *is* one, of course, but you'll never know it."

"Never know it?" Boyne pulled her up. "But what in the world constitutes a ghost except the fact of its being known for one?"

"I can't say. But that's the story."

"That there's a ghost, but that nobody knows it's a ghost?"

"Well—not till afterward, at any rate."

"Till afterward?"

"Not till long long afterward."

"But if it's once been identified as an unearthly visitant, why hasn't it *signalement* been handed down in the family? How has it managed to preserve its incognito?"

Alida could only shake her head. "Don't ask me. But it has."

"And then suddenly"—Mary spoke up as if from cavernous depths of divination—"suddenly, long afterward, one says to one's self *'That was it'?*"

She was startled at the sepulchral sound with which her question fell on the banter of the other two, and she saw the shadow of the same surprise flit across Alida's pupils. "I suppose so. One just has to wait."

"Oh, hang waiting!" Ned broke in. "Life's too short for a ghost who can only be enjoyed in retrospect. Can't we do better than that, Mary?"

But it turned out that in the event they were not destined to, for within three months of their conversation with Mrs. Stair they were settled at Lyng, and the life they had yearned for, to the point of planning it in advance in all its daily details, had actually begun for them.

It was to sit, in the thick December dusk, by just such a wide-hooded fireplace, under just such black oak rafters, with the sense that beyond the mullioned panes the downs were darkened to a deeper solitude; it was for the ultimate indulgence of such sensations that Mary Boyne, abruptly exiled from New York by her husband's business, had endured for nearly fourteen years the soul-deadening ugliness of a Middle Western town, and that Boyne had ground on doggedly at his engineering till, with a suddenness that still made her blink, the prodigious windfall of the Blue Star Mine had put them at a stroke in possession of life and the leisure to taste it. They had never for a moment meant their new state to be one of idleness; but they meant to give themselves only to harmonious activities. She had her vision of painting and gardening (against a background of grey walls), he dreamed of the production of his long-planned book on the "Economic Basis of Culture"; and with such absorbing work ahead no existence could be too sequestered: they could not get far enough from the world, or plunge deep enough into the past.

Dorsetshire had attracted them from the first by an air of remoteness out of all proportion to its geographical position. But to the Boynes it was one of the ever-recurring wonders of the whole incredibly compressed island—a nest of counties, as they put it—that for the production of its effects so little of a given quality went so far: that so few miles made a distance, and so short a distance a difference.

"It's that," Ned had once enthusiastically explained, "that gives such depth to their effects, such relief to their contrasts. They've been able to lay the butter so thick on every delicious mouthful."

The butter had certainly been laid on thick at Lyng: the old house hidden under a shoulder of the downs had almost all the finer marks of commerce with a protracted past. The mere fact that it was neither large nor exceptional made it, to the Boynes, abound the more completely in its special charm—the charm of having been for centuries a deep dim reservoir of life. The life had probably not been of the most vivid order: for long periods, no doubt, it had fallen as noiselessly into the past as the quiet drizzle of autumn fell, hour after hour, into the fish pond between the yews; but these backwaters of existence sometimes breed, in their sluggish depths, strange acuities of emotion, and Mary Boyne had felt from the first mysterious stir of intenser memories.

The feeling had never been stronger than on this particular afternoon when, waiting in the library for the lamps to come, she rose from her seat and stood among the shadows of the hearth. Her husband had gone off, after luncheon, for one of his long tramps on the downs. She had noticed of late that he preferred to go alone; and, in the tried security of their personal relations, had been driven to conclude that his book was bothering him, and that he needed the afternoons to turn over in solitude the problems left from the morning's work. Certainly the book was not going as smoothly as she had thought it would, and there were lines of perplexity between his eyes such as had never been there in his engineering days. He had often, then, looked fagged to the verge of illness, but the native demon of worry had never branded his brow. Yet the few pages he had so far read to her—the introduction, and a summary of the opening chapter—showed a firm hold on his subject, and an increasing confidence in his powers.

The fact threw her into deeper perplexity, since, now that he had done with business and its disturbing contingencies, the one other possible source of anxiety was eliminated. Unless it were his health, then? But physically he had gained since they had come to Dorsetshire, grown robuster, ruddier, and fresher eyed. It was only within the last week that she had felt in him the undefinable change which made her restless in his absence, and as tongue-tied in his presence as though it were *she* who had a secret to keep from him!

The thought that there *was* a secret somewhere between them struck her with a sudden rap of wonder, and she looked about her down the long room.

"Can it be the house?" she mused.

The room itself might have been full of secrets. They seemed to be piling themselves up, as evening fell, like the layers and layers of velvet shadow dropping from the low ceiling, the rows of books, the smoke-blurred sculpture of the hearth.

"Why, of course—the house is haunted!" she reflected.

The ghost—Alida's imperceptible ghost—after figuring largely in the banter of their first month or two at Lyng, had been gradually left aside as too ineffectual for imaginative use. Mary had, indeed, as became the tenant of a haunted house, made the customary inquiries among her rural neighbors, but, beyond a vague "They do say so,

Ma'am," the villagers had nothing to impart. The elusive specter had apparently never had sufficient identity for a legend to crystallize about it, and after a time the Boynes had set the matter down to their profit-and-loss account, agreeing that Lyng was one of the few houses good enough in itself to dispense with supernatural enhancements.

"And I suppose, poor ineffectual demon, that's why it beats its beautiful wings in vain in the void," Mary had laughingly concluded.

"Or, rather," Ned answered in the same strain, "why, amid so much that's ghostly, it can never affirm its separate existence as *the* ghost." And thereupon their invisible housemate had finally dropped out of their references, which were numerous enough to make them soon unaware of the loss.

Now, as she stood on the hearth, the subject of their earlier curiosity revived in her with a new sense of its meaning—a sense gradually acquired through daily contact with the scene of the lurking mystery. It was the house itself, of course, that possessed the ghost-seeing faculty, that communed visually but secretly with its own past; if one could only get into close enough communion with the house, one might surprise its secret, and acquire the ghost sight on one's own account. Perhaps, in his long hours in this very room, where she never trespassed till the afternoon, her husband *had* acquired it already, and was silently carrying about the weight of whatever it had revealed to him. Mary was too well versed in the code of the spectral world not to know that one could not talk about the ghosts one saw: to do so was almost as great a breach of taste as to name a lady in a club. But this explanation did not really satisfy her. "What, after all, except for the fun of the shudder," she reflected, "would he really care for any of their old ghosts?" And thence she was thrown back once more on the fundamental dilemma: the fact that one's greater or less susceptibility to spectral influences had no particular bearing on the case, since, when one *did* see a ghost at Lyng, one did not know it.

"Not till long afterward," Alida Stair had said. Well, supposing Ned *had* seen one when they first came, and had known only within the last week what had happened to him? More and more under the spell of the hour, she threw back her thoughts to the early days of their tenancy, but at first only to recall a lively confusion of unpacking, settling, arranging of books, and calling to each other from remote corners of the house as, treasure after treasure, it revealed itself to them. It was in this particular connection that she presently recalled a certain soft afternoon of the previous October, when, passing from the first rapturous flurry of exploration to a detailed inspection of the old house, she had pressed (like a novel heroine) a panel that opened on a flight of corkscrew stairs leading to a flat ledge of the roof—the roof which, from below, seemed to slope away on all sides too abruptly for any but practiced feet to scale.

The view from this hidden coign was enchanting, and she had flown down to snatch Ned from his papers and give him the freedom of her discovery. She remembered still how, standing at her side, he had passed his arm about her while their gaze flew to the long tossed horizon line of the downs, and then dropped contentedly back to trace the arabesque of yew hedges about the fish pond, and the shadow of the cedar on the lawn.

"And now the other way," he had said, turning her about within his arm; and closely pressed to him, she had absorbed, like some long satisfying draught, the picture of the grey-walled court, the squat lions on the gates, and the lime avenue reaching up to the highroad under the downs.

It was just then, while they gazed and held each other, that she had felt his arm relax, and heard a sharp "Hullo!"that made her turn to glance at him.

Distinctly, yes, she now recalled that she had seen, as she glanced, a shadow of anxiety, of perplexity, rather, fall across his face; and, following his eyes, had beheld the figure of a man—a man in loose greyish clothes, as it appeared to her—who was sauntering down the lime avenue to the court with the doubtful gait of a stranger who seeks his way. Her shortsighted eyes had given her but a blurred impression of slightness and greyishness, with something foreign, or at least unlocal, in the cut of the figure or its dress; but her husband had apparently seen more—seen enough to make him push past her with a hasty "Wait!" and dash down the stairs without pausing to give her a hand.

A slight tendency to dizziness obliged her, after a provisional clutch at the chimney against which they had been leaning, to follow him first more cautiously; and when she had reached the landing she paused again, for a less definite reason, leaning over the banister to strain her eyes through the silence of the brown sun-flecked depths. She lingered there till, somewhere in those depths, she heard the closing of a door; then, mechanically impelled, she went down the shallow flights of steps till she reached the lower hall.

The front door stood open on the sunlight of the court, and hall and court were empty. The library door was open, too, and after listening in vain for any sound of voices within, she crossed the threshold, and found her husband alone, vaguely fingering the papers on his desk.

He looked up, as if surprised at her entrance, but the shadow of anxiety had passed from his face, leaving it even, as she fancied, a little brighter and clearer than usual.

"What was it? Who was it?" she asked.

"Who?" he repeated, with the surprise still all on his side.

"The man we saw coming toward the house."

He seemed to reflect. "The man? Why, I thought I saw Peters; I dashed after him to say a word about the stable drains, but he had disappeared before I could get down."

"Disappeared? But he seemed to be walking so slowly when we saw him."

Boyne shrugged his shoulders. "So I thought; but he must have got up steam in the interval. What do you say to our trying a scramble up Meldon Steep before sunset?"

That was all. At the time the occurrence had been less than nothing, had, indeed, been immediately obliterated by the magic of their first vision from Meldon Steep, a height which they had dreamed of climbing ever since they had first seen its bare spine rising above the roof of Lyng. Doubtless it was the mere fact of the other incident's having occurred on the very day of their ascent to Meldon that had kept it stored away in the fold of memory from which it now emerged; for in itself it had no mark of the portentous. At the moment there could have been nothing more natural than that Ned should dash himself from the roof in the pursuit of dilatory tradesmen. It was the period when they were always on the watch for one or the other of the specialists employed about the place; always lying in wait for them, and rushing out at them with questions, reproaches, or reminders. And certainly in the distance the grey figure had looked like Peters.

Yet now, as she reviewed the scene, she felt her husband's explanation of it to have been invalidated by the look of anxiety on his face. Why had the familiar appearance of Peters made him anxious? Why, above all, if it was of such prime necessity to confer with him on the subject of the stable drains, had the failure to find him produced such a look of relief? Mary could not say that any one of these questions had occurred to her at the time, yet, from the promptness with which they now marshalled themselves at her summons, she had a sense that they must all along have been there, waiting their hour.

## II

Weary with her thoughts, she moved to the window. The library was now quite dark, and she was surprised to see how much faint light the outer world still held.

As she peered out into it across the court, a figure shaped itself far down the perspective of bare limes: it looked a mere blot of deeper grey in the greyness, and for an instant, as it moved toward her, her heart thumped to the thought "It's the ghost!"

She had time, in that long instant, to feel suddenly that the man of whom, two months earlier, she had had a distant vision from the roof, was now, at his predestined hour, about to reveal himself as *not* having been Peters; and her spirit sank under the impending fear of the disclosure. But almost with the next tick of the clock the figure, gaining substance and character, showed itself even to her weak sight as her husband's; and she turned to meet him, as he entered, with the confession of her folly.

"It's really too absurd," she laughed out, "but I never *can* remember!"

"Remember what?" Boyne questioned as they drew together.

"That when one sees the Lyng ghost one never knows it."

Her hand was on his sleeve, and he kept it there, but with no response in his gesture or in the lines of his preoccupied face.

"Did you think you'd seen it?" he asked, after an appreciable interval.

"Why, I actually took *you* for it, my dear, in my mad determination to spot it!"

"Me—just now?" His arm dropped away, and he turned from her with a faint echo of her laugh. "Really, dearest, you'd better give it up, if that's the best you can do."

"Oh, yes, I give it up. Have *you?*" she asked, turning round on him abruptly.

The parlormaid had entered with letters and a lamp, and the light struck up into Boyne's face as he bent above the tray she presented.

"Have *you?*" Mary perversely insisted, when the servant had disappeared on her errand of illumination.

"Have I what?" he rejoined absently, the light bringing out the sharp stamp of worry between his brows as he turned over the letters.

"Given up trying to see the ghost." Her heart beat a little at the experiment she was making.

Her husband, laying his letters aside, moved away into the shadow of the hearth.

"I never tried," he said, tearing open the wrapper of a newspaper.

"Well, of course," Mary persisted, "the exasperating thing is that there's no use trying, since one can't be sure till so long afterward."

He was unfolding the paper as if he had hardly heard her; but after a pause, during which the sheets rustled spasmodically between his hands, he looked up to ask, "Have you any idea *how long?*"

Mary had sunk into a low chair beside the fireplace. From her seat she glanced over, startled, at her husband's profile, which was projected against the circle of lamplight.

"No; none. Have *you?*" she retorted, repeating her former phrase with an added stress of intention.

Boyne crumpled the paper into a bunch, and then, inconsequently, turned back with it toward the lamp.

"Lord, no! I only meant," he exclaimed, with a faint tinge of impatience, "is there any legend, any tradition, as to that?"

"Not that I know of," she answered; but the impulse to add "What makes you ask?" was checked by the reappearance of the parlormaid, with tea and a second lamp.

With the dispersal of shadows, and the repetition of the daily domestic office, Mary Boyne felt herself less oppressed by that sense of something mutely imminent which had darkened her afternoon. For a few moments she gave herself to the details of her task, and when she looked up from it she was struck to the point of bewilderment by the change in her husband's face. He had seated himself near the farther lamp, and was absorbed in the perusal of his letters; but was it something he had found in them, or merely the shifting of her own point of view, that had restored his features to their normal aspect? The longer she looked the more definitely the change affirmed itself. The lines of tension had vanished, and such traces of fatigue as lingered were of the kind easily attributable to steady mental effort. He glanced up, as if drawn by her gaze, and met her eyes with a smile.

"I'm dying for my tea, you know; and here's a letter for you," he said.

She took the letter he held out in exchange for the cup she proffered him, and, returning to her seat, broke the seal with the languid gesture of the reader whose interests are all enclosed in the circle of one cherished presence.

Her next conscious motion was that of starting to her feet, the letter falling to them as she rose, while she held out to her husband a newspaper clipping.

"Ned! What's this? What does it mean?"

He had risen at the same instant, almost as if hearing her cry before she uttered it; and for a perceptible space of time he and she studied each other, like adversaries watching for an advantage, across the space between her chair and his desk.

"What's that? You fairly made me jump!" Boyne said at length, moving toward her with a sudden half-exasperated laugh. The shadow of apprehension was on his face again, not now a look of fixed foreboding, but a shifting vigilance of lips and eyes that gave her the sense of his feeling himself invisibly surrounded.

Her hand shook so that she could hardly give him the clipping.

"This article—from the *Waukesha Sentinel*—that a man named Elwell has brought suit against you—that there was something wrong about the Blue Star Mine. I can't understand more than half."

They continued to face each other as she spoke, and to her astonishment she saw that her words had the almost immediate effect of dissipating the strained watchfulness of his look.

"Oh, *that!*" He glanced down the printed slip, and then folded it with the gesture of one who handles something harmless and familiar. "What's the matter with you this afternoon, Mary? I thought you'd got bad news."

She stood before him with her undefinable terror subsiding slowly under the reassurance of his tone.

"You knew about this, then—it's all right?"

"Certainly I knew about it; and it's all right."

"But what *is* it? I don't understand. What does this man accuse you of?"

"Pretty nearly every crime in the calendar." Boyne had tossed the clipping down, and thrown himself into an armchair near the fire. "Do you want to hear the story? It's not particularly interesting—just a squabble over interests in the Blue Star."

"But who is this Elwell? I don't know the name."

"Oh, he's a fellow I put into it—gave him a hand up. I told you all about him at the time."

"I dare say. I must have forgotten." Vainly she strained back among her memories. "But if you helped him, why does he make this return?"

"Probably some shyster lawyer got hold of him and talked him over. It's all rather technical and complicated. I thought that kind of thing bored you."

His wife felt a sting of compunction. Theoretically, she deprecated the American wife's detachment from her husband's professional interests, but in practice she had always found it difficult to fix her attention on Boyne's report of the transactions in which his varied interests involved him. Besides, she had felt during their years of exile, that, in a community where the amenities of living could be obtained only at the cost of efforts as arduous as her husband's professional labor, such brief leisure as he and she could command should be used as an escape from immediate preoccupations, a flight to the life they always dreamed of living. Once or twice, now that this new life had actually drawn its magic circle about them, she had asked herself if she had done right; but hitherto such conjectures had been no more than the retrospective excursions of an active fancy. Now, for the first time, it startled her a little to find how little she knew of the material foundation on which her happiness was built.

She glanced at her husband, and was again reassured by the composure of his face; yet she felt the need of more definite grounds for her reassurance.

"But doesn't this suit worry you? Why have you never spoken to me about it?"

He answered both questions at once. "I didn't speak of it at first because it *did* worry me—annoyed me, rather. But it's all ancient history now. Your correspondent must have got hold of a back number of the *Sentinel*."

She felt a quick thrill of relief. "You mean it's over? He's lost his case?"

There was a just perceptible delay in Boyne's reply. "The suit's been withdrawn—that's all."

But she persisted, as if to exonerate herself from the inward charge of being too easily put off. "Withdrawn it because he saw he had no chance?"

"Oh, he had no chance," Boyne answered.

She was still struggling with a dimly felt perplexity at the back of her thoughts.

"How long ago was it withdrawn?"

He paused, as if with a slight return to his former uncertainty. "I've just had the news now; but I've been expecting it."

"Just now—in one of your letters?"

"Yes; in one of my letters."

She made no answer, and was aware only, after a short interval of waiting, that he had risen, and, strolling across the room, had placed himself on the sofa at her side. She felt him, as he did so, pass an arm about her, she felt his hand seek hers and clasp it, and turning slowly, drawn by the warmth of his cheek, she met his smiling eyes.

"It's all right—it's all right?" she questioned, through the flood of her dissolving doubts; and "I give you my word it was never righter!" he laughed back at her, holding her close.

III

One of the strangest things she was afterward to recall out of all the next day's strangeness was the sudden and complete recovery of her sense of security.

It was in the air when she woke in her low-ceiled, dusky room; it went with her downstairs to the breakfast table, flashed out at her from the fire, and reduplicated itself from the flanks of the urn and the sturdy flutings of the Georgian teapot. It was as if in some roundabout way, all her diffused fears of the previous day, with their moment of sharp concentration about the newspaper article—as if this dim questioning of the future, and startled return upon the past, had between them liquidated the arrears of some haunting moral obligation. If she had indeed been careless of her husband's affairs, it was, her new state seemed to prove, because her faith in him instinctively justified such carelessness; and his right to her faith had now affirmed itself in the very face of menace and suspicion. She had never seen him more untroubled, more naturally and unconsciously himself, than after the cross-examination to which she had subjected him: it was almost as if he had been aware of her doubts, and had wanted the air cleared as much as she did.

It was as clear, thank heaven, as the bright outer light that surprised her almost with a touch of summer when she issued from the house for her daily round of the gardens. She had left Boyne at his desk, indulging herself, as she passed the library door, by a last peep at his quiet face, where he bent, pipe in mouth, about his papers; and now she had her own morning's task to perform. The task involved, on such charmed winter days, almost as much happy loitering about the different quarters of her domain as if spring were already at work there. There were such endless possibilities still before her, such opportunities to bring out the latent graces of the old place, without a single irreverent touch of alteration, that the winter was all too short to plan what spring and autumn executed. And her recovered sense of safety gave, on this particular morning, a peculiar zest to her progress through the sweet still place. She went first to the kitchen garden, where the espaliered pear trees drew complicated patterns on the walls, and pigeons were fluttering and preening about the silvery-slated roof of their cot. There was something wrong about the piping of the hot-house, and she was expecting an authority from Dorchester, who was to drive out between trains and make a diagnosis of the boiler. But when she dipped into the damp heat of the greenhouses, among the spiced scents and waxy pinks and reds of old-fashioned exotics—even the flora of Lyng was in the note!—she learned that the great man had not arrived, and, the day being too rare to waste in an artificial atmosphere, she came out again and paced along the springy turf of the bowling green to the gardens behind the house. At their farther end rose a grass terrace, looking across the fish pond and yew hedges to the long house front with its twisted chimney stacks and blue roof angles all drenched in the pale gold moisture of the air.

Seen thus, across the level tracery of the gardens, it sent her, from open windows and hospitably smoking chimneys, the look of some warm human presence, of a mind slowly ripened on a sunny wall of experience. She had never before had such a sense of her intimacy with it, such a conviction that its secrets were all beneficent, kept, as they said to children, "for one's good," such a trust in its power to gather up her life and Ned's into the harmonious pattern of the long long story it sat there weaving in the sun.

She heard steps behind her, and turned, expecting to see the gardener accompanied by the engineer from Dorchester. But only one figure was in sight, that of a youngish slightly built man, who, for reasons she could not on the spot have given, did not remotely resemble her notion of an authority on hothouse boilers. The newcomer, on seeing her, lifted his hat, and paused with the air of a gentleman—perhaps a traveler—who wishes to make it known that his intrusion is involuntary. Lyng occasionally attracted the more cultivated traveler, and Mary half expected to see the stranger dissemble a camera, or justify his presence by producing it. But he made no gesture of any sort, and after a moment she asked, in a tone responding to the courteous hesitation of his attitude: "Is there anyone you wish to see?"

"I came to see Mr. Boyne," he answered. His intonation, rather than his accent, was faintly American, and Mary, at the note, looked at him more closely. The brim of his soft felt hat cast a shade on his face, which, thus obscured, wore to her shortsighted gaze a look of seriousness, as of a person arriving on business, and civilly but firmly aware of his rights.

Past experience had made her equally sensible to such claims; but she was jealous of her husband's morning hours, and doubtful of his having given anyone the right to intrude on them.

"Have you an appointment with my husband?" she asked.

The visitor hesitated, as if unprepared for the question.

"I think he expects me," he replied.

It was Mary's turn to hesitate. "You see this is his time for work: he never sees anyone in the morning."

He looked at her a moment without answering; then, as if accepting her decision, he began to move away. As he turned, Mary saw him pause and glance up at the peaceful house front. Something in his air suggested weariness and disappointment, the dejection of the traveler who has come from far off and whose hours are limited by the timetable. It occurred to her that if this were the case her refusal might have made his errand vain, and a sense of compunction caused her to hasten after him.

"May I ask if you have come a long way?"

He gave her the same grave look. "Yes—I have come a long way."

"Then, if you'll go to the house, no doubt my husband will see you now. You'll find him in the library."

She did not know why she had added the last phrase, except from a vague impulse to atone for her previous inhospitality. The visitor seemed about to express his thanks, but her attention was distracted by the approach of the gardener with a companion who bore all the marks of being the expert from Dorchester.

"This way," she said, waving the stranger to the house; and an instant later she had forgotten him in the absorption of her meeting with the boiler maker.

The encounter led to such far-reaching results that the engineer ended by finding it expedient to ignore his train, and Mary was beguiled into spending the remainder of the morning in absorbed confabulation among the flower pots. When the colloquy ended, she was surprised to find that it was nearly luncheon time, and she half expected, as she hurried back to the house, to see her husband coming out to meet her. But she found no one in the court but an undergardener raking the gravel, and the hall, when she entered it, was so silent that she guessed Boyne to be still at work.

Not wishing to disturb him, she turned into the drawing room, and there, at her writing table, lost herself in renewed calculations of the outlay to which the morning's conference had pledged her. The fact that she could permit herself such follies had not yet lost its novelty; and somehow, in contrast to the vague fears of the previous days, it now seemed an element of her recovered security, of the sense that, as Ned had said, things in general had never been "righter."

She was still luxuriating in a lavish play of figures when the parlormaid, from the threshold, roused her with an inquiry as to the expediency of serving luncheon. It was one of their jokes that Trimmle announced luncheon as if she were divulging a state secret, and Mary, intent upon her papers, merely murmured an absent-minded assent.

She felt Trimmle wavering doubtfully on the threshold, as if in rebuke of such unconsidered assent; then her retreating steps sounded down the passage, and Mary, pushing away her papers, crossed the hall and went to the library door. It was still closed, and she wavered in her turn, disliking to disturb her husband, yet anxious that he should not exceed his usual measure of work. As she stood there, balancing her impulses, Trimmle returned with the announcement of luncheon, and Mary, thus impelled, opened the library door.

Boyne was not at his desk, and she peered about her, expecting to discover him before the bookshelves, somewhere down the length of the room; but her call brought no response, and gradually it became clear to her that he was not there.

She turned back to the parlormaid.

"Mr. Boyne must be upstairs. Please tell him that luncheon is ready."

Trimmle appeared to hesitate between the obvious duty of obedience and an equally obvious conviction of the foolishness of the injunction laid on her. The struggle resulted in her saying: "If you please, Madam, Mr. Boyne's not upstairs."

"Not in his room? Are you sure?"

"I'm sure, Madam."

Mary consulted the clock. "Where is he, then?"

"He's gone out," Trimmle announced, with the superior air of one who has respectfully waited for the question that a well-ordered mind would have put first.

Mary's conjecture had been right, then. Boyne must have gone to the gardens to meet her, and since she had missed him, it was clear that he had taken the shorter way by the south door, instead of going round to the court. She crossed the hall to the French window opening directly on the yew garden, but the parlormaid, after another moment of inner conflict, decided to bring out: "Please, Madam, Mr. Boyne didn't go that way."

Mary turned back. "Where *did* he go? And when?"

"He went out of the front door, up the drive, Madam." It was a matter of principle with Trimmle never to answer more than one question at a time.

"Up the drive? At this hour?" Mary went to the door herself, and glanced across the court through the tunnel of bare limes. But its perspective was as empty as when she had scanned it on entering.

"Did Mr. Boyne leave no message?"

Trimmle seemed to surrender herself to a last struggle with the forces of chaos.

"No, Madam. He just went out with the gentleman."

"The gentleman? What gentleman?" Mary wheeled about, as if to front this new factor.

"The gentleman who called, Madam," said Trimmle resignedly.

"When did a gentleman call? Do explain yourself, Trimmle!"

Only the fact that Mary was very hungry, and that she wanted to consult her husband about the greenhouses, would have caused her to lay so unusual an injunction on her attendant; and even now she was detached enough to note in Trimmle's eye the dawning defiance of the respectful subordinate who has been pressed too hard.

"I couldn't exactly say the hour, Madam, because I didn't let the gentleman in," she replied, with an air of discreetly ignoring the irregularity of her mistress's course.

"You didn't let him in?"

"No, Madam. When the bell rang I was dressing, and Agnes—"

"Go and ask Agnes, then," said Mary.

Trimmle still wore her look of patient magnanimity. "Agnes would not know, Madam, for she had unfortunately burnt her hand in trimming the wick of the new lamp from town"—Trimmle, as Mary was aware, had always been opposed to the new lamp—"and so Mrs. Dockett sent the kitchenmaid instead."

Mary looked again at the clock. "It's after two! Go and ask the kitchenmaid if Mr. Boyne left any word."

She went into luncheon without waiting, and Trimmle presently brought her there the kitchenmaid's statement that the gentleman had called about eleven o'clock, and that Mr. Boyne had gone out with him without leaving any message. The kitchenmaid did not even know the caller's name, for he had written it on a slip of paper, which he had folded and handed to her, with the injunction to deliver it at once to Mr. Boyne.

Mary finished her luncheon, still wondering, and when it was over, and Trimmle had brought the coffee to the drawing room, her wonder had deepened to a first faint tinge of disquietude. It was unlike Boyne to absent himself without explanation at so unwonted an hour, and the difficulty of identifying the visitor whose summons he had apparently obeyed made his disappearance the more unaccountable. Mary Boyne's experience as the wife of a busy engineer, subject to sudden calls and compelled to keep irregular hours, had trained her to the philosophic acceptance of surprises; but since Boyne's withdrawal from business he had adopted a Benedictine regularity of life. As if to make up for the dispersed and agitated years, with their "stand-up" lunches, and dinners rattled down to the joltings of the dining cars, he cultivated the last refinements of punctuality and monotony, discouraging his wife's fancy for the unexpected, and declaring that to a delicate taste there were infinite gradations of pleasure in the recurrences of habit.

Still, since no life can completely defend itself from the unforeseen, it was evident that all Boyne's precautions would sooner or later prove unavailable, and Mary concluded that he had cut short a tiresome visit by walking with his caller to the station, or at least accompanying him for part of the way.

This conclusion relieved her from further preoccupation, and she went out herself to take up her conference with the gardener. Thence she walked to the village post office, a mile or so away; and when she turned toward home the early twilight was setting in.

She had taken a footpath across the downs, and as Boyne, meanwhile, had probably returned from the station by the highroad, there was little likelihood of their meeting. She felt sure, however, of his having reached the house before her; so sure that, when she entered it herself, without even pausing to inquire of Trimmle, she made directly for the library. But the library was still empty, and with an unwonted exactness of visual memory she observed that the papers on her husband's desk lay precisely as they had lain when she had gone in to call him to luncheon.

Then of a sudden she was seized by a vague dread of the unknown. She had closed the door behind her on entering, and as she stood alone in the long silent room, her dread seemed to take shape and sound, to be there breathing and lurking among the shadows. Her shortsighted eyes strained through them, half-discerning an actual presence, something aloof, that watched and knew; and in the recoil from that intangible presence she threw herself on the bell rope and gave it a sharp pull.

The sharp summons brought Trimmle in precipitately with a lamp, and Mary breathed again at this sobering reappearance of the usual.

"You may bring tea if Mr. Boyne is in," she said, to justify her ring.

"Very well, Madam. But Mr. Boyne is not in," said Trimmle, putting down the lamp.

"Not in? You mean he's come back and gone out again?"

"No, Madam. He's never been back."

The dread stirred again, and Mary knew that now it had her fast.

"Not since he went out with—the gentleman?"

"Not since he went out with the gentleman."

"But who *was* the gentleman?" Mary insisted, with the shrill note of someone trying to be heard through a confusion of noises.

"That I couldn't say, Madam." Trimmle, standing there by the lamp, seemed suddenly to grow less round and rosy, as though eclipsed by the same creeping shade of apprehension.

"But the kitchenmaid knows—wasn't it the kitchenmaid who let him in?"

"She doesn't know either, Madam, for he wrote his name on a folded paper."

Mary, through her agitation, was aware that they were both designating the unknown visitor by a vague pronoun, instead of the conventional formula which, till then, had kept their allusions within the bounds of conformity. And at the same moment her mind caught at the suggestion of the folded paper.

"But he must have a name! Where's the paper?"

She moved to the desk, and began to turn over the documents that littered it. The first that caught her eye was an unfinished letter in her husband's hand, with his pen lying across it, as though dropped there at a sudden summons.

"My dear Parvis"—who was Parvis?—"I have just received your

letter announcing Elwell's death, and while I suppose there is now no further risk of trouble, it might be safer—"

She tossed the sheet aside, and continued her search; but no folded paper was discoverable among the letters and pages of manuscript which had been swept together in a heap, as if by a hurried or a startled gesture.

"But the kitchenmaid *saw* him. Send her here," she commanded, wondering at her dullness in not thinking sooner of so simple a solution.

Trimmle vanished in a flash, as if thankful to be out of the room, and when she reappeared, conducting the agitated underling, Mary had regained her self-possession, and had her questions ready.

The gentleman was a stranger, yes—that she understood. But what had he said? And, above all, what had he looked like? The first question was easily enough answered, for the disconcerting reason that he had said so little—had merely asked for Mr. Boyne, and, scribbling something on a bit of paper, had requested that it should at once be carried in to him.

"Then you don't know what he wrote? You're not sure it *was* his name?"

The kitchenmaid was not sure, but supposed it was, since he had written it in answer to her inquiry as to whom she should announce.

"And when you carried the paper in to Mr. Boyne, what did he say?"

The kitchenmaid did not think that Mr. Boyne had said anything, but she could not be sure, for just as she had handed him the paper and he was opening it, she had become aware that the visitor had followed her into the library, and she had slipped out, leaving the two gentlemen together.

"But then, if you left them in the library, how do you know that they went out of the house?"

This question plunged the witness into a momentary inarticulateness, from which she was rescued by Trimmle, who, by means of ingenious circumlocutions, elicited the statement that before she could cross the hall to the back passage she had heard the two gentlemen behind her, and had seen them go out of the front door together.

"Then, if you saw the strange gentleman twice, you must be able to tell me what he looked like."

But with this final challenge to her powers of expression it became clear that the limit of the kitchenmaid's endurance had been reached. The obligation of going to the front door to "show in" a visitor was in itself so subversive of the fundamental order of things that it had thrown her faculties into hopeless disarray, and she could only stammer out, after various panting efforts: "His hat, mum, was different-like, as you might say—"

"Different? How different?" Mary flashed out, her own mind, in the same instant, leaping back to an image left on it that morning, and then lost under layers of subsequent impressions.

"His hat had a wide brim, you mean, and his face was pale—a youngish face?" Mary pressed her, with a white-lipped intensity of interrogation. But if the kitchenmaid found any adequate answer to this challenge, it was swept away for her listener down the rushing current of her own convictions. The stranger—the stranger in the garden! Why had Mary not thought of him before? She needed no one now to tell her that it was he who had called for her husband and gone away with him. But who was he, and why had Boyne obeyed him?

IV

It leaped out at her suddenly, like a grin out of the dark, that they had often called England so little—"such a confoundedly hard place to get lost in."

*A confoundedly hard place to get lost in!* That had been her husband's phrase. And now, with the whole machinery of official investigation sweeping its flashlights from shore to shore, and across the dividing straits; now, with Boyne's name blazing from the walls of every town and village, his portrait (how that wrung her!) hawked up and down the country like the image of a hunted criminal; now the little compact populous island, so policed, surveyed, and administered, revealed itself as a Sphinxlike guardian of abysmal mysteries, staring back into his wife's anguished eyes as if with the wicked joy of knowing something they would never know!

In the fortnight since Boyne's disappearance there had been no word of him, no trace of his movements. Even the usual misleading reports that raise expectancy in tortured bosoms had been few and fleeting. No one but the kitchenmaid had seen Boyne leave the house, and no one else had seen "the gentleman" who accompanied him. All inquiries in the neighborhood failed to elicit the memory of a stranger's presence that day in the neighborhood of Lyng. And no one had met Edward Boyne, either alone or in company, in any of the neighboring

villages, or on the road across the downs, or at either of the local
railway stations. The sunny English noon had swallowed him as completely as if he had gone out into Cimmerian night.

Mary, while every official means of investigation was working at
its highest pressure, had ransacked her husband's papers for any trace of
antecedent complications, of entanglements or obligations unknown to
her, that might throw a ray into the darkness. But if any such had
existed in the background of Boyne's life, they had vanished like the
slip of paper on which the visitor had written his name. There
remained no possible thread of guidance except—if it were indeed an
exception—the letter which Boyne had apparently been in the act of
writing when he received his mysterious summons. That letter, read
and reread by his wife, and submitted by her to the police, yielded little
enough to feed conjecture.

"I have just heard of Elwell's death, and while I suppose there is
now no further risk of trouble, it might be safer—" That was all. The
"risk of trouble" was easily explained by the newspaper clipping which
had apprised Mary of the suit brought against her husband by one of his
associates in the Blue Star enterprise. The only new information conveyed by the letter was the fact of its showing Boyne, when he wrote
it, to be still apprehensive of the results of the suit, though he had told
his wife that it had been withdrawn, and though the letter itself proved
that the plaintiff was dead. It took several days of cabling to fix the
identity of the "Parvis" to whom the fragment was addressed, but even
after these inquiries had shown him to be a Waukesha lawyer, no new
facts concerning the Elwell suit were elicited. He appeared to have had
no direct concern in it, but to have been conversant with the facts
merely as an acquaintance, and possible intermediary; and he declared
himself unable to guess with what object Boyne intended to seek his
assistance.

This negative information, sole fruit of the first fortnight's search,
was not increased by a jot during the slow weeks that followed. Mary
knew that the investigations were still being carried on, but she had a
vague sense of their gradually slackening, as the actual march of time
seemed to slacken. It was as though the days, flying horror-struck from
the shrouded image of the one inscrutable day, gained assurance as the
distance lengthened, till at last they fell back into their normal gait. And
so with the human imaginations at work on the dark event. No doubt
it occupied them still, but week by week and hour by hour it grew less
absorbing, took up less space, was slowly but inevitably crowded out of

the foreground of consciousness by the new problems perpetually bubbling up from the cloudy caldron of human experience.

Even Mary Boyne's consciousness gradually felt the same lowering of velocity. It still swayed with the incessant oscillations of conjecture; but they were slower, more rhythmical in their beat. There were even moments of weariness when, like the victim of some poison which leaves the brain clear, but holds the body motionless, she saw herself domesticated with the Horror, accepting its perpetual presence as one of the fixed conditions of life.

These moments lengthened into hours and days, till she passed into a phase of stolid acquiescence. She watched the routine of daily life with the incurious eye of a savage on whom the meaningless processes of civilization make but the faintest impression. She had come to regard herself as part of the routine, a spoke of the wheel, revolving with its motion; she felt almost like the furniture of the room in which she sat, an insensate object to be dusted and pushed about with the chairs and tables. And this deepening apathy held her fast at Lyng, in spite of the entreaties of friends and the usual medical recommendation of "change." Her friends supposed that her refusal to move was inspired by the belief that her husband would one day return to the spot from which he had vanished, and a beautiful legend grew up about this imaginary state of waiting. But in reality she had no such belief: the depths of anguish enclosing her were no longer lighted by flashes of hope. She was sure that Boyne would never come back, that he had gone out of her sight as completely as if Death itself had waited that day on the threshold. She had even renounced, one by one, the various theories as to his disappearance which had been advanced by the press, the police, and her own agonized imagination. In sheer lassitude her mind turned from these alternatives of horror, and sank back into the blank fact that he was gone.

No, she would never know what had become of him—no one would ever know. But the house *knew*; the library in which she spent her long lonely evenings knew. For it was here that the last scene had been enacted, here that the stranger had come, and spoken the word which had caused Boyne to rise and follow him. The floor she trod had felt his tread; the books on the shelves had seen his face; and there were moments when the intense consciousness of the old dusky walls seemed about to break out into some audible revelation of their secret. But the revelation never came, and she knew it would never come. Lyng was not one of the garrulous old houses that betray the secrets entrusted to them. Its very legend proved that it had always been the mute accomplice, the incorruptible custodian, of the mysteries it had surprised. And Mary Boyne, sitting face to face with its silence, felt the futility of seeking to break it by any human means.

## V

"I don't say it *wasn't* straight, and yet I don't say it *was* straight. It was business."

Mary, at the words, lifted her head with a start, and looked intently at the speaker.

When, half an hour before, a card with "Mr. Parvis" on it had been brought up to her, she had been immediately aware that the name had been a part of her consciousness ever since she had read it at the head of Boyne's unfinished letter. In the library she had found awaiting her a small sallow man with a bald head and gold eyeglasses, and it sent a tremor through her to know that this was the person to whom her husband's last known thought had been directed.

Parvis, civilly, but without vain preamble—in the manner of a man who has his watch in his hand—had set forth the object of his visit. He had "run over" to England on business, and finding himself in the neighborhood of Dorchester, had not wished to leave it without paying his respects to Mrs. Boyne; and without asking her, if the occasion offered, what she meant to do about Bob Elwell's family.

The words touched the spring of some obscure dread in Mary's bosom. Did her visitor, after all, know what Boyne had meant by his unfinished phrase? She asked for an elucidation of his question, and noticed at once that he seemed surprised at her continued ignorance of the subject. Was it possible that she really knew as little as she said?

"I know nothing—you must tell me," she faltered out; and her visitor thereupon proceeded to unfold his story. It threw, even to her confused perceptions, and imperfectly initiated vision, a lurid glare on the whole hazy episode of the Blue Star Mine. Her husband had made his money in that brilliant speculation at the cost of "getting ahead" of someone less alert to seize the chance; and the victim of his ingenuity was young Robert Elwell, who had "put him on" to the Blue Star scheme.

Parvis, at Mary's first cry, had thrown her a sobering glance through his impartial glasses.

"Bob Elwell wasn't smart enough, that's all; if he had been, he might have turned round and served Boyne the same way. It's the kind of thing that happens every day in business. I guess it's what the scientists call the survival of the fittest—see?" said Mr. Parvis, evidently pleased with the aptness of his analogy.

Mary felt a physical shrinking from the next question she tried to frame: it was as though the words on her lips had a taste that nauseated her.

"But then—you accuse my husband of doing something dishonorable?"

Mr. Parvis surveyed the question dispassionately. "Oh, no, I don't. I don't even say it wasn't straight." He glanced up and down the long lines of books, as if one of them might have supplied him with the definition he sought. "I don't say it *wasn't* straight, and yet I don't say it *was* straight. It was business." After all, no definition in his category could be more comprehensive than that.

Mary sat staring at him with a look of terror. He seemed to her like the indifferent emissary of some evil power.

"But Mr. Elwell's lawyers apparently did not take your view, since I suppose the suit was withdrawn by their advice."

"Oh, yes; they knew he hadn't a leg to stand on, technically. It was when they advised him to withdraw the suit that he got desperate. You see, he'd borrowed most of the money he lost in the Blue Star, and he was up a tree. That's why he shot himself when they told him he had no show."

The horror was sweeping over Mary in great deafening waves.

"He shot himself? He killed himself because of *that?*"

"Well, he didn't kill himself, exactly. He dragged on two months before he died." Parvis emitted the statement as unemotionally as a gramophone grinding out its record.

"You mean that he tried to kill himself, and failed? And tried again?"

"Oh, he didn't have to *try* again," said Parvis grimly.

They sat opposite each other in silence, he swinging his eyeglasses thoughtfully about his finger, she, motionless, her arms stretched along her knees in an attitude of rigid tension.

"But if you knew all this," she began at length, hardly able to force her voice above a whisper, "how is it that when I wrote you at the time of my husband's disappearance you said you didn't understand his letter?"

Parvis received this without perceptible embarrassment: "Why, I didn't understand it—strictly speaking. And it wasn't the time to talk about it, if I had. The Elwell business was settled when the suit was withdrawn. Nothing I could have told you would have helped you to find your husband."

Mary continued to scrutinize him. "Then why are you telling me now?"

Still Parvis did not hesitate. "Well, to begin with, I supposed you knew more than you appear to—I mean about the circumstances of Elwell's death. And then people are talking of it now; the whole matter's been raked up again. And I thought if you didn't know you ought to."

She remained silent, and he continued: "You see, it's only come out lately what a bad state Elwell's affairs were in. His wife's a proud woman, and she fought on as long as she could, going out to work, and taking sewing at home when she got too sick—something with the heart, I believe. But she had his mother to look after, and the children, and she broke down under it, and finally had to ask for help. That called attention to the case, and the papers took it up, and a subscription was started. Everybody out there liked Bob Elwell, and most of the prominent names in the place are down on the list, and people began to wonder why—"

Parvis broke off to fumble in an inner pocket. "Here," he continued, "here's an account of the whole thing from the *Sentinel*—a little sensational, of course. But I guess you'd better look it over."

He held out a newspaper to Mary, who unfolded it slowly, remembering, as she did so, the evening when, in that same room, the perusal of a clipping from the *Sentinel* had first shaken the depths of her security.

As she opened the paper, her eyes, shrinking from the glaring headlines, "Widow of Boyne's Victim Forced to Appeal for Aid," ran down the column of text to two portraits inserted in it. The first was her husband's, taken from a photograph made the year they had come to England. It was the picture of him that she liked best, the one that stood on the writing table upstairs in her bedroom. As the eyes in the photograph met hers, she felt it would be impossible to read what was said of him, and closed her lids with the sharpness of the pain.

"I thought if you felt disposed to put your name down—" she heard Parvis continue.

She opened her eyes with an effort, and they fell on the other portrait. It was that of a youngish man, slightly built, with features somewhat blurred by the shadow of a projecting hat brim. Where had she seen that outline before? She stared at it confusedly, her heart hammering in her ears. Then she gave a cry.

"This is the man—the man who came for my husband!"

She heard Parvis start to his feet, and was dimly aware that she had slipped backward into the corner of the sofa, and that he was bending above her in alarm. She straightened herself, and reached out for the paper, which she had dropped.

"It's the man! I should know him anywhere!" she persisted in a voice that sounded to her own ears like a scream.

Parvis's answer seemed to come to her from far off, down endless fog-muffled windings.

"Mrs. Boyne, you're not very well. Shall I call somebody? Shall I get a glass of water?"

"No, no, no!" She threw herself toward him, her hand frantically clutching the newspaper. "I tell you, it's the man! I *know* him! He spoke to me in the garden!"

Parvis took the journal from her, directing his glasses to the portrait. "It can't be, Mrs. Boyne. It's Robert Elwell."

"Robert Elwell?" Her white stare seemed to travel into space. "Then it was Robert Elwell who came for him."

"Came for Boyne? The day he went away from here?" Parvis's voice dropped as hers rose. He bent over, laying a fraternal hand on her, as if to coax her gently back into her seat. "Why, Elwell was dead! Don't you remember?"

Mary sat with her eyes fixed on the picture, unconscious of what he was saying.

"Don't you remember Boyne's unfinished letter to me—the one you found on his desk that day? It was written just after he'd heard of Elwell's death." She noticed an odd shake in Parvis's unemotional voice. "Surely you remember!" he urged her.

Yes, she remembered: that was the profoundest horror of it. Elwell had died the day before her husband's disappearance; and this was Elwell's portrait; and it was the portrait of the man who had spoken to her in the garden. She lifted her head and looked slowly about the library. The library could have borne witness that it was also the portrait of the man who had come in that day to call Boyne from his unfinished letter. Through the misty surgings of her brain she heard the faint boom of half-forgotten words—words spoken by Alida Stair on the lawn at Pangbourne before Boyne and his wife had ever seen the house at Lyng, or had imagined that they might one day live there.

"This was the man who spoke to me," she repeated.

She looked again at Parvis. He was trying to conceal his disturbance under what he probably imagined to be an expression of indulgent commiseration; but the edges of his lips were blue. "He thinks me mad; but I'm not mad," she reflected; and suddenly there flashed upon her a way of justifying her strange affirmation.

She sat quiet, controlling the quiver of her lips, and waiting till she could trust her voice; then she said, looking straight at Parvis: "Will you answer me one question, please? When was it that Robert Elwell tried to kill himself?"

"When—when?" Parvis stammered.

"Yes; the date. Please try to remember."

She saw that he was growing still more afraid of her. "I have a reason," she insisted.

"Yes, yes. Only I can't remember. About two months before, I should say."

"I want the date," she repeated.

Parvis picked up the newspaper. "We might see here," he said, still humoring her. He ran his eyes down the page. "Here it is. Last October— the  "

She caught the words from him. "The 20th, wasn't it?" With a sharp look at her, he verified. "Yes, the 20th. Then you *did* know?"

"I know now." Her gaze continued to travel past him. "Sunday, the 20th—that was the day he came first."

Parvis's voice was almost inaudible. "Came *here* first?"

"Yes."

"You saw him twice, then?"

"Yes, twice." She just breathed it at him. "He came first on the 20th of October. I remember the date because it was the day we went up Meldon Steep for the first time." She felt a faint gasp of inward laughter at the thought that but for that she might have forgotten.

Parvis continued to scrutinize her, as if trying to intercept her gaze.

"We saw him from the roof," she went on. "He came down the lime avenue toward the house. He was dressed just as he is in that picture. My husband saw him first. He was frightened, and ran down ahead of me; but there was no one there. He had vanished."

"Elwell had vanished?" Parvis faltered.

"Yes." Their two whispers seemed to grope for each other. "I couldn't think what had happened. I see now. He *tried* to come then; but he wasn't dead enough—he couldn't reach us. He had to wait for two months to die; and then he came back again—and Ned went with him."

She nodded at Parvis with the look of triumph of a child who has worked out a difficult puzzle. But suddenly she lifted her hands with a desperate gesture, pressing them to her temples.

"Oh, my God! I sent him to Ned—I told him where to go! I sent him to this room!" she screamed.

She felt the walls of books rush toward her, like inward falling ruins; and she heard Parvis, a long way off, through the ruins, crying to her, and struggling to get at her. But she was numb to his touch, she did not know what he was saying. Through the tumult she heard but one clear note, the voice of Alida Stair, speaking on the lawn at Pangbourne.

"You won't know till afterward," it said. "You won't know till long, long afterward."

# GERTRUDE ATHERTON
## The Striding Place

Weigall, continental and detached, tired early of grouse-shooting. To stand propped, against a sod fence while his host's workmen routed up the birds with long poles and drove them towards the waiting guns, made him feel himself a parody on the ancestors who had roamed the moors and forests of this West Riding of Yorkshire in hot pursuit of game worth the killing. But when in England in August he always accepted whatever proffered for the season, and invited his host to shoot pheasants on his estates in the South. The amusements of life, he argued, should be accepted with the same philosophy as its ills.

It had been a bad day. A heavy rain had made the moor so spongy that it fairly sprang beneath the feet. Whether or not the grouse had haunts of their own, wherein they were immune from rheumatism, the bag had been small. The women, too, were an unusually dull lot, with the exception of a new-minded *débutante* who bothered Weigall at dinner by demanding the verbal restoration of the vague paintings on the vaulted roof above them.

But it was no one of these things that sat on Weigall's mind as, when the other men went up to bed, he let himself out of the castle and sauntered down to the river. His intimate friend, the companion of his boyhood, the chum of his college days, his fellow-traveler in many lands, the man for whom he possessed stronger affection than for all men, had mysteriously disappeared two days ago, and his track might have sprung to the upper air for all trace he had left behind him. He had been a guest on the adjoining estate during the past week, shooting with the fervor of the true sportsman, making love in the intervals to Adeline Cavan, and apparently in the best of spirits. As far as was known there was nothing to lower his mental mercury, for his rent-roll was a large one, Miss Cavan blushed whenever he looked at her, and, being one of the best shots in England, he was never happier than in August. The suicide theory was preposterous, all agreed, and there was as little reason to believe him murdered. Nevertheless, he had walked out of March Abbey two nights ago without hat or overcoat, and had not been seen since.

The country was being patrolled night and day. A hundred keepers and workmen were beating the woods and poking the bogs on the moors, but as yet not so much as a handkerchief had been found.

Weigall did not believe for a moment that Wyatt Gifford was dead, and although it was impossible not to be affected by the general uneasiness, he was disposed to be more angry than frightened. At Cambridge Gifford had been an incorrigible practical joker, and by no means had outgrown the habit; it would be like him to cut across the country in his evening clothes, board a cattle-train, and amuse himself touching up the picture of the sensation in West Riding.

However, Weigall's affection for his friend was too deep to companion with tranquillity in the present state of doubt, and, instead of going to bed early with the other men, he determined to walk until ready for sleep. He went down to the river and followed the path through the woods. There was no moon, but the stars sprinkled their cold light upon the pretty belt of water flowing placidly past wood and ruin, between green masses of overhanging rocks or sloping banks tangled with tree and shrub, leaping occasionally over stones with the harsh notes of an angry scold, to recover its equanimity the moment the way was clear again.

It was very dark in the depths where Weigall trod. He smiled as he recalled a remark of Gifford's: "An English wood is like a good many other things in life—very promising at a distance, but a mellow mockery when you get within. You see daylight on both sides, and the sun freckles the very bracken. Our woods need the night to make them seem what they ought to be—what they once were, before our ancestors' descendants demanded so much more money, in these so much more various days." Weigall strolled along, smoking, and thinking of his friend, his pranks—many of which had done more credit to his imagination than this—and recalling conversations that had lasted the night through. Just before the end of the London season they had walked the streets one hot night after a party, discussing the various theories of the soul's destiny. That afternoon they had met at the coffin of a college friend whose mind had been a blank for the past three years. Some months previously they had called at the asylum to see him. His expression had been senile, his face imprinted with the record of debauchery. In death the face was placid, intelligent, without ignoble lineation—the face of the man they had known at college. Weigall and Gifford had had no time to comment there, and the afternoon and evening were full; but, coming forth from the house of festivity together, they had reverted almost at once to the topic.

"I cherish the theory," Gifford had said, "that the soul sometimes lingers in the body after death. During madness, of course, it is an impotent prisoner, albeit a conscious one. Fancy its agony, and its horror! What more natural than that, when the lifespark goes out, the tortured soul should take possession of the vacant skull and triumph once more for a few hours while old friends look their last? It has had time to repent while compelled to crouch and behold the result of its work, and it has shrived itself into a state of comparative purity. If I had my way, I should stay inside my bones until the coffin had gone into its niche, that I might obviate for my poor old comrade the tragic impersonality of death. And I should like to see justice done to it, as it were to see it lowered among its ancestors with the ceremony and solemnity that are its due. I am afraid that if I dissevered myself too quickly, I should yield to curiosity and hasten to investigate the mysteries of space."

"You believe in the soul as an independent entity, then—that it and the vital principle are not one and the same?"

"Absolutely. The body and soul are twins, life comrades—sometimes friends, sometimes enemies, but always loyal in the last instance. Some day, when I am tired of the world, I shall go to India and become a mahatma, solely for the pleasure of receiving proof during life of this independent relationship."

"Suppose you were not sealed up properly, and returned after one of your astral flights to find your earthly part unfit for habitation? It is an experiment I don't think I should care to try, unless even juggling with soul and flesh had palled."

"That would not be an uninteresting predicament. I should rather enjoy experimenting with broken machinery."

The high wild roar of water smote suddenly upon Weigall's ear and checked his memories. He left the wood and walked out on the huge slippery stones which nearly close the River Wharfe at this point, and watched the waters boil down into the narrow pass with their furious untiring energy. The black quiet of the woods rose high on either side. The stars seemed colder and whiter just above. On either hand the perspective of the river might have run into a rayless cavern. There was no lonelier spot in England, nor one which had the right to claim so many ghosts, if ghosts there were.

Weigall was not a coward, but he recalled uncomfortably the tales of those that had been done to death in the Strid.* Wordsworth's Boy of Egremond had been disposed of by the practical Whitaker; but countless others, more venturesome than wise, had gone down into that narrow boiling course, never to appear in the still pool a few yards beyond. Below the great rocks which form the walls of the Strid was believed to be a natural vault, on to whose shelves the dead were drawn. The spot had an ugly fascination. Weigall stood, visioning skeletons, uncoffined and green, the home of the eyeless things which had devoured all that had covered and filled that rattling symbol of man's mortality; then fell to wondering if any one had attempted to leap the Strid of late. It was covered with slime; he had never seen it look so treacherous.

He shuddered and turned away, impelled, despite his manhood, to flee the spot. As he did so, something tossing in the foam below the fall—something as white, yet independent of it—caught his eye and arrested his step. Then he saw that it was describing a contrary motion to the rushing water—an upward backward motion. Weigall stood rigid, breathless; he fancied he heard the crackling of his hair. Was that a hand? It thrust itself still higher above the boiling foam, turned side-wise, and four frantic fingers were distinctly visible against the black rock beyond.

Weigall's superstitious terror left him. A man was there, struggling to free himself from the suction beneath the Strid, swept down, doubt-less, but a moment before his arrival, perhaps as he stood with his back to the current.

He stepped as close to the edge as he dared. The hand doubled as if in imprecation, shaking savagely in the face of that force which leaves

---

*"This striding place is called the 'Strid,'
   A name which it took of yore;
A thousand years hath it borne the name,
   And it shall a thousand more."

its creatures to immutable law; then spread wide again, clutching, expanding, crying for help as audibly as the human voice.

Weigall dashed to the nearest tree, dragged and twisted off a branch with his strong arms, and returned as swiftly to the Strid. The hand was in the same place, still gesticulating as wildly; the body was undoubtedly caught in the rocks below, perhaps already half-way along one of those hideous shelves. Weigall let himself down upon a lower rock, braced his shoulder against the mass beside him, then, leaning out over the water, thrust the branch into the hand. The fingers clutched it convulsively. Weigall tugged powerfully, his own feet dragged perilously near the edge. For a moment he produced no impression, then an arm shot above the waters.

The blood sprang to Weigall's head; he was choked with the impression that the Strid had him in her roaring hold, and he saw nothing. Then the mist cleared. The hand and arm were nearer, although the rest of the body was still concealed by the foam. Weigall peered out with distended eyes. The meager light revealed in the cuffs links of a peculiar device. The fingers clutching the branch were as familiar.

Weigall forgot the slippery stones, the terrible death if he stepped too far. He pulled with passionate will and muscle. Memories flung themselves into the hot light of his brain, trooping rapidly upon each other's heels, as in the thought of the drowning. Most of the pleasures of his life, good and bad, were identified in some way with this friend. Scenes of college days, of travel, where they had deliberately sought adventure and stood between one another and death upon more occasions than one, of hours of delightful companionship among the treasures of art, and others in the pursuit of pleasure, flashed like the changing particles of a kaleidoscope. Weigall had loved several women; but he would have flouted in these moments the thought that he had ever loved any woman as he loved Wyatt Gifford. There were so many charming women in the world, and in the thirty-two years of his life he had never known another man to whom he had cared to give his intimate friendship.

He threw himself on his face. His wrists were cracking, the skin was torn from his hands. The fingers still gripped the stick. There was life in them yet.

Suddenly something gave way. The hand swung about, tearing the branch from Weigall's grasp. The body had been liberated and flung outward, though still submerged by the foam and spray.

Weigall scrambled to his feet and sprang along the rocks, knowing that the danger from suction was over and that Gifford must be carried straight to the quiet pool. Gifford was a fish in the water and could live under it longer than most men. If he survived this, it would not be the first time that his pluck and science had saved him from drowning.

Weigall reached the pool. A man in his evening clothes floated on it, his face turned towards a projecting rock over which his arm had fallen, upholding the body. The hand that had held the branch hung limply over the rock, its white reflection visible in the black water. Weigall plunged into the shallow pool, lifted Gifford in his arms and returned to the bank. He laid the body down and threw off his coat that he might be the freer to practise the methods of resuscitation. He was glad of the moment's respite. The valiant life in the man might have been exhausted in that last struggle. He had not dared to look at his face, to put his ear to the heart. The hesitation lasted but a moment. There was no time to lose.

He turned to his prostrate friend. As he did so, something strange and disagreeable smote his senses. For a half-moment he did not appreciate its nature. Then his teeth clacked together, his feet, his outstretched arms pointed towards the woods. But he sprang to the side of the man and bent down and peered into his face. There was no face.

# SHERWOOD ANDERSON
## Death in the Woods

### I

She was an old woman and lived on a farm near the town in which I lived. All country and small-town people have seen such old women, but no one knows much about them. Such an old woman comes into town driving an old worn-out horse or she comes afoot carrying a basket. She may own a few hens and have eggs to sell. She brings them in a basket and takes them to a grocer. There she trades them in. She gets some salt pork and some beans. Then she gets a pound or two of sugar and some flour.

Afterwards she goes to the butcher's and asks for some dog-meat. She may spend ten or fifteen cents, but when she does she asks for something. Formerly the butchers gave liver to anyone who wanted to carry it away. In our family we were always having it. Once one of my brothers got a whole cow's liver at the slaughterhouse near the fair grounds in our town. We had it until we were sick of it. It never cost a cent. I have hated the thought of it ever since.

The old farm woman got some liver and a soup-bone. She never visited with anyone, and as soon as she got what she wanted she lit out for home. It made quite a load for such an old body. No one gave her a lift. People drive right down a road and never notice an old woman like that.

There was such an old woman who used to come into town past our house one summer and fall when I was a young boy and was sick with what was called inflammatory rheumatism. She went home later carrying a heavy pack on her back. Two or three large gaunt-looking dogs followed at her heels.

The old woman was nothing special. She was one of the nameless ones that hardly anyone knows, but she got into my thoughts. I have just suddenly now, after all these years, remembered her and what happened. It is a story. Her name was Grimes, and she lived with her husband and son in a small unpainted house on the bank of a small creek four miles from town.

The husband and son were a tough lot. Although the son was but twenty-one, he had already served a term in jail. It was whispered about that the woman's husband stole horses and ran them off to some other county. Now and then, when a horse turned up missing, the man had also disappeared. No one ever caught him. Once, when I was loafing at Tom Whitehead's livery-barn, the man came there and sat on the bench in front. Two or three other men were there, but no one spoke to him. He sat for a few minutes and then got up and went away. When he was leaving he turned around and stared at the men. There was a look of defiance in his eyes. "Well, I have tried to be friendly. You don't want to talk to me. It has been so wherever I have gone in this town. If, some day, one of your fine horses turns up missing, well, then what?" He did not say anything actually. "I'd like to bust one of you on the jaw," was about what his eyes said. I remember how the look in his eyes made me shiver.

The old man belonged to a family that had had money once. His name was Jake Grimes. It all comes back clearly now. His father, John Grimes, had owned a sawmill when the country was new, and had made money. Then he got to drinking and running after women. When he died there wasn't much left.

Jake blew in the rest. Pretty soon there wasn't any more lumber to cut and his land was nearly all gone.

He got his wife off a German farmer, for whom he went to work one June day in the wheat harvest. She was a young thing then and scared to death. You see, the farmer was up to something with the girl—she was, I think, a bound girl[1] and his wife had her suspicions. She took it out on the girl when the man wasn't around. Then, when the wife had to go off to town for supplies, the farmer got after her. She told young Jake that nothing really ever happened, but he didn't know whether to believe it or not.

---

[1] A girl contracted to a period of service.

He got her pretty easy himself, the first time he was out with her. He wouldn't have married her if the German farmer hadn't tried to tell him where to get off. He got her to go riding with him in his buggy one night when he was threshing on the place, and then he came for her the next Sunday night.

She managed to get out of the house without her employer's seeing, but when she was getting into the buggy he showed up. It was almost dark, and he just popped up suddenly at the horse's head. He grabbed the horse by the bridle and Jake got out his buggy-whip.

They had it out all right! The German was a tough one. Maybe he didn't care whether his wife knew or not. Jake hit him over the face and shoulders with the buggy-whip, but the horse got to acting up and he had to get out.

Then the two men went for it. The girl didn't see it. The horse started to run away and went nearly a mile down the road before the girl got him stopped. Then she managed to tie him to a tree beside the road. (I wonder how I know all this. It must have stuck in my mind from small-town tales when I was a boy.) Jake found her there after he got through with the German. She was huddled up in the buggy seat, crying, scared to death. She told Jake a lot of stuff, how the German had tried to get her, how he chased her once into the barn, how another time, when they happened to be alone in the house together, he tore her dress open clear down the front. The German, she said, might have got her that time if he hadn't heard his old woman drive in at the gate. She had been off to town for supplies. Well, she would be putting the horse in the barn. The German managed to sneak off to the fields without his wife seeing. He told the girl he would kill her if she told. What could she do? She told a lie about ripping her dress in the barn when she was feeding the stock. I remember now that she was a bound girl and did not know where her father and mother were. Maybe she did not have any father. You know what I mean.

Such bound children were often enough cruelly treated. They were children who had no parents, slaves really. There were very few orphan homes then. They were legally bound into some home. It was a matter of pure luck how it came out.


II


She married Jake and had a son and daughter, but the daughter died.

Then she settled down to feed stock. That was her job. At the German's place she had cooked the food for the German and his wife. The wife was a strong woman with big hips and worked most of the time in the fields with her husband. She fed them and fed the cows in the barn, fed the pigs, the horses and the chickens. Every moment of every day, as a young girl, was spent feeding something.

Then she married Jake Grimes and he had to be fed. She was a slight thing, and when she had been married for three or four years, and after the two children were born, her slender shoulders became stooped.

Jake always had a lot of big dogs around the house, that stood near the unused sawmill near the creek. He was always trading horses when he wasn't stealing something and had a lot of poor bony ones about. Also he kept three or four pigs and a cow. They were all pastured in the few acres left of the Grimes place and Jake did little enough work.

He went into debt for a threshing outfit and ran it for several years, but it did not pay. People did not trust him. They were afraid he would steal the grain at night. He had to go a long way off to get work and it cost too much to get there. In the winter he hunted and cut a little firewood, to be sold in some nearby town. When the son grew up he was just like the father. They got drunk together. If there wasn't anything to eat in the house when they came home the old man gave his old woman a cut over the head. She had a few chickens of her own and had to kill one of them in a hurry. When they were all killed she wouldn't have any eggs to sell when she went to town, and then what would she do?

She had to scheme all her life about getting things fed, getting the pigs fed so they would grow fat and could be butchered in the fall. When they were butchered her husband took most of the meat off to town and sold it. If he did not do it first the boy did. They fought sometimes and when they fought the old woman stood aside trembling.

She had got the habit of silence anyway—that was fixed. Sometimes, when she began to look old—she wasn't forty yet—and when the husband and son were both off, trading horses or drinking or hunting or stealing, she went around the house and the barnyard muttering to herself.

How was she going to get everything fed?—that was her problem. The dogs had to be fed. There wasn't enough hay in the barn for the horses and the cow. If she didn't feed the chickens how could they lay eggs? Without eggs to sell how could she get things in town, things she had to have to keep the life of the farm going? Thank heaven, she did not have to feed her husband—in a certain way. That hadn't lasted long after their marriage and after the babies came. Where he went on his long trips she did not know. Sometimes he was gone from home for weeks, and after the boy grew up they went off together.

They left everything at home for her to manage and she had no money. She knew no one. No one ever talked to her in town. When it was winter she had to gather sticks of wood for her fire, had to try to keep the stock fed with very little grain.

The stock in the barn cried to her hungrily, the dogs followed her about. In the winter the hens laid few enough eggs. They huddled in the corners of the barn and she kept watching them. If a hen lays an egg in the barn in the winter and you do not find it, it freezes and breaks.

One day in winter the old woman went off to town with a few eggs and the dogs followed her. She did not get started until nearly three o'clock and the snow was heavy. She hadn't been feeling very well for several days and so she went muttering along, scantily clad, her shoulders stooped. She had an old grain bag in which she carried her eggs, tucked away down in the bottom. There weren't many of them, but in winter the price of eggs is up. She would get a little meat in exchange for the eggs, some salt pork, a little sugar, and some coffee perhaps. It might be the butcher would give her a piece of liver.

When she had got to town and was trading in her eggs the dogs lay by the door outside. She did pretty well, got the things she needed, more than she had hoped. Then she went to the butcher and he gave her some liver and some dog-meat.

It was the first time anyone had spoken to her in a friendly way for a long time. The butcher was alone in his shop when she came in and was annoyed by the thought of such a sick-looking old woman out on such a day. It was bitter cold and the snow, that had let up during the afternoon, was falling again. The butcher said something about her husband and her son, swore at them, and the old woman stared at him, a look of mild surprise in her eyes as he talked. He said that if either the husband or the son were going to get any of the liver or the heavy bones with scraps of meat hanging to them that he had put into the grain bag, he'd see him starve first.

Starve, eh? Well, things had to be fed. Men had to be fed, and the horses that weren't any good but maybe could be traded off, and the poor thin cow that hadn't given any milk for three months.

Horses, cows, pigs, dogs, men.

## III

The old woman had to get back before darkness came if she could. The dogs followed at her heels, sniffing at the heavy grain bag she had fastened on her back. When she got to the edge of town she stopped by a fence and tied the bag on her back with a piece of rope she had carried in her dress-pocket for just that purpose. That was an easier way to carry it. Her arms ached. It was hard when she had to crawl over fences and once she fell over and landed in the snow. The dogs went frisking about. She had to struggle to get to her feet again, but she made it. The point of climbing over the fences was that there was a short cut over a hill and through a woods. She might have gone around by the road, but it was a mile farther that way. She was afraid she couldn't make it. And then, besides, the stock had to be fed. There was a little hay left and a little corn. Perhaps her husband and son would bring some home when they came. They had driven off in the only buggy the Grimes family had, a rickety thing, a rickety horse hitched to the buggy, two other rickety horses led by halters. They were going to trade horses, get a little money if they could. They might come home drunk. It would be well to have something in the house when they came back.

The son had an affair on with a woman at the county seat, fifteen miles away. She was a rough enough woman, a tough one. Once, in the summer, the son had brought her to the house. Both she and the son had been drinking. Jake Grimes was away and the son and his woman ordered the old woman about like a servant. She didn't mind much; she was used to it. Whatever happened she never said anything. That was her way of getting along. She had managed that way when she was a young girl at the German's and ever since she had married Jake. That time her son brought his woman to the house they stayed all night, sleeping together just as though they were married. It hadn't shocked the old woman, not much. She had got past being shocked early in life.

With the pack on her back she went painfully along across an open field, wading in the deep snow, and got into the woods.

There was a path, but it was hard to follow. Just beyond the top of the hill, where the woods was thickest, there was a small clearing. Had someone once thought of building a house there? The clearing was as large as a building lot in town, large enough for a house and a garden. The path ran along the side of the clearing, and when she got there the old woman sat down to rest at the foot of a tree.

It was a foolish thing to do. When she got herself placed, the pack against the tree's trunk, it was nice, but what about getting up again? She worried about that for a moment and then quietly closed her eyes.

She must have slept for a time. When you are about so cold you can't get any colder. The afternoon grew a little warmer and the snow came thicker than ever. Then after a time the weather cleared. The moon even came out.

There were four Grimes dogs that had followed Mrs. Grimes into town, all tall gaunt fellows. Such men as Jake Grimes and his son always keep just such dogs. They kick and abuse them, but they stay. The Grimes dogs, in order to keep from starving, had to do a lot of foraging for themselves, and they had been at it while the old woman slept with her back to the tree at the side of the clearing. They had been chasing rabbits in the woods and in adjoining fields and in their ranging had picked up three other farm dogs.

After a time all the dogs came back to the clearing. They were excited about something. Such nights, cold and clear and with a moon, do things to dogs. It may be that some old instinct, come down from the time when they were wolves and ranged the woods in packs on winter nights, comes back into them.

The dogs in the clearing, before the old woman, had caught two or three rabbits and their immediate hunger had been satisfied. They began to play, running in circles in the clearing. Round and round they ran, each dog's nose at the tail of the next dog. In the clearing, under the snow-laden trees and under the wintry moon they made a strange picture, running thus silently, in a circle their running had beaten in the soft snow. The dogs made no sound. They ran around and around in the circle.

It may have been that the old woman saw them doing that before she died. She may have awakened once or twice and looked at the strange sight with dim old eyes.

She wouldn't be very cold now, just drowsy. Life hangs on a long time. Perhaps the old woman was out of her head. She may have dreamed of her girlhood, at the German's, and before that, when she was a child and before her mother lit out and left her.

Her dreams couldn't have been very pleasant. Not many pleasant things had happened to her. Now and then one of the Grimes dogs left the running circle and came to stand before her. The dog thrust his face close to her face. His red tongue was hanging out.

The running of the dogs may have been a kind of death ceremony. It may have been that the primitive instinct of the wolf, having been aroused in the dogs by the night and the running, made them somehow afraid.

"Now we are no longer wolves. We are dogs, the servants of men. Keep alive, man! When man dies we become wolves again."

When one of the dogs came to where the old woman sat with her back against the tree and thrust his nose close to her face he seemed satisfied and went back to run with the pack. All the Grimes dogs did it at some time during the evening, before she died. I knew all about it afterward, when I grew to be a man, because once in a woods in Illinois, on another winter night, I saw a pack of dogs act just like that. The dogs were waiting for me to die as they had waited for the old woman that night when I was a child, but when it happened to me I was a young man and had no intention whatever of dying.

The old woman died softly and quietly. When she was dead and when one of the Grimes dogs had come to her and had found her dead all the dogs stopped running.

They gathered about her.

Well, she was dead now. She had fed the Grimes dogs when she was alive, what about now?

There was the pack on her back, the grain bag containing the piece of salt pork, the liver the butcher had given her, the dog-meat, the soup-bones. The butcher in town, having been suddenly overcome with a feeling of pity, had loaded her grain bag heavily. It had been a big haul for the old woman.

It was a big haul for the dogs now.


IV

One of the Grimes dogs sprang suddenly out from among the others and began worrying the pack on the old woman's back. Had the dogs really been wolves that one would have been the leader of the pack. What he did, all the others did.

All of them sank their teeth into the grain bag the old woman had fastened with ropes to her back.

They dragged the old woman's body out into the open clearing. The worn-out dress was quickly torn from her shoulders. When she was found, a day or two later, the dress had been torn from her body clear to the hips, but the dogs had not touched her body. They had got the meat out of the grain bag, that was all. Her body was frozen stiff when it was found, and the shoulders were so narrow and the body so slight that in death it looked like the body of some charming young girl.

Such things happened in towns of the Middle West, on farms near town, when I was a boy. A hunter out after rabbits found the old woman's body and did not touch it. Something, the beaten round path in the little snow-covered clearing, the silence of the place, the place where the dogs had worried the body trying to pull the grain bag away or tear it open—something startled the man and he hurried off to town.

I was in Main Street with one of my brothers who was town newsboy and who was taking the afternoon papers to the stores. It was almost night.

The hunter came into a grocery and told his story. Then he went to a hardware shop and into a drugstore. Men began to gather on the sidewalks. Then they started out along the road to the place in the woods.

My brother should have gone on about his business of distributing papers but he didn't. Everyone was going to the woods. The undertaker went and the town marshal. Several men got on a dray and rode out to where the path left the road and went into the woods, but the horses weren't very sharply shod and slid about on the slippery roads. They made no better time than those of us who walked.

The town marshal was a large man whose leg had been injured in the Civil War. He carried a heavy cane and limped rapidly along the road. My brother and I followed at his heels, and as we went other men and boys joined the crowd.

It had grown dark by the time we got to where the old woman had left the road but the moon had come out. The marshal was thinking there might have been a murder. He kept asking the hunter questions. The hunter went along with his gun across his shoulders, a dog following at his heels. It isn't often a rabbit hunter has a chance to be so conspicuous. He was taking full advantage of it, leading the procession with the town marshal. "I didn't see any wounds. She was a beautiful young girl. Her face was buried in the snow. No, I didn't know her." As a matter of fact, the hunter had not looked closely at the body. He had been frightened. She might have been murdered and someone might spring out from behind a tree and murder him. In a woods, in the late afternoon, when the trees are all bare and there is white snow on the ground, when all is silent, something creepy steals over the mind and body. If something strange or uncanny has happened in the neighborhood all you think about is getting away from there as fast as you can.

The crowd of men and boys had got to where the old woman had crossed the field and went, following the marshal and the hunter, up the slight incline and into the woods.

My brother and I were silent. He had his bundle of papers in a bag slung across his shoulder. When he got back to town he would have to go on distributing his papers before he went home to supper. If I went along, as he had no doubt already determined I should, we would both be late. Either mother or our older sister would have to warm our supper.

Well, we would have something to tell. A boy did not get such a chance very often. It was lucky we just happened to go into the grocery when the hunter came in. The hunter was a country fellow. Neither of us had ever seen him before.

Now the crowd of men and boys had got to the clearing. Darkness comes quickly on such winter nights, but the full moon made everything clear. My brother and I stood near the tree, beneath which the old woman had died.

She did not look old, lying there in that light, frozen and still. One of the men turned her over in the snow and I saw everything. My body trembled with some strange mystical feeling and so did my brother's. It might have been the cold.

Neither of us had ever seen a woman's body before. It may have been the snow, clinging to the frozen flesh, that made it look so white and lovely, so like marble. No woman had come with the party from town; but one of the men, he was the town blacksmith, took off his overcoat and spread it over her. Then he gathered her into his arms and started off to town, all the others following silently. At that time no one knew who she was.

V

I had seen everything, had seen the oval in the snow, like a miniature race track, where the dogs had run, had seen how the men were mystified, had seen the white bare young-looking shoulders, had heard the whispered comments of the men.

The men were simply mystified. They took the body to the undertaker's, and when the blacksmith, the hunter, the marshal and several others had got inside they closed the door. If father had been there perhaps he could have got in, but we boys couldn't.

I went with my brother to distribute the rest of his papers and when we got home it was my brother who told the story.

I kept silent and went to bed early. It may have been I was not satisfied with the way he told it.

Later, in the town, I must have heard other fragments of the old woman's story. She was recognized the next day and there was an investigation.

The husband and son were found somewhere and brought to town and there was an attempt to connect them with the woman's death, but it did not work. They had perfect enough alibis. However, the town was against them. They had to get out. Where they went I never heard.

I remember only the picture there in the forest, the men standing about, the naked girlish-looking figure, face down in the snow, the tracks made by the running dogs and the clear cold winter sky above. White fragments of clouds were drifting across the sky. They went racing across the little open space among the trees.

The scene in the forest had become for me, without my knowing it, the foundation for the real story I am now trying to tell. The fragments, you see, had to be picked up slowly, long afterwards.

Things happened. When I was a young man I worked on the farm of a German. The hired-girl was afraid of her employer. The farmer's wife hated her.

I saw things at that place. Once later, I had a half-uncanny, mystical adventure with dogs in an Illinois forest on a clear, moonlit winter night. When I was a schoolboy, and on a summer day, I went with a boy friend out along a creek some miles from town and came to the house where the old woman had lived. No one had lived in the house since her death. The doors were broken from the hinges; the window lights were all broken. As the boy and I stood in the road outside, two dogs, just roving farm dogs no doubt, came running around the corner of the house. The dogs were tall, gaunt fellows and came down to the fence and glared through at us, standing in the road.

The whole thing, the story of the old woman's death, was to me as I grew older like music heard from far off. The notes had to be picked up slowly one at a time. Something had to be understood.

The woman who died was one destined to feed animal life. Anyway, that is all she ever did. She was feeding animal life before she was born, as a child, as a young woman working on the farm of the German, after she married, when she grew old and when she died. She fed animal life in cows, in chickens, in pigs, in horses, in dogs, in men. Her daughter had died in childhood and with her one son she had no articulate relations. On the night when she died she was hurrying homeward, bearing on her body food for animal life.

She died in the clearing in the woods and even after her death continued feeding animal life.

You see it is likely that, when my brother told the story, that night when we got home and my mother and sister sat listening, I did not think he got the point. He was too young and so was I. A thing so complete has its own beauty.

I shall not try to emphasize the point. I am only explaining why I was dissatisfied then and have been ever since. I speak of that only that you may understand why I have been impelled to try to tell the simple story over again.

# H. P. LOVECRAFT
## The Outsider

That night the Baron dreamt of many a wo;
And all his warrior-guests, with shade and form
Of witch, and demon, and large coffin-worm,
Were long be-nightmared.

KEATS

Unhappy is he to whom the memories of childhood bring only
fear and sadness. Wretched is he who looks back upon lone hours
in vast and dismal chambers with brown hangings and maddening
rows of antique books, or upon awed watches in twilight groves
of grotesque, gigantic, and vine-encumbered trees that silently
wave twisted branches far aloft. Such a lot the gods gave to me—
to me, the dazed, the disappointed; the barren, the broken. And yet
I am strangely content and cling desperately to those sere memories, when my mind momentarily threatens to reach beyond to *the
other.*

I know not where I was born, save that the castle was infinitely
old and infinitely horrible, full of dark passages and having high ceil-
ings where the eye could find only cobwebs and shadows. The stones
in the crumbling corridors seemed always hideously damp, and there
was an accursed smell everywhere, as of the piled-up corpses of dead
generations. It was never light, so that I used sometimes to light
candles and gaze steadily at them for relief, nor was there any sun out-
doors, since the terrible trees grew high above the topmost accessible
tower. There was one black tower which reached above the trees into
the unknown outer sky, but that was partly ruined and could not be
ascended save by a well-nigh impossible climb up the sheer wall, stone
by stone.

I must have lived years in this place, but I cannot measure the
time. Beings must have cared for my needs, yet I cannot recall any

person except myself, or anything alive but the noiseless rats and bats and spiders. I think that whoever nursed me must have been shockingly aged, since my first conception of a living person was that of somebody mockingly like myself, yet distorted, shrivelled, and decaying like the castle. To me there was nothing grotesque in the bones and skeletons that strewed some of the stone crypts deep down among the foundations. I fantastically associated these things with everyday events, and thought them more natural than the coloured pictures of living beings which I found in many of the mouldy books. From such books I learned all that I know. No teacher urged or guided me, and I do not recall hearing any human voice in all those years—not even my own; for although I had read of speech, I had never thought to try to speak aloud. My aspect was a matter equally unthought of, for there were no mirrors in the castle, and I merely regarded myself by instinct as akin to the youthful figures I saw drawn and painted in the books. I felt conscious of youth because I remembered so little.

Outside, across the putrid moat and under the dark mute trees, I would often lie and dream for hours about what I read in the books; and would longingly picture myself amidst gay crowds in the sunny world beyond the endless forests. Once I tried to escape from the forest, but as I went farther from the castle the shade grew denser and the air more filled with brooding fear; so that I ran frantically back lest I lose my way in a labyrinth of nighted silence.

So through endless twilights I dreamed and waited, though I knew not what I waited for. Then in the shadowy solitude my longing for light grew so frantic that I could rest no more, and I lifted entreating hands to the single black ruined tower that reached above the forest into the unknown outer sky. And at last I resolved to scale that tower, fall though I might; since it were better to glimpse the sky and perish, than to live without ever beholding day.

In the dank twilight I climbed the worn and aged stone stairs till I reached the level where they ceased, and thereafter clung perilously to small footholds leading upward. Ghastly and terrible was that dead, stairless cylinder of rock; black, ruined, and deserted, and sinister with startled bats whose wings made no noise. But more ghastly and terrible still was the slowness of my progress; for climb as I might, the darkness overhead grew no thinner, and a new chill as of haunted and venerable mould assailed me. I shivered as I wondered why I did not reach the light, and would have looked down had I dared. I fancied that night had come suddenly upon me, and vainly groped with one free hand for a window embrasure, that I might peer out and above, and try to judge the height I had attained.

All at once, after an infinity of awesome, sightless, crawling up that concave and desperate precipice, I felt my head touch a solid thing, and I knew I must have gained the roof, or at least some kind of floor. In the darkness I raised my free hand and tested the barrier, finding it stone and immovable. Then came a deadly circuit of the tower, clinging to whatever holds the slimy wall could give; till finally my testing hand found the barrier yielding, and I turned upward again, pushing the slab or door with my head as I used both hands in my fearful ascent. There was no light revealed above, and as my hands went higher I knew that my climb was for the nonce ended; since the slab was the trap-door of an aperture leading to a level stone surface of greater circumference than the lower tower, no doubt the floor of some lofty and capacious observation chamber. I crawled through carefully, and tried to prevent the heavy slab from falling back into place, but failed in the latter attempt. As I lay exhausted on the stone floor I heard the eerie echoes of its fall, hoped when necessary to pry it up again.

Believing I was now at prodigious height, far above the accursed branches of the wood, I dragged myself up from the floor and fumbled about for windows, that I might look for the first time upon the sky, and the moon and stars of which I had read. But on every hand I was disappointed; since all that I found were vast shelves of marble, bearing odious oblong boxes of disturbing size. More and more I reflected, and wondered what hoary secrets might abide in this high apartment so many aeons cut off from the castle below. Then unexpectedly my hands came upon a doorway, where hung a portal of stone, rough with strange chiselling. Trying it, I found it locked; but with a supreme burst of strength I overcame all obstacles and dragged it open inward. As I did so there came to me the purest ecstasy I have ever known; for shining tranquilly through an ornate grating of iron, and down a short stone passageway of steps that ascended from the newly found doorway, was the radiant full moon, which I had never before seen save in dreams and in vague visions I dared not call memories.

Fancying now that I had attained the very pinnacle of the castle, I commenced to rush up the few steps beyond the door; but the sudden veiling of the moon by a cloud caused me to stumble, and I felt my way more slowly in the dark. It was still very dark when I reached the grating—which I tried carefully and found unlocked, but which I did not open for fear of falling from the amazing height to which I had climbed. Then the moon came out.

Most demoniacal of all shocks is that of the abysmally unexpected and grotesquely unbelievable. Nothing I had before undergone could compare in terror with what I now saw; with the bizarre marvels that sight implied. The sight itself was as simple as it was stupefying, for it was merely this: instead of a dizzying prospect of treetops seen from a lofty eminence, there stretched around me on the level through the grating nothing less than *the solid ground*, decked and diversified by marble slabs and columns, and overshadowed by an ancient stone church, whose ruined spire gleamed spectrally in the moonlight.

Half unconscious, I opened the grating and staggered out upon the white gravel path that stretched away in two directions. My mind, stunned and chaotic as it was, still held the frantic craving for light; and not even the fantastic wonder which had happened could stay my course. I neither knew nor cared whether my experience was insanity, dreaming, or magic; but was determined to gaze on brilliance and gaiety at any cost. I knew not who I was or what I was, or what my surroundings might be; though as I continued to stumble along I became conscious of a kind of fearsome latent memory that made my progress not wholly fortuitous. I passed under an arch out of that region of slabs and columns, and wandered through the open country; sometimes following the visible road, but sometimes leaving it curiously to tread across meadows where only occasional ruins bespoke the ancient presence of a forgotten road. Once I swam across a swift river where crumbling, mossy masonry told of a bridge long vanished.

Over two hours must have passed before I reached what seemed to be my goal, a venerable ivied castle in a thickly wooded park, maddeningly familiar, yet full of perplexing strangeness to me. I saw that the moat was filled in, and that some of the well-known towers were demolished; whilst new wings existed to confuse the beholder. But what I observed with chief interest and delight were the open windows—gorgeously ablaze with light and sending forth sound of the gayest revelry. Advancing to one of these I looked in and saw an oddly dressed company indeed; making merry, and speaking brightly to one another. I had never, seemingly, heard human speech before and could guess only vaguely what was said. Some of the faces seemed to hold expressions that brought up incredibly remote recollections, others were utterly alien.

I now stepped through the low window into the brilliantly lighted room, stepping as I did so from my single bright moment of hope to my blackest convulsion of despair and realization. The nightmare was quick to come, for as I entered, there occurred immediately one of the most terrifying demonstrations I had ever conceived. Scarcely had I crossed the sill when there descended upon the whole company a sudden and unheralded fear of hideous intensity, distorting every face and evoking the most horrible screams from nearly every throat. Flight was universal, and in the clamour and panic several fell in a swoon and were dragged away by their madly fleeing companions. Many covered their eyes with their hands, and plunged blindly and awkwardly in their race to escape, overturning furniture and stumbling against the walls before they managed to reach one of the many doors.

The cries were shocking; and as I stood in the brilliant apartment alone and dazed, listening to their vanishing echoes, I trembled at the thought of what might be lurking near me unseen. At a casual inspection the room seemed deserted, but when I moved towards one of the alcoves I thought I detected a presence there—a hint of motion beyond the golden-arched doorway leading to another and somewhat similar room. As I approached the arch I began to perceive the presence more clearly; and then, with the first and last sound I ever uttered—a ghastly ululation that revolted me almost as poignantly as its noxious cause—I beheld in full, frightful vividness the inconceivable, indescribable, and unmentionable monstrosity which had by its simple appearance changed a merry company to a herd of delirious fugitives.

I cannot even hint what it was like, for it was a compound of all that is unclean, uncanny, unwelcome, abnormal, and detestable. It was the ghoulish shade of decay, antiquity, and dissolution; the putrid, dripping eidolon of unwholesome revelation, the awful baring of that which the merciful earth should always hide. God knows it was not of this world—or no longer of this world—yet to my horror I saw in its eaten-away and bone-revealing outlines a leering, abhorrent travesty on the human shape; and in its mouldy, disintegrating apparel an unspeakable quality that chilled me even more.

I was almost paralysed, but not too much so to make a feeble effort towards flight; a backward stumble which failed to break the spell in which the nameless, voiceless monster held me. My eyes bewitched by the glassy orbs which stared loathsomely into them, refused to close; though they were mercifully blurred, and showed the terrible object but indistinctly after the first shock. I tried to raise my hand to shut out the sight, yet so stunned were my nerves that my arm could not fully obey my will. The attempt, however, was enough to disturb my balance; so that I had to stagger forward several steps to avoid falling. As I did so I became suddenly and agonizingly aware of the *nearness* of the carrion thing, whose hideous hollow breathing I half fancied I could hear. Nearly mad, I found myself yet able to throw out a hand to ward off the foetid apparition which pressed so close; when in one cataclysmic second of cosmic nightmarishness and hellish accident *my fingers touched the rotting outstretched paw of the monster beneath the golden arch.*

I did not shriek, but all the fiendish ghouls that ride the night-wind shrieked for me as in that same second there crashed down upon my mind a single fleeting avalanche of soul-annihilating memory. I knew in that second all that had been; I remembered beyond the frightful castle and the trees, and recognized the altered edifice in which I now stood; I recognized, most terrible of all, the unholy abomination that stood leering before me as I withdrew my sullied fingers from its own.

But in the cosmos there is balm as well as bitterness, and that balm is nepenthe. In the supreme horror of that second I forgot what had horrified me, and the burst of black memory vanished in a chaos of echoing images. In a dream I fled from that haunted and accursed pile, and ran swiftly and silently in the moonlight. When I returned to the churchyard place of marble and went down the steps I found the stone trap-door immovable; but I was not sorry, for I had hated the antique castle and the trees. Now I ride with the mocking and friendly ghouls on the night-wind, and play by day amongst the catacombs of Nephren-Ka in the sealed and unknown valley of Hadoth by the Nile. I know that light is not for me, save that of the moon over the rock tombs of Neb, nor any gaiety save the unnamed feasts of Nitokris beneath the Great Pyramid; yet in my new wildness and freedom I almost welcome the bitterness of alienage.

For although nepenthe has calmed me, I know always that I am an outsider; a stranger in this century and among those who are still men. This I have known ever since I stretched out my fingers to the abomination within that great gilded frame; stretched out my fingers and touched *a cold and unyielding surface of polished glass.*

# WILLIAM FAULKNER
## A Rose for Emily

# I

When Miss Emily Grierson died, our whole town went to her funeral: the men through a sort of respectful affection for a fallen monument, the women mostly out of curiosity to see the inside of her house, which no one save an old manservant—a combined gardener and cook—had seen in at least ten years.

It was a big, squarish frame house that had once been white, decorated with cupolas and spires and scrolled balconies in the heavily lightsome style of the seventies, set on what had once been our most select street. But garages and cotton gins had encroached and obliterated even the august names of that neighborhood; only Miss Emily's house was left, lifting its stubborn and coquettish decay above the cotton wagons and the gasoline pumps—an eyesore among eyesores. And now Miss Emily had gone to join the representatives of those august names where they lay in the cedar-bemused cemetery among the ranked and anonymous graves of Union and Confederate soldiers who fell at the battle of Jefferson.

Alive, Miss Emily had been a tradition, a duty, and a care; a sort of hereditary obligation upon the town, dating from that day in 1894 when Colonel Sartoris, the mayor—he who fathered the edict that no Negro woman should appear on the streets without an apron—remitted her taxes, the dispensation dating from the death of her father on into perpetuity. Not that Miss Emily would have accepted charity. Colonel Sartoris invented an involved tale to the effect that Miss Emily's father had loaned money to the town, which the town, as a matter of business, preferred this way of repaying. Only a man of Colonel Sartoris' generation and thought could have invented it, and only a woman could have believed it.

When the next generation, with its more modern ideas, became mayors and aldermen, this arrangement created some little dissatisfaction. On the first of the year they mailed her a tax notice. February came, and there was no reply. They wrote her a formal letter, asking her to call at the sheriff's office at her convenience. A week later the mayor wrote her himself, offering to call or to send his car for her, and received in reply a note on paper of an archaic shape, in a thin, flowing calligraphy in faded ink, to the effect that she no longer went out at all. The tax notice was also enclosed, without comment.

They called a special meeting of the Board of Aldermen. A deputation waited upon her, knocked at the door through which no visitor had passed since she ceased giving china-painting lessons eight or ten years earlier. They were admitted by the old Negro into a dim hall from which a stairway mounted into still more shadow. It smelled of dust and disuse—a close, dank smell. The Negro led them into the parlor. It was furnished in heavy, leather-covered furniture. When the Negro opened the blinds of one window, a faint dust rose sluggishly about their thighs, spinning with slow motes in the single sun-ray. On a tarnished gilt easel before the fireplace stood a crayon portrait of Miss Emily's father.

They rose when she entered—a small, fat woman in black, with a thin gold chain descending to her waist and vanishing into her belt, leaning on an ebony cane with a tarnished gold head. Her skeleton was small and spare; perhaps that was why what would have been merely plumpness in another was obesity in her. She looked bloated, like a body long submerged in motionless water, and of that pallid hue. Her eyes, lost in the fatty ridges of her face, looked like two small pieces of coal pressed into a lump of dough as they moved from one face to another while the visitors stated their errand.

She did not ask them to sit. She just stood in the door and listened quietly until the spokesman came to a stumbling halt. Then they could hear the invisible watch ticking at the end of the gold chain.

Her voice was dry and cold. "I have no taxes in Jefferson. Colonel Sartoris explained it to me. Perhaps one of you can gain access to the city records and satisfy yourselves."

"But we have. We are the city authorities, Miss Emily. Didn't you get a notice from the sheriff, signed by him?"

"I received a paper, yes," Miss Emily said. "Perhaps he considers himself the sheriff. . . . I have no taxes in Jefferson."

"But there is nothing on the books to show that, you see. We must go by the—"

"See Colonel Sartoris. I have no taxes in Jefferson."

"But, Miss Emily—"

"See Colonel Sartoris." (Colonel Sartoris had been dead almost ten years.) "I have no taxes in Jefferson. Tobe!" The Negro appeared. "Show these gentlemen out."

## II

So she vanquished them, horse and foot, just as she had vanquished their fathers thirty years before about the smell. That was two years after her father's death and a short time after her sweetheart—the one we believed would marry her—had deserted her. After her father's death she went out very little; after her sweetheart went away, people hardly saw her at all. A few of the ladies had the temerity to call, but were not received, and the only sign of life about the place was the Negro man—a young man then—going in and out with a market basket.

"Just as if a man—any man—could keep a kitchen properly," the ladies said; so they were not surprised when the smell developed. It was another link between the gross, teeming world and the high and mighty Griersons.

A neighbor, a woman, complained to the mayor, Judge Stevens, eighty years old.

"But what will you have me do about it, madam?" he said.

"Why, send her word to stop it," the woman said. "Isn't there a law?"

"I'm sure that won't be necessary," Judge Stevens said. "It's probably just a snake or a rat that nigger of hers killed in the yard. I'll speak to him about it."

The next day he received two more complaints, one from a man who came in diffident deprecation. "We really must do something about it, Judge. I'd be the last one in the world to bother Miss Emily, but we've got to do something." That night the Board of Aldermen met—three gray-beards and one younger man, a member of the rising generation.

"It's simple enough," he said. "Send her word to have her place cleaned up. Give her a certain time to do it in, and if she don't . . ."

"Dammit, sir," Judge Stevens said, "will you accuse a lady to her face of smelling bad?"

So the next night, after midnight, four men crossed Miss Emily's lawn and slunk about the house like burglars, sniffing along the base of the brickwork and at the cellar openings while one of them performed a regular sowing motion with his hand out of a sack slung from his shoulder. They broke open the cellar door and sprinkled lime there, and in all the outbuildings. As they recrossed the lawn, a window that had been dark was lighted and Miss Emily sat in it, the light behind her, and her upright torso motionless as that of an idol. They crept quietly across the lawn and into the shadow of the locusts that lined the street. After a week or two the smell went away.

That was when people had begun to feel really sorry for her. People in our town, remembering how old lady Wyatt, her great-aunt, had gone completely crazy at last, believed that the Griersons held themselves a little too high for what they really were. None of the young men were quite good enough for Miss Emily and such. We had long thought of them as a tableau; Miss Emily a slender figure in white in the background, her father a spraddled silhouette in the foreground, his back to her and clutching a horsewhip, the two of them framed by the back-flung front door. So when she got to be thirty and was still single, we were not pleased exactly, but vindicated; even with insanity in the family she wouldn't have turned down all of her chances if they had really materialized.

When her father died, it got about that the house was all that was left to her; and in a way, people were glad. At last they could pity Miss Emily. Being left alone, and a pauper, she had become humanized. Now she too would know the old thrill and the old despair of a penny more or less.

The day after his death all the ladies prepared to call at the house and offer condolence and aid, as is our custom. Miss Emily met them at the door, dressed as usual and with no trace of grief on her face. She told them that her father was not dead. She did that for three days, with the ministers calling on her, and the doctors, trying to persuade her to let them dispose of the body. Just as they were about to resort to law and force, she broke down, and they buried her father quickly.

We did not say she was crazy then. We believed she had to do that. We remembered all the young men her father had driven away, and we knew that with nothing left, she would have to cling to that which had robbed her, as people will.

## III

She was sick for a long time. When we saw her again, her hair was cut short, making her look like a girl, with a vague resemblance to those angels in colored church windows—sort of tragic and serene.

The town had just let the contracts for paving the sidewalks, and in the summer after her father's death they began to work. The construction company came with niggers and mules and machinery, and a foreman named Homer Barron, a Yankee—a big, dark, ready man, with a big voice and eyes lighter than his face. The little boys would follow in groups to hear him cuss the niggers, and the niggers singing in time to the rise and fall of picks. Pretty soon he knew everybody in town. Whenever you heard a lot of laughing anywhere about the square, Homer Barron would be in the center of the group. Presently we began to see him and Miss Emily on Sunday afternoons driving in the yellow-wheeled buggy and the matched team of bays from the livery stable.

At first we were glad that Miss Emily would have an interest, because the ladies all said, "Of course a Grierson would not think seriously of a Northerner, a day laborer." But there were still others, older people, who said that even grief could not cause a real lady to forget *noblesse oblige*—without calling it *noblesse oblige*. They just said, "Poor Emily. Her kinsfolk should come to her." She had some kin in Alabama; but years ago her father had fallen out with them over the estate of old lady Wyatt, the crazy woman, and there was no communication between the two families. They had not even been represented at the funeral.

And as soon as the old people said, "Poor Emily," the whispering began. "Do you suppose it's really so?" they said to one another. "Of course it is. What else could . . ." This behind their hands; rustling of craned silk and satin behind jalousies closed upon the sun of Sunday afternoon as the thin, swift clop-clop-clop of the matched team passed: "Poor Emily."

She carried her head high enough—even when we believed that she was fallen. It was as if she demanded more than ever the recognition of her dignity as the last Grierson; as if it had wanted that touch of earthiness to reaffirm her imperviousness. Like when she bought the rat poison, the arsenic. That was over a year after they had begun to say "Poor Emily," and while the two female cousins were visiting her.

"I want some poison," she said to the druggist. She was over thirty then, still a slight woman, though thinner than usual, with cold, haughty black eyes in a face the flesh of which was strained across the temples and about the eyesockets as you imagine a lighthouse-keeper's face ought to look. "I want some poison," she said.

"Yes, Miss Emily. What kind? For rats and such? I'd recom——"

"I want the best you have. I don't care what kind."

The druggist named several. "They'll kill anything up to an elephant. But what you want is——"

"Arsenic," Miss Emily said. "Is that a good one?"

"Is . . . arsenic? Yes, ma'am. But what you want——"

"I want arsenic."

The druggist looked down at her. She looked back at him, erect, her face like a strained flag. "Why, of course," the druggist said. "If that's what you want. But the law requires you to tell what you are going to use it for."

Miss Emily just stared at him, her head tilted back in order to look him eye for eye, until he looked away and went and got the arsenic and wrapped it up. The Negro delivery boy brought her the package; the druggist didn't come back. When she opened the package at home there was written on the box, under the skull and bones: "For rats."

IV

So the next day we all said, "She will kill herself"; and we said it would be the best thing. When she had first begun to be seen with Homer Barron, we had said, "She will marry him." Then we said, "She will persuade him yet," because Homer himself had remarked— he liked men, and it was known that he drank with the younger men in the Elk's Club—that he was not a marrying man. Later we said, "Poor Emily," behind the jalousies as they passed on Sunday afternoon in the glittering buggy, Miss Emily with her head high and Homer Barron with his hat cocked and a cigar in his teeth, reins and whip in a yellow glove.

Then some of the ladies began to say that it was a disgrace to the town and a bad example to the young people. The men did not want to interfere, but at last the ladies forced the Baptist minister—Miss

Emily's people were Episcopal—to call upon her. He would never divulge what happened during that interview, but he refused to go back again. The next Sunday they again drove about the streets, and the following day the minister's wife wrote to Miss Emily's relations in Alabama.

So she had blood-kin under her roof again and we sat back to watch developments. At first nothing happened. Then we were sure that they were to be married. We learned that Miss Emily had been to the jeweler's and ordered a man's toilet set in silver, with the letters H.B. on each piece. Two days later we learned that she had bought a complete outfit of men's clothing, including a nightshirt, and we said, "They are married." We were really glad. We were glad because the two female cousins were even more Grierson than Miss Emily had ever been.

So we were not surprised when Homer Barron—the streets had been finished some time since—was gone. We were a little disappointed that there was not a public blowing-off, but we believed that he had gone on to prepare for Miss Emily's coming, or to give her a chance to get rid of the cousins. (By that time it was a cabal, and we were all Miss Emily's allies to help circumvent the cousins.) Sure enough, after another week they departed. And, as we had expected all along, within three days Homer Barron was back in town. A neighbor saw the Negro man admit him at the kitchen door at dusk one evening.

And that was the last we saw of Homer Barron. And of Miss Emily for some time. The Negro man went in and out with the market basket, but the front door remained closed. Now and then we would see her at a window for a moment as the men did that night when they sprinkled the lime, but for almost six months she did not appear on the streets. Then we knew that this was to be expected too; as if that quality of her father which had thwarted her woman's life so many times had been too virulent and too furious to die.

When we next saw Miss Emily, she had grown fat and her hair was turning gray. During the next few years it grew grayer and grayer until it attained an even pepper-and-salt iron-gray, when it ceased turning. Up to the day of her death at seventy-four it was still that vigorous iron-gray, like the hair of an active man.

From that time on her front door remained closed, save for a period of six or seven years, when she was about forty, during which she gave lessons in china-painting. She fitted up a studio in one of the downstairs rooms, where the daughters and granddaughters of Colonel Sartoris' contemporaries were sent to her with the same regularity and in the same spirit that they were sent on Sundays with a twenty-five-cent piece for the collection plate. Meanwhile her taxes had been remitted.

Then the newer generation became the backbone and the spirit of the town, and the painting pupils grew up and fell away and did not send their children to her with boxes of color and tedious brushes and pictures cut from the ladies' magazines. The front door closed upon the last one and remained closed for good. When the town got free postal delivery Miss Emily alone refused to let them fasten the metal numbers above her door and attach a mailbox to it. She would not listen to them.

Daily, monthly, yearly we watched the Negro grow grayer and more stooped, going in and out with the market basket. Each December we sent her a tax notice, which would be returned by the post office a week later, unclaimed. Now and then we would see her in one of the downstairs windows—she had evidently shut up the top floor of the house—like the carven torso of an idol in a niche, looking or not looking at us, we could never tell which. Thus she passed from generation to generation—dear, inescapable, impervious, tranquil, and perverse.

And so she died. Fell ill in the house filled with dust and shadows, with only a doddering Negro man to wait on her. We did not even know she was sick; we had long since given up trying to get any information from the Negro. He talked to no one, probably not even to her, for his voice had grown harsh and rusty, as if from disuse.

She died in one of the downstairs rooms, in a heavy walnut bed with a curtain, her gray head propped on a pillow yellow and moldy with age and lack of sunlight.

## V

The Negro met the first of the ladies at the front door and let them in, with their hushed, sibilant voices and their quick, curious glances, and then he disappeared. He walked right through the house and out the back and was not seen again.

The two female cousins came at once. They held the funeral on the second day, with the town coming to look at Miss Emily beneath a mass of bought flowers, with the crayon face of her father musing profoundly above the bier and the ladies sibilant and macabre; and the very old men—some in their brushed Confederate uniforms—on the porch and the lawn, talking of Miss Emily as if she had been a contemporary of theirs, believing that they had danced with her and courted her perhaps, confusing time with its mathematical progression, as the old do, to whom all the past is not a diminishing road, but, instead, a huge meadow which no winter ever quite touches, divided from them now by the narrow bottleneck of the most recent decade of years.

Already we knew that there was one room in that region above stairs which no one had seen in forty years, and which would have to be forced. They waited until Miss Emily was decently in the ground before they opened it.

The violence of breaking down the door seemed to fill this room with pervading dust. A thin, acrid pall as of the tomb seemed to lie everywhere upon this room decked and furnished as for a bridal: upon the valance curtains of faded rose color, upon the rose-shaded lights, upon the dressing table, upon the delicate array of crystal and the man's toilet things backed with tarnished silver, silver so tarnished that the monogram was obscured. Among them lay a collar and tie, as if they had just been removed, which, lifted, left upon the surface a pale crescent in the dust. Upon a chair hung the suit, carefully folded; beneath it the two mute shoes and the discarded socks.

The man himself lay in the bed.

For a long while we just stood there, looking down at the profound and fleshless grin. The body had apparently once lain in the attitude of an embrace, but now the long sleep that outlasts love, that conquers even the grimace of love, had cuckolded him. What was left of him, rotted beneath what was left of the nightshirt, had become inextricable from the bed in which he lay; and upon him and upon the pillow beside him lay that even coating of the patient and biding dust.

Then we noticed that in the second pillow was the indentation of a head. One of us lifted something from it, and leaning forward, that faint and invisible dust dry and acrid in the nostrils, we saw a long strand of iron-gray hair.

# AUGUST DERLETH
## The Lonesome Place

You who sit in your houses of nights, you who sit in the theaters, you who are gay at dances and parties—all you who are enclosed by four walls—you have no conception of what goes on outside in the dark. In the lonesome places. And there are so many of them, all over—in the country, in the small towns, in the cities. If you were out in the evenings, in the night, you would know about them, you would pass them and wonder, perhaps, and if you were a small boy you might be frightened . . . frightened the way Johnny Newell and I were frightened, the way thousands of small boys from one end of the country to the other are being frightened when they have to go out alone at night, past lonesome places, dark and lightless, somber and haunted. . . .

I want you to understand that if it had not been for the lonesome place at the grain elevator, the place with the big old trees and the sheds up close to the sidewalk, and the piles of lumber—if it had not been for that place Johnny Newell and I would never have been guilty of murder. I say it even if there is nothing the law can do about it. They cannot touch us, but it is true, and I know, and Johnny knows, but we never talk about it, we never say anything; it is just something we keep here, behind our eyes, deep in our thoughts where it is a fact which is lost among thousands of others, but no less there, something we know beyond cavil.

It goes back a long way. But as time goes, perhaps it is not long. We were young, we were little boys in a small town. Johnny lived three houses away and across the street from me, and both of us lived in the block west of the grain elevator. We were never afraid to go past the lonesome place together. But we were not often together. Sometimes one of us had to go that way alone, sometimes the other. I went that way most of the time—there was no other, except to go far around, because that was the straight way down town, and I had to walk there, when my father was too tired to go.

In the evenings it would happen like this. My mother would discover that she had no sugar or salt or bologna, and she would say, "Steve, you go down town and get it. Your father's too tired."

I would say, "I don't wanna."

She would say, "You go."

I would say, "I can go in the morning before school."

She would say, "You go now. I don't want to hear another word out of you. Here's the money."

And I would have to go.

Going down was never quite so bad, because most of the time there was still some afterglow in the west, and a kind of pale light lay there, a luminousness, like part of the day lingering there, and all around town you could hear the kids hollering in the last hour they had to play, and you felt somehow not alone, you could go down into that dark place under the trees and you would never think of being lonesome. But when you came back—that was different. When you came back the afterglow was gone; if the stars were out, you could never see them for the trees; and though the streetlights were on—the old-fashioned lights arched over the crossroads—not a ray of them penetrated the lonesome place near the elevator. There it was, half a block long, black as black could be, dark as the deepest night, with the shadows of the trees making it a solid place of darkness, with the faint glow of light where a streetlight pooled at the end of the street, far away it seemed, and that other glow behind, where the other corner light lay.

And when you came that way you walked slower and slower. Behind you lay the brightly lit stores; all along the way there had been houses, with lights in the windows and music playing and voices of people sitting to talk on their porches—but up there, ahead of you, there was the lonesome place, with no house nearby, and up beyond it the tall, dark grain elevator, gaunt and forbidding, the lonesome place of trees and sheds and lumber, in which anything might be lurking, anything at all, the lonesome place where you were sure that something haunted the darkness waiting for the moment and the hour and the night when you came through to burst forth from its secret place and leap upon you, tearing you and rending you and doing unmentionable things before it had done with you.

That was the lonesome place. By day it was oak and maple trees over a hundred years old, low enough so that you could almost touch the big spreading limbs; it was sheds and lumber piles that were seldom disturbed; it was a sidewalk and long grass, never mowed or kept down until late fall, when somebody burned it off; it was a shady place in the hot summer days where some cool air always lingered. You were never afraid of it by day, but by night it was a different place; for then it was lonesome, away from sight or sound, a place of darkness and strangeness, a place of terror for little boys haunted by a thousand fears.

And every night, coming home from town, it happened like this. I would walk slower and slower, the closer I got to the lonesome place. I would think of every way around it. I would keep hoping somebody would come along, so that I could walk with him. Mr. Newell, maybe, or old Mrs. Potter, who lived farther up the street, or Reverend Bislor, who lived at the end of the block beyond the grain elevator. But nobody ever came. At this hour it was too soon after supper for them to go out, or, already out, too soon for them to return. So I walked slower and slower, until I got to the edge of the lonesome place—and then I ran as fast as I could, sometimes with my eyes closed.

Oh, I knew what was there, all right. I knew there was something in that dark, lonesome place. Perhaps it was the bogey-man. Sometimes my grandmother spoke of him, of how he waited in dark places for bad boys and girls. Perhaps it was an ogre. I knew about ogres in the books of fairy tales. Perhaps it was something else, something worse. I ran. I ran hard. Every blade of grass, every leaf, every twig that touched me was Its hand reaching for me. The sound of my footsteps slapping the sidewalk were Its steps pursuing. The hard breathing which was my own became Its breathing in Its frenetic struggle to reach me, to rend and tear me, to imbue my soul with terror.

I would burst out of that place like a flurry of wind, fly past the gaunt elevator, and not pause until I was safe in the yellow glow of the familiar streetlight. And then, in a few steps, I was home.

And mother would say, "For the Lord's sake, have you been running on a hot night like this?"

I would say, "I hurried."

"You didn't have to hurry that much. I don't need it till breakfast time."

And I would say, "I could-a got it in the morning. I could-a run down before breakfast. Next time, that's what I'm gonna do."

Nobody would pay any attention.

Some nights Johnny had to go down town, too. Things then weren't the way they are today, when every woman makes a ritual of afternoon shopping and seldom forgets anything; in those days, they didn't go down town so often, and when they did, they had such lists they usually forgot something. And after Johnny and I had been through the lonesome place on the same night, we compared notes next day.

"Did you see anything?" he would ask.

"No, but I heard it," I would say.

"I felt it," he would whisper tensely. "It's got big, flat clawed feet. You know what's the ugliest feet around?"

"Sure, one of those stinking yellow soft-shelled turtles."

"It's got feet like that. Oh, ugly, and soft, and sharp claws! I saw one out of the corner of my eye," he would say.

"Did you see its face?" I would ask.

"It ain't got no face. Cross my heart an' hope to die, there ain't no face. That's worse'n if there was one."

Oh, it was a horrible beast—not an animal, not a man—that lurked in the lonesome place and came forth predatorily at night, waiting for us to pass. It grew like this, out of our mutual experiences. We discovered that it had scales, and a great long tail, like a dragon. It breathed from somewhere, hot as fire, but it had no face and no mouth in it, just a horrible opening in its throat. It was as big as an elephant, but it did not look like anything so friendly. It belonged there in the lonesome place; it would never go away; that was its home, and it had to wait for its food to come to it—the unwary boys and girls who had to pass through the lonesome place at night.

How I tried to keep from going near the lonesome place after dark!

"Why can't Mady go?" I would ask.

"Mady's too little," mother would answer.

"I'm not so big."

"Oh, shush! You're a big boy now. You're going to be seven years old. Just think of it."

"I don't think seven is old," I would say. I didn't, either. Seven wasn't nearly old enough to stand up against what was in the lonesome place.

"Your Sears Roebuck pants are long ones," she would say.

"I don't care about any old Sears Roebuck pants. I don't wanna go."

"I want you to go. You never get up early enough in the morning."

"But I will. I promise I will. I promise, Ma!" I would cry out.

"Tomorrow morning it will be a different story. No, you go."

That was the way it went every time. I had to go. And Mady was the only one who guessed. " 'Fraidy cat," she would whisper. Even she never really knew. She never had to go through the lonesome place after dark. They kept her at home. She never knew how something could lie up in those old trees, lie right along those old limbs across the sidewalk and drop down without a sound, clawing and tearing, something without a face, with ugly clawed feet like a soft-shelled turtle's, with scales and a tail like a dragon, something as big as a house, all black, like the darkness in that place.

But Johnny and I knew.

"It almost got me last night," he would say, his voice low, looking anxiously out of the woodshed where we sat as if It might hear us.

"Gee, I'm glad it didn't," I would say. "What was it like?"

"Big and black. Awful black. I looked around when I was running, and all of a sudden there wasn't any light way back at the other end. Then I knew it was coming. I ran like everything to get out of there. It was almost on me when I got away. Look there!"

And he would show me a rip in his shirt where a claw had come down.

"And you?" he would ask excitedly, big-eyed. "What about you?"

"It was back behind the lumber piles when I came through," I said. "I could just feel it waiting. I was running, but it got right up—you look, there's a pile of lumber tipped over there."

And we would walk down into the lonesome place in midday and look. Sure enough, there would be a pile of lumber tipped over, and we would look to where something had been lying down, the grass all pressed down. Sometimes we would find a handkerchief and wonder whether It had caught somebody; then we would go home and wait to hear if anyone was missing, speculating apprehensively all the way home whether It had got Mady or Christine or Helen, or any one of the girls in our class or Sunday School, or whether maybe It had got

Miss Doyle, the young primary-grades teacher who had to walk that way sometimes after supper. But no one was ever reported missing, and the mystery grew. Maybe It had got some stranger who happened to be passing by and didn't know about the Thing that lived there in the lonesome place. We were sure It had got somebody. It scared us, bad, and after something like this I hated all the more to go down town after supper, even for candy or ice cream.

"Some night I won't come back, you'll see," I would say.

"Oh, don't be silly," my mother would say.

"You'll see. You'll see. It'll get me next, you'll see."

"What'll get you?" she would ask offhandedly.

"Whatever it is out there in the dark," I would say.

"There's nothing out there but the dark," she would say.

"What about the bogey-man?" I would protest.

"They caught him," she would say. "A long time ago. He's locked up for good."

But Johnny and I knew better. His parents didn't know, either. The minute he started to complain, his dad reached for a hickory switch they kept behind the door. He had to go out fast and never mind what was in the lonesome place.

What do grown-up people know about the things boys are afraid of? Oh, hickory switches and such like, they know that. But what about what goes on in their minds when they have to come home alone at night through the lonesome places? What do they know about lonesome places where no light from the street corner ever comes? What do they know about a place and time when a boy is very small and very alone, and the night is as big as the town, and the darkness is the whole world? When grownups are big, old people who cannot understand anything, no matter how plain? A boy looks up and out, but he can't look very far when the trees bend down over and press close, when the sheds rear up along one side and the trees on the other, when the darkness lies like a cloud along the sidewalk and the arc lights are far, far away. No wonder then that Things grow in the darkness of lonesome places the way It grew in that dark place near the grain elevator. No wonder a boy runs like the wind until his heartbeats sound like a drum and push up to suffocate him.

"You're white as a sheet," mother would say sometimes. "You've been running again."

"Yes," I would say. "I've been running." But I never said why; I knew they wouldn't believe me; I knew nothing I could say would convince them about the Thing that lived back there, down the block, down past the grain elevator in that dark, lonesome place.

"You don't have to run," my father would say. "Take it easy."

"I ran," I would say. But I wanted in the worst way to say I had to run and to tell them why I had to; but I knew they wouldn't believe me any more than Johnny's parents believed him when he told them, as he did once.

He got a licking with a strap and had to go to bed.

I never got licked. I never told them.

But now it must be told, now it must be set down.

For a long time we forgot about the lonesome place. We grew older and we grew bigger. We went on through school into high school, and somehow we forgot about the Thing in the lonesome place. That place never changed. The trees grew older. Sometimes the lumber piles were bigger or smaller. Once the sheds were painted— red, like blood. Seeing them that way the first time, I remembered. Then I forgot again. We took to playing baseball and basketball and football. We began to swim in the river and to date the girls. We never talked about the Thing in the lonesome place any more, and when we went through there at night it was like something forgotten that lurked back in a corner of the mind. We thought of something we ought to remember, but never could quite remember; that was the way it seemed—like a memory locked away, far away in childhood. We never ran through that place, and sometimes it was even a good place to walk through with a girl, because she always snuggled up close and said how spooky it was there under the overhanging trees. But even then we never lingered there, not exactly lingered; we didn't run through there, but we walked without faltering or loitering, no matter how pretty a girl she was.

The years went past, and we never thought about the lonesome place again.

We never thought how there would be other little boys going through it at night, running with fast-beating hearts, breathless with terror, anxious for the safety of the arc light beyond the margin of the shadow which confined the dweller in that place, the light-fearing creature that haunted the dark, like so many terrors dwelling in similar lonesome places in the cities and small towns and countrysides all over the world, waiting to frighten little boys and girls, waiting to invade them with horror and unshakable fear—waiting for something more. . . .

Three nights ago little Bobby Jeffers was killed in the lonesome place. He was all mauled and torn and partly crushed, as if something big had fallen on him. Johnny, who was on the Village Board, went to look at the place, and after he had been there, he telephoned me to go, too, before other people walked there.

I went down and saw the marks, too. It was just as the coroner said, only not an "animal of some kind," as he put it. Something with a dragging tail, with scales, with great clawed feet—and I knew it had no face.

I knew, too, that Johnny and I were guilty. We had murdered Bobby Jeffers because the thing that killed him was the thing Johnny and I had created out of our childhood fears and left in that lonesome place to wait for some scared little boy at some minute in some hour during some dark night, a little boy who, like fat Bobby Jeffers, couldn't run as fast as Johnny and I could run.

And the worst is not that there is nothing to do, but that the lonesome place is being changed. The village is cutting down some of the trees now, removing the sheds, and putting up a streetlight in the middle of that place; it will not be dark and lonesome any longer, and the Thing that lives there will have to go somewhere else, where people are unsuspecting, to some other lonesome place in some other small town or city or countryside, where It will wait as It did here, for some frightened little boy or girl to come along, waiting in the dark and the lonesomeness . . .

# E. B. WHITE
## The Door

Everything (he kept saying) is something it isn't. And everybody is always somewhere else. Maybe it was the city, being in the city, that made him feel how queer everything was and that it was something else. Maybe (he kept thinking) it was the names of the things. The names were tex and frequently koid. Or they were flex and oid, or they were duroid (sani) or flexsan (duro), but everything was glass (but not quite glass) and the thing that you touched (the surface, washable, crease-resistant) was rubber, only it wasn't quite rubber and you didn't quite touch it but almost. The wall, which was glass but thrutex, turned out on being approached not to be a wall, it was something else, it was an opening or doorway—and the doorway (through which he saw himself approaching) turned out to be something else, it was a wall. And what he had eaten not having agreed with him.

He was in a washable house, but he wasn't sure. Now about those rats, he kept saying to himself. He meant the rats that the Professor had driven crazy by forcing them to deal with problems which were beyond the scope of rats, the insoluble problems. He meant the rats that had been trained to jump at the square card with the circle in the middle, and the card (because it was something it wasn't) would give way and let the rat into a place where the food was, but then one day it would be a trick played on the rat, and the card would be changed, and the rat would jump but the card wouldn't give way, and it was an impossible situation (for a rat) and the rat would go insane and into its eyes would come the unspeakably bright imploring look of the frustrated, and after the convulsions were over and the frantic racing around, then the passive stage would set in and the willingness to let anything be done to it, even if it was something else.

He didn't know which door (or wall) or opening in the house to jump at, to get through, because one was an opening that wasn't a door (it was a void, or koid) and the other was a wall that wasn't an opening, it was a sanitary cupboard of the same color. He caught a glimpse of his eyes staring into his eyes, in the thrutex, and in them was the expression he had seen in the picture of the rats—weary after convulsions and the frantic racing around, when they were willing and did not mind having anything done to them. More and more (he kept saying) I am confronted by a problem which is incapable of solution (for this time even if he chose the right door, there would be no food behind it) and that is what madness is, and things seeming different from what they are. He heard, in the house where he was, in the city to which he had gone (as toward a door which might, or might not, give way), a noise—not a loud noise but more of a low prefabricated humming. It came from a place in the base of the wall (or stat) where the flue carrying the filterable air was, and not far from the Minipiano, which was made of the same material nail-brushes are made of, and which was under the stairs. "This, too, has been tested," she said, pointing, but not at it, "and found viable." It wasn't a loud noise, he kept thinking, sorry that he had seen his eyes, even though it was through his own eyes that he had seen them.

First will come the convulsions (he said), then the exhaustion, then the willingness to let anything be done. "And you better believe it *will* be."

All his life he had been confronted by situations which were incapable of being solved, and there was a deliberateness behind all this, behind this changing of the card (or door), because they would always wait till you had learned to jump at the certain card (or door)—the one with the circle—and then they would change it on you. There have been so many doors changed on me, he said, in the last twenty years, but it is now becoming clear that it is an impossible situation, and the question is whether to jump again, even though they ruffle you in the rump with the blast of air—to make you jump. He wished he wasn't standing by the Minipiano. First they would teach you the prayers and the Psalms, and that would be the right door (the one with the circle), and the long sweet words with the holy sound, and that would be the one to jump at to get where the food was. Then one day you jumped and it didn't give way, so that all you got was the bump on the nose, and the first bewilderment, the first young bewilderment.

I don't know whether to tell her about the door they substituted or not, he said, the one with the equation on it and the picture of the amoeba reproducing itself by division. Or the one with the photostatic copy of the check for thirty-two dollars and fifty cents. But the jumping was so long ago, although the bump is . . . how those old wounds hurt! Being crazy this way wouldn't be so bad if only, if only. If only when you put your foot forward to take a step, the ground wouldn't come up to meet your foot the way it does. And the same way in the street (only I may never get back to the street unless I jump at the right door), the curb coming up to meet your foot, anticipating ever so delicately the weight of the body, which is somewhere else. "We could take your name," she said, "and send it to you." And it wouldn't be so bad if only you could read a sentence all the way through without jumping (your eye) to something else on the same page; and then (he kept thinking) there was that man out in Jersey, the one who started to chop his trees down, one by one, the man who began talking about how he would take his house to pieces, brick by brick, because he faced a problem incapable of solution, probably, so he began to hack at the trees in the yard, began to pluck with trembling fingers at the bricks in the house. Even if a house is not washable, it is worth taking down. It is not till later that the exhaustion sets in.

But it is inevitable that they will keep changing the doors on you, he said, because that is what they are for; and the thing is to get used to it and not let it unsettle the mind. But that would mean not jumping, and you can't. Nobody can not jump. There will be no not-jumping. Among rats, perhaps, but among people never. Everybody has to keep jumping at a door (the one with the circle on it) because that is the way everybody is, specially some people. You wouldn't want me, standing here, to tell you, would you, about my friend the poet (deceased) who said, "My heart has followed all my days something I cannot name"? (It had the circle on it.) And like many poets, although few so beloved, he is gone. It killed him, the jumping. First, of course, there were the preliminary bouts, the convulsions, and the calm and the willingness.

I remember the door with the picture of the girl on it (only it was spring), her arms outstretched in loveliness, her dress (it was the one with the circle on it) uncaught, beginning the slow, clear, blinding cascade—and I guess we would all like to try that door again, for it seemed like the way and for a while it was the way, the door would open and you would go through winged and exalted (like any rat) and the food would be there, the way the Professor had it arranged, everything O.K., and you had chosen the right door for the world was young. The time they changed that door on me, my nose bled for a hundred hours—how do you like that, Madam? Or would you prefer to show me further through this so strange house, or you could take my name and send it to me, for although my heart has followed all my days something I cannot name, I am tired of the jumping and I do not know which way to go, Madam, and I am not even sure that I am not tried beyond the endurance of man (rat, if you will) and have taken leave of sanity. What are you following these days, old friend, after your recovery from the last bump? What is the name, or is it something you cannot name? The rats have a name for it by this time, perhaps, but I don't know what they call it. I call it plexikoid and it comes in sheets, something like insulating board, unattainable and ugli-proof.

And there was the man out in Jersey, because I keep thinking about his terrible necessity and the passion and trouble he had gone to all those years in the indescribable abundance of a householder's detail, building the estate and the planting of the trees and in spring the lawn-dressing and in fall the bulbs for the spring burgeoning, and the watering of the grass on the long light evenings in summer and the gravel for the driveway (all had to be thought out, planned) and the decorative borders, probably, the perennials and the bug spray, and the building of the house from the plans of the architect, first the sills, then the studs, then the full corn in the ear, the floors laid on the floor timbers, smoothed, and then the carpets upon the smooth floors and the curtains and the rods there for. And then, almost without warning, he would be jumping at the same old door and it wouldn't give: they had changed it on him, making life no longer supportable under the elms in the elm shade, under the maples in the maple shade.

"Here you have the maximum of openness in a small room."

It was impossible to say (maybe it was the city) what made him feel the way he did, and I am not the only one either, he kept thinking—ask any doctor if I am. The doctors, they know how many there are, they even know where the trouble is only they don't like to tell you about the prefrontal lobe because that means making a hole in your skull and removing the work of centuries. It took so long coming, this lobe, so many, many years. (Is it something you read in the paper, perhaps?) And now, the strain being so great, the door having been changed by the Professor once too often . . . but it only means a whiff of ether, a few deft strokes, and the higher animal becomes a little easier in his mind and more like the lower one. From now on, you see, that's the way it will be, the ones with the small prefrontal lobes will win because the other ones are hurt too much by this incessant bumping. They can stand just so much, eh, Doctor? (And what is that, pray, that you have in your hand?) Still, you never can tell, eh, Madam?

He crossed (carefully) the room, the thick carpet under him softly, and went toward the door carefully, which was glass and he could see himself in it, and which, at his approach, opened to allow him to pass through; and beyond he half expected to find one of the old doors that he had known, perhaps the one with the circle, the one with the girl her arms outstretched in loveliness and beauty before him. But he saw instead a moving stairway, and descended in light (he kept thinking) to the street below and to the other people. As he stepped off, the ground came up slightly, to meet his foot.

# SHIRLEY JACKSON
## The Lovely House

## I

The house in itself was, even before anything had happened there, as lovely a thing as she had ever seen. Set among its lavish grounds, with a park and a river and a wooded hill surrounding it, and carefully planned and tended gardens close upon all sides, it lay upon the hills as though it were something too precious to be seen by everyone; Margaret's very coming there had been a product of such elaborate arrangement, and such letters to and fro, and such meetings and hopings and wishings, that when she alighted with Carla Montague at the doorway of Carla's home, she felt that she too had come home, to a place striven for and earned. Carla stopped before the doorway and stood for a minute, looking first behind her, at the vast reaching gardens and the green lawn going down to the river, and the soft hills beyond, and then at the perfect grace of the house, showing so clearly the long-boned structure within, the curving staircases and the arched doorways and the tall thin lines of steadying beams, all of it resting back against the hills, and up, past rows of windows and the flying lines of the roof, on, to the tower—Carla stopped, and looked, and smiled, and then turned and said, "Welcome, Margaret."

"It's a lovely house," Margaret said, and felt that she had much better have said nothing.

The doors were opened and Margaret, touching as she went the warm head of a stone faun beside her, passed inside. Carla, following, greeted the servants by name, and was welcomed with reserved pleasure; they stood for a minute on the rose and white tiled floor. "Again, welcome, Margaret," Carla said.

Far ahead of them the great stairway soared upward, held to the hall where they stood by only the slimmest of carved balustrades; on Margaret's left hand a tapestry moved softly as the door behind was closed. She could see the fine threads of the weave, and the light colors, but she could not have told the picture unless she went far away, perhaps as far away as the staircase, and looked at it from there; perhaps, she thought, from halfway up the stairway this great hall, and perhaps the whole house, is visible, as a complete body of story together, all joined and in sequence. Or perhaps I shall be allowed to move slowly from one thing to another, observing each, or would that take all the time of my visit?

"I never saw anything so lovely," she said to Carla, and Carla smiled.

"Come and meet my mama," Carla said.

They went through doors at the right, and Margaret, before she could see the light room she went into, was stricken with fear at meeting the owners of the house and the park and the river, and as she went beside Carla she kept her eyes down.

"Mama," said Carla, "this is Margaret, from school."

"Margaret," said Carla's mother, and smiled at Margaret kindly. "We are very glad you were able to come."

She was a tall lady wearing pale green and pale blue, and Margaret said as gracefully as she could, "Thank you, Mrs. Montague; I am very grateful for having been invited."

"Surely," said Mrs. Montague softly, "surely my daughter's friend Margaret from school should be welcome here; surely we should be grateful that she has come."

"Thank you, Mrs. Montague," Margaret said, not knowing how she was answering, but knowing that she was grateful.

When Mrs. Montague turned her kind eyes on her daughter, Margaret was at last able to look at the room where she stood next to her friend; it was a pale green and a pale blue long room with tall windows that looked out onto the lawn and the sky, and thin colored china ornaments on the mantel. Mrs. Montague had left her needlepoint when they came in and from where Margaret stood she could see the pale sweet pattern from the underside; all soft colors it was, melting into one another endlessly, and not finished. On the table nearby were books, and one large book of sketches that were most certainly Carla's;

Carla's harp stood next to the windows, and beyond one window were marble steps outside, going shallowly down to a fountain, where water moved in the sunlight. Margaret thought of her own embroidery—a pair of slippers she was working for her friend—and knew that she should never be able to bring it into this room, where Mrs. Montague's long white hands rested on the needlepoint frame, soft as dust on the pale colors.

"Come," said Carla, taking Margaret's hand in her own. "Mama has said that I might show you some of the house."

They went out again into the hall, across the rose and white tiles which made a pattern too large to be seen from the floor, and through a doorway where tiny bronze fauns grinned at them from the carving. The first room that they went into was all gold, with gilt on the window frames and on the legs of the chairs and tables, and the small chairs standing on the yellow carpet were made of gold brocade with small gilded backs, and on the wall were more tapestries showing the house as it looked in the sunlight with even the trees around it shining, and these tapestries were let into the wall and edged with thin gilded frames.

"There is so much tapestry," Margaret said.

"In every room," Carla agreed. "Mama has embroidered all the hangings for her own room, the room where she writes her letters. The other tapestries were done by my grandmamas and my great-grandmamas and my great-great-grandmamas."

The next room was silver, and the small chairs were of silver brocade with narrow silvered backs, and the tapestries on the walls of this room were edged with silver frames and showed the house in moonlight, with the white light shining on the stones and the windows glittering.

"Who uses these rooms?" Margaret asked.

"No one," Carla said.

They passed then into a room where everything grew smaller as they looked at it: the mirrors on both sides of the room showed the door opening and Margaret and Carla coming through, and then, reflected, a smaller door opening and a small Margaret and a smaller Carla coming through, and then, reflected again, a still smaller door and Margaret and Carla, and so on, endlessly, Margaret and Carla diminishing and reflecting. There was a table here and nesting under it another lesser table, and under that another one, and another under that one, and on the greatest table lay a carved wooden bowl holding within it another carved wooden bowl, and another within that, and another within that one. The tapestries in this room were of the house reflected in the lake, and the tapestries themselves were reflected, in and out, among the mirrors on the wall, with the house in the tapestries reflected in the lake.

This room frightened Margaret rather, because it was so difficult for her to tell what was in it and what was not, and how far in any direction she might easily move, and she backed out hastily, pushing Carla behind her. They turned from here into another doorway which led them out again into the great hall under the soaring staircase, and Carla said, "We had better go upstairs and see your room; we can see more of the house another time. We have *plenty* of time, after all," and she squeezed Margaret's hand joyfully.

They climbed the great staircase, and passed, in the hall upstairs, Carla's room, which was like the inside of a shell in pale colors, with lilacs on the table, and the fragrance of the lilacs followed them as they went down the halls.

The sound of their shoes on the polished floor was like rain, but the sun came in on them wherever they went. "Here," Carla said, opening a door, "is where we have breakfast when it is warm; here," opening another door, "is the passage to the room where Mama does her letters. And that—" nodding, "—is the stairway to the tower, and *here* is where we shall have dances when my brother comes home."

"A real tower?" Margaret said.

"And *here*," Carla said, "is the old schoolroom, and my brother and I studied here before he went away, and I stayed on alone studying here until it was time for me to come to school and meet *you*."

"Can we go up into the tower?" Margaret asked.

"Down here, at the end of the hall," Carla said, "is where all my grandpapas and my grandmamas and my great-great-grandpapas and grandmamas live." She opened the door to the long gallery, where pictures of tall old people in lace and pale waistcoats leaned down to stare at Margaret and Carla. And then, to a walk at the top of the house, where they leaned over and looked at the ground below and the tower above, and Margaret looked at the gray stone of the tower and wondered who lived there, and Carla pointed out where the river ran far below, far away, and said they should walk there tomorrow.

"When my brother comes," she said, "he will take us boating on the river."

In her room, unpacking her clothes, Margaret realized that her white dress was the only one possible for dinner, and thought that she would have to send home for more things; she had intended to wear her ordinary gray downstairs most evenings before Carla's brother came, but knew she could not when she saw Carla in light blue, with pearls around her neck. When Margaret and Carla came into the drawing room before dinner Mrs. Montague greeted them very kindly, and asked had Margaret seen the painted room, or the room with the tiles?

"We had no time to go near that part of the house at all," Carla said.

"After dinner, then," Mrs. Montague said, putting her arm affectionately around Margaret's shoulders, "we will go and see the painted room and the room with the tiles, because they are particular favorites of mine."

"Come and meet my papa," Carla said.

The door was just opening for Mr. Montague, and Margaret, who felt almost at ease now with Mrs. Montague, was frightened again of Mr. Montague, who spoke loudly and said, "So this is m'girl's friend from school? Lift up your head, girl, and let's have a look at you." When Margaret looked up blindly, and smiled weakly, he patted her cheek and said, "We shall have to make you look bolder before you leave us," and then he tapped his daughter on the shoulder and said she had grown to a monstrous fine girl.

They went in to dinner, and on the walls of the dining room were tapestries of the house in the seasons of the year, and the dinner service was white china with veins of gold running through it, as though it had been mined and not molded. The fish was one Margaret did not recognize, and Mr. Montague very generously insisted upon serving her himself without smiling at her ignorance. Carla and Margaret were each given a glassful of pale spicy wine.

"When my brother comes," Carla said to Margaret, "we will not dare be so quiet at table." She looked across the white cloth to Margaret, and then to her father at the head, to her mother at the foot, with the long table between them, and said, "My brother can make us laugh all the time."

"Your mother will not miss you for these summer months?" Mrs. Montague said to Margaret.

"She has my sisters, ma'am," Margaret said, "and I have been away at school for so long that she has learned to do without me."

"We mothers never learn to do without our daughters," Mrs.

Montague said, and looked fondly at Carla. "Or our sons," she added with a sigh.

"When my brother comes," Carla said, "you will see what this house can be like with life in it."

"When does he come?" Margaret asked.

"One week," Mr. Montague said, "three days, and four hours."

When Mrs. Montague rose, Margaret and Carla followed her, and Mr. Montague rose gallantly to hold the door for them all.

That evening Carla and Margaret played and sang duets, although Carla said that their voices together were too thin to be appealing without a deeper voice accompanying, and that when her brother came they should have some splendid trios. Mrs. Montague compli mented their singing, and Mr. Montague fell asleep in his chair.

Before they went upstairs Mrs. Montague reminded herself of her promise to show Margaret the painted room and the room with the tiles, and so she and Margaret and Carla, holding their long dresses up away from the floor in front so that their skirts whispered behind them, went down a hall and through a passage and down another hall, and through a room filled with books and then through a painted door into a tiny octagonal room where each of the sides were paneled and painted, with pink and blue and green and gold small pictures of shepherds and nymphs, lambs and fauns, playing on the broad green lawns by the river, with the house standing lovely behind them. There was nothing else in the little room, because seemingly the paintings were furniture enough for one room, and Margaret felt surely that she could stay happily and watch the small painted people playing, without ever seeing anything more of the house. But Mrs. Montague led her on, into the room of the tiles, which was not exactly a room at all, but had one side all glass window looking out onto the same lawn of the pictures in the octagonal room. The tiles were set into the floor of this room, in tiny bright spots of color which showed, when you stood back and looked at them, that they were again a picture of the house, only now the same materials that made the house made the tiles, so that the tiny windows were tiles of glass, and the stones of the tower were chips of gray stone, and the bricks of the chimneys were chips of brick.

Beyond the tiles of the house Margaret, lifting her long skirt as she walked, so that she should not brush a chip of the tower out of place, stopped and said, "What is *this*?" And stood back to see, and then knelt down and said, "*What* is this?"

"Isn't she enchanting?" said Mrs. Montague, smiling at Margaret, "I've always loved her."

"I was wondering what Margaret would say when she saw it," said Carla, smiling also.

It was a curiously made picture of a girl's face, with blue chip eyes and a red chip mouth, staring blindly from the floor, with long light braids made of yellow stone chips going down evenly on either side of her round cheeks.

"She is pretty," said Margaret, stepping back to see her better. "What does it say underneath?"

She stepped back again, holding her head up and back to read the letters, pieced together with stone chips and set unevenly in the floor. "Here was Margaret," it said, "who died for love."

## II

There was, of course, not time to do everything. Before Margaret had seen half the house, Carla's brother came home. Carla came running up the great staircase one afternoon calling, "Margaret, Margaret, he's come," and Margaret, running down to meet her, hugged her and said, "I'm so glad."

He had certainly come, and Margaret, entering the drawing room shyly behind Carla, saw Mrs. Montague with tears in her eyes and Mr. Montague standing straighter and prouder than before, and Carla said, "Brother, here is Margaret."

He was tall and haughty in uniform, and Margaret wished she had met him a little later, when she had perhaps been to her room again, and perhaps tucked up her hair. Next to him stood his friend, a captain, small and dark and bitter, and smiling bleakly upon the family assembled. Margaret smiled back timidly at them both, and stood behind Carla.

Everyone then spoke at once. Mrs. Montague said, "We've missed you so," and Mr. Montague said, "Glad to have you back, m'boy," and Carla said, "We shall have such times—I've promised Margaret—" and Carla's brother said, "So this is Margaret?" and the dark captain said, "I've been wanting to come."

It seemed that they all spoke at once, every time; there would be a long waiting silence while all of them looked around with joy at being together, and then suddenly everyone would have found something to say. It was so at dinner. Mrs. Montague said, "You're not eating enough," and "You used to be more fond of pomegranates," and Carla said, "We're to go boating," and "We'll have a dance, won't we?" and "Margaret and I insist upon a picnic," and "I saved the river for my brother to show to Margaret." Mr. Montague puffed and laughed and passed the wine, and Margaret hardly dared lift her eyes. The black captain said, "Never realized what an attractive old place it could be, after all," and Carla's brother said, "There's much about the house I'd like to show Margaret."

After dinner they played charades, and even Mrs. Montague did Achilles with Mr. Montague, holding his heel and both of them laughing and glancing at Carla and Margaret and the captain. Carla's brother leaned on the back of Margaret's chair and once she looked up at him and said, "No one ever calls you by name. Do you actually have a name?"

"Paul," he said.

The next morning they walked on the lawn, Carla with the captain and Margaret with Paul. They stood by the lake, and Margaret looked at the pure reflection of the house and said, "It almost seems as though we could open a door and go in."

"There," said Paul, and he pointed with his stick at the front entrance, "there is where we shall enter, and it will swing open for us with an underwater crash."

"Margaret," said Carla, laughing, "you say odd things, sometimes. If you tried to go into *that* house, you'd be in the lake."

"Indeed, and not like it much, at all," the captain added.

"Or would you have the side door?" asked Paul, pointing with his stick.

"I think I prefer the front door," said Margaret.

"But you'd be drowned," Carla said. She took Margaret's arm as they started back toward the house, and said, "We'd make a scene for a tapestry right now, on the lawn before the house."

"Another tapestry?" said the captain, and grimaced.

They played croquet, and Paul hit Margaret's ball toward a wicket, and the captain accused her of cheating prettily. And they played word games in the evening, and Margaret and Paul won, and everyone said Margaret was so clever. And they walked endlessly on the lawns before the house, and looked into the still lake, and watched the reflection of the house in the water, and Margaret chose a room in the reflected house for her own, and Paul said she should have it.

"That's the room where Mama writes her letters," said Carla, looking strangely at Margaret.

"Not in our house in the lake," said Paul.

"And I suppose if you like it she would lend it to you while you stay," Carla said.

"Not at all," said Margaret amiably. "I think I should prefer the tower anyway."

"Have you seen the rose garden?" Carla asked.

"Let me take you there," said Paul.

Margaret started across the lawn with him, and Carla called to her, "Where are you off to now, Margaret?"

"Why, to the rose garden," Margaret called back, and Carla said, staring, "You are really very odd, sometimes, Margaret. And it's growing colder, far too cold to linger among the roses," and so Margaret and Paul turned back.

Mrs. Montague's needlepoint was coming on well. She had filled in most of the outlines of the house, and was setting in the windows. After the first small shock of surprise, Margaret no longer wondered that Mrs. Montague was able to set out the house so well without a pattern or a plan; she did it from memory and Margaret, realizing this for the first time, thought "How amazing," and then "But of course how else *would* she do it?"

To see a picture of the house, Mrs. Montague needed only to lift her eyes in any direction, but, more than that, she had of course never used any other model for her embroidery; she had of course learned the faces of the house better than the faces of her children. The dreamy life of the Montagues in the house was most clearly shown Margaret as she watched Mrs. Montague surely and capably building doors and windows, carvings and cornices, in her embroidered house, smiling tenderly across the room to where Carla and the captain bent over a book together, while her fingers almost of themselves turned the edge of a carving Margaret had forgotten or never known about until, leaning over the back of Mrs. Montague's chair, she saw it form itself under Mrs. Montague's hands.

The small thread of days and sunlight, then, that bound Margaret to the house, was woven here as she watched. And Carla, lifting her head to look over, might say, "Margaret, do come and look, here. Mother is always at her work, but my brother is rarely home."

They went for a picnic, Carla and the captain and Paul and Margaret, and Mrs. Montague waved to them from the doorway as they

left, and Mr. Montague came to his study window and lifted his hand
to them. They chose to go to the wooded hill beyond the house,
although Carla was timid about going too far away—"I always like to
be where I can see the roofs, at least," she said—and sat among the
trees, on moss greener than Margaret had ever seen before, and spread
out a white cloth and drank red wine.

It was a very proper forest, with neat trees and the green moss,
and an occasional purple or yellow flower growing discreetly away
from the path. There was no sense of brooding silence, as there sometimes is with trees about, and Margaret realized, looking up to see the
sky clearly between the branches, that she had seen this forest in the
tapestries in the breakfast room, with the house shining in the sunlight
beyond.

"Doesn't the river come through here somewhere?" she asked,
hearing, she thought, the sound of it through the trees. "I feel so comfortable here among these trees, so at home."

"It is possible," said Paul, "to take a boat from the lawn in front of
the house and move without sound down the river, through the trees,
past the fields and then, for some reason, around past the house again.
The river, you see, goes almost around the house in a great circle. We
are very proud of that."

"The river *is* nearby," said Carla. "It goes almost completely
around the house."

"Margaret," said the captain. "You must not look rapt on a picnic
unless you are contemplating nature."

"I was, as a matter of fact," said Margaret. "I was contemplating a
caterpillar approaching Carla's foot."

"Will you come and look at the river?" said Paul, rising and
holding his hand out to Margaret. "I think we can see much of its great
circle from near here."

"Margaret," said Carla as Margaret stood up, "you are *always*
wandering off."

"I'm coming right back," Margaret said, with a laugh. "It's only
to look at the river."

"Don't be away long," Carla said. "We must be getting back
before dark."

The river as it went through the trees was shadowed and cool,
broadening out into pools where only the barest movement disturbed
the ferns along its edge, and where small stones made it possible to step
out and see the water all around, from a precarious island, and where

without sound a leaf might be carried from the limits of sight to the limits of sight, moving swiftly but imperceptibly and turning a little as it went.

"Who lives in the tower, Paul?" asked Margaret, holding a fern and running it softly over the back of her hand. "I know someone lives there, because I saw someone moving at the window once."

"Not *lives* there," said Paul, amused. "Did you think we kept a political prisoner locked away?"

"I thought it might be the birds, at first," Margaret said, glad to be describing this to someone.

"No," said Paul, still amused. "There's an aunt, or a great-aunt, or perhaps even a great-great-great-aunt. She doesn't live there, at all, but goes there because she says she cannot *endure* the sight of tapestry." He laughed. "She has filled the tower with books, and a huge old cat, and she may practice alchemy there, for all anyone knows. The reason you've never seen her would be that she has one of her spells of hiding away. Sometimes she is downstairs daily."

"Will I ever meet her?" Margaret asked wonderingly.

"Perhaps," Paul said. "She might take it into her head to come down formally one night to dinner. Or she might wander carelessly up to you where you sat on the lawn, and introduce herself. Or you might never see her, at that."

"Suppose I went up to the tower?"

Paul glanced at her strangely. "I suppose you could, if you wanted to," he said. "*I've* been there."

"Margaret," Carla called through the woods. "Margaret, we shall be late if you do not give up brooding by the river."

All this time, almost daily, Margaret was seeing new places in the house: the fan room, where the most delicate filigree fans had been set into the walls with their fine ivory sticks painted in exquisite miniature; the small room where incredibly perfect wooden and glass and metal fruits and flowers and trees stood on glittering glass shelves, lined up against the windows. And daily she passed and repassed the door behind which lay the stairway to the tower, and almost daily she stepped carefully around the tiles on the floor which read "Here was Margaret, who died for love."

It was no longer possible, however, to put off going to the tower. It was no longer possible to pass the doorway several times a day and do no more than touch her hand secretly to the panels, or perhaps set her head against them and listen, to hear if there were footsteps up or down, or a voice calling her. It was not possible to pass the doorway once more, and so in the early morning Margaret set her hand firmly to the door and pulled it open, and it came easily, as though relieved that at last, after so many hints and insinuations, and so much waiting and such helpless despair, Margaret had finally come to open it.

The stairs beyond, gray stone and rough, were, Margaret thought, steep for an old lady's feet, but Margaret went up effortlessly, though timidly. The stairway turned around and around, going up to the tower, and Margaret followed, setting her feet carefully upon one step after another, and holding her hands against the warm stone wall on either side, looking forward and up, expecting to be seen or spoken to before she reached the top; perhaps, she thought once, the walls of the tower were transparent and she was clearly, ridiculously visible from the outside, and Mrs. Montague and Carla, on the lawn—if indeed they ever looked upward to the tower—might watch her and turn to one another with smiles, saying, "There is Margaret, going up to the tower at last," and, smiling, nod to one another.

The stairway ended, as she had not expected it would, in a heavy wooden door, which made Margaret, standing on the step below to find room to raise her hand and knock, seem smaller, and even standing at the top of the tower she felt that she was not really tall.

"Come in," said the great aunt's voice, when Margaret had knocked twice; the first knock had been received with an expectant silence, as though inside someone had said inaudibly, "Is that someone knocking at *this* door?" and then waited to be convinced by a second knock; and Margaret's knuckles hurt from the effort of knocking to be heard through a heavy wooden door. She opened the door awkwardly from below—how much easier this all would be, she thought, if I knew the way—went in, and said politely, before she looked around, "I'm Carla's friend. They said I might come up to the tower to see it, but of course if you would rather I went away I shall." She had planned to say this more gracefully, without such an implication that invitations to the tower were issued by the downstairs Montagues, but the long climb and her being out of breath forced her to say everything at once, and she had really no time for the sounding periods she had composed.

In any case the great-aunt said politely—she was sitting at the other side of the round room, against the window, and she was not very clearly visible—"I am amazed that they told you about me at all. However, since you are here I cannot pretend that I really object to having you; you may come in and sit down."

Margaret came obediently into the room and sat down on the stone bench which ran all the way around the tower room, under the windows which of course were on all sides and open to the winds, so that the movement of the air through the tower room was insistent and constant, making talk difficult and even distinguishing objects a matter of some effort.

As though it were necessary to establish her position in the house emphatically and immediately, the old lady said, with a gesture and a grin, "My tapestries," and waved at the windows. She seemed to be not older than a great-aunt, although perhaps too old for a mere aunt, but her voice was clearly able to carry through the sound of the wind in the tower room and she seemed compact and strong beside the window, not at all as though she might be dizzy from looking out, or tired from the stairs.

"May I look out the window?" Margaret asked, almost of the cat, which sat next to her and regarded her without friendship, but without, as yet, dislike.

"Certainly," said the great-aunt. "Look out the windows, by all means."

Margaret turned on the bench and leaned her arms on the wide stone ledge of the window, but she was disappointed. Although the tops of the trees did not reach halfway up the tower, she could see only branches and leaves below and no sign of the wide lawns or the roofs of the house or the curve of the river.

"I hoped I could see the way the river went, from here."

"The river doesn't *go* from here," said the old lady, and laughed.

"I mean," Margaret said, "they told me that the river went around in a curve, almost surrounding the house."

"Who told you?" said the old lady.

"Paul."

"I see," said the old lady. "*He's* back, is he?"

"He's been here for several days, but he's going away again soon."

"And what's *your* name?" asked the old lady, leaning forward.

"Margaret."

"I see," said the old lady again. "That's my name, too," she said.

Margaret thought that "How nice" would be an inappropriate reply to this, and something like "Is it?" or "Just imagine" or "What a coincidence" would certainly make her feel more foolish than she believed she really was, so she smiled uncertainly at the old lady and dismissed the notion of saying "What a lovely name."

"He should have come and gone sooner," the old lady went on, as though to herself. "Then we'd have it all behind us."

"Have all *what* behind us?" Margaret asked, although she felt that she was not really being included in the old lady's conversation with herself, a conversation that seemed—and probably was—part of a larger conversation which the old lady had with herself constantly and on larger subjects than the matter of Margaret's name, and which even Margaret, intruder as she was, and young, could not be allowed to interrupt for very long. "Have all *what* behind us?" Margaret asked insistently.

"I say," said the old lady, turning to look at Margaret, "he should have come and gone already, and we'd all be well out of it by now."

"I see," said Margaret. "Well, I don't think he's going to be here much longer. He's talking of going." In spite of herself, her voice trembled a little. In order to prove to the old lady that the trembling in her voice was imaginary, Margaret said almost defiantly, "It will be very lonely here after he has gone."

"We'll be well out of it, Margaret, you and I," the old lady said. "Stand away from the window, child, you'll be wet."

Margaret realized with this that the storm, which had—she knew now—been hanging over the house for long sunny days had broken, suddenly, and that the wind had grown louder and was bringing with it through the windows of the tower long stinging rain. There were drops on the cat's black fur, and Margaret felt the side of her face wet. "Do your windows close?" she asked. "If I could help you—?"

"*I* don't mind the rain," the old lady said. "It wouldn't be the first time it's rained around the tower."

"*I* don't mind it," Margaret said hastily, drawing away from the window. She realized that she was staring back at the cat, and added nervously, "Although, of course, getting wet is—" She hesitated and the cat stared back at her without expression. "I mean," she said apologetically, "some people don't *like* getting wet."

The cat deliberately turned its back on her and put its face closer to the window.

"What were you saying about Paul?" Margaret asked the old lady, feeling somehow that there might be a thin thread of reason tangling the old lady and the cat and the tower and the rain, and even, with abrupt clarity, defining Margaret herself and the strange hesitation which had caught at her here in the tower. "He's going away soon, you know."

"It would have been better if it were over with by now," the old lady said. "These things don't take really long, you know, and the sooner the better, I say."

"I suppose *that's* true," Margaret said intelligently.

"After all," said the old lady dreamily, with raindrops in her hair, "we don't always see ahead, into things that are going to happen."

Margaret was wondering how soon she might politely go back downstairs and dry herself off, and she meant to stay politely only so long as the old lady seemed to be talking, however remotely, about Paul. Also, the rain and the wind were coming through the window onto Margaret in great driving gusts, as though Margaret and the old lady and the books and the cat would be washed away, and the top of the tower cleaned of them.

"I *would* help you if I could," the old lady said earnestly to Margaret, raising her voice almost to a scream to be heard over the wind and the rain. She stood up to approach Margaret, and Margaret, thinking she was about to fall, reached out a hand to catch her. The cat stood up and spat, the rain came through the window in a great sweep, and Margaret, holding the old lady's hands, heard through the sounds of the wind the equal sounds of all the voices in the world, and they called to her saying, "Goodbye, goodbye," and "All is lost" and another voice saying, "I will always remember you," and still another called, "It is so dark." And, far away from the others, she could hear a voice calling, "Come back, come back." Then the old lady pulled her hands away from Margaret and the voices were gone. The cat shrank back and the old lady looked coldly at Margaret and said, "As I was saying, I would help you if I *could*."

"I'm so sorry," Margaret said weakly. "I thought you were going to fall."

"Goodbye," said the old lady.

III

At the ball Margaret wore a gown of thin blue lace that belonged to Carla, and yellow roses in her hair, and she carried one of the fans from the fan room, a daintily painted ivory thing which seemed indestructible, since she dropped it twice, and which had a tiny picture of the house painted on its ivory sticks, so that when the fan was closed the house was gone. Mrs. Montague had given it to her to carry, and had given Carla another, so that when Margaret and Carla passed one another dancing, or met by the punch bowl or in the halls, they said happily to one another, "Have you still got your fan? I gave mine to someone to hold for a minute; I showed mine to everyone. Are you still carrying your fan? I've got *mine.*"

Margaret danced with strangers and with Paul, and when she danced with Paul they danced away from the others, up and down the long gallery hung with pictures, in and out between the pillars which led to the great hall opening into the room of the tiles. Near them danced ladies in scarlet silk, and green satin, and white velvet, and Mrs. Montague, in black with diamonds at her throat and on her hands, stood at the top of the room and smiled at the dancers, or went on Mr. Montague's arm to greet guests who came laughingly in between the pillars looking eagerly and already moving in time to the music as they walked. One lady wore white feathers in her hair, curling down against her shoulder; another had a pink scarf over her arms, and it floated behind her as she danced. Paul was in his haughty uniform, and Carla wore red roses in her hair and danced with the captain.

"Are you really going tomorrow?" Margaret asked Paul once during the evening; she knew that he was, but somehow asking the question—which she had done several times before—established a communication between them, of his right to go and her right to wonder, which was sadly sweet to her.

"I *said* you might meet the great-aunt," said Paul, as though in answer; Margaret followed his glance, and saw the old lady of the tower. She was dressed in yellow satin, and looked very regal and proud as she moved through the crowd of dancers, drawing her skirt aside if any of them came too close to her. She was coming toward Margaret and Paul where they sat on small chairs against the wall, and when she came close enough she smiled, looking at Paul, and said to him, holding out her hands, "I am very glad to see you, my dear."

Then she smiled at Margaret and Margaret smiled back, thankful that the old lady held out no hands to her.

"Margaret told me you were here," the old lady said to Paul, "and I came down to see you once more."

"I'm happy that you did," Paul said. "I wanted to see you so much that I almost came to the tower."

They both laughed and Margaret, looking from one to the other of them, wondered at the strong resemblance between them. Margaret sat very straight and stiff on her narrow chair, with her blue lace skirt falling charmingly around her and her hands folded neatly in her lap, and listened to their talk. Paul had found the old lady a chair and they sat with their heads near together, looking at one another as they talked, and smiling.

"You look very fit," the old lady said. "Very fit indeed." She sighed.

"You look wonderfully well," Paul said.

"Oh, well," said the old lady. "I've aged. I've aged, I know it."

"So have I," said Paul.

"Not noticeably," said the old lady, shaking her head and regarding him soberly for a minute. "*You* never will, I suppose."

At that moment the captain came up and bowed in front of Margaret, and Margaret, hoping that Paul might notice, got up to dance with him.

"I saw you sitting there alone," said the captain, "and I seized the precise opportunity I have been awaiting all evening."

"Excellent military tactics," said Margaret, wondering if these remarks had not been made a thousand times before, at a thousand different balls.

"I could be a splendid tactician," said the captain gallantly, as though carrying on his share of the echoing conversation, the words spoken under so many glittering chandeliers, "if my objective were always so agreeable to me."

"I saw you dancing with Carla," said Margaret.

"Carla," he said, and made a small gesture that somehow showed Carla as infinitely less than Margaret. Margaret knew that she had seen him make the same gesture to Carla, probably with reference to Margaret. She laughed.

"I forget what I'm supposed to say now," she told him.

"You're supposed to say," he told her seriously, " 'And do you really leave us so soon?' "

"And do you really leave us so soon?" said Margaret obediently.

"The sooner to return," he said, and tightened his arm around her waist. Margaret said, it being her turn, "We shall miss you very much."

"*I* shall miss *you*," he said, with a manly air of resignation.

They danced two waltzes, after which the captain escorted her handsomely back to the chair from which he had taken her, next to which Paul and the old lady continued in conversation, laughing and gesturing. The captain bowed to Margaret deeply, clicking his heels.

"May I leave you alone for a minute or so?" he asked. "I believe Carla is looking for me."

"I'm perfectly all right here," Margaret said. As the captain hurried away she turned to hear what Paul and the old lady were saying.

"I remember, I remember," said the old lady laughing, and she tapped Paul on the wrist with her fan. "I never imagined there would be a time when I should find it funny."

"But it *was* funny," said Paul.

"We were so young," the old lady said. "I can hardly remember."

She stood up abruptly, bowed to Margaret, and started back across the room among the dancers. Paul followed her as far as the doorway and then left her to come back to Margaret. When he sat down next to her he said, "So you met the old lady?"

"I went to the tower," Margaret said.

"She told me," he said absently, looking down at his gloves. "Well," he said finally, looking up with an air of cheerfulness. "Are they *never* going to play a waltz?"

Shortly before the sun came up over the river the next morning they sat at breakfast, Mr. and Mrs. Montague at the ends of the table, Carla and the captain, Margaret and Paul. The red roses in Carla's hair had faded and been thrown away, as had Margaret's yellow roses, but both Carla and Margaret still wore their ball gowns, which they had been wearing for so long that the soft richness of them seemed natural, as though they were to wear nothing else for an eternity in the house, and the gay confusion of helping one another dress, and admiring one another, and straightening the last folds to hang more gracefully, seemed all to have happened longer ago than memory, to be perhaps a dream that might never have happened at all, as perhaps the figures in the tapestries on the walls of the dining room might remember, secretly, an imagined process of dressing themselves and coming with laughter and light voices to sit on the lawn where they were woven. Margaret, looking at Carla, thought that she had never seen Carla so familiarly as in this soft white gown, with her hair dressed high on her head—had it really been curled and pinned that way? Or had it always, forever, been so?—and the fan in her hand—had she not always had that fan, held just so?—and when Carla turned her head slightly on her long neck she captured the air of one of the portraits in the long gallery. Paul and the captain were still somehow trim in their uniforms; they were leaving at sunrise.

"Must you really leave this morning?" Margaret whispered to Paul.

"You are all kind to stay up and say goodbye," said the captain, and he leaned forward to look down the table at Margaret, as though it were particularly kind of her.

"Every time my son leaves me," said Mrs. Montague, "it is as though it were the first time."

Abruptly, the captain turned to Mrs. Montague and said, "I noticed this morning that there was a bare patch on the grass before the door. Can it be restored?"

"I had not known," Mrs. Montague said, and she looked nervously at Mr. Montague, who put his hand quietly on the table and said, "We hope to keep the house in good repair so long as we are able."

"But the broken statue by the lake?" said the captain. "And the tear in the tapestry behind your head?"

"It is wrong of you to notice these things," Mrs. Montague said, gently.

"What can I do?" he said to her. "It is impossible not to notice these things. The fish are dying, for instance. There are no grapes in the arbor this year. The carpet is worn to thread near your embroidery frame," he bowed to Mrs. Montague, "and in the house itself—" bowing to Mr. Montague, "—there is a noticeable crack over the window of the conservatory, a crack in the solid stone. Can you repair that?"

Mr. Montague said weakly, "It is very wrong of you to notice these things. Have you neglected the sun, and the bright perfection of the drawing room? Have you been recently to the gallery of portraits? Have you walked on the green portions of the lawn, or only watched for the bare places?"

"The drawing room is shabby," said the captain softly. "The green brocade sofa is torn a little near the arm. The carpet has lost its luster. The gilt is chipped on four of the small chairs in the gold room, the silver paint scratched in the silver room. A tile is missing from the face of Margaret, who died for love, and in the great gallery the paint has faded slightly on the portrait of—" bowing to Mr. Montague, "—your great-great-great-grandfather, sir."

Mr. Montague and Mrs. Montague looked at one another, and

then Mrs. Montague said, "Surely it is not necessary to reproach *us* for these things?"

The captain reddened and shook his head.

"My embroidery is very nearly finished," Mrs. Montague said. "I have only to put the figures into the foreground."

"I shall mend the brocade sofa," said Carla.

The captain glanced once around the table, and sighed. "I must pack," he said. "We cannot delay our duties even though we have offended lovely women." Mrs. Montague, turning coldly away from him, rose and left the table, with Carla and Margaret following.

Margaret went quickly to the tile room, where the white face of Margaret who died for love stared eternally into the sky beyond the broad window. There was indeed a tile missing from the wide white cheek, and the broken spot looked like a tear, Margaret thought; she kneeled down and touched the tile face quickly to be sure that it was not a tear.

Then she went slowly back through the lovely rooms, across the broad rose and white tiled hall, and into the drawing room, and stopped to close the tall doors behind her.

"There really is a tile missing," she said.

Paul turned and frowned; he was standing alone in the drawing room, tall and bright in his uniform, ready to leave. "You are mistaken," he said. "It is not possible that anything should be missing."

"I saw it."

"It is not *true*, you know," he said. He was walking quickly up and down the room, slapping his gloves on his wrist, glancing nervously, now and then, at the door, at the tall windows opening out onto the marble stairway. "The house is the same as ever," he said. "It does not change."

"But the worn carpet . . ." It was under his feet as he walked.

"Nonsense," he said violently. "Don't you think I'd know my own house? I care for it constantly, even when *they* forget; without this house I could not exist; do you think it would begin to crack while I am here?"

"How can you keep it from aging? Carpets *will* wear, you know, and unless they are replaced . . ."

"Replaced?" He stared as though she had said something evil. "What could replace anything in this house?" He touched Mrs. Montague's embroidery frame, softly. "All we can do is add to it."

There was a sound outside; it was the family coming down the great stairway to say goodbye. He turned quickly and listened, and it seemed to be the sound he had been expecting. "I will always remember you," he said to Margaret, hastily, and turned again toward the tall windows. "Goodbye."

"It is so dark," Margaret said, going beside him. "You will come back?"

"I will come back," he said sharply. "Goodbye." He stepped across the sill of the window onto the marble stairway outside; he was black for a moment against the white marble, and Margaret stood still at the window watching him go down the steps and away through the gardens. "Lost, lost," she heard faintly, and, from far away, "all is lost."

She turned back to the room, and, avoiding the worn spot in the carpet and moving widely around Mrs. Montague's embroidery frame, she went to the great doors and opened them. Outside, in the hall with the rose and white tiled floor, Mr. and Mrs. Montague and Carla were standing with the captain.

"Son," Mrs. Montague was saying. "When will you be back?"

"Don't *fuss* at me," the captain said. "I'll be back when I can."

Carla stood silently, a little away. "Please be careful," she said, and, "Here's Margaret, come to say goodbye to you, brother."

"Don't linger, m'boy," said Mr. Montague. "Hard on the women."

"There are so many things Margaret and I planned for you while you were here," Carla said to her brother. "The time has been so short."

Margaret, standing beside Mrs. Montague, turned to Carla's brother *(and Paul; who was Paul?)* and said "Goodbye." He bowed to her and moved to go to the door with his father.

"It is hard to see him go," Mrs. Montague said. "And we do not know when he will come back." She put her hand gently on Margaret's shoulder. "We must show you more of the house," she said. "I saw you one day try the door of the ruined tower; have you seen the hall of flowers? Or the fountain room?"

"When my brother comes again," Carla said, "we shall have a musical evening, and perhaps he will take us boating on the river."

"And my visit?" said Margaret smiling. "Surely there will be an end to my visit?"

Mrs. Montague, with one last look at the door from which Mr. Montague and the captain had gone, dropped her hand from Margaret's shoulder and said, "I must go to my embroidery. I have neglected it while my son was with us."

"You will not leave us before my brother comes again?" Carla asked Margaret.

"I have only to put the figures into the foreground," Mrs. Montague said, hesitating on her way to the drawing room. "I shall have you exactly if you sit on the lawn near the river."

"We shall be models of stillness," said Carla, laughing. "Margaret, will you come and sit beside me on the lawn?"

# PAUL BOWLES
## Allal

He was born in the hotel where his mother worked. The hotel had only three dark rooms which gave on a courtyard behind the bar. Beyond was another smaller patio with many doors. This was where the servants lived, and where Allal spent his childhood.

The Greek who owned the hotel had sent Allal's mother away. He was indignant because she, a girl of fourteen, had dared to give birth while she was working for him. She would not say who the father was, and it angered him to reflect that he himself had not taken advantage of the situation while he had had the chance. He gave the girl three months' wages and told her to go home to Marrakech. Since the cook and his wife liked the girl and offered to let her live with them for a while, he agreed that she might stay on until the baby was big enough to travel. She remained in the back patio for a few months with the cook and his wife, and then one day she disappeared, leaving the baby behind. No one heard of her again.

As soon as Allal was old enough to carry things, they set him to work. It was not long before he could fetch a pail of water from the well behind the hotel. The cook and his wife were childless, so that he played alone.

When he was somewhat older he began to wander over the empty tableland outside. There was nothing else up here but the barracks, and they were enclosed by a high blind wall of red adobe. Everything else was below in the valley: the town, the gardens, and the river winding southward among the thousands of palm trees. He could sit on a point of rock far above and look down at the people walking in the alleys of the town. It was only later that he visited the place and saw what the inhabitants were like. Because he had been left behind by his mother they called him a son of sin, and laughed when they looked at him. It seemed to him that in this way they hoped to make him into a shadow, in order not to have to think of him as real and alive. He awaited with dread the time when he would have to go each morning to the town and work. For the moment he helped in the kitchen and served the officers from the barracks, along with the few motorists who passed through the region. He got small tips in the restaurant, and free food and lodging in a cell of the servants' quarters, but the Greek gave him no wages. Eventually he reached an age when this situation seemed shameful, and he went of his own accord to the town below and began to work, along with other boys of his age, helping to make the mud bricks people used for building their houses.

Living in the town was much as he had imagined it would be. For two years he stayed in a room behind a blacksmith's shop, leading a life without quarrels, and saving whatever money he did not have to spend to keep himself alive. Far from making any friends during this time, he formed a thorough hatred for the people of the town, who never allowed him to forget that he was a son of sin, and therefore not like others, but *meskhot* damned. Then he found a small house, not much more than a hut, in the palm groves outside the town. The rent was low and no one lived nearby. He went to live there, where the only sound was the wind in the trees, and avoided the people of the town when he could.

One hot summer evening shortly after sunset he was walking under the arcades that faced the town's main square. A few paces ahead of him an old man in a white turban was trying to shift a heavy sack from one shoulder to the other. Suddenly it fell to the ground, and Allal stared as two dark forms flowed out of it and disappeared into the shadows. The old man pounced upon the sack and fastened the top of it, at the same time beginning to shout: Look out for the snakes! Help me find my snakes!

Many people turned quickly around and walked back the way they had come. Others stood at some distance, watching. A few called to the old man: Find your snakes fast and get them out of here! Why are they here? We don't want snakes in this town!

Hopping up and down in his anxiety, the old man turned to Allal. Watch this for me a minute, my son. He pointed at the sack lying on the earth at his feet, and snatching up a basket he had been carrying, went swiftly around the corner into an alley. Allal stood where he was. No one passed by.

It was not long before the old man returned, panting with triumph. When the onlookers in the square saw him again, they began to call out, this time to Allal: Show that *berrani* the way out of the town! He has no right to carry those things in here. Out! Out!

Allal picked up the big sack and said to the old man: Come on.

They left the square and went through the alleys until they were at the edge of town. The old man looked up then, saw the palm trees black against the fading sky ahead, and turned to the boy beside him.

Come on, said Allal again, and he went to the left along the rough path that led to his house. The old man stood perplexed.

You can stay with me tonight, Allal told him.

And these? he said, pointing first at the sack and then at the basket. They have to be with me.

Allal grinned. They can come.

When they were sitting in the house Allal looked at the sack and the basket. I'm not like the rest of them here, he said.

It made him feel good to hear the words being spoken. He made a contemptuous gesture. Afraid to walk through the square because of a snake. You saw them.

The old man scratched his chin. Snakes are like people, he said. You have to get to know them. Then you can be their friends.

Allal hesitated before he asked: Do you ever let them out?

Always, the old man said with energy. It's bad for them to be inside like this. They've got to be healthy when they get to Taroudant, or the man there won't buy them.

He began a long story about his life as a hunter of snakes, explaining that each year he made a voyage to Taroudant to see a man who bought them for the Aissaoua snake charmers in Marrakech. Allal made tea while he listened, and brought out a bowl of kif paste to eat with the tea. Later, when they were sitting comfortably in the midst of the pipe smoke, the old man chuckled. Allal turned to look at him.

Shall I let them out?

Fine!

But you must sit and keep quiet. Move the lamp nearer.

He untied the sack, shook it a bit, and returned to where he had been sitting. Then in silence Allal watched the long bodies move cautiously out into the light. Among the cobras were others with markings so delicate and perfect that they seemed to have been designed and painted by an artist. One reddish-gold serpent, which coiled itself lazily in the middle of the floor, he found particularly beautiful. As he stared at it, he felt a great desire to own it and have it always with him.

The old man was talking. I've spent my whole life with snakes, he said. I could tell you some things about them. Did you know that if you give them *majoun* you can make them do what you want, and without saying a word? I swear by Allah!

Allal's face assumed a doubtful air. He did not question the truth of the other's statement, but rather the likelihood of his being able to put the knowledge to use. For it was at that moment that the idea of actually taking the snake first came into his head. He was thinking that whatever he was to do must be done quickly, for the old man would be leaving in the morning. Suddenly he felt a great impatience.

Put them away so I can cook dinner, he whispered. Then he sat admiring the ease with which the old man picked up each one by its head and slipped it into the sack. Once again he dropped two of the snakes into the basket, and one of these, Allal noted, was the red one. He imagined he could see the shining of its scales through the lid of the basket.

As he set to work preparing the meal Allal tried to think of other things. Then, since the snake remained in his mind in spite of everything, he began to devise a way of getting it. While he squatted over the fire in a corner, he mixed some kif paste in a bowl of milk and set it aside.

The old man continued to talk. That was good luck, getting the two snakes back like that, in the middle of the town. You can never be sure what people are going to do when they find out you're carrying snakes. Once in El Kelaa they took all of them and killed them, one after the other, in front of me. A year's work. I had to go back home and start all over again.

Even as they ate, Allal saw that his guest was growing sleepy. How will things happen? he wondered. There was no way of knowing beforehand precisely what he was going to do, and the prospect of having to handle the snake worried him. It could kill me, he thought.

Once they had eaten, drunk tea and smoked a few pipes of kif, the old man lay back on the floor and said he was going to sleep. Allal sprang up. In here! he told him, and led him to his own mat in an alcove. The old man lay down and swiftly fell asleep.

Several times during the next half hour Allal went to the alcove and peered in, but neither the body in its burnoose nor the head in its turban had stirred.

First he got out his blanket, and after tying three of its corners together, spread it on the floor with the fourth corner facing the basket. Then he set the bowl of milk and kif paste on the blanket. As he loosened the strap from the cover of the basket the old man coughed. Allal stood immobile, waiting to hear the cracked voice speak. A small breeze had sprung up, making the palm branches rasp one against the other, but there was no further sound from the alcove. He crept to the far side of the room and squatted by the wall, his gaze fixed on the basket.

Several times he thought he saw the cover move slightly, but each time he decided he had been mistaken. Then he caught his breath. The shadow along the base of the basket was moving. One of the creatures had crept out from the far side. It waited for a while before continuing into the light, but when it did, Allal breathed a prayer of thanks. It was the red and gold one.

When finally it decided to go to the bowl, it made a complete tour around the edge, looking in from all sides, before lowering its head toward the milk. Allal watched, fearful that the foreign flavor of the kif paste might repel it. The snake remained there without moving.

He waited a half hour or more. The snake stayed where it was, its head in the bowl. From time to time, Allal glanced at the basket, to be certain that the second snake was still in it. The breeze went on, rubbing the palm branches together. When he decided it was time, he rose slowly, and keeping an eye on the basket where apparently the other snake still slept, he reached over and gathered together the three tied corners of the blanket. Then he lifted the fourth corner, so that both the snake and the bowl slid to the bottom of the improvised sack. The snake moved slightly, but he did not think it was angry. He knew exactly where he would hide it: between some rocks in the dry riverbed.

Holding the blanket in front of him he opened the door and stepped out under the stars. It was not far up the road, to a group of high palms, and then to the left down into the oued. There was a space between the boulders where the bundle would be invisible. He pushed it in with care, and hurried back to the house. The old man was asleep.

There was no way of being sure that the other snake was still in the basket, so Allal picked up his burnoose and went outside. He shut the door and lay down on the ground to sleep.

Before the sun was in the sky the old man was awake, lying in the alcove coughing. Allal jumped up, went inside, and began to make a fire in the *mijmah*. A minute later he heard the other exclaim: They're loose again! Out of the basket! Stay where you are and I'll find them.

It was not long before the old man grunted with satisfaction. I have the black one! he cried. Allal did not look up from the corner where he crouched, and the old man came over, waving a cobra. Now I've got to find the other one.

He put the snake away and continued to search. When the fire was blazing, Allal turned and said: Do you want me to help you look for it?

No, no! Stay where you are.

Allal boiled the water and made the tea, and still the old man was crawling on his knees, lifting boxes and pushing sacks. His turban had slipped off and his face ran with sweat.

Come and have tea, Allal told him.

The old man did not seem to have heard him at first. Then he rose and went into the alcove, where he rewound his turban. When he came out he sat down with Allal, and they had breakfast.

Snakes are very clever, the old man said. They can get into places that don't exist. I've moved everything in this house.

After they had finished eating, they went outside and looked for the snake between the close-growing trunks of the palms near the house. When the old man was convinced that it was gone, he went sadly back in.

That was a good snake, he said at last. And now I'm going to Taroudant.

They said good-bye, and the old man took his sack and basket and started up the road toward the highway.

All day long as he worked, Allal thought of the snake, but it was not until sunset that he was able to go to the rocks in the oued and pull out the blanket. He carried it back to the house in a high state of excitement.

Before he untied the blanket, he filled a wide dish with milk and kif paste, and set it on the floor. He ate three spoonfuls of the paste himself and sat back to watch, drumming on the low wooden tea table with his fingers. Everything happened just as he had hoped. The snake came slowly out of the blanket, and very soon had found the dish and was drinking the milk. As long as it drank he kept drumming; when it had finished and raised its head to look at him, he stopped, and it crawled back inside the blanket.

Later that evening he put down more milk, and drummed again on the table. After a time the snake's head appeared, and finally all of it, and the entire pattern of action was repeated.

That night and every night thereafter, Allal sat with the snake, while with infinite patience he sought to make it his friend. He never attempted to touch it, but soon he was able to summon it, keep it in front of him for as long as he pleased, merely by tapping on the table, and dismiss it at will. For the first week or so he used the kif paste; then he tried the routine without it. In the end the results were the same. After that he fed it only milk and eggs.

Then one evening as his friend lay gracefully coiled in front of him, he began to think of the old man, and formed an idea that put all other things out of his mind. There had not been any kif paste in the house for several weeks, and he decided to make some. He bought the ingredients the following day, and after work he prepared the paste. When it was done, he mixed a large amount of it in a bowl with milk and set it down for the snake. Then he himself ate four spoonfuls, washing them down with tea.

He quickly undressed, and moving the table so that he could reach it, stretched out naked on a mat near the door. This time he continued to tap on the table, even after the snake had finished drinking the milk. It lay still, observing him, as if it were in doubt that the familiar drumming came from the brown body in front of it.

Seeing that even after a long time it remained where it was, staring at him with its stony yellow eyes, Allal began to say to it over and over: Come here. He knew it could not hear his voice, but he believed it could feel his mind as he urged it. You can make them do what you want, without saying a word, the old man had told him.

Although the snake did not move, he went on repeating his command, for by now he knew it was going to come. And after another long wait, all at once it lowered its head and began to move toward him. It reached his hip and slid along his leg. Then it climbed up his leg and lay for a time across his chest. Its body was heavy and tepid, its scales wonderfully smooth. After a time it came to rest, coiled in the space between his head and his shoulder.

By this time the kif paste had completely taken over Allal's mind. He lay in a state of pure delight, feeling the snake's head against his own, without a thought save that he and the snake were together. The patterns forming and melting behind his eyelids seemed to be the same ones that covered the snake's back. Now and then in a huge frenzied movement they all swirled up and shattered into fragments which swiftly became one great yellow eye, split through the middle by the narrow vertical pupil that pulsed with his own heartbeat. Then the eye would recede, through shifting shadow and sunlight, until only the designs of the scales were left, swarming with renewed insistence as they merged and separated. At last the eye returned, so huge this time that it had no edge around it, its pupil dilated to form an aperture almost wide enough for him to enter. As he stared at the blackness within, he understood that he was being slowly propelled toward the opening. He put out his hands to touch the polished surface of the eye on each side, and as he did this he felt the pull from within. He slid through the crack and was swallowed by darkness.

On awakening Allal felt that he had returned from somewhere far away. He opened his eyes and saw, very close to him, what looked like the flank of an enormous beast, covered with coarse stiff hair. There was a repeated vibration in the air, like distant thunder curling around the edges of the sky. He sighed, or imagined that he did, for his breath made no sound. Then he shifted his head a bit, to try and see beyond the mass of hair beside him. Next he saw the ear, and he knew he was looking at his own head from the outside. He had not expected this; he had hoped only that his friend would come in and share his mind with him. But it did not strike him as being at all strange; he merely said to himself that now he was seeing through the eyes of the snake, rather than through his own.

Now he understood why the serpent had been so wary of him: from here the boy was a monstrous creature, with all the bristles on his head and his breathing that vibrated inside him like a far-off storm.

He uncoiled himself and glided across the floor to the alcove. There was a break in the mud wall wide enough to let him out. When he had pushed himself through, he lay full length on the ground in the crystalline moonlight, staring at the strangeness of the landscape, where shadows were not shadows.

He crawled around the side of the house and started up the road toward the town, rejoicing in a sense of freedom different from any he had ever imagined. There was no feeling of having a body, for he was perfectly contained in the skin that covered him. It was beautiful to caress the earth with the length of his belly as he moved along the silent road, smelling the sharp veins of wormwood in the wind. When the voice of the Muezzin floated out over the countryside from the mosque, he could not hear it, or know that within the hour the night would end.

On catching sight of a man ahead, he left the road and hid behind a rock until the danger had passed. But then as he approached the town there began to be more people, so that he let himself down into the *seguia*, the deep ditch that went along beside the road. Here the stones and clumps of dead plants impeded his progress. He was still struggling along the floor of the *seguia*, pushing himself around the rocks and through the dry tangles of matted stalks left by the water, when dawn began to break.

The coming of daylight made him anxious and unhappy. He clambered up the bank of the *seguia* and raised his head to examine the road. A man walking past saw him, stood quite still, and then turned and ran back. Allal did not wait; he wanted now to get home as fast as possible.

Once he felt the thud of a stone as it struck the ground somewhere behind him. Quickly he threw himself over the edge of the *seguia* and rolled squirming down the bank. He knew the terrain here: where the road crossed the oued, there were two culverts not far apart. A man stood at some distance ahead of him with a shovel, peering down into the *seguia*. Allal kept moving, aware that he would reach the first culvert before the man could get to him.

The floor of the tunnel under the road was ribbed with hard little waves of sand. The smell of the mountains was in the air that moved through. There were places in here where he could have hidden, but he kept moving, and soon reached the other end. Then he continued to the second culvert and went under the road in the other direction, emerging once again into the *seguia*. Behind him several men had gathered at the entrance to the first culvert. One of them was on his knees, his head and shoulders inside the opening.

He now set out for the house in a straight line across the open ground, keeping his eye on the clump of palms beside it. The sun had just come up, and the stones began to cast long bluish shadows. All at once a small boy appeared from behind some nearby palms, saw him, and opened his eyes and mouth wide with fear. He was so close that Allal went straight to him and bit him in the leg. The boy ran wildly toward the group of men in the *seguia*.

Allal hurried on to the house, looking back only as he reached the hole between the mud bricks. Several men were running among the trees toward him. Swiftly he glided through into the alcove. The brown body still lay near the door. But there was no time, and Allal needed time to get back to it, to lie close to its head and say: Come here.

As he stared out into the room at the body, there was a great pounding on the door. The boy was on his feet at the first blow, as if a spring had been released, and Allal saw with despair the expression of total terror in his face, and the eyes with no mind behind them. The boy stood panting, his fists clenched. The door opened and some of the men peered inside. Then with a roar the boy lowered his head and rushed through the doorway. One of the men reached out to seize him, but lost his balance and fell. An instant later all of them turned and began to run through the palm grove after the naked figure.

Even when, from time to time, they lost sight of him, they could hear the screams, and then they would see him, between the palm trunks, still running. Finally he stumbled and fell face downward. It was then that they caught him, bound him, covered his nakedness, and took him away, to be sent one day soon to the hospital at Berrechid.

That afternoon the same group of men came to the house to carry out the search they had meant to make earlier. Allal lay in the alcove, dozing. When he awoke, they were already inside. He turned and crept to the hole. He saw the man waiting there, a club in his hand.

The rage had always been in his heart; now it burst forth. As if his body were a whip, he sprang into the room. The men nearest him were on their hands and knees, and Allal had the joy of pushing his fangs into two of them before a third severed his head with an axe.

# ISAAC BASHEVIS SINGER
## The Reencounter

The telephone rang and Dr. Max Greitzer woke up. On the night table the clock showed fifteen minutes to eight. "Who could be calling so early?" he murmured. He picked up the phone and a woman's voice said, "Dr. Greitzer, excuse me for calling at this hour. A woman who was once dear to you has died. Liza Nestling."

"My God!"

"The funeral is today at eleven. I thought you would want to know."

"You are right. Thank you. Thank you. Liza Nestling played a major role in my life. May I ask whom I am speaking to?"

"It doesn't matter. Liza and I became friends after you two separated. The service will be in Gutgestalt's funeral parlor. You know the address?"

"Yes, thank you."

The woman hung up.

Dr. Greitzer lay still for a while. So Liza was gone. Twelve years had passed since their breaking up. She had been his great love. Their affair lasted about fifteen years—no, not fifteen; thirteen. The last two had been filled with so many misunderstandings and complications, with so much madness, that words could not describe them. The same powers that built this love destroyed it entirely. Dr. Greitzer and Liza Nestling never met again. They never wrote to one another. From a friend of hers he learned that she was having an affair with a would-be theater director, but that was the only word he had about her. He hadn't even known that Liza was still in New York.

Dr. Greitzer was so distressed by the bad news that he didn't remember how he got dressed that morning or found his way to the funeral parlor. When he arrived, the clock across the street showed twenty-five to nine. He opened the door, and the receptionist told him that he had come too early. The service would not take place until eleven o'clock.

"Is it possible for me to see her now?" Max Greitzer asked. "I am a very close friend of hers, and . . ."

"Let me ask if she's ready." The girl disappeared behind a door.

Dr. Greitzer understood what she meant. The dead are elaborately fixed up before they are shown to their families and those who attend the funeral.

Soon the girl returned and said, "It's all right. Fourth floor, room three."

A man in a black suit took him up in the elevator and opened the door to room number 3. Liza lay in a coffin opened to her shoulders, her face covered with gauze. He recognized her only because he knew it was she. Her black hair had the dullness of dye. Her cheeks were rouged, and the wrinkles around her closed eyes were hidden under makeup. On her reddened lips there was a hint of a smile. How do they produce a smile? Max Greitzer wondered. Liza had once accused him of being a mechanical person, a robot with no emotion. The accusation was false then, but now, strangely, it seemed to be true. He was neither dejected nor frightened.

The door to the room opened and a woman with an uncanny resemblance to Liza entered. "It's her sister, Bella," Max Greitzer said to himself. Liza had often spoken about her younger sister, who lived in California, but he had never met her. He stepped aside as the woman approached the coffin. If she burst out crying, he would be nearby to comfort her. She showed no special emotion, and he decided to leave her with her sister, but it occurred to him that she might be afraid to stay alone with a corpse, even her own sister's.

After a few moments, she turned and said, "Yes, it's her."

"I expect you flew in from California," Max Greitzer said, just to say something.

"From California?"

"Your sister was once close to me. She often spoke about you. My name is Max Greitzer."

The woman stood silent and seemed to ponder his words. Then she said, "You're mistaken."

"Mistaken? You aren't her sister, Bella?"

"Don't you know that Max Greitzer died? There was an obituary in the newspapers."

Max Greitzer tried to smile. "Probably another Max Greitzer." The moment he uttered these words, he grasped the truth: he and Liza were both dead—the woman who spoke to him was not Bella but Liza herself. He now realized that if he were still alive he would be shaken with grief. Only someone on the other side of life could accept with such indifference the death of a person he had once loved. Was what he was experiencing the immortality of the soul, he wondered. If he were able, he would laugh now, but the illusion of body had vanished; he and Liza no longer had material substance. Yet they were both present. Without a voice he asked, "Is this possible?"

He heard Liza answer in her smart style, "If it is so, it must be possible." She added, "For your information, your body is lying here too."

"How did it happen? I went to sleep last night a healthy man."

"It wasn't last night and you were not healthy. A degree of amnesia seems to accompany this process. It happened to me a day ago and therefore—"

"I had a heart attack?"

"Perhaps."

"What happened to *you*?" he asked.

"With me, everything takes a long time. How did you hear about me, anyway?" she added.

"I thought I was lying in bed. Fifteen minutes to eight, the telephone rang and a woman told me about you. She refused to give her name."

"Fifteen minutes to eight, your body was already here. Do you want to go look at yourself? I've seen you. You are in number 5. They made a *krasavetz* out of you."

He hadn't heard anyone say *krasavetz* for years. It meant a beautiful man. Liza had been born in Russia and she often used this word.

"No. I'm not curious."

In the chapel it was quiet. A clean-shaven rabbi with curly hair and a gaudy tie made a speech about Liza. "She was an intellectual woman in the best sense of the word," he said. "When she came to America, she worked all day in a shop and at night she attended college, graduating with high honors. She had bad luck and many things in her life went awry, but she remained a lady of high integrity."

"I never met that man. How could he know about me?" Liza asked.

"Your relatives hired him and gave him the information," Greitzer said.

"I hate these professional compliments."

"Who's the fellow with the gray mustache on the first bench?" Max Greitzer asked.

Liza uttered something like a laugh. "My has-been husband."

"You were married? I heard only that you had a lover."

"I tried everything, with no success whatsoever."

"Where would you like to go?" Max Greitzer asked.

"Perhaps to your service."

"Absolutely not."

"What state of being is this?" Liza asked. "I see everything. I recognize everyone. There is my Aunt Reizl. Right behind her is my Cousin Becky. I once introduced you to her."

"Yes, true."

"The chapel is half empty. From the way I acted toward others in such circumstances, it is what I deserve. I'm sure that for you the chapel will be packed. Do you want to wait and see?"

"I haven't the slightest desire to find out."

The rabbi had finished his eulogy and a cantor recited "God Full of Mercy." His chanting was more like crying and Liza said, "My own father wouldn't have gone into such lamentations."

"Paid tears."

"I've had enough of it," Liza said. "Let's go."

They floated from the funeral parlor to the street. There, six limousines were lined up behind the hearse. One of the chauffeurs was eating a banana.

"Is this what they call death?" Liza asked. "It's the same city, the same streets, the same stores. I seem the same, too."

"Yes, but without a body."

"What am I then? A soul?"

"Really, I don't know what to tell you," Max Greitzer said. "Do you feel any hunger?"

"Hunger? No."

"Thirst?"

"No. No. What do you say to all this?"

"The unbelievable, the absurd, the most vulgar superstitions are proving to be true," Max Greitzer said.

"Perhaps we will find there is even a Hell and a Paradise."

"Anything is possible at this point."

"Perhaps we will be summoned to the Court on High after the burial and asked to account for our deeds?"

"Even this can be."

"How does it come about that we are together?"

"Please, don't ask any more questions. I know as little as you."

"Does this mean that all the philosophic works you read and wrote were one big lie?"

"Worse—they were sheer nonsense."

At that moment, four pallbearers carried out the coffin holding Liza's body. A wreath lay on top, with an inscription in gold letters: "To the unforgettable Liza in loving memory."

"Whose wreath is that?" Liza asked, and she answered herself, "For this he's not stingy."

"Would you like to go with them to the cemetery?" Max Greitzer asked.

"No—what for? That phony cantor may recite a whining Kaddish after me."

"What do you want to do?"

Liza listened to herself. She wanted nothing. What a peculiar state, not to have a single wish. In all the years she could remember, her will, her yearnings, her fears, tormented her without letting up. Her dreams were full of desperation, ecstasy, wild passions. More than any other catastrophe, she dreaded the final day, when all that has been is extinguished and the darkness of the grave begins. But here she was, remembering the past, and Max Greitzer was again with her. She said to him, "I imagined that the end would be much more dramatic."

"I don't believe this is the end," he said. "Perhaps a transition between two modes of existence."

"If so, how long will it last?"

"Since time has no validity, duration has no meaning."

"Well, you've remained the same with your puzzles and paradoxes. Come, we cannot just stay here if you want to avoid seeing your mourners," Liza said. "Where should we go?"

"You lead."

Max Greitzer took her astral arm and they began to rise without purpose, without destination. As they might have done from an airplane, they looked down at the earth and saw cities, rivers, fields, lakes—everything but human beings.

"Did you say something?" Liza asked.

And Max Greitzer answered, "Of all my disenchantments, immortality is the greatest."

# WILLIAM GOYEN
## In the Icebound Hothouse

It is true that I have not been able to utter more than a madman's sound since my eyes beheld the sight. I've lost speech. And so they have asked me to write. Since you are a poet, write, they told me. Little do they know what they might get. Little, even, do I.

So I'm writing this in the Detention House, where they're holding me until I can give word. Little do they know what I might give. Little, even, do I. A "suspicious witness" they name me. I am, certainly, a witness—or was. But was there no "suspicious witness" for *me*? To help me explain? Maybe the dead naked girl was my witness. Had she watched from the high window of the Biology Lab? As I loitered near the icebound hothouse? As I knocked on the ice-armored door? As I peered through the ice-ribboned windows; as I waved to the sullen Nurseryman inside? No use wasting time on that, her lips are forever sealed, cold, kissless and silent. But the dead naked girl certainly was my key to the hothouse; it was she who, at last, gave me entrance, opened the icebound door barred to me heretofore. Through her death. Before my eyes, at the sound of crashing glass, sprang open the door, shattering ice over me. I got in! Oh I got into the hothouse all right. Her sacrifice! The diving girl's sacrifice! I notice as I write how my mind throws rapid thoughts. Not like my mind. Which usually operates in languor; at slow bubble; and darkening and thickening, like a custard at simmer. Symptom of my bad head.

But would not working among green things make for a certain bliss? Harmony, peacefulness? What had disturbed the Nurseryman that he was drunken among his growing things? A crocked Nurseryman in the hothouse! Drunk among his plants, drunk in the greenhouse. Drunk in the shooting galaxy of Fuchsias, knocking his head into the Comet blossoms. His drunken breath scalding the Maidenhair Fern; alcohol fumes over the Babybreath. Pissed among the tuberous Begonias.

Seedsman in a warm nursery of sprouts and tendrils, so close to the making of leaf and bud, to the workings of bulb and seed, wouldn't you think the nursing man might be tranquil? What ate at you, green man, that you drowned your sorrows? What blighted your joy, nurse, that you sought relief in the deadening of it? What is the canker worm that ate at your roots? If you, among healing flowers and leaf, got a kind of madness, what about us lost in the bloomless? If the green be mad, then what of the dry? What does it mean that the garden is greening and the gardener withering? For if the gardener walk dumb, be two sheets in the wind, what of us, who speak and are sober and have no garden? "In a world of grief and pain, flowers bloom, even so," to quote an old saying. Even so.

Even so, I was haunted by the drunken Nurseryman. Plotzed, smashed, a bag on. The Phlox grows so straight and is so festered with blossoms: what of the afflicted hand that shakes as it tends, and scatters the blossoms? How can a quivering hand tie a leaning stem? Without a clear head—hung over in the greenhouse—can bulbs be sorted? In a plague of Whitebug was both nurse and patient afflicted? Then who nurses the nurse?

There for most of the month of January, everything was frozen cracking silver. We'd had a "silver freeze": rain all night, a sudden drop in temperature, everything brittle, silvery, ice-encased, breakable trees cracking, streets and sidewalks paved with ice, houses like iced cakes. Fierce, burning world, untraversable, a harsh world of thorns, daggers, blades. Passing every frozen morning in this silver winter, the elegant greenhouse, tropical oasis on that desert campus, in the month of January when everything was frozen silver, I saw him weaving inside the ice-gripped glass. Under a frozen sky I moved like a cripple over the frozen land. The greenhouse was a cake of ice decorated with blooms and silver windows. I could hardly see through the panes with their white icing. Yet inside I saw glimmering colors, salmon and rose and purple and red, glimmering in the roselight lampglow. I was drawn to the glow and laureate warmth of the icebound hothouse. The vision in the frozen hothouse! Glimmering and locked in the icestorm.

And through the window I saw the figure of the Nurseryman. Drunk! Worming his way under hanging baskets of showering blooms, staggering around fountains of lace-leaves, lurching through fountainous palms. An evil figure? Would he harm the growing, the blooming? This lone figure, moving among the glowing blooms—he haunted me, haunts me yet. Even now.

Why does the Nurseryman drink? I questioned. Has a giant Begonia, that he nursed almost upon his bosom for weeks when it was sick, died? Has a Maidenhair Fern, fragile as a mist sprayed from an atomizer, evaporated? Did the death of delicate things drive the gardener to bottle? But does he not know, has he not heard that all flowering things fade and die? That the grass withereth when the wind blows over? All things die? Does he not know? I asked the dark of night. Living among green (the most perishable color), was he not accustomed to daily yellowing (leaf) and graying (frond); all things die . . . ? Did insidious insects arrive? That unstoppable march through the ages, millions of legs, millions of antennae moving through the centuries. Did bugs come? And do quick damage, effect sleight-of-hand change on a tray of Pansies so perfect-looking that a gardener would believe they were changeless, like china flowers? Did a dragon worm get to the Ficus tree and draw its infernal saw across the root; did a viper-like insect, thick as a snake, hatch in the very soil that caressed and gently clasped the Tree of Eden plant and in a time when it had gained its power, strengthening itself as the buds fattened, strike with one strike at the bulb of the Tree and bring an end to it? What losses a gardener suffers! But was the gardener not accustomed to devastation by insect? What was the canker eating at the roots of the Nurseryman? Did he reach for the bottle instead of the bug killer? I cannot yet understand this gardener. In his greenhouse all was order. Cleanliness; not one leaf on the floor. The rows of green were neat. But he was disordered. And lurching a little. Yet he never fell over a little cradle of nursing seedlings or crashed against a hanging *Habernaria grandiflora*. He moved cautiously through the rainy tropical leaves and the sunny blooms far away from the blue sea whose light had nourished them and given them color, far away from the hot noons, from the rain wilderness and mossy coves and humid crevices, from soft shadows of hidden glens. Like a ghost he was here, gone, then there. Sometimes I'd see his shadow falling over the green; sometimes he seemed like a statue standing in the shadow of huge leaves, head bowed, fixed like stone.

But why was I banned? Why did the Nurseryman say *no* to me;

why did he turn me away when I waved to him, knocking at the bound door that was garlanded with flowers of ice? Why did he turn me away? At the first rejection, when he held up his rough Nurseryman's hand, big as a spade yet gentle enough to touch a bluet without bruising it—when he raised his big hand before me saying *no!* no admittance to the hothouse, I stepped back surprised by the inhospitality—if not cruelty—of being turned away and with that old feeling of expulsion that stabbed me. But I tried again. And again. Each time that the Nurseryman repulsed me he grew more passionate, darker, more threatening—more desperate each day. Why? Each time he reeled more, swooned more. Sometimes his rubeate face would be close to the icy glass of the door and it wavered and glowered through the frozen water. His features were then distorted and a little monstrous. His eyes were dark shadows, his face fiery and forlorn; he seemed a man of sorrows. Sometimes he seemed almost ready to admit me, to open the frozen crystal door to the faery bower of the hothouse. O tender nurse of this forbidden garden, what have you to say?

But what were my feelings as this strange denying relationship grew? At the beginning it was clear to me that I rankled because a figure of power had denied me. Defiance heated me. Rebellion dizzied me. I'd throw a stone through a window, climb to the top of the Biology Lab, which was on the top floor of a building that rose up beside the greenhouse, and drop something—hurl a chair—through the glass roof, and let in the freezing air and so burn the warm flowers, vandalizing the beautiful thing I was denied. Once because the first-grade class didn't elect a boy to be the one to take home for the weekend the class goldfish—a dreaming delicate creature wafting on golden wings through a green waving paradise—but chose a girl, the boy reached into the bowl and squished the golden fish through his fingers like pudding. I felt like that—again—after all these years. Also—beauty denied. I defied those who had held back from me, who had given me the pain of feeling not-taken. Whatever their reason, I had fallen into states of rage and accusation. Not chosen, kept outside—these feelings gave me such heartbreak at first that I wanted to vanish and hide. So abandoned, I thought I'd die, and wished to. But I rose up in defiance.

My next visit to the greenhouse was around midnight (the first had been at twilight). I had to get in. The cold was so bitter. Yet the icebound hothouse was glowing like a radiant stove. I felt that I was dying. My room in the Guest House was bleak with chill; the awful pictures of founders and donors were glaring with comfort and satisfaction. I had felt quite mad in that room of transients' odors and early American pewter, those white curtains scalloped at the bay window, that chintz. If only the Nurseryman would let me in. From the freezing cold outside I saw him in the distance in a drunken trance, there by the sunny orange tree. Seeing me, his old enemy, he held fast for a moment and I thought he was about to come to me to give me, at last, welcome—in a split second a look of yielding, of need, of almost reaching out, had crossed his body. But in another moment up slowly came the awful interdicting hand. I only showed him, in my answer, my own face of need; and then I went away.

The third time was in the early morning at daybreak. As I stood at the ice-veiled glass door, it happened. I saw it chute. Something like the rushing sound of wings drew my glance upwards. Whatever was falling from the top of the Biology Building in another second crashed through the glass roof of the hothouse. A plume of silver steam rose and floated over the broken greenhouse. Some pressure sprang open the frozen door like a miracle, and I entered, at last, the ripe heat of the Nursery. I was admitted. I was in. The smell of humid mulch and sticky seed was close to the smell of sex, genital and just used. I was for a moment almost overcome with the eroticness of it.

And then the fog rose from the ground and from the very leaves and through the fog I saw the body. The body lay face up, flat on its back. It lay out like an anatomy lesson figure. Arms outstretched, legs spread. Who had leaped from the Biology Building into the frozen lake of the glass roof of the greenhouse? To crash and die among the ferns and blooming Oleander in the frozen month of January? And naked? My God this white body of marble skin and coal-black finest hair lying splashed among the curling ferns. Just as the diver must have envisioned it—if she had planned the leap and had not simply insanely hurled herself down. My door-opener, my admitter. She died for me, I thought.

The drunken gardener edged out of the steaming gloom of a far corner. He shook all over and now could not move, frozen with fear in the hothouse, fixed to the ground near the Camellias. Did he think the body had dropped out of the sky? Fallen like a lavish blossom, some human-like blossom that had been torn loose by the Nurseryman's jerking hand? When I came through the fog to him and we were face to face, the look between us showed how deep had been our knowledge of each other, and then he staggered free and began fidgeting mechanically about the greenhouse like a toy man. He simply bobbled and jacked round and round the greenhouse, in and out of corners and along green byways, a berserk fox-trotter. I saw the body of the young woman whole and unbroken except for a wisp of purplish blood in the corner of her pale-lipped mouth. Flesh among greengrowing things. Leaf and skin. It was the sound that I was still hearing in my ears. Flesh against glass. Stone, rock breaking through glass is different. Flesh and bone crashing through glass, as though against water—you know, without looking, that it is a body hitting the water.

Gazing down upon the greenhouse in winter might have been a bewitching experience for somebody. Rosy in the black nighttime, it would glow below through the frosty glass like a sherbet, like a giant bouquet, like some centerpiece on the white snow table of the field it rested in. Such a delectable vision, such a faery confection of glass, ice, roseglow and bloom, might finally have drawn the gazer into it. Or did Nature? Was Nature arranging a still life *(nature mort!)* in the greenhouse? Adding flesh, skin, bone, hair. But there it lay, dazzling piece of mortality, delivered to the Nurseryman and me, *ex machina*.

Now I saw the Nurseryman begin to shuffle slowly towards me and the fallen body. There he stood gazing down upon the figure for the longest time. He gazed and gazed, as the fog floated up from the freezing once-warm earth of the Nursery. Was it somebody come back? Returned to collect an old debt? Somebody leaving themselves on the Nurseryman's doorstep . . . a self-delivered foundling? How to read the answer in the gardener's eyes. Those eyes! The look of Cain was in those green orbs. I watched them change as they gazed on: now hazel, now blue, now palest green. Chameleon eyes hath the Nurseryman. Or at least half that murderer brother's look—a look of horror and a look of madness—the brute look of the ages: killer's brother. But I saw the other half of the Nurseryman's look—the lover brother's, the keeper's, Abel's look of brotherly tenderness. I, brother to each brother, one-time looker through the iced glass of the forbidden greenhouse, bundled in wool, booted feet grinding on ice, hooded with animal fur to my brow, outsider refused entry, had now arrived within.

A "Visiting Poet" is what I am. Walking around an ancient university with a hole in my breast. And not even on the faculty of this venerable institution. Visiting. Being an "invited" poet keeps me from belonging to any staff. I am a wanderer-visitor to various seats of learning, sitting in a temporary Chair. A One-Year Chair, a One-Term Chair. An academic year here, a semester there. Worst of all—surprise!—I'm not even a functioning poet. I have not produced a poem

for some years. The flow has—temporarily, one hopes—frozen, shall
we say. I just can't for the time being—give. Yet I go on, in the company of beginner poets in classrooms, speaking of what I can't do.
Impotence instructing love. What has frozen the juices, stopped the
flow in the Poet-in-Residence with the hole in his breast? You ask?
Should I have an answer? If I had an answer I might go to work on it.
Maybe a loss of faith? I don't know. Something's stopped. The battery
fell out somewhere along the way. Where's the power? Also I became
grubby. The shine gone. I felt molty. The flower off me. I felt dry.
Love! Love unreturned. Do you know, *est-ce que vous savez*, you who
took me from the icebound hothouse and now "detain" me, are you
acquainted with fouled love? You will answer that that is a sentimental
question, even unscrupulous under the circumstances. "Unscrupulous"
indeed! Well, that's *your* word, not mine. I'm not trying to work up
pity; nor am I trying to build up a case of self-pity, God forbid. But a
poet is a person of love, whether he's producing, at the moment, or
not; a person with love to give. He's also somebody who needs to get
love back—for Christ's sake. You back there who the hell did you
think I was, somebody giving all that passion and not getting anything
back? How long did you think I could go on like that? I must admit it
was my choice to go on like that. I kept hoping you'd change. That
you'd come to me. Give me *something back*. And so I went on; giving,
giving; went on too far, went into a territory where I couldn't turn
back, where I was lost; a territory that was dark and where I felt dark
feelings toward you, resentment and hate. My God, I who could love
you so much. I, torn lover, who wanted to put you together with
tender hands and wanted to tear you apart with the hands of a savage.
Love not got back! You somewhere! Perverter! Spoiler! Perverting
what was beautiful, fouling what was beautiful. Fouler! Fouler! Fouler!
I don't know what kept me from striking you in those days. Because of
your fear, your little lack of courage, your selfish little fear. And I keep
walking around with a hole in my breast. I could have talked to the
Nurseryman about this. We could have had conversations in the
deepest nights and in the veiled and humid morning twilights in
the healing flower-hung bloom-graced grottos and little primrose
bowers, Wisteria arbors of the Nursery. He might have taken my
sorrow, smoothed a little my anger, given me some of the wisdom of a
gardener, helped me understand the fouling of passion, the spoiling of
love. I might have shown him the photographs, the letters, even some
of my early poems written in the gone days of my passion and tender

love, while they were still pure feeling in me, poetry, before I found a
fouling object. Love indeed! Poem-crusher! Poetry-robber! I could
have spoken of betrayal, of the knife-cut of tepid love, the stabbing
dagger of half-baked feeling. The Nurseryman might have begun to
drink less whiskey. He might have felt needed, of service beyond the
watering of mute blossoms, the feeding of dumb stalks. Does nobody
give a penny in Hell for another's woes? If he did not, if the gardener-
Nurseryman did not, and put concern and caring for his brothers into
the bottle, at least he could have allowed me the company of flowers,
passing blooms for a passing visitor. Well he didn't. Even so. He'd
probably have annoyed me with drunken slobberings, baby speech.
And he couldn't have heard me or would've half-heard me ringing
with booze like doorbells in his ears. But I don't know anything and
this is all only conjecture. And it doesn't matter now.

But what was between those two, Nurseryman and dead girl,
beautiful figure laid out almost obscenely in the leaves and blooms?
And why was this sight chosen for me to see, why was I selected as a
witness to it? I, no more than a passerby, enchanted by a glowing hothouse in the frozen winter, somehow possessed by a drunken
Nurseryman who denied me hospitality when I most needed welcome.
Or was there nothing between the two, were they strangers? And
therefore was it a murder? Murder in the Biology Lab and at daybreak
and the body hurled below, into the greenhouse. There was no stab
wound on the perfect body; no prints of a squeezing hand on the fair
throat. The classic mound that swelled gently from the bottom of the
belly seemed chaste. The fair beautiful body seemed whole and perfect,
had fallen, even through glass, whole and perfect, like fruit unbruised—
plucked rather than fallen fruit. Was there a sign of struggle in the Laboratory? Paraphernalia overturned? Did Somebody in the heat of
quarrel push her through the window? Was there a face of horror at
the window when the body fell? Now I saw what passion burned in
the Nurseryman's heart. Like a heaving bull. Panting and groaning, he
fell upon the naked girl and clutching her to his body rolled and wal-
lowed on the hothouse floor. If she had not already been dead, he
might have killed her with his very body. Until the figure of the man
and girl, combined into one strange being, half-clothed, with one head
of wild and furious hair, lay still under the palms. I managed to take
steps, but it was as though each step would draw up the very ground
with it, as though my feet were magnets. I dragged closer and knelt to
look upon this figure of violence. I saw surely that the Nurseryman was

dead. I could not bring myself to touch him to see if he was breathing, but I saw no signs of breathing, heard no breath. The Nurseryman of the cold *No!*, the gardener of the icebound hothouse, had died of passion. I opened my mouth but I could not say any word. Could I have spoken, would I have greeted, at last, the Nurseryman now joined to the body of my admitter to the hothouse? The odd still figure, lasciviously spent, beautiful with white buttocks and tressed with flowing hair, and terrible, too, like a slain beast upon the floor come from the wilds into this fragile garden of poetry and blooming summer, this figure was mine. As though I had created it.

I do not know why I picked up a little spade and slid it as if I were scooping something from the softest part of the flesh of the Nurseryman where his heart hung in the dark of his breast. The spade no doubt dug his heartless heart half out. Had I withdrawn the little scoop it might have spooned out the enigmatic heart to me, like a boiled egg. I wanted the No-man's heart, now not so much in vengeance as in calm curiosity. Almost scientifically. The heart images! I imagined his heart might look like a bell. A bell aloft in the tower of his lungs. A bulb, buried in the depth of his root-veined breast. Testicles, that hung under the shaft of his neck. My God the images. Violence has brought me images. I craved the heart of the dead Nurseryman. They dug out Shelley's heart. They fought on the shore for Shelley's heart. O gardener of this garden, O lost nurse of this Nursery, unhappy and inhospitable host of the icebound greenhouse, what would your heart be like?

And there, shrouded in the warm gathering fog, I sat down with this figure, settled, now, in some kind of understanding far beyond anything I could utter, of the fallen naked girl and the passion-stilled, heart-spaded Nurseryman, and in some kind of joining of them; for strangely I felt the third, we were, somehow, beyond anything I could explain if even I had words, a trio, our experience together and one with the other would never be known but had brought us together in this union, dark brother, wild sister. And there I remained until someone would come. I felt the killing cold creeping in upon the hothouse, and the fog was wrapping us around.

But what could I have to say to those who, hearing the dawn crash, arrived to behold this vision under the palms? And, sleep-thickened, wondered of me what had happened? I was as dumb and as frozen as the gardener had been, I could have been a statue there among the steaming palms. Some did, however, when they got their senses back, recognize the young woman—a sophomore biology student from a neighboring state. The two bodies were so clenched together that they removed them as one, covered with a blanket and carried out into the cold. The little spade made a tent of the blanket as they carried the figure of violence out into the morning cold.

As they took me out of the greenhouse, a chilling vapor rose from the sodden ground. Outside I turned and saw the ruined hothouse. The blooming colors were darkened and already the leaves were blackening in poisonous blotches as if some acid had burned them, and it had only been the winter cold that had touched them. The Nursery was fouled.

My throat felt of iron; my tongue was like a club. I gargled to the questions asked of me. But my case in my head was that the girl stabbed with the spade the violating Nurseryman as I passed by and I'd broken in to be of help. This is a lie I now confess, albeit a lie never told. How can I explain what happened? You expect me to, you, my Captors. But I am afraid and speechless and have no knowledge of anything; I need a friend, someone to help me. I knew I was done for and, without words, I crowed and crooned like a baby and rocked my head No! No! when you came to tell me of my fingerprints on the spade that must have left a moon-shaped scar in the heart of the Nurseryman. The old moon in the new moon's arms. I had never thought of the heart as a moon. Moon in my breast! O moon of my heart! Maybe my old wild poetry will come again to me.

I want to go home! That house rises before me, built once more. Again on the pit floor of my life, it blows into shape before me. That house. It seemed perfect in its simplicity. Its quietness within itself. The humility of it, resting there shady under the trees; the dirt yard, the noble footworn steps. It seemed my last innocence and one of the few beautiful things of openness and plainness that I knew—the woodfire's throbbing glow rosying the room where I slept with my mother while the wind crackled the frozen branches at the window; the peaceful woodfirelight-blessed room, the warmth of the simple room in that strong sure house. Surely it led me to poetry, for it had given me early deep feeling, mornings of unnameable feelings in the silver air, nights of visions after stories told by the lamplight. But oh I see that it held a shadowed life. Even at the best of times the light in that life was contending with a shadow that came back and back and back. "I can never quite get this little handmirror clear," my mother said, "that was my mother's—and her mother's. Out of a lot of lost stuff, or broken, this little mirror has come through. But there's always been a faint little cast on it that I can never get off, can clean and clean; can hardly see it but it's there; you can wipe it off and look back at it later and there it is, come back, that cast, just right there, there in the left-hand corner, see it? Wonder what it is, guess it's in the very glass."

On the frosted frontdoor pane was the figure of a mysterious rider with a plumed hat astride a phantom horse the color of a cloud, silver-gray, with plumed cloud-colored mane and plumed silver tail—a Prince? a Knight? But why, I wonder now, was he rearing back as if startled by the knocker at the door, challenging the arriver at the door, "Who are you and why have you come here?" Who put the rider there? Who of my ancestors put the rider there? Why, there were warm stories told at night, loving as often as fearful, as often gay as melancholy. Who among the old dwellers of these rooms was dark? Who put the dark host at the door, rearing suspicious horse and suspicious plumed dark rider shying back from the homeless traveler, from the guest half-welcome? Even for me when sometimes I returned and came, once more, to that door, tired and wanting home. Even there. Even then. O rider I am done for, the brothers in me have for the last time fought, the dark one won, darkness prevailed, O rider why did I ever come to this university, O why did I not resign when I saw the emptiness of this school, the failed professors, these classes in poetry, these students, this town, the depth of my loneliness and hunger?

# JOHN CHEEVER
## The Enormous Radio

Jim and Irene Westcott were the kind of people who seem to strike that satisfactory average of income, endeavor, and respectability that is reached by the statistical reports in college alumni bulletins. They were the parents of two young children, they had been married nine years, they lived on the twelfth floor of an apartment house near Sutton Place, they went to the theatre on an average of 10.3 times a year, and they hoped someday to live in Westchester. Irene Westcott was a pleasant, rather plain girl with soft brown hair and a wide, fine forehead upon which nothing at all had been written, and in the cold weather she wore a coat of fitch skins dyed to resemble mink. You could not say that Jim Westcott looked younger than he was, but you could at least say of him that he seemed to feel younger. He wore his graying hair cut very short, he dressed in the kind of clothes his class had worn at Andover, and his manner was earnest, vehement, and intentionally naïve. The Westcotts differed from their friends, their classmates, and their neighbors only in an interest they shared in serious music. They went to a great many concerts—although they seldom mentioned this to anyone—and they spent a good deal of time listening to music on the radio.

Their radio was an old instrument, sensitive, unpredictable, and beyond repair. Neither of them understood the mechanics of radio—or of any of the other appliances that surrounded them—and when the instrument faltered, Jim would strike the side of the cabinet with his hand. This sometimes helped. One Sunday afternoon, in the middle of a Schubert quartet, the music faded away altogether. Jim struck the cabinet repeatedly, but there was no response; the Schubert was lost to them forever. He promised to buy Irene a new radio, and on Monday when he came home from work he told her that he had got one. He refused to describe it, and said it would be a surprise for her when it came.

The radio was delivered at the kitchen door the following afternoon, and with the assistance of her maid and the handyman Irene uncrated it and brought it into the living room. She was struck at once with the physical ugliness of the large gumwood cabinet. Irene was proud of her living room, she had chosen its furnishings and colors as carefully as she chose her clothes, and now it seemed to her that the new radio stood among her intimate possessions like an aggressive intruder. She was confounded by the number of dials and switches on the instrument panel, and she studied them thoroughly before she put the plug into a wall socket and turned the radio on. The dials flooded with a malevolent green light, and in the distance she heard the music of a piano quintet. The quintet was in the distance for only an instant; it bore down upon her with a speed greater than light and filled the apartment with the noise of music amplified so mightily that it knocked a china ornament from a table to the floor. She rushed to the instrument and reduced the volume. The violent forces that were snared in the ugly gumwood cabinet made her uneasy. Her children came home from school then, and she took them to the Park. It was not until later in the afternoon that she was able to return to the radio.

The maid had given the children their suppers and was supervising their baths when Irene turned on the radio, reduced the volume, and sat down to listen to a Mozart quintet that she knew and enjoyed. The music came through clearly. The new instrument had a much purer tone, she thought, than the old one. She decided that tone was most important and that she could conceal the cabinet behind a sofa. But as soon as she had made her peace with the radio, the interference began. A crackling sound like the noise of a burning powder fuse began to accompany the singing of the strings. Beyond the music, there was a rustling that reminded Irene unpleasantly of the sea, and as the quintet progressed, these noises were joined by many others. She tried all the dials and switches but nothing dimmed the interference, and she sat down, disappointed and bewildered, and tried to trace the flight of the melody. The elevator shaft in her building ran beside the living-room wall, and it was the noise of the elevator that gave her a clue to the character of the static. The rattling of the elevator cables and the opening and closing of the elevator doors were reproduced in her loudspeaker, and, realizing that the radio was sensitive to electrical currents of all sorts, she began to discern through the Mozart the ringing of telephone bells, the dialing of phones, and the lamentation of a vacuum cleaner. By listening more carefully, she was able to distinguish doorbells, elevator bells, electric razors, and Waring mixers, whose sounds had been picked up from the apartments that surrounded hers and transmitted through her loudspeaker. The powerful and ugly instrument, with its mistaken sensitivity to discord, was more than she could hope to master, so she turned the thing off and went into the nursery to see her children.

When Jim Westcott came home that night, he went to the radio confidently and worked the controls. He had the same sort of experience Irene had had. A man was speaking on the station Jim had chosen, and his voice swung instantly from the distance into a force so powerful that it shook the apartment. Jim turned the volume control and reduced the voice. Then, a minute or two later, the interference began. The ringing of telephones and doorbells set in, joined by the rasp of the elevator doors and the whir of cooking appliances. The character of the noise had changed since Irene had tried the radio earlier; the last of the electric razors was being unplugged, the vacuum cleaners had all been returned to their closets, and the static reflected that change in pace that overtakes the city after the sun goes down. He fiddled with the knobs but couldn't get rid of the noises, so he turned the radio off and told Irene that in the morning he'd call the people who had sold it to him and give them hell.

The following afternoon, when Irene returned to the apartment from a luncheon date, the maid told her that a man had come and fixed the radio. Irene went into the living room before she took off her hat or her furs and tried the instrument. From the loudspeaker came a recording of the "Missouri Waltz." It reminded her of the thin, scratchy music from an old-fashioned phonograph that she sometimes heard across the lake where she spent her summers. She waited until the waltz had finished, expecting an explanation of the recording, but there was none. The music was followed by silence, and then the plaintive and scratchy record was repeated. She turned the dial and got a satisfactory burst of Caucasian music—the thump of bare feet in the dust and the rattle of coin jewelry—but in the background she could hear the ringing of bells and a confusion of voices. Her children came home from school then, and she turned off the radio and went to the nursery.

When Jim came home that night, he was tired, and he took a bath and changed his clothes. Then he joined Irene in the living room. He had just turned on the radio when the maid announced dinner, so he left it on, and he and Irene went to the table.

Jim was too tired to make even a pretense of sociability, and there was nothing about the dinner to hold Irene's interest, so her attention wandered from the food to the deposits of silver polish on the candlesticks and from there to the music in the other room. She listened for a few minutes to a Chopin prelude and then was surprised to hear a man's voice break in. "For Christ's sake, Kathy," he said, "do you always have to play the piano when I get home?" The music stopped abruptly. "It's the only chance I have," a woman said. "I'm at the office all day." "So am I," the man said. He added something obscene about an upright piano, and slammed a door. The passionate and melancholy music began again.

"Did you hear that?" Irene asked.

"What?" Jim was eating his dessert.

"The radio. A man said something while the music was still going on—something dirty."

"It's probably a play."

"I don't think it *is* a play," Irene said.

They left the table and took their coffee into the living room. Irene asked Jim to try another station. He turned the knob. "Have you seen my garters?" a man asked. "Button me up," a woman said. "Have you seen my garters?" the man said again. "Just button me up and I'll find your garters," the woman said. Jim shifted to another station. "I wish you wouldn't leave apple cores in the ashtrays," a man said. "I hate the smell."

"This is strange," Jim said.

"Isn't it?" Irene said.

Jim turned the knob again. " 'On the coast of Coromandel where the early pumpkins blow,' " a woman with a pronounced English accent said, " 'in the middle of the woods lived the Yonghy-Bonghy-Bò. Two old chairs, and half a candle, one old jug without a handle . . .' "

"My God!" Irene cried. "That's the Sweeneys' nurse."

" 'These were all his worldly goods,' " the British voice continued.

"Turn that thing off," Irene said. "Maybe they can hear *us*." Jim switched the radio off. "That was Miss Armstrong, the Sweeneys' nurse," Irene said. "She must be reading to the little girl. They live in 17-B. I've talked with Miss Armstrong in the Park. I know her voice very well. We must be getting other people's apartments."

"That's impossible," Jim said.

"Well, that was the Sweeneys' nurse," Irene said hotly. "I know her voice. I know it very well. I'm wondering if they can hear us."

Jim turned the switch. First from a distance and then nearer, nearer, as if borne on the wind came the pure accents of the Sweeneys' nurse again: " '*Lady Jingly! Lady Jingly!* ' " she said, " '*sitting where the pumpkins blow, will you come and be my wife?* said the Yonghy-Bonghy-Bò . . .' "

Jim went over to the radio and said "Hello" loudly into the speaker.

" '*I am tired of living singly,* ' " the nurse went on, " '*on this coast so wild and shingly, I'm a-weary of my life; if you'll come and be my wife, quite serene would be my life . . .* ' "

"I guess she can't hear us," Irene said. "Try something else."

Jim turned to another station, and the living room was filled with the uproar of a cocktail party that had overshot its mark. Someone was playing the piano and singing the "Whiffenpoof Song," and the voices that surrounded the piano were vehement and happy. "Eat some more sandwiches," a woman shrieked. There were screams of laughter and a dish of some sort crashed to the floor.

"Those must be the Fullers, in 11-E," Irene said. "I knew they were giving a party this afternoon. I saw her in the liquor store. Isn't this too divine? Try something else. See if you can get those people in 18-C."

The Westcotts overheard that evening a monologue on salmon fishing in Canada, a bridge game, running comments on home movies of what had apparently been a fortnight at Sea Island, and a bitter family quarrel about an overdraft at the bank. They turned off their radio at midnight and went to bed, weak with laughter. Sometime in the night, their son began to call for a glass of water and Irene got one and took it to his room. It was very early. All the lights in the neighborhood were extinguished, and from the boy's window she could see the empty street. She went into the living room and tried the radio. There was some faint coughing, a moan, and then a man spoke. "Are you all right, darling?" he asked. "Yes," a woman said wearily. "Yes,

I'm all right, I guess," and then she added with great feeling, "But, you know, Charlie, I don't feel like myself any more. Sometimes there are about fifteen or twenty minutes in the week when I feel like myself. I don't like to go to another doctor, because the doctor's bills are so awful already, but I just don't feel like myself, Charlie. I just never feel like myself." They were not young, Irene thought. She guessed from the timbre of their voices that they were middle-aged. The restrained melancholy of the dialogue and the draft from the bedroom window made her shiver, and she went back to bed.

The following morning, Irene cooked breakfast for the family— the maid didn't come up from her room in the basement until ten— braided her daughter's hair, and waited at the door until her children and her husband had been carried away in the elevator. Then she went into the living room and tried the radio. "I don't want to go to school," a child screamed. "I hate school. I won't go to school. I hate school." "You will go to school," an enraged woman said. "We paid eight hundred dollars to get you into that school and you'll go if it kills you." The next number on the dial produced the worn record of the "Missouri Waltz." Irene shifted the control and invaded the privacy of several breakfast tables. She overheard demonstrations of indigestion, carnal love, abysmal vanity, faith, and despair. Irene's life was nearly as simple and sheltered as it appeared to be, and the forthright and some-times brutal language that came from the loudspeaker that morning astonished and troubled her. She continued to listen until her maid came in. Then she turned off the radio quickly, since this insight, she realized, was a furtive one.

Irene had a luncheon date with a friend that day, and she left her apartment at a little after twelve. There were a number of women in the elevator when it stopped at her floor. She stared at their handsome and impassive faces, their furs, and the cloth flowers in their hats. Which one of them had been to Sea Island? she wondered. Which one had overdrawn her bank account? The elevator stopped at the tenth floor and a woman with a pair of Skye terriers joined them. Her hair was rigged high on her head and she wore a mink cape. She was hum-ming the "Missouri Waltz."

Irene had two Martinis at lunch, and she looked searchingly at her friend and wondered what her secrets were. They had intended to go shopping after lunch, but Irene excused herself and went home. She told the maid that she was not to be disturbed; then she went into the living room, closed the doors, and switched on the radio. She heard, in the course of the afternoon, the halting conversation of a woman entertaining her aunt, the hysterical conclusion of a luncheon party, and a hostess briefing her maid about some cocktail guests. "Don't give the best Scotch to anyone who hasn't white hair," the hostess said. "See if you can get rid of that liver paste before you pass those hot things, and could you lend me five dollars? I want to tip the elevator man."

As the afternoon waned, the conversations increased in intensity From where Irene sat, she could see the open sky above the East River. There were hundreds of clouds in the sky, as though the south wind had broken the winter into pieces and were blowing it north, and on her radio she could hear the arrival of cocktail guests and the return of children and businessmen from their schools and offices. "I found a good-sized diamond on the bathroom floor this morning," a woman said. "It must have fallen out of that bracelet Mrs. Dunston was wearing last night." "We'll sell it," a man said. "Take it down to the jeweler on Madison Avenue and sell it. Mrs. Dunston won't know the difference, and we could use a couple of hundred bucks . . ." " 'Oranges and lemons, say the bells of St. Clement's,' " the Sweeneys' nurse sang. " 'Halfpence and farthings, say the bells of St. Martin's. When will you pay me? say the bells at old Bailey . . .' " "It's not a hat," a woman cried, and at her back roared a cocktail party. "It's not a hat, it's a love affair. That's what Walter Florell said. He said it's not a hat, it's a love affair," and then, in a lower voice, the same woman added, "Talk to somebody, for Christ's sake, honey, talk to somebody. If she catches you standing here not talking to anybody, she'll take us off her invitation list, and I love these parties."

The Westcotts were going out for dinner that night, and when Jim came home, Irene was dressing. She seemed sad and vague, and he brought her a drink. They were dining with friends in the neighborhood, and they walked to where they were going. The sky was broad and filled with light. It was one of those splendid spring evenings that excite memory and desire, and the air that touched their hands and faces felt very soft. A Salvation Army band was on the corner playing "Jesus Is Sweeter." Irene drew on her husband's arm and held him there for a minute, to hear the music. "They're really such nice people, aren't they?" she said. "They have such nice faces. Actually, they're so much nicer than a lot of the people we know." She took a bill from her purse and walked over and dropped it into the tambourine. There was in her face, when she returned to her husband, a look of radiant melancholy that he was not familiar with. And her conduct at the dinner party that night seemed strange to him, too. She interrupted her hostess rudely and stared at the people across the table from her with an intensity for which she would have punished her children.

It was still mild when they walked home from the party, and Irene looked up at the spring stars. " 'How far that little candle throws its beams,' " she exclaimed. " 'So shines a good deed in a naughty world.' " She waited that night until Jim had fallen asleep, and then went into the living room and turned on the radio.

Jim came home at about six the next night. Emma, the maid, let him in, and he had taken off his hat and was taking off his coat when Irene ran into the hall. Her face was shining with tears and her hair was disordered. "Go up to 16-C, Jim!" she screamed. "Don't take off your coat. Go up to 16-C. Mr. Osborn's beating his wife. They've been quarreling since four o'clock, and now he's hitting her. Go up there and stop him."

From the radio in the living room, Jim heard screams, obscenities, and thuds. "You know you don't have to listen to this sort of thing," he said. He strode into the living room and turned the switch. "It's indecent," he said. "It's like looking in windows. You know you don't have to listen to this sort of thing. You can turn it off."

"Oh, it's so horrible, it's so dreadful," Irene was sobbing. "I've been listening all day, and it's so depressing."

"Well, if it's so depressing, why do you listen to it? I bought this damned radio to give you some pleasure," he said. "I paid a great deal of money for it. I thought it might make you happy. I wanted to make you happy."

"Don't, don't, don't, don't quarrel with me," she moaned, and laid her head on his shoulder. "All the others have been quarreling all day. Everybody's been quarreling. They're all worried about money. Mrs. Hutchinson's mother is dying of cancer in Florida and they don't have enough money to send her to the Mayo Clinic. At least, Mr. Hutchinson says they don't have enough money. And some woman in this building is having an affair with the handyman—with that hideous handyman. It's too disgusting. And Mrs. Melville has heart trouble and Mr. Hendricks is going to lose his job in April and Mrs. Hendricks is horrid about the whole thing and that girl who plays the 'Missouri Waltz' is a whore, a common whore, and the elevator man has tuberculosis and Mr. Osborn has been beating Mrs. Osborn." She wailed, she trembled with grief and checked the stream of tears down her face with the heel of her palm.

"Well, why do you have to listen?" Jim asked again. "Why do you have to listen to this stuff if it makes you so miserable?"

"Oh, don't, don't, don't," she cried. "Life is too terrible, too sordid and awful. But we've never been like that, have we, darling? Have we? I mean, we've always been good and decent and loving to one another, haven't we? And we have two children, two beautiful children. Our lives aren't sordid, are they, darling? Are they?" She flung her arms around his neck and drew his face down to hers. "We're happy, aren't we, darling? We are happy, aren't we?"

"Of course we're happy," he said tiredly. He began to surrender his resentment. "Of course we're happy. I'll have that damned radio fixed or taken away tomorrow." He stroked her soft hair. "My poor girl," he said.

"You love me, don't you?" she asked. "And we're not hypercritical or worried about money or dishonest, are we?"

"No, darling," he said.

A man came in the morning and fixed the radio. Irene turned it on cautiously and was happy to hear a California-wine commercial and a recording of Beethoven's Ninth Symphony, including Schiller's "Ode to Joy." She kept the radio on all day and nothing untoward came from the speaker.

A Spanish suite was being played when Jim came home. "Is everything all right?" he asked. His face was pale, she thought. They had some cocktails and went in to dinner to the "Anvil Chorus" from *Il Trovatore*. This was followed by Debussy's "La Mer."

"I paid the bill for the radio today," Jim said. "It cost four hundred dollars. I hope you'll get some enjoyment out of it."

"Oh, I'm sure I will," Irene said.

"Four hundred dollars is a good deal more than I can afford," he went on. "I wanted to get something that you'd enjoy. It's the last extravagance we'll be able to indulge in this year. I see that you haven't paid your clothing bills yet. I saw them on your dressing table." He looked directly at her. "Why did you tell me you'd paid them? Why did you lie to me?"

"I just didn't want you to worry, Jim," she said. She drank some water. "I'll be able to pay my bills out of this month's allowance. There were the slipcovers last month, and that party."

"You've got to learn to handle the money I give you a little more intelligently, Irene," he said. "You've got to understand that we won't have as much money this year as we had last. I had a very sobering talk with Mitchell today. No one is buying anything. We're spending all our time promoting new issues, and you know how long that takes. I'm not getting any younger, you know. I'm thirty-seven. My hair will be gray next year. I haven't done as well as I'd hoped to do. And I don't suppose things will get any better."

"Yes, dear," she said.

"We've got to start cutting down," Jim said. "We've got to think of the children. To be perfectly frank with you, I worry about money a great deal. I'm not at all sure of the future. No one is. If anything should happen to me, there's the insurance, but that wouldn't go very far today. I've worked awfully hard to give you and the children a comfortable life," he said bitterly. "I don't like to see all of my energies, all of my youth, wasted in fur coats and radios and slipcovers and—"

"Please, Jim," she said. "Please. They'll hear us."

"*Who'll hear us?* Emma can't hear us."

"The radio."

"Oh, I'm sick!" he shouted. "I'm sick to death of your apprehensiveness. The radio can't hear us. Nobody can hear us. And what if they can hear us? Who cares?"

Irene got up from the table and went into the living room. Jim went to the door and shouted at her from there. "Why are you so Christly all of a sudden? What's turned you overnight into a convent girl? You stole your mother's jewelry before they probated her will. You never gave your sister a cent of that money that was intended for her—not even when she needed it. You made Grace Howland's life miserable, and where was all your piety and your virtue when you went to that abortionist? I'll never forget how cool you were. You packed your bag and went off to have that child murdered as if you were going to Nassau. If you'd had any reasons, if you'd had any good reasons—"

Irene stood for a minute before the hideous cabinet, disgraced and sickened, but she held her hand on the switch before she extinguished the music and the voices, hoping that the instrument might speak to her kindly, that she might hear the Sweeneys' nurse. Jim continued to shout at her from the door. The voice on the radio was suave and noncommittal. "An early-morning railroad disaster in Tokyo," the loud-speaker said, "killed twenty-nine people. A fire in a Catholic hospital near Buffalo for the care of blind children was extinguished early this morning by nuns. The temperature is forty-seven. The humidity is eighty-nine."

# RAY BRADBURY
## The Veldt

"George, I wish you'd look at the nursery."

"What's wrong with it?"

"I don't know."

"Well, then."

"I just want you to look at it, is all, or call a psychologist in to look at it."

"What would a psychologist want with a nursery?"

"You know very well what he'd want." His wife paused in the middle of the kitchen and watched the stove busy humming to itself, making supper for four.

"It's just that the nursery is different now than it was."

"All right, let's have a look."

They walked down the hall of their soundproofed Happylife Home, which had cost them thirty thousand dollars installed, this house which clothed and fed and rocked them to sleep and played and sang and was good to them. Their approach sensitized a switch somewhere and the nursery light flicked on when they came within ten feet of it. Similarly, behind them, in the halls, lights went on and off as they left them behind, with a soft automaticity.

"Well," said George Hadley.

They stood on the thatched floor of the nursery. It was forty feet across by forty feet long and thirty feet high; it had cost half again as much as the rest of the house. "But nothing's too good for our children," George had said.

The nursery was silent. It was empty as a jungle glade at hot high noon. The walls were blank and two dimensional. Now, as George and Lydia Hadley stood in the center of the room, the walls began to purr and recede into crystalline distance, it seemed, and presently an African veldt appeared, in three dimensions, on all sides, in color, reproduced to the final pebble and bit of straw. The ceiling above them became a deep sky with a hot yellow sun.

George Hadley felt the perspiration start on his brow.

"Let's get out of this sun," he said. "This is a little too real. But I don't see anything wrong."

"Wait a moment, you'll see," said his wife.

Now the hidden odorophonics were beginning to blow a wind of odor at the two people in the middle of the baked veldtland. The hot straw smell of lion grass, the cool green smell of the hidden water hole, the great rusty smell of animals, the smell of dust like a red paprika in the hot air. And now the sounds: the thump of distant antelope feet on grassy sod, the papery rustling of vultures. A shadow passed through the sky. The shadow flickered on George Hadley's upturned, sweating face.

"Filthy creatures," he heard his wife say.

"The vultures."

"You see, there are the lions, far over, that way. Now they're on their way to the water hole. They've just been eating," said Lydia. "I don't know what."

"Some animal." George Hadley put his hand up to shield off the burning light from his squinted eyes. "A zebra or a baby giraffe, maybe."

"Are you sure?" His wife sounded peculiarly tense.

"No, it's a little late to be sure," he said, amused. "Nothing over there I can see but cleaned bone, and the vultures dropping for what's left."

"Did you hear that scream?" she asked.

"No."

"About a minute ago?"

"Sorry, no."

The lions were coming. And again George Hadley was filled with admiration for the mechanical genius who had conceived this room. A miracle of efficiency selling for an absurdly low price. Every home should have one. Oh, occasionally they frightened you with their clinical accuracy, they startled you, gave you a twinge, but most of the time what fun for everyone, not only your own son and daughter, but for yourself when you felt like a quick jaunt to a foreign land, a quick change of scenery. Well, here it was!

And here were the lions now, fifteen feet away, so real, so feverishly and startlingly real that you could feel the prickling fur on your hand, and your mouth was stuffed with the dusty upholstery smell of their heated pelts, and the yellow of them was in your eyes like the yellow of an exquisite French tapestry, the yellows of lions and summer grass, and the sound of the matted lion lungs exhaling on the silent noontide, and the smell of meat from the panting, dripping mouths.

The lions stood looking at George and Lydia Hadley with terrible green-yellow eyes.

"Watch out!" screamed Lydia.

The lions came running at them.

Lydia bolted and ran. Instinctively, George sprang after her. Outside, in the hall, with the door slammed, he was laughing and she was crying, and they both stood appalled at the other's reaction.

"George!"

"Lydia! Oh, my dear poor sweet Lydia!"

"They almost got us!"

"Walls, Lydia, remember; crystal walls, that's all they are. Oh, they look real, I must admit—Africa in your parlor—but it's all dimensional, superreactionary, supersensitive color film and mental tape film behind glass screens. It's all odorophonics and sonics, Lydia. Here's my handkerchief."

"I'm afraid." She came to him and put her body against him and cried steadily. "Did you see? Did you *feel*? It's too real."

"Now, Lydia . . ."

"You've got to tell Wendy and Peter not to read any more on Africa."

"Of course—of course." He patted her.

"Promise?"

"Sure."

"And lock the nursery for a few days until I get my nerves settled."

"You know how difficult Peter is about that. When I punished him a month ago by locking the nursery for even a few hours—the tantrum he threw! And Wendy too. They *live* for the nursery."

"It's got to be locked, that's all there is to it."

"All right." Reluctantly he locked the huge door. "You've been working too hard. You need a rest."

"I don't know—I don't know," she said, blowing her nose, sitting down in a chair that immediately began to rock and comfort her. "Maybe I don't have enough to do. Maybe I have time to think too much. Why don't we shut the whole house off for a few days and take a vacation?"

"You mean you want to fry my eggs for me?"

"Yes." She nodded.

"And darn my socks?"

"Yes." A frantic, watery-eyed nodding.

"And sweep the house?"

"Yes, yes—oh, yes!"

"But I thought that's why we bought this house, so we wouldn't have to do anything?"

"That's just it. I feel like I don't belong here. The house is wife and mother now, and nursemaid. Can I compete with an African veldt? Can I give a bath and scrub the children as efficiently or quickly as the automatic scrub bath can? I cannot. And it isn't just me. It's you. You've been awfully nervous lately."

"I suppose I have been smoking too much."

"You look as if you didn't know what to do with yourself in this house, either. You smoke a little more every morning and drink a little more every afternoon and need a little more sedative every night. You're beginning to feel unnecessary too."

"Am I?" He paused and tried to feel into himself to see what was really there.

"Oh, George!" She looked beyond him, at the nursery door. "Those lions can't get out of there, can they?"

He looked at the door and saw it tremble as if something had jumped against it from the other side.

"Of course not," he said.

At dinner they ate alone, for Wendy and Peter were at a special plastic carnival across town and had televised home to say they'd be late, to go ahead eating. So George Hadley, bemused, sat watching the dining-room table produce warm dishes of food from its mechanical interior.

"We forgot the ketchup," he said.

"Sorry," said a small voice within the table, and ketchup appeared.

As for the nursery, thought George Hadley, it won't hurt for the children to be locked out of it awhile. Too much of anything isn't good for anyone. And it was clearly indicated that the children had been spending a little too much time on Africa. That *sun*. He could feel it on his neck, still, like a hot paw. And the *lions*. And the smell of blood. Remarkable how the nursery caught the telepathic emanations of the children's minds and created life to fill their every desire. The children thought lions, and there were lions. The children thought zebras, and there were zebras. Sun—sun. Giraffes—giraffes. Death and death.

That *last*. He chewed tastelessly on the meat that the table had cut for him. Death thoughts. They were awfully young, Wendy and Peter, for death thoughts. Or, no, you were never too young, really. Long before you knew what death was you were wishing it on someone else. When you were two years old you were shooting people with cap pistols.

But this—the long, hot African veldt—the awful death in the jaws of a lion. And repeated again and again.

"Where are you going?"

He didn't answer Lydia. Preoccupied, he let the lights glow softly on ahead of him, extinguish behind him as he padded to the nursery door. He listened against it. Far away, a lion roared.

He unlocked the door and opened it. Just before he stepped inside, he heard a faraway scream. And then another roar from the lions, which subsided quickly.

He stepped into Africa. How many times in the last year had he opened this door and found Wonderland, Alice, the Mock Turtle, or Aladdin and his Magical Lamp, or Jack Pumpkinhead of Oz, or Dr. Doolittle, or the cow jumping over a very real-appearing moon—all the delightful contraptions of a make-believe world. How often had he seen Pegasus flying in the sky ceiling, or seen fountains of red fireworks, or heard angel voices singing. But now, this yellow hot Africa, this bake oven with murder in the heat. Perhaps Lydia was right. Perhaps they needed a little vacation from the fantasy which was growing a bit too real for ten-year-old children. It was all right to exercise one's mind with gymnastic fantasies, but when the lively child mind settled on *one* pattern . . . ? It seemed that, at a distance, for the past month, he had heard lions roaring, and smelled their strong odor seeping as far away as his study door. But, being busy, he had paid it no attention.

George Hadley stood on the African grassland alone. The lions looked up from their feeding, watching him. The only flaw to the illusion was the open door through which he could see his wife, far down the dark hall, like a framed picture, eating her dinner abstractedly.

"Go away," he said to the lions.

They did not go.

He knew the principle of the room exactly. You sent out your thoughts. Whatever you thought would appear.

"Let's have Aladdin and his lamp," he snapped.

The veldtland remained; the lions remained.

"Come on, room! I demand Aladdin!" he said.

Nothing happened. The lions mumbled in their baked pelts.

"Aladdin!"

He went back to dinner. "The fool room's out of order," he said. "It won't respond."

"Or—"

"Or what?"

"Or it *can't* respond," said Lydia, "because the children have thought about Africa and lions and killing so many days that the room's in a rut."

"Could be."

"Or Peter's set it to remain that way."

"Set it?"

"He may have got into the machinery and fixed something."

"Peter doesn't know machinery."

"He's a wise one for ten. That I.Q. of his—"

"Nevertheless—"

"Hello, Mom. Hello, Dad."

The Hadleys turned. Wendy and Peter were coming in the front door, cheeks like peppermint candy, eyes like bright blue agate marbles, a smell of ozone on their jumpers from their trip in the helicopter.

"You're just in time for supper," said both parents.

"We're full of strawberry ice cream and hot dogs," said the children, holding hands. "But we'll sit and watch."

"Yes, come tell us about the nursery," said George Hadley.

The brother and sister blinked at him and then at each other. "Nursery?"

"All about Africa and everything," said the father with false joviality.

"I don't understand," said Peter.

"Your mother and I were just traveling through Africa with rod and reel; Tom Swift and his Electric Lion," said George Hadley.

"There's no Africa in the nursery," said Peter simply.

"Oh, come now, Peter. We know better."

"I don't remember any Africa," said Peter to Wendy. "Do you?"

"No."

"Run see and come tell."

She obeyed.

"Wendy, come back here!" said George Hadley, but she was gone. The house lights followed her like a flock of fireflies. Too late, he realized he had forgotten to lock the nursery door after his last inspection.

"Wendy'll look and come tell us," said Peter.

"She doesn't have to tell *me*. I've seen it."

"I'm sure you're mistaken, Father."

"I'm not, Peter. Come along now."

But Wendy was back. "It's not Africa," she said breathlessly.

"We'll see about this," said George Hadley, and they all walked down the hall together and opened the nursery door.

There was a green, lovely forest, a lovely river, a purple mountain, high voices singing, and Rima, lovely and mysterious, lurking in the trees with colorful flights of butterflies, like animated bouquets, lingering in her long hair. The African veldtland was gone. The lions were gone. Only Rima was here now, singing a song so beautiful that it brought tears to your eyes.

George Hadley looked in at the changed scene. "Go to bed," he said to the children.

They opened their mouths.

"You heard me," he said.

They went off to the air closet, where a wind sucked them like brown leaves up the flue to their slumber rooms.

George Hadley walked through the singing glade and picked up something that lay in the corner near where the lions had been. He walked slowly back to his wife.

"What is that?" she asked.

"An old wallet of mine," he said.

He showed it to her. The smell of hot grass was on it and the smell of a lion. There were drops of saliva on it, it had been chewed, and there were blood smears on both sides.

He closed the nursery door and locked it, tight.

★ ★ ★

In the middle of the night he was still awake and he knew his wife was awake. "Do you think Wendy changed it?" she said at last, in the dark room.

"Of course."

"Made it from a veldt into a forest and put Rima there instead of lions?"

"Yes."

"Why?"

"I don't know. But it's staying locked until I find out."

"How did your wallet get there?"

"I don't know anything," he said, "except that I'm beginning to be sorry we bought that room for the children. If children are neurotic at all, a room like that—"

"It's supposed to help them work off their neuroses in a healthful way."

"I'm starting to wonder." He stared at the ceiling.

"We've given the children everything they ever wanted. Is this our reward—secrecy, disobedience?"

"Who was it said, 'Children are carpets, they should be stepped on occasionally'? We've never lifted a hand. They're insufferable—let's admit it. They come and go when they like; they treat us as if we were offspring. They're spoiled and we're spoiled."

"They've been acting funny ever since you forbade them to take the rocket to New York a few months ago."

"They're not old enough to do that alone, I explained."

"Nevertheless, I've noticed they've been decidedly cool toward us since."

"I think I'll have David McClean come tomorrow morning to have a look at Africa."

"But it's not Africa now, it's *Green Mansions* country and Rima."

"I have a feeling it'll be Africa again before then."

A moment later they heard the screams.

Two screams. Two people screaming from downstairs. And then a roar of lions.

"Wendy and Peter aren't in their rooms," said his wife.

He lay in his bed with his beating heart. "No," he said. "They've broken into the nursery."

"Those screams—they sound familiar."

"Do they?"

"Yes, awfully."

And although their beds tried very hard, the two adults couldn't be rocked to sleep for another hour. A smell of cats was in the night air.

"Father?" said Peter.

"Yes."

Peter looked at his shoes. He never looked at his father anymore, nor at his mother. "You aren't going to lock up the nursery for good, are you?"

"That all depends."

"On what?" snapped Peter.

"On you and your sister. If you intersperse this Africa with a little variety—oh, Sweden perhaps, or Denmark or China—"

"I thought we were free to play as we wished."

"You are, within reasonable bounds."

"What's wrong with Africa, Father?"

"Oh, so now you admit you have been conjuring up Africa, do you?"

"I wouldn't want the nursery locked up," said Peter coldly. "Ever."

"Matter of fact, we're thinking of turning the whole house off for about a month. Live sort of a carefree one-for-all existence."

"That sounds dreadful! Would I have to tie my own shoes instead of letting the shoe tier do it? And brush my own teeth and comb my hair and give myself a bath?"

"It would be fun for a change, don't you think?"

"No, it would be horrid. I didn't like it when you took out the picture painter last month."

"That's because I wanted you to learn to paint all by yourself, son."

"I don't want to do anything but look and listen and smell; what else *is* there to do?"

"All right, go play in Africa."

"Will you shut off the house sometime soon?"

"We're considering it."

"I don't think you'd better consider it any more, Father."

"I won't have any threats from my son!"

"Very well." And Peter strolled off to the nursery.

"Am I on time?" said David McClean.

"Breakfast?" asked George Hadley.

"Thanks, had some. What's the trouble?"

"David, you're a psychologist."

"I should hope so."

"Well, then, have a look at our nursery. You saw it a year ago when you dropped by; did you notice anything peculiar about it then?"

"Can't say I did; the usual violence, a tendency toward a slight paranoia here or there, usual in children because they feel persecuted by parents constantly, but, oh, really nothing."

They walked down the hall. "I locked the nursery up," explained the father, "and the children broke back into it during the night. I let them stay so they could form the patterns for you to see."

There was a terrible screaming from the nursery.

"There it is," said George Hadley. "See what you make of it."

They walked in on the children without rapping.

The screams had faded. The lions were feeding.

"Run outside a moment, children," said George Hadley. "No, don't change the mental combination. Leave the walls as they are. Get!"

With the children gone, the two men stood studying the lions clustered at a distance, eating with great relish whatever it was they had caught.

"I wish I knew what it was," said George Hadley. "Sometimes I can almost see. Do you think if I brought high-powered binoculars here and—"

David McClean laughed dryly. "Hardly." He turned to study all four walls. "How long has this been going on?"

"A little over a month."

"It certainly doesn't *feel* good."

"I want facts, not feelings."

"My dear George, a psychologist never saw a fact in his life. He only hears about feelings; vague things. This doesn't feel good, I tell you. Trust my hunches and my instincts. I have a nose for something bad. This is very bad. My advice to you is to have the whole damn room torn down and your children brought to me every day during the next year for treatment."

"Is it that bad?"

"I'm afraid so. One of the original uses of these nurseries was so that we could study the patterns left on the walls by the child's mind, study at our leisure, and help the child. In this case, however, the room has become a channel toward—destructive thoughts, instead of a release away from them."

"Didn't you sense this before?"

"I sensed only that you had spoiled your children more than most. And now you're letting them down in some way. What way?"

"I wouldn't let them go to New York."

"What else?"

"I've taken a few machines from the house and threatened them, a month ago, with closing up the nursery unless they did their homework. I did close it for a few days to show I meant business."

"Ah, ha!"

"Does that mean anything?"

"Everything. Where before they had a Santa Claus now they have a Scrooge. Children prefer Santas. You've let this room and this house replace you and your wife in your children's affections. This room is their mother and father, far more important in their lives than their real parents. And now you come along and want to shut it off. No wonder there's hatred here. You can feel it coming out of the sky. Feel that sun. George, you'll have to change your life. Like too many others, you've built it around creature comforts. Why, you'd starve tomorrow if something went wrong in your kitchen. You wouldn't know how to tap an egg. Nevertheless, turn everything off. Start new. It'll take time. But we'll make good children out of bad in a year, wait and see."

"But won't the shock be too much for the children, shutting the room up abruptly, for good?"

"I don't want them going any deeper into this, that's all."

The lions were finished with their red feast.

The lions were standing on the edge of the clearing watching the two men.

"Now *I'm* feeling persecuted," said McClean. "Let's get out of here. I never have cared for these damned rooms. Make me nervous."

"The lions look real, don't they?" said George Hadley. "I don't suppose there's any way—"

"What?"

"—that they could *become* real?"

"Not that I know."

"Some flaw in the machinery, a tampering or something?"

"No."

They went to the door.

"I don't imagine the room will like being turned off," said the father.

"Nothing ever likes to die—even a room."

"I wonder if it hates me for wanting to switch it off?"

"Paranoia is thick around here today," said David McClean. "You can follow it like a spoor. Hello." He bent and picked up a bloody scarf. "This yours?"

"No." George Hadley's face was rigid. "It belongs to Lydia."

They went to the fuse box together and threw the switch that killed the nursery.

The two children were in hysterics. They screamed and pranced and threw things. They yelled and sobbed and swore and jumped at the furniture.

"You can't do that to the nursery, you can't!"

"Now, children."

The children flung themselves onto a couch, weeping.

"George," said Lydia Hadley, "turn on the nursery, just for a few moments. You can't be so abrupt."

"No."

"You can't be so cruel."

"Lydia, it's off, and it stays off. And the whole damn house dies as of here and now. The more I see of the mess we've put ourselves in, the more it sickens me. We've been contemplating our mechanical, electronic navels for too long. My God, how we need a breath of honest air!"

And he marched about the house turning off the voice clocks, the stoves, the heaters, the shoe shiners, the shoe lacers, the body scrubbers and swabbers and massagers, and every other machine he could put his hand to.

The house was full of dead bodies, it seemed. It felt like a mechanical cemetery. So silent. None of the humming hidden energy of machines waiting to function at the tap of a button.

"Don't let them do it!" wailed Peter at the ceiling, as if he was talking to the house, the nursery. "Don't let Father kill everything." He turned to his father. "Oh, I hate you!"

"Insults won't get you anywhere."

"I wish you were dead!"

"We were, for a long while. Now we're going to really start living. Instead of being handled and massaged, we're going to *live*."

Wendy was still crying and Peter joined her again. "Just a

moment, just one moment, just another moment of nursery," they wailed.

"Oh, George," said the wife, "it can't hurt."

"All right—all right, if they'll just shut up. One minute, mind you, and then off forever."

"Daddy, Daddy, Daddy!" sang the children, smiling with wet faces.

"And then we're going on a vacation. David McClean is coming back in half an hour to help us move out and get to the airport. I'm going to dress. You turn the nursery on for a minute, Lydia, just a minute, mind you."

And the three of them went babbling off while he let himself be vacuumed upstairs through the air flue and set about dressing himself. A minute later Lydia appeared.

"I'll be glad when we get away," she sighed.

"Did you leave them in the nursery?"

"I wanted to dress too. Oh, that horrid Africa. What can they see in it?"

"Well, in five minutes we'll be on our way to Iowa. Lord, how did we ever get in this house? What prompted us to buy a nightmare?"

"Pride, money, foolishness."

"I think we'd better get downstairs before those kids get engrossed with those damned beasts again."

Just then they heard the children calling, "Daddy, Mommy, come quick—quick!"

They went downstairs in the air flue and ran down the hall. The children were nowhere in sight. "Wendy? Peter!"

They ran into the nursery. The veldtland was empty save for the lions waiting, looking at them. "Peter, Wendy?"

The door slammed.

"Wendy, Peter!"

George Hadley and his wife whirled and ran back to the door.

"Open the door!" cried George Hadley, trying the knob. "Why, they've locked it from the outside! Peter!" He beat at the door. "Open up!"

He heard Peter's voice outside, against the door.

"Don't let them switch off the nursery and the house," he was saying.

Mr. and Mrs. George Hadley beat at the door. "Now, don't be

ridiculous, children. It's time to go. Mr. McClean'll be here in a minute and . . ."

And then they heard the sounds.

The lions on three sides of them, in the yellow veldt grass, padding through the dry straw, rumbling and roaring in their throats.

The lions.

Mr. Hadley looked at his wife and they turned and looked back at the beasts edging slowly forward, crouching, tails stiff.

Mr. and Mrs. Hadley screamed.

And suddenly they realized why those other screams had sounded familiar.

"Well, here I am," said David McClean in the nursery doorway. "Oh, hello." He stared at the two children seated in the center of the open glade eating a little picnic lunch. Beyond them was the water hole and the yellow veldtland; above was the hot sun. He began to perspire. "Where are your father and mother?"

The children looked up and smiled. "Oh, they'll be here directly."

"Good, we must get going." At a distance, Mr. McClean saw the lions fighting and clawing and then quieting down to feed in silence under the shady trees.

He squinted at the lions with his hand up to his eyes.

Now the lions were done feeding. They moved to the water hole to drink.

A shadow flickered over Mr. McClean's hot face. Many shadows flickered. The vultures were dropping down the blazing sky.

"A cup of tea?" asked Wendy in the silence.

# W. S. MERWIN
## The Dachau Shoe

My cousin Gene (he's really only a second cousin) has a shoe he picked up at Dachau. It's a pretty worn-out shoe. It wasn't top quality in the first place, he explained. The sole is cracked clear across and has pulled loose from the upper on both sides, and the upper is split at the ball of the foot. There's no lace and there's no heel.

He explained he didn't steal it because it must have belonged to a Jew who was dead. He explained that he wanted some little thing. He explained that the Russians looted everything. They just took anything. He explained that it wasn't top quality to begin with. He explained that the guards or the kapos would have taken it if it had been any good. He explained that he was lucky to have got anything. He explained that it wasn't wrong because the Germans were defeated. He explained that everybody was picking up something. A lot of guys wanted flags or daggers or medals or things like that, but that kind of thing didn't appeal to him so much. He kept it on the mantelpiece for a while but he explained that it wasn't a trophy.

He explained that it's no use being vindictive. He explained that he wasn't. Nobody's perfect. Actually we share a German grandfather. But he explained that this was the reason why we had to fight that war. What happened at Dachau was a crime that could not be allowed to pass. But he explained that we could not really do anything to stop it while the war was going on because we had to win the war first. He explained that we couldn't always do just what we would have liked to do. He explained that the Russians killed a lot of Jews too. After a couple of years he put the shoe away in a drawer. He explained that the dust collected in it.

Now he has it down in the cellar in a box. He explains that the central heating makes it crack worse. He'll show it to you, though, any time you ask. He explains how it looks. He explains how it's hard to take it in, even for him. He explains how it was raining, and there weren't many things left when he got there. He explains how there wasn't anything of value and you didn't want to get caught taking anything of that kind, even if there had been. He explains how everything inside smelled. He explains how it was just lying out in the mud, probably right where it had come off. He explains that he ought to keep it. A thing like that.

You really ought to go and see it. He'll show it to you. All you have to do is ask. It's not that it's really a very interesting shoe when you come right down to it but you learn a lot from his explanations.

## W. S. MERWIN
### The Approved

This one I was allowed to know. His face was a triangle standing on its point, hiding a parade of hollows. He was allowed to know other schoolfellows. And I was allowed to know him. Sometimes we pretended to a liking which neither of us felt, because it was approved. But no one could walk far on that surface.

He was respectable. At that age. His conduct at school was indeed better than mine, who was allowed to know only him. I with my one-legged japes, ill-timed, the delight of no one, like irrelevant misquotations from a foreign language. Little shames for which I was not otherwise punished because of some undefinable privilege that hedged me around, like a correspondence between a parent and the authorities, which is a great pointer of fingers. But he made no awkward sallies, played the games, was not considered the most cowardly, in fact excelled at catching a ball, and in class answered as well as I did, with the hollows prompting him.

For he too had a source of privilege. It was not his mother alone, who worked all day at a notions counter, suffered with her feet, and heaved herself up on Sundays in the choir to take solo parts in the anthems, her voice like an empty powder box. She was married to his privilege, she was its daughter as well, and while I knew her she became its mother.

I was allowed to visit their house. He was allowed to go where he pleased and I was allowed to visit him in the dark sagging unpainted building smelling of cats, where the grandmother sat in the kitchen year after year, clutching herself and crying, clinging to the privilege. For they were Death's family. No one contested it. Death visited other dwellings in other streets but that was all in a day's work, and he came back to them to sleep.

Death was the grandmother's father, born in the old country, and she clung to him and showed his picture and told of the food he liked and of how he missed his home. Then Death was the grandmother's husband, also born in the old country, and she showed his picture, so like the other, one man at two different ages, both of them clearly Death, both of them forms of the same presence, the same exaltation. It had brought the old country with it, a weight in a locked trunk on its back, and at night it stretched its legs in the house and the windows rattled and the cats clawed silently at the doors. And Death was the mother's husband, as she had not understood until too late. She never showed his picture. She brought up his two sons and struggled to turn them into repetitions of him. And so it transpired with the elder, who of the two seemed less like him, but who was still a child when he lay in Death's bed like his father and his grandfather and all the other males of the family except the one whom I was allowed to know, and the privilege washed over him like an arm of the sea. In Death's room in which he himself had reverently suspended from the ceiling the paper airplanes which he had made with tireless care. They turned slowly above him—pieces of his memory. In Death's room with its pictures of Death at all ages, and its lace from the old country, and its gray wallpaper.

I was allowed to know the youngest because it was a nice family. And because of the privilege. Sometimes we imagined that we liked each other, because it was approved. But we never came to trust each other, to laugh, to be content. He was not Death, but one of Death's only sons.

# W. S. MERWIN
## Spiders I Have Known

The one no bigger than the head of a pencil, that emerged from the forehead of the new dentist perhaps an inch above his left eyebrow, ran down to the eyebrow and along it and dropped from the side of his face to the little scalloped glass tray on which the dentist was selecting a drill. It then disappeared. From my sight at least. I did not wish to call the dentist's attention to it at that precise moment. Besides I recognized that it was a perfectly harmless variety.

I would have been ashamed to be afraid.

The one that I found had taken up residence in a bundle of letters only a few months old. It was smaller than the wolf spiders that live in some of the corners and do no harm at all. It was also darker than they, and heavily—beautifully—furred. Some of its children clung to it like troops of tiny dust-colored anthropoids, and others had taken up lodgings in several of the larger envelopes. I looked up the species. Its bite is not poisonous, if I identified it correctly. I devoted some time to trying to remember which letters those were, who had written them, what they had said, whether I had answered them, and how things now stood, as a result, with each of the correspondents.

I would have been afraid to be ashamed.

The one that hung in the old apple tree that spring when we returned at last to the farm by the lake with its old garden into which I had been allowed to run, alone, with only a perfunctory word of caution from my mother, a word whose real purpose had been to dispel the attention of my father. The blossoms were just opening on the tree and the air rushed past me carrying them with it as though I were on a swing, when suddenly there it was in front of me, as big as my face, against the bright sky the color and depth of the fenders of the new car. The whole web was swaying gently in the wind. The abdomen had a kind of face on it. No, not a face, a mask. In orange and yellow. I knew it was a kind that was more afraid of me than I was of it.

I was ashamed.

The one that ran across each of my footprints in turn as I was crossing the dry bit on my way back, when you were sick and we didn't know how it would go after that, but maybe it wasn't working at all. I had the medicines but not much faith in them. It came to the edge of each footprint, hesitated, and then shot across like a woman with a baby, afraid of snipers, or a good child caught in a cloudburst. I couldn't understand how it kept up with me. My hands were full. You were in pain. I didn't want to stop. It's bad luck to harm them. Poor things. Besides, the danger of that species has been greatly exaggerated.

I would have been ashamed.

# W. S. MERWIN
## Postcards from the Maginot Line

This morning there was another one in the mail. A slightly blurred and clumsily retouched shot of some of the fortifications, massive and scarcely protruding from the enormous embankments. The guns—the few that can be seen—look silly, like wax cigars. The flag looks like a lead soldier's, with the paint put on badly. The whole thing might be a model.

But there have been the others. Many of them. For the most part seen from the exterior, from all angles—head-on, perspectives facing north and facing south, looking out from the top of the embankments, even one from above. They might all have been taken from a model, in fact, but when they are seen together that impression fades. And then there are the interiors. Officers' quarters which, the legend says, are hundreds of feet below ground. Views of apparently endless corridors into which little ramps of light descend at intervals; panels of dials of different sizes, with black patches on them that have been censored out. It was rather startling to notice a small flicker of relief at the sight of the black patches: it had seemed somehow imprudent to make public display of so much of the defenses.

A few of the cards have shown other, related subjects: a mezzotint of Maginot as a child in the 1880's, a view of the house where he grew up, with his portrait in an oval inset above it, pictures of villages near the line of fortifications, with their churches, and old men sitting under trees, and cows filing through the lanes, and monuments from other wars. They have all been marked, front and back, in heavy black letters

THE MAGINOT LINE, and the legend in each case has made the relation clear. And the postmarks are all from there.

They have been coming for months, at least once a week. All signed simply "Pierre." Whoever he is. He certainly seems to know me, or know about me—referring to favorite authors, incidents from my childhood, friends I have not seen for years. He says repeatedly that he is comfortable there. He praises what he calls the tranquillity of the life. He says, as though referring to an old joke, that with my fondness for peace I would like it. He says war is unthinkable. A thing of the past. He describes the flowers in the little beds. He describes the social life. He tells what he is reading. He asks why I never write. He asks why none of us ever write. He says we have nothing to fear.

# SYLVIA PLATH
## Johnny Panic and the Bible of Dreams

Every day from nine to five I sit at my desk facing the door of the office and type up other people's dreams. Not just dreams. That wouldn't be practical enough for my bosses. I type up also people's daytime complaints: trouble with mother, trouble with father, trouble with the bottle, the bed, the headache that bangs home and blacks out the sweet world for no known reason. Nobody comes to our office unless they have troubles. Troubles that can't be pinpointed by Wassermanns or Wechsler-Bellevues alone.

Maybe a mouse gets to thinking pretty early on how the whole world is run by these enormous feet. Well, from where I sit, I figure the world is run by one thing and this one thing only. Panic with a dog-face, devil-face, hag-face, whore-face, panic in capital letters with no face at all—it's the same Johnny Panic, awake or asleep.

When people ask me where I work, I tell them I'm Assistant to the Secretary in one of the Out-Patient Departments of the Clinics Building of the City Hospital. This sounds so be-all end-all they seldom get around to asking me more than what I do, and what I do is mainly type up records. On my own hook though, and completely under cover, I am pursuing a vocation that would set these doctors on their ears. In the privacy of my one-room apartment I call myself secretary to none other than Johnny Panic himself.

Dream by dream I am educating myself to become that rare character, rarer, in truth, than any member of the Psychoanalytic Institute, a dream connoisseur. Not a dream stopper, a dream explainer, an exploiter of dreams for the crass practical ends of health and happiness, but an unsordid collector of dreams for themselves alone. A lover of dreams for Johnny Panic's sake, the Maker of them all.

There isn't a dream I've typed up in our record books that I don't know by heart. There isn't a dream I haven't copied out at home into Johnny Panic's Bible of Dreams.

This is my real calling.

Some nights I take the elevator up to the roof of my apartment building. Some nights, about three a.m. Over the trees at the far side of the park the United Fund torch flare flattens and recovers under some witchy invisible push and here and there in the hunks of stone and brick I see a light. Most of all, though, I feel the city sleeping. Sleeping from the river on the west to the ocean on the east, like some rootless island rockabying itself on nothing at all.

I can be tight and nervy as the top string on a violin, and yet by the time the sky begins to blue I'm ready for sleep. It's the thought of all those dreamers and what they're dreaming wears me down till I sleep the sleep of fever. Monday to Friday what do I do but type up those same dreams. Sure, I don't touch a fraction of them the city over, but page by page, dream by dream, my Intake books fatten and weigh down the bookshelves of the cabinet in the narrow passage running parallel to the main hall, off which passage the doors to all the doctors' little interviewing cubicles open.

I've got a funny habit of identifying the people who come in by their dreams. As far as I'm concerned, the dreams single them out more than any Christian name. This one guy, for example, who works for a ball-bearing company in town, dreams every night how he's lying on his back with a grain of sand on his chest. Bit by bit this grain of sand grows bigger and bigger till it's big as a fair-sized house and he can't draw breath. Another fellow I know of has had a certain dream ever since they gave him ether and cut out his tonsils and adenoids when he was a kid. In this dream he's caught in the rollers of a cotton mill, fighting for his life. Oh, he's not alone, although he thinks he is. A lot of people these days dream they're being run over or eaten by machines. They're the cagey ones who won't go on the subway or the elevators. Coming back from my lunch hour in the hospital cafeteria I often pass them, puffing up the unswept stone stairs to our office on the fourth floor. I wonder, now and then, what dreams people had before ball bearings and cotton mills were invented.

I've a dream of my own. My one dream. A dream of dreams.

In this dream there's a great half-transparent lake stretching away in every direction, too big for me to see the shores of it, if there are any shores, and I'm hanging over it, looking down from the glass belly of some helicopter. At the bottom of the lake—so deep I can only guess at the dark masses moving and heaving—are the real dragons. The ones that were around before men started living in caves and cooking meat over fires and figuring out the wheel and the alphabet. Enormous isn't the word for them; they've got more wrinkles than Johnny Panic himself. Dream about these long enough and your feet and hands shrivel away when you look at them too closely. The sun shrinks to the size of an orange, only chillier, and you've been living in Roxbury since the last ice age. No place for you but a room padded soft as the first room you knew of, where you can dream and float, float and dream, till at last you actually are back among those great originals and there's no point in any dreams at all.

It's into this lake people's minds run at night, brooks and gutter trickles to one borderless common reservoir. It bears no resemblance to those pure sparkling-blue sources of drinking water the suburbs guard more jealously than the Hope diamond in the middle of pine woods and barbed fences.

It's the sewage farm of the ages, transparence aside.

Now the water in this lake naturally stinks and smokes from what dreams have been left sogging around in it over the centuries. When you think how much room one night of dream props would take up for one person in one city, and that city a mere pinprick on a map of the world, and when you start multiplying this space by the population of the world, and that space by the number of nights there have been since the apes took to chipping axes out of stone and losing their hair, you have some idea what I mean. I'm not the mathematical type: my head starts splitting when I get only as far as the number of dreams going on during one night in the State of Massachusetts.

By this time, I already see the surface of the lake swarming with snakes, dead bodies puffed as blowfish, human embryos bobbing around in laboratory bottles like so many unfinished messages from the great I Am. I see whole storehouses of hardware: knives, paper cutters, pistons and cogs and nutcrackers; the shiny fronts of cars looming up, glass-eyed and evil-toothed. Then there's the spider-man and the web-footed man from Mars, and the simple, lugubrious vision of a human face turning aside forever, in spite of rings and vows, to the last lover of all.

One of the most frequent shapes in this backwash is so commonplace it seems silly to mention. It's a grain of dirt. The water is thick with these grains. They seep in among everything else and revolve under some queer power of their own, opaque, ubiquitous. Call the water what you will, Lake Nightmare, Bog of Madness, it's here the sleeping people lie and toss together among the props of their worst dreams, one great brotherhood, though each of them, waking, thinks himself singular, utterly apart.

This is my dream. You won't find it written up in any casebook. Now the routine in our office is very different from the routine in Skin Clinic, for example, or in Tumor. The other clinics have strong similarities to each other; none are like ours. In our clinic, treatment doesn't get prescribed. It is invisible. It goes right on in those little cubicles, each with its desk, its two chairs, its window and its door with the opaque glass rectangle set in the wood. There is a certain spiritual purity about this kind of doctoring. I can't help feeling the special privilege of my position as Assistant Secretary in the Adult Psychiatric Clinic. My sense of pride is borne out by the rude invasions of other clinics into our cubicles on certain days of the week for lack of space elsewhere: our building is a very old one, and the facilities have not expanded with the expanding needs of the time. On these days of overlap the contrast between us and the other clinics is marked.

On Tuesdays and Thursdays, for instance, we have lumbar punctures in one of our offices in the morning. If the practical nurse chances to leave the door of the cubicle open, as she usually does, I can glimpse the end of the white cot and the dirty yellow-soled bare feet of the patient sticking out from under the sheet. In spite of my distaste at this sight, I can't keep my eyes away from the bare feet, and I find myself glancing back from my typing every few minutes to see if they are still there, if they have changed their position at all. You can understand what a distraction this is in the middle of my work. I often have to reread what I have typed several times, under the pretense of careful proofreading, in order to memorize the dreams I have copied down from the doctor's voice over the audiograph.

Nerve Clinic next door, which tends to the grosser, more unimaginative end of our business, also disturbs us in the mornings. We use their offices for therapy in the afternoon, as they are only a morning clinic, but to have their people crying, or singing, or chattering loudly in Italian or Chinese, as they often do, without break for four hours at a stretch every morning, is distracting to say the least.

In spite of such interruptions by other clinics, my own work is advancing at a great rate. By now I am far beyond copying only what comes after the patient's saying: "I have this dream, Doctor." I am at the point of re-creating dreams that are not even written down at all. Dreams that shadow themselves forth in the vaguest way, but are themselves hid, like a statue under red velvet before the grand unveiling.

To illustrate. This woman came in with her tongue swollen and stuck out so far she had to leave a party she was giving for twenty friends of her French-Canadian mother-in-law and be rushed to our Emergency Ward. She thought she didn't want her tongue to stick out and, to tell the truth, it was an exceedingly embarrassing affair for her, but she hated that French-Canadian mother-in-law worse than pigs, and her tongue was true to her opinion, even if the rest of her wasn't. Now she didn't lay claim to any dreams. I have only the bare facts above to begin with, yet behind them I detect the bulge and promise of a dream.

So I set myself to uprooting this dream from its comfortable purchase under her tongue.

Whatever the dream I unearth, by work, taxing work, and even by a kind of prayer, I am sure to find a thumbprint in the corner, a malicious detail to the right of center, a bodiless midair Cheshire cat grin, which shows the whole work to be gotten up by the genius of Johnny Panic, and him alone. He's sly, he's subtle, he's sudden as thunder, but he gives himself away only too often. He simply can't resist melodrama. Melodrama of the oldest, most obvious variety.

I remember one guy, a stocky fellow in a nail-studded black leather jacket, running straight in to us from a boxing match at Mechanics Hall, Johnny Panic hot at his heels. This guy, good Catholic though he was, young and upright and all, had one mean fear of death. He was actually scared blue he'd go to hell. He was a pieceworker at a fluorescent light plant. I remember this detail because I thought it funny he should work there, him being so afraid of the dark as it turned out. Johnny Panic injects a poetic element in this business you don't often find elsewhere. And for that he has my eternal gratitude.

I also remember quite clearly the scenario of the dream I had worked out for this guy: a gothic interior in some monastery cellar, going on and on as far as you could see, one of those endless perspectives between two mirrors, and the pillars and walls were made of nothing but human skulls and bones, and in every niche there was a body laid out, and it was the Hall of Time, with the bodies in the foreground still warm, discoloring and starting to rot in the middle distance, and the bones emerging, clean as a whistle, in a kind of white futuristic glow at the end of the line. As I recall, I had the whole scene lighted, for the sake of accuracy, not with candles, but with the ice-bright fluorescence that makes skin look green and all the pink and red flushes dead black-purple.

You ask, how do I know this was the dream of the guy in the black leather jacket? I don't know. I only believe this was his dream, and I work at belief with more energy and tears and entreaties than I work at re-creating the dream itself.

My office, of course, has its limitations. The lady with her tongue stuck out, the guy from Mechanics Hall—these are our wildest ones. The people who have really gone floating down toward the bottom of that boggy lake come in only once, and are then referred to a place more permanent than our office which receives the public from nine to five, five days a week only. Even those people who are barely able to walk about the streets and keep working, who aren't yet halfway down in the lake, get sent to the Out-Patient Department at another hospital specializing in severer cases. Or they may stay a month or so in our own Observation Ward in the central hospital which I've never seen.

I've seen the secretary of that ward, though. Something about her merely smoking and drinking her coffee in the cafeteria at the ten o'clock break put me off so I never went to sit next to her again. She has a funny name I don't ever quite remember correctly, something really odd, like Miss Milleravage. One of those names that seem more like a pun mixing up Milltown and Ravage than anything in the city phone directory. But not so odd a name, after all, if you've ever read through the phone directory, with its Hyman Diddlebockers and Sasparilla Greenleafs. I read through the phone book once, never mind when, and it satisfied a deep need in me to realize how many people aren't called Smith.

Anyhow, this Miss Milleravage is a large woman, not fat, but all sturdy muscle and tall on top of it. She wears a gray suit over her hard bulk that reminds me vaguely of some kind of uniform, without the details of cut having anything strikingly military about them. Her face, hefty as a bullock's, is covered with a remarkable number of tiny maculae, as if she'd been lying under water for some time and little algae had latched on to her skin, smutching it over with tobacco-browns and greens. These moles are noticeable mainly because the skin around them is so pallid. I sometimes wonder if Miss Milleravage has ever seen the wholesome light of day. I wouldn't be a bit surprised if she'd been brought up from the cradle with the sole benefit of artificial lighting.

Byrna, the secretary in Alcoholic Clinic just across the hall from us, introduced me to Miss Milleravage with the gambit that I'd "been in England too."

Miss Milleravage, it turned out, had spent the best years of her life in London hospitals.

"Had a friend," she boomed in her queer, doggish basso, not favoring me with a direct look, "a nurse at Bart's. Tried to get in touch with her after the war, but the head of the nurses had changed, everybody'd changed, nobody'd heard of her. She must've gone down with the old head nurse, rubbish and all, in the bombings." She followed this with a large grin.

Now I've seen medical students cutting up cadavers, four stiffs to a classroom, about as recognizably human as Moby Dick, and the students playing catch with the dead men's livers. I've heard guys joke about sewing a woman up wrong after a delivery at the charity ward of the Lying-In. But I wouldn't want to see what Miss Milleravage would write off as the biggest laugh of all time. No thanks and then some. You could scratch her eyes with a pin and swear you'd struck solid quartz.

My boss has a sense of humor too, only it's gentle. Generous as Santa on Christmas Eve.

I work for a middle-aged lady named Miss Taylor who is the Head Secretary of the clinic and has been since the clinic started thirty-three years ago—the year of my birth, oddly enough. Miss Taylor knows every doctor, every patient, every outmoded appointment slip, referral slip and billing procedure the hospital has ever used or thought of using. She plans to stick with the clinic until she's farmed out in the green pastures of Social Security checks. A woman more dedicated to her work I never saw. She's the same way about statistics as I am about dreams: if the building caught fire she would throw every last one of those books of statistics to the firemen below at the serious risk of her own skin.

I get along extremely well with Miss Taylor. The one thing I never let her catch me doing is reading the old record books. I have actually very little time for this. Our office is busier than the stock exchange with the staff of twenty-five doctors in and out, medical students in training, patients, patients' relatives, and visiting officials from other clinics referring patients to us, so even when I'm covering the office alone, during Miss Taylor's coffee break and lunch hour, I seldom get to dash down more than a note or two.

This kind of catch-as-catch-can is nerve-racking, to say the least. A lot of the best dreamers are in the old books, the dreamers that come in to us only once or twice for evaluation before they're sent elsewhere. For copying out these dreams I need time, a lot of time. My circumstances are hardly ideal for the unhurried pursuit of my art. There is, of course, a certain derring-do in working under such hazards, but I long for the rich leisure of the true connoisseur who indulges his nostrils above the brandy snifter for an hour before his tongue reaches out for the first taste.

I find myself all too often lately imagining what a relief it would be to bring a briefcase into work, big enough to hold one of those thick, blue, cloth-bound record books full of dreams. At Miss Taylor's lunch time, in the lull before the doctors and students crowd in to take their afternoon patients, I could simply slip one of the books, dated ten or fifteen years back, into my briefcase, and leave the briefcase under my desk till five o'clock struck. Of course, odd-looking bundles are inspected by the doorman of the Clinics Building and the hospital has its own staff of police to check up on the multiple varieties of thievery that go on, but for heaven's sake, I'm not thinking of making off with typewriters or heroin. I'd only borrow the book overnight and slip it back on the shelf first thing the next day before anybody else came in. Still, being caught taking a book out of the hospital would probably mean losing my job and all my source material with it.

This idea of mulling over a record book in the privacy and comfort of my own apartment, even if I have to stay up night after night for this purpose, attracts me so much I become more and more impatient with my usual method of snatching minutes to look up dreams in Miss Taylor's half-hours out of the office.

The trouble is, I can never tell exactly when Miss Taylor will come back to the office. She is so conscientious about her job she'd be likely to cut her half hour at lunch short and her twenty minutes at coffee shorter, if it weren't for her lame left leg. The distinct sound of this lame leg in the corridor warns me of her approach in time for me to whip the record book I'm reading into my drawer out of sight and pretend to be putting down the final flourishes on a phone message or some such alibi. The only catch, as far as my nerves are concerned, is that Amputee Clinic is around the corner from us in the opposite direction from Nerve Clinic and I've gotten really jumpy due to a lot of false alarms where I've mistaken some pegleg's hitching step for the step of Miss Taylor herself returning early to the office.

On the blackest days, when I've scarcely time to squeeze one dream out of the old books and my copywork is nothing but weepy college sophomores who can't get a lead in *Camino Real*, I feel Johnny Panic turn his back, stony as Everest, higher than Orion, and the motto of the great Bible of Dreams, "Perfect fear casteth out all else," is ash and lemon water on my lips. I'm a wormy hermit in a country of prize pigs so corn-happy they can't see the slaughterhouse at the end of the track. I'm Jeremiah vision-bitten in the Land of Cockaigne.

What's worse: day by day I see these psyche-doctors studying to win Johnny Panic's converts from him by hook, crook, and talk, talk, talk. Those deep-eyed, bush-bearded dream collectors who preceded me in history, and their contemporary inheritors with their white jackets and knotty-pine-paneled offices and leather couches, practiced and still practice their dream-gathering for worldly ends: health and money, money and health. To be a true member of Johnny Panic's congregation one must forget the dreamer and remember the dream: the dreamer is merely a flimsy vehicle for the great Dream Maker himself. This they will not do. Johnny Panic is gold in the bowels, and they try to root him out by spiritual stomach pumps.

Take what happened to Harry Bilbo. Mr. Bilbo came into our office with the hand of Johnny Panic heavy as a lead coffin on his shoulder. He had an interesting notion about the filth in this world. I figured him for a prominent part in Johnny Panic's Bible of Dreams, Third Book of Fear, Chapter Nine on Dirt, Disease and General Decay. A friend of Harry's blew a trumpet in the Boy Scout band when they were kids. Harry Bilbo'd also blown on his friend's trumpet. Years later the friend got cancer and died. Then, one day not so long ago, a cancer doctor came into Harry's house, sat down in a chair, passed the top of the morning with Harry's mother and, on leaving, shook her hand and opened the door for himself. Suddenly Harry Bilbo wouldn't blow trumpets or sit down on chairs or shake hands if all the cardinals of Rome took to blessing him twenty-four hours around the clock for fear of catching cancer. His mother had to go turning the TV knobs and water faucets on and off and opening doors for him. Pretty soon Harry stopped going to work because of the spit and dog turds in the street. First that stuff gets on your shoes and then when you take your shoes off it gets on your hands and then at dinner it's a quick trip into your mouth and not a hundred Hail Marys can keep you from the chain reaction.

The last straw was, Harry quit weight lifting in the public gym when he saw this cripple exercising with the dumbbells. You can never tell what germs cripples carry behind their ears and under their fingernails. Day and night Harry Bilbo lived in holy worship of Johnny Panic, devout as any priest among censers and sacraments. He had a beauty all his own.

Well, these white-coated tinkerers managed, the lot of them, to talk Harry into turning on the TV himself, and the water faucets, and to opening closet doors, front doors, bar doors. Before they were through with him, he was sitting down on movie-house chairs, and benches all over the Public Garden, and weight lifting every day of the week at the gym in spite of the fact another cripple took to using the rowing machine. At the end of his treatment he came in to shake hands with the Clinic Director. In Harry Bilbo's own words, he was "a changed man." The pure Panic light had left his face. He went out of the office doomed to the crass fate these doctors call health and happiness.

About the time of Harry Bilbo's cure a new idea starts nudging at the bottom of my brain. I find it hard to ignore as those bare feet sticking out of the lumbar puncture room. If I don't want to risk carrying a record book out of the hospital in case I get discovered and fired and have to end my research forever, I can really speed up work by staying in the Clinics Building overnight. I am nowhere near exhausting the clinic's resources and the piddling amount of cases I am able to read in Miss Taylor's brief absences during the day are nothing to what I could get through in a few nights of steady copying. I need to accelerate my work if only to counteract those doctors.

Before I know it, I am putting on my coat at five and saying good-night to Miss Taylor, who usually stays a few minutes' overtime to clear up the day's statistics, and sneaking around the corner into the ladies' room. It is empty. I slip into the patients' john, lock the door from the inside, and wait. For all I know, one of the clinic cleaning ladies may try to knock the door down, thinking some patient's passed out on the seat. My fingers are crossed. About twenty minutes later the door of the lavatory opens and someone limps over the threshold like a chicken favoring a bad leg. It is Miss Taylor, I can tell by the resigned sigh as she meets the jaundiced eye of the lavatory mirror. I hear the click-cluck of various touch-up equipment on the bowl, water sloshing, the scritch of a comb in frizzed hair, and then the door is closing with a slow-hinged wheeze behind her.

I am lucky. When I come out of the ladies' room at six o'clock the corridor lights are off and the fourth-floor hall is as empty as church on Monday. I have my own key to our office; I come in first every morning, so that's no trouble. The typewriters are folded back into the desks, the locks are on the dial phones, all's right with the world.

Outside the window the last of the winter light is fading. Yet I do not forget myself and turn on the overhead bulb. I don't want to be spotted by any hawk-eyed doctor or janitor in the hospital buildings across the little courtyard. The cabinet with the record books is in the windowless passage opening onto the doctors' cubicles, which have windows overlooking the courtyard. I make sure the doors to all the cubicles are shut. Then I switch on the passage light, a sallow twenty-five-watt affair blackening at the top. Better than an altarful of candles to me at this point, though. I didn't think to bring a sandwich. There is an apple in my desk drawer left over from lunch, so I reserve that for whatever pangs I may feel about one o'clock in the morning, and get out my pocket notebook. At home every evening it is my habit to tear out the notebook pages I've written on at the office during the day and pile them up to be copied in my manuscript. In this way I cover my tracks so no one idly picking up my notebook at the office could ever guess the type or scope of my work.

I begin systematically by opening the oldest book on the bottom shelf. The once-blue cover is no-color now, the pages are thumbed and blurry carbons, but I'm humming from foot to topknot: this dream book was spanking new the day I was born. When I really get organized I'll have hot soup in a thermos for the dead-of-winter nights, turkey pies and chocolate éclairs. I'll bring hair curlers and four changes of blouse to work in my biggest handbag on Monday mornings so no one will notice me going downhill in looks and start suspecting unhappy love affairs or pink affiliations or my working on dream books in the clinic four nights a week.

Eleven hours later. I am down to apple core and seeds and in the month of May, 1931, with a private nurse who has just opened a laundry bag in her patient's closet and found five severed heads in it, including her mother's.

A chill air touches the nape of my neck. From where I am sitting cross-legged on the floor in front of the cabinet, the record book heavy on my lap, I notice out of the corner of my eye that the door of the cubicle beside me is letting in a little crack of blue light. Not only along the floor, but up the side of the door too. This is odd since I made sure from the first that all the doors were shut tight. The crack of blue light is widening and my eyes are fastened to two motionless shoes in the doorway, toes pointing toward me.

They are brown leather shoes of a foreign make, with thick elevator soles. Above the shoes are black silk socks through which shows a pallor of flesh. I get as far as the gray pinstriped trouser cuffs.

"Tch, tch," chides an infinitely gentle voice from the cloudy regions above my head. "Such an uncomfortable position! Your legs must be asleep by now. Let me help you up. The sun will be rising shortly."

Two hands slip under my arms from behind and I am raised, wobbly as an unset custard, to my feet, which I cannot feel because my legs are, in fact, asleep. The record book slumps to the floor, pages splayed.

"Stand still a minute." The Clinic Director's voice fans the lobe of my right ear. "Then the circulation will revive."

The blood in my not-there legs starts pinging under a million sewing-machine needles and a vision of the Clinic Director acid-etches itself on my brain. I don't even need to look around: fat pot-belly buttoned into his gray pinstriped waistcoat, woodchuck teeth yellow and buck, every-color eyes behind the thick-lensed glasses quick as minnows.

I clutch my notebook. The last floating timber of the *Titanic*.

What does he know, what does he know?

Everything.

"I know where there is a nice hot bowl of chicken noodle soup." His voice rustles, dust under the bed, mice in straw. His hand welds onto my left upper arm in fatherly love. The record book of all the dreams going on in the city of my birth at my first yawp in this world's air he nudges under the bookcase with a polished toe.

We meet nobody in the dawn-dark hall. Nobody on the chill

stone stair down to the basement corridors where Billy the Record Room Boy cracked his head skipping steps one night on a rush errand.

I begin to double-quickstep so he won't think it's me he's hustling. "You can't fire me," I say calmly. "I quit."

The Clinic Director's laugh wheezes up from his accordion-pleated bottom gut. "We mustn't lose you so soon." His whisper snakes off down the whitewashed basement passages, echoing among the elbow pipes, the wheelchairs and stretchers beached for the night along the steam-stained walls. "Why, we need you more than you know."

We wind and double and my legs keep time with his until we come, somewhere in those barren rat tunnels, to an all-night elevator run by a one-armed Negro. We get on, and the door grinds shut like the door on a cattle car, and we go up and up. It is a freight elevator, crude and clanky, a far cry from the plush passenger lifts I am used to in the Clinics Building.

We get off at an indeterminate floor. The Clinic Director leads me down a bare corridor lit at intervals by socketed bulbs in little wire cages on the ceiling. Locked doors set with screened windows line the hall on either hand. I plan to part company with the Clinic Director at the first red Exit sign, but on our journey there are none. I am in alien territory, coat on the hanger in the office, handbag and money in my top desk drawer, notebook in my hand, and only Johnny Panic to warm me against the ice age outside.

Ahead a light gathers, brightens. The Clinic Director, puffing slightly at the walk, brisk and long, to which he is obviously unaccustomed, propels me around a bend and into a square, brilliantly lit room.

"Here she is."

"The little witch!"

Miss Milleravage hoists her tonnage up from behind the steel desk facing the door.

The walls and the ceiling of the room are riveted metal battleship plates. There are no windows.

From small, barred cells lining the sides and back of the room I see Johnny Panic's top priests staring out at me, arms swaddled behind their backs in the white Ward nightshirts, eyes redder than coals and hungry-hot.

They welcome me with queer croaks and grunts, as if their tongues were locked in their jaws. They have no doubt heard of my work by way of Johnny Panic's grapevine and want to know how his apostles thrive in the world.

I lift my hands to reassure them, holding up my notebook, my voice loud as Johnny Panic's organ with all stops out.

"Peace! I bring to you . . ."

The Book.

"None of that old stuff, sweetie." Miss Milleravage is dancing out at me from behind her desk like a trick elephant.

The Clinic Director closes the door to the room.

The minute Miss Milleravage moves I notice what her hulk has been hiding from view behind the desk—a white cot high as a man's waist with a single sheet stretched over the mattress, spotless and drumskin tight. At the head of the cot is a table on which sits a metal box covered with dials and gauges.

The box seems to be eyeing me, copperhead-ugly, from its coils of electric wires, the latest model in Johnny-Panic-Killers.

I get ready to dodge to one side. When Miss Milleravage grabs, her fat hand comes away with a fist full of nothing. She starts for me again, her smile heavy as dogdays in August.

"None of that. None of that. I'll have that little black book."

Fast as I run around the high white cot, Miss Milleravage is so fast you'd think she wore rollerskates. She grabs and gets. Against her great bulk I beat my fists, and against her whopping milkless breasts, until her hands on my wrists are iron hoops and her breath hushabyes me with a love-stink fouler than Undertaker's Basement.

"My baby, my own baby's come back to me . . ."

"She," says the Clinic Director, sad and stern, "has been making time with Johnny Panic again."

"Naughty naughty."

The white cot is ready. With a terrible gentleness Miss Milleravage takes the watch from my wrist, the rings from my fingers, the hairpins from my hair. She begins to undress me. When I am bare, I am anointed on the temples and robed in sheets virginal as the first snow.

Then, from the four corners of the room and from the door behind me come five false priests in white surgical gowns and masks whose one lifework is to unseat Johnny Panic from his own throne. They extend me full-length on my back on the cot. The crown of wire is placed on my head, the wafer of forgetfulness on my tongue. The masked priests move to their posts and take hold: one of my left leg, one of my right, one of my right arm, one of my left. One behind my head at the metal box where I can't see.

From their cramped niches along the wall, the votaries raise their voices in protest. They begin the devotional chant:

> The only thing to love is Fear itself
> Love of Fear is the beginning of wisdom.
> The only thing to love is Fear itself.
> May Fear and Fear and Fear be
> everywhere.

There is no time for Miss Milleravage or the Clinic Director or the priests to muzzle them.

The signal is given.

The machine betrays them.

At the moment when I think I am most lost the face of Johnny Panic appears in a nimbus of arc lights on the ceiling overhead. I am shaken like a leaf in the teeth of glory. His beard is lightning. Lightning is in his eye. His Word charges and illumines the universe.

The air crackles with his blue-tongued lightning-haloed angels.

His love is the twenty-story leap, the rope at the throat, the knife at the heart.

He forgets not his own.

# ROBERT COOVER
## In Bed One Night

So one night he comes in from using the bathroom takes off his clothes
stretches scratches himself puts on his pajamas yawns sets the alarm
turns down the sheets crawls into bed fumbles for the lightswitch above
him bumps something soft with his elbow which turns out to be a pale
whitehaired lady in a plain gray nightgown lying in bed beside him
*wha—?!* he cries out in alarm and demanding an explanation is told she
has been assigned to his bed by the social security it's the shortage she
says the s's not coming out just right her teeth he sees now in a glass of
water on the nighttable private beds are a luxury the world can no
longer afford she explains adding that she hopes he won't kick during
the night because of her brother who has only one leg is ailing poor
soul and is sleeping at the foot of the bed (this is true he feels him there
sees him knobby old gent in a cloth cap and long underwear one leg
empty pinned up to the rear flap) all of which takes him by surprise and
with a gasp he says so to which the old lady replies in her prim toothless
way that yes yes life in the modern world what there is left of it is not
always easy young man it's what they call the progress of civilized
paradox she's heard about it on the television but at least he still has his
own bed has he not he's after all luckier than most naming no names
(she sighs) even if it is only a three-quarters and a bit tight for five
and—*five!!* he cries rearing up in panic *five*—? and sure enough there
they are two more three in fact how did he miss them before a skinny
oriental huddling down behind the old lady dishwater hands shifty eyes
antiseptic smell quivering taut as a mainspring and on this side just

arriving a heavybellied worker in oily overalls staggering toward the
bed with a fat woman tottering on stiletto heels huge but squeezed
shinily into a tight green dress hair undone eyes wet their faces smeared
with sweat and paint and cockeyed the—look out!—both of them as
they—*crash!*—hit the nighttable send it flying lamp waterglass teeth and
all upsetting the old lady needless to say who goes crawling around on
the splashed bed on her hands and knees looking for the teeth spluttering petulantly through her flabby lips that woman's not allowed here
it's not fair they said five! the worker paying no mind or too drunk to
hear hauling off his overalls kicking them aside his underwear belching
growling pushing the woman toward the bed cracking her big ass
soundly when she hesitates making her yelp with pain not here Duke
not with that old lady watching shut up goddamn you I don't ask for
much the old lady is complaining still scratching about for her dentures
justice that's all a little respect dignity a dress rips the worker blows a
beery fart it's a hard thing growing old but I don't ask for any prizes—
pwitheth she says—and look at that chink Duke look at his goddamn
eyes bug what's he staring at but the worker just grunts irritably and
shoves her roughly onto the bed and onto its erstwhile owner now too
overcome by the well-meant outrages of a world turned to rubble and
mercy even to move ah me! all this order he thinks as the worker
plummets down upon them both like a felled tree and commences to
fumble groggily for the bawling fat woman's seat of bliss (he could
show him where it is but if he doesn't know how to ask politely then
to hell with him) all this desperate husbandry this tender regulation of
woe the whore on him weeping and groaning now ass high and soft
legs flailing believe me says the old lady crankily still on her bony knees
if I don't find my dentures there'll be the dickens to pay I mean it—my
*denthyurth* she says—it ain't fair complains the old man at the foot of
the bed him having a woman all to hisself that ain't square ignore them
Albert says the old lady don't encourage them she's not even supposed
to be here I know my rights insists the old man and gets a foot in the
face for them they's a law—*splut! kaff!*—he squawks disappearing over
the foot of the bed which is now rocking and creaking fearsomely with
the mighty thrashing about of the drunken lovers linked up on top of
what on a different occasion might loosely be thought of as the host
knocking his wind out whap whump oh Duke my god Duke gasp!
Albert—? a sweet stink rising are you all right Albert? and true the
pounding friction wet and massive giving him a certain local pleasure
for all the burden of it but it does not console him what can? sunk as he

is in the dark corruptions of nostalgia dreaming of the good old days get back up here Albert you'll catch your death oh Christ Duke—slop! slap!—kill that—*pant!*—kill that chink Duke break his fucking neck pop his yellow eyes out yes alas those days of confusion profligacy ruthless solitude tears come to his eyes just thinking about them as the old man reappears at the foot crawling hand over hand the pin that was holding up his empty pantleg between his teeth the old lady remonstrating no violence now please the oriental crouching tremulous on the pillow by the headboard with a knife a gentle answer Albert turneth away—screams groans grunts the worker roaring in pain and rage oh my god Duke! but he wipes away the foolish tears angry with his own weakness forget those days they're gone and just as well he lectures himself as a pale woman enters with three runnynosed kids clinging to her limp skirts there's been some mistake but we're awfully tired sir just a little corner—? yes forget those stupid times get some sleep and then tomorrow it's down to the social security for a new bed assignment a pretty lady maybe to hear his case Duke? report the losses tidy up wash the sheets out are you okay? say something Duke and lulled by the heavy rhythms of fucking and weeping the kids wrestling their mother whispering at them to settle down or the nice man will ask them to leave the old lady's gummy scolding he drifts off dreaming of a short queue happy accidents and wondering if he Duke? remembered to switch off the bathroom light *aack!* screw the cap back on the toothpaste *now* what have you done Albert oh no! *thwallowed the pin—?!*

# URSULA K. LE GUIN
## Schrödinger's Cat

As things appear to be coming to some sort of climax, I have withdrawn to this place. It is cooler here, and nothing moves fast.

On the way here I met a married couple who were coming apart. She had pretty well gone to pieces, but he seemed, at first glance, quite hearty. While he was telling me that he had no hormones of any kind, she pulled herself together and, by supporting her head in the crook of her right knee and hopping on the toes of the right foot, approached us shouting, "Well what's *wrong* with a person trying to express themselves?" The left leg, the arms, and the trunk, which had remained lying in the heap, twitched and jerked in sympathy. "Great legs," the husband pointed out, looking at the slim ankle. "My wife has great legs."

A cat has arrived, interrupting my narrative. It is a striped yellow tom with white chest and paws. He has long whiskers and yellow eyes. I never noticed before that cats had whiskers above their eyes; is that normal? There is no way to tell. As he has gone to sleep on my knee, I shall proceed.

Where?

Nowhere, evidently. Yet the impulse to narrate remains. Many things are not worth doing, but almost anything is worth telling. In any case, I have a severe congenital case of *Ethica laboris puritanica*, or Adam's Disease. It is incurable except by total decapitation. I even like to dream when asleep, and to try and recall my dreams: it assures me that I haven't wasted seven or eight hours just lying there. Now here I am, lying, here. Hard at it.

Well, the couple I was telling you about finally broke up. The pieces of him trotted around bouncing and cheeping, like little chicks, but she was finally reduced to nothing but a mass of nerves: rather like fine chicken wire, in fact, but hopelessly tangled.

So I came on, placing one foot carefully in front of the other, and grieving. This grief is with me still. I fear it is part of me, like foot or loin or eye, or may even be myself: for I seem to have no other self, nothing further, nothing that lies outside the borders of grief.

Yet I don't know what I grieve for: my wife? my husband? my children, or myself? I can't remember. Most dreams are forgotten, try as one will to remember. Yet later music strikes the note, and the harmonic rings along the mandolin strings of the mind, and we find tears in our eyes. Some note keeps playing that makes me want to cry; but what for? I am not certain.

The yellow cat, who may have belonged to the couple that broke up, is dreaming. His paws twitch now and then, and once he makes a small, suppressed remark with his mouth shut. I wonder what a cat dreams of, and to whom he was speaking just then. Cats seldom waste words. They are quiet beasts. They keep their counsel, they reflect. They reflect all day, and at night their eyes reflect. Overbred Siamese cats may be as noisy as little dogs, and then people say, "They're talking," but the noise is farther from speech than is the deep silence of the hound or the tabby. All this cat can say is meow, but maybe in his silences he will suggest to me what it is that I have lost, what I am grieving for. I have a feeling that he knows. That's why he came here. Cats look out for Number one.

It was getting awfully hot. I mean, you could touch less and less. The stove burners, for instance. Now I know that stove burners always used to get hot; that was their final cause, they existed in order to get hot. But they began to get hot without having been turned on. Electric units or gas rings, there they'd be when you came into the kitchen for breakfast, all four of them glaring away, the air above them shaking like clear jelly with the heat waves. It did no good to turn them off, because they weren't on in the first place. Besides, the knobs and dials were also hot, uncomfortable to the touch.

Some people tried hard to cool them off. The favorite technique was to turn them on. It worked sometimes, but you could not count on it. Others investigated the phenomenon, tried to get at the root of it, the cause. They were probably the most frightened ones, but man is most human at his most frightened. In the face of the hot stove burners they acted with exemplary coolness. They studied, they observed. They were like the fellow in Michelangelo's *Last Judgment*, who has clapped his hands over his face in horror as the devils drag him down to Hell—but only over one eye. The other eye is busy looking. It's all he can do, but he does it. He observes. Indeed, one wonders if Hell would exist, if he did not look at it. However, neither he, nor the people I am talking about, had enough time left to do much about it. And then finally of course there were the people who did not try to do or think anything about it at all.

When the water came out of the cold-water taps hot one morning, however, even people who had blamed it all on the Democrats began to feel a more profound unease. Before long, forks and pencils and wrenches were too hot to handle without gloves; the cars were really terrible. It was like opening the door of an oven going full blast, to open the door of your car. And by then, other people almost scorched your fingers off. A kiss was like a branding iron. Your child's hair flowed along your hand like fire.

Here, as I said, it is cooler; and, as a matter of fact, this animal is cool. A real cool cat. No wonder it's pleasant to pet his fur. Also he moves slowly, at least for the most part, which is all the slowness one can reasonably expect of a cat. He hasn't that frenetic quality most creatures acquired—all they did was ZAP and gone. They lacked presence. I suppose birds always tended to be that way, but even the hummingbird used to halt for a second in the very center of his metabolic frenzy, and hang, still as a hub, present, above the fuchsias—then gone again, but you knew something was there besides the blurring brightness. But it got so that even robins and pigeons, the heavy impudent birds, were a blur; and as for swallows, they cracked the sound barrier. You knew of swallows only by the small, curved sonic booms that looped about the eaves of old houses in the evening.

Worms shot like subway trains through the dirt of gardens, among the writhing roots of roses.

You could scarcely lay a hand on children, by then: too fast to catch, too hot to hold. They grew up before your eyes.

But then, maybe that's always been true.

I was interrupted by the cat, who woke and said meow once, then jumped down from my lap and leaned against my legs diligently. This is a cat who knows how to get fed. He also knows how to jump. There was a lazy fluidity to his leap, as if gravity affected him less than it does other creatures. As a matter of fact there were some localised cases, just before I left, of the failure of gravity; but this quality in the cat's leap was something quite else. I am not yet in such a state of confusion that I can be alarmed by grace. Indeed, I found it reassuring. While I was opening a can of sardines, a person arrived.

Hearing the knock, I thought it might be the mailman. I miss mail very much, so I hurried to the door and said, "Is it the mail?"

A voice replied, "Yah!" I opened the door. He came in, almost pushing me aside in his haste. He dumped down an enormous knapsack he had been carrying, straightened up, massaged his shoulders, and said, "Wow!"

"How did you get here?"

He stared at me and repeated, "How?"

At this my thoughts concerning human and animal speech recurred to me, and I decided that this was probably not a man, but a small dog. (Large dogs seldom go yah, wow, how, unless it is appropriate to do so.)

"Come on, fella," I coaxed him. "Come, come on, that's a boy, good doggie!" I opened a can of pork and beans for him at once, for he looked half starved. He ate voraciously, gulping and lapping. When it was gone he said "Wow!" several times. I was just about to scratch him behind the ears when he stiffened, his hackles bristling, and growled deep in his throat. He had noticed the cat.

The cat had noticed him some time before, without interest, and was now sitting on a copy of *The Well-Tempered Clavier* washing sardine oil off its whiskers.

"Wow!" the dog, whom I had thought of calling Rover, barked. "Wow! Do you know what that is? *That's Schrödinger's cat!*"

"No it's not, not any more; it's my cat," I said, unreasonably offended.

"Oh, well, Schrödinger's dead, of course, but it's his cat. I've seen hundreds of pictures of it. Erwin Schrödinger, the great physicist, you know. Oh, wow! To think of finding it here!"

The cat looked coldly at him for a moment, and began to wash its left shoulder with negligent energy. An almost religious expression had come into Rover's face. "It was meant," he said in a low, impressive tone. "Yah. It was *meant*. It can't be a mere coincidence. It's too improbable. Me, with the box; you, with the cat; to meet—

here—now." He looked up at me, his eyes shining with happy fervor. "Isn't it wonderful?" he said. "I'll get the box set up right away." And he started to tear open his huge knapsack.

While the cat washed its front paws, Rover unpacked. While the cat washed its tail and belly, regions hard to reach gracefully, Rover put together what he had unpacked, a complex task. When he and the cat finished their operations simultaneously and looked at me, I was impressed. They had come out even, to the very second. Indeed it seemed that something more than chance was involved. I hoped it was not myself.

"What's that?" I asked, pointing to a protuberance on the outside of the box. I did not ask what the box was as it was quite clearly a box.

"The gun," Rover said with excited pride.

"The gun?"

"To shoot the cat."

"To shoot the cat?"

"Or to *not shoot* the cat. Depending on the photon."

"The photon?"

"Yah! It's Schrödinger's great Gedankenexperiment. You see, there's a little emitter here. At Zero Time, five seconds after the lid of the box is closed, it will emit one photon. The photon will strike a half-silvered mirror. The quantum mechanical probability of the photon passing through the mirror is exactly one half, isn't it? So! If the photon passes through, the trigger will be activated and the gun will fire. If the photon is deflected, the trigger will not be activated and the gun will not fire. Now, you put the cat in. The cat is in the box. You close the lid. You go away! You stay away! What happens?" Rover's eyes were bright.

"The cat gets hungry?"

"The cat gets shot—or not shot," he said, seizing my arm, though not, fortunately, in his teeth. "But the gun is silent, perfectly silent. The box is soundproof. There is no way to know whether or not the cat has been shot, until you lift the lid of the box. There is *no* way! Do you see how central this is to the whole of quantum theory? Before Zero Time the whole system, on the quantum level or on our level, is nice and simple. But after Zero Time the whole system can be represented only by a linear combination of two waves. We cannot predict the behavior of the photon, and thus, once it has behaved, we cannot predict the state of the system it has determined. We cannot predict it! God plays dice with the world! So it is beautifully demonstrated that if you desire certainty, any certainty, you must create it yourself!"

"How?"

"By lifting the lid of the box, of course," Rover said, looking at me with sudden disappointment, perhaps a touch of suspicion, like a Baptist who finds he has been talking church matters not to another Baptist as he thought, but a Methodist, or even, God forbid, an Episcopalian. "To find out whether the cat is dead or not."

"Do you mean," I said carefully, "that until you lift the lid of the box, the cat has neither been shot nor not been shot?"

"Yah!" Rover said, radiant with relief, welcoming me back to the fold. "Or maybe, you know, both."

"But why does opening the box and looking reduce the system back to one probability, either live cat or dead cat? Why don't we get included in the system when we lift the lid of the box?"

There was a pause. "How?" Rover barked, distrustfully.

"Well, we would involve ourselves in the system, you see, the superposition of two waves. There's no reason why it should only exist *inside* an open box, is there? So when we came to look, there we would be, you and I, both looking at a live cat, and both looking at a dead cat. You see?"

A dark cloud lowered on Rover's eyes and brow. He barked twice in a subdued, harsh voice, and walked away. With his back turned to me he said in a firm, sad tone, "You must not complicate the issue. It is complicated enough."

"Are you sure?"

He nodded. Turning, he spoke pleadingly. "Listen. It's all we have—the box. Truly it is. The box. And the cat. And they're here. The box, the cat, at last. Put the cat in the box. Will you? Will you let me put the cat in the box?"

"No," I said, shocked.

"Please. Please. Just for a minute. Just for half a minute! Please let me put the cat in the box!"

"Why?"

"I can't stand this terrible uncertainty," he said, and burst into tears.

I stood some while indecisive. Though I felt sorry for the poor son of a bitch, I was about to tell him, gently, No; when a curious thing happened. The cat walked over to the box, sniffed around it, lifted his tail and sprayed a corner to mark his territory, and then lightly, with that marvellous fluid ease, leapt into it. His yellow tail just flicked the edge of the lid as he jumped, and it closed, falling into place with a soft, decisive click.

"The cat is in the box," I said.

"The cat is in the box," Rover repeated in a whisper, falling to his knees. "Oh, wow. Oh, wow. Oh, wow."

There was silence then: deep silence. We both gazed, I afoot, Rover kneeling, at the box. No sound. Nothing happened. Nothing would happen. Nothing would ever happen, until we lifted the lid of the box.

"Like Pandora," I said in a weak whisper. I could not quite recall Pandora's legend. She had let all the plagues and evils out of the box, of course, but there had been something else, too. After all the devils were let loose, something quite different, quite unexpected, had been left. What had it been? Hope? A dead cat? I could not remember.

Impatience welled up in me. I turned on Rover, glaring. He returned the look with expressive brown eyes. You can't tell me dogs haven't got souls.

"Just exactly what are you trying to prove?" I demanded.

"That the cat will be dead, or not dead," he murmured submissively. "Certainty. All I want is certainty. To know for *sure* that God *does* play dice with the world."

I looked at him for a while with fascinated incredulity. "Whether he does, or doesn't," I said, "do you think he's going to leave you a note about it in the box?" I went to the box, and with a rather dramatic gesture, flung the lid back. Rover staggered up from his knees, gasping, to look. The cat was, of course, not there.

Rover neither barked, nor fainted, nor cursed, nor wept. He really took it very well.

"Where is the cat?" he asked at last.

"Where is the box?"

"Here."

"Where's here?"

"Here is now."

"We used to think so," I said, "but really we should use larger boxes."

He gazed about him in mute bewilderment, and did not flinch even when the roof of the house was lifted off just like the lid of a box, letting in the unconscionable, inordinate light of the stars. He had just time to breathe, "Oh, wow!"

I have identified the note that keeps sounding. I checked it on the mandolin before the glue melted. It is the note A, the one that drove the composer Schumann mad. It is a beautiful, clear tone, much clearer now that the stars are visible. I shall miss the cat. I wonder if he found what it was we lost?

I had followed my man here. Everything he did was mysterious to me, and his predilection for the Water Works this November day was no less so. A square, granite building, flat-roofed, with crenelated turrets at the corners, it stood hard by the reservoir on a high plain overlooking the city from the north. There was an abundance of windows through which, however, no light seemed to pass. I saw reflected the sky behind me, a tumultuous thing of billowing shapes of gray tumbling through vaults of pink sunset and with black rain clouds sailing overhead like an armada.

His carriage was in the front yard. His horse pawed the stony ground and swung its head about to look at me.

The reservoir behind the building, five or six city blocks in area, was cratered in an embankment that went up from the ground at an angle suggesting the pyramidal platform of an ancient civilization, Mayan perhaps. On Sundays in warm weather, people came here from the city and climbed the embankment, calling out to one another as they rose to the sight of a squared expanse of water. This day it was his alone. I heard the violent chop, the insistent slap of the tides against the cobblestone.

He stood a ways out in the darkening day; he was studying something upon the water, my black-bearded captain. He held his hat brim. The corner of his long coat took the wind and pressed against his leg.

I was sure he knew of my presence. Indeed, for some days I had sensed from his actions a mad presumption of partnership, as if he

engaged in his enterprises for our mutual benefit. I climbed the
embankment a hundred or so yards to his east and faced into the wind
to see the object of his attention.

It was a toy boat under sail, rising and falling in heavy swells at
alarming heel, disappearing and then reappearing all atumble, water
pouring off her sides.

We watched her for several minutes. She disappeared and rose
and again disappeared. There was a rhythm in this to lull the perception, and some moments passed before I realized, waiting for her rising,
that I waited in vain. I was as struck in the chest with the catastrophe as
if I had stood on some cliff and watched the sea take a sailing vessel.

When I thought to look for my man, he was running across the
wide moat of hardened earth that led to the rear gates of the Water
Works. I followed. Inside the building I felt the chill of entombed air
and I heard the orchestra of water hissing and roaring in its fall. I ran
down a stone corridor and found another that offered passage to the left
or right. I listened. I heard his steps clearly, a metallic rap of heels
echoing from my right. At the end of the dark conduit was a flight of
iron stairs rising circularly about a black steel gear shaft. Around I went,
rising, and reaching the top story, I found the view opening out from a
catwalk over a vast inner pool of roiling water. This hellish churn
pounded up a mineral mist, like a fifth element, in whose sustenance
there grew on the blackened stone face of the far wall a profusion of
moss and slime.

Above me was a skylight of translucent glass. By its dim light I discovered him not five feet from where I stood. He was bent over the rail
with a rapt expression of the most awful intensity. I thought he would
topple, so unaware of himself did he seem in that moment. I found the
sight of him in his passion almost unendurable. So again I looked at
what he was seeing, and there below, in the yellowing rush of spumed
currents and water plunging into its mechanical harness, a small human
body was pressed against the machinery of one of the sluicegates, its
clothing caught as in some hinge, and the child, for it was a miniature
like the ship in the reservoir, went slamming about, first one way and
then the next, as if in mute protest, trembling and shaking and ani-
mating by its revulsion the death that had already overtaken it. Someone
shouted, and after a moment I saw, as if they had separated from the
stone, three uniformed men poised on a lower ledge. They were well
apprised of the situation. They were heaving on a line strung from a
pulley fixed in the far wall, and by this means advancing a towline

attached to the wall below my catwalk where I could not see. But now into view he came, another of the water workers, suspended from a sling by the ankles, his hands outstretched as he waited to be aligned so that he could free the flow of this obstruction.

And then he had him, raised from the water by his shirt, an urchin, anywhere from four to eight I would have said, drowned blue, and then by the ankles and shoes, and so suspended, both, they swung back across the pouring currents rhythmically, like performing aerialists, till they were out of sight below me.

I wondered, perhaps from the practiced quality of their maneuver, if the water workers were not accustomed to such impediments. A few minutes later, in the yard under the darkened sky, I watched my man load the wrapped corpse into his carriage, shut the door smartly, and leap then to the high seat, where he commanded his horse with a great rolling snap of the reins. And off it went, the bright black wheel spokes brought to a blur as the dead child was raced to the city.

The rain had begun. I went back in and felt the oppression of a universe of water, inside and out, over the dead and the living.

The water workers were dividing some treasure among themselves. They wore the dark-blue uniform with the high collar of the city employee, but amended with rough sweaters under the tunics and with trousers tucked into their high boots. It was not an enviable employment here. I could imagine in human lungs the same flora that grew on stone. Their faces were bright and flushed, their blood urged to the skin by the chill and their skin brought to a high glaze by the mist.

They saw me and made a great show of not caring. They broke out the whiskey for their tin cups. There is such a cherishing of ritual too among firemen and gravediggers.

# HARLAN ELLISON
## Shattered Like a Glass Goblin

So it was there, eight months later, that Rudy found her; in that huge and ugly house off Western Avenue in Los Angeles; living with them, *all* of them; not just Jonah, but all of them.

It was November in Los Angeles, near sundown, and unaccountably chill even for the fall in that place always near the sun. He came down the sidewalk and stopped in front of the place. It was gothic hideous, with the grass half-cut and the rusted lawnmower sitting in the middle of an unfinished swath. Grass cut as if a placating gesture to the outraged tenants of the two lanai apartment houses that loomed over that squat structure on either side. (Yet how strange . . . the apartment buildings were taller, the old house hunched down between them, but *it* seemed to dominate *them*. How odd.)

Cardboard covered the upstairs windows.

A baby carriage was overturned on the front walk.

The front door was ornately carved.

Darkness seemed to breathe heavily.

Rudy shifted the duffel bag slightly on his shoulder. He was afraid of the house. He was breathing more heavily as he stood there, and a panic he could never have described tightened the fat muscles on either side of his shoulderblades. He looked up into the corners of the darkening sky, seeking a way out, but he could only go forward. Kristina was in there.

Another girl answered the door.

She looked at him without speaking, her long blonde hair half-obscuring her face; peering out from inside the veil of Clairol and dirt.

When he asked a second time for Kris, she wet her lips in the corners, and a tic made her cheek jump. Rudy set down the duffel bag with a whump. "Kris, please," he said urgently.

The blonde girl turned away and walked back into the dim hallways of the terrible old house. Rudy stood in the open doorway, and suddenly, as if the blonde girl had been a barrier to it, and her departure had released it, he was assaulted, like a smack in the face, by a wall of pungent scent. It was marijuana.

He reflexively inhaled, and his head reeled. He took a step back, into the last inches of sunlight coming over the lanai apartment building, and then it was gone, and he was still buzzing, and moved forward, dragging the duffel bag behind him.

He did not remember closing the front door, but when he looked, some time later, it was closed behind him.

He found Kris on the third floor, lying against the wall of a dark closet, her left hand stroking a faded pink rag rabbit, her right hand at her mouth, the little finger crooked, the thumb-ring roach holder half-obscured as she sucked up the last wonders of the joint. The closet held an infinitude of odors—dirty sweat socks as pungent as stew, fleece jackets on which the rain had dried to mildew, a mop gracious with its scent of old dust hardened to dirt, the overriding weed smell of what she had been at for no one knew how long—and it held her. As pretty as pretty could be.

"Kris?"

Slowly, her head came up, and she saw him. Much later, she tracked and focused and she began to cry. "Go away."

In the limpid silences of the whispering house, back and above him in the darkness, Rudy heard the sudden sound of leather wings beating furiously for a second, then nothing.

Rudy crouched down beside her, his heart grown twice its size in his chest. He wanted so desperately to reach her, to talk to her. "Kris . . . please . . ." She turned her head away, and with the hand that had been stroking the rabbit she slapped at him awkwardly, missing him.

For an instant, Rudy could have sworn he heard the sound of someone counting heavy gold pieces, somewhere off to his right, down a passageway of the third floor. But when he half-turned, and looked out through the closet door, and tried to focus his hearing on it, there was no sound to home in on.

Kris was trying to crawl back farther into the closet. She was trying to smile.

He turned back; on hands and knees he moved into the closet after her.

"The rabbit," she said, languorously. "You're crushing the rabbit." He looked down, his right knee was lying on the soft matted-fur head of the pink rabbit. He pulled it out from under his knee and threw it into a corner of the closet. She looked at him with disgust. "You haven't changed, Rudy. Go away."

"I'm outta the army, Kris," Rudy said gently. "They let me out on a medical. I want you to come back, Kris, please."

She would not listen, but pulled herself away from him, deep into the closet, and closed her eyes. He moved his lips several times, as though trying to recall words he had already spoken, but there was no sound, and he lit a cigarette, and sat in the open doorway of the closet, smoking and waiting for her to come back to him. He had waited eight months for her to come back to him, since he had been inducted and she had written him telling him, *Rudy, I'm going to live with Jonah at The Hill.*

There was the sound of something very tiny, lurking in the infinitely black shadow where the top step of the stairs from the second floor met the landing. It giggled in a glass harpsichord trilling. Rudy knew it was giggling at *him*, but he could discern no movement from that corner.

Kris opened her eyes and stared at him with distaste. "Why did you come here?"

"Because we're gonna be married."

"Get out of here."

"I love you, Kris. Please."

She kicked out at him. It didn't hurt, but it was meant to. He backed out of the closet slowly.

Jonah was down in the living room. The blonde girl who had answered the door was trying to get his pants off him. He kept shaking his head no, and trying to fend her off with a weak-wristed hand. The record player under the brick-and-board bookshelves was playing Simon & Garfunkel, "The Big Bright Green Pleasure Machine."

"Melting," Jonah said gently. "Melting," and he pointed toward the big, foggy mirror over the fireplace mantel. The fireplace was crammed with unburned wax milk cartons, candy bar wrappers, newspapers from the underground press, and kitty litter. The mirror was dim and chill. *"Melting!"* Jonah yelled suddenly, covering his eyes.

"Oh shit!" the blonde girl said, and threw him down, giving up at last. She came toward Rudy.

"What's wrong with him?" Rudy asked.

"He's freaking out again. Christ, what a drag he can be."

"Yeah, but what's *happening* to him?"

She shrugged. "He sees his face melting, that's what he says."

"Is he on marijuana?"

The blonde girl looked at him with sudden distrust. "Mari—? Hey, who *are* you?"

"I'm a friend of Kris's."

The blonde girl assayed him for a moment more, then by the way her shoulders dropped and her posture relaxed, she accepted him. "I thought you might've just walked in, you know, maybe the Laws. You know?"

There was a Middle Earth poster on the wall behind her, with its brightness faded in a long straight swath where the sun caught it every morning. He looked around uneasily. He didn't know what to do.

"I was supposed to marry Kris. Eight months ago," he said.

"You want to fuck?" asked the blonde girl. "When Jonah trips he turns off. I been drinking Coca-Cola all morning and all day, and I'm really horny."

Another record dropped onto the turntable and Stevie Wonder blew hard into his harmonica and started singing, "I Was Born to Love Her."

"I was engaged to Kris," Rudy said, feeling sad. "We was going to be married when I got out of basic. But she decided to come over here with Jonah, and I didn't want to push her. So I waited eight months, but I'm out of the army now."

"Well, *do* you or *don't* you?"

Under the dining room table. She put a satin pillow under her. It said: *Souvenir of Niagara Falls, New York.*

When he went back into the living room, Jonah was sitting up on the sofa, reading Hesse's *Magister Ludi.*

"Jonah?" Rudy said. Jonah looked up. It took him a while to recognize Rudy.

When he did, he patted the sofa beside him, and Rudy came and sat down.

"Hey, Rudy, where y'been?"

"I've been in the army."

"Wow."

"Yeah, it was awful."

"You out now? I mean for good?"

Rudy nodded. "Uh-huh. Medical."

"Hey, that's good."

They sat quietly for a while. Jonah started to nod, and then said to himself, "You're not very tired."

Rudy said, "Jonah, hey listen, what's the story with Kris? You know, we was supposed to get married about eight months ago."

"She's around someplace," Jonah answered.

Out of the kitchen, through the dining room where the blonde girl lay sleeping under the table, came the sound of something wild, tearing at meat. It went on for a long time, but Rudy was looking out the front window, the big bay window. There was a man in a dark gray suit standing talking to two policemen on the sidewalk at the edge of the front walk leading up to the front door. He was pointing at the big, old house.

"Jonah, can Kris come away now?"

Jonah looked angry. "Hey, listen, man, nobody's *keeping* her here. She's been grooving with all of us and she likes it. Go ask her. Christ, don't bug *me!*"

The two cops were walking up to the front door.

Rudy got up and went to answer the doorbell.

They smiled at him when they saw his uniform.

"May I help you?" Rudy asked them.

The first cop said, "Do you live here?"

"Yes," said Rudy. "My name is Rudolph Boekel. May I help you?"

"We'd like to come inside and talk to you."

"Do you have a search warrant?"

"We don't want to search, we only want to talk to you. Are you in the army?"

"Just discharged. I came home to see my family."

"Can we come in?"

"No, sir."

The second cop looked troubled. "Is this the place they call 'The Hill'?"

"Who?" Rudy asked, looking perplexed.

"Well, the neighbors said this was 'The Hill' and there were some pretty wild parties going on here."

"Do you hear any partying?"

The cops looked at each other. Rudy added, "It's always very quiet here. My mother is dying of cancer of the stomach."

They let Rudy move in, because he was able to talk to people who came to the door from the outside. Aside from Rudy, who went out to get food, and the weekly trips to the unemployment line, no one left The Hill. It was usually very quiet.

Except sometimes there was a sound of growling in the back hall leading up to what had been a maid's room; and the splashing from the basement, the sound of wet things on bricks.

It was a self-contained little universe, bordered on the north by acid and mescaline, on the south by pot and peyote, on the east by speed and redballs, on the west by downers and amphetamines. There were eleven people living in The Hill. Eleven, and Rudy.

He walked through the halls, and sometimes found Kris, who would not talk to him, save once, when she asked him if he'd ever been heavy behind *anything* except love. He didn't know what to answer her, so he only said, "Please," and she called him a square and walked off toward the stairway leading to the dormered attic.

Rudy had heard squeaking from the attic. It had sounded to him like the shrieking of mice being torn to pieces. There were cats in the house.

He did not know why he was there, except that he didn't understand why *she* wanted to stay. His head always buzzed and he sometimes felt that if he just said the right thing, the right way, Kris would come away with him. He began to dislike the light. It hurt his eyes.

No one talked to anyone else very much. There was always a struggle to keep high, to keep the *group high* as elevated as possible. In that way they cared for each other.

And Rudy became their one link with the outside. He had written to someone—his parents, a friend, a bank, someone—and now there was money coming in. Not much, but enough to keep the food stocked, and the rent paid. But he insisted Kris be nice to him.

They all made her be nice to him, and she slept with him in the little room on the second floor where Rudy had put his newspapers and his duffel bag. He lay there most of the day, when he was not out on errands for The Hill, and he read the smaller items about train wrecks and molestations in the suburbs. And Kris came to him and they made love of a sort.

One night she convinced him he should "make it, heavy behind acid" and he swallowed fifteen hundred mikes cut with Methedrine, in two big gel caps, and she was stretched out like taffy for six miles. He was a fine copper wire charged with electricity, and he pierced her flesh. She wriggled with the current that flowed through him, and became softer yet. He sank down through the softness, and carefully observed the intricate wood-grain effect her teardrops made as they rose in the mist around him. He was down-drifting slowly, turning and turning, held by a whisper of blue that came out of his body like a spiderweb. The sound of her breathing in the moist crystal pillared cavity that went down and down was the sound of the very walls themselves, and when he touched them with his warm metal fingertips she drew in breath heavily, forcing the air up around him as he sank down, twisting slowly in a veil of musky looseness.

There was an insistent pulsing growing somewhere below him, and he was afraid of it as he descended, the high pitched whining of something threatening to shatter. He felt panic. Panic gripped him, flailed at him, his throat constricted, he tried to grasp the veil and it tore away in his hands; then he was falling, faster now, much faster, and *afraid!*

Violet explosions all around him and the shrieking of something that wanted him, that was seeking him, pulsing deeply in the throat of an animal he could not name, and he heard her shouting, heard her wail and pitch beneath him and a terrible crushing feeling in him . . .

And then there was silence.

That lasted for a moment.

And then there was soft music that demanded nothing but inattention. So they lay there, fitted together, in the heat of the tiny room, and they slept for some hours.

After that, Rudy seldom went out into the light. He did the shopping at night, wearing shades. He emptied the garbage at night, and he swept down the front walk, and did the front lawn with scissors because the lawnmower would have annoyed the residents of the lanai apartments (who no longer complained, because there was seldom a sound from The Hill).

He began to realize he had not seen some of the eleven young people who lived in The Hill for a long time. But the sounds from above and below and around him in the house grew more frequent.

Rudy's clothes were too large for him now. He wore only underpants. His hands and feet hurt. The knuckles of his fingers were larger, from cracking them, and they were always an angry crimson.

His head always buzzed. The thin perpetual odor of pot had saturated into the wood walls and the rafters. He had an itch on the outside of his ears he could not quell. He read newspapers all the time, old newspapers whose items were embedded in his memory. He remembered a job he had once held as a garage mechanic, but that seemed a very long time ago. When they cut off the electricity in The Hill, it didn't bother Rudy, because he preferred the dark. But he went to tell the eleven.

He could not find them.

They were all gone. Even Kris, who should have been there somewhere.

He heard the moist sounds from the basement and went down with fur and silence into the darkness. The basement had been flooded. One of the eleven was there. His name was Teddy. He was attached to the slime-coated upper wall of the basement, hanging close to the stone, pulsing softly and giving off a thin purple light, purple as a bruise. He dropped a rubbery arm into the water, and let it hang there, moving idly with the tideless tide. Then something came near it, and he made a *sharp* movement, and brought the thing up still writhing in his rubbery grip, and inched it along the wall to a dark, moist spot on his upper surface, near the veins that covered its length, and pushed the thing at the dark-blood spot, where it shrieked with a terrible sound, and went in and there was a sucking noise, then a swallowing sound.

Rudy went back upstairs. On the first floor he found the one who was the blonde girl, whose name was Adrianne. She lay out thin and white as a tablecloth on the dining room table as three of the others he had not seen in a very long while put their teeth into her, and through their hollow sharp teeth they drank up the yellow fluid from the bloated pus-pockets that had been her breasts and her buttocks. Their faces were very white and their eyes were like soot-smudges.

Climbing to the second floor, Rudy was almost knocked down by the passage of something that had been Victor, flying on heavily ribbed leather wings. It carried a cat in its jaws.

He saw the thing on the stairs that sounded as though it was counting heavy gold pieces. It was not counting heavy gold pieces. Rudy could not look at it; it made him feel sick.

He found Kris in the attic, in a corner breaking the skull and sucking out the moist brains of a thing that giggled like a harpsichord.

"Kris, we have to go away," he told her. She reached out and touched him, snapping her long, pointed, dirty fingernails against him. He rang like crystal.

In the rafters of the attic Jonah crouched, gargoyled and sleeping. There was a green stain on his jaws, and something stringy in his claws.

"Kris, please," he said urgently.

His head buzzed.

His ears itched.

Kris sucked out the last of the mellow good things in the skull of the silent little creature, and scraped idly at the flaccid body with hairy hands. She settled back on her haunches, and her long, hairy muzzle came up.

Rudy scuttled away.

He ran loping, his knuckles brushing the attic floor as he scampered for safety. Behind him, Kris was growling. He got down to the second floor and then to the first, and tried to climb up on the Morris chair to the mantel, so he could see himself in the mirror, by the light of the moon, through the fly-blown window. But Naomi was on the window, lapping up the flies with her tongue.

He climbed with desperation, wanting to see himself. And when he stood before the mirror, he saw that he was transparent, that there was nothing inside him, that his ears had grown pointed and had hair on their tips; his eyes were as huge as a tarsier's and the reflected light hurt him.

Then he heard the growling behind and below him.

The little glass goblin turned, and the werewolf rose up on its hind legs and touched him till he rang like fine crystal.

And the werewolf said with very little concern, "Have you ever grooved heavy behind *anything* except love?"

"Please!" the little glass goblin begged, just as the great hairy paw slapped him into a million coruscating rainbow fragments all expanding consciously into the tight little enclosed universe that was The Hill, all buzzing highly contacted and tingling off into a darkness that began to seep out through the silent wooden walls . . .

# DON DeLILLO
## Human Moments in World War III

A note about Vollmer. He no longer describes the earth as a library globe or a map that has come alive, as a cosmic eye staring into deep space. This last was his most ambitious fling at imagery. The war has changed the way he sees the earth. The earth is land and water, the dwelling place of mortal men, in elevated dictionary terms. He doesn't see it anymore (storm-spiraled, sea-bright, breathing heat and haze and color) as an occasion for picturesque language, for easeful play or speculation.

At two hundred and twenty kilometers we see ship wakes and the larger airports. Icebergs, lightning bolts, sand dunes. I point out lava flows and cold-core eddies. That silver ribbon off the Irish coast, I tell him, is an oil slick.

This is my third orbital mission, Vollmer's first. He is an engineering genius, a communications and weapons genius, and maybe other kinds of genius as well. As mission specialist I'm content to be in charge. (The word "specialist," in the peculiar usage of Colorado Command, refers here to someone who does not specialize.) Our spacecraft is designed primarily to gather intelligence. The refinement of the quantum burn technique enables us to make frequent adjustments of orbit without firing rockets every time. We swing out into high wide trajectories, the whole earth as our psychic light, to inspect unmanned and possibly hostile satellites. We orbit tightly, snugly, take intimate looks at surface activities in untraveled places.

The banning of nuclear weapons has made the world safe for war.

I try not to think big thoughts or submit to rambling abstractions. But the urge sometimes comes over me. Earth orbit puts men into philosophical temper. How can we help it? We see the planet complete, we have a privileged vista. In our attempts to be equal to the experience, we tend to meditate importantly on subjects like the human condition. It makes a man feel *universal*, floating over the continents, seeing the rim of the world, a line as clear as a compass arc, knowing it is just a turning of the bend to Atlantic twilight, to sediment plumes and kelp beds, an island chain glowing in the dusky sea.

I tell myself it is only scenery. I want to think of our life here as ordinary, as a housekeeping arrangement, an unlikely but workable setup caused by a housing shortage or spring floods in the valley.

Vollmer does the systems checklist and goes to his hammock to rest. He is twenty-three years old, a boy with a longish head and close-cropped hair. He talks about northern Minnesota as he removes the objects in his personal preference kit, placing them on an adjacent Velcro surface for tender inspection. I have a 1901 silver dollar in my personal preference kit. Little else of note. Vollmer has graduation pictures, bottle caps, small stones from his backyard. I don't know whether he chose these items himself or whether they were pressed on him by parents who feared that his life in space would be lacking in human moments.

Our hammocks are human moments, I suppose, although I don't know whether Colorado Command planned it that way. We eat hot dogs and almond crunch bars and apply lip balm as part of the presleep checklist. We wear slippers at the firing panel. Vollmer's football jersey is a human moment. Outsized, purple and white, of polyester mesh, bearing the number 79, a big man's number, a prime of no particular distinction, it makes him look stoop-shouldered, abnormally long-framed.

"I still get depressed on Sundays," he says.

"Do we have Sundays here?"

"No, but they have them there and I still feel them. I always know when it's Sunday."

"Why do you get depressed?"

"The slowness of Sundays. Something about the glare, the smell of warm grass, the church service, the relatives visiting in nice clothes. The whole day kind of lasts forever."

"I didn't like Sundays either."

"They were slow but not lazy-slow. They were long and hot, or long and cold. In summer my grandmother made lemonade. There was a routine. The whole day was kind of set up beforehand and the routine almost never changed. Orbital routine is different. It's satisfying. It gives our time a shape and substance. Those Sundays were shapeless despite the fact you knew what was coming, who was coming, what we'd all say. You knew the first words out of the mouth of each person before anyone spoke. I was the only kid in the group. People were happy to see me. I used to want to hide."

"What's wrong with lemonade?" I ask.

A battle management satellite, unmanned, reports high-energy laser activity in orbital sector Dolores. We take out our laser kits and study them for half an hour. The beaming procedure is complex and because the panel operates on joint control only we must rehearse the sets of established measures with the utmost care.

A note about the earth. The earth is the preserve of day and night. It contains a sane and balanced variation, a natural waking and sleeping, or so it seems to someone deprived of this tidal effect.

This is why Vollmer's remark about Sundays in Minnesota struck me as interesting. He still feels, or claims he feels, or thinks he feels, that inherently earthbound rhythm.

To men at this remove, it is as though things exist in their particular physical form in order to reveal the hidden simplicity of some powerful mathematical truth. The earth reveals to us the simple awesome beauty of day and night. It is there to contain and incorporate these conceptual events.

Vollmer in his shorts and suction clogs resembles a high-school swimmer, all but hairless, an unfinished man not aware he is open to cruel scrutiny, not aware he is without devices, standing with arms folded in a place of echoing voices and chlorine fumes. There is something stupid in the sound of his voice. It is too direct, a deep voice from high in the mouth, well back in the mouth, slightly insistent, a little loud. Vollmer has never said a stupid thing in my presence. It is just his voice that is stupid, a grave and naked bass, a voice without inflection or breath.

We are not cramped here. The flight deck and crew quarters are thoughtfully designed. Food is fair to good. There are books, video-cassettes, news and music. We do the manual checklists, the oral checklists, the simulated firings with no sign of boredom or carelessness. If anything, we are getting better at our tasks all the time. The only danger is conversation.

I try to keep our conversations on an everyday plane. I make it a point to talk about small things, routine things. This makes sense to me. It seems a sound tactic, under the circumstances, to restrict our talk to familiar topics, minor matters. I want to build a structure of the commonplace. But Vollmer has a tendency to bring up enormous subjects. He wants to talk about war and the weapons of war. He wants to discuss global strategies, global aggressions. I tell him now that he has stopped describing the earth as a cosmic eye, he wants to see it as a game board or computer model. He looks at me plain-faced and tries to get me in a theoretical argument: selection space-based attacks versus long drawn-out well-modulated land-sea-air engagements. He quotes experts, mentions sources. What am I supposed to say? He will suggest that people are disappointed in the war. The war is dragging into its third week. There is a sense in which it is worn out, played out. He gathers this from the news broadcasts we periodically receive. Something in the announcer's voice hints at a let-down, a fatigue, a faint bitterness about—*something*. Vollmer is probably right about this. I've heard it myself in the tone of the broadcaster's voice, in the voice of Colorado Command, despite the fact that our news is censored, that they are not telling us things they feel we shouldn't know, in our special situation, our exposed and sensitive position. In his direct and stupid-sounding and uncannily perceptive way, young Vollmer says that people are not enjoying this war to the same extent that people have always enjoyed and nourished themselves on war, as a heightening, a periodic intensity. What I object to in Vollmer is that he often shares my deep-reaching and most reluctantly held convictions. Coming from that mild face, in that earnest resonant run-on voice, these ideas unnerve and worry me as they never do when they remain unspoken. Vollmer's candor exposes something painful.

It is not too early in the war to discern nostalgic references to earlier wars. All wars refer back. Ships, planes, entire operations are named after ancient battles, simpler weapons, what we perceive as conflicts of nobler intent. This recon-interceptor is called Tomahawk II. When I sit at the firing panel I look at a photograph of Vollmer's granddad when he was a young man in sagging khakis and a shallow helmet, standing in a bare field, a rifle strapped to his shoulder. This is a human moment and it reminds me that war, among other things, is a form of longing.

We dock with the command station, take on food, exchange videocassettes. The war is going well, they tell us, although it isn't likely they know much more than we do.

Then we separate.

The maneuver is flawless and I am feeling happy and satisfied, having resumed human contact with the nearest form of the outside world, having traded quips and manly insults, traded voices, traded news and rumors—buzzes, rumbles, scuttlebutt. We stow our supplies of broccoli and apple cider and fruit cocktail and butterscotch pudding. I feel a homey emotion, putting away the colorfully packaged goods, a sensation of prosperous well-being, the consumer's solid comfort.

Vollmer's T-shirt bears the word *Inscription*.

"People had hoped to be caught up in something bigger than themselves," he says. "They thought it would be a shared crisis. They could feel a sense of shared purpose, shared destiny. Like a snowstorm that blankets a large city—but lasting months, lasting years, carrying everyone along, creating fellow-feeling where there was only suspicion and fear. Strangers talking to each other, meals by candlelight when the power fails. The war would ennoble everything we say and do. What was impersonal would become personal. What was solitary would be shared. But what happens when the sense of shared crisis begins to dwindle much sooner than anyone expected? We begin to think the feeling lasts longer in snowstorms."

A note about selective noise. Forty-eight hours ago I was monitoring data on the mission console when a voice broke in on my report to Colorado Command. The voice was unenhanced, heavy with static. I checked my headset, checked the switches and lights. Seconds later the command signal resumed and I heard our flight dynamics officer ask me to switch to the redundant sense frequencer. I did this but it only caused the weak voice to return, a voice that carried with it a strange and unspecifiable poignancy. I seemed somehow to recognize it. I don't mean I knew who was speaking. It was the tone I recognized, the touching quality of some half-remembered and tender event, even through the static, the sonic mist.

In any case, Colorado Command resumed transmission in a matter of seconds.

"We have a deviate, Tomahawk."

"We copy. There's a voice."

"We have gross oscillation here."

"There's some interference. I have gone redundant but I'm not sure it's helping."

"We are clearing an outframe to locate source."

"Thank you, Colorado."

"It is probably just selective noise. You are negative red on the step-function quad."

"It was a voice," I told them.

"We have just received an affirm on selective noise."

"I could hear words, in English."

"We copy selective noise."

"Someone was talking, Colorado."

"What do you think selective noise is?"

"I don't know what it is."

"You are getting a spill from one of the unmanneds."

"If it's an unmanned, how could it be sending a voice?"

"It is not a voice as such, Tomahawk. It is selective noise. We have some real firm telemetry on that."

"It sounded like a voice."

"It is supposed to sound like a voice. But it is not a voice as such. It is enhanced."

"It sounded unenhanced. It sounded human in all sorts of ways."

"It is signals and they are spilling from geosynchronous orbit. This is your deviate. You are getting voice codes from twenty-two thousand miles. It is basically a weather report. We will correct, Tomahawk. In the meantime, advise you stay redundant."

About ten hours later Vollmer heard the voice. Then he heard two or three other voices. They were people speaking, people in conversation. He gestured to me as he listened, pointed to the headset, then raised his shoulders, held his hands apart to indicate surprise and bafflement. In the swarming noise (as he said later), it wasn't easy to get the drift of what people were saying. The static was frequent, the references were somewhat elusive, but Vollmer mentioned how intensely affecting these voices were, even when the signals were at their weakest. One thing he did know: it wasn't selective noise. A quality of purest, sweetest sadness issued from remote space. He wasn't sure but he thought there was also a background noise integral to the conversation. Laughter. The sound of people laughing.

In other transmissions we've been able to recognize theme music, an announcer's introduction, wisecracks and bursts of applause, commercials for products whose long-lost brand names evoke the golden antiquity of great cities buried in sand and river silt.

Somehow we are picking up signals from radio programs of forty, fifty, sixty years ago.

Our current task is to collect imagery data on troop deployment. Vollmer surrounds his Hasselblad, engrossed in some microadjustment. There is a seaward bulge of stratocumulus. Sunglint and littoral drift. I see blooms of plankton in a blue of such Persian richness it seems as animal rapture, a color-change to express some form of intuitive delight. As the surface features unfurl, I list them aloud by name. It is the only game I play in space, reciting the earth-names, the nomenclature of contour and structure. Glacial scour, moraine debris. Shatter-coning at the edge of a multi-ring impact site. A resurgent caldera, a mass of castellated rimrock. Over the sand seas now. Parabolic dunes, star dunes, straight dunes with radial crests. The emptier the land, the more luminous and precise the names for its features. Vollmer says the thing science does best is name the features of the world.

He has degrees in science and technology. He was a scholarship winner, an honors student, a research assistant. He ran science projects, read technical papers in the deep-pitched earnest voice that rolls off the roof of his mouth. As mission specialist (generalist), I sometimes resent his nonscientific perceptions, the glimmerings of maturity and balanced judgment. I am beginning to feel slightly preempted. I want him to stick to systems, onboard guidance, data parameters. His human insights make me nervous.

"I'm happy," he says.

These words are delivered with matter-of-fact finality and the simple statement affects me powerfully. It frightens me in fact. What does he mean he's happy? Isn't happiness totally outside our frame of reference? How can he think it is possible to be happy here? I want to say to him, "This is just a housekeeping arrangement, a series of more or less routine tasks. Attend to your tasks, do your testing, run through your checklists." I want to say, "Forget the measure of our vision, the sweep of things, the war itself, the terrible death. Forget the over-

arching night, the stars as static points, as mathematical fields. Forget
the cosmic solitude, the upwelling awe and dread."

I want to say, "Happiness is not a fact of this experience, at least
not to the extent that one is bold enough to speak of it."

Laser technology contains a core of foreboding and myth. It is a clean
sort of lethal package we are dealing with, a well-behaved beam of
photons, an engineered coherence, but we approach the weapon with
our minds full of ancient warnings and fears. (There ought to be a term
for this ironic condition: primitive fear of the weapons we are advanced
enough to design and produce.) Maybe this is why the project man-
agers were ordered to work out a firing procedure that depends on the
coordinated actions of two men—two temperaments, two souls—
operating the controls together. Fear of the power of light, the pure
stuff of the universe.

A single dark mind in a moment of inspiration might think it lib-
erating to fling a concentrated beam at some lumbering humpbacked
Boeing making its commercial rounds at thirty thousand feet.

Vollmer and I approach the firing panel. The panel is designed in
such a way that the joint operators must sit back to back. The reason
for this, although Colorado Command never specifically said so, is to
keep us from seeing each other's face. Colorado wants to be sure that
weapons personnel in particular are not influenced by each other's tics
and perturbations. We are back to back, therefore, harnessed in our
seats, ready to begin. Vollmer in his purple and white jersey, his fleeced
pad-abouts.

This is only a test.

I start the playback. At the sound of a prerecorded voice command, we each insert a modal key in its proper slot. Together we count
down from five and then turn the keys one-quarter left. This puts the
system in what is called an open-minded mode. We count down from
three. The enhanced voice says, *You are open-minded now.*

Vollmer speaks into his voiceprint analyzer.

"This is code B for bluegrass. Request voice identity clearance."

We count down from five and then speak into our voiceprint
analyzers. We say whatever comes into our heads. The point is simply
to produce a voiceprint that matches the print in the memory bank.
This ensures that the men at the panel are the same men authorized to
be there when the system is in an open-minded mode.

This is what comes into my head: "I am standing at the corner of

Fourth and Main, where thousands are dead of unknown causes, their scorched bodies piled in the street."

We count down from three. The enhanced voice says, *You are cleared to proceed to lock-in position.*

We turn our modal keys half right. I activate the logic chip and study the numbers on my screen. Vollmer disengages voiceprint and puts us in voice circuit rapport with the onboard computer's sensing mesh. We count down from five. The enhanced voice says, *You are locked in now.*

"Random factor seven," I say. "Problem seven. Solution seven."

Vollmer says, "Give me an acronym."

"BROWN, for Bearing Radius Oh White Nine."

My color-spec lights up brown. The numbers on my display screen read 2, 18, 15, 23, 14. These are the alphanumeric values of the letters in the acronym BROWN as they appear in unit succession.

The logic-gate opens. The enhanced voice says, *You are logical now.*

As we move from one step to the next, as the colors, numbers, characters, lights and auditory signals indicate that we are proceeding correctly, a growing satisfaction passes through me—the pleasure of elite and secret skills, a life in which every breath is governed by specific rules, by patterns, codes, controls. I try to keep the results of the operation out of my mind, the whole point of it, the outcome of these sequences of precise and esoteric steps. But often I fail. I let the image in, I think the thought, I even say the word at times. This is confusing, of course. I feel tricked. My pleasure feels betrayed, as if it had a life of its own, a childlike or intelligent-animal existence independent of the man at the firing panel.

We count down from five. Vollmer releases the lever that unwinds the systems-purging disc. My pulse marker shows green at three-second intervals. We count down from three. We turn the modal keys three-quarters right. I activate the beam sequencer. We turn the keys one-quarter right. We count down from three. Bluegrass music plays over the squawk box. The enhanced voice says, *You are moded to fire now.*

We study our world map kits.

"Don't you sometimes feel a power in you?" Vollmer says. "An extreme state of good health, sort of. An *arrogant* healthiness. That's it. You are feeling so good you begin thinking you're a little superior to other people. A kind of life-strength. An optimism about yourself that you generate almost at the expense of others. Don't you sometimes feel this?"

(Yes, as a matter of fact.)

"There's probably a German word for it. But the point I want to make is that this powerful feeling is so—I don't know—*delicate.* That's it. One day you feel it, the next day you are suddenly puny and doomed. A single little thing goes wrong, you feel doomed, you feel utterly weak and defeated and unable to act powerfully or even sensibly. Everyone else is lucky, you are unlucky, hapless, sad, ineffectual and doomed."

(Yes, yes.)

By chance we are over the Missouri River now, looking toward the Red Lakes of Minnesota. I watch Vollmer go through his map kit, trying to match the two worlds. This is a deep and mysterious happiness, to confirm the accuracy of a map. He seems immensely satisfied. He keeps saying, *"That's it, that's it."*

Vollmer talks about childhood. In orbit he has begun to think about his early years for the first time. He is surprised at the power of these memories. As he speaks he keeps his head turned to the window. Minnesota is a human moment. Upper Red Lake, Lower Red Lake. He clearly feels he can see himself there.

"Kids don't take walks," he says. "They don't sunbathe or sit on the porch."

He seems to be saying that children's lives are too well-supplied to accommodate the spells of reinforced being that the rest of us depend on. A deft enough thought but not to be pursued. It is time to prepare for a quantum burn.

We listen to the old radio shows. Light flares and spreads across the blue-banded edge, sunrise, sunset, the urban grids in shadow. A man and woman trade well-timed remarks, light, pointed, bantering. There is a sweetness in the tenor voice of the young man singing, a simple vigor that time and distance and random noise have enveloped in eloquence and yearning. Every sound, every lilt of strings has this veneer of age. Vollmer says he remembers these programs, although of course he has never heard them before. What odd happenstance, what flourish or grace of the laws of physics, enables us to pick up these signals? Traveled voices, chambered and dense. At times they have the detached and surreal quality of aural hallucination, voices in attic rooms, the complaints of dead relatives. But the sound effects are full of urgency and verve. Cars turn dangerous corners, crisp gunfire fills the night. It was, it is, wartime. Wartime for Duz and Grape-Nuts Flakes. Comedians make fun of the way the enemy talks. We hear hysterical mock German, moonshine Japanese. The cities are in light, the listening millions, fed, met comfortably in drowsy rooms, at war, as the night comes softly down. Vollmer says he recalls specific moments, the comic inflections, the announcer's fat-man laughter. He recalls individual voices rising from the laughter of the studio audience, the cackle of a St. Louis businessman, the brassy wail of a high-shouldered blonde, just arrived in California, where women wear their hair this year in aromatic bales.

Vollmer drifts across the wardroom, upside-down, eating an almond crunch.

He sometimes floats free of his hammock, sleeping in a fetal crouch, bumping into walls, adhering to a corner of the ceiling grid.

"Give me a minute to think of the name," he says in his sleep.

He says he dreams of vertical spaces from which he looks, as a boy, at—*something*. My dreams are the heavy kind, the kind that are hard to wake from, to rise out of. They are strong enough to pull me back down, dense enough to leave me with a heavy head, a drugged and bloated feeling. There are episodes of faceless gratification, vaguely disturbing.

"It's almost unbelievable when you think of it, how they live there in all that ice and sand and mountainous wilderness. Look at it," he says. "Huge barren deserts, huge oceans. How do they endure all those terrible things? The floods alone. The earthquakes alone make it crazy to live there. Look at those fault systems. They're so big, there's so many of them. The volcanic eruptions alone. What could be more frightening than a volcanic eruption? How do they endure avalanches, year after year, with numbing regularity? It's hard to believe people live there. The floods alone. You can see whole huge discolored areas, all flooded out, washed out. How do they survive, where do they go? Look at the cloud buildups. Look at that swirling storm center. What about the people who live in the path of a storm like that? It must be packing incredible winds. The lightning alone. People exposed on beaches, near trees and telephone poles. Look at the cities with their spangled lights spreading in all directions. Try to imagine the crime and violence. Look at the smoke pall hanging low. What does that mean in terms of respiratory disorders? It's crazy. Who would live there? The deserts, how they encroach. Every year they claim more and more arable land. How enormous those snowfields are. Look at the massive storm fronts over the ocean. There are ships down there, small craft some of them. Try to imagine the waves, the rocking. The hurricanes alone. The tidal waves. Look at those coastal communities exposed to tidal waves. What could be more frightening than a tidal wave? But they live there, they stay there. Where could they go?"

I want to talk to him about calorie intake, the effectiveness of the earplugs and nasal decongestants. The earplugs are human moments. The apple cider and the broccoli are human moments. Vollmer himself is a human moment, never more so than when he forgets there is a war.

The close-cropped hair and longish head. The mild blue eyes that bulge slightly. The protuberant eyes of long-bodied people with stooped shoulders. The long hands and wrists. The mild face. The easy face of a handyman in a panel truck that has an extension ladder fixed to the roof and a scuffed license plate, green and white, with the state motto beneath the digits. That kind of face.

He offers to give me a haircut. What an interesting thing a haircut is, when you think of it. Before the war there were time slots reserved for such activities. Houston not only had everything scheduled well in advance but constantly monitored us for whatever meager feedback might result. We were wired, taped, scanned, diagnosed, and metered. We were men in space, objects worthy of the most scrupulous care, the deepest sentiments and anxieties.

Now there is a war. Nobody cares about my hair, what I eat, how I feel about the spacecraft's decor, and it is not Houston but Colorado we are in touch with. We are no longer delicate biological specimens adrift in an alien environment. The enemy can kill us with its photons, its mesons, its charged particles faster than any calcium deficiency or trouble of the inner ear, faster than any dusting of micrometeoroids. The emotions have changed. We've stopped being candidates for an embarrassing demise, the kind of mistake or unforeseen event that tends to make a nation grope for the appropriate response. As men in war we can be certain, dying, that we will arouse uncomplicated sorrows, the open and dependable feelings that grateful nations count on to embellish the simplest ceremony.

★　　★　　★

A note about the universe. Vollmer is on the verge of deciding that our planet is alone in harboring intelligent life. We are an accident and we happened only once. (What a remark to make, in egg-shaped orbit, to someone who doesn't want to discuss the larger questions.) He feels this way because of the war.

The war, he says, will bring about an end to the idea that the universe swarms, as they say, with life. Other astronauts have looked past the star-points and imagined infinite possibility, grape-clustered worlds teeming with higher forms. But this was before the war. Our view is changing even now, his and mine, he says, as we drift across the firmament.

Is Vollmer saying that cosmic optimism is a luxury reserved for periods between world wars? Do we project our current failure and despair out toward the star clouds, the endless night? After all, he says, where are they? If they exist, why has there been no sign, not one, not any, not a single indication that serious people might cling to, not a whisper, a radio pulse, a shadow? The war tells us it is foolish to believe.

Our dialogues with Colorado Command are beginning to sound like computer-generated tea-time chat. Vollmer tolerates Colorado's jargon only to a point. He is critical of their more debased locutions and doesn't mind letting them know. Why, then, if I agree with his views on this matter, am I becoming irritated by his complaints? Is he too young to champion the language? Does he have the experience, the professional standing to scold our flight dynamics officer, our conceptual paradigm officer, our status consultants on waste-management systems and evasion-related zonal options? Or is it something else completely, something unrelated to Colorado Command and our communications with them? Is it the sound of his voice? Is it just his *voice* that is driving me crazy?

Vollmer has entered a strange phase. He spends all his time at the window now, looking down at the earth. He says little or nothing. He simply wants to look, do nothing but look. The oceans, the continents, the archipelagos. We are configured in what is called a cross-orbit series and there is no repetition from one swing around the earth to the next. He sits there looking. He takes meals at the window, does checklists at the window, barely glancing at the instruction sheets as we pass over tropical storms, over grass fires and major ranges. I keep waiting for him to return to his prewar habit of using quaint phrases to describe the earth. It's a beach ball, a sun-ripened fruit. But he simply looks out the window, eating almond crunches, the wrappers floating away. The view clearly fills his consciousness. It is powerful enough to silence him, to still the voice that rolls off the roof of his mouth, to leave him turned in the seat, twisted uncomfortably for hours at a time.

The view is endlessly fulfilling. It is like the answer to a lifetime of questions and vague cravings. It satisfies every childlike curiosity, every muted desire, whatever there is in him of the scientist, the poet, the primitive seer, the watcher of fire and shooting stars, whatever obsessions eat at the night side of his mind, whatever sweet and dreamy yearning he has ever felt for nameless places faraway, whatever earth-sense he possesses, the neural pulse of some wilder awareness, a sympathy for beasts, whatever belief in an immanent vital force, the Lord of Creation, whatever secret harboring of the idea of human oneness, whatever wishfulness and simplehearted hope, whatever of too much and not enough, all at once and little by little, whatever burning urge to escape responsibility and routine, escape his own overspecialization, the circumscribed and inward-spiraling self, whatever remnants of his boyish longing to fly, his dreams of strange spaces and eerie heights, his fantasies of happy death, whatever indolent and sybaritic leanings, lotus-eater, smoker of grasses and herbs, blue-eyed gazer into space— all these are satisfied, all collected and massed in that living body, the sight he sees from the window.

"It is just so interesting," he says at last. "The colors and all."

The colors and all.

# JOHN L'HEUREUX
## The Anatomy of Desire

Because Hanley's skin had been stripped off by the enemy, he could find no one who was willing to be with him for long. The nurses were obligated, of course, to see him now and then, and sometimes the doctor, but certainly not the other patients and certainly not his wife and children. He was raw, he was meat, and he would never be any better. He had a great and natural desire, therefore, to be possessed by someone.

He would walk around on his skinned feet, leaving bloody footprints up and down the corridors, looking for someone to love him.

"You're not supposed to be out here," the nurse said. And she added, somehow making it sound kind, "You untidy the floor, Hanley."

"I want to be loved by someone," he said. "I'm human too. I'm like you."

But he knew he was not like her. Everybody called her the saint.

"Why couldn't it be you?" he said.

She was swabbing his legs with blood retardant, a new discovery that kept Hanley going. It was one of those miracle medications that just grew out of the war.

"I wasn't chosen," she said. "I have my skin."

"No," he said. "I mean why couldn't it be you who will love me, possess me? I have desires too," he said.

She considered this as she swabbed his shins and the soles of his feet.

"I have no desires," she said. "Or only one. It's the same thing."

He looked at her loving face. It was not a pretty face, but it was saintly.

"Then you will?" he said.

"If I come to know sometime that I must," she said.

The enemy had not chosen Hanley, they had just lucked upon him sleeping in his trench. They were a raid party of four, terrified and obedient, and they had been told to bring back an enemy to serve as an example of what is done to infiltrators.

They dragged Hanley back across the line and ran him, with his hands tied behind his back, the two kilometers to the general's tent.

The general dismissed the guards because he was very taken with Hanley. He untied the cords that bound his wrists and let his arms hang free. Then slowly, ritually, he tipped Hanley's face toward the light and examined it carefully. He kissed him on the brow and on the cheek and finally on the mouth. He gazed deep and long into Hanley's eyes until he saw his own reflection there looking back. He traced the lines of Hanley's eyebrows, gently, with the tip of his index finger. "Such a beautiful face," he said in his own language. He pressed his palms lightly against Hanley's forehead, against his cheekbones, his jaw. With his little finger he memorized the shape of Hanley's lips, the laugh lines at his eyes, the chin. The general did Hanley's face very thoroughly. Afterward he did some things down below, and so just before sunrise when the time came to lead Hanley out to the stripping post, he told the soldiers with the knives: "This young man could be my own son; so spare him here and here."

The stripping post stood dead-center in the line of barbed wire only a few meters beyond the range of gunfire. A loudspeaker was set up and began to blare the day's message. "This is what happens to infiltrators. No infiltrators will be spared." And then as troops from both sides watched through binoculars, the enemy cut the skin from Hanley's body, sparing—as the general had insisted—his face and his genitals. They were skilled men and the skin was stripped off expeditiously and they hung it, headless, on the barbed wire as an example. They lay Hanley himself on the ground where he could die.

He was rescued a little after noon when the enemy, for no good reason, went into sudden retreat.

Hanley was given emergency treatment at the field unit, and when they had done what they could for him, they sent him on to the vets' hospital. At least there, they told each other, he will be attended by the saint.

It was quite some time before the saint said yes, she would love him.

"Not just love me. Possess me."

"There are natural reluctancies," she said. "There are personal peculiarities," she said. "You will have to have patience with me."

"You're supposed to be a saint," he said.

So she lay down with him in his bloody bed and he found great satisfaction in holding this small woman in his arms. He kissed her and caressed her and felt young and whole again. He did not miss his wife and children. He did not miss his skin.

The saint did everything she must. She told him how handsome he was and what pleasure he gave her. She touched him in the way he liked best. She said he was her whole life, her fate. And at night when he woke her to staunch the blood, she whispered how she needed him, how she could not live without him.

This went on for some time.

The war was over and the occupying forces had made the general mayor of the capital city. He was about to run for senator and wanted his past to be beyond the reproach of any investigative committee. He wrote Hanley a letter which he sent through the International Red Cross.

"You could have been my own son," he said. "What we do in war is what we have to do. We do not choose cruelty or violence. I did only what was my duty."

"I am in love and I am loved," Hanley said. "Why isn't this enough?"

The saint was swabbing his chest and belly with blood retardant.

"Nothing is ever enough," she said.

"I love, but I am not possessed by love," he said. "I want to be surrounded by you. I want to be enclosed. I want to be enveloped. I don't have the words for it. But do you understand?"

"You want to be possessed," she said.

"I want to be inside you."

And so they made love, but afterward he said, "That was not enough. That is only a metaphor for what I want."

★  ★  ★

The general was elected senator and was made a trustee of three nuclear-arms conglomerates. But he was not well. And he was not sleeping well.

He wrote to Hanley, "I wake in the night and see your face before mine. I feel your forehead pressing against my palms. I taste your breath. I did only what I had to do. You could have been my son."

"I know what I want," Hanley said.
"If I can do it, I will," the saint said.
"I want your skin."

And so she lay down on the long white table, shuddering, while Hanley made his first incision. He cut along the shoulders and then down the arms and back up, then down the sides and the legs to the feet. It took him longer than he had expected. The saint shivered at the cold touch of the knife and she sobbed once at the sight of the blood, but by the time Hanley lifted the shroud of skin from her crimson body, she was resigned, satisfied even.

Hanley had spared her face and her genitals.

He spread the skin out to dry and, while he waited, he swabbed her raw body carefully with blood retardant. He whispered little words of love and thanks and desire for her. A smile played about her lips, but she said nothing.

It would be a week before he could put on her skin.

The general wrote to Hanley one last letter. "I can endure no more. I am possessed by you."

Hanley put on the skin of the saint. His genitals fitted nicely through the gap he had left and the skin at his neck matched hers exactly. He walked the corridors and for once left no bloody tracks behind. He stood before mirrors and admired himself. He touched his breasts and his belly and his thighs and there was no blood on his hands.

"Thank you," he said to her. "It is my heart's desire fulfilled. I am inside you. I am possessed by you."

And then, in the night, he kissed her on the brow and on the cheek and finally on the mouth. He gazed deep and long into her eyes. He traced the lines of her eyebrows gently, with the tip of his index finger. "Such a beautiful face," he said. He pressed his palms lightly against her forehead, her cheekbones, her jaw. With his little finger he memorized the shape of her lips.

And then it was that Hanley, loved, desperate to possess and be possessed, staring deep into the green and loving eyes of the saint, saw that there can be no possession, there is only desire. He plucked at his empty skin, and wept.

# RAYMOND CARVER
## Little Things

Early that day the weather turned and the snow was melting into dirty water. Streaks of it ran down from the little shoulder-high window that faced the back yard. Cars slushed by on the street outside, where it was getting dark. But it was getting dark on the inside too.

He was in the bedroom pushing clothes into a suitcase when she came to the door.

I'm glad you're leaving! I'm glad you're leaving! she said. Do you hear?

He kept on putting his things into the suitcase.

Son of a bitch! I'm so glad you're leaving! She began to cry. You can't even look at me in the face, can you?

Then she noticed the baby's picture on the bed and picked it up.

He looked at her and she wiped her eyes and stared at him before turning and going back to the living room.

Bring that back, he said.

Just get your things and get out, she said.

He did not answer. He fastened the suitcase, put on his coat, looked around the bedroom before turning off the light. Then he went out to the living room.

She stood in the doorway of the little kitchen, holding the baby.

I want the baby, he said.

Are you crazy?

No, but I want the baby. I'll get someone to come by for his things.

You're not touching this baby, she said.

The baby had begun to cry and she uncovered the blanket from around his head.

Oh, oh, she said, looking at the baby.

He moved toward her.

For God's sake! she said. She took a step back into the kitchen.

I want the baby.

Get out of here.

She turned and tried to hold the baby over in a corner behind the stove.

But he came up. He reached across the stove and tightened his hands on the baby.

Let go of him, he said.

Get away, get away! she cried.

The baby was red-faced and screaming. In the scuffle they knocked down a flower pot that hung behind the stove.

He crowded her into the wall then, trying to break her grip. He held on to the baby and pushed with all his weight.

Let go of him, he said.

Don't, she said. You're hurting the baby, she said.

I'm not hurting the baby, he said.

The kitchen window gave no light. In the near-dark he worked on her fisted fingers with one hand and with the other hand he gripped the screaming baby up under an arm near the shoulder.

She felt her fingers being forced open. She felt the baby going from her.

No! she screamed just as her hands came loose.

She would have it, this baby. She grabbed for the baby's other arm. She caught the baby around the wrist and leaned back.

But he would not let go. He felt the baby slipping out of his hands and he pulled back very hard.

In this matter, the issue was decided.

# JOYCE CAROL OATES
## The Temple

There, again, the vexing, mysterious sound!—a faint mewing cry followed by a muffled scratching, as of something being raked by nails, or claws. At first the woman believed the sound must be coming from somewhere inside the house, a small animal, perhaps a squirrel, trapped in the attic beneath the eaves, or in a remote corner of the earthen-floored cellar; after she searched the house thoroughly, she had to conclude that it emanated from somewhere outside, at the bottom of the old garden, perhaps. It was far more distinct at certain times than at others, depending upon the direction and velocity of the wind.

How like a baby's cry, terribly distressing to hear! and the scratching, which came in spasmodic, desperate flurries, was yet more distressing, evoking an obscure horror.

The woman believed she'd first begun hearing the sound at the time of the spring thaw in late March, when melting ice dripped in a continuous arhythmic delirium from chimneys, roofs, eaves, trees. With the coming of warm weather, her bedroom window open to the night, her sleep was increasingly disturbed.

She had no choice, then, did she?—she must trace the sound to its origin. She set about the task calmly enough one morning, stepping out into unexpectedly bright, warm sunshine, and making her way into the lush tangle of vegetation that had been her mother's garden of thirty years before. The mewing sound, the scratching—it seemed to be issuing from the very bottom of the garden, close by a stained concrete drainage ditch that marked the end of the property. As soon as she listened for it, however, it ceased.

How steady the woman's heartbeat, amid the quickening pulse of a May morning.

Out of the old garage, that had once been a stable, the woman got a shovel, a spade, a rake, these implements festooned in cobwebs and dust, and began to dig. It was awkward work and her soft hands ached after only minutes, so she returned to the garage to fetch gardening gloves these too covered in cobwebs and dust, and stiffened with dirt. The mid-morning sun was ablaze so she located an old straw hat of her mother's: it fitted her head oddly, as if its band had been sweated through and dried, stiffened asymmetrically.

So she set again to work. First, she dug away sinewy weeds and vines, chicory, wild mustard, tall grasses, in the area out of which the cry had emanated; she managed to uncover the earth, which was rich with compost, very dark, moist. Almost beneath her feet, the plaintive mewing sounded! "Yes. Yes. I'm here," she whispered. She paused, very excited; she heard a brief flurry of scratching, then silence. "I'm here, now." She grunted as she pushed the shovel into the earth, urging it downward with her weight, her foot; it was a pity she'd so rarely used gardening implements, in all of her fifty years. She was a naturally graceful woman so out of her element here she felt ludicrous to herself, like a beast on its hind legs.

She dug. She spaded, and raked. She dug again, deepening and broadening the hole which was like a wound in the jungle-like vegetation. Chips and shards of aged brick, glass, stones were uncovered, striking the shovel. Beetles scurried away, their shells glinting darkly in the sunshine. Earthworms squirmed, some of them cut cruelly in two. For some time the woman worked in silence, hearing only her quickened heartbeat and a roaring pulse in her ears; then, distinctly, with the impact of a shout, there came the pleading cry again, so close she nearly dropped the shovel.

At last, covered in sweat, her hands shaking, the woman struck something solid. She dropped to her knees and groped in the moist dark earth and lifted something round and hollow—a human skull? But it was small, hardly half the size of an adult's skull.

"My God!" the woman whispered.

Squatting then above the jagged hole, turning the skull in her fingers. How light it was! The color of parchment, badly stained from the soil. She brushed bits of damp earth away, marveling at the subtle contours of the cranium. Not a hair remained. The delicate bone was cracked in several places and its texture minutely scarified, like a ceramic glaze. A few of the teeth were missing, but most appeared to be intact, though caked with dirt. The perfectly formed jaws, the slope of the cheekbones! The empty eye sockets, so round . . . The woman lifted the skull to stare into the sockets as if staring into mirror-eyes, eyes of an eerie transparency. A kind of knowledge passed between her and these eyes yet she did not know: was this a child's skull? had a child been buried here, it must have been decades ago, on her family's property? Unnamed, unmarked? Unacknowledged? Unknown?

For several fevered hours the woman dug deeper into the earth. She was panting in the overhead sun, which seemed to penetrate the straw hat as if it were made of gauze; her sturdy body was clammy with sweat. She discovered a number of scattered bones—a slender forearm, curving ribs, part of a hand, fingers—these too parchment-colored, child-sized. What small, graceful fingers! How they had scratched, clawed, for release! Following this morning, forever, the finger bones would be at peace.

By early afternoon, the woman gave up her digging. She could find no more of the skeleton than a dozen or so random bones.

She went up to the house, and returned quickly, eagerly, with a five-foot runner of antique velvet cloth, a deep wine color, in which to carry the skull and bones up to the house. For no one must see. No one must know. "*I* am here, *I* will always be here," the woman promised. "*I* will never abandon you." She climbed to the second floor of the house, and in her bedroom at the rear she lay the velvet runner on a table beside her bed and beneath a bay window through whose diamond-shaped, leaded panes a reverent light would fall. Tenderly, meticulously, the woman arranged the skull and bones into the shape of a human being. Though most of the skeleton was missing, it would never seem to the woman's loving eye that this was so.

In this way the woman's bedroom became a secret temple. On the velvet cloth the skull and bones, unnamed, would be discovered after the woman's death, but that was a long way off.

# ANNE RICE
## "Freniere" (from *Interview with the Vampire*)

"But, let me describe New Orleans, as it was then, and as it was to become, so you can understand how simple our lives were. There was no city in America like New Orleans. It was filled not only with the French and Spanish of all classes who had formed in part its peculiar aristocracy, but later with immigrants of all kinds, the Irish and the German in particular. Then there were not only the black slaves, yet unhomogenized and fantastical in their different tribal garb and manners, but the great growing class of the free people of color, those marvellous people of our mixed blood and that of the islands, who produced a magnificent and unique caste of craftsmen, artists, poets, and renowned feminine beauty. And then there were the Indians, who covered the levee on summer days selling herbs and crafted wares. And drifting through all, through this medley of languages and colors, were the people of the port, the sailors of ships, who came in great waves to spend their money in the cabarets, to buy for the night the beautiful women both dark and light, to dine on the best of Spanish and French cooking and drink the imported wines of the world. Then add to these, within years after my transformation, the Americans, who built the city up river from the old French Quarter with magnificent Grecian houses which gleamed in the moonlight like temples. And, of course, the planters, always the planters, coming to town with their families in shining landaus to buy evening gowns and silver and gems, to crowd the narrow streets on the way to the old French Opera House and the Théâtre d'Orléans and the St. Louis

Cathedral, from whose open doors came the chants of High Mass over the crowds of the Place d'Armes on Sundays, over the noise and bickering of the French Market, over the silent, ghostly drift of the ships along the raised waters of the Mississippi, which flowed against the levee above the ground of New Orleans itself, so that the ships appeared to float against the sky.

"This was New Orleans, a magical and magnificent place to live. In which a vampire, richly dressed and gracefully walking through the pools of light of one gas lamp after another might attract no more notice in the evening than hundreds of other exotic creatures—if he attracted any at all, if anyone stopped to whisper behind a fan, 'That man . . . how pale, how he gleams . . . how he moves. It's not natural!' A city in which a vampire might be gone before the words had even passed the lips, seeking out the alleys in which he could see like a cat, the darkened bars in which sailors slept with their heads on the table, great high-ceilinged hotel rooms where a lone figure might sit, her feet upon the embroidered cushion, her legs covered with a lace counterpane, her head bent under the tarnished light of a single candle, never seeing the great shadow move across the plaster flowers of the ceiling, never seeing the long white finger reached to press the fragile flame.

"Remarkable, if for nothing else, because of this, that all of those men and women who stayed for any reason left behind them some monument, some structure of marble and brick and stone that still stands; so that even when the gas lamps went out and the planes came in and the office buildings crowded the blocks of Canal Street, something irreducible of beauty and romance remained; not in every street perhaps, but in so many that the landscape is for me the landscape of those times always, and walking now in the starlit streets of the Quarter or the Garden District I am in those times again. I suppose that is the nature of the monument. Be it a small house or a mansion of Corinthian columns and wrought-iron lace. The monument does not say that this or that man walked here. No, that what he felt in one time in one spot continues. The moon that rose over New Orleans then still rises. As long as the monuments stand, it still rises. The feeling, at least here . . . and there . . . it remains the same."

The vampire appeared sad. He sighed, as if he doubted what he had just said. "What was it?" he asked suddenly as if he were slightly tired. "Yes, money. Lestat and I had to make money. And I was telling you that he could steal. But it was investment afterwards that mattered. What we accumulated we must use. But I go ahead of myself. I killed animals. But I'll get to that in a moment. Lestat killed humans all the time, sometimes two or three a night, sometimes more. He would drink from one just enough to satisfy a momentary thirst, and then go on to another. The better the human, as he would say in his vulgar way, the more he liked it. A fresh young girl, that was his favorite food the first of the evening; but the triumphant kill for Lestat was a young man. A young man around your age would have appealed to him in particular."

"Me?" the boy whispered. He had leaned forward on his elbows to peer into the vampire's eyes, and now he drew up.

"Yes," the vampire went on, as if he hadn't observed the boy's change of expression. "You see, they represented the greatest loss to Lestat, because they stood on the threshold of the maximum possibility of life. Of course, Lestat didn't understand this himself. I came to understand it. Lestat understood nothing.

"I shall give you a perfect example of what Lestat liked. Up the river from us was the Freniere plantation, a magnificent spread of land which had great hopes of making a fortune in sugar, just shortly after the refining process had been invented. I presume you know sugar was refined in Louisiana. There is something perfect and ironic about it, this land which I loved producing refined sugar. I mean this more unhappily than I think you know. This refined sugar is a poison. It was like the essence of life in New Orleans, so sweet that it can be fatal, so richly enticing that all other values are forgotten. . . . But as I was saying, up river from us lived the Frenieres, a great old French family which had produced in this generation five young women and one young man. Now, three of the young women were destined not to marry, but two were young enough still and all depended upon the young man. He was to manage the plantation as I had done for my mother and sister; he was to negotiate marriages, to put together dowries when the entire fortune of the place rode precariously on the next year's sugar crop; he was to bargain, fight, and keep at a distance the entire material world for the world of Freniere. Lestat decided he wanted him. And when fate alone nearly cheated Lestat, he went wild. He risked his own life to get the Freniere boy, who had become involved in a duel. He had insulted a young Spanish Creole at a ball. The whole thing was nothing, really; but like most young Creoles this one was willing to die for nothing. They were both willing to die for nothing. The Freniere household was in an uproar. You must understand, Lestat knew this perfectly. Both of us had hunted the Freniere plantation, Lestat for slaves and chicken thieves and me for animals."

"You were killing *only* animals?"

"Yes. But I'll come to that later, as I said. We both knew the plantation, and I had indulged in one of the greatest pleasures of a vampire, that of watching people unbeknownst to them. I knew the Freniere sisters as I knew the magnificent rose trees around my brother's oratory. They were a unique group of women. Each in her own way was as smart as the brother; and one of them, I shall call her Babette, was not only as smart as her brother, but far wiser. Yet none had been educated to care for the plantation; none understood even the simplest facts about its financial state. All were totally dependent upon young Freniere, and all knew it. And so, larded with their love for him, their passionate belief that he hung the moon and that any conjugal love they might ever know would only be a pale reflection of their love for him, larded with this was a desperation as strong as the will to survive. If Freniere died in the duel, the plantation would collapse. Its fragile economy, a life of splendor based on the perennial mortgaging of the next year's crop, was in his hands alone. So you can imagine the panic and misery in the Freniere household the night that the son went to town to fight the appointed duel. And now picture Lestat, gnashing his teeth like a comic-opera devil because he was not going to kill the young Freniere."

"You mean then . . . that you *felt* for the Freniere women?"

"I felt for them totally," said the vampire. "Their position was agonizing. And I felt for the boy. That night he locked himself in his father's study and made a will. He knew full well that if he fell under the rapier at four a.m. the next morning, his family would fall with him. He deplored his situation and yet could do nothing to help it. To run out on the duel would not only mean social ruin for him, but would probably have been impossible. The other young man would have pursued him until he was forced to fight. When he left the plantation at midnight, he was staring into the face of death itself with the character of a man who, having only one path to follow, has resolved to follow it with perfect courage. He would either kill the Spanish boy or die; it was unpredictable, despite all his skill. His face reflected a depth of feeling and wisdom I'd never seen on the face of any of Lestat's struggling victims. I had my first battle with Lestat then and there. I'd prevented him from killing the boy for months, and now he meant to kill him before the Spanish boy could.

"We were on horseback, racing after the young Freniere towards New Orleans, Lestat bent on overtaking him, I bent on overtaking Lestat. Well, the duel, as I told you, was scheduled for four a.m. On the edge of the swamp just beyond the city's northern gate. And arriving there just shortly before four, we had precious little time to return to Pointe du Lac, which meant our own lives were in danger. I was incensed at Lestat as never before, and he was determined to get the boy. 'Give him his chance!' I was insisting, getting hold of Lestat before he could approach the boy. It was midwinter, bitter-cold and damp in the swamps, one volley of icy rain after another sweeping the clearing where the duel was to be fought. Of course, I did not fear these elements in the sense that you might; they did not numb me, nor threaten me with mortal shivering or illness. But vampires feel cold as acutely as humans, and the blood of the kill is often the rich, sensual alleviation of that cold. But what concerned me that morning was not the pain I felt, but the excellent cover of darkness these elements provided, which made Freniere extremely vulnerable to Lestat's attack. All he need do would be step away from his two friends towards the swamp and Lestat might take him. And so I physically grappled with Lestat. I held him."

"But towards all this you had detachment, distance?"

"Hmmm . . ." the vampire sighed. "Yes. I had it, and with it a supremely resolute anger. To glut himself upon the life of an entire family was to me Lestat's supreme act of utter contempt and disregard for all he should have seen with a vampire's depth. So I held him in the dark, where he spit at me and cursed at me; and young Freniere took his rapier from his friend and second and went out on the slick, wet grass to meet his opponent. There was a brief conversation, then the duel commenced. In moments, it was over. Freniere had mortally wounded the other boy with a swift thrust to the chest. And he knelt in the grass, bleeding, dying, shouting something unintelligible at Freniere. The victor simply stood there. Everyone could see there was no sweetness in the victory. Freniere looked on death as if it were an abomination. His companions advanced with their lanterns, urging him to come away as soon as possible and leave the dying man to his friends. Meantime, the wounded one would allow no one to touch him. And then, as Freniere's group turned to go, the three of them walking heavily towards their horses, the man on the ground drew a pistol. Perhaps I alone could see this in the powerful dark. But, in any event, I shouted to Freniere as I ran towards the gun. And this was all that Lestat needed. While I was lost in my clumsiness, distracting Freniere and going for the gun itself, Lestat, with his years of experience and superior speed, grabbed the young man and spirited him into the cypresses. I doubt his friends even knew what had happened. The pistol had gone off, the wounded man had collapsed, and I was tearing through the near-frozen marshes shouting for Lestat.

"Then I saw him. Freniere lay sprawled over the knobbed roots of a cypress, his boots deep in the murky water, and Lestat was still bent over him, one hand on the hand of Freniere that still held the foil. I went to pull Lestat off, and that right hand swung at me with such lightning speed I did not see it, did not know it had struck me until I found myself in the water also; and, of course, by the time I recovered, Freniere was dead. I saw him as he lay there, his eyes closed, his lips utterly still as if he were just sleeping. 'Damn you!' I began cursing Lestat. And then I started, for the body of Freniere had begun to slip down into the marsh. The water rose over his face and covered him completely. Lestat was jubilant; he reminded me tersely that we had less than an hour to get back to Pointe du Lac, and he swore revenge on me. 'If I didn't like the life of a Southern planter, I'd finish you tonight. I know a way,' he threatened me. 'I ought to drive your horse into the swamps. You'd have to dig yourself a hole and smother!' He rode off.

"Even over all these years, I feel that anger for him like a white-hot liquid filling my veins. I saw then what being a vampire meant to him."

"He was just a killer," the boy said, his voice reflecting some of the vampire's emotion. "No regard for anything."

"No. Being a vampire for him meant revenge. Revenge against life itself. Every time he took a life it was revenge. It was no wonder, then, that he appreciated nothing. The nuances of vampire existence weren't even available to him because he was focused with a maniacal vengeance upon the mortal life he'd left. Consumed with hatred, he looked back. Consumed with envy, nothing pleased him unless he could take it from others; and once having it, he grew cold and dissatisfied, not loving the thing for itself; and so he went after something else. Vengeance, blind and sterile and contemptible.

"But I've spoken to you about the Freniere sisters. It was almost half past five when I reached their plantation. Dawn would come shortly after six, but I was almost home. I slipped onto the upper gallery of their house and saw them all gathered in the parlor; they had never even dressed for bed. The candles burnt low, and they sat already as mourners, waiting for the word. They were all dressed in black, as was their at-home custom, and in the dark the black shapes of their dresses massed together with their raven hair, so that in the glow of the candles their faces appeared as five soft, shimmering apparitions, each uniquely sad, each uniquely courageous. Babette's face alone appeared resolute. It was as if she had already made up her mind to take the burdens of Freniere if her brother died, and she had that same expression on her face now which had been on her brother's when he mounted to leave for the duel. What lay ahead of her was nearly impossible. What lay ahead was the final death of which Lestat was guilty. So I did something then which caused me great risk. I made myself known to her. I did this by playing the light. As you can see, my face is very white and has a smooth, highly reflective surface, rather like that of polished marble."

"Yes," the boy nodded, and appeared flustered. "It's very . . . beautiful, actually," said the boy. "I wonder if . . . but what happened?"

"You wonder if I was a handsome man when I was alive," said the vampire. The boy nodded. "I was. Nothing structurally is changed in me. Only I never knew that I was handsome. Life whirled about me a wind of petty concerns, as I've said. I gazed at nothing, not even a mirror . . . especially not a mirror . . . with a free eye. But this is what happened. I stepped near to the pane of glass and let the light touch my face. And this I did at a moment when Babette's eyes were turned towards the panes. Then I appropriately vanished.

"Within seconds all the sisters knew a 'strange creature' had been seen, a ghostlike creature, and the two slave maids steadfastly refused to investigate. I waited out these moments impatiently for just that which I wanted to happen: Babette finally took a candelabrum from a side table, lit the candles and, scorning everyone's fear, ventured out onto the cold gallery alone to see what was there, her sisters hovering in the door like great, black birds, one of them crying that the brother was dead and she had indeed seen his ghost. Of course, you must understand that Babette, being as strong as she was, never once attributed what she saw to imagination or to ghosts.

I let her come the length of the dark gallery before I spoke to her, and even then I let her see only the vague outline of my body beside one of the columns. 'Tell your sisters to go back,' I whispered to her. 'I come to tell you of your brother. Do as I say.' She was still for an instant, and then she turned to me and strained to see me in the dark. 'I have only a little time. I would not harm you for the world,' I said. And she obeyed. Saying it was nothing, she told them to shut the door, and they obeyed as people obey who not only need a leader but are desperate for one. Then I stepped into the light of Babette's candles."

The boy's eyes were wide. He put his hand to his lips. "Did you look to her . . . as you do to me?" he asked.

"You ask that with such innocence," said the vampire. "Yes, I suppose I certainly did. Only, by candlelight I always had a less supernatural appearance. And I made no pretense with her of being an ordinary creature. 'I have only minutes,' I told her at once. 'But what I have to tell you is of the greatest importance. Your brother fought bravely and won the duel—but wait. You must know now, he is dead. Death was proverbial with him, the thief in the night about which all his goodness or courage could do nothing. But this is not the principal thing which I came to tell you. It is this. You can rule the plantation and you can save it. All that is required is that you let no one convince you otherwise. You must assume his position despite any outcry, any talk of convention, any talk of propriety or common sense. You must listen to nothing. The same land is here now that was here yesterday morning when your brother slept above. Nothing is changed. You must take his place. If you do not, the land is lost and the family is lost. You will be five women on a small pension doomed to live but half or less of what life could give you. Learn what you must know. Stop at nothing until you have the answers. And take my visitation to you to be your courage whenever you waver. You must take the reins of your own life. Your brother is dead.'

"I could see by her face that she had heard every word. She would have questioned me had there been time, but she believed me when I said there was not. Then I used all my skill to leave her so swiftly I appeared to vanish. From the garden I saw her face above in the glow of her candles. I saw her search the dark for me, turning around and around. And then I saw her make the Sign of the Cross and walk back to her sisters within."

The vampire smiled. "There was absolutely no talk on the river coast of any strange apparition to Babette Freniere, but after the first mourning and sad talk of the women left all alone, she became the scandal of the neighborhood because she chose to run the plantation on her own. She managed an immense dowry for her younger sister, and was married herself in another year. And Lestat and I almost never exchanged words."

# PETER STRAUB
## A Short Guide to the City

The viaduct killer, named for the location where his victims' bodies have been discovered, is still at large. There have been six victims to date, found by children, people exercising their dogs, lovers, or—in one instance—by policemen. The bodies lay sprawled, their throats slashed, partially sheltered by one or another of the massive concrete supports at the top of the slope beneath the great bridge. We assume that the viaduct killer is a resident of the city, a voter, a renter or property owner, a product of the city's excellent public school system, perhaps even a parent of children who even now attend one of its seven elementary schools, three public high schools, two parochial schools, or single nondenominational private school. He may own a boat or belong to the Book-of-the-Month Club, he may frequent one or another of its many bars and taverns, he may have subscription tickets to the concert series put on by the city symphony orchestra. He may be a factory worker with a library ticket. He owns a car, perhaps two. He may swim in one of the city's public pools or the vast lake, punctuated with sailboats, during the hot moist August of the city.

For this is a Midwestern city, northern, with violent changes of season. The extremes of climate, from ten or twenty below zero to up around one hundred in the summer, cultivate an attitude of acceptance in its citizens, of insularity—it looks inward, not out, and few of its children leave for the more temperate, uncertain, and experimental cities of the eastern or western coasts. The city is proud of its modesty—it cherishes the ordinary, or what it sees as the ordinary, which is not.

(It has had the same mayor for twenty-four years, a man of limited-to-average intelligence who has aged gracefully and has never had any other occupation of any sort.)

Ambition, the yearning for fame, position, and achievement, is discouraged here. One of its citizens became the head of a small foreign state, another a famous bandleader, yet another a Hollywood staple who for decades played the part of the star's best friend and confidant; this, it is felt, is enough, and besides, all of these people are now dead. The city has no literary tradition. Its only mirror is provided by its two newspapers, which have thick sports sections and are comfortable enough to be read in bed.

The city's characteristic mode is *denial*. For this reason, an odd fabulousness permeates every quarter of the city, a receptiveness to fable, to the unrecorded. A river runs through the center of the business district, as the Liffey runs through Dublin, the Seine through Paris, the Thames through London, and the Danube through Budapest, though our river is smaller and less consequential than any of these.

Our lives are ordinary and exemplary, the citizens would say. We take part in the life of the nation, history courses through us for all our immunity to the national illnesses: it is even possible that in our ordinary lives . . . We too have had our pulse taken by the great national seers and opinion-makers, for in us you may find . . .

Forty years ago, in winter, the body of a woman was found on the banks of the river. She had been raped and murdered, cast out of the human community—a prostitute, never identified—and the noises of struggle that must have accompanied her death went unnoticed by the patrons of the Green Woman Taproom, located directly above that point on the river where her body was discovered. It was an abnormally cold winter that year, a winter of shared misery, and within the Green Woman the music was loud, feverish, festive.

In that community, which is Irish and lives above its riverfront shops and bars, neighborhood children were supposed to have found a winged man huddling in a packing case, an aged man, half-starved, speaking a strange language none of the children knew. His wings were ragged and dirty, many of the feathers as cracked and threadbare as those of an old pigeon's, and his feet were dirty and swollen. *Ull! Li! Gack!* the children screamed at him, mocking the sounds that came from his mouth. They pelted him with rocks and snowballs, imagining that he had crawled up from that same river which sent chill damp— a damp as cold as cancer—into their bones and bedrooms, which gave them earaches and chilblains, which in summer bred rats and mosquitos.

One of the city's newspapers is Democratic, the other Republican. Both papers ritually endorse the mayor, who though consummately political has no recognizable politics. Both of the city's newspapers also support the Chief of Police, crediting him with keeping the city free of the kind of violence that has undermined so many other American cities. None of our citizens goes armed, and our church attendance is still far above the national average.

We are ambivalent about violence.

We have very few public statues, mostly of Civil War generals. On the lakefront, separated from the rest of the town by a six-lane expressway, stands the cube-like structure of the Arts Center, otherwise called the War Memorial. Its rooms are hung with mediocre paintings before which schoolchildren are led on tours by their teachers, most of whom were educated in our local school system.

Our teachers are satisfied, decent people, and the statistics about alcohol and drug abuse among both students and teachers are very encouraging.

There is no need to linger at the War Memorial.

Proceeding directly north, you soon find yourself among the orderly, impressive precincts of the wealthy. It was in this sector of the town, known generally as the East Side, that the brewers and tanners who made our city's first great fortunes set up their mansions. Their houses have a northern, Germanic, even Baltic look which is entirely appropriate to our climate. Of gray stone or red brick, the size of factories or prisons, these stately buildings seem to conceal that vein of fantasy that is actually our most crucial inheritance. But it may be that the style of life—the invisible, hidden life—of these inbred merchants is itself fantastic: the multitude of servants, the maids and coachmen, the cooks and laundresses, the private zoos, the elaborate dynastic marriages and fleets of cars, the rooms lined with silk wallpaper, the twenty-course meals, the underground wine cellars and bomb shelters. . . . Of course we do not know if all of these things are true, or even if some of them are true. Our society folk keep to themselves, and what we know of them we learn chiefly from the newspapers, where they are pictured at their balls, standing with their beautiful daughters before fountains of champagne. The private zoos have been broken up long ago. As citizens, we are free to walk down the avenues, past the magnificent houses, and to peer in through the gates at their coach houses and lawns. A uniformed man polishes a car, four tall young people in white play tennis on a private court.

The viaduct killer's victims have all been adult women.

While you continue moving north you will find that as the houses diminish in size the distance between them grows greater. Through the houses, now without gates and coach houses, you can glimpse a sheet of flat grayish-blue—the lake. The air is free, you breathe it in. That is freedom, breathing this air from the lake. Free people may invent themselves in any image, and you may imagine yourself a prince of the earth, walking with an easy stride. Your table is set with linen, china, crystal, and silver, and as you dine, as the servants pass among you with the serving trays, the talk is educated, enlightened, without prejudice of any sort. The table talk is mainly about ideas, it is true, ideas of a conservative cast. You deplore violence, you do not recognize it.

Further north lie suburbs, which are uninteresting.

If from the War Memorial you proceed south, you cross the viaduct. Beneath you is a valley—the valley is perhaps best seen in the dead of winter. All of our city welcomes winter, for our public buildings are gray stone fortresses which, on days when the temperature dips below zero and the old gray snow of previous storms swirls in the avenues, seem to blend with the leaden air and become dreamlike and cloudy. This is how they were meant to be seen. The valley is called . . . it is called the Valley. Red flames tilt and waver at the tops of columns, and smoke pours from factory chimneys. The trees seem to be black. In the winter, the smoke from the factories becomes solid, like dark gray glaciers, and hangs in the dark air in defiance of gravity, like wings that are a light feathery gray at their tips and darken imperceptibly toward black, toward pitchy black at the point where these great frozen glaciers, these dirigibles, would join the body at the shoulder. The bodies of the great birds to which these wings are attached must be imagined.

In the old days of the city, the time of the private zoos, wolves were bred in the Valley. Wolves were in great demand in those days. Now the wolf-ranches have been entirely replaced by factories, by rough taverns owned by retired shop foremen, by spurs of the local railroad line, and by narrow streets lined with rickety frame houses and shoe-repair shops. Most of the old wolf-breeders were Polish, and though their kennels, grassy yards, and barbed-wire exercise runs have disappeared, at least one memory of their existence endures: the Valley's street signs are in the Polish language. Tourists are advised to skirt the Valley, and it is always recommended that photographs be confined to the interesting views obtained by looking down from the viaduct. The more courageous visitors, those in search of pungent experience, are cautiously directed to the taverns of the ex-foremen, in particular the oldest of these (the Rusty Nail and the Brace 'n' Bit), where the wooden floors have so softened and furred with lavings and scrubbings that the boards have come to resemble the pelts of long narrow short-haired animals. For the intrepid, these words of caution: do not dress conspicuously, and carry only small amounts of cash. Some working knowledge of Polish is also advised.

Continuing further south, we come to the Polish district proper, which also houses pockets of Estonians and Lithuanians. More than the city's sadly declining downtown area, this district has traditionally been regarded as the city's heart, and has remained unchanged for more than a hundred years. Here the visitor may wander freely among the markets and street fairs, delighting in the sight of well-bundled children rolling hoops, patriarchs in tall fur hats and long beards, and women gathering around the numerous communal water pumps. The sausages and stuffed cabbage sold at the food stalls may be eaten with impunity, and the local beer is said to be of an unrivaled purity. Violence in this district is invariably domestic, and the visitor may feel free to enter the frequent political discussions, which in any case partake of a nostalgic character. In late January or early February the "South Side" is at its best, with the younger people dressed in multilayered heavy woolen garments decorated with the "reindeer" or "snowflake" motif, and the older women of the community seemingly vying to see which of them can outdo the others in the thickness, blackness, and heaviness of her outergarments and in the severity of the traditional head scarf known as the babushka. In late winter the neatness and orderliness of these colorful folk may be seen at its best, for the wandering visitor will often see the bearded paterfamilias sweeping and shoveling not only his immaculate bit of sidewalk (for these houses are as close together as those of the wealthy along the lakefront, so near to one another that until very recently telephone service was regarded as an irrelevance), but his tiny front lawn as well, with its Marian shrines, crèches, ornamental objects such as elves, trolls, postboys, etc. It is not unknown for residents here to proffer the stranger an invitation to inspect their houses, in order to display the immaculate condition of the kitchen with its well-blackened wood stove and polished ornamental tiles, and perhaps even extend a thimble-glass of their own peach or plum brandy to the thirsty visitor.

Alcohol, with its associations of warmth and comfort, is ubiquitous here, and it is the rare family that does not devote some portion of the summer to the preparation of that winter's plenty.

For these people, violence is an internal matter, to be resolved within or exercised upon one's own body and soul or those of one's immediate family. The inhabitants of these neat, scrubbed little houses with their statues of Mary and cathedral tiles, the descendants of the hard-drinking wolf-breeders of another time, have long since abandoned the practice of crippling their children to ensure their continuing exposure to parental values, but self-mutilation has proved more difficult to eradicate. Few blind themselves now, but many a grandfather conceals a three-fingered hand within his embroidered mitten. Toes are another frequent target of self-punishment, and the prevalence of cheerful, even boisterous shops, always crowded with old men telling stories, which sell the hand-carved wooden legs known as "pegs" or "dollies," speaks of yet another.

No one has ever suggested that the viaduct killer is a South Side resident.

The South Siders live in a profound relationship to violence, and its effects are invariably implosive rather than explosive. Once a decade, perhaps twice a decade, one member of a family will realize, out of what depths of cultural necessity the outsider can only hope to imagine, that the whole family must die—*be sacrificed*, to speak with greater accuracy. Axes, knives, bludgeons, bottles, babushkas, ancient derringers, virtually every imaginable implement has been used to carry out this aim. The houses in which this act of sacrifice has taken place are immediately if not instantly cleaned by the entire neighborhood, acting in concert. The bodies receive a Catholic burial in consecrated ground, and a mass is said in honor of both the victims and their murderer. A picture of the departed family is installed in the church which abuts Market Square, and for a year the house is kept clean and dust-free by the grandmothers of the neighborhood. Men young and old will quietly enter the house, sip the brandy of the "removed," as they are called, meditate, now and then switch on the wireless or the television set, and reflect on the darkness of earthly life. The departed are frequently said to appear to friends and neighbors, and often accurately predict the coming of storms and assist in the location of lost household objects, a treasured button or Mother's sewing needle. After the year has elapsed, the house is sold, most often to a young couple, a young blacksmith or market vendor and his bride, who find the furniture and even the clothing of the "removed" welcome additions to their small household.

Further south are suburbs and impoverished hamlets, which do not compel a visit.

Immediately west of the War Memorial is the city's downtown. Before its decline, this was the city's business district and administrative center, and the monuments of its affluence remain. Marching directly west on the wide avenue which begins at the expressway are the Federal Building, the Post Office, and the great edifice of City Hall. Each is an entire block long and constructed of granite blocks quarried far north in the state. Flights of marble stairs lead up to the massive doors of these structures, and crystal chandeliers can be seen through many of the windows. The facades are classical and severe, uniting in an architectural landscape of granite revetments and colonnades of pillars. (Within, these grand and inhuman buildings have long ago been carved and partitioned into warrens illuminated by bare light bulbs or flickering fluorescent tubing, each tiny office with its worn counter for petitioners and a stamped sign proclaiming its function: Tax & Excise, Dog Licenses, Passports, Graphs & Charts, Registry of Notary Publics, and the like. The larger rooms with chandeliers which face the avenue, reserved for civic receptions and banquets, are seldom used.)

In the next sequence of buildings are the Hall of Records, the Police Headquarters, and the Criminal Courts Building. Again, wide empty marble steps lead up to massive bronze doors, rows of columns, glittering windows which on wintry days reflect back the gray empty sky. Local craftsmen, many of them descendants of the city's original French settlers, forged and installed the decorative iron bars and grilles on the facade of the Criminal Courts Building.

After we pass the massive, nearly windowless brick facades of the Gas and Electric buildings, we reach the arching metal drawbridge over the river. Looking downriver, we can see its muddy banks and the lights of the terrace of the Green Woman Taproom, now a popular gathering place for the city's civil servants. (A few feet further east is the spot from which a disgruntled lunatic attempted and failed to assassinate President Dwight D. Eisenhower.) Further on stand the high cement walls of several breweries. The drawbridge has not been raised since 1956, when a corporate yacht passed through.

Beyond the drawbridge lies the old mercantile center of the city, with its adult bookstores, pornographic theaters, coffee shops, and its rank of old department stores. These now house discount outlets selling roofing tiles, mufflers and other auto parts, plumbing equipment, and cut-rate clothing, and most of their display windows have been boarded or bricked in since the civic disturbances of 1968. Various civic plans have failed to revive this area, though the cobblestones and gas street lamps installed in the optimistic mid-seventies can for the most part still be seen. Connoisseurs of the poignant will wish to take a moment to appreciate them, though they should seek to avoid the bands of ragged children that frequent this area at nightfall, for though these children are harmless they can become pressing in their pleas for small change.

Many of these children inhabit dwellings they have constructed themselves in the vacant lots between the adult bookstores and fast-food outlets of the old mercantile district, and the "tree houses" atop mounds of tires, most of them several stories high and utilizing fire escapes and flights of stairs scavenged from the old department stores, are of some architectural interest. The stranger should not attempt to penetrate these "children's cities," and on no account should offer them any more than the pocket change they request or display a camera, jewelry, or an expensive wristwatch. The truly intrepid tourist seeking excitement may hire one of these children to guide him to the diversions of his choice. Two dollars is the usual gratuity for this service.

It is not advisable to purchase any of the goods the children themselves may offer for sale, although they have been affected by the same self-consciousness evident in the impressive buildings on the other side of the river and do sell picture postcards of their largest and most eccentric constructions. It may be that the naive architecture of these tree houses represents the city's most authentic artistic expression, and the postcards, amateurish as most of them are, provide interesting, perhaps even valuable, documentation of this expression of what may be called folk art.

These industrious children of the mercantile area have ritualized their violence into highly formalized tattooing and "spontaneous" forays and raids into the tree houses of opposing tribes during which only superficial injuries are sustained, and it is not suspected that the viaduct killer comes from their number.

Further west are the remains of the city's museum and library, devastated during the civic disturbances, and beyond these picturesque, still-smoking hulls lies the ghetto. It is not advised to enter the ghetto on foot, though the tourist who has arranged to rent an automobile may safely drive through it after he has negotiated his toll at the gate house. The ghetto's residents are completely self-sustaining, and the attentive tourist who visits this district will observe the multitude of tents housing hospitals, wholesale food and drug warehouses, and the like. Within the ghetto are believed to be many fine poets, painters, and musicians, as well as the historians known as "memorists," who are the district's living encyclopedias and archivists. The "memorist's" tasks include the memorization of the works of the area's poets, painters, etc., for the district contains no printing presses or art supply shops, and these inventive and self-reliant people have devised this method of preserving their works. It is not believed that a people capable of inventing the genre of "oral painting" could have spawned the viaduct killer, and in any case no ghetto resident is permitted access to any other area of the city.

The ghetto's relationship to violence is unknown.

Further west the annual snowfall increases greatly, for seven months of the year dropping an average of two point three feet of snow each month upon the shopping malls and paper mills which have concentrated here. Dust storms are common during the summers, and certain infectious viruses, to which the inhabitants have become immune, are carried in the water.

Still further west lies the Sports Complex.

The tourist who has ventured thus far is well advised to turn back at this point and return to our beginning, the War Memorial. Your car may be left in the ample and clearly posted parking lot on the Memorial's eastern side. From the Memorial's wide empty terraces, you are invited to look southeast, where a great unfinished bridge crosses half the span to the hamlets of Wyatt and Arnoldville. Construction was abandoned on this noble civic project, subsequently imitated by many cities in our western states and in Australia and Finland, immediately after the disturbances of 1968, when its lack of utility became apparent. When it was noticed that many families chose to eat their bag lunches on the Memorial's lakeside terraces in order to gaze silently at its great interrupted arc, the bridge was adopted as the symbol of the city, and its image decorates the city's many flags and medals.

The "Broken Span," as it is called, which hangs in the air like the great frozen wings above the Valley, serves no function but the symbolic. In itself and entirely by accident this great non-span memorializes violence, not only by serving as a reference to the workmen who lost their lives during its construction (its nonconstruction). It is not rounded or finished in any way, for labor on the bridge ended abruptly, even brutally, and from its truncated floating end dangle lengths of rusting iron webbing, thick wire cables weighted by chunks of cement, and bits of old planking material. In the days before access to the un-bridge was walled off by an electrified fence, two or three citizens each year elected to commit their suicides by leaping from the end of the span; and one must resort to a certain lexical violence when referring to it. Ghetto residents are said to have named it "Whitey," and the tree-house children call it "Ursula," after one of their own killed in the dis-turbances. South Siders refer to it as "The Ghost," civil servants, "The Beast," and East Siders simply as "that thing." The "Broken Span" has the violence of all unfinished things, of everything interrupted or left undone. In violence there is often the quality of *yearning*—the yearning for completion. For closure. For that which is absent and would if pre-sent bring to fulfillment. For the body without which the wing is a use-less frozen ornament. It ought not to go unmentioned that most of the city's residents have never seen the "bridge" except in its representa-tions, and for this majority the "bridge" is little more or less than a myth, being without any actual referent. It is pure idea.

Violence, it is felt though unspoken, is the physical form of sen sitivity. The city believes this. Incompletion, the lack of referent which strands you in the realm of pure idea, demands release from itself. We are above all an American city, and what we believe most deeply we . . .

The victims of the viaduct killer, that citizen who excites our attention, who makes us breathless with outrage and causes our police force to ransack the humble dwellings along the riverbank, have all been adult women. These women in their middle years are taken from their lives and set like statues beside the pillar. Each morning there is more pedestrian traffic on the viaduct, in the frozen mornings men (mainly men) come with their lunches in paper bags, walking slowly along the cement walkway, not looking at one another, barely knowing what they are doing, looking down over the edge of the viaduct, looking away, dawdling, finally leaning like fishermen against the railing, waiting until they can no longer delay going to their jobs.

The visitor who has done so much and gone so far in this city may turn his back on the "Broken Span," the focus of civic pride, and look in a southwesterly direction past the six lanes of the expressway, perhaps on tiptoe (children may have to mount one of the convenient retaining walls). The dull flanks of the viaduct should just now be visible, with the heads and shoulders of the waiting men picked out in the gray air like brush strokes. The quality of their yearning, its expectancy, is visible even from here.

# STEVEN MILLHAUSER
## In the Penny Arcade

In the summer of my twelfth birthday, I stepped from August sunshine into the shadows of the penny arcade. My father and mother had agreed to wait outside, on a green bench beside the brilliant white ticket booth. Even as I entered the shade cast by the narrow overhang, I imagined my mother gazing anxiously after me from under her wide-brimmed summer hat, as if she might lose me forever in that intricate darkness, while my father, supporting the sun-polished bowl of his pipe with one hand, and frowning as if angrily in the intense light, for he refused to wear either a hat or sunglasses, had already begun studying the signs on the dart-and-balloon booth and the cotton-candy stand, in order to demonstrate to me that he was not overly anxious on my account. After all, I was a big boy now. I had not been to the amusement park for two years. I had dreamed of it all that tense, enigmatic summer, when the world seemed hushed and expectant, as if on the verge of revealing an overwhelming secret. Inside the penny arcade I saw at once that the darkness was not dark enough. I had remembered a plunge into the enticing darkness of movie theaters on hot bright summer afternoons, but here sunlight entered through the open doorway shaded by the narrow overhanging roof. Through a high window a shaft of sunlight fell, looking as if it had been painted with a wide brush onto the dusty air. Among the mysterious ringing of bells, the clanks, the metallic whirrings of the penny arcade I could hear the bright, prancing, secretly mournful music of the merry-go-round and the cries and clatter of the distant roller coaster.

The darkness seemed thicker toward the back of the penny arcade, as if it had retreated from the open doorway and gathered more densely there. Slowly I made my way deeper in. Tough teenagers with hair slicked back on both sides stood huddled over the pinball machines. In their dangerous hair, rich with violence, I could see the deep lines made by their combs, like knife cuts in wood. I passed a glass case containing a yellow toy derrick sitting on a heap of prizes: plastic rings, flashlight pens, little games with holes and silver balls, black rubber tarantulas, red-hots and licorice pipes. Before the derrick a father held up a little blond girl in red shorts and a blue T-shirt; working the handle, she tried to make the jaws of the derrick close over a prize, which kept slipping back into the pile. Nearby, a small boy sat gripping a big black wheel that controlled a car racing on a screen. A tall muscular teenager with a blond crewcut and sullen gray eyes stood bent over a pinball machine that showed luminous Hawaiian girls with red flowers in their gleaming black hair; each time his finger pushed the button, a muscle tensed visibly in his dark, bare upper arm. For a moment I was tempted by the derrick, but at once despised my childishness and continued on my way. It was not prizes I had come out of the sun for. It was something else I had come for, something mysterious and elusive that I could scarcely name. Tense with longing, with suppressed excitement, and with the effort of appearing tough, dangerous, and inconspicuous, I came at last to the old fortune teller in her glass booth.

Through the dusty glass I saw that she had aged. Her red turban was streaked with dust, one of her pale blue eyes had nearly faded away, and her long, pointing finger, suspended above a row of five dusty and slightly upcurled playing cards, was chipped at the knuckle. A crack showed in the side of her nose. Her one good eye had a vague and vacant look, as if she had misplaced something and could no longer remember what it was. She looked as if the long boredom of uninterrupted meditation had withered her spirit. A decayed spiderweb stretched between her sleeve and wrist.

I remembered how I had once been afraid of looking into her eyes, unwilling to be caught in that deep, mystical gaze. Feeling betrayed and uneasy, I abandoned her and went off in search of richer adventures.

The merry-go-round music had stopped, and far away I heard the cry: "Three tries for two bits! Everybody a winner!" I longed to escape from these sounds, into the lost beauty and darkness of the penny arcade. I passed several dead-looking games and rounded the corner of a big machine that printed your name on a disk of metal. I found him standing against the wall, beside a dusty pinball machine with a piece of tape over its coin-slot. No one seemed to be paying attention to him. He was wearing a black cowboy hat pulled low over his forehead, a black shirt, wrinkled black pants, and black, cracked boots with nickel-colored spurs. He had long black sideburns and a thin black mustache. His black belt was studded with white wooden bullets. In the center of his chest was a small red target. He stood with one arm held away from his side, the hand gripping a black pistol that pointed down. Facing him stood a post to which was attached a holster with a gun. From the butt of the gun came a coiled black rubber wire that ran into the post. A faded sign gave directions in tiny print. I slid the holster to hip level and, stepping up against it, practiced my draw. Then I placed a dime carefully in the shallow depression of the coin-slot, pushed the metal tongue in and out, and grasped the gun. I heard a whirring sound. Suddenly someone began to speak; I looked quickly about, but the voice came from the cowboy's stomach. I had forgotten. Slowly, wearily, as if dragging their way reluctantly up from a deep well, the words struggled forth. "All . . . right . . . you . . . dirty . . . side . . . winder. . . . Drrrrraw!" I drew my gun and shot him in the heart. The cowboy stood dully staring at me, as if he were wondering without interest why I had just killed him. Then slowly, slowly, he began to raise his gun. I could feel the strain of that slow raising in my own tensed arm. When the gun was pointing a little to the left of my stomach, he stopped. I heard a dim, soft bang. Wearily, as if from far away, he said: "Take . . . that . . . you . . . low . . . down . . . varmint." Slowly he began to lower his burdensome gun. When the barrel was pointing downward, I heard the whirring stop. I looked about; a little girl holding a candied apple in a fat fist stared up at me without expression. In rage and sorrow I strode away.

I passed the little men with boxing gloves standing stiffly in their glass case, but I knew better than to try to stir them into sluggish and inept life. A desolation had fallen over the creatures of the penny arcade. Even the real, live people strolling noisily about had become infected with the general woodenness; their laughter sounded forced, their gestures seemed exaggerated and unconvincing. I felt caught in an atmosphere of decay and disappointment. I felt that if I could not find whatever it was I was looking for, my entire life would be harmed. Making my way along narrow aisles flanked by high, clattering games, I

turned left and right among them, scorning their unmysterious pleasures, until at last I came to a section of old machines, in a dusky recess
near the back of the hall.

The machines stood close together, as if huddling in dark, disrepu-
table comradeship, yet with a careless and indifferent air among them.
Three older boys, one of whom had a pack of cigarettes tucked into
the rolled-up sleeve of his T-shirt, stood peering into three viewers. I
chose a machine as far from them as possible. A faded picture in dim
colors showed a woman with faded yellow hair standing with her back
to me and looking over her shoulder with a smile. She was wearing a
tall white hat that had turned nearly gray, a faded white tuxedo jacket,
faded black nylon stockings with a black line up the back, and faded red
high-heels. In one hand she held a cane with which she reached behind
her, lifting slightly the back of her jacket to reveal the tense top of one
stocking and the bottom of a faded garter. With a feeling of oppression
I placed my dime in the slot and leaned my face onto the metal viewer.
Its edges pressed against the bones of my face as if it had seized me and
pulled me close. I pushed the metal tongue in and out; for a moment
nothing happened. Then a title appeared: A DAY AT THE CIRCUS. It
vanished to reveal a dim woman in black-and-white who was standing
on a horse in an outdoor ring surrounded by well-dressed men and
women. She was wearing a tight costume with a little skirt and did not
look like the woman in the picture. As the horse trotted slowly round
and round the ring, sometimes leaping jerkily forward as the film
jerkily unreeled, she stood on one leg and reached out the other leg
behind her. Once she jumped in the air and landed looking the other
way, and once she stood on her hands. The men and women strained
to see past each other's shoulders; sometimes they looked at each other
and nodded vigorously. I waited for something to happen, for some
unspoken promise to be fulfilled, but all at once the movie ended. Desperately dissatisfied I tried to recall the troubling, half-naked woman I
had seen two years earlier, but my memory was vague and uncertain;
perhaps I had not even dared to peer into the forbidden viewer.

I left the machines and began walking restlessly through the loud
hall, savoring its shame, its fall from mystery. It seemed to me that I
must have walked into the wrong arcade; I wondered whether there
was another one in a different part of the amusement park, the true
penny arcade that had enchanted my childhood. It seemed as though a
blight had overtaken the creatures of this hall: they were sickly, wasted
versions of themselves. Perhaps they were impostors, who had treach-

erously overthrown the true creatures and taken their place. Anxiously I continued my sad wandering, searching for something I could no longer understand—a nuance, a mystery, a dark glimmer. Under a pin-ball machine I saw a cone of paper covered with sticky pink wisps. An older boy in jeans and a white T-shirt, wearing a dark-green canvas apron divided into pockets bulging with coins, looked sharply about for customers who needed change. I came to a shadowy region at the back of the hall; there was no one about. I noticed that the merry-go-round music had stopped again. The machines in this region had an old and melancholy look. I passed them without interest, turned a corner, and saw before me a dark alcove.

A thick rope of blue velvet, attached to two posts, stretched in a curve before the opening. In the darkness within I saw a jumble of dim shapes, some covered with cloths like furniture in a closed room in a decaying mansion in a movie. I felt something swell within me, as if my temples would burst; at the same time I was extraordinarily calm. I knew that these must be the true machines and creatures of the penny arcade, and that for some unaccountable reason they had been removed to make way for the sad impostors whose shameful performance I had witnessed. I looked quickly behind me; I could barely breathe. With a feeling that at any moment I might dissolve, I stepped over the rope and entered the forbidden dark.

It was too dark for me to see clearly, but some other sense was so heightened that I was almost painfully alert. I could feel the mystery of these banished machines, their promise of rich and intricate excite-ments. I could not understand why they had been set apart in this enchanted cavern, but I had no doubt that here was the lost penny arcade, crowded with all that I had longed for and almost forgotten. With fearful steps I came to a machine carelessly covered with a cloth; peering intensely at the exposed portion, I caught a glimpse of cracked glass. At that moment I heard a sound behind me, and in terror I whirled around.

No one was there. A hush had fallen over the penny arcade. I hurried to the rope and stepped into safety. At first I thought the hall had become strangely deserted, but I saw several people walking slowly and quietly about. It appeared that one of those accidental hushes had fallen over things, as sometimes happens in a crowd: the excitement dies down, for an instant the interwoven cries and voices become unraveled, quietness pours into the suddenly open spaces from which it had been excluded. In that hush, anything might happen. All my senses had burst wide open. I was so tense with inner excitement, which pressed against my temples, that it seemed as if I would expand to fill the entire hall.

Through an intervening maze of machines I could see the black hat brim and black elbow of the distant cowboy. In the tremulous stillness, which at any moment might dissolve, he seemed to await me.

Even as I approached I sensed that he had changed. He seemed more sure of himself, and he looked directly at me. His mouth wore an expression of faint mockery. I could feel his whole nature expanding and unfolding within him. From the shadow of his hat brim his eyes blazed darkly; for a moment I had the sensation of someone behind me. I turned, and saw in the glass booth across the hall the fortune teller staring at me with piercing blue eyes. Between her and the cowboy I could feel a dark complicity. Somewhere I heard a gentle creaking, and I became aware of small, subtle motions all about me. The creatures of the penny arcade were waking from their wooden torpor. At first I could not see an actual motion, but I realized that the position of the little boxers had changed slightly, that the fortune teller had raised a warning finger. Secret signals were passing back and forth. I heard another sound, and saw a little hockey player seated at the side of his painted wooden field. I turned back to the cowboy; he looked at me with ferocity and contempt. His black eyes blazed. I could see one of his hands quiver with alertness. A muscle in his cheek tensed. My temples were throbbing, I could scarcely breathe. I sensed that at any moment something forbidden was going to happen. I looked at his gun, which was now in his holster. I raised my eyes; he was ready. As if mesmerized I put a dime in the slot and pushed the tongue in and out. For a moment he stared at me in cool fury. All at once he drew and fired—with such grace and swiftness, such deeply soothing swiftness, that something relaxed far back in my mind. I drew and fired, wondering whether I was already dead. He stood still, gazing at me with sudden calm. Grasping his stomach with both hands, he staggered slowly back, looking at me with an expression of flawless and magnificent malice. Gracefully he slumped to one knee, and bowed his unforgiving head as if in prayer; and falling slowly onto his side, he rolled onto his back with his arms outspread.

At once he rose, slapped dust from his pants, and returned to his original position. Radiant with spite, noble with venomous rancor, he looked at me with fierce amusement; I felt he was mocking me in some inevitable way. I knew that I hadn't a moment to lose, that I must seize

my chance before it was too late. Tearing my eyes from his, I left him there in the full splendor of his malevolence.

Through the quiet hall I rushed furiously along. I came to a dusky recess near the back; no one was there. Thrusting in my dime, I pressed my hot forehead onto the cool metal. It was just as I thought: the woman slipped gracefully from her horse and, curtseying to silent applause, made her way through the crowd. She entered a dim room containing a bed with a carved mahogany headboard, and a tall swivel mirror suspended on a frame. She smiled at herself in the mirror, as if acknowledging that at last she had entered into her real existence. With a sudden rapid movement she began removing her costume. Beneath her disguise she was wearing a long jacket and a pair of black nylon stockings. Turning her back to the mirror and smiling over her shoulder, she lifted her jacket with the hook of her cane to reveal the top of her taut, dazzling stocking and a glittering garter. Teasingly she lifted it a little higher, then suddenly threw away the cane and began to unbutton her jacket. She frowned down and fumbled with the thick, clumsy buttons as I watched with tense impatience; as the jacket came undone I saw something dim and shadowy beneath. At last she slipped out of the jacket, revealing a shimmering white slip which came to her knees. Quickly pulling the slip over her head, so that her face was concealed for a moment, she revealed a flowery blouse above a gleaming black girdle. Gripping the top of the girdle she began to peel it down, but it clung to her so tightly that she had to keep shifting her weight from leg to leg, her face grew dark, suddenly the girdle slipped off and revealed yet another tight and glimmering garment beneath, faster and faster she struggled out of her underwear, tossing each piece aside and revealing new and unsuspected depths of silken concealment, and always I had the sense that I was coming closer and closer to a dark mystery that cunningly eluded me. Prodigal and exuberant in her undressing, she offered a rich revelation of half-glimpses, an abundance of veiled and dusky disclosures. She blossomed with shimmer, silk, and shadow, ushering me into a lush and intricate realm of always more dangerous exposures which themselves proved to be new and dazzling concealments. Exhausted by these intensities, I watched her anxiously yet with growing languor, as if something vital in the pit of my stomach were being drawn forth and spun into the shimmer of her inexhaustible disrobings. She herself was lost in a feverish ecstasy, in the midst of which I detected a sadness, as if with each gesture she were grandly discarding parts of her life. I felt a melting languor, a feverish

melancholy, until I knew that at any moment—"Hey!" I tore my face
away. A boy in a yellow T-shirt was shouting at his friend. People
strolled about, bells rang, children shouted in the penny arcade. Bright,
prancing, sorrowful music from the merry-go-round turned round and
round in the air. With throbbing temples I walked into the more open
part of the arcade. The cowboy stood frozen in place, four boys in
high-school jackets stood turning the rods from which the little hockey
players hung down. Two small boys stood over the little boxers, who
jerkily performed their motions. I turned around: in the dark alcove,
before which stretched a blue velvet rope, I saw a collection of old,
broken pinball machines. Across the hall the faded fortune teller sat
dully in her dusty glass cage. A weariness had settled over the penny
arcade. I felt tired and old, as if nothing could ever happen here. The
strange hush, the waking of the creatures from their wooden slumber,
seemed dim and uncertain, as if it had taken place long ago.

It was time to leave. Sadly I walked over to the wooden cowboy
in his dusty black hat. I looked at him without forgiveness, taking
careful note of the paint peeling from his hands. A boy of about my age
stood before him, ready to draw. When the wooden figure began to
speak, the boy burst into loud, mocking laughter. I felt the pain of
that laughter burning in my chest, and I glanced reproachfully at the
cowboy; from under the shadows of his hat his dull eyes seemed to
acknowledge me. Slowly, jerkily, he began to raise his wooden arm.
The lifting caused his head to shift slightly, and for an instant he cast at
me a knowing gaze. An inner excitement seized me. Giving him a
secret salute, I began walking rapidly about, as if stillness could not
contain such illuminations.

All at once I had understood the secret of the penny arcade.

I understood with the force of an inner blow that the creatures of
the penny arcade had lost their freedom under the constricting gaze of
all those who no longer believed in them. Their majesty and mystery
had been crushed down by the shrewd, oppressive eyes of countless
visitors who looked at them without seeing their fertile inner nature.
Gradually worn down into a parody of themselves, restricted to three
or four preposterous wooden gestures, they yet contained within themselves the life that had once been theirs. Under the nourishing gaze of
one who understood them, they might still spring into a semblance of
their former selves. During the strange hush that had fallen over the
arcade, the creatures had been freed from the paralyzing beams of commonplace attention that held them down as surely as the little ropes

held down Gulliver in my illustrated book. I recognized that I myself had become part of the conspiracy of dullness, and that only in a moment of lavish awareness, which had left me confused and exhausted, had I seen truly. They had not betrayed me: I had betrayed them. I saw that I was in danger of becoming ordinary, and I understood that from now on I would have to be vigilant.

For this was the only penny arcade, the true penny arcade. There was no other.

Turning decisively, I walked toward the entrance and stepped into the dazzle of a perfect August afternoon. My mother and father shimmered on their bench, as if they were dissolving into light. In the glittering sandy dust beside their bench I saw the blazing white top of an ice-cream cup. My father was looking at his watch, my mother's face was turning toward me with a sorrowful expression that had already begun to change to deepest joy. A smell of saltwater from the beach beyond the park mingled with a smell of asphalt and cotton candy. Over the roof of the dart-and-balloon booth, silver airplanes were sailing lazily round and round at the ends of black cables in the brilliant blue sky. Shaking my head as if to clear it of shadows, I prepared myself to greet the simple pleasures of the sun.

# STEPHEN KING
## The Reach

"The Reach was wider in those days," Stella Flanders told her great-grand-children in the last summer of her life, the summer before she began to see ghosts. The children looked at her with wide, silent eyes, and her son, Alden, turned from his seat on the porch where he was whittling. It was Sunday, and Alden wouldn't take his boat out on Sundays no matter how high the price of lobster was.

"What do you mean, Gram?" Tommy asked, but the old woman did not answer. She only sat in her rocker by the cold stove, her slippers bumping placidly on the floor.

Tommy asked his mother: "What does she mean?"

Lois only shook her head, smiled, and sent them out with pots to pick berries.

Stella thought: She's forgot. Or did she ever know?

The Reach had been wider in those days. If anyone knew it was so, that person was Stella Flanders. She had been born in 1884, she was the oldest resident of Goat Island, and she had never once in her life been to the mainland.

*Do you love?* This question had begun to plague her, and she did not even know what it meant.

Fall set in, a cold fall without the necessary rain to bring a really fine color to the trees, either on Goat or on Raccoon Head across the Reach. The wind blew long, cold notes that fall, and Stella felt each note resonate in her heart.

On November 19, when the first flurries came swirling down out of a sky the color of white chrome, Stella celebrated her birthday. Most of the village turned out. Hattie Stoddard came, whose mother had died of pleurisy in 1954 and whose father had been lost with the *Dancer* in 1941. Richard and Mary Dodge came, Richard moving slowly up the path on his cane, his arthritis riding him like an invisible passenger. Sarah Havelock came, of course; Sarah's mother Annabelle had been Stella's best friend. They had gone to the island school together, grades one to eight, and Annabelle had married Tommy Frane, who had pulled her hair in the fifth grade and made her cry, just as Stella had married Bill Flanders, who had once knocked all of her schoolbooks out of her arms and into the mud (but she had managed not to cry). Now both Annabelle and Tommy were gone and Sarah was the only one of their seven children still on the island. Her husband, George Havelock, who had been known to everyone as Big George, had died a nasty death over on the mainland in 1967, the year there was no fishing. An ax had slipped in Big George's hand, there had been blood—too much of it!—and an island funeral three days later. And when Sarah came in to Stella's party and cried, "Happy birthday, Gram!" Stella hugged her tight and closed her eyes.

(*do you do you love?*)

but she did not cry.

There was a tremendous birthday cake. Hattie had made it with her best friend, Vera Spruce. The assembled company bellowed out "Happy Birthday to You" in a combined voice that was loud enough to drown out the wind . . . for a little while, anyway. Even Alden sang, who in the normal course of events would sing only "Onward, Christian Soldiers" and the doxology in church and would mouth the words of all the rest with his head hunched and his big old jug ears just as red as tomatoes. There were ninety-five candles on Stella's cake, and even over the singing she heard the wind, although her hearing was not what it once had been.

She thought the wind was calling her name.

*"I was not the only one," she would have told Lois's children if she could. "In my day there were many that lived and died on the island. There was no mail boat in those days; Bull Symes used to bring the mail when there was mail. There was no ferry, either. If you had business on the Head, your man took you in the lobster boat. So far as I know, there wasn't a flushing toilet on the island until 1946. 'Twas Bull's boy Harold that put in the first one*

*the year after the heart attack carried Bull off while he was out dragging traps.*
*I remember seeing them bring Bull home. I remember that they brought him*
*up wrapped in a tarpaulin, and how one of his green boots poked out. I*
*remember . . .*

  *And they would say: "What, Gram? What do you remember?"*
  *How would she answer them? Was there more?*

On the first day of winter, a month or so after the birthday party, Stella
opened the back door to get stovewood and discovered a dead sparrow
on the back stoop. She bent down carefully, picked it up by one foot,
and looked at it.

  "Frozen," she announced, and something inside her spoke
another word. It had been forty years since she had seen a frozen
bird—1938. The year the Reach had frozen.

  Shuddering, pulling her coat closer, she threw the dead sparrow in
the old rusty incinerator as she went by it. The day was cold. The sky
was a clear, deep blue. On the night of her birthday four inches of
snow had fallen, had melted, and no more had come since then. "Got
to come soon," Larry McKeen down at the Goat Island Store said
sagely, as if daring winter to stay away.

  Stella got to the woodpile, picked herself an armload and carried
it back to the house. Her shadow, crisp and clean, followed her.

  As she reached the back door, where the sparrow had fallen, Bill
spoke to her—but the cancer had taken Bill twelve years before.
"Stella," Bill said, and she saw his shadow fall beside her, longer but just
as clear-cut, the shadow-bill of his shadow-cap twisted jauntily off to
one side just as he had always worn it. Stella felt a scream lodged in her
throat. It was too large to touch her lips.

  "Stella," he said again, "when you comin across to the mainland?
We'll get Norm Jolley's old Ford and go down to Bean's in Freeport
just for a lark. What do you say?"

  She wheeled, almost dropping her wood, and there was no one
there. Just the dooryard sloping down to the hill, then the wild white
grass, and beyond all, at the edge of everything, clear-cut and somehow
magnified, the Reach . . . and the mainland beyond it.

*"Gram, what's the Reach?" Lona might have asked . . . although she never*
*had. And she would have given them the answer any fisherman knew by rote: a*
*Reach is a body of water between two bodies of land, a body of water which is*
*open at either end. The old lobsterman's joke went like this: know how to read*

*y'compass when the fog comes, boys; between Jonesport and London there's a mighty long Reach.*

*"Reach is the water between the island and the mainland," she might have amplified, giving them molasses cookies and hot tea laced with sugar. "I know that much. I know it as well as my husband's name . . . and how he used to wear his hat."*

*"Gram?" Lona would say. "How come you never been across the Reach?"*

*"Honey," she would say, "I never saw any reason to go."*

In January, two months after the birthday party, the Reach froze for the first time since 1938. The radio warned islanders and mainlanders alike not to trust the ice, but Stewie McClelland and Russell Bowie took Stewie's Bombardier Skiddoo out anyway after a long afternoon spent drinking Apple Zapple wine, and sure enough, the skiddoo went into the Reach. Stewie managed to crawl out (although he lost one foot to frostbite). The Reach took Russell Bowie and carried him away.

That January 25 there was a memorial service for Russell. Stella went on her son Alden's arm, and he mouthed the words to the hymns and boomed out the doxology in his great tuneless voice before the benediction. Stella sat afterward with Sarah Havelock and Hattie Stoddard and Vera Spruce in the glow of the wood fire in the town-hall basement. A going-away party for Russell was being held, complete with Za-Rex punch and nice little cream-cheese sandwiches cut into triangles. The men, of course, kept wandering out back for a nip of something a bit stronger than Za-Rex. Russell Bowie's new widow sat red-eyed and stunned beside Ewell McCracken, the minister. She was seven months big with child—it would be her fifth—and Stella, half-dozing in the heat of the woodstove, thought: *She'll be crossing the Reach soon enough, I guess. She'll move to Freeport or Lewiston and go for a waitress, I guess.*

She looked around at Vera and Hattie, to see what the discussion was.

"No, I didn't hear," Hattie said. "What *did* Freddy say?"

They were talking about Freddy Dinsmore, the oldest man on the island (two years younger'n me, though, Stella thought with some satisfaction), who had sold out his store to Larry McKeen in 1960 and now lived on his retirement.

"Said he'd never seen such a winter," Vera said, taking out her knitting. "He says it is going to make people sick."

Sarah Havelock looked at Stella, and asked if Stella had ever seen such a winter. There had been no snow since that first little bit; the ground lay crisp and bare and brown. The day before, Stella had walked thirty paces into the back field, holding her right hand level at the height of her thigh, and the grass there had snapped in a neat row with a sound like breaking glass.

"No," Stella said. "The Reach froze in '38, but there was snow that year. Do you remember Bull Symes, Hattie?"

Hattie laughed. "I think I still have the black-and-blue he gave me on my sit-upon at the New Year's party in '53. He pinched me *that* hard. What about him?"

"Bull and my own man walked across to the mainland that year," Stella said. "That February of 1938. Strapped on snowshoes, walked across to Dorrit's Tavern on the Head, had them each a shot of whiskey, and walked back. They asked me to come along. They were like two little boys off to the sliding with a toboggan between them."

They were looking at her, touched by the wonder of it. Even Vera was looking at her wide-eyed, and Vera had surely heard the tale before. If you believed the stories, Bull and Vera had once played some house together, although it was hard, looking at Vera now, to believe she had ever been so young.

"And you didn't go?" Sarah asked, perhaps seeing the reach of the Reach in her mind's eye, so white it was almost blue in the heatless winter sunshine, the sparkle of the snow crystals, the mainland drawing closer, walking across, yes, walking across the ocean just like Jesus-out-of-the-boat, leaving the island for the one and only time in your life on *foot*—

"No," Stella said. Suddenly she wished she had brought her own knitting. "I didn't go with them."

"Why *not*?" Hattie asked, almost indignantly.

"It was washday," Stella almost snapped, and then Missy Bowie, Russell's widow, broke into loud, braying sobs. Stella looked over and there sat Bill Flanders in his red-and-black-checked jacket, hat cocked to one side, smoking a Herbert Tareyton with another tucked behind his ear for later. She felt her heart leap into her chest and choke between beats.

She made a noise, but just then a knot popped like a rifle shot in the stove, and neither of the other ladies heard.

"Poor *thing*," Sarah nearly cooed.

"Well shut of that good-for-nothing," Hattie grunted. She searched for the grim depth of the truth concerning the departed Russell Bowie and found it: "Little more than a tramp for pay, that man. She's well out of *that* two-hoss trace."

Stella barely heard these things. There sat Bill, close enough to the Reverend McCracken to have tweaked his nose if he so had a mind; he looked no more than forty, his eyes barely marked by the crow's-feet that had later sunk so deep, wearing his flannel pants and his gum-rubber boots with the gray wool socks folded neatly down over the tops.

"We're waitin on you, Stel," he said. "You come on across and see the mainland. You won't need no snowshoes this year."

There he sat in the town-hall basement, big as Billy-be-damned, and then another knot exploded in the stove and he was gone. And the Reverend McCracken went on comforting Missy Bowie as if nothing had happened.

That night Vera called up Annie Phillips on the phone, and in the course of the conversation mentioned to Annie that Stella Flanders didn't look well, not at all well.

"Alden would have a scratch of a job getting her off-island if she took sick," Annie said. Annie liked Alden because her own son Toby had told her Alden would take nothing stronger than beer. Annie was strictly temperance, herself.

"Wouldn't get her off 'tall unless she was in a coma," Vera said, pronouncing the word in the downeast fashion: *comer*. "When Stella says 'Frog,' Alden jumps. Alden ain't but half-bright, you know. Stella pretty much runs him."

"Oh, ayuh?" Annie said.

Just then there was a metallic crackling sound on the line. Vera could hear Annie Phillips for a moment longer—not the words, just the sound of her voice going on behind the crackling—and then there was nothing. The wind had gusted up high and the phone lines had gone down, maybe into Godlin's Pond or maybe down by Borrow's Cove, where they went into the Reach sheathed in rubber. It was possible that they had gone down on the other side, on the Head . . . and some might even have said (only half-joking) that Russell Bowie had reached up a cold hand to snap the cable, just for the hell of it.

Not 700 feet away Stella Flanders lay under her puzzle-quilt and listened to the dubious music of Alden's snores in the other room. She

listened to Alden so she wouldn't have to listen to the wind . . . but she
heard the wind anyway, oh yes, coming across the frozen expanse of
the Reach, a mile and a half of water that was now overplated with ice,
ice with lobsters down below, and groupers, and perhaps the twisting,
dancing body of Russell Bowie, who used to come each April with his
old Rogers rototiller and turn her garden.

*Who'll turn the earth this April?* she wondered as she lay cold and
curled under her puzzle-quilt. And as a dream in a dream, her voice
answered her voice: *Do you love?* The wind gusted, rattling the storm
window. It seemed that the storm window was talking to her, but she
turned her face away from its words. And did not cry.

*"But, Gram," Lona would press (she never gave up, not that one, she was like
her mom, and her grandmother before her), "you still haven't told why you
never went across."*

*"Why, child, I have always had everything I wanted right here
on Goat."*

*"But it's so small. We live in Portland. There's buses, Gram!"*

*"I see enough of what goes on in cities on the TV. I guess I'll stay
where I am."*

*Hal was younger, but somehow more intuitive; he would not press her as
his sister might, but his question would go closer to the heart of things: "You
never wanted to go across, Gram? Never?"*

*And she would lean toward him, and take his small hands, and tell him
how her mother and father had come to the island shortly after they were married, and how Bull Symes's grandfather had taken Stella's father as a 'prentice
on his boat. She would tell him how her mother had conceived four times but
one of her babies had miscarried and another had died a week after birth—she
would have left the island if they could have saved it at the mainland hospital,
but of course it was over before that was even thought of.*

*She would tell them that Bill had delivered Jane, their grandmother,
but not that when it was over he had gone into the bathroom and first puked
and then wept like a hysterical woman who had her monthlies p'ticularly
bad. Jane, of course, had left the island at fourteen to go to high school; girls
didn't get married at fourteen anymore, and when Stella saw her go off in the
boat with Bradley Maxwell, whose job it had been to ferry the kids back and
forth that month, she knew in her heart that Jane was gone for good,
although she would come back for a while. She would tell them that
Alden had come along ten years later, after they had given up, and as if to
make up for his tardiness, here was Alden still, a lifelong bachelor, and in*

*some ways Stella was grateful for that because Alden was not terribly bright
and there are plenty of women willing to take advantage of a man with a
slow brain and a good heart (although she would not tell the children that
last, either).*

*She would say: "Louis and Margaret Godlin begat Stella Godlin, who
became Stella Flanders; Bill and Stella Flanders begat Jane and Alden Flanders
and Jane Flanders became Jane Wakefield; Richard and Jane Wakefield begat
Lois Wakefield, who became Lois Perrault; David and Lois Perrault begat
Lona and Hal. Those are your names, children: you are Godlin-Flanders-
Wakefield-Perrault. Your blood is in the stones of this island, and I stay here
because the mainland is too far to reach. Yes, I love; I have loved, anyway, or
at least tried to love, but memory is so wide and so deep, and I cannot cross.
Godlin-Flanders-Wakefield-Perrault . . ."*

That was the coldest February since the National Weather Service
began keeping records, and by the middle of the month the ice covering the Reach was safe. Snowmobiles buzzed and whined and sometimes turned over when they climbed the ice-heaves wrong. Children
tried to skate, found the ice too bumpy to be any fun, and went back to
Godlin's Pond on the far side of the hill, but not before little Justin
McCracken, the minister's son, caught his skate in a fissure and broke
his ankle. They took him over to the hospital on the mainland where a
doctor who owned a Corvette told him, "Son, it's going to be as good
as new."

Freddy Dinsmore died very suddenly just three days after Justin
McCracken broke his ankle. He caught the flu late in January, would
not have the doctor, told everyone it was "Just a cold from goin out to
get the mail without m'scarf," took to his bed, and died before anyone
could take him across to the mainland and hook him up to all those
machines they have waiting for guys like Freddy. His son George, a
tosspot of the first water even at the advanced age (for tosspots,
anyway) of sixty-eight, found Freddy with a copy of the *Bangor Daily
News* in one hand and his Remington, unloaded, near the other.
Apparently he had been thinking of cleaning it just before he died.
George Dinsmore went on a three-week toot, said toot financed by
someone who knew that George would have his old dad's insurance
money coming. Hattie Stoddard went around telling anyone who
would listen that old George Dinsmore was a sin and a disgrace, no
better than a tramp for pay.

There was a lot of flu around. The school closed for two weeks that February instead of the usual one because so many pupils were out sick. "No snow breeds germs," Sarah Havelock said.

Near the end of the month, just as people were beginning to look forward to the false comfort of March, Alden Flanders caught the flu himself. He walked around with it for nearly a week and then took to his bed with a fever of a hundred and one. Like Freddy, he refused to have the doctor, and Stella stewed and fretted and worried. Alden was not as old as Freddy, but that May he would turn sixty.

The snow came at last. Six inches on Valentine's Day, another six on the twentieth, and a foot in a good old norther on the leap, February 29. The snow lay white and strange between the cove and the mainland, like a sheep's meadow where there had been only gray and surging water at this time of year since time out of mind. Several people walked across to the mainland and back. No snowshoes were necessary this year because the snow had frozen to a firm, glittery crust. They might take a knock of whiskey, too, Stella thought, but they would not take it at Dorrit's. Dorrit's had burned down in 1958.

And she saw Bill all four times. Once he told her: "Y'ought to come soon, Stella. We'll go steppin. What do you say?"

She could say nothing. Her fist was crammed deep into her mouth.

*"Everything I ever wanted or needed was here," she would tell them. "We had the radio and now we have the television, and that's all I want of the world beyond the Reach. I had my garden year in and year out. And lobster? Why, we always used to have a pot of lobster stew on the back of the stove and we used to take it off and put it behind the door in the pantry when the minister came calling so he wouldn't see we were eating 'poor man's soup.'*

*"I have seen good weather and bad, and if there were times when I wondered what it might be like to actually be in the Sears store instead of ordering from the catalogue, or to go into one of those Shaw's markets I see on TV instead of buying at the store here or sending Alden across for something special like a Christmas capon or an Easter ham . . . or if I ever wanted, just once, to stand on Congress Street in Portland and watch all the people in their cars and on the sidewalks, more people in a single look than there are on the whole island these days . . . if I ever wanted those things, then I wanted this more. I am not strange. I am not peculiar, or even very eccentric for a woman of my years. My mother sometimes used to say, 'All the difference in the world is between work*

*and want,' and I believe that to my very soul. I believe it is better to plow deep than wide.*

*"This is my place, and I love it."*

One day in middle March, with the sky as white and lowering as a loss of memory, Stella Flanders sat in her kitchen for the last time, laced up her boots over her skinny calves for the last time, and wrapped her bright red woolen scarf (a Christmas present from Hattie three Christmases past) around her neck for the last time. She wore a suit of Alden's long underwear under her dress. The waist of the drawers came up to just below the limp vestiges of her breasts, the shirt almost down to her knees.

Outside, the wind was picking up again, and the radio said there would be snow by afternoon. She put on her coat and her gloves. After a moment of debate, she put a pair of Alden's gloves on over her own. Alden had recovered from the flu, and this morning he and Harley Blood were over rehanging a storm door for Missy Bowie, who had had a girl. Stella had seen it, and the unfortunate little mite looked just like her father.

She stood at the window for a moment, looking out at the Reach, and Bill was there as she had suspected he might be, standing about halfway between the island and the Head, standing on the Reach just like Jesus-out-of-the-boat, beckoning to her, seeming to tell her by gesture that the time was late if she ever intended to step a foot on the mainland in this life.

"If it's what you want, Bill," she fretted in the silence. "God knows I don't."

But the wind spoke other words. She did want to. She wanted to have this adventure. It had been a painful winter for her—the arthritis which came and went irregularly was back with a vengeance, flaring the joints of her fingers and knees with red fire and blue ice. One of her eyes had gotten dim and blurry (and just the other day Sarah had mentioned—with some unease—that the firespot that had been there since Stella was sixty or so now seemed to be growing by leaps and bounds). Worst of all, the deep, gripping pain in her stomach had returned, and two mornings before she had gotten up at five o'clock, worked her way along the exquisitely cold floor into the bathroom, and had spat a great wad of bright red blood into the toilet bowl. This morning there had been some more of it, foul-tasting stuff, coppery and shuddersome.

The stomach pain had come and gone over the last five years, sometimes better, sometimes worse, and she had known almost from the beginning that it must be cancer. It had taken her mother and father and her mother's father as well. None of them had lived past seventy, and so she supposed she had beat the tables those insurance fellows kept by a carpenter's yard.

"You eat like a horse," Alden told her, grinning, not long after the pains had begun and she had first observed the blood in her morning stool. "Don't you know that old fogies like you are supposed to be peckish?"

"Get on or I'll swat ye!" Stella had answered, raising a hand to her gray-haired son, who ducked, mock-cringed, and cried: "Don't, Ma! I take it back!"

Yes, she had eaten hearty, not because she wanted to, but because she believed (as many of her generation did), that if you fed the cancer it would leave you alone. And perhaps it worked, at least for a while; the blood in her stools came and went, and there were long periods when it wasn't there at all. Alden got used to her taking second helpings (and thirds, when the pain was particularly bad), but she never gained a pound.

Now it seemed the cancer had finally gotten around to what the froggies called the *pièce de résistance*.

She started out the door and saw Alden's hat, the one with the fur-lined ear flaps, hanging on one of the pegs in the entry. She put it on—the bill came all the way down to her shaggy salt-and-pepper eyebrows—and then looked around one last time to see if she had forgotten anything. The stove was low, and Alden had left the draw open too much again—she told him and told him, but that was one thing he was just never going to get straight.

"Alden, you'll burn an extra quarter-cord a winter when I'm gone," she muttered, and opened the stove. She looked in and a tight, dismayed gasp escaped her. She slammed the door shut and adjusted the draw with trembling fingers. For a moment—just a moment—she had seen her old friend Annabelle Frane in the coals. It was her face to the life, even down to the mole on her cheek.

And had Annabelle winked at her?

She thought of leaving Alden a note to explain where she had gone, but she thought perhaps Alden would understand, in his own slow way.

Still writing notes in her head—*Since the first day of winter I have been seeing your father and he says dying isn't so bad; at least I think that's it*—Stella stepped out into the white day.

The wind shook her and she had to rest Alden's cap on her head before the wind could steal it for a joke and cartwheel it away. The cold seemed to find every chink in her clothing and twist into her; damp March cold with wet snow on its mind.

She set off down the hill toward the cove, being careful to walk on the cinders and clinkers that George Dinsmore had spread. Once George had gotten a job driving plow for the town of Raccoon Head, but during the big blow of '77 he had gotten smashed on rye whiskey and had driven the plow smack through not one, not two, but three power poles. There had been no lights over the Head for five days. Stella remembered now how strange it had been, looking across the Reach and seeing only blackness. A body got used to seeing that brave little nestle of lights. Now George worked on the island, and since there was no plow, he didn't get into much hurt.

As she passed Russell Bowie's house, she saw Missy, pale as milk, looking out at her. Stella waved. Missy waved back.

*She would tell them this:*

*"On the island we always watched out for our own. When Gerd Henreid broke the blood vessel in his chest that time, we had covered-dish suppers one whole summer to pay for his operation in Boston—and Gerd came back alive, thank God. When George Dinsmore ran down those power poles and the Hydro slapped a lien on his home, it was seen to that the Hydro had their money and George had enough of a job to keep him in cigarettes and booze . . . why not? He was good for nothing else when his workday was done, although when he was on the clock he would work like a dray-horse. That one time he got into trouble was because it was at night, and night was always George's drinking time. His father kept him fed, at least. Now Missy Bowie's alone with another baby. Maybe she'll stay here and take her welfare and ADC money here, and most likely it won't be enough, but she'll get the help she needs. Probably she'll go, but if she stays she'll not starve . . . and listen, Lona and Hal: if she stays, she may be able to keep something of this small world with the little Reach on one side and the big Reach on the other, something it would be too easy to lose hustling hash in Lewiston or donuts in Portland or drinks at the Nashville North in Bangor. And I am old enough not to beat around the bush about what that something might be: a way of being and a way of living—a feeling."*

*They had watched out for their own in other ways as well, but she would not tell them that. The children would not understand, nor would Lois and David, although Jane had known the truth. There was Norman and Ettie Wilson's baby that was born a mongoloid, its poor dear little feet turned in, its bald skull lumpy and cratered, its fingers webbed together as if it had dreamed too long and too deep while swimming that interior Reach; Reverend McCracken had come and baptized the baby, and a day later Mary Dodge came, who even at that time had midwived over a hundred babies, and Norman took Ettie down the hill to see Frank Child's new boat and although she could barely walk, Ettie went with no complaint, although she had stopped in the door to look back at Mary Dodge, who was sitting calmly by the idiot baby's crib and knitting. Mary had looked up at her and when their eyes met, Ettie burst into tears. "Come on," Norman had said, upset. "Come on, Ettie, come on." And when they came back an hour later the baby was dead, one of those crib-deaths, wasn't it merciful he didn't suffer. And many years before that, before the war, during the Depression, three little girls had been molested coming home from school, not badly molested, at least not where you could see the scar of the hurt, and they all told about a man who offered to show them a deck of cards he had with a different kind of dog on each one. He would show them this wonderful deck of cards, the man said, if the little girls would come into the bushes with him, and once in the bushes this man said, "But you have to touch this first." One of the little girls was Gert Symes, who would go on to be voted Maine's Teacher of the Year in 1978, for her work at Brunswick High. And Gert, then only five years old, told her father that the man had some fingers gone on one hand. One of the other little girls agreed that this was so. The third remembered nothing. Stella remembered Alden going out one thundery day that summer without telling her where he was going, although she asked. Watching from the window, she had seen Alden meet Bull Symes at the bottom of the path, and then Freddy Dinsmore had joined them and down at the cove she saw her own husband, whom she had sent out that morning just as usual, with his dinner pail under his arm. More men joined them, and when they finally moved off she counted just one under a dozen. The Reverend McCracken's predecessor had been among them. And that evening a fellow named Daniels was found at the foot of Slyder's Point, where the rocks poke out of the surf like the fangs of a dragon that drowned with its mouth open. This Daniels was a fellow Big George Havelock had hired to help him put new sills under his house and a new engine in his Model A truck. From New Hampshire he was, and he was a sweet-talker who had found other odd jobs to do when the work at the Have-locks' was done . . . and in church, he could carry a tune! Apparently, they said, Daniels had been walking up on top of Slyder's Point and had slipped, tumbling all the way to the bottom. His neck was broken and his head was bashed in. As he had no people that anyone knew of, he was buried on the island, and the Reverend McCracken's predecessor gave the graveyard eulogy, saying as how this Daniels had been a hard worker and a good help even though he was two fingers shy on his right hand. Then he read the benediction and the graveside group had gone back to the town-hall basement where they drank Za-Rex punch and ate cream-cheese sandwiches, and Stella never asked her men where they had gone on the day Daniels fell from the top of Slyder's Point.*

*"Children," she would tell them, "we always watched out for our own. We had to, for the Reach was wider in those days and when the wind roared and the surf pounded and the dark came early, why, we felt very small—no more than dust motes in the mind of God. So it was natural for us to join hands, one with the other.*

*"We joined hands, children, and if there were times when we wondered what it was all for, or if there was ary such a thing as love at all, it was only because we had heard the wind and the waters on long winter nights, and we were afraid.*

*"No, I've never felt I needed to leave the island. My life was here. The Reach was wider in those days."*

Stella reached the cove. She looked right and left, the wind blowing her dress out behind her like a flag. If anyone had been there she would have walked further down and taken her chance on the tumbled rocks, although they were glazed with ice. But no one was there and she walked out along the pier, past the old Symes boathouse. She reached the end and stood there for a moment, head held up, the wind blowing past the padded flaps of Alden's hat in a muffled flood.

Bill was out there, beckoning. Beyond him, beyond the Reach, she could see the Congo Church over there on the Head, its spire almost invisible against the white sky.

Grunting, she sat down on the end of the pier and then stepped onto the snow crust below. Her boots sank a little; not much. She set Alden's cap again—how the wind wanted to tear it off!—and began to walk toward Bill. She thought once that she would look back, but she did not. She didn't believe her heart could stand that.

She walked, her boots crunching into the crust, and listened to the faint thud and give of the ice. There was Bill, further back now but still beckoning. She coughed, spat blood onto the white snow that covered the ice. Now the Reach spread wide on either side and she could, for the first time in her life, read the "Stanton's Bait and Boat" sign over there without Alden's binoculars. She could see the cars passing to and fro on the Head's main street and thought with real wonder: *They can go as far as they want . . . Portland . . . Boston . . . New York City. Imagine!* And she could almost do it, could almost imagine a road that simply rolled on and on, the boundaries of the world knocked wide.

A snowflake skirled past her eyes. Another. A third. Soon it was snowing lightly and she walked through a pleasant world of shifting bright white; she saw Raccoon Head through a gauzy curtain that sometimes almost cleared. She reached up to set Alden's cap again and snow puffed off the bill into her eyes. The wind twisted fresh snow up in filmy shapes, and in one of them she saw Carl Abersham, who had gone down with Hattie Stoddard's husband on the *Dancer.*

Soon, however, the brightness began to dull as the snow came harder. The Head's main street dimmed, dimmed, and at last was gone. For a time longer she could make out the cross atop the church, and then that faded out too, like a false dream. Last to go was that bright yellow-and-black sign reading "Stanton's Bait and Boat," where you could also get engine oil, flypaper, Italian sandwiches, and Budweiser to go.

Then Stella walked in a world that was totally without color, a gray-white dream of snow. *Just like Jesus-out-of-the-boat,* she thought, and at last she looked back but now the island was gone, too. She could see her tracks going back, losing definition until only the faint half-circles of her heels could be seen . . . and then nothing. Nothing at all.

She thought: *It's a whiteout. You got to be careful, Stella, or you'll never get to the mainland. You'll just walk around in a big circle until you're worn out and then you'll freeze to death out here.*

She remembered Bill telling her once that when you were lost in the woods, you had to pretend that the leg which was on the same side of your body as your smart hand was lame. Otherwise that smart leg would begin to lead you and you'd walk in a circle and not even realize it until you came around to your backtrail again. Stella didn't believe she could afford to have that happen to her. Snow today, tonight, and tomorrow, the radio had said, and in a whiteout such as this, she would not even know if she came around to her backtrail, for the wind and the fresh snow would erase it long before she could return to it.

Her hands were leaving her in spite of the two pairs of gloves she wore, and her feet had been gone for some time. In a way, this was almost a relief. The numbness at least shut the mouth of her clamoring arthritis.

Stella began to limp now, making her left leg work harder. The arthritis in her knees had not gone to sleep, and soon they were screaming at her. Her white hair flew out behind her. Her lips had drawn back from her teeth (she still had her own, all save four) and she looked straight ahead, waiting for that yellow-and-black sign to materialize out of the flying whiteness.

It did not happen.

Sometime later, she noticed that the day's bright whiteness had begun to dull to a more uniform gray. The snow fell heavier and thicker than ever. Her feet were still planted on the crust but now she was walking through five inches of fresh snow. She looked at her watch, but it had stopped. Stella realized she must have forgotten to wind it that morning for the first time in twenty or thirty years. Or had it just stopped for good? It had been her mother's and she had sent it with Alden twice to the Head, where Mr. Dostie had first marveled over it and then cleaned it. Her watch, at least, had been to the mainland.

She fell down for the first time some fifteen minutes after she began to notice the day's growing grayness. For a moment she remained on her hands and knees, thinking it would be so easy just to stay here, to curl up and listen to the wind, and then the determination that had brought her through so much reasserted itself and she got up, grimacing. She stood in the wind, looking straight ahead, willing her eyes to see . . . but they saw nothing.

*Be dark soon.*

Well, she had gone wrong. She had slipped off to one side or the other. Otherwise she would have reached the mainland by now. Yet she didn't believe she had gone so far wrong that she was walking parallel to the mainland or even back in the direction of Goat. An interior navigator in her head whispered that she had overcompensated and slipped off to the left. She believed she was still approaching the mainland but was now on a costly diagonal.

That navigator wanted her to turn right, but she would not do that. Instead, she moved straight on again, but stopped the artificial limp. A spasm of coughing shook her, and she spat bright red into the snow.

Ten minutes later (the gray was now deep indeed, and she found herself in the weird twilight of a heavy snowstorm) she fell again, tried to get up, failed at first, and finally managed to gain her feet. She stood swaying in the snow, barely able to remain upright in the wind, waves of faintness rushing through her head, making her feel alternately heavy and light.

Perhaps not all the roaring she heard in her ears was the wind, but it surely was the wind that finally succeeded in prying Alden's hat from her head. She made a grab for it, but the wind danced it easily out of her reach and she saw it only for a moment, flipping gaily over and over into the darkening gray, a bright spot of orange. It struck the snow, rolled, rose again, was gone. Now her hair flew around her head freely.

"It's all right, Stella," Bill said. "You can wear mine."

She gasped and looked around in the white. Her gloved hands had gone instinctively to her bosom, and she felt sharp fingernails scratch at her heart.

She saw nothing but shifting membranes of snow—and then, moving out of that evening's gray throat, the wind screaming through it like the voice of a devil in a snowy tunnel, came her husband. He was at first only moving colors in the snow: red, black, dark green, lighter green; then these colors resolved themselves into a flannel jacket with a flapping collar, flannel pants, and green boots. He was holding his hat out to her in a gesture that appeared almost absurdly courtly, and his face was Bill's face, unmarked by the cancer that had taken him (had that been all she was afraid of? that a wasted shadow of her husband would come to her, a scrawny concentration-camp figure with the skin pulled taut and shiny over the cheekbones and the eyes sunken deep in the sockets?) and she felt a surge of relief.

"Bill? Is that really you?"

"Course."

"Bill," she said again, and took a glad step toward him. Her legs betrayed her and she thought she would fall, fall right through him—he was, after all, a ghost—but he caught her in arms as strong and as competent as those that had carried her over the threshold of the house that she had shared only with Alden in these latter years. He supported her, and a moment later she felt the cap pulled firmly onto her head.

"Is it really you?" she asked again, looking up into his face, at the crow's-feet around his eyes which hadn't sunk deep yet, at the spill of snow on the shoulders of his checked hunting jacket, at his lively brown hair.

"It's me," he said. "It's all of us."

He half-turned with her and she saw the others coming out of the snow that the wind drove across the Reach in the gathering darkness.

A cry, half joy, half fear, came from her mouth as she saw Madeline
Stoddard, Hattie's mother, in a blue dress that swung in the wind like a
bell, and holding her hand was Hattie's dad, not a mouldering skeleton
somewhere on the bottom with the *Dancer*, but whole and young. And
there, behind those two—

"Annabelle!" she cried. "Annabelle Frane, is it you?"

It *was* Annabelle; even in this snowy gloom Stella recognized the
yellow dress Annabelle had worn to Stella's own wedding, and as she
struggled toward her dear friend, holding Bill's arm, she thought that
she could smell roses.

*"Annabelle!"*

"We're almost there now, dear," Annabelle said, taking her other
arm. The yellow dress, which had been considered Daring in its day
(but, to Annabelle's credit and to everyone else's relief, not quite a
Scandal), left her shoulders bare, but Annabelle did not seem to feel the
cold. Her hair, a soft, dark auburn, blew long in the wind. "Only a
little further."

She took Stella's other arm and they moved forward again. Other
figures came out of the snowy night (for it *was* night now). Stella
recognized many of them, but not all. Tommy Frane had joined
Annabelle; Big George Havelock, who had died a dog's death in the
woods, walked behind Bill; there was the fellow who had kept the
lighthouse on the Head for most of twenty years and who used to
come over to the island during the cribbage tournament Freddy Dinsmore held every February—Stella could almost but not quite
remember his name. And there was Freddy himself! Walking off to one
side of Freddy, by himself and looking bewildered, was Russell Bowie.

"Look, Stella," Bill said, and she saw black rising out of the gloom
like the splintered prows of many ships. It was not ships, it was split and
fissured rock. They had reached the Head. They had crossed the
Reach.

She heard voices, but was not sure they actually spoke:

*Take my hand, Stella—*

*(do you)*

*Take my hand, Bill—*

*(oh do you do you)*

*Annabelle . . . Freddy . . . Russell . . . John . . . Ettie . . . Frank . . .*
*take my hand, take my hand . . . my hand . . .*

*(do you love)*

"Will you take my hand, Stella?" a new voice asked.

She looked around and there was Bull Symes. He was smiling kindly at her and yet she felt a kind of terror in her at what was in his eyes and for a moment she drew away, clutching Bill's hand on her other side the tighter.

"Is it—"

"Time?" Bull asked. "Oh, ayuh, Stella, I guess so. But it don't hurt. At least, I never heard so. All that's before."

She burst into tears suddenly—all the tears she had never wept— and put her hand in Bull's hand. "Yes," she said, "yes I will, yes I did, yes I do."

They stood in a circle in the storm, the dead of Goat Island, and the wind screamed around them, driving its packet of snow, and some kind of song burst from her. It went up into the wind and the wind carried it away. They all sang then, as children will sing in their high, sweet voices as a summer evening draws down to summer night. They sang, and Stella felt herself going to them and with them, finally across the Reach. There was a bit of pain, but not much; losing her maiden-head had been worse. They stood in a circle in the night. The snow blew around them and they sang. They sang, and—

*—and Alden could not tell David and Lois, but in the summer after Stella died, when the children came out for their annual two weeks, he told Lona and Hal. He told them that during the great storms of winter the wind seems to sing with almost human voices, and that sometimes it seemed to him he could almost make out the words: "Praise God from whom all blessings flow/Praise Him, ye creatures here below . . ."*

*But he did not tell them (imagine slow, unimaginative Alden Flanders saying such things aloud, even to the children!) that sometimes he would hear that sound and feel cold even by the stove; that he would put his whittling aside, or the trap he had meant to mend, thinking that the wind sang in all the voices of those who were dead and gone . . . that they stood somewhere out on the Reach and sang as children do. He seemed to hear their voices and on these nights he sometimes slept and dreamed that he was singing the doxology, unseen and unheard, at his own funeral.*

*There are things that can never be told, and there are things, not exactly secret, that are not discussed. They had found Stella frozen to death on the mainland a day after the storm had blown itself out. She was sitting on a natural chair of rock about one hundred yards south of the Raccoon Head town limits, frozen just as neat as you please. The doctor who owned the Corvette said that he was frankly amazed. It would have been a walk of over four miles, and the autopsy required by law in the case of an unattended, unusual death had shown an advanced cancerous condition—in truth, the old woman had been riddled with it. Was Alden to tell David and Lois that the cap on her head had not been his? Larry McKeen had recognized that cap. So had John Bensohn. He had seen it in their eyes, and he supposed they had seen it in his. He had not lived long enough to forget his dead father's cap, the look of its bill or the places where the visor had been broken.*

*"These are things made for thinking on slowly," he would have told the children if he had known how. "Things to be thought on at length, while the hands do their work and the coffee sits in a solid china mug nearby. They are questions of Reach, maybe: do the dead sing? And do they love the living?"*

*On the nights after Lona and Hal had gone back with their parents to the mainland in Al Curry's boat, the children standing astern and waving good-bye, Alden considered that question, and others, and the matter of his father's cap.*

*Do the dead sing? Do they love?*

*On those long nights alone, with his mother Stella Flanders at long last in her grave, it often seemed to Alden that they did both.*

# CHARLES JOHNSON
## Exchange Value

Me and my brother, Loftis, came in by the old lady's window. There was some kinda boobytrap—boxes of broken glass—that shoulda warned us Miss Bailey wasn't the easy mark we made her to be. She been living alone for twenty years in 4-B down the hall from Loftis and me, long before our folks died—a hincty, halfbald West Indian woman with a craglike face, who kept her door barricaded, shutters closed, and wore the same sorry-looking outfit—black wingtip shoes, cropfingered gloves in winter, and a man's floppy hat—like maybe she dressed half-asleep or in a dark attic. Loftis, he figured Miss Bailey had some grandtheft dough stashed inside, jim, or leastways a shoebox full of money, 'cause she never spent a nickel on herself, not even for food, and only left her place at night.

Anyway, we figured Miss Bailey was gone. Her mailbox be full, and Pookie White, who run the Thirty-ninth Street Creole restaurant, he say she ain't dropped by in days to collect the handouts he give her so she can get by. So here's me and Loftis, tipping around Miss Bailey's blackdark kitchen. The floor be littered with fruitrinds, roaches, old food furred with blue mold. Her dirty dishes be stacked in a sink feathered with cracks, and it looks like the old lady been living, lately, on Ritz crackers and Department of Agriculture (Welfare Office) peanut butter. Her toilet be stopped up, too, and, on the bathroom floor, there's five Maxwell House coffee cans full of shit. Me, I was closing her bathroom door when I whiffed this evil smell so bad, so thick, I could hardly breathe, and what air I breathed was stifling, like solid fluid in my throatpipes, like broth or soup. "Cooter," Loftis whisper, low, across the room, "you smell that?" He went right on sniffing it, like people do for some reason when something be smelling stanky, then took out his headrag and held it over his mouth. "Smells like something crawled up in here and died!" Then, head low, he slipped his long self into the living room. Me, I stayed by the window, gulping for air, and do you know why?

You oughta know, up front, that I ain't too good at this gangster stuff, and I had a real bad feeling about Miss Bailey from the get-go. Mama used to say it was Loftis, not me, who'd go places—I see her standing at the sideboard by the sink now, big as a Frigidaire, white flour to her elbows, a washtowel over her shoulder, while we ate a breakfast of cornbread and syrup. Loftis, he graduated fifth at DuSable High School, had two gigs and, like Papa, he be always wanting the things white people had out in Hyde Park, where Mama did daywork sometimes. Loftis, he be the kind of brother who buys *Esquire*, sews Hart, Schaffner & Marx labels in Robert Hall suits, talks properlike, packs his hair with Murray's; and he took classes in politics and stuff at the Black People's Topographical Library in the late 1960s. At thirty, he make his bed military-style, reads *Black Scholar* on the bus he takes to the plant, and, come hell or high water, plans to make a Big Score. Loftis, he say I'm 'bout as useful on a hustle—or when it comes to getting ahead—as a headcold, and he says he has to count my legs sometimes to make sure I ain't a mule, seeing how, for all my eighteen years, I can't keep no job and sorta stay close to home, watching TV, or reading *World's Finest* comic books, or maybe just laying dead, listening to music, imagining I see faces or foreign places in water stains on the wallpaper, 'cause some days, when I remember Papa, then Mama, killing theyselves for chump change—a pitiful li'l bowl of porridge—I get to thinking that even if I ain't had all I wanted, maybe I've had, you know, all I'm ever gonna get.

"Cooter," Loftis say from the living room. "You best get in here quick."

Loftis, he'd switched on Miss Bailey's bright, overhead living room lights, so for a second I couldn't see and started coughing—the smell be so powerful it hit my nostrils like coke—and when my eyes cleared, shapes come forward in the light, and I thought for an instant like I'd slipped in space. I seen why Loftis called me, and went back two steps. See, 4-B's so small if you ring Miss Bailey's doorbell, the toilet'd flush. But her living room, webbed in dust, be filled to the max with dollars of all denominations, stacks of stock in General Motors, Gulf Oil, and 3M Company in old White Owl cigar boxes, battered purses, or bound in pink rubber bands. It be like the kind of cubbyhole kids play in, but filled with . . . *things*: everything, like a world inside the world, you take it from me, so like picturebook scenes of plentiful-ness you could seal yourself off in here and settle forever. Loftis and me both drew breath suddenly. There be unopened cases of Jack Daniel's, three safes cemented to the floor, hundreds of matchbooks, unworn clothes, a fuel-burning stove, dozens of wedding rings, rubbish, World War II magazines, a carton of a hundred canned sardines, mink stoles, old rags, a birdcage, a bucket of silver dollars, thousands of books, paintings, quarters in tobacco cans, two pianos, glass jars of pennies, a set of bagpipes, an almost complete Model A Ford dappled with rust, and, I swear, three sections of a dead tree.

"Damn!" My head be light; I sat on an up-ended peach crate and picked up a bottle of Jack Daniel's.

"Don't you touch *anything*!" Loftis, he panting a little; he slap both hands on a table. "Not until we inventory this stuff."

"Inventory? Aw, Lord, Loftis," I say, "something ain't *right* about this stash. There could be a curse on it. . . ."

"Boy, sometime you act weak-minded."

"For real, Loftis, I got a feeling. . . ."

Loftis, he shucked off his shoes, and sat down heavily on the lumpy arm of a stuffed chair. "Don't say *any*thing." He chewed his knuckles, and for the first time Loftis looked like he didn't know his next move. "Let me think, okay?" He squeezed his nose in a way he has when thinking hard, sighed, then stood up and say, "There's some-thing you better see in that bedroom yonder. Cover up your mouth."

"Loftis, I ain't going in there."

He look at me right funny then. "She's a miser, that's all. She saves things."

"But a tree?" I say. "Loftis, a *tree* ain't normal!"

"Cooter, I ain't gonna tell you twice."

Like always, I followed Loftis, who swung his flashlight from the plant—he a night watchman—into Miss Bailey's bedroom, but me, I'm thinking how trippy this thing is getting, remembering how, last year, when I had a paper route, the old lady, with her queer, crablike walk, pulled my coat for some change in the hallway, and when I give her a handful of dimes, she say, like one of them spooks on old-time radio, "Thank you, Co-o-oter," then gulped the coins down like aspirin, no lie, and scurried off like a hunchback. Me, I wanted no parts of this squirrely old broad, but Loftis, he holding my wrist now, beaming his light onto a low bed. The room had a funny, museumlike smell. Real sour. It was full of dirty laundry. And I be sure the old lady's stuff had a terrible string attached when Loftis, looking away, lifted her bedsheets and a knot of black flies rose. I stepped back and held my breath. Miss Bailey be in her long-sleeved flannel nightgown, bloated, like she'd been blown up by a bicycle pump, her old face caved in with rot, fly-blown, her fingers big and colored like spoiled bananas. Her wristwatch be ticking softly beside a half-eaten hamburger. Above the bed, her wall had roaches squashed in little swirls of bloodstain. Maggots clustered in her eyes, her ears, and one fist-sized rat hissed inside her flesh. My eyes snapped shut. My knees failed; then I did a Hollywood faint. When I surfaced, Loftis, he be sitting beside me in the living room, where he'd drug me, reading a wrinkled, yellow article from the *Chicago Daily Defender*.

"Listen to this," Loftis say. " 'Elnora Bailey, forty-five, a Negro housemaid in the Highland Park home of Henry Conners, is the beneficiary of her employer's will. An old American family, the Conners arrived in this country on the *Providence* shortly after the voyage of the *Mayflower*. The family flourished in the early days of the 1900s.'. . ." He went on, getting breath: " 'A distinguished and wealthy industrialist, without heirs or a wife, Conners willed his entire estate to Miss Bailey of 3347 North Clark Street for her twenty years of service to his family.'. . ." Loftis, he give that Geoffrey Holder laugh of his, low and deep; then it eased up his throat until it hit a high note and tipped his head back onto his shoulders. "Cooter, that was before we was born! Miss Bailey kept this in the Bible next to her bed."

Standing, I braced myself with one hand against the wall. "She didn't earn it?"

"Naw." Loftis, he folded the paper—"Not one penny"—and stuffed it in his shirt pocket. His jaw looked tight as a horseshoe. "Way *I* see it," he say, "this was her one shot in a lifetime to be rich, but being country, she had backward ways and blew it." Rubbing his hands, he stood up to survey the living room. "Somebody's gonna find Miss Bailey soon, but if we stay on the case—Cooter, don't square up on me now—we can tote everything to our place before daybreak. Best we start with the big stuff."

"But why didn't she *use* it, huh? Tell me that?"

Loftis, he don't pay me no mind. When he gets an idea in his head, you can't dig it out with a chisel. How long it took me and Loftis to inventory, then haul Miss Bailey's queer old stuff to our crib, I can't say, but that cranky old ninnyhammer's hoard come to $879,543 in cash money, thirty-two bank books (some deposits be only $5), and me, I wasn't sure I was dreaming or what, but I suddenly flashed on this feeling, once we left her flat, that all the fears Loftis and me had about the future be gone, 'cause Miss Bailey's property was the past— the power of that fellah Henry Conners trapped like a bottle spirit— which we could live off, so it was the future, too, pure potential: can *do.* Loftis got to talking on about how that piano we pushed home be equal to a thousand bills, jim, which equals, say, a bad TEAC A-3340 tape deck, or a down payment on a deuce-and-a-quarter. Its value be (Loftis say) that of a universal standard of measure, relational, unreal as number, so that tape deck could turn, magically, into two gold lamé suits, a trip to Tijuana, or twenty-five blow jobs from a ho—we had $879,543 worth of wishes, if you can deal with that. Be like Miss Bailey's stuff is raw energy, and Loftis and me, like wizards, could transform her stuff into anything else at will. All we had to do, it seemed to me, was decide exactly what to exchange it for.

While Loftis studied this over (he looked funny, like a potato trying to say something, after the inventory, and sat, real quiet, in the kitchen), I filled my pockets with fifties, grabbed me a cab downtown to grease, yum, at one of them high-hat restaurants in the Loop. . . . But then I thought better of it, you know, like I'd be out of place—just another jig putting on airs—and scarfed instead at a ribjoint till both my eyes bubbled. This fat lady making fishburgers in the back favored an old hardleg baby-sitter I once had, a Mrs. Paine who made me eat ocher, and I wanted so bad to say, "Loftis and me Got Ovuh," but I couldn't put that in the wind, could I, so I hatted up. Then I copped a boss silk necktie, cashmere socks, and a whistle-slick maxi leather jacket on State Street, took cabs *every*where, but when I got home that evening, a funny, Pandora-like feeling hit me. I took off the jacket, boxed it—it looked trifling in the hallway's weak light—and, tired, turned my key in the door. I couldn't get in. Loftis, he'd changed the lock and, when he finally let me in, looking vaguer, crabby, like something out of the Book of Revelations, I seen this elaborate, booby-trapped tunnel of cardboard and razor blades behind him, with a two-foot space just big enough for him or me to crawl through. That wasn't all. Two bags of trash from the furnace room downstairs be sitting inside the door. Loftis, he give my leather jacket this evil look, hauled me inside, and hit me upside my head.

"How much this thing set us back?"

"Two fifty." My jaws got tight; I toss him my receipt. "You want me to take it back? Maybe I can get something else. . . ."

Loftis, he say, not to me, but to the receipt, "Remember the time Mama give me that ring we had in the family for fifty years? And I took it to Merchandise Mart and sold it for a few pieces of candy?" He hitched his chair forward and sat with his elbows on his knees. "That's what you did, Cooter. You crawled into a Clark bar." He commence to rip up my receipt, then picked up his flashlight and keys. "As soon as you buy something you *lose* the power to buy something." He button up his coat with holes in the elbows, showing his blue shirt, then turned 'round at the tunnel to say, "Don't touch Miss Bailey's money, or drink her splo, or do *any*thing until I get back."

"Where you going?"

"To work. It's Wednesday, ain't it?"

"You going to work?"

"Yeah."

"You got to go *really?* Loftis," I say, "what you brang them bags of trash in here for?"

"It ain't trash!" He cut his eyes at me. "There's good clothes in there. Mr. Peterson tossed them out, he don't care, but I saw some use in them, that's all."

"Loftis . . ."

"Yeah?"

"What we gonna do with all this money?"

Loftis pressed his fingers to his eyelids, and for a second he looked caged, or like somebody'd kicked him in his stomach. Then he cut me some slack: "Let me think on it tonight—it don't pay to rush—then we can TCB, okay?"

Five hours after Loftis leave for work, that old blister Mr. Peterson, our landlord, he come collecting rent, find Mrs. Bailey's body in apartment 4-B, and phoned the fire department. Me, I be folding my new jacket in tissue paper to keep it fresh, adding the box to Miss Bailey's unsunned treasures when two paramedics squeezed her on a long stretcher through a crowd in the hallway. See, I had to pin her from the stairhead, looking down one last time at this dizzy old lady, and I seen something in her face, like maybe she'd been poor as Job's turkey for thirty years, suffering that special Negro fear of using up what little we get in this life—Loftis, he call that entropy—believing in her belly, and for all her faith, jim, that there just ain't no more coming tomorrow from grace, or the Lord, or from her own labor, like she can't kill nothing, and won't nothing die . . . so when Conners will her his wealth, it put her through changes, she be spellbound, possessed by the promise of life, panicky about depletion, and locked now in the past 'cause *every* purchase, you know, has to be a poor buy: a loss of life. Me, I wasn't worried none. Loftis, he got a brain trained by years of talking trash with people in Frog Hudson's barbershop on Thirty-fifth Street. By morning, I knew, he'd have some kinda wheeze worked out.

But Loftis, he don't come home. Me, I got kinda worried. I listen to the hi-fi all day Thursday, only pawing outside to peep down the stairs, like that'd make Loftis come sooner. So Thursday go by; and come Friday the head's out of kilter—first there's an ogrelike belch from the toilet bowl, then water bursts from the bathroom into the kitchen—and me, I can't call the super (How do I explain the tunnel?), so I gave up and quit bailing. But on Saturday, I could smell greens cooking next door. Twice I almost opened Miss Bailey's sardines, even though starving be less an evil than eating up our stash, but I waited till it was dark and, with my stomach talking to me, stepped outside to Pookie White's, lay a hard-luck story on him, and Pookie, he give me some jambalaya and gumbo. Back home in the living room, finger-feeding myself, barricaded in by all that hope-made material, the Kid felt like a king in his counting room, and I copped some Zs in an armchair till I heard the door move on its hinges, then bumping in the tunnel, and a heavy-footed walk thumped into the bedroom.

"Loftis?" I rubbed my eyes. "You back?" It be Sunday morning. Six-thirty sharp. Darkness dissolved slowly into the strangeness of twilight, with the rays of sunlight surging at exactly the same angle they fall each evening, as if the hour be an island, a moment outside time. Me, I'm afraid Loftis gonna fuss 'bout my not straightening up, letting things go. I went into the bathroom, poured water in the one-spigot washstand—brown rust come bursting out in flakes—and rinsed my face. "Loftis, you supposed to be home four days ago. Hey," I say, toweling my face, "you okay?" How come he don't answer me? Wiping my hands on the seat of my trousers, I tipped into Loftis's room. He sleeping with his mouth open. His legs be drawn up, both fists clenched between his knees. He'd kicked his blanket on the floor. In his sleep, Loftis laughed, or moaned, it be hard to tell. His eyelids, not quite shut, show slits of white. I decided to wait till Loftis wake up for his decision, but turning, I seen his watch, keys, and what looked in the first stain of sunlight to be a carefully wrapped piece of newspaper on his nightstand. The sunlight swelled to a bright shimmer, focusing the bedroom slowly like solution do a photographic image in the developer. And then something so freakish went down I ain't sure it took place. Fumble-fingered, I unfolded the paper, and inside be a blemished penny. It be like suddenly somebody slapped my head from behind. Taped on the penny be a slip of paper, and on the paper be the note "Found while walking down Devon Avenue." I hear Loftis mumble like he trapped in a nightmare. "Hold tight," I whisper. "It's all right." Me, I wanted to tell Loftis how Miss Bailey looked four days ago, that maybe it didn't have to be like that for us—did it?—because we could change. Couldn't we? Me, I pull his packed sheets over him, wrap up the penny, and, when I locate Miss Bailey's glass jar in the living room, put it away carefully, for now, with the rest of our things.

# JOHN CROWLEY
## Snow

I don't think Georgie would ever have got one for herself: She was at once unsentimental and a little in awe of death. No, it was her first husband—an immensely rich and (from Georgie's description) a strangely weepy guy—who had got it for her. Or for himself, actually, of course. He was to be the beneficiary. Only he died himself shortly after it was installed. If *installed* is the right word. After he died, Georgie got rid of most of what she'd inherited from him, liquidated it, it was cash that she had liked best about that marriage anyway; but the Wasp couldn't really be got rid of. Georgie ignored it.

In fact the thing really was about the size of a wasp of the largest kind, and it had the same lazy and mindless flight. And of course it really was a bug, not of the insect kind but of the surveillance kind. And so its name fit all around: one of those bits of accidental poetry the world generates without thinking. O Death, where is thy sting?

Georgie ignored it, but it was hard to avoid; you had to be a little careful around it; it followed Georgie at a variable distance, depending on her motions and the number of other people around her, the level of light, and the tone of her voice. And there was always the danger you might shut it in a door or knock it down with a tennis racket. It cost a fortune (if you count the access and the perpetual-care contract, all prepaid), and though it wasn't really fragile, it made you nervous.

It wasn't recording all the time. There had to be a certain amount of light, though not much. Darkness shut it off. And then sometimes it would get lost. Once when we hadn't seen it hovering around for a time,

I opened a closet door, and it flew out, unchanged. It went off looking for her, humming softly. It must have been shut in there for days.

Eventually it ran out, or down. A lot could go wrong, I suppose, with circuits that small, controlling that many functions. It ended up spending a lot of time bumping gently against the bedroom ceiling, over and over, like a winter fly. Then one day the maid swept it out from under the bureau, a husk. By that time it had transmitted at least eight thousand hours (eight thousand was the minimum guarantee) of Georgie: of her days and hours, her comings in and her goings out, her speech and motion, her living self—all on file, taking up next to no room, at The Park. And then, when the time came, you could go there, to The Park, say on a Sunday afternoon; and in quiet landscaped surroundings (as The Park described it) you would find her personal resting chamber; and there, in privacy, through the miracle of modern information storage and retrieval systems, you could access her: her alive, her as she was in every way, never changing or growing any older, fresher (as The Park's brochure said) than in memory ever green.

I married Georgie for her money, the same reason she married her first, the one who took out The Park's contract for her. She married me, I think, for my looks; she always had a taste for looks in men. I wanted to write. I made a calculation that more women than men make, and decided that to be supported and paid for by a rich wife would give me freedom to do so, to "develop." The calculation worked out no better for me than it does for most women who make it. I carried a typewriter and a case of miscellaneous paper from Ibiza to Gstaad to Bali to London, and typed on beaches, and learned to ski. Georgie liked me in ski clothes.

Now that those looks are all but gone, I can look back on myself as a young hunk and see that I was in a way a rarity, a type that you also run into often among women and less among men, the beauty unaware of his beauty, aware that he affects women profoundly and more or less instantly but doesn't know why; thinks he is being listened to and understood, that his soul is being seen, when all that's being seen is long-lashed eyes and a strong, square, tanned wrist turning in a lovely gesture, stubbing out a cigarette. Confusing. By the time I figured out why I had for so long been indulged and cared for and listened to, why I was interesting, I wasn't as interesting as I had been. At about the same time I realized I wasn't a writer at all. Georgie's investment stopped looking as good to her, and my calculation had ceased to add up; only by that time I had come, pretty unexpectedly, to love Georgie

a lot, and she just as unexpectedly had come to love and need me too, as much as she needed anybody. We never really parted, even though when she died I hadn't seen her for years. Phone calls, at dawn or four a.m. because she never, for all her travel, really grasped that the world turns and cocktail hour travels around with it.

She was a crazy, wasteful, happy woman, without a trace of malice or permanence or ambition in her—easily pleased and easily bored and strangely serene despite the hectic pace she kept up. She cherished things and lost them and forgot them: things, days, people. She had fun, though, and I had fun with her; that was her talent and her destiny, not always an easy one. Once, hung over in a New York hotel, watching a sudden snowfall out the immense window, she said to me, "Charlie, I'm going to die of fun."

And she did. Snow-foiling in Austria, she was among the first to get one of those snow leopards, silent beasts as fast as speedboats. Alfredo called me in California to tell me, but with the distance and his accent and his eagerness to tell me *he* wasn't to blame, I never grasped the details. I was still her husband, her closest relative, heir to the little she still had, and beneficiary, too, of The Park's access concept. Fortunately, The Park's services included collecting her from the morgue in Gstaad and installing her in her chamber at The Park's California unit. Beyond signing papers and taking delivery when Georgie arrived by freight airship at Van Nuys, there was nothing for me to do. The Park's representative was solicitous and made sure I understood how to go about accessing Georgie, but I wasn't listening. I am only a child of my time, I suppose. Everything about death, the fact of it, the fate of the remains, and the situation of the living faced with it, seems grotesque to me, embarrassing, useless. And everything done about it only makes it more grotesque, more useless: Someone I loved is dead; let me therefore dress in clown's clothes, talk backwards, and buy expensive machinery to make up for it. I went back to L.A.

A year or more later, the contents of some safe-deposit boxes of Georgie's arrived from the lawyer's: some bonds and such stuff, and a small steel case, velvet lined, that contained a key, a key deeply notched on both sides and headed with smooth plastic, like the key to an expensive car.

Why did I go to The Park that first time? Mostly because I had forgotten about it: getting that key in the mail was like coming across a pile of old snapshots you hadn't cared to look at when they were new but which after they have aged come to contain the past, as they did not contain the present. I was curious.

I understood very well that The Park and its access concept were very probably only another cruel joke on the rich, preserving the illusion that they can buy what can't be bought, like the cryonics fad of thirty years before. Once in Ibiza, Georgie and I met a German couple who also had a contract with The Park; their Wasp hovered over them like a Paraclete and made them self-conscious in the extreme—they seemed to be constantly rehearsing the eternal show being stored up for their descendants. Their deaths had taken over their lives, as though they were pharaohs. Did they, Georgie wondered, exclude the Wasp from their bedroom? Or did its presence there stir them to greater efforts, proofs of undying love and admirable vigor for the unborn to see?

No, death wasn't to be cheated that way, any more than by pyramids, by masses said in perpetuity. It wasn't Georgie saved from death that I would find. But there were eight thousand hours of her life with me, genuine hours, stored there more carefully than they could be in my porous memory; Georgie hadn't excluded the Wasp from her bedroom, our bedroom, and she who had never performed for anybody could not have conceived of performing for it. And there would be me, too, undoubtedly, caught unintentionally by the Wasp's attention: out of those thousands of hours there would be hundreds of myself, and myself had just then begun to be problematic to me, something that had to be figured out, something about which evidence had to be gathered and weighed. I was thirty-eight years old.

That summer, then, I borrowed a Highway Access Permit (the old HAPpy card of those days) from a county lawyer I knew and drove the coast highway up to where The Park was, at the end of a pretty beach road, all alone above the sea. It looked from the outside like the best, most peaceful kind of Italian country cemetery, a low stucco wall topped with urns, amid cypresses, an arched gate in the center. A small brass plaque on the gate: PLEASE USE YOUR KEY. The gate opened, not to a square of shaded tombstones but onto a ramped corridor going down: The cemetery wall was an illusion, the works were underground. Silence, or nameless Muzak like silence; solitude—either the necessary technicians were discreetly hidden or none were needed. Certainly the access concept turned out to be simplicity itself, in operation anyway. Even I, who am an idiot about information technology, could tell that. The Wasp was genuine state-of-the-art stuff, but what we mourners got was as ordinary as home movies, as old letters tied up in ribbon.

A display screen near the entrance told me down which corridor to find Georgie, and my key let me into a small screening room where there was a moderate-size TV monitor, two comfortable chairs, and dark walls of chocolate-brown carpeting. The sweet-sad Muzak. Georgie herself was evidently somewhere in the vicinity, in the wall or under the floor, they weren't specific about the charnel-house aspect of the place. In the control panel before the TV were a keyhole for my key and two bars: ACCESS and RESET.

I sat, feeling foolish and a little afraid, too, made more uncomfortable by being so deliberately soothed by neutral furnishings and sober tools. I imagined, around me, down other corridors, in other chambers, that others communed with their dead as I was about to do; that the dead were murmuring to them beneath the stream of Muzak; that they wept to see and hear, as I might. But I could hear nothing. I turned my key in its slot, and the screen lit up. The dim lights dimmed further, and the Muzak ceased. I pushed ACCESS, obviously the next step. No doubt all these procedures had been explained to me long ago at the dock when Georgie in her aluminum box was being off-loaded, and I hadn't listened. And on the screen she turned to look at me—only not at me, though I started and drew breath—at the Wasp that watched her.

She was in mid-sentence, mid-gesture. Where? When? *Or put it on the same card with the others,* she said, turning away. Someone said something, Georgie answered, and stood up, the Wasp panning and moving erratically with her, like an amateur with a home-video camera. A white room, sunlight, wicker. Ibiza. Georgie wore a cotton blouse, open; from a table she picked up lotion, poured some on her hand, and rubbed it across her freckled breastbone. The meaningless conversation about putting something on a card went on, ceased. I watched the room, wondering what year, what season I had stumbled into. Georgie pulled off her shirt—her small round breasts tipped with large, childlike nipples, child's breasts she still had at forty, shook delicately. And she went out onto the balcony, the Wasp following, blinded by sun, adjusting. *If you want to do it that way,* someone said. The someone crossed the screen, a brown blur, naked. It was me. Georgie said: *Oh, look, hummingbirds.*

She watched them, rapt, and the Wasp crept close to her cropped blond head, rapt too, and I watched her watch. She turned away, rested her elbows on the balustrade. I couldn't remember this day. How should I? One of hundreds, of thousands. . . . She looked out to the bright sea, wearing her sleepwalking face, mouth partly open, and absently stroked her breast with her oiled hand. An iridescent glitter among the flowers was the hummingbird.

Without really knowing what I did—I felt hungry, suddenly,

hungry for pastness, for more—I touched the RESET bar. The balcony in Ibiza vanished, the screen glowed emptily. I touched ACCESS.

At first there was darkness, a murmur; then a dark back moved away from before the Wasp's eye, and a dim scene of people resolved itself. Jump. Other people, or the same people, a party? Jump. Apparently the Wasp was turning itself on and off according to the changes in light levels here, wherever *here* was. Georgie in a dark dress having her cigarette lit: brief flare of the lighter. She said *Thanks*. Jump. A foyer or hotel lounge. Paris? The Wasp jerkily sought for her among people coming and going; it couldn't make a movie, establishing shots, cutaways—it could only doggedly follow Georgie, like a jealous husband, seeing nothing else. This was frustrating. I pushed RESET. ACCESS. Georgie brushed her teeth, somewhere, somewhen.

I understood, after one or two more of these terrible leaps. Access was random. There was no way to dial up a year, a day, a scene. The Park had supplied no program, none; the eight thousand hours weren't filed at all; they were a jumble, like a lunatic's memory, like a deck of shuffled cards. I had supposed, without thinking about it, that they would begin at the beginning and go on till they reached the end. Why didn't they?

I also understood something else. If access was truly random, if I truly had no control, then I had lost as good as forever those scenes I had seen. Odds were on the order of eight thousand to one (more? far more? probabilities are opaque to me) that I would never light on them again by pressing this bar. I felt a pang of loss for that afternoon in Ibiza. It was doubly gone now. I sat before the empty screen, afraid to touch ACCESS again, afraid of what I would lose.

I shut down the machine (the light level in the room rose, the Muzak poured softly back in) and went out into the halls, back to the display screen in the entranceway. The list of names slowly, greenly, rolled over like the list of departing flights at an airport. Code numbers were missing from beside many, indicating perhaps that they weren't yet in residence, only awaited. In the *D*s, only three names, and DIRECTOR—hidden among them as though he were only another of the dead. A chamber number. I went to find it, and went in.

The director looked more like a janitor or a night watchman, the semi-retired type you often see caretaking little-visited places. He wore a brown smock like a monk's robe, and was making coffee in a corner of his small office, out of which little business seemed to be done. He looked up startled, caught out, when I entered.

"Sorry," I said, "but I don't think I understand this system right."

"A problem?" he said. "Shouldn't be a problem." He looked at me a little wide-eyed and shy, hoping not to be called on for anything difficult. "Equipment's all working?"

"I don't know," I said. "It doesn't seem that it could be." I described what I thought I had learned about The Park's access concept. "That can't be right, can it?" I said. "That access is totally random . . ."

He was nodding, still wide-eyed, paying close attention.

"Is it?" I asked.

"Is it what?"

"Random."

"Oh, yes. Yes, sure. If everything's in working order."

I could think of nothing to say for a moment, watching him nod reassuringly. Then: "Why?" I asked. "I mean why is there no way at all to, to organize, to have some kind of organized access to the material?" I had begun to feel that sense of grotesque foolishness in the presence of death, as though I were haggling over Georgie's effects. "That seems stupid, if you'll pardon me."

"Oh no, oh no," he said. "You've read your literature? You've read all your literature?"

"Well, to tell the truth . . ."

"It's all just as described," the director said. "I can promise you that. If there's any problem at all . . ."

"Do you mind," I said, "if I sit down?" I smiled. He seemed so afraid of me and my complaint, of me as mourner, possibly grief-crazed and unable to grasp the simple limits of his responsibilities to me, that he needed soothing himself. "I'm sure everything's fine," I said. "I just don't think I understand. I'm kind of dumb about these things."

"Sure. Sure. Sure." He regretfully put away his coffee makings and sat behind his desk, lacing his fingers together like a consultant. "People get a lot of satisfaction out of the access here," he said, "a lot of comfort, if they take it in the right spirit." He tried a smile. I wondered what qualifications he had had to show to get this job. "The random part. Now, it's all in the literature. There's the legal aspect—you're not a lawyer are you, no, no, sure, no offense. You see, the material here isn't *for* anything, except, well, except for communing. But suppose the stuff were programmed, searchable. Suppose there was a problem about taxes or inheritance or so on. There could be subpoenas, lawyers all over the place, destroying the memorial concept completely."

I really hadn't thought of that. Built-in randomness saved past lives from being searched in any systematic way. And no doubt saved The Park from being in the records business and at the wrong end of a lot of suits. "You'd have to watch the whole eight thousand hours," I said, "and even if you found what you were looking for there'd be no way to replay it. It would have gone by." It would slide into the random past even as you watched it, like that afternoon in Ibiza, that party in Paris. Lost.

He smiled and nodded. I smiled and nodded.

"I'll tell you something," he said. "They didn't predict that. The randomness. It was a side effect, an effect of the storage process. Just luck." His grin turned down, his brows knitted seriously. "See, we're storing here at the molecular level. We have to go that small, for space problems. I mean your eight-thousand-hour guarantee. If we had gone tape or conventional, how much room would it take up? If the access concept caught on. A lot of room. So we went vapor-trap and endless-tracking. Size of my thumbnail. It's all in the literature." He looked at me strangely. I had a sudden intense sensation that I was being fooled, tricked, that the man before me in his smock was no expert, no technician; he was a charlatan, or maybe a madman impersonating a director and not belonging here at all. It raised the hair on my neck, and passed. "So the randomness," he was saying. "It was an effect of going molecular. Brownian movement. All you do is lift the endless tracking for a microsecond and you get a rearrangement at the molecular level. We don't randomize. The molecules do it for us."

I remembered Brownian movement, just barely, from physics class. The random movement of molecules, the teacher said; it has a mathematical description. It's like the movement of dust motes you see swimming in a shaft of sunlight, like the swirl of snowflakes in a glass paperweight that shows a cottage being snowed on. "I see," I said. "I guess I see."

"Is there," he said, "any other problem?" He said it as though there might be some other problem and that he knew what it might be and that he hoped I didn't have it. "You understand the system, key lock, two bars, ACCESS, RESET. . . ."

"I understand," I said. "I understand now."

"Communing," he said, standing, relieved, sure I would be gone soon. "I understand. It takes a while to relax into the communing concept."

"Yes," I said. "It does."

I wouldn't learn what I had come to learn, whatever that was. The Wasp had not been good at storage after all, no, no better than my young soul had been. Days and weeks had been missed by its tiny eye. It hadn't seen well, and in what it had seen it had been no more able to distinguish the just-as-well-forgotten from the unforgettable than my own eye had been. No better and no worse—the same.

And yet, and yet—she stood up in Ibiza and dressed her breasts with lotion, and spoke to me: *Oh, look, hummingbirds.* I had forgotten, and the Wasp had not; and I owned once again what I hadn't known I had lost, hadn't known was precious to me.

The sun was setting when I left The Park, the satin sea foaming softly, randomly around the rocks.

I had spent my life waiting for something, not knowing what, not even knowing I waited. Killing time. I was still waiting. But what I had been waiting for had already occurred and was past.

It was two years, nearly, since Georgie had died: two years until, for the first and last time, I wept for her; for her, and for myself.

Of course I went back. After a lot of work and correctly placed dollars, I netted a HAPpy card of my own. I had time to spare, like a lot of people then, and often on empty afternoons (never on Sunday) I would get out onto the unpatched and weed-grown freeway and glide up the coast. The Park was always open. I relaxed into the communing concept.

Now, after some hundreds of hours spent there underground, now when I have long ceased to go through those doors (I have lost my key, I think; anyway I don't know where to look for it), I know that the solitude I felt myself to be in was real. The watchers around me, the listeners I sensed in other chambers, were mostly my imagination. There was rarely anyone there. These tombs were as neglected as any tombs anywhere usually are. Either the living did not care to attend much on the dead—when have they ever?—or the hopeful buyers of the contracts had come to discover the flaw in the access concept: as I discovered it, in the end.

ACCESS, and she takes dresses one by one from her closet, and holds them against her body, and studies the effect in a tall mirror, and puts them back again. She had a funny face, which she never made except when looking at herself in the mirror, a face made for no one but herself, that was actually quite unlike her. The mirror Georgie.

RESET.

ACCESS. By a bizarre coincidence here she is looking in another mirror. I think the Wasp could be confused by mirrors. She turns away, the Wasp adjusts; there is someone asleep, tangled in bedclothes on a big hotel bed, morning, a room-service cart. Oh: the Algonquin: myself. Winter. Snow is falling outside the tall window. She searches her handbag, takes out a small vial, swallows a pill with coffee, holding the cup by its body and not its handle. I stir, show a tousled head of hair. Conversation—unintelligible. Gray room, whitish snow light, color degraded. Would I now (I thought, watching us) reach out for her? Would I in the next hour take her, or she me, push aside the bedclothes, open her pale pajamas? She goes into the john, shuts the door. The Wasp watches stupidly, excluded, transmitting the door.

RESET, finally.

But what (I would wonder) if I had been patient, what if I had watched and waited?

Time, it turns out, takes an unconscionable time. The waste, the footless waste—it's no spectator sport. Whatever fun there is in sitting idly looking at nothing and tasting your own being for a whole afternoon, there is no fun in replaying it. The waiting is excruciating. How often, in five years, in eight thousand hours of daylight or lamplight, might we have coupled, how much time expended in lovemaking? A hundred hours, two hundred? Odds were not high of my coming on such a scene; darkness swallowed most of them, and the others were lost in the interstices of endless hours spent shopping, reading, on planes and in cars, asleep, apart. Hopeless.

ACCESS. She has turned on a bedside lamp. Alone. She hunts amid the Kleenex and magazines on the bedside table, finds a watch, looks at it dully, turns it right side up, looks again, and puts it down. Cold. She burrows in the blankets, yawning, staring, then puts out a hand for the phone but only rests her hand on it, thinking. Thinking at four a.m. She withdraws her hand, shivers a child's deep, sleepy shiver, and shuts off the light. A bad dream. In an instant it's morning, dawn; the Wasp slept, too. She sleeps soundly, unmoving, only the top of her blond head showing out of the quilt—and will no doubt sleep so for hours, watched over more attentively, more fixedly, than any peeping Tom could ever have watched over her.

RESET.

ACCESS.

"I can't hear as well as I did at first," I told the director. "And the definition is getting softer."

"Oh sure," the director said. "That's really in the literature. We have to explain that carefully. That this might be a problem."

"It isn't just my monitor?" I asked. "I thought it was probably only the monitor."

"No, no, not really, no," he said. He gave me coffee. We'd gotten to be friendly over the months. I think, as well as being afraid of me, he was glad I came around now and then; at least one of the living came here, one at least was using the services. "There's a *slight* degeneration that does occur."

"Everything seems to be getting gray."

His face had shifted into intense concern, no belittling this problem. "Mm-hm, mm-hm, see, at the molecular level where we're at, there is degeneration. It's just in the physics. It randomizes a little over time. So you lose—you don't lose a minute of what you've got, but you lose a little definition. A little color. But it levels off."

"It does?"

"We think it does. Sure it does, we promise it does. We *predict* that it will."

"But you don't know."

"Well, well you see we've only been in this business a short while. This concept is new. There were things we couldn't know." He still looked at me, but seemed at the same time to have forgotten me. Tired. He seemed to have grown colorless himself lately, old, losing definition. "You might start getting some snow," he said softly.

ACCESS RESET ACCESS.

A gray plaza of herringbone-laid stones, gray, clicking palms. She turns up the collar of her sweater, narrowing her eyes in a stern wind. Buys magazines at a kiosk: *Vogue, Harper's, La Moda. Cold*, she says to the kiosk girl. *Frio.* The young man I was takes her arm; they walk back along the beach, which is deserted and strung with cast seaweed, washed by a dirty sea. Winter in Ibiza. We talk, but the Wasp can't hear, the sea's sound confuses it; it seems bored by its duties and lags behind us.

RESET.

ACCESS. The Algonquin, terribly familiar: morning, winter. She turns away from the snowy window. Myself in bed . . . and for a moment watching this I felt suspended between two mirrors, reflected endlessly. I had seen this before; I had lived it once and remembered it once, and remembered the memory, and here it was again, or could it be nothing but another morning, a similar morning? There were far more than one like this, in this place. But no; she turns from the window, she gets out her vial of pills, picks up the coffee cup by its body: I had seen this moment before, not months before, weeks before, here in this chamber. I had come upon the same scene twice.

What are the odds of it, I wondered, what are the odds of coming upon the same minutes again, these minutes.

I stir within the bedclothes.

I leaned forward to hear, this time, what I would say; it was something like *but fun anyway*, or something.

*Fun*, she says, laughing, harrowed, the degraded sound a ghost's twittering. *Charlie, someday I'm going to die of fun.*

She takes her pill. The Wasp follows her to the john, and is shut out.

Why am I here? I thought, and my heart was beating hard and slow. What am I here for? What?

RESET.

ACCESS.

Silvered icy streets, New York, Fifth Avenue. She is climbing shouting from a cab's dark interior. *Just don't shout at me,* she shouts at someone, her mother I never met, a dragon. She is out and hurrying away down the sleety street with her bundles, the Wasp at her shoulder. I could reach out and touch her shoulder and make her turn and follow me out.

Walking away, lost in the colorless press of traffic and people, impossible to discern within the softened snowy image.

Something was very wrong.

Georgie hated winter, she escaped it most of the time we were together, about the first of the year beginning to long for the sun that had gone elsewhere; Austria was all right for a few weeks, the toy villages and sugar snow and bright, sleek skiers were not really the winter she feared, though even in fire-warmed chalets it was hard to get her naked without gooseflesh and shudders from some draft only she could feel. We were chaste in winter. So Georgie escaped it: Antigua and Bali and two months in Ibiza when the almonds blossomed. It was continual false, flavorless spring all winter long.

How often could snow have fallen when the Wasp was watching her?

Not often; countable times, times I could count up myself if I could remember as the Wasp could. Not often. Not always.

"There's a problem," I said to the director.

"It's peaked out, has it?" he said. "That definition problem?"

"Well, no," I said. "Actually, it's gotten worse."

He was sitting behind his desk, arms spread wide across his chair's back, and a false, pinkish flush to his cheeks like undertaker's makeup. Drinking.

"Hasn't peaked out, huh?" he said.

"That's not the problem," I said. "The problem is the access. It's not random like you said."

"Molecular level," he said. "It's in the physics."

"You don't understand. It's not getting more random. It's getting less random. It's getting selective. It's freezing up."

"No no no," he said dreamily. "Access is random. Life isn't all summer and fun, you know. Into each life some rain must fall."

I sputtered, trying to explain. "But but but . . ."

"You know," he said. "I've been thinking of getting out of access." He pulled open a drawer in the desk before him; it made an empty sound. He stared within it dully for a moment, and shut it. "The Park's been good for me, but I'm just not used to this. Used to be you thought you could render a service, you know? Well, hell, you know, you've had fun, what do you care."

He *was* mad. For an instant I heard the dead around me; I tasted on my tongue the stale air of underground.

"I remember," he said, tilting back in his chair and looking elsewhere, "many years ago, I got into access. Only we didn't call it that then. What I did was, I worked for a stock-footage house. It was going out of business like they all did, like this place here is going to do, shouldn't say that, but you didn't hear it. Anyway, it was a big warehouse with steel shelves for miles, filled with film cans, film cans filled with old plastic film, you know? Film of every kind. And movie people, if they wanted old scenes of past time in their movies, would call up and ask for what they wanted, find me this, find me that. And we had everything, every kind of scene, but you know what the hardest thing to find was? Just ordinary scenes of daily life. I mean people just doing things and living their lives. You know what we *did* have? Speeches. People giving speeches. Like presidents. You could have hours of speeches, but not just people, whatchacallit, oh, washing clothes, sitting in a park . . ."

"It might just be the reception," I said. "Somehow."

He looked at me for a long moment as though I had just arrived. "Anyway," he said at last, turning away again, "I was there awhile learning the ropes. And producers called and said, 'Get me this, get me that.' And one producer was making a film, some film of the past, and he wanted old scenes, *old*, of people long ago, in the summer; having fun; eating ice cream; swimming in bathing suits; riding in convertibles. Fifty years ago. Eighty years ago."

He opened his empty drawer again, found a toothpick, and began to use it.

"So I accessed the earliest stuff. Speeches. More speeches. But I found a scene here and there—people in the street, fur coats, window-shopping, traffic. Old people, I mean they were young then, but people of the past; they have these pinched kind of faces, you get to know them. Sad, a little. On city streets, hurrying, holding their hats. Cities were sort of black then, in film; black cars in the streets, black derby hats. Stone.

"Well, it wasn't what they wanted. I found summer for them, color summer, but new. They wanted old. I kept looking back. I kept looking, I did. The further back I went, the more I saw these pinched faces, black cars, black streets of stone. Snow. There isn't any summer there."

With slow gravity he rose and found a brown bottle and two coffee cups. He poured sloppily. "So it's not your reception," he said. "Film takes longer, I guess, but it's the physics. All in the physics. A word to the wise is sufficient."

The liquor was harsh, a cold distillate of past sunlight. I wanted to go, get out, not look back. I would not stay watching until there was only snow.

"So I'm getting out of access," the director said. "Let the dead bury the dead, right? Let the dead bury the dead."

I didn't go back. I never went back, though the highways opened again and The Park isn't far from the town I've settled in. Settled; the right word. It restores your balance, in the end, even in a funny way your cheerfulness, when you come to know, without regrets, that the best thing that's going to happen in your life has already happened. And I still have some summer left to me.

I think there are two different kinds of memory, and only one kind gets worse as I get older: the kind where, by an effort of will, you can reconstruct your first car or your Service serial number or the name and figure of your high school physics teacher—a Mr. Holm, in a gray suit, a bearded guy, skinny, about thirty. The other kind doesn't worsen; if anything it grows more intense. The sleepwalking kind, the kind you stumble into as into rooms with secret doors and suddenly find yourself sitting not on your front porch but in a classroom, you can't at first think where or when, and a bearded, smiling man is turning in his hand a glass paperweight, inside which a little cottage stands in a swirl of snow.

There is no access to Georgie, except that now and then, unpredictably, when I'm sitting on the porch or pushing a grocery cart or standing at the sink, a memory of that kind will visit me, vivid and startling, like a hypnotist's snap of fingers. Or like that funny experience you sometimes have, on the point of sleep, of hearing your name called softly and distinctly by someone who is not there.

# THOMAS LIGOTTI
## The Last Feast of Harlequin

*To the Memory of H. P. Lovecraft*

### I

My interest in the town of Mirocaw was first aroused when I heard that an annual festival was held there which promised to include, to some extent, the participation of clowns among its other elements of pageantry. A former colleague of mine, who is now attached to the anthropology department of a distant university, had read one of my recent articles ("The Clown Figure in American Media," *Journal of Popular Culture*), and wrote to me that he vaguely remembered reading or being told of a town somewhere in the state that held a kind of "Fool's Feast" every year, thinking that this might be pertinent to my peculiar line of study. It was, of course, more pertinent than he had reason to think, both to my academic aims in this area and to my personal pursuits.

Aside from my teaching, I had for some years been engaged in various anthropological projects with the primary ambition of articulating the significance of the clown figure in diverse cultural contexts. Every year for the past twenty years I have attended the pre-Lenten festivals that are held in various places throughout the southern United States. Every year I learned something more concerning the esoterics of celebration. In these studies I was an eager participant—along with playing my part as an anthropologist, I also took a place behind the clownish mask myself. And I cherished this role as I did nothing else in my life. To me the title of Clown has always carried connotations of a noble sort. I was an adroit jester, strangely enough, and had always taken pride in the skills I worked so diligently to develop.

I wrote to the State Department of Recreation, indicating what information I desired and exposing an enthusiastic urgency which came naturally to me on this topic. Many weeks later I received a tan envelope imprinted with a government logo. Inside was a pamphlet that catalogued all of the various seasonal festivities of which the state was officially aware, and I noted in passing that there were as many in late autumn and winter as in the warmer seasons. A letter inserted within the pamphlet explained to me that, according to their voluminous records, no festivals held in the town of Mirocaw had been officially registered. Their files, nonetheless, could be placed at my disposal if I should wish to research this or similar matters in connection with some definite project. At the time this offer was made I was already laboring under so many professional and personal burdens that, with a weary hand, I simply deposited the envelope and its contents in a drawer, never to be consulted again.

Some months later, however, I made an impulsive digression from my responsibilities and, rather haphazardly, took up the Mirocaw project. This happened as I was driving north one afternoon in late summer with the intention of examining some journals in the holdings of a library at another university. Once out of the city limits the scenery changed to sunny fields and farms, diverting my thoughts from the signs that I passed along the highway. Nevertheless, the subconscious scholar in me must have been regarding these with studious care. The name of a town loomed into my vision. Instantly the scholar retrieved certain records from some deep mental drawer, and I was faced with making a few hasty calculations as to whether there was enough time and motivation for an investigative side trip. But the exit sign was even hastier in making its appearance, and I soon found myself leaving the highway, recalling the roadsign's promise that the town was no more than seven miles east.

These seven miles included several confusing turns, the forced taking of a temporarily alternate route, and a destination not even visible until a steep rise had been fully ascended. On the descent another helpful sign informed me that I was within the city limits of Mirocaw. Some scattered houses on the outskirts of the town were the first structures I encountered. Beyond them the numerical highway became Townshend Street, the main avenue of Mirocaw.

The town impressed me as being much larger once I was within its limits than it had appeared from the prominence just outside. I saw that the general hilliness of the surrounding countryside was also an internal feature of Mirocaw. Here, though, the effect was different. The parts of the town did not look as if they adhered very well to one another. This condition might be blamed on the irregular topography of the town. Behind some of the old stores in the business district, steeply roofed houses had been erected on a sudden incline, their peaks appearing at an extraordinary elevation above the lower buildings. And because the foundations of these houses could not be glimpsed, they conveyed the illusion of being either precariously suspended in air, threatening to topple down, or else constructed with an unnatural loftiness in relation to their width and mass. This situation also created a weird distortion of perspective. The two levels of structures overlapped each other without giving a sense of depth, so that the houses, because of their higher elevation and nearness to the foreground buildings, did not appear diminished in size as background objects should. Consequently, a look of flatness, as in a photograph, predominated in this area. Indeed, Mirocaw could be compared to an album of old snapshots, particularly ones in which the camera had been upset in the process of photography, causing the pictures to develop on angle: a cone-roofed turret, like a pointed hat jauntily askew, peeked over the houses on a neighboring street; a billboard displaying a group of grinning vegetables tipped its contents slightly westward; cars abutting steep curbs seemed to be flying skyward in the glare-distorted windows of a five-and-ten; people leaned lethargically as they trod up and down sidewalks; and on that sunny day the clock tower, which at first I mistook for a church steeple, cast a long shadow that seemed to extend an impossible distance and wander into unlikely places in its progress across the town. I should say that perhaps the disharmonies of Mirocaw are more acutely affecting my imagination in retrospect than they were on that first day, when I was primarily concerned with locating the city hall or some other center of information.

I pulled around a corner and parked. Sliding over to the other side of the seat, I rolled down the window and called to a passerby: "Excuse me, sir," I said. The man, who was shabbily dressed and very old, paused for a moment without approaching the car. Though he had apparently responded to my call, his vacant expression did not betray the least awareness of my presence, and for a moment I thought it just a coincidence that he halted on the sidewalk at the same time I addressed him. His eyes were focused somewhere beyond me with a weary and imbecilic gaze. After a few moments he continued on his way and I said nothing to call him back, even though at the last second his face

began to appear dimly familiar. Someone else finally came along who was able to direct me to the Mirocaw City Hall and Community Center.

The city hall turned out to be the building with the clock tower. Inside I stood at a counter behind which some people were working at desks and walking up and down a back hallway. On one wall was a poster for the state lottery: a jack-in-the-box with both hands grasping green bills. After a few moments, a tall, middle-aged woman came over to the counter.

"Can I help you?" she asked in a neutral, bureaucratic voice.

I explained that I had heard about the festival—saying nothing about being a nosy academic—and asked if she could provide me with further information or direct me to someone who could.

"Do you mean the one held in the winter?" she asked.

"How many of them are there?"

"Just that one."

"I suppose, then, that that's the one I mean." I smiled as if sharing a joke with her.

Without another word, she walked off into the back hallway. While she was absent I exchanged glances with several of the people behind the counter who periodically looked up from their work.

"There you are," she said when she returned, handing me a piece of paper that looked like the product of a cheap copy machine. *Please Come to the Fun*, it said in large letters. *Parades*, it went on, *Street Masquerade*, *Bands*, *The Winter Raffle*, and *The Coronation of the Winter Queen*. The page continued with the mention of a number of miscellaneous festivities. I read the words again. There was something about that imploring little "please" at the top of the announcement that made the whole affair seem like a charity function.

"When is it held? It doesn't say when the festival takes place."

"Most people already know that." She abruptly snatched the page from my hands and wrote something at the bottom. When she gave it back to me, I saw "Dec. 19–21" written in blue-green ink. I was immediately struck by an odd sense of scheduling on the part of the festival committee. There was, of course, solid anthropological and historical precedent for holding festivities around the winter solstice, but the timing of this particular event did not seem entirely practical.

"If you don't mind my asking, don't these days somewhat conflict with the regular holiday season? I mean, most people have enough going on at that time."

"It's just tradition," she said, as if invoking some venerable ancestry behind her words.

"That's very interesting," I said as much to myself as to her.

"Is there anything else?" she asked.

"Yes. Could you tell me if this festival has anything to do with clowns? I see there's something about a masquerade."

"Yes, of course there are some people in . . . costumes. I've never been in that position myself . . . that is, yes, there are clowns of a sort."

At that point my interest was definitely aroused, but I was not sure how much further I wanted to pursue it. I thanked the woman for her help and asked the best way to get back to the highway, not anxious to retrace the labyrinthine route by which I had entered the town. I walked back to my car with a whole flurry of half-formed questions, and as many vague and conflicting answers, cluttering my mind.

The directions the woman gave me necessitated passing through the south end of Mirocaw. There were not many people moving about in this section of town. Those that I did see, shuffling lethargically down a block of battered storefronts, exhibited the same sort of forlorn expression and manner as the old man from whom I had asked directions earlier. I must have been passing through a central artery of this area, for on either side stretched street after street of poorly tended yards and houses bowed with age and indifference. When I came to a stop at a streetcorner, one of the citizens of this slum passed in front of my car. This lean, morose, and epicene person turned my way and sneered outrageously with a taut little mouth, yet seemed to be looking at no one in particular. After progressing a few streets farther, I came to a road that led back to the highway. I felt detectably more comfortable as soon as I found myself traveling once again through the expanses of sun-drenched farmlands.

I reached the library with more than enough time for my research, and so I decided to make a scholarly detour to see what material I could find that might illuminate the winter festival held in Mirocaw. The library, one of the oldest in the state, included in its holding the entire run of the Mirocaw *Courier*. I thought this would be an excellent place to start. I soon found, however, that there was no handy way to research information from this newspaper, and I did not want to engage in a blind search for articles concerning a specific subject.

I next turned to the more organized resources of the newspapers for the larger cities located in the same county, which incidentally

shares its name with Mirocaw. I uncovered very little about the town, and almost nothing concerning its festival, except in one general article on annual events in the area that erroneously attributed to Mirocaw a "large Middle-Eastern community" which every spring hosted a kind of ethnic jamboree. From what I had already observed, and from what I subsequently learned, the citizens of Mirocaw were solidly mid-western-American, the probable descendants in a direct line from some enterprising pack of New Englanders of the last century. There was one brief item devoted to a Mirocavian event, but this merely turned out to be an obituary notice for an old woman who had quietly taken her life around Christmas time. Thus, I returned home that day all but empty handed on the subject of Mirocaw.

However, it was not long afterward that I received another letter from the former colleague of mine who had first led me to seek out Mirocaw and its festival. As it happened, he rediscovered the article that caused him to stir my interest in a local "Fool's Feast." This article had its sole appearance in an obscure festschrift of anthropology studies published in Amsterdam twenty years ago. Most of these papers were in Dutch, a few in German, and only one was in English: "The Last Feast of Harlequin: Preliminary Notes on a Local Festival." It was exciting, of course, finally to be able to read this study, but even more exciting was the name of its author: Dr. Raymond Thoss.

## II

Before proceeding any further, I should mention something about Thoss, and inevitably about myself. Over two decades ago, at my alma mater in Cambridge, Mass., Thoss was a professor of mine. Long before playing a role in the events I am about to describe, he was already one of the most important figures in my life. A striking personality, he inevitably influenced everyone who came in contact with him. I remember his lectures on social anthropology, how he turned that dim room into a brilliant and profound circus of learning. He moved in an uncannily brisk manner. When he swept his arm around to indicate some common term on the blackboard behind him, one felt he was pre-senting nothing less than an item of fantastic qualities and secret value. When he replaced his hand in the pocket of his old jacket this fleet-ing magic was once again stored away in its wellworn pouch, to be retrieved at the sorcerer's discretion. We sensed he was teaching us more than we could possibly learn, and that he himself was in possession of greater and deeper knowledge than he could possibly impart. On one occasion I summoned up the audacity to offer an interpretation—which was somewhat opposed to his own—regarding the tribal clowns of the Hopi Indians. I implied that personal experience as an amateur clown and special devotion to this study provided me with an insight possibly more valuable than his own. It was then he disclosed, casually and very obiter dicta, that he had actually acted in the role of one of these masked tribal fools and had celebrated with them the dance of the *kachinas*. In revealing these facts, however, he somehow managed not to add to the humiliation I had already inflicted upon myself. And for this I was grateful to him.

Thoss's activities were such that he sometimes became the object of gossip or romanticized speculation. He was a fieldworker par excellence, and his ability to insinuate himself into exotic cultures and situations, thereby gaining insights where other anthropologists merely collected data, was renowned. At various times in his career there had been rumors of his having "gone native" à la the Frank Hamilton Cushing legend. There were hints, which were not always irresponsible or cheaply glamorized, that he was involved in projects of a freakish sort, many of which focused on New England. It is a fact that he spent six months posing as a mental patient at an institution in western Massachusetts, gathering information on the "culture" of the psychically disturbed. When his book *Winter Solstice: The Longest Night of a Society* was published, the general opinion was that it was disappointingly subjective and impressionistic, and that, aside from a few moving but "poetically obscure" observations, there was nothing at all to give it value. Those who defended Thoss claimed he was a kind of super-anthropologist: while much of his work emphasized his own mind and feelings, his experience had in fact penetrated to a rich core of hard data which he had yet to disclose in objective discourse. As a student of Thoss, I tended to support this latter estimation of him. For a variety of tenable and untenable reasons, I believed Thoss capable of unearthing hitherto inaccessible strata of human existence. So it was gratifying at first that this article entitled "The Last Feast of Harlequin" seemed to uphold the Thoss mystique, and in an area I personally found captivating.

Much of the content of the article I did not immediately comprehend, given its author's characteristic and often strategic obscurities. On first reading, the most interesting aspect of this brief study—the "notes" encompassed only twenty pages—was the general mood of the piece. Thoss's eccentricities were definitely present in these pages, but only as a struggling inner force which was definitely contained—incarcerated, I might say—by the somber rhythmic movements of his prose and by some gloomy references he occasionally called upon. Two references in particular shared a common theme. One was a quotation from Poe's "The Conqueror Worm," which Thoss employed as a rather sensational epigraph. The point of the epigraph, however, was nowhere echoed in the text of the article save in another passing reference. Thoss brought up the well-known genesis of the modern Christmas celebration, which of course descends from the Roman Saturnalia. Then, making it clear he had not yet observed the Mirocaw festival and had only gathered its nature from various informants, he established that it too contained many, even more overt, elements of the Saturnalia. Next he made what seemed to me a trivial and purely linguistic observation, one that had less to do with his main course of argument than it did with the equally peripheral Poe epigraph. He briefly mentioned that an early sect of the Syrian Gnostics called themselves "Saturnians" and believed, among other religious heresies, that mankind was created by angels who were in turn created by the Supreme Unknown. The angels, however, did not possess the power to make their creation an erect being and for a time he crawled upon the earth like a worm. Later, the Creator remedied this grotesque state of affairs. At the time I supposed that the symbolic correspondences of mankind's origins and ultimate condition being associated with worms, combined with a year-end festival recognizing the winter death of the earth, was the gist of this Thossian "insight," a poetic but scientifically valueless observation.

Other observations he made on the Mirocaw festival were also strictly etic; in other words, they were based on second-hand sources, hearsay testimony. Even at that juncture, however, I felt Thoss knew more than he disclosed; and, as I later discovered, he had indeed included information on certain aspects of Mirocaw which suggested he was already in possession of several keys which for the moment he was keeping securely in his own pocket. By then I myself possessed a most revealing morsel of knowledge. A note to the "Harlequin" article apprised the reader that the piece was only a fragment in rude form of a more wide-ranging work in preparation. This work was never seen by the world. My former professor had not published anything since his withdrawal from academic circulation some twenty years ago. Now I suspected where he had gone.

For the man I had asked for directions on the streets of Mirocaw, the man with the disconcertingly lethargic gaze, had very much resembled a superannuated version of Dr. Raymond Thoss.

### III

And now I have a confession to make. Despite my reasons for being enthusiastic about Mirocaw and its mysteries, especially its relationship to both Thoss and my own deepest concerns as a scholar—I contemplated the days ahead of me with no more than a feeling of frigid numbness and often with a sense of profound depression. Yet I had no reason to be surprised at this emotional state, which had little relevance to the outward events in my life but was determined by inward conditions that worked according to their own, quite enigmatic, seasons and cycles. For many years, at least since my university days, I have suffered from this dark malady, this recurrent despondency in which I would become buried when it came time for the earth to grow cold and bare and the skies heavy with shadows. Nevertheless, I pursued my plans, though somewhat mechanically, to visit Mirocaw during its festival days, for I superstitiously hoped that this activity might diminish the weight of my seasonal despair. In Mirocaw would be parades and parties and the opportunity to play the clown once again.

For weeks in advance I practiced my art, even perfecting a new feat of juggling magic, which was my special forte in foolery. I had my costumes cleaned, purchased fresh makeup, and was ready. I received permission from the university to cancel some of my classes prior to the holiday, explaining the nature of my project and the necessity of arriving in the town a few days before the festival began, in order to do some preliminary research, establish informants, and so on. Actually my plan was to postpone any formal inquiry until after the festival and to involve myself beforehand as much as possible in its activities. I would, of course, keep a journal during this time.

There was one resource I did want to consult, however. Specifically, I returned to that outstate library to examine those issues of the Mirocaw *Courier* dating from December two decades ago. One story in particular confirmed a point Thoss made in the "Harlequin" article, though the event it chronicled must have taken place after Thoss had written his study.

The *Courier* story appeared two weeks after the festival had ended for that year and was concerned with the disappearance of a woman named Elizabeth Beadle, the wife of Samuel Beadle, a hotel owner in Mirocaw. The county authorities speculated that this was another instance of the "holiday suicides" which seemed to occur with inordinate seasonal regularity in the Mirocaw region. Thoss documented this situation in his "Harlequin" article, though I suspected that today these deaths would be neatly categorized under the heading "seasonal affective disorder." In any case, the authorities searched a half-frozen lake near the outskirts of Mirocaw where they had found many successful suicides in years past. This year, however, no body was discovered. Alongside the article was a picture of Elizabeth Beadle. Even in the grainy microfilm reproduction one could detect a certain vibrancy and vitality in Mrs. Beadle's face. That an hypothesis of "holiday suicide" should be so readily posited to explain her disappearance seemed strange and in some way unjust.

Thoss, in his brief article, wrote that every year there occurred changes of a moral or spiritual cast which seemed to affect Mirocaw along with the usual winter metamorphosis. He was not precise about its origin or nature but stated, in typically mystifying fashion, that the effect of this "subseason" on the town was conspicuously negative. In addition to the number of suicides actually accomplished during this time, there was also a rise in treatment of "hypochondriacal" conditions, which was how the medical men of twenty years past characterized these cases in discussions with Thoss. This state of affairs would gradually worsen and finally reach a climax during the days scheduled for the Mirocaw festival. Thoss speculated that given the secretive nature of small towns, the situation was probably even more intensely pronounced than casual investigation could reveal.

The connection between the festival and this insidious subseasonal climate in Mirocaw was a point on which Thoss did not come to any rigid conclusions. He did write, nevertheless, that these two "climatic aspects" had had a parallel existence in the town's history as far back as available records could document. A late nineteenth-century history of Mirocaw County speaks of the town by its original name of New Colstead, and castigates the townspeople for holding a "ribald and soulless feast" to the exclusion of normal Christmas observances. (Thoss comments that the historian had mistakenly fused two distinct aspects of the season, their actual relationship being essentially antagonistic.) The "Harlequin" article did not trace the festival to its earliest appearance (this may not have been possible), though Thoss emphasized the New

England origins of Mirocaw's founders. The festival, therefore, was one imported from this region and could reasonably be extended at least a century; that is, if it had not been brought over from the Old World, in which case its roots would become indefinite until further research could be done. Surely Thoss's allusion to the Syrian Gnostics suggested the latter possibility could not entirely be ruled out.

But it seemed to be the festival's source in New England that nourished Thoss's speculations. He wrote of this patch of geography as if it were an acceptable place to end the search. For him, the very words "New England" seemed to be stripped of all traditional connotations and had come to imply nothing less than a gateway to all lands, both known and suspected, and even to ages beyond the civilized history of the region. Having been educated partly in New England, I could somewhat understand this sentimental exaggeration, for indeed there are places that seem archaic beyond chronological measure, appearing to transcend relative standards of time and achieving a kind of absolute antiquity which cannot be logically fathomed. But how this vague suggestion related to a small town in the Midwest I could not imagine. Thoss himself observed that the residents of Mirocaw did not betray any mysteriously primitive consciousness. On the contrary, they appeared superficially unaware of the genesis of their winter merrymaking. That such a tradition had endured through the years, however, even eclipsing the conventional Christmas holiday, revealed a profound awareness of the festival's meaning and function.

I cannot deny that what I had learned about the Mirocaw festival did inspire a trite sense of fate, especially given the involvement of such an important figure from my past as Thoss. It was the first time in my academic career that I knew myself to be better suited than anyone else to discern the true meaning of scattered data, even if I could only attribute this special authority to chance circumstances.

Nevertheless, as I sat in that library on a morning in mid-December I doubted for a moment the wisdom of setting out for Mirocaw rather than returning home, where the more familiar *rite de passage* of winter depression awaited me. My original scheme was to avoid the cyclical blues the season held for me, but it seemed this was also a part of the history of Mirocaw, only on a much larger scale. My emotional instability, however, was exactly what qualified me most for the particular field work ahead, though I did not take pride or consolation in the fact. And to retreat would have been to deny myself an opportunity that might never offer itself again. In retrospect, there seems to have been no fortuitous resolution to the decision I had to make. As it happened, I went ahead to the town.

## IV

Just past noon, on December 18, I started driving toward Mirocaw. A blur of dull, earthen-coloured scenery extended in every direction. The snowfalls of late autumn had been sparse, and only a few white patches appeared in the harvested fields along the highway. The clouds were gray and abundant. Passing by a stretch of forest, I noticed the black, ragged clumps of abandoned nests clinging to the twisted mesh of bare branches. I thought I saw black birds skittering over the road ahead, but they were only dead leaves and they flew into the air as I drove by.

I approached Mirocaw from the south, entering the town from the direction I had left it on my visit the previous summer. This took me once again through that part of town which seemed to exist on the wrong side of some great invisible wall dividing the desirable sections of Mirocaw from the undesirable. As lurid as this district had appeared to me under the summer sun, in the thin light of that winter afternoon it degenerated into a pale phantom of itself. The frail stores and starved-looking houses suggested a borderline region between the material and nonmaterial worlds, with one sardonically wearing the mask of the other. I saw a few gaunt pedestrians who turned as I passed by, though seemingly not *because* I passed by, making my way up to the main street of Mirocaw.

Driving up the steep rise of Townshend Street, I found the sights there comparatively welcoming. The rolling avenues of the town were in readiness for the festival. Streetlights had their poles raveled with evergreen, the fresh boughs proudly conspicuous in a barren season. On the doors of many of the businesses on Townshend were holly wreaths, equally green but observably plastic. However, although there was nothing unusual in this traditional greenery of the season, it soon became apparent to me that Mirocaw had quite abandoned itself to this particular symbol of Yuletide. It was garishly in evidence everywhere. The windows of stores and houses were framed in green lights, green streamers hung down from storefront awnings, and the beacons of the Red Rooster Bar were peacock green floodlights. I supposed the residents of Mirocaw desired these decorations, but the effect was one of excess. An eerie emerald haze permeated the town, and faces looked slightly reptilian.

At the time I assumed that the prodigious evergreen, holly wreaths, and colored lights (if only of a single color) demonstrated an emphasis on the vegetable symbols of the Nordic Yuletide, which would inevitably be muddled into the winter festival of any northern country just as they had been adopted for the Christmas season. In his "Harlequin" article Thoss wrote of the pagan aspect of Mirocaw's festival, likening it to the ritual of a fertility cult, with probable connections to chthonic divinities at some time in the past. But Thoss had mistaken, as I had, what was only part of the festival's significance for the whole.

The hotel at which I had made reservations was located on Townshend. It was an old building of brown brick, with an arched doorway and a pathetic coping intended to convey an impression of neoclassicism. I found a parking space in front and left my suitcases in the car.

When I first entered the hotel lobby it was empty. I thought perhaps the Mirocaw festival would have attracted enough visitors to at least bolster the business of its only hotel, but it seemed I was mistaken. Tapping a little bell, I leaned on the desk and turned to look at a small, traditionally decorated Christmas tree on a table near the entranceway. It was complete with shiny, egg-fragile bulbs; miniature candy canes; flat, laughing Santas with arms wide; a star on top nodding awkwardly against the delicate shoulder of an upper branch; and colored lights that bloomed out of flower-shaped sockets. For some reason this seemed to me a sorry little piece.

"May I help you?" said a young woman arriving from a room adjacent to the lobby.

I must have been staring rather intently at her, for she looked away and seemed quite uneasy. I could hardly imagine what to say to her or how to explain what I was thinking. In person she immediately radiated a chilling brilliance of manner and expression. But if this woman had not committed suicide twenty years before, as the newspaper article had suggested, neither had she aged in that time.

"Sarah," called a masculine voice from the invisible heights of a stairway. A tall, middle-aged man came down the steps. "I thought you were in your room," said the man, whom I took to be Samuel Beadle. Sarah, not Elizabeth, Beadle glanced sideways in my direction to indicate to her father that she was conducting the business of the hotel. Beadle apologized to me, and then excused the two of them for a moment while they went off to one side to continue their exchange.

I smiled and pretended everything was normal, while trying to remain within earshot of their conversation. They spoke in tones that suggested their conflict was a familiar one: Beadle's overprotective concern with his daughter's whereabouts and Sarah's frustrated understanding of certain restrictions placed upon her. The conversation ended, and Sarah ascended the stairs, turning for a moment to give me a facial pantomime of apology for the unprofessional scene that had just taken place.

"Now, sir, what can I do for you?" Beadle asked, almost demanded.

"Yes, I have a reservation. Actually, I'm a day early, if that doesn't present a problem." I gave the hotel the benefit of the doubt that its business might have been secretly flourishing.

"No problem at all, sir," he said, presenting me with the registration form, and then a brass-colored key dangling from a plastic disc bearing the number 44.

"Luggage?"

"Yes, it's in my car."

"I'll give you a hand with that."

While Beadle was settling me in my fourth-floor room it seemed an opportune moment to broach the subject of the festival, the holiday suicides, and perhaps, depending upon his reaction, the fate of his wife. I needed a respondent who had lived in the town for a good many years and who could enlighten me about the attitude of Mirocavians toward their season of sea-green lights.

"This is just fine," I said about the clean but somber room. "Nice view. I can see the bright green lights of Mirocaw just fine from up here. Is the town usually all decked out like this? For the festival, I mean."

"Yes, sir, for the festival," he replied mechanically.

"I imagine you'll probably be getting quite a few of us out-of-towners in the next couple days."

"Could be. Is there anything else?"

"Yes, there is. I wonder if you could tell me something about the festivities."

"Such as . . ."

"Well, you know, the clowns and so forth."

"Only clowns here are the ones that're . . . well, picked out, I suppose you would say."

"I don't understand."

"Excuse me, sir. I'm very busy right now. Is there anything else?"

I could think of nothing at the moment to perpetuate our conversation. Beadle wished me a good stay and left.

I unpacked my suitcases. In addition to regular clothing I had also brought along some of the items from my clown's wardrobe. Beadle's comment that clowns were "picked out" here left me wondering exactly what purpose these street masqueraders served in the festival. The clown figure has had so many meanings in different times and cultures. The jolly, well-loved joker familiar to most people is actually but one aspect of this protean creature. Madmen, hunchbacks, amputees, and other abnormals were once considered natural clowns; they were elected to fulfil a comic role which could allow others to see them as ludicrous rather than as terrible reminders of the forces of disorder in the world. But sometimes a cheerless jester was required to draw attention to this same disorder, as in the case of King Lear's morbid and honest fool, who of course was eventually hanged, and so much for his clownish wisdom. Clowns have often had ambiguous and sometimes contradictory roles to play. Thus, I knew enough not to brashly jump into costume and cry out, "Here I am again!"

That first day in Mirocaw I did not stray far from the hotel. I read and rested for a few hours and then ate at a nearby diner. Through the window beside my table I watched the winter night turn the soft green glow of the town into a harsh and almost totally new color as it contrasted with the darkness. The streets of Mirocaw seemed to me unusually busy for a small town at evening. Yet it was not the kind of activity one normally sees before an approaching Christmas holiday. This was not a crowd of bustling shoppers loaded with bright bags of presents. Their arms were empty, their hands shoved deep in their pockets against the cold, which nevertheless had not driven them to the solitude of their presumably warm houses. I watched them enter and exit store after store without buying; many merchants remained open late, and even the places that were closed had left their neons illuminated. The faces that passed the window of the diner were possibly just stiffened by the cold, I thought; frozen into deep frowns and nothing else. In the same window I saw the reflection of my own face. It was not the face of an adept clown; it was slack and flabby and at that moment seemed the face of someone less than alive. Outside was the town of

Mirocaw, its streets dipping and rising with a lunatic severity, its citizens packing the sidewalks, its heart bathed in green: as promising a field of professional and personal challenge as I had ever encountered—and I was bored to the point of dread. I hurried back to my hotel room.

"Mirocaw has another coldness within its cold," I wrote in my journal that night. "Another set of buildings and streets that exists behind the visible town's facade like a world of disgraceful back alleys." I went on like this for about a page, across which I finally engraved a big "X." Then I went to bed.

In the morning I left my car at the hotel and walked toward the main business district a few blocks away. Mingling with the good people of Mirocaw seemed like the proper thing to do at that point in my scientific sojourn. But as I began laboriously walking up Townshend (the sidewalks were cramped with wandering pedestrians), a glimpse of someone suddenly replaced my haphazard plan with a more specific and immediate one. Through the crowd and about fifteen paces ahead was my goal.

"Dr. Thoss," I called.

His head almost seemed to turn and look back in response to my shout, but I could not be certain. I pushed past several warmly wrapped bodies and green-scarved necks. Only to find that the object of my pursuit appeared to be maintaining the same distance from me, though I did not know if this was being done deliberately or not. At the next corner, the dark-coated Thoss abruptly turned right onto a steep street which led downward directly toward the dilapidated south end of Mirocaw. When I reached the corner I looked down the sidewalk and could see him very clearly from above. I also saw how he managed to stay so far ahead of me in a mob that had impeded my own progress. For some reason the people on the sidewalk made room so that he could move past them easily, without the usual jostling of bodies. It was not a dramatic physical avoidance, though it seemed nonetheless intentional. Fighting the tight fabric of the throng, I continued to follow Thoss, losing and regaining sight of him.

By the time I reached the bottom of the sloping street the crowd had thinned out considerably, and after walking a block or so farther I found myself practically a lone pedestrian pacing behind a distant figure that I hoped was still Thoss. He was now walking quite swiftly and in a way that seemed to acknowledge my pursuit of him, though really it felt as if he were leading me as much as I was chasing him. I called his name a few more times at a volume he could not have failed to hear, assuming that deafness was not one of the changes to have come over him; he was, after all, not a young man, nor even a middle-aged one any longer.

Thoss suddenly crossed in the middle of the street. He walked a few more steps and entered a signless brick building between a liquor store and a repair shop of some kind. In the "Harlequin" article Thoss had mentioned that the people living in this section of Mirocaw maintained their own businesses, and that these were patronized almost exclusively by residents of the area. I could well believe this statement when I looked at these little sheds of commerce, for they had the same badly weathered appearance as their clientele. The formidable shoddiness of these buildings notwithstanding, I followed Thoss into the plain brick shell of what had been, or possibly still was, a diner.

Inside it was unusually dark. Even before my eyes made the adjustment I sensed that this was not a thriving restaurant cozily cluttered with chairs and tables—as was the establishment where I had eaten the night before—but a place with only a few disarranged furnishings, and very cold. It seemed colder, in fact, than the winter streets outside.

"Dr. Thoss?" I called toward a lone table near the center of the long room. Perhaps four or five were sitting around the table, with some others blending into the dimness behind them. Scattered across the top of the table were some books and loose papers. Seated there was an old man indicating something in the pages before him, but it was not Thoss. Beside him were two youths whose wholesome features distinguished them from the grim weariness of the others. I approached the table and they all looked up at me. None of them showed a glimmer of emotion except the two boys, who exchanged worried and guilt-ridden glances with each other, as if they had been discovered in some shameful act. They both suddenly burst from the table and ran into the dark background, where a light appeared briefly as they exited by a back door.

"I'm sorry," I said diffidently. "I thought I saw someone I knew come in here."

They said nothing. Out of a back room others began to emerge, no doubt interested in the source of the commotion. In a few moments the room was crowded with these tramp-like figures, all of them gazing emptily in the dimness. I was not at this point frightened of them; at least I was not afraid they would do me any physical harm. Actually, I felt as if it was quite within my power to pummel them easily into submission, their mousy faces almost inviting a succession of firm blows. But there were so many of them.

They slid slowly toward me in a worm-like mass. Their eyes seemed empty and unfocused, and I wondered a moment if they were even aware of my presence. Nevertheless, I was the center upon which their lethargic shuffling converged, their shoes scuffing softly along the bare floor. I began to deliver a number of hasty inanities as they continued to press toward me, their weak and unexpectedly odorless bodies nudging against mine. (I understood now why the people along the sidewalks seemed to instinctively avoid Thoss.) Unseen legs seemed to become entangled with my own; I staggered and then regained my balance. This sudden movement aroused me from a kind of mesmeric daze which I must have fallen into without being aware of it. I had intended to leave that dreary place long before events had reached such a juncture, but for some reason I could not focus my intentions strongly enough to cause myself to act. My mind had been drifting farther away as these slavish things approached. In a sudden surge of panic I pushed through their soft ranks and was outside.

The open air revived me to my former alertness, and I immediately started pacing swiftly up the hill. I was no longer sure that I had not simply imagined what had seemed, and at the same time did not seem, like a perilous moment. Had their movements been directed toward a harmful assault, or were they trying merely to intimidate me? As I reached the green-glazed main street of Mirocaw I really could not be sure what had just happened.

The sidewalks were still jammed with a multitude of pedestrians, but now they seemed to be moving and chattering in a more lively way. There was a kind of vitality that could only be attributed to the imminent festivities. A group of young men had begun celebrating prematurely and strode noisily across the street at midpoint, obviously intoxicated. From the laughter and joking among the still sober citizens I gathered that, mardi-gras style, public drunkenness was within the traditions of this winter festival. I looked for anything to indicate the beginnings of the Street Masquerade, but saw nothing: no brightly garbed harlequins or snow-white pierrots. Were the ceremonies even now in preparation for the coronation of the Winter Queen? "The Winter Queen," I wrote in my journal. "Figure of fertility invested with symbolic powers of revival and prosperity. Elected in the manner of a high school prom queen. Check for possible consort figure in the form of a representative from the underworld."

In the pre-darkness hours of December 19 I sat in my hotel room and wrote and thought and organized. I did not feel too badly, all things considered. The holiday excitement which was steadily rising in the streets below my window was definitely infecting me. I forced myself to take a short nap in anticipation of a long night. When I awoke, Mirocaw's annual feast had begun.

V

Shouting, commotion, carousing. Sleepily I went to the window and looked out over the town. It seemed all the lights of Mirocaw were shining, save in that section down the hill which became part of the black void of winter. And now the town's greenish tinge was even more pronounced, spreading everywhere like a great green rainbow that had melted from the sky and endured, phosphorescent, into the night. In the streets was the brightness of an artificial spring. The byways of Mirocaw vibrated with activity: on a nearby corner a brass band blared; marauding cars blew their horns and were sometimes mounted by laughing pedestrians; a man emerged from the Red Rooster Bar, threw up his arms, and crowed. I looked closely at the individual celebrants, searching for the vestments of clowns. Soon, delightedly, I saw them. The costume was red and white, with matching cap, and the face painted a noble alabaster. It almost seemed to be a clownish incarnation of that white-bearded and black-booted Christmas fool.

This particular fool, however, was not receiving the affection and respect usually accorded to a Santa Claus. My poor fellow-clown was in the middle of a circle of revelers who were pushing him back and forth from one to the other. The object of this abuse seemed to accept it somewhat willingly, but this little game nevertheless appeared to have humiliation as its purpose. "Only clowns here are the one's that're picked out," echoed Beadle's voice in my memory. "Picked *on*" seemed closer to the truth.

Packing myself in some heavy clothes, I went out into the green gleaming streets. Not far from the hotel I was stumbled into by a character with a wide blue and red grin and bright baggy clothes. Actually he had been shoved into me by some youths outside a drugstore.

"See the freak," said an obese and drunken fellow. "See the freak fall."

My first response was anger, and then fear as I saw two others flanking the fat drunk. They walked toward me and I tensed myself for a confrontation.

"This is a disgrace," one said, the neck of a wine bottle held loosely in his left hand.

But it was not to me they were speaking; it was to the clown, who had been pushed to the sidewalk. His three persecutors helped him up with a sudden jerk and then splashed wine in his face. They ignored me altogether.

"Let him loose," the fat one said. "Crawl away, freak. Oh, he flies!"

The clown trotted off, becoming lost in the throng.

"Wait a minute," I said to the rowdy trio, who had started lumbering away. I quickly decided that it would probably be futile to ask them to explain what I had just witnessed, especially amid the noise and confusion of the festivities. In my best jovial fashion I proposed we all go someplace where I could buy them each a drink. They had no objection and in a short while we were all squeezed around a table in the Red Rooster.

Over several drinks I explained to them that I was from out of town, which pleased them no end for some reason. I told them there were some things I did not understand about their festival.

"I don't think there's anything *to* understand," the fat one said. "It's just what you see."

I asked him about the people dressed as clowns.

"Them? They're the freaks. It's their turn this year. Everyone takes their turn. Next year it might be mine. Or *yours*," he said, pointing at one of his friends across the table. "And when we find out which one you are—"

"You're not smart enough," said the defiant potential freak.

This was an important point: the fact that individuals who play the clowns remain, or at least attempted to remain, anonymous. This arrangement would help remove inhibitions a resident of Mirocaw might have about abusing his own neighbor or even a family relation. From what I later observed, the extent of this abuse did not go beyond a kind of playful roughhousing. And even so, it was only the occasional group of rowdies who actually took advantage of this aspect of the festival, the majority of the citizens very much content to stay on the sidelines.

As far as being able to illuminate the meaning of this custom, my three young friends were quite useless. To them it was amusement, as I imagine it was to the majority of Mirocavians. This was understandable. I suppose the average person would not be able to explain exactly how the profoundly familiar Christmas holiday came to be celebrated in its present form.

I left the bar alone and not unaffected by the drinks I had consumed there. Outside, the general merrymaking continued. Loud music emanated from several quarters. Mirocaw had fully transformed itself from a sedate small town to an enclave of Saturnalia within the dark immensity of a winter night. But Saturn is also the planetary symbol of melancholy and sterility, a clash of opposites contained within that single word. And as I wandered half-drunkenly down the street, I discovered that there was a conflict within the winter festival itself. This discovery indeed appeared to be that secret key which Thoss withheld in his study of the town. Oddly enough, it was through my unfamiliarity with the outward nature of the festival that I came to know its true nature.

I was mingling with the crowd on the street, warmly enjoying the confusion around me, when I saw a strangely designed creature lingering on the corner up ahead. It was one of the Mirocaw clowns. Its clothes were shabby and nondescript, almost in the style of a tramp-type clown, but not humorously exaggerated enough. The face, though, made up for the lackluster costume. I had never seen such a strange conception for a clown's countenance. The figure stood beneath a dim streetlight, and when it turned its head my way I realized why it seemed familiar. The thin, smooth, and pale head; the wide eyes; the oval-shaped features resembling nothing so much as the skull-faced, screaming creature in that famous painting (memory fails me). This clownish imitation rivalled the original in suggesting stricken realms of abject horror and despair: an inhuman likeness more proper to something under the earth than upon it.

From the first moment I saw this creature, I thought of those inhabitants of the ghetto down the hill. There was the same nauseating passivity and languor in its bearing. Perhaps if I had not been drinking earlier I would not have been bold enough to take the action I did. I decided to join in one of the upstanding traditions of the winter festival, for it annoyed me to see this morbid impostor of a clown standing up. When I reached the corner I laughingly pushed myself into the creature—"Whoops!"—who stumbled backward and ended up on the sidewalk. I laughed again and looked around for approval from the festivalers in the vicinity. No one, however, seemed to appreciate or even acknowledge what I had done. They did not laugh with me or point with amusement, but only passed by, perhaps walking a little faster until they were some distance from this streetcorner incident. I realized instantly I had violated some tacit rule of behaviour, though I had thought my action well within the common practice. The thought occurred to me that I might even be apprehended and prosecuted for what in any other circumstances was certainly a criminal act. I turned around to help the clown back to his feet, hoping to somehow redeem my offense, but the creature was gone. Solemnly I walked away from the scene of my inadvertent crime and sought other streets away from its witnesses.

Along the various back avenues of Mirocaw I wandered, pausing exhaustedly at one point to sit at the counter of a small sandwich shop that was packed with customers. I ordered a cup of coffee to revive my overly alcoholed system. Warming my hands around the cup and sipping slowly from it, I watched the people outside as they passed the front window. It was well after midnight but the thick flow of passersby gave no indication that anyone was going home early. A carnival of profiles filed past the window and I was content simply to sit back and observe, until finally one of these faces made me start. It was that frightful little clown I had roughed up earlier. But although its face was familiar in its ghastly aspect, there was something different about it. And I wondered that there should be two such hideous freaks.

Quickly paying the man at the counter, I dashed out to get a second glimpse of the clown, who was now nowhere in sight. The dense crowd kept me from pursuing this figure with any speed, and I wondered how the clown could have made its way so easily ahead of me. Unless the crowd had instinctively allowed this creature to pass unhindered through its massive ranks, as it did for Thoss. In the process of searching for this particular freak, I discovered that interspersed among the celebrating populace of Mirocaw, which included the sanctioned festival clowns, there was not one or two, but a considerable number of these pale, wraith-like creatures. And they all drifted along the streets unmolested by even the rowdiest of revelers. I now understood one of the taboos of the festival. These other clowns were not to

be disturbed and should even be avoided, much as were the residents of
the slum at the edge of town. Nevertheless, I felt instinctively that the
two groups of clowns were somehow identified with each other, even
if the ghetto clowns were not welcome at Mirocaw's winter festival.
Indeed, they were not simply part of the community and celebrating
the season in their own way. To all appearances, this group of melancholy mummers constituted nothing less than an entirely independent
festival—a festival within a festival.

Returning to my room, I entered my suppositions into the
journal I was keeping for this venture. The following are excerpts:

> There is a superstitiousness displayed by the residents of Mirocaw
> with regard to these people from the slum section, particularly as
> they lately appear in those dreadful faces signifying their own fes-
> tival. What is the relationship between these simultaneous celebra-
> tions? Did one precede the other? If so, which? My opinion at this
> point—and I claim no conclusiveness for it—is that Mirocaw's
> winter festival is the later manifestation, that it appeared after the fes-
> tival of those depressingly pallid clowns, in order to cover it up or
> mitigate its effect. The holiday suicides come to mind, and the sub-
> climate Thoss wrote about, the disappearance of Elizabeth Beadle
> twenty years ago, and my own experience with this pariah clan
> existing outside yet within the community. Of my own experience
> with this emotionally deleterious subseason I would rather not speak
> at this time. Still not able to say whether or not my usual winter
> melancholy is the cause. On the general subject of mental health,
> I must consider Thoss's book about his stay in a psychiatric hospi-
> tal (in western Mass., almost sure of that. Check on this book &
> Mirocaw's New England roots). The winter solstice is tomorrow,
> albeit sometime past midnight (how blurry these days and nights are
> becoming!). It is, of course, the day of the year in which night hours
> surpass daylight hours by the greatest margin. Note what this has to
> do with the suicides and a rise in psychic disorder. Recalling Thoss's
> list of documented suicides in his article, there seemed to be a recur-
> rence of specific family names, as there very likely might be for any
> kind of data collected in a small town. Among these names was a
> Beadle or two. Perhaps, then, there is a genealogical basis for the sui-
> cides which has nothing to do with Thoss's mystical subclimate,
> which is a colorful idea to be sure and one that seems fitting for this
> town of various outward and inward aspects, but is not a conception
> that can be substantiated.

One thing that seems certain, however, is the division of Mirocaw into two very distinct types of citizenry, resulting in two festivals and the appearance of similar clowns—a term now used in an extremely loose sense. But there is a connection, and I believe I have some idea of what it is. I said before that the normal residents of the town regard those from the ghetto, and especially their clown figures, with superstition. Yet it's more than that: there is fear, perhaps a kind of hatred—the particular kind of hatred resulting from some powerful and irrational memory. What threatens Mirocaw I think I can very well understand. I recall the incident earlier today in that vacant diner. "Vacant" is the appropriate word here, despite its contradiction of fact. The congregation of that half-lit room formed less a presence than an absence, even considering the oppressive number of them. Those eyes that did not or could not focus on anything, the pining lassitude of their faces, the lazy march of their feet. I was spiritually drained when I ran out of there. I then understood why these people and their activities are avoided.

I cannot question the wisdom of these ancestral Mirocavians who began the tradition of the winter festival and gave the town a pretext for celebration and social intercourse at a time when the consequences of brooding isolation are most severe, those longest and darkest days of the solstice. A mood of Christmas joviality obviously would not be sufficient to counter the menace of this season. But even so, there are still the suicides of individuals who are somehow cut off, I imagine, from the vitalizing activities of the festival.

It is the nature of this insidious subseason that seems to determine the outward forms of Mirocaw's winter festival: the optimistic greenery in a period of gray dormancy; the fertile promise of the Winter Queen; and, most interesting to my mind, the clowns. The bright clowns of Mirocaw who are treated so badly; they appear to serve as substitute figures for those dark-eyed mummers of the slums. Since the latter are feared for some power or influence they possess, they may still be symbolically confronted and conquered through their counterparts, who are elected for precisely this function. If I am right about this, I wonder to what extent there is a conscious awareness among the town's populace of this indirect show of aggression. Those three young men I spoke with tonight did not seem to possess much insight beyond seeing that there was a certain amount of robust fun in the festival's tradition. For that matter, how much awareness is there on the *other side* of these two antagonistic festivals? Too horrible to think of such a thing, but I must wonder if, for all their apparent aimlessness, those inhabitants of the ghetto are not the only ones who know what they are about. No denying that behind those inhumanly limp expressions there seems to lie a kind of obnoxious intelligence.

Now I realize the confusion of my present state, but as I wobbled from street to street tonight, watching those oval-mouthed clowns, I could not help feeling that all the merrymaking in Mirocaw was somehow allowed only by their sufferance. This I hope is no more than a fanciful Thossian intuition, the sort of idea that is curious and thought-provoking without ever seeming to gain the benefit of proof. I know my mind is not entirely lucid, but I feel that it may be possible to penetrate Mirocaw's many complexities and illuminate the hidden side of the festival season. In particular I must look for the significance of the other festival. Is it also some kind of fertility celebration? From what I have seen, the tenor of this "celebrating" sub-group is one of *anti*-fertility, if anything. How have they managed to keep from dying out completely over the years? How do they maintain their numbers?

But I was too tired to formulate any more of my sodden speculations. Falling onto my bed, I soon became lost in dreams of streets and faces.

## VI

I was, of course, slightly hung over when I woke up late the next morning. The festival was still going strong, and loud blaring music outside roused me from a nightmare. It was a parade. A number of floats proceeded down Townshend, a familiar color predominating. There were theme floats of pilgrims and Indians, cowboys and Indians, and clowns of an orthodox type. In the middle of it all was the Winter Queen herself, freezing atop an icy throne. She waved in all directions. I even imagined she waved up at my dark window.

In the first few groggy moments of wakefulness I had no sympathy with my excitation of the previous night. But I discovered that my former enthusiasm had merely lain dormant, and soon returned with an even greater intensity. Never before had my mind and senses been so active during this usually inert time of year. At home I would have been playing lugubrious old records and looking out the window quite a bit. I was terribly grateful in a completely abstract way for my commitment to a meaningful mania. And I was eager to get to work after I had had some breakfast at the coffee shop.

When I got back to my room I discovered the door was unlocked. And there was something written on the dresser mirror. The

writing was red and greasy, as if done with a clown's make-up pencil—
my own, I realized. I read the legend, or rather I should say *riddle*, several
times: "What buries itself before it is dead?" I looked at it for quite a
while, very shaken at how vulnerable my holiday fortifications were.
Was this supposed to be a warning of some kind? A threat to the effect
that if I persisted in a certain course I would end up prematurely interred?
I would have to be careful, I told myself. My resolution was to let
nothing deter me from the inspired strategy I had conceived for myself. I
wiped the mirror clean, for it was now needed for other purposes.

　　I spent the rest of the day devising a very special costume and the
appropriate face to go with it. I easily shabbied up my overcoat with a
torn pocket or two and a complete set of stains. Combined with blue
jeans and a pair of rather scuffed-up shoes, I had a passable costume for
a derelict. The face, however, was more difficult, for I had to experiment from memory. Remembering the screaming pierrot in that
painting ( *The Scream*, I now recall), helped me quite a bit. At nightfall I
exited the hotel by the back stairway.

　　It was strange to walk down the crowded street in this gruesome
disguise. Though I thought I would feel conspicuous, the actual experience was very close, I imagined, to one of complete invisibility. No one
looked at me as I strolled by, or as they strolled by, or as we strolled
by each other. I was a phantom—perhaps the ghost of festivals past, or
those yet to come.

　　I had no clear idea where my disguise would take me that
night, only vague expectations of gaining the confidence of my
fellow specters and possibly in some way coming to know their
secrets. For a while I would simply wander around in that lacka-
daisical manner I had learned from them, following their lead in any
way they might indicate. And for the most part, this meant doing
almost nothing and doing it silently. If I passed one of my kind on
the sidewalk there was no speaking, no exchange of knowing looks,
no recognition at all that I was aware of. We were there on the
streets of Mirocaw to create a presence and nothing more. At least,
this is how I came to feel about it. As I drifted along with my bodiless invisibility, I felt myself more and more becoming an empty,
floating shape, seeing without being seen and walking without the
interference of those grosser creatures who shared my world. It
was not an experience completely without interest or even pleasure.
The clown's shibboleth of "here we are again" took on a new
meaning for me as I felt myself a novitiate of a more rarified order of

harlequinry. And very soon the opportunity to make further progress along this path presented itself.

On the other side of the street, going the opposite direction, a pickup truck slowly passed, gently parting a sea of zigging and zagging celebrants. The cargo in the back of this truck was curious, for it was made up entirely of my fellow sectarians. Further down the street the truck stopped and another of them boarded it over the back gate. One block down I saw still another get on. Two blocks down, the truck made a U-turn at an intersection and headed in my direction.

I stood at the curb as I had seen the others do. I was not sure the truck would pick me up, thinking that somehow they knew I was an imposter. The truck did, however, slow down, almost coming to a stop when it reached me. The others were crowded on the floor of the truck bed. Most of them were just staring into nothingness with the usual indifference I had come to expect from their kind. But a few actually glanced at me with some anticipation. For a second I hesitated, not sure I wanted to pursue this ruse any further. At the last moment, some impulse sent me climbing up the back of the truck and squeezing myself in among the others.

There were only a few more to pick up before the truck headed for the outskirts of Mirocaw and beyond. At first I tried to maintain a clear orientation with respect to the town. But as we took turn after turn through the darkness of narrow country roads, I found myself unable to preserve any sense of direction. The majority of the others in the back of the truck exhibited no apparent awareness of their fellow passengers. Guardedly, I looked from face to ghostly face. A few of them spoke in short whispered phrases to others close by. I could not make out what they were saying but the tone of their voices was one of innocent normalcy, as if they were not of the hardened slum-herd of Mirocaw. Perhaps, I thought, these were thrill-seekers who had disguised themselves as I had done, or, more likely, initiates of some kind. Possibly they had received prior instructions at such meetings as I had stumbled onto the day before. It was also likely that among this crew were those very boys I had frightened into a precipitate exit from that old diner.

The truck was now speeding along a fairly open stretch of country, heading toward those higher hills that surrounded the now distant town of Mirocaw. The icy wind whipped around us, and I could not keep myself from trembling with cold. This definitely betrayed me as one of the newcomers among the group, for the two bodies that pressed against mine were rigidly still and even seemed to be radiating a frigidity of their own. I glanced ahead at the darkness into which we were rapidly progressing.

We had left all open country behind us now, and the road was enclosed by thick woods. The mass of bodies in the truck leaned into each other as we began traveling up a steep incline. Above us, at the top of the hill, were lights shining somewhere within the woods. When the road levelled off the truck made an abrupt turn, steering into what I thought was the roadside blackness or a great ditch. There was an unpaved path, however, upon which the truck proceeded toward the glowing in the near distance.

This glowing became brighter and sharper as we approached, flickering upon the trees and revealing stark detail where there had formerly been only smooth darkness. As the truck pulled into a clearing and came to a stop, I saw a loose assembly of figures, many of which held lanterns that beamed with a dazzling and frosty light. I stood up in the back of the truck to unboard as the others were doing. Glancing around from that height I saw approximately thirty more of those cadaverous clowns milling about. One of my fellow passengers spied me lingering in the truck and in a strangely high-pitched whisper told me to hurry, explaining something about the "apex of darkness." I thought again about this solstice night; it was technically the longest period of darkness of the year, even if not by a very significant margin from many other winter nights. Its true significance, though, was related to considerations having little to do with either statistics or the calendar.

I went over to the place where the others were forming into a tighter crowd, and in which there was a sense of expectancy in the subtle gestures and expressions of its individual members. Glances were now exchanged, the hand of one lightly touched the shoulder of another, and a pair of circled eyes gazed over to where two figures were setting their lanterns on the ground about six feet apart. The illumination of these lanterns revealed an opening in the earth. Eventually the awareness of everyone was focused on this roundish pit, and as if by prearranged signal we all began huddling around it. The only sounds were those of the wind and our own movements as we crushed frozen leaves and sticks underfoot.

Finally, when we had all surrounded this gaping hole, the first one jumped in, leaving our sight for a moment but then reappearing to take hold of a lantern which another one handed him from above. The miniature abyss filled with light, and I could see it was no more than six feet deep. Near the base of its inner wall the mouth of a tunnel was carved out. The figure holding the lantern stooped a little and disappeared into the passage.

One by one, then, the members of the crowd leaped into the darkness of this pit, and every fifth one took a lantern. I kept to the back of the group, for whatever subterranean activities were going to take place, I was sure I wanted to be on their periphery. When only about ten of us remained on the ground above, I maneuvered to let four of them precede me so that as the fifth I might receive a lantern. This was exactly how it worked out, for after I had leaped to the bottom of the hole a light was ritually handed down to me. Turning about face, I quickly entered the passageway. At that point I shook so with cold that I was neither curious nor afraid, but only grateful for the shelter.

I entered a long, gently sloping tunnel, just high enough for me to stand upright. It was considerably warmer down there than outside in the cold darkness of the woods. After a few moments I had sufficiently thawed out so that my concerns shifted from those of physical comfort to a sudden and justified preoccupation with my survival. As I walked I held my lantern close to the sides of the tunnel. They were relatively smooth and even, as if the passage had not been made by manual digging but had been burrowed by something which left behind a clue to its dimensions in the tunnel's size and shape. This delirious idea came to me when I recalled the message that had been left on my bedroom mirror: "What buries itself before it is dead?"

I had to hurry along to keep up with those uncanny spelunkers who preceded me. The lanterns ahead bobbed with every step of their bearers, the lumbering procession seeming less and less real the farther we marched into that snug little tunnel. At some point I noticed the line ahead of me growing shorter. The processions were emptying out into a cavernous chamber where I, too, soon arrived. This area was about thirty feet in height, its other dimensions approximating those of a large ballroom. Gazing into the distance above made me uncomfortably aware of how far we had descended into the earth. Unlike the smooth sides of the tunnel, the walls of this cavern looked jagged and irregular, as though they had been gnawed at. The earth had been removed, I assumed, either through the tunnel from which we had emerged, or else by way of one of the many other black openings that I saw around the edges of the chamber, for possibly they too led back to the surface.

But the structure of this chamber occupied my mind a great deal less than did its occupants. There to meet us on the floor of the great cavern was what must have been the entire slum population of Mirocaw, and more, all with the same eerily wide-eyed and oval-mouthed faces. They formed a circle around an altar-like object which had some kind of dark, leathery covering draped over it. Upon the altar, another covering of the same material concealed a lumpy form beneath.

And behind this form, looking down upon the altar, was the only figure whose face was not greased with makeup.

He wore a long snowy robe that was the same color as the wispy hair berimming his head. His arms were calmly at his sides. He made no movement. The man I once believed would penetrate great secrets stood before us with the same professorial bearing that had impressed me so many years ago, yet now I felt nothing but dread at the thought of what revelations lay pocketed within the abysmal folds of his magisterial attire. Had I really come here to challenge such a formidable figure? The name by which I knew him seemed itself insufficient to designate one of his stature. Rather I should name him by his other incarnations: god of all wisdom, scribe of all sacred books, father of all magicians, thrice great and more—rather I should call him *Thoth.*

He raised his cupped hands to his congregation and the ceremony was underway.

It was all very simple. The entire assembly, which had remained speechless until this moment, broke out in the most horrendous high-pitched singing that can be imagined. It was a choir of sorrow, of shrieking, delirium, and of shame. The cavern rang shrilly with the dissonant, whining chorus. My voice, too, was added to the congregation's, trying to blend with their maimed music. But my singing could not imitate theirs, having a huskiness unlike their cacaphonous keening wail. To keep from exposing myself as an intruder I continued to mouth their words without sound. These words were a revelation of the moody malignancy which until then I had no more than sensed whenever in the presence of these figures. They were singing to the "unborn in paradise," to the "pure unlived lives." They sang a dirge for existence, for all its vital forms and seasons. Their ideals were those of darkness, chaos, and a melancholy half-existence consecrated to all the many shapes of death. A sea of thin, bloodless faces trembled and screamed with perverted hopes. And the robed, guiding figure at the heart of all this—elevated over the course of twenty years to the status of high priest—was the man from whom I had taken so many of my own life's principles. It would be useless to describe what I felt at that moment and a waste of the time I need to describe the events which followed.

The singing abruptly stopped and the towering white-haired figure began to speak. He was welcoming those of the new generation— twenty winters had passed since the "Pure Ones" had expanded their ranks. The word "pure" in this setting was a violence to what sense and composure I still retained, for nothing could have been more foul than what was to come. Thoss—and I employ this defunct identity only as a convenience—closed his sermon and moved back toward the dark-skinned altar. There, with all the flourish of his former life, he drew back the topmost covering. Beneath it was a limp-limbed effigy, a collapsed puppet sprawled upon the slab. I was standing toward the rear of the congregation and attempted to keep as close to the exit passage as I could. Thus, I did not see everything as clearly as I might have.

Thoss looked down over the crooked, doll-like form and then out at the gathering. I even imagined that he made knowing eye-contact with myself. He spread his arms and a stream of continuous and unintelligible words flowed from his moaning mouth. The congregation began to stir, not greatly but perceptibly. Until that moment there was a limit to what I believed was the evil of these people. They were, after all, only that. They were merely morbid, self-tortured souls with strange beliefs. If there was anything I had learned in all my years as an anthropologist it was that the world is infinitely rich in strange ideas, even to the point where the concept of strangeness itself had little meaning for me. But with the scene I then witnessed, my conscience bounded into a realm from which it will never return.

For now was the transformation scene, the culmination of every harlequinade.

It began slowly. There was increasing movement among those on the far side of the chamber from where I stood. Someone had fallen to the floor and the others in the area backed away. The voice at the altar continued its chanting. I tried to gain a better view but there were too many of them around me. Through the mass of obstructing bodies I caught only glimpses of what was taking place.

The one who had swooned to the floor of the chamber seemed to be losing all former shape and proportion. I thought it was a clown's trick. They were clowns, were they not? I myself could make four white balls transform into four black balls as I juggled them. And this was not my most astonishing feat of clownish magic. And is there not always a sleight-of-hand inherent in all ceremonies, often dependent on the transported delusions of the celebrants? This was a good show, I thought, and giggled to myself. The transformation scene of Harlequin throwing off his fool's facade. O God, Harlequin, do not move like that! Harlequin, where are your arms? And your legs have melted together and have begun squirming upon the floor. What horrible, mouthing umbilicus is that where your face should be? *What is it that buries itself before it is dead?* The almighty serpent of wisdom—the Conqueror Worm.

It now started happening all around the chamber. Individual members of the congregation would gaze emptily—caught for a moment in a frozen trance—and then collapse to the floor to begin the sickening metamorphosis. This happened with ever-increasing frequency the louder and more frantic Thoss chanted his insane prayer or curse. Then there began a writhing movement toward the altar, and Thoss welcomed the things as they curled their way to the altar-top. I knew now what lax figure lay upon it.

This was Kora and Persephone, the daughter of Ceres and the Winter Queen: the child abducted into the underworld of death. Except this child had no supernatural mother to save her, no living mother at all. For the sacrifice I witnessed was an echo of one that had occurred twenty years before, the carnival feast of the preceding generation—O *carne vale!* Now both mother and daughter had become victims of this subterranean sabbath. I finally realized this truth when the figure stirred upon the altar, lifted its head of icy beauty, and screamed at the sight of mute mouths closing around her.

I ran from the chamber into the tunnel. (There was nothing else that could be done, I have obsessively told myself.) Some of the others who had not yet changed began to pursue me. They would have caught up to me, I have no doubt, for I fell only a few yards into the passage. And for a moment I imagined that I too was about to undergo a transformation, but I had not been prepared as the others had been. When I heard the approaching footsteps of my pursuers I was sure there was an even worse fate facing me upon the altar. But the footsteps ceased and retreated. They had received an order in the voice of their high priest. I too heard the order, though I wish I had not, for until then I had imagined that Thoss did not remember who I was. It was that voice which taught me otherwise.

For the moment I was free to leave. I struggled to my feet and, having broken my lantern in the fall, retraced my way back through cloacal blackness.

Everything seemed to happen very quickly once I emerged from the tunnel and climbed up from the pit. I wiped the reeking grease-paint from my face as I ran through the woods and back to the road. A passing car stopped, though I gave it no other choice except to run me down.

"Thank you for stopping."

"What the hell are you doing out here?" the driver asked.

I caught my breath. "It was a joke. The festival. Friends thought it would be funny . . . Please drive on."

My ride let me off about a mile out of town, and from there I could find my way. It was the same way I had come into Miro-caw on my first visit the summer before. I stood for a while at the summit of that high hill just outside the city limits, looking down upon the busy little hamlet. The intensity of the festival had not abated, and would not until morning. I walked down toward the welcoming glow of green, slipped through the festivities unnoticed, and returned to the hotel. No one saw me go up to my room. Indeed, there was an atmosphere of absence and abandonment through that building, and the desk in the lobby was unattended.

I locked the door to my room and collapsed upon the bed.

## VII

When I awoke the next morning I saw from my window that the town and surrounding countryside had been visited during the night by a snowstorm, one which was entirely unpredicted. The snow was still falling and blowing and gathering on the now deserted streets of Mirocaw. The festival was over. Everyone had gone home.

And this was exactly my own intention. Any action on my part concerning what I had seen the night before would have to wait until I was away from the town. I am still not sure it will do the slightest good to speak up like this. Any accusations I could make against the slum populous of Mirocaw would be resisted, as well they should be, as unbelievable. Perhaps in a very short while none of this will be my concern.

With packed suitcases in both hands I walked up to the front desk to check out. The man behind the desk was not Beadle and he had to fumble around to find my bill.

"Here we are. Everything all right?"

"Fine," I answered. "Is Mr. Beadle around?"

"No, I'm afraid he's not back yet. Been out all night looking for his daughter. She's a very popular girl, being the Winter Queen and all that nonsense. Probably find she was at a party somewhere."

A little noise came out of my throat.

I threw my suitcases in the back seat of my car and got behind the wheel. On that morning nothing I could recall seemed real to me. The snow was falling and I watched it through my windshield, slow and silent and entrancing. I started up my car, routinely glancing in my rear view mirror. What I saw there is now vividly framed in my mind, as it was framed in the back window of my car when I turned to verify its reality.

In the middle of the street behind me, standing ankle-deep in snow, was Thoss and another figure. When I looked closely at the other I recognized him as one of the boys whom I surprised in that diner. But he had now taken on a corrupt and listless resemblance to his new family. Both he and Thoss stared at me, making no attempt to forestall my departure. Thoss knew that this was unnecessary.

I had to carry the image of those two dark figures in my mind as I drove back home. But only now has the full weight of my experience descended upon me. So far I have claimed illness in order to avoid my teaching schedule. To face the normal flow of life as I had formerly known it would be impossible. I am now very much under the influence of a season and a climate far colder and more barren than all the winters in human memory. And mentally retracing past events does not seem to have helped; I can feel myself sinking deeper into a velvety white abyss.

At certain times I could almost dissolve entirely into this inner realm of awful purity and emptiness. I remember those invisible moments when in disguise I drifted through the streets of Mirocaw, untouched by the drunken, noisy forms around me: untouchable. But instantly I recoil at this grotesque nostalgia, for I realize what is happening and what I do not want to be true, though Thoss proclaimed it was. I recall his command to those others as I lay helplessly prone in the tunnel. They could have apprehended me, but Thoss, my old master called them back. His voice echoed throughout that cavern, and it now reverberates within my own psychic chambers of memory.

"He is one of us," it said. "He has *always* been one of us."

It is this voice which now fills my dreams and my days and my long winter nights. I have seen you, Dr. Thoss, through the snow outside my window. Soon I will celebrate, alone, that last feast which will kill your words, only to prove how well I have learned their truth.

# BREECE D'J PANCAKE
## Time and Again

Mr. Weeks called me out again tonight, and I look back down the hall of my house. I left the kitchen light burning. This is an empty old house since the old lady died. When Mr. Weeks doesn't call, I write everybody I know about my boy. Some of my letters always come back, and the folks who write back say nobody knows where he got off to. I can't help but think he might come home at night when I am gone, so I let the kitchen light burn and go on out the door.

The cold air is the same, and the snow pellets my cap, sifts under my collar. I hear my hogs come grunting from their shed, thinking I have come to feed them. I ought to feed them better than that awful slop, but I can't until I know my boy is safe. I told him not to go and look, that the hogs just squeal because I never kill them. They always squeal when they are happy, but he went and looked. Then he ran off someplace.

I brush the snow from my road plow's windshield and climb in. The vinyl seats are cold, but I like them. They are smooth and easy cleaned. The lug wrench is where it has always been beside my seat. I heft it, put it back. I start the salt spreader, lower my shear, and head out to clean the mountain road.

The snow piles in a wall against the berm. No cars move. They are stranded at the side, and as I plow past them, a line falls in behind me, but they always drop back. They don't know how long it takes the salt to work. They are common fools. They rush around in such weather and end up dead. They never sit still and wait for the salt to work.

I think I am getting too old to do this anymore. I wish I could rest and watch my hogs get old and die. When the last one is close to dying, I will feed him his best meal and leave the gate open. But that will most likely not happen, because I know this stretch of Route 60 from Ansted to Gauley, and I do a good job. Mr. Weeks always brags on what a good job I do, and when I meet the other truck plowing the uphill side of this road, I will honk. That will be Mr. Weeks coming up from Gauley. I think how I never met Mr. Weeks in my life but in a snowplow. Sometimes I look out to Sewel Mountain and see snow coming, then I call Mr. Weeks. But we are not friends. We don't come around each other at all. I don't even know if he's got family.

I pass the rest stop at Hawks Nest, and a new batch of fools line up behind me, but pretty soon I am alone again. As I plow down the grade toward Chimney Corners, my lights are the only ones on the road, and the snow takes up the yellow spinning of my dome light and the white curves of my headlights. I smile at the pretties they make, but I am tired and wish I was home. I worry about the hogs. I should have given them more slop, but when the first one dies, the others will eat him quick enough.

I make the big turn at Chimney Corners and see a hitchhiker standing there. His front is clean, and he looks half frozen, so I stop to let him in.

He says, "Hey, thank you, Mister."

"How far you going?"

"Charleston."

"You got family there?" I say.

"Yessir."

"I only go to Gauley Bridge, then I turn around."

"That's fine," he says. He is a polite boy.

The fools pack up behind me, and my low gears whine away from them. Let them fall off the mountain for all I care.

"This is not good weather to be on the road," I say.

"Sure ain't, but a fellow's got to get home."

"Why didn't you take a bus?"

"Aw, buses stink," he says. My boy always talked like that.

"Where you been?"

"Roanoke. Worked all year for a man. He give me Christmastime and a piece of change."

"He sounds like a good man."

"You bet. He's got this farm outside of town—horses—you ain't seen such horses. He's gonna let me work the horses next year."

"I have a farm, but I only have some hogs left."

"Hogs is good business," he says.

I look at him. "You ever see a hog die?" I look back at the road snow.

"Sure."

"Hogs die hard. I seen people die in the war easier than a hog at a butchering."

"Never noticed. We shot and stuck them pretty quick. They do right smart jerking around, but they're dead by then."

"Maybe."

"What can you do with a hog if you don't butcher him? Sell him?"

"My hogs are old hogs. Not good for anything. I just been letting them die. I make my money on this piece of road every winter. Don't need much."

He says, "Ain't got any kids?"

"My boy run off when my wife died. But that was considerable time ago."

He is quiet a long time. Where the road is patched, I work my shear up, and go slower to let more salt hit behind. In my mirror, I see the lights of cars sneaking up behind me.

Then of a sudden the hitchhiker says, "What's your boy do now?"

"He was learning a mason's trade when he run off."

"Makes good money."

"I don't know. He was only a hod carrier then."

He whistles. "I done that two weeks this summer. I never been so sore."

"It's hard work," I say. I think, this boy has good muscles if he can carry hod.

I see the lights of Mr. Weeks's snowplow coming toward us. I gear into first. I am not in a hurry. "Scrunch down," I say. "I'd get in trouble for picking you up."

The boy hunkers in the seat, and the lights from Mr. Weeks's snowplow shine into my cab. I wave into the lights, not seeing Mr. Weeks, and we honk when we pass. Now I move closer to center. I want to do a good job and get all the snow, but when the line of cars behind Mr. Weeks comes toward me, I get fidgety. I don't want to cause any accidents. The boy sits up and starts talking again, and it makes me jittery.

"I was kinda scared about coming through Fayette County," he says.

"Uh-huh," I say. I try not to brush any cars.

"Damn, but a lot of hitchhikers gets killed up here."

A man lays on his horn as he goes past, but I have to get what Mr. Weeks left, and I am always too close to center.

The boy says, "That soldier's bones—Jesus, but that was creepy."

The last car edges by, but my back and shoulders are shaking and I sweat.

"That soldier," he says. "You know about that?"

"I don't know."

"They found his duffel bag at the bottom of Lovers' Leap. All his grip was in there, and his bones, too."

"I remember. That was too bad." The snow makes such nice pictures in my headlights, and it rests me to watch them.

"There was a big retard got killed up here, too. He was the only one they ever found with all his meat on. Rest of them, they just find their bones."

"They haven't found any in years," I say. This snow makes me think of France. It was snowing like this when they dropped us over France. I yawn.

"I don't know," he says. "Maybe the guy who done them all in is dead."

"I figure so," I say.

The hill bottoms out slowly, and we drive on to Gauley, clearing the stretch beside New River. The boy is smoking and taking in the snow.

"It snowed like this in France the winter of 'forty-four," I say. "I was in the paratroops, and they dropped us where the Germans were thick. My platoon took a farmhouse without a shot."

"Damn," he says. "Did you knife them?"

"Snapped their necks," I say, and I see my man tumble into the sty. People die so easy.

We come to Gauley, where the road has already been cleared by the other trucks. I pull off, and the line of cars catches up, sloshing by. I grip the wrench.

"Look under the seat for my flashlight, boy."

He bends forward, grabbing under the seat, and his head is turned from me. But I am way too tired now, and I don't want to clean the seat. "She ain't there, Mister."

"Well," I say. I look at the lights of the cars. They are fools.

"Thanks again," he says. He hops to the ground, and I watch him walking backward, thumbing. I am almost too tired to drive home. I sit and watch this boy walking backward until a car stops for him. I think, he is a polite boy, and lucky to get rides at night.

All the way up the mountain, I count the men in France, and I have to stop and count again. I never get any farther than that night it snowed. Mr. Weeks passes me and honks, but I don't honk. Time and again, I try to count and can't.

I pull up beside my house. My hogs run from their shelter in the backyard and grunt at me. I stand by my plow and look at the first rims of light around Sewel Mountain through the snowy limbs of the trees. Cars hiss by on the clean road. The kitchen light still burns, and I know the house is empty. My hogs stare at me, snort beside their trough. They are waiting for me to feed them, and I walk to their pen.

# LISA TUTTLE
## Replacements

Walking through grey north London to the tube station, feeling guilty that he hadn't let Jenny drive him to work and yet relieved to have escaped another pointless argument, Stuart Holder glanced down at a pavement covered in a leaf-fall of fast-food cartons and white paper bags and saw, amid the dog turds, beer cans and dead cigarettes, something horrible.

It was about the size of a cat, naked looking, with leathery, hairless skin and thin, spiky limbs that seemed too frail to support the bulbous, ill-proportioned body. The face, with tiny bright eyes and a wet slit of a mouth, was like an evil monkey's. It saw him and moved in a crippled, spasmodic way. Reaching up, it made a clotted, strangled noise. The sound touched a nerve, like metal between the teeth, and the sight of it, mewling and choking and scrabbling, scaly claws flexing and wriggling, made him feel sick and terrified. He had no phobias, he found insects fascinating, not frightening, and regularly removed, unharmed, the spiders, wasps and mayflies which made Jenny squeal or shudder helplessly.

But this was different. This wasn't some rare species of wingless bat escaped from a zoo, it wasn't something he would find pictured in any reference book. It was something that should not exist, a mistake, something alien. It did not belong in his world.

A little snarl escaped him and he took a step forward and brought his foot down hard.

The small, shrill scream lanced through him as he crushed it beneath his shoe and ground it into the road.

Afterwards, as he scraped the sole of his shoe against the curb to clean it, nausea overwhelmed him. He leaned over and vomited helplessly into a red-and-white-striped box of chicken bones and crumpled paper.

He straightened up, shaking, and wiped his mouth again and again with his pocket handkerchief. He wondered if anyone had seen, and had a furtive look around. Cars passed at a steady crawl. Across the road a cluster of schoolgirls dawdled near a man smoking in front of a newsagent's, but on this side of the road the fried chicken franchise and bathroom suppliers had yet to open for the day and the nearest pedestrians were more than a hundred yards away.

Until that moment, Stuart had never killed anything in his life. Mosquitoes and flies of course, other insects probably, a nest of hornets once, that was all. He had never liked the idea of hunting, never lived in the country. He remembered his father putting out poisoned bait for rats, and he remembered shying bricks at those same vermin on a bit of waste ground where he had played as a boy. But rats weren't like other animals; they elicited no sympathy. Some things had to be killed if they would not be driven away.

He made himself look to make sure the thing was not still alive. Nothing should be left to suffer. But his heel had crushed the thing's face out of recognition, and it was unmistakably dead. He felt a cool tide of relief and satisfaction, followed at once, as he walked away, by a nagging uncertainty, the imminence of guilt. Was he right to have killed it, to have acted on violent, irrational impulse? He didn't even know what it was. It might have been somebody's pet.

He went hot and cold with shame and self-disgust. At the corner he stopped with five or six others waiting to cross the road and because he didn't want to look at them he looked down.

And there it was, alive again.

He stifled a scream. No, of course it was not the same one, but another. His leg twitched; he felt frantic with the desire to kill it, and the terror of his desire. The thin wet mouth was moving as if it wanted to speak.

As the crossing-signal began its nagging blare he tore his eyes away from the creature squirming at his feet. Everyone else had started to cross the street, their eyes, like their thoughts, directed ahead. All except one. A woman in a smart business suit was standing still on the pavement, looking down, a sick fascination on her face.

As he looked at her looking at it, the idea crossed his mind that he should kill it for her, as a chivalric, protective act. But she wouldn't see it that way. She would be repulsed by his violence. He didn't want her to think he was a monster. He didn't want to be the monster who had exulted in the crunch of fragile bones, the flesh and viscera merging pulpily beneath his shoe.

He forced himself to look away, to cross the road, to spare the alien life. But he wondered, as he did so, if he had been right to spare it.

Stuart Holder worked as an editor for a publishing company with offices an easy walk from St. Paul's. Jenny had worked there, too, as a secretary, when they met five years ago. Now, though, she had quite a senior position with another publishing house, south of the river, and recently they had given her a car. He had been supportive of her ambitions, supportive of her learning to drive, and proud of her on all fronts when she succeeded, yet he was aware, although he never spoke of it, that something about her success made him uneasy. One small, niggling, insecure part of himself was afraid that one day she would realize she didn't need him anymore. That was why he picked at her, and second-guessed her decisions when she was behind the wheel and he was in the passenger seat. He recognized this as he walked briskly through more crowded streets towards his office, and he told himself he would do better. He would have to. If anything drove them apart it was more likely to be his behavior than her career. He wished he had accepted her offer of a ride today. Better any amount of petty irritation between husband and wife than to be haunted by the memory of that tiny face, distorted in the death he had inflicted. Entering the building, he surreptitiously scraped the sole of his shoe against the carpet.

Upstairs two editors and one of the publicity girls were in a huddle around his secretary's desk; they turned on him the guilty-defensive faces of women who have been discussing secrets men aren't supposed to know.

He felt his own defensiveness rising to meet theirs as he smiled. "Can I get any of you chaps a cup of coffee?"

"I'm sorry, Stuart, did you want . . . ?" As the others faded away, his secretary removed a stiff white paper bag with the NEXT logo printed on it from her desktop.

"Joke, Frankie, joke." He always got his own coffee because he liked the excuse to wander, and he was always having to reassure her that she was not failing in her secretarial duties. He wondered if Next sold sexy underwear, decided it would be unkind to tease her further.

He felt a strong urge to call Jenny and tell her what had happened, although he knew he wouldn't be able to explain, especially not over the phone. Just hearing her voice, the sound of sanity, would be a comfort, but he restrained himself until just after noon, when he made the call he made every day.

Her secretary told him she was in a meeting. "Tell her Stuart rang," he said, knowing she would call him back as always.

But that day she didn't. Finally, at five minutes to five, Stuart rang his wife's office and was told she had left for the day.

It was unthinkable for Jenny to leave work early, as unthinkable as for her not to return his call. He wondered if she was ill. Although he usually stayed in the office until well after six, now he shoved a manuscript in his briefcase and went out to brave the rush hour.

He wondered if she was mad at him. But Jenny didn't sulk. If she was angry she said so. They didn't lie or play those sorts of games with each other, pretending not to be in, "forgetting" to return calls.

As he emerged from his local underground station Stuart felt apprehensive. His eyes scanned the pavement and the gutters, and once or twice the flutter of paper made him jump, but of the creatures he had seen that morning there were no signs. The body of the one he had killed was gone, perhaps eaten by a passing dog, perhaps returned to whatever strange dimension had spawned it. He noticed, before he turned off the high street, that other pedestrians were also taking a keener than usual interest in the pavement and the edge of the road, and that made him feel vindicated somehow.

London traffic being what it was, he was home before Jenny. While he waited for the sound of her key in the lock he made himself a cup of tea, cursed, poured it down the sink, and had a stiff whisky instead. He had just finished it and was feeling much better when he heard the street door open.

"Oh!" The look on her face reminded him unpleasantly of those women in the office this morning, making him feel like an intruder in his own place. Now Jenny smiled, but it was too late. "I didn't expect you to be here so early."

"Nor me. I tried to call you, but they said you'd left already. I wondered if you were feeling all right."

"I'm fine!"

"You look fine." The familiar sight of her melted away his irritation. He loved the way she looked: her slender, boyish figure, her close-cropped, curly hair, her pale complexion and bright blue eyes.

Her cheeks now had a slight hectic flush. She caught her bottom lip between her teeth and gave him an assessing look before coming straight out with it. "How would you feel about keeping a pet?"

Stuart felt a horrible conviction that she was not talking about a dog or a cat. He wondered if it was the whisky on an empty stomach which made him feel dizzy.

"It was under my car. If I hadn't happened to notice something moving down there I could have run over it." She lifted her shoulders in a delicate shudder.

"Oh, God, Jenny, you haven't brought it home!"

She looked indignant. "Well, of course I did! I couldn't just leave it in the street—somebody else might have run it over."

Or stepped on it, he thought, realizing now that he could never tell Jenny what he had done. That made him feel even worse, but maybe he was wrong. Maybe it was just a cat she'd rescued. "What is it?"

She gave a strange, excited laugh. "I don't know. Something very rare, I think. Here, look." She slipped the large, woven bag off her shoulder, opening it, holding it out to him. "Look. Isn't it the sweetest thing?"

How could two people who were so close, so alike in so many ways, see something so differently? He only wanted to kill it, even now, while she had obviously fallen in love. He kept his face carefully neutral although he couldn't help flinching from her description. "Sweet?"

It gave him a pang to see how she pulled back, holding the bag protectively close as she said, "Well, I know it's not pretty, but so what? I thought it was horrible, too, at first sight. . . ." Her face clouded, as if she found her first impression difficult to remember, or to credit, and her voice faltered a little. "But then, then I realized how helpless it was. It needed me. It can't help how it looks. Anyway, doesn't it kind of remind you of the Psammead?"

"The what?"

"Psammead. You know, *The Five Children and It?*"

He recognized the title but her passion for old-fashioned children's books was something he didn't share. He shook his head impatiently. "That thing didn't come out of a book, Jen. You found it in the street and you don't know what it is or where it came from. It could be dangerous, it could be diseased."

"Dangerous," she said in a withering tone.

"You don't know."

"I've been with him all day and he hasn't hurt me, or anybody else at the office, he's perfectly happy being held, and he likes being scratched behind the ears."

He did not miss the pronoun shift. "It might have rabies."

"Don't be silly."

"Don't *you* be silly; it's not exactly native, is it? It might be carrying all sorts of foul parasites from South America or Africa or wherever."

"Now you're being racist. I'm not going to listen to you. *And* you've been drinking." She flounced out of the room.

If he'd been holding his glass still he might have thrown it. He closed his eyes and concentrated on breathing in and out slowly. This was worse than any argument they'd ever had, the only crucial disagreement of their marriage. Jenny had stronger views about many things than he did, so her wishes usually prevailed. He didn't mind that. But this was different. He wasn't having that creature in his home. He had to make her agree.

Necessity cooled his blood. He had his temper under control when his wife returned. "I'm sorry," he said, although she was the one who should have apologized. Still looking prickly, she shrugged and would not meet his eyes. "Want to go out to dinner tonight?"

She shook her head. "I'd rather not. I've got some work to do."

"Can I get you something to drink? I'm only one whisky ahead of you, honest."

Her shoulders relaxed. "I'm sorry. Low blow. Yeah, pour me one. And one for yourself." She sat down on the couch, her bag by her feet. Leaning over, reaching inside, she cooed, "Who's my little sweetheart, then?"

Normally he would have taken a seat beside her. Now, though, he eyed the pale, misshapen bundle on her lap and, after handing her a glass, retreated across the room. "Don't get mad, but isn't having a pet one of those things we discuss and agree on beforehand?"

He saw the tension come back into her shoulders, but she went on stroking the thing, keeping herself calm. "Normally, yes. But this is special. I didn't plan it. It happened, and now I've got a responsibility to him. Or her." She giggled. "We don't even know what sex you are, do we, my precious?"

He said carefully, "I can see that you had to do something when you found it, but keeping it might not be the best thing."

"I'm not going to put it out in the street."

"No, no, but . . . don't you think it would make sense to let a professional have a look at it? Take it to a vet, get it checked out . . . maybe it needs shots or something."

She gave him a withering look and for a moment he faltered, but then he rallied. "Come on, Jenny, be reasonable! You can't just drag some strange animal in off the street and keep it, just like that. You don't even know what it eats."

"I gave it some fruit at lunch. It ate that. Well, it sucked out the juice. I don't think it can chew."

"But you don't know, do you? Maybe the fruit juice was just an aperitif, maybe it needs half its weight in live insects every day, or a couple of small, live mammals. Do you really think you could cope with feeding it mice or rabbits fresh from the pet shop every week?"

"Oh, Stuart."

"Well? Will you just take it to a vet? Make sure it's healthy? Will you do that much?"

"And then I can keep it? If the vet says there's nothing wrong with it, and it doesn't need to eat anything too impossible?"

"Then we can talk about it. Hey, don't pout at me; I'm not your father, I'm not telling you what to do. We're partners, and partners don't make unilateral decisions about things that affect them both; partners discuss things and reach compromises and . . ."

"There can't be any compromise about this."

He felt as if she'd doused him with ice water. "What?"

"Either I win and I keep him or you win and I give him up. Where's the compromise?"

This was why wars were fought, thought Stuart, but he didn't say it. He was the picture of sweet reason, explaining as if he meant it, "The compromise is that we each try to see the other person's point. You get the animal checked out, make sure it's healthy and I, I'll keep an open mind about having a pet, and see if I might start liking . . . him. Does he have a name yet?"

Her eyes flickered. "No . . . we can choose one later, together. If we keep him."

He still felt cold and, although he could think of no reason for it, he was certain she was lying to him.

In bed that night as he groped for sleep Stuart kept seeing the tiny, hideous face of the thing screaming as his foot came down on it. That moment of blind, killing rage was not like him. He couldn't deny he had done it, or how he had felt, but now, as Jenny slept innocently beside him, as the creature she had rescued, a twin to his victim, crouched alive in the bathroom, he tried to remember it differently.

In fantasy, he stopped his foot, he controlled his rage and, staring at the memory of the alien animal, he struggled to see past his anger and his fear, to see through those fiercer masculine emotions and find his way to Jenny's feminine pity. Maybe his intuition had been wrong and hers was right. Maybe, if he had waited a little longer, instead of lashing out, he would have seen how unnecessary his fear was.

Poor little thing, poor little thing. It's helpless, it needs me, it's harmless so I won't harm it.

Slowly, in imagination, he worked towards that feeling, *her* feeling, and then, suddenly, he was there, through the anger, through the fear, through the hate to . . . not love, he couldn't say that, but compassion. Glowing and warm, compassion filled his heart and flooded his veins, melting the ice there and washing him out into the sea of sleep, and dreams where Jenny smiled and loved him and there was no space between them for misunderstanding.

He woke in the middle of the night with a desperate urge to pee. He was out of bed in the dark hallway when he remembered what was waiting in the bathroom. He couldn't go back to bed with the need unsatisfied, but he stood outside the bathroom door, hand hovering over the light switch on this side, afraid to turn it on, open the door, go in.

It wasn't, he realized, that he was afraid of a creature no bigger than a football and less likely to hurt him; rather, he was afraid that he might hurt it. It was a stronger variant of that reckless vertigo he had felt sometimes in high places, the fear, not of falling, but of throwing oneself off, of losing control and giving in to self-destructive urges. He didn't *want* to kill the thing—had his own feelings not undergone a sea change, Jenny's love for it would have been enough to stop him—but something, some dark urge stronger than himself, might make him.

Finally he went down to the end of the hall and outside to the weedy, muddy little area which passed for the communal front garden and in which the rubbish bins, of necessity, were kept, and, shivering in his thin cotton pajamas in the damp, chilly air, he watered the sickly forsythia, or whatever it was, that Jenny had planted so optimistically last winter.

When he went back inside, more uncomfortable than when he had gone out, he saw the light was on in the bathroom, and as he approached the half-open door, he heard Jenny's voice, low and soothing. "There, there. Nobody's going to hurt you, I promise. You're safe here. Go to sleep now. Go to sleep."

He went past without pausing, knowing he would be viewed as an intruder, and got back into bed. He fell asleep, lulled by the meaningless murmur of her voice, still waiting for her to join him.

Stuart was not used to doubting Jenny, but when she told him she had visited a veterinarian who had given her new pet a clean bill of health, he did not believe her.

In a neutral tone he asked, "Did he say what kind of animal it was?"

"He didn't know."

"He didn't know what it was, but he was sure it was perfectly healthy."

"God, Stuart, what do you want? It's obvious to everybody but you that my little friend is healthy and happy. What do you want, a birth certificate?"

He looked at her "friend," held close against her side, looking squashed and miserable. "What do you mean, 'everybody'?"

She shrugged. "Everybody at work. They're all jealous as anything." She planted a kiss on the thing's pointy head. Then she looked at him, and he realized that she had not kissed him, as she usually did, when he came in. She'd been clutching that thing the whole time. "I'm going to keep him," she said quietly. "If you don't like it, then . . ." Her pause seemed to pile up in solid, transparent blocks between them. "Then, I'm sorry, but that's how it is."

So much for an equal relationship, he thought. So much for sharing. Mortally wounded, he decided to pretend it hadn't happened. "Want to go out for Indian tonight?"

She shook her head, turning away. "I want to stay in. There's something on telly. You go on. You could bring me something back, if you wouldn't mind. A spinach bahjee and a couple of nans would do me."

"And what about . . . something for your little friend?"

She smiled a private smile. "He's all right. I've fed him already." Then she raised her eyes to his and acknowledged his effort. "Thanks."

He went out and got take-away for them both, and stopped at the off-license for the Mexican beer Jenny favored. A radio in the off-license was playing a sentimental song about love that Stuart remembered from his earliest childhood: his mother used to sing it. He was shocked to realize he had tears in his eyes.

That night Jenny made up the sofa bed in the spare room, explaining, "He can't stay in the bathroom; it's just not satisfactory, you know it's not."

"He needs the bed?"

"I do. He's confused, everything is new and different, I'm the one thing he can count on. I have to stay with him. He needs me."

"He needs you? What about me?"

"Oh, Stuart," she said impatiently. "You're a grown man. You can sleep by yourself for a night or two."

"And that thing can't?"

"Don't call him a thing."

"What am I supposed to call it? Look, you're not its mother—it doesn't need you as much as you'd like to think. It was perfectly all right in the bathroom last night—it'll be fine in here on its own."

"Oh? And what do you know about it? You'd like to kill him, wouldn't you? Admit it."

"No," he said, terrified that she had guessed the truth. If she knew how he had killed one of those things she would never forgive him. "It's not true, I don't—I couldn't hurt it any more than I could hurt you."

Her face softened. She believed him. It didn't matter how he felt about the creature. Hurting it, knowing how she felt, would be like committing an act of violence against her, and they both knew he wouldn't do that. "Just for a few nights, Stuart. Just until he settles in."

He had to accept that. All he could do was hang on, hope that she still loved him and that this wouldn't be forever.

The days passed. Jenny no longer offered to drive him to work. When he asked her, she said it was out of her way and with traffic so bad a detour would make her late. She said it was silly to take him the short distance to the station, especially as there was nowhere she could safely stop to let him out, and anyway the walk would do him good. They were all good reasons, which he had used in the old days himself, but her excuses struck him painfully when he remembered how eager she had once been for his company, how ready to make any detour for his sake. Her new pet accompanied her everywhere, even to work, snug in the little nest she had made for it in a woven carrier bag.

"Of course things are different now. But I haven't stopped loving you," she said when he tried to talk to her about the breakdown of their marriage. "It's not like I've found another man. This is something completely different. It doesn't threaten you; you're still my husband."

But it was obvious to him that a husband was no longer something she particularly valued. He began to have fantasies about killing it. Not, this time, in a blind rage, but as part of a carefully thought-out plan. He might poison it, or spirit it away somehow and pretend it had run away. Once it was gone he hoped Jenny would forget it and be his again.

But he never had a chance. Jenny was quite obsessive about the thing, as if it were too valuable to be left unguarded for a single minute. Even when she took a bath, or went to the toilet, the creature was with her, behind the locked door of the bathroom. When he offered to look after it for her for a few minutes she just smiled, as if the idea was manifestly ridiculous, and he didn't dare insist.

So he went to work, and went out for drinks with colleagues, and spent what time he could with Jenny, although they were never alone. He didn't argue with her, although he wasn't above trying to move her to pity if he could. He made seemingly casual comments designed to convince her of his change of heart so that eventually, weeks or months from now, she would trust him and leave the creature with him—and then, later, perhaps, they could put their marriage back together.

One afternoon, after an extended lunch break, Stuart returned to the office to find one of the senior editors crouched on the floor beside his secretary's empty desk, whispering and chuckling to herself.

He cleared his throat nervously. "Linda?"

She lurched back on her heels and got up awkwardly. She blushed and ducked her head as she turned, looking very unlike her usual high-powered self. "Oh, uh, Stuart, I was just—"

Frankie came in with a pile of photocopying. "Uh-huh," she said loudly.

Linda's face got even redder. "Just going," she mumbled, and fled.

Before he could ask, Stuart saw the creature, another crippled bat-without-wings, on the floor beside the open bottom drawer of

Frankie's desk. It looked up at him, opened its slit of a mouth and gave a sad little hiss. Around one matchstick-thin leg it wore a fine golden chain which was fastened at the other end to the drawer.

"Some people would steal anything that's not chained down," said Frankie darkly. "People you wouldn't suspect."

He stared at her, letting her see his disapproval, his annoyance, disgust, even. "Animals in the office aren't part of the contract, Frankie."

"It's not an animal."

"What is it, then?"

"I don't know. You tell me."

"It doesn't matter what it is, you can't have it here."

"I can't leave it at home."

"Why not?"

She turned away from him, busying herself with her stacks of paper. "I can't leave it alone. It might get hurt. It might escape."

"Chance would be a fine thing."

She shot him a look, and he was certain she knew he wasn't talking about *her* pet. He said, "What does your boyfriend think about it?"

"I don't have a boyfriend." She sounded angry but then, abruptly, the anger dissipated, and she smirked. "I don't have to have one, do I?"

"You can't have that animal here. Whatever it is. You'll have to take it home."

She raised her fuzzy eyebrows. "Right now?"

He was tempted to say yes, but thought of the manuscripts that wouldn't be sent out, the letters that wouldn't be typed, the delays and confusions, and he sighed. "Just don't bring it back again. All right?"

"Yowza."

He felt very tired. He could tell her what to do but she would no more obey than would his wife. She would bring it back the next day and keep bringing it back, maybe keeping it hidden, maybe not, until he either gave in or was forced into firing her. He went into his office, closed the door, and put his head down on his desk.

That evening he walked in on his wife feeding the creature with her blood.

It was immediately obvious that it was that way round. The creature might be a vampire—it obviously was—but his wife was no helpless victim. She was wide awake and in control, holding the creature firmly, letting it feed from a vein in her arm.

She flinched as if anticipating a shout, but he couldn't speak. He watched what was happening without attempting to interfere and gradually she relaxed again, as if he wasn't there.

When the creature, sated, fell off, she kept it cradled on her lap and reached with her other hand for the surgical spirit and cotton wool on the table, moistened a piece of cotton wool and tamped it to the tiny wound. Then, finally, she met her husband's eyes.

"He has to eat," she said reasonably. "He can't chew. He needs blood. Not very much, but . . ."

"And he needs it from you? You can't . . . ?"

"I can't hold down some poor scared rabbit or dog for him, no." She made a shuddering face. "Well, really, think about it. You know how squeamish I am. This is so much easier. It doesn't hurt."

It hurts me, he thought, but couldn't say it. "Jenny . . ."

"Oh, don't start," she said crossly. "I'm not going to get any disease from it, and he doesn't take enough to make any difference. Actually, I like it. We both do."

"Jenny, please don't. Please. For me. Give it up."

"No." She held the scraggy, ugly thing close and gazed at Stuart like a dispassionate executioner. "I'm sorry, Stuart, I really am, but this is nonnegotiable. If you can't accept that you'd better leave."

This was the showdown he had been avoiding, the end of it all. He tried to rally his arguments and then he realized he had none. She had said it. She had made her choice, and it was nonnegotiable. And he realized, looking at her now, that although she reminded him of the woman he loved, he didn't want to live with what she had become.

He could have refused to leave. After all, he had done nothing wrong. Why should he give up his home, this flat which was half his? But he could not force Jenny out onto the streets with nowhere to go; he still felt responsible for her.

"I'll pack a bag, and make a few phone calls," he said quietly. He knew someone from work who was looking for a lodger, and if all else failed, his brother had a spare room. Already, in his thoughts, he had left.

He ended up, once they'd sorted out their finances and formally separated, in a flat just off the Holloway Road, near Archway. It was not too far to walk if Jenny cared to visit, which she never did. Sometimes he called on her, but it was painful to feel himself an unwelcome visitor in the home they once had shared.

He never had to fire Frankie; she handed in her notice a week later, telling him she'd been offered an editorial job at The Women's Press. He wondered if pets in the office were part of the contract over there.

He never learned if the creatures had names. He never knew where they had come from, or how many there were. Had they fallen only in Islington? (Frankie had a flat somewhere off Upper Street.) He never saw anything on the news about them, or read any official confirmation of their existence, but he was aware of occasional oblique references to them in other contexts, occasional glimpses.

One evening, coming home on the tube, he found himself looking at the woman sitting opposite. She was about his own age, probably in her early thirties, with strawberry blond hair, greenish eyes, and an almost translucent complexion. She was strikingly dressed in high, soft-leather boots, a long black woolen skirt, and an enveloping cashmere cloak of cranberry red. High on the cloak, below and to the right of the fastening at the neck, was a simple, gold circle brooch. Attached to it he noticed a very fine golden chain which vanished inside the cloak, like the end of a watch fob.

He looked at it idly, certain he had seen something like it before, on other women, knowing it reminded him of something. The train arrived at Archway, and as he rose to leave the train, so did the attractive woman. Her stride matched his. They might well leave the station together. He tried to think of something to say to her, some pretext for striking up a conversation. He was after all a single man again now, and she might be a single woman. He had forgotten how single people in London contrived to meet.

He looked at her again, sidelong, hoping she would turn her head and look at him. With one slender hand she toyed with her gold chain. Her cloak fell open slightly as she walked, and he caught a glimpse of the creature she carried beneath it, close to her body, attached by a slender golden chain.

He stopped walking and let her get away from him. He had to rest for a little while before he felt able to climb the stairs to the street.

By then he was wondering if he had really seen what he thought he had seen. The glimpse had been so brief. But he had been deeply shaken by what he saw or imagined, and he turned the wrong way outside the station. When he finally realized, he was at the corner of Jenny's road, which had once also been his. Rather than retrace his steps, he decided to take the turning and walk past her house.

Lights were on in the front room, the curtains drawn against the early winter dark. His footsteps slowed as he drew nearer. He felt such a longing to be inside, back home, belonging. He wondered if she would be pleased at all to see him. He wondered if she ever felt lonely, as he did.

Then he saw the tiny, dark figure between the curtains and the window. It was spread-eagled against the glass, scrabbling uselessly; inside, longing to be out.

As he stared, feeling its pain as his own, the curtains swayed and opened slightly as a human figure moved between them. He saw the woman reach out and pull the creature away from the glass, back into the warm, lighted room with her, and the curtains fell again, shutting him out.

# MELISSA PRITCHARD
## Spirit Seizures

BASED ON *THE WATSEKA WONDER*,
AN AUTHENTICATED NARRATIVE OF SPIRIT MANIFESTATION
BY DR. E. W. STEVENS, 1908

*July 1882: The Binning farm three miles outside Watseka, Illinois—*

Purplish soil receded in motionless, combed waves from around the
frame house. The ripening corn surged, had an oily river sheen over
it. . . .

Holding her newest baby, Lurancy walked again to the road's
edge, shielding her eyes, her sunbonnet tied but swinging against her
damp back. Deep clay ruts crisscrossed the road, old wheel ruts, but no
dust was building in the distance, no buggy approached from town.
Mr. Asa B. Roff, a wealthy lawyer, and his wife, Anne, former residents of Watseka, had come from Emporia, Kansas, to visit their eldest
daughter. News that they would also be visiting the Binnings had bred
a quarrel with Lurancy's husband. Thomas had gone down to the river
to fish and lay traps, and to evade further argument. That morning
Lurancy had attended both to the baby and their daughter, Lucia, with
overscrupulous attention, had stiffly set down Thomas's plate of breakfast, avoided watching him eat.

Thomas Binning. In overalls and cracked shoes, that black shingle
of hair laid flat across his broad plank of forehead, that infrequent
laughter forever reminding her of a saw drawn backward. Now he was
coldly separate; her hands served, his took. There could be little else
with the Roffs about to visit them again.

Two summers before, the Roffs had returned to Watseka from
their new home in Emporia. Lurancy Vennum Binning, as a new

bride, had been proud to show her new home, that first child lifting up her belly. Thomas had nearly undone that pride, sitting in their barren front parlor, his knees sprung like an iron scissors, his hands flopped like wrung hens. He sat, stonily ignorant, in that darkened room with Mr. and Mrs. Roff and their daughter Minerva, leaving with a hard curse when Minerva Roff tremblingly proposed that the soul of her sister Mary be brought forward through the able instrument of their dear Lurancy.

Lurancy had already confessed to Thomas about the summer she was thirteen, the night in July 1877 when the voices had started. Hissing voices, breaths clawing over her face . . . *Lurancy, Rancy* . . . a dissonant choir of the dead stopped only by her mother's presence. Then followed seizures, trances, ecstasies, her body rigid while her voice roamed among the contents of heaven. Dead but unreconciled souls borrowed her voice, pressed grievance through her, sour from desuetude.

With everyone, family, physicians, ministers, neighbors, banded under the sad resolve to commit Lurancy Vennum to the Springfield asylum, the Roffs, whose own daughter Mary had been subject to similar seizures before she died in 1865, brought a spiritualist down from Janesville. In the presence of Dr. E. W. Stevens, Mr. and Mrs. Vennum, and Asa Roff, the soul of Mary Roff, dead twelve years, asserted its benign, wonderful residence within Lurancy's flesh. From February to May 1878, Mary's spirit read like wildest news out of the living envelope of Lurancy Vennum. While living at the Vennum house, Mary asked repeatedly to be taken home. With the Vennums' consent, Mary was returned "home," to the Roffs. In late May this personality, soul, or spirit of Mary Roff vacated Lurancy Vennum and willingly returned to "heaven and angels." Lurancy was escorted back to the Vennum house, recovered in all her senses.

Thomas Binning had understood nothing. Lurancy's voice had boiled through him, leaving him empty of all but the most sedimentary opinion that spiritualists were deluded fools. He cared for Lurancy Vennum only as he knew her, present before his eyes. Ordinary.

Churned white butter, a sweaty caul over it, hung down the well. Two cakes, wrapped in cloth pale as cerements, lay like tiny mummies across the cookstove. Lurancy went out to cut oxeye sunflower, unrolling gaudy bunches of it from her apron, placing them in a stone crock on the kitchen windowsill and a pewter pitcher in the front parlor. The house otherwise stood plain, unsoftened by material prosperity.

(Lurancy's family had moved from Milford to Watseka the summer she turned seven, the same summer Martin Meara was hanged for tying his son across a hot stove because he had not, it was said by way of explanation, plowed his day's portion. Townspeople, mostly men and boys, had ridden out to see the hanging, brought back pieces of the hackberry tree. Hackberry branches, to be whittled by morbid hands, or thrillingly revolved down in dusty, worn pockets.)

Out on the porch steps Lurancy shook out her wavy black hair (*troughed as a washboard*, her mother would say), refastened it with the several tortoise combs her mother had given her on her wedding day. Lucia ran about on the planked porch, cradling the wood doll Thomas had fashioned for her. A wasp tagged near and Lurancy slapped at it with the hem of her gingham dress as she went past, joggling the baby, pacing restlessly from porch side to porch side, from road's edge to house and back, waiting for her friends. . . .

Pinned beneath a glary noon light, Lurancy held the baby in one arm, yanked the wooden wagon along with the other, Lucia bobbing in it, her sunbonnet hiding her diamond fleck of face, the picnic hamper rocking beside her. In the hamper Lurancy had put cold chicken, bread and butter slices, raspberries, and, in a conciliatory mood, one of the company cakes. The rift with Thomas had broken her peace, and she had no temperament to sustain any quarrel.

Scores of crows were raiding the white, blowing wheat. In turn, they would eat the grasshoppers. To everything a season and time. A solitary crow hopped boldly near them; Lucia cried out, afraid of the obsidian bird and its rapacious sideways eye.

The meadow was full-lit, porous and greenly translucent as a luna moth's wing. Clover was rampant, its puffy thick heads slewed like hail. The Iroquois River glittered behind a long shoulder of trees, a black collar tatted out of the trunks and shade running along its bottom. Dragonflies clicked, netted iridescence passing through a hot canvas of air. Lurancy stopped to pick some tickseed, the tattered gold ruffs and red eye. When Lucia complained, Lurancy set down the flowers, the baby, and lifted her from the wagon, helping her ruck up her skirts and squat. Sweet-smelling urine pooled into the seeding grasses.

Lurancy pulled the wagon toward a familiar break in the trees, the elms and maples, to the narrow path down which Thomas would have gone to fish.

His back was to them, standing by the dun, high-banked river, water both she and her brothers had been baptized in.

Thomas.

From his face, turned first on Lucia, then to herself, Lurancy perceived, and gratefully, that he had no stock in further argument.

They sat peaceably, ate what she had brought. She opened her dress to feed the baby. Thomas had caught a string of fish, shot two mallards, drakes.

The Roffs have not come.

Maybe they lost their way? He was teasing, yet so honestly hopeful that she laughed.

You should use the mallard or the fish if they'll be staying over for supper, Rancy.

Yes.

She knotted back her skirts, rinsed the pewter dishes in the river. Thomas stood nearby, holding the baby; when she lost a dish to the current, he retrieved it for her.

Thomas had begun, lately, to talk of homesteading. Selling the farm. Of Kansas. Moving to some treeless spot, worlds from anybody, living most likely in a sod hut. Where her life would ebb with the bearing of child upon child. With helping Thomas to tame a bit of tough prairie. Well, she had chosen him. Now he picked the course and rigor of their lives. The Roffs would come, stir up her old self, jog her longing for those wide, fertile talks about spirit worlds, angels, and spirit guides, all things which Thomas opposed, even cursed. (What you cannot see, do you think you are to know, imagine that you know?)

Lucia clasped the lank bouquet as the wagon rose and dipped through the meadow. The baby, shaded by the hamper, slept. Over where the farm lay, the sky was a massive block of gray-purple. By the river it would still be sunny and hot. Wind tossed like a wall of water over them. Lurancy's muslin apron buffeted fitfully. Lucia began to cry, covering her ears at the first crack of thunder. A blue skeletal jig of lightning flared. Lurancy dragged at the wagon as fast as she dared without throwing the baby. She could see the wash, make out her own dress and one of Lucia's a-skip on the line as if they were partnered at a town dance. Rain like a scatter of buckshot hit at her face. Pull up your bonnet, Lucia, she yelled over the wind, then pulled up her own.

The air was thick with a greenish, moldery light. Another

heaving split of thunder, sounding like a house collapsed, with a crackle of husk beneath it. Trees blew, heeled in one direction, suddenly weak-seeming.

Lurancy strained to make out the shape of an unfamiliar object outside their house. The buggy, the Roffs' buggy, empty, stood outside their porch, the horses' heads dejected, rain stippling their reddish hides. It seemed the whole awash world of the dead had come with these people who would have cause to greet her, perhaps even to love her, then set about drawing their dead child's spirit like spittled thread through the blunt eye of able Lurancy Binning.

Lurancy willed her spirit to loft, untenant, so Mary Roff might enter, impetuously, this world.

> *for all flesh is like*
> *grass*
> *and all its glory like the flower of*
> *grass*
> *but the grass withers, the flower falls*
> *but the word of the Lord will endure*
> *for ever*

Lurancy picked up the baby, grabbed Lucia by the hand, and even with skirts nearly anchored by cold rain and hemmed by river clay, the near-empty vessel of Lurancy Binning pitched lightly up the wide solid steps her husband had built for her, to seek some short respite with those he refused to understand.

1889: DR.RICHARD HODGSON, OF THE SOCIETY FOR PSYCHICAL RESEARCH, LISTENS TO MINERVA ALTER, FORTY-SIX YEARS OLD AND SISTER TO MARY ROFF

. . . Of us five Roff children, Mary stood forth, from the very beginning, as peculiar. Subject to fits, black pressing moods. Which grew increasingly worse, don't you see, to the point where Mother and Father tried a great many things to cure her. As a girl I can recall the house being overtaken by doctors, ministers, faith healers of all kinds. One remedy working, then another, then nothing.

Mary, when she was well, had a great attachment to music. Solemn dreary tunes out of our Methodist hymnal pleased her most. We tried to tease her out of her preference for such dirges. "What sad, sobering music for a pretty child, Mary," our mother would say, but Mary would turn with her dark eyes from the piano, fix us with those impenetrable eyes. "But it is the exact pace and lyric which pleases me, Mother."

Would you like me to play one of Mary's hymns for you, Doctor? This is the exact piano she used to sit down to. Father gave it to Dr. Alter and myself when they moved out to Emporia. At the time Mary's spirit took up lodging in Miss Vennum, it was nearly the first object she recognized with affection when she stepped back into our family home. But it had been twelve years since her death, don't you see, so her fingers would not work over the keys with any of the grace they had once possessed, and for that she sweetly and, faintly troubled, apologized. . . .

Here, if I remember, is a favorite of Mary's before she died, aged eighteen years:

> *How blest is our brother bereft*
> *Of all that could burthen his mind!*
> *How easy the soul, that hath left*
> *The wearisome body behind!*
>
> *This languishing head is at rest,*
> *Its thinking and aching are o'er,*
> *This quiet immovable breast*
> *Is heaved by affliction no more. . . .*

For over a year Mary was sent off to Peoria, to the water cures. Again, it seemed to help, until the melancholia and fits returned. Most of our backwoods physicians still treated any overstimulation of the body by leeching. Mary herself took to placing leeches against her temples, to take away the "lump of pain," as she called it. There the leeches would lie, growing from cool to warm, flat to swollen, till they dropped off, all sated. And Mary would collect them into jars, treat them almost as her playthings (*rusty-black, wormy, eyeless creatures, like something the Devil might scheme to create*). Dr. Alter never held to the idea of cupping or leeching, thought it old-fashioned and dangerous to debilitate a weak person with fasting or draining of vital blood.

. . . Why yes, Dr. Hodgson, I do remember that one particular afternoon you refer to. Awful. Awful, discovering my sister in the backyard, just under some bushes. All bloody, nearly dead. She'd taken a kitchen knife and gone into the yard, deliberately cut into her arm. You must have heard then, Doctor, that part of the story where Mary's spirit, while in the bodily vehicle of Miss Vennum, went to show Dr. Stevens the knife scar along her arm, then remembered, saying, oh, this is not the one, that other arm is in the ground, then described to him her burial, named the mourners standing about her grave. . . .

Oh, stories did circulate and abound, details of Mary's spirit-return, her uncanny recall of old neighbors, past occasions, things no one but Mary Roff herself could have recalled.

Before passing back into the Borderland that May of 1878, Mary wanted Lurancy to be given certain small tokens, a few cards, some marbles, 25¢, Mary, you see, being grateful to Lurancy. This I did.

The first time I met my sister after her death? That would be February 1878: Mother and I were walking down Sixth Street to pay a visit to the Vennums, having heard about their oldest girl's strange seizures so much like Mary's had been, her repeated claim to be Mary Roff. Before Mother, I noticed the girl leaning out from the top story of their small, rather shabby house, waving and calling "Nervie, Nervie!" Always Mary's nickname for me. The voice was exactly Mary's.

At our parents' house over those next three months, Mary and I spent many hours recalling childhood; or rather, Mary remembered while I affirmed. Pranks, for instance the time she and one of our younger cousins tried to rub a made-up ointment into the sore eyes of one of our hens. She remembered that.

Mary's spirit, at the beginning, refused food. At table she bowed her head, murmuring that she supped in heaven; but as the body of Miss Vennum regained its vigor, so did Mary begin to eat. That spring I accompanied Mother and Mary into many of our finest homes in Watseka. I was accustomed soon enough to being overlooked while all flocked to see the proof of Mary in young Lurancy Vennum . . . and rarely were disappointed.

In the years before her death, Mary was famous in Watseka and beyond for her fits and clairvoyances. Blindfolded, she read newspapers aloud, read sealed letters, then arranged boxes of letters alphabetically, things of that sort. Newspapermen, well-to-do townspeople, even Mayor Secrets and his wife, all paid ceaseless visits to our home, until our very lives revolved around Mary's peculiar orb, and by her reflection we were cast into that same unnatural light.

After she died, July the 5th, 1865, our lives took up some normalcy. I met Dr. Alter, we were married, I continued teaching Sunday school. He practiced the medicine he'd learned on the East Coast and in Boston. He was popular here in Watseka, with his new ideas and theories . . . yet these couldn't save our own children. When black diphtheria came through Milford, then Watseka, we watched our innocent children, six of our seven, sicken and succumb. Three taken in the span of one night. Dr. Alter made a slit in Ada's windpipe, trying to bring air to her lungs; without result he did the same for little Charles. Which of us was the more bereft by the loss in one week, of six of our children, myself still nursing Asa, who died in my arms, or my husband, being unable to save one of them? It was quick, beyond control; he was as helpless as I was.

If you would be so kind as to follow me, Dr. Hodgson, to the table over by the window, you can see what gives me peace at times. . . . This is hair from each one of our children. Ada's. Frederick's. Here is Maude's. Mary's. Charlie. Even little Asa, who had such a crop of it and so black. As they died in turn, Mother went into their rooms for me, cutting their hair. I plait and twist, like this, shaping the hair into patterns, bouquets. . . . When I finished that first time, pain welled up and so maddeningly that I was compelled to tear the bouquet apart, almost frantically, and begin again.

More often than Dr. Alter, I visit the grave beds at Oak Hill (*those pickets, a pale set of tongues swelling up from the earth*).

Yes. Well yes, he did. A seventh child, Robert, did survive. With his wife and five children he lives just outside Milford, a carpenter. Robert was left to raise, but I hadn't much heart for it. . . . Looking at him, I saw the others. Wondered why him spared, and not even my favorite. Many families lost children that winter; I suppose we were not singled out except in the extremity of our loss.

I have heard, as others have written it to me, that Lurancy Binning lives out in Kansas, Rawlins County, mother to six or seven. Those episodes in her early life nearly forgotten, occupied as she is with the obligations of rearing children, raising up living children . . .

As a physician, of course, my husband has slipped back into the lively stream of need and fulfillment of need. But since Mary, since my own children were taken, I savor so little. The spiritual cannot console me, perhaps from being overlong exposed to it. I am most content up at Oak Hill. Or in turning their hair to glinting shapes, vines.

I am removed from nature's lures, numb to its cruel trees, cruel birds, cruel river water, to its food, or to any fine thing. A bead-strand of monotony before my eyes. I have, as you see for yourself, been carted off by grief.

I would gain no benefit by lying to you or to anyone about my sister Mary. I care little what others beyond this place say of the case of Mary Roff or the "Watseka Wonder," as Miss Vennum is at times called. Mary's soul returned to us that one time, then briefly, twice more, when Mother and Father and I visited the Binning farm. Lurancy's husband, unaccustomed to our spiritualist beliefs, was neither welcoming nor hospitable; yet she seemed exceedingly joyful to see us. I remember that. How she pressed her children upon me, quite thoughtlessly (*agonizing, the sight of tiny, still-animate faces*).

I will walk with you over to our family home. You will want to talk with my brother and his family. No, I prefer not. I will go on to Oak Hill.

(*Where all one day will assemble in plain, purblind rows, under sober in eloquent stone, our lives reduced to that faint quaver of rumour . . . where some hundred years from now, we may persist, a source of curiosity and likely, some little disbelief . . .*)

Well now.

It has been nearly a lifting of some burden, to speak to you of these things.

## MARY ROFF

*I'm gonna take a trip on that old gospel ship*
*I'm goin' far beyond the sky*
*I'm gonna shout and sing, til the bell done ring*
*When I bid this world good-bye*

What is a House but a hundred boards upended and smacked together, the ten hammers which plowed the humid air, the cracking of hammers, the thundering which resides in the air around the loosening nails, the dark fingerspaces between . . . ? And what is a town but fifty such buildings, lined up and stopping short . . . ending with my House, which goes only so far across the thickened ground to overlook the flat river. . . .? What is a town such as this but a hastily reassembled forest, trees felled, taken into measured pieces and put back together in such a way that they might move about in them secretly, sleep, fight, take supper, increase their poor numbers, instead of standing outside, looking up a solid, impenetrable trunk, awed and displaced?

And what is Bodily Flesh but a house so lightly mortised as to permit an occasional strike of soul to flash through like summer lightning? Mary Roff. I was that white, half-empty pitcher, born unwhole, unfinished, as a baby comes without its hearing or its proper sight, missing some symmetry of limb, so I did enter the clayey sphere of weights and dimensions, unfinished. No one saw that I was a soul not fixedly mortised. That older, swifter souls slid in and out of me, bats in an abandoned and shifting outbuilding. I was an incompleteness pouring like oil or watered wine between two vessels, a shiny arc rocking between one named assembly of flesh and another, and near the end, poured from Mary into Lurancy, and back from Lurancy poured yet again into Mary . . . a child's game, going in and out the windows. . . .

> *If you are ashamed of me, you ought not to be*
> *And you'd better have a care,*
> *If too much fault you find, you'll sure be left behind*
> *When I'm sailing through the air*

And what was Lurancy Vennum Binning but that vulnerable, slight growth latched on to by heavy, malevolent souls, then turned by me into a woman yoked to toil, to the magnetism of scraping her nourishment from dirt? I was glad for her to have husband-love and child-love, what I never knew, being encumbered by an oppression of spirits all crowding into the closet of one body as if it were some great vibrating hall.

And what, then, of Nervie, my sister Nervie, but a high-spirited woman, unable to tolerate either flesh or spirit, a woman possessed of no convictions but those passive ones of grief and loss—she grew attached to loss, dependent on sorrow, came to love them dearer than anything.

What is Soul or Spirit but Mystery, a Glory Ship, that Rumor founded by tales such as mine—Mad Mary Roff—tales bringing not confirmation but bare continuance of hope . . . instructing humanity in its keenest question: But if a man die, shall he live again?

*I have good news to bring*
*And that is why I sing,*
*All my joys with you I'll share*
*I'm gonna take a trip on that old Gospel Ship*
*And go sailing through the air*

# NANCY ETCHEMENDY
## Cat in Glass

I was once a respectable woman. Oh yes, I know that's what they all say when they've reached a pass like mine: I was well educated, well traveled, had lovely children and a nice husband with a good financial mind. How can anyone have fallen so far, except one who deserved to anyway? I've had time aplenty to consider the matter, lying here eyeless in this fine hospital bed while the stench of my wounds increases. The matrons who guard my room are tight-lipped. But I heard one of them whisper yesterday, when she thought I was asleep, "Jesus, how could anyone do such a thing?" The answer to all these questions is the same. I have fallen so far, and I have done what I have done, to save us each and every one from the *Cat in Glass*.

My entanglement with the cat began fifty-two years ago, when my sister, Delia, was attacked by an animal. It happened on an otherwise ordinary spring afternoon. There were no witnesses. My father was still in his office at the college, and I was dawdling along on my way home from first grade at Chesly Girls' Day School, counting cracks in the sidewalk. Delia, younger than I by three years, was alone with Fiona, the Irish woman who kept house for us. Fiona had just gone outside for a moment to hang laundry. She came in to check on Delia, and discovered a scene of almost unbelievable carnage. Oddly, she had heard no screams.

As I ran up the steps and opened our door, I heard screams indeed. Not Delia's—for Delia had nothing left to scream with—but

Fiona's, as she stood in the front room with her hands over her eyes. She couldn't bear the sight. Unfortunately, six-year-olds have no such compunction. I stared long and hard, sick and trembling, yet entranced.

From the shoulders up, Delia was no longer recognizable as a human being. Her throat had been shredded and her jaw ripped away. Most of her hair and scalp were gone. There were long, bloody furrows in the creamy skin of her arms and legs. The organdy pinafore in which Fiona had dressed her that morning was clotted with blood, and the blood was still coming. Some of the walls were even spattered with it where the animal, whatever it was, had worried her in its frenzy. Her fists and heels banged jerkily against the floor. Our pet dog, Freddy, lay beside her, also bloody, but quite limp. Freddy's neck was broken.

I remember slowly raising my head—I must have been in shock by then—and meeting the bottomless gaze of the glass cat that sat on the hearth. Our father, a professor of art history, was very proud of this sculpture, for reasons I did not understand until many years later. I only knew that it was valuable and we were not allowed to touch it. A chaotic feline travesty, it was not the sort of thing you would want to touch anyway. Though basically catlike in shape, it bristled with transparent threads and shards. There was something at once wild and vaguely human about its face. I had never liked it much, and Delia had always been downright frightened of it. On this day, as I looked up from my little sister's ruins, the cat seemed to glare at me with bright, terrifying satisfaction.

I had experienced, a year before, the thing every child fears most: the death of my mother. It had given me a kind of desperate strength, for I thought, at the tender age of six, that I had survived the worst life had to offer. Now, as I returned the mad stare of the glass cat, it came to me that I was wrong. The world was a much more evil place than I had ever imagined, and nothing would ever be the same again.

Delia died officially in the hospital a short time later. After a cursory investigation, the police laid the blame on Freddy. I still have the newspaper clipping, yellow now, and held together with even yellower cellophane tape. "The family dog lay dead near the victim, blood smearing its muzzle and forepaws. Sergeant Morton theorizes that the dog, a pit bull terrier and member of a breed specifically developed for vicious fighting, turned killer and attacked its tragic young owner. He also suggests that the child, during the death struggle, flung the murderous beast away with enough strength to break its neck."

Even I, a little girl, knew that this "theory" was lame; the neck of a pit bull is an almost impossible thing to break, even by a large, determined man. And Freddy, in spite of his breeding, had always been gentle, even protective, with us. Simply stated, the police were mystified, and this was the closest thing to a rational explanation they could produce. As far as they were concerned, that was the end of the matter. In fact, it had only just begun.

I was shipped off to my Aunt Josie's house for several months. What Father did during this time, I never knew, though I now suspect he spent those months in a sanatorium. In the course of a year, he had lost first his wife and then his daughter. Delia's death alone was the kind of outrage that might permanently have unhinged a lesser man. But a child has no way of knowing such things. I was bitterly angry at him for going away. Aunt Josie, though kind and good-hearted, was a virtual stranger to me, and I felt deserted. I had nightmares in which the glass cat slunk out of its place by the hearth and prowled across the countryside. I would hear its hard claws ticking along the floor outside the room where I slept. At those times, half-awake and screaming in the dark, no one could have comforted me except Father.

When he did return, the strain of his suffering showed. His face was thin and weary, and his hair dusted with new gray, as if he had stood outside too long on a frosty night. On the afternoon of his arrival, he sat with me on Aunt Josie's sofa, stroking my cheek while I cuddled gladly, my anger at least temporarily forgotten in the joy of having him back.

His voice, when he spoke, was as tired as his face. "Well, my darling Amy, what do you suppose we should do now?"

"I don't know," I said. I assumed that, as always in the past, he had something entertaining in mind—that he would suggest it, and then we would do it.

He sighed. "Shall we go home?"

I went practically rigid with fear. "Is the cat still there?"

Father looked at me, frowning slightly. "Do we have a cat?"

I nodded. "The big glass one."

He blinked, then made the connection. "Oh, the Chelichev, you mean? Well . . . I suppose it's still there. I hope so, in fact."

I clung to him, scrambling halfway up his shoulders in my panic. I could not manage to speak. All that came out of my mouth was an erratic series of whimpers.

"Shhhh, shhhh," said Father. I hid my face in the starched white cloth of his shirt, and heard him whisper, as if to himself, "How can a glass cat frighten a child who's seen the things you've seen?"

"I hate him! He's glad Delia died. And now he wants to get *me*."

Father hugged me fiercely. "You'll never see him again. I promise you," he said. And it was true, at least as long as he lived.

So the Chelichev *Cat in Glass* was packed away in a box and put into storage with the rest of our furnishings. Father sold the house, and we traveled for two years. When the horror had faded sufficiently, we returned home to begin a new life. Father went back to his professorship, and I to my studies at Chesly Girls' Day School. He bought a new house. The glass cat was not among the items he had sent up from storage. I did not ask him why. I was just as happy to forget about it, and forget it I did.

I neither saw the glass cat nor heard of it again until many years later. I was a grown woman by then, a schoolteacher in a town far from the one in which I'd spent my childhood. I was married to a banker, and had two lovely daughters and even a cat, which I finally permitted in spite of my abhorrence for them, because the girls begged so hard for one. I thought my life was settled, that it would progress smoothly toward a peaceful old age. But this was not to be. The glass cat had other plans.

The chain of events began with Father's death. It happened suddenly, on a snowy afternoon, as he graded papers in the tiny, snug office he had always had on campus. A heart attack, they said. He was found seated at his desk, Erik Satie's Dadaist composition "La Belle Excentrique" still spinning on the turntable of his record player.

I was not at all surprised to discover that he had left his affairs in some disarray. It's not that he had debts or was a gambler. Nothing so serious. It's just that order was slightly contrary to his nature. I remember once, as a very young woman, chiding him for the modest level of chaos he preferred in his life. "Really, Father," I said. "Can't you admire Dadaism without living it?" He laughed and admitted that he didn't seem able to.

As Father's only living relative, I inherited his house and other property, including his personal possessions. There were deeds to be transferred, insurance reports to be filed, bills and loans to be paid. He did have an attorney, an old school friend of his who helped a great deal in organizing the storm of paperwork from a distance. The attorney also arranged for the sale of the house and hired someone to clean it out and ship the contents to us. In the course of the winter, a steady stream of cartons containing everything from scrapbooks to Chinese miniatures arrived at our doorstep. So I thought nothing of it when a large box labeled "fragile" was delivered one day by registered courier. There was a note from the attorney attached, explaining that he had just discovered it in a storage warehouse under Father's name, and had had them ship it to me unopened.

It was a dismal February afternoon, a Friday. I had just come home from teaching. My husband, Stephen, had taken the girls to the mountains for a weekend of skiing, a sport I disliked. I had stayed behind and was looking forward to a couple of days of quiet solitude. The wind drove spittles of rain at the windows as I knelt on the floor of the front room and opened the box. I can't explain to you quite what I felt when I pulled away the packing paper and found myself face-to-face with the glass cat. Something akin to uncovering a nest of cockroaches in a drawer of sachet, I suppose. And that was swiftly followed by a horrid and minutely detailed mental re-creation of Delia's death.

I swallowed my screams, struggling to replace them with something rational. "It's merely a glorified piece of glass." My voice bounced off the walls in the lonely house, hardly comforting.

I had an overpowering image of something inside me, something dark and featureless except for wide white eyes and scrabbling claws. *Get us out of here!* it cried, and I obliged, seizing my coat from the closet hook and stumbling out into the wind.

I ran in the direction of town, slowing only when one of my shoes fell off and I realized how I must look. Soon I found myself seated at a table in a diner, warming my hands in the steam from a cup of coffee, trying to convince myself that I was just being silly. I nursed the coffee as long as I could. It was dusk by the time I felt able to return home. There I found the glass cat, still waiting for me.

I turned on the radio for company and made a fire in the fireplace. Then I sat down before the box and finished unpacking it. The sculpture was as horrible as I remembered, truly ugly and disquieting. I might never have understood why Father kept it if he had not enclosed this letter of explanation, neatly handwritten on his college stationery:

To whom it may concern:

This box contains a sculpture, *Cat in Glass*, designed and executed by the late Alexander Chelichev. Because of Chelichev's standing as a noted forerunner of Dadaism, a historical account of *Cat*'s genesis may be of interest to scholars.

I purchased *Cat* from the artist himself at his Zurich loft in December 1915, two months before the violent rampage that resulted in his confinement in a hospital for the criminally insane, and well before his artistic importance was widely recognized. (For the record, the asking price was forty-eight Swiss francs, plus a good meal with wine.) It is known that Chelichev had a wife and two children elsewhere in the city at that time, though he lived with them only sporadically. The following is the artist's statement about *Cat in Glass*, transcribed as accurately as possible from a conversation we held during dinner.

"I have struggled with the Devil all my life. He wants no rules. No order. His presence is everywhere in my work. I was beaten as a child, and when I became strong enough, I killed my father for it. I see you are skeptical, but it is true. Now I am a grown man, and I find my father in myself. I have a wife and children, but I spend little time with them because I fear the father-devil in me. I do not beat my children. Instead, I make this cat. Into the glass I have poured this madness of mine. Better there than in the eyes of my daughters."

It is my belief that *Cat in Glass* was Chelichev's last finished creation.

Sincerely,
Lawrence Waters
Professor of Art History

I closed the box, sealed it with the note inside, and spent the next two nights in a hotel, pacing the floor, sleeping little. The following Monday, Stephen took the cat to an art dealer for appraisal. He came home late that afternoon excited and full of news about the great Alexander Chelichev.

He made himself a gin and tonic as he expounded. "That glass cat is priceless, Amy. Did you realize? If your father had sold it, he'd have been independently wealthy. He never let on."

I was putting dinner on the table. The weekend had been a terrible strain. This had been a difficult day on top of it—snowy, and the children in my school class were wild with pent-up energy. So were our daughters, Eleanor and Rose, aged seven and four, respectively. I could hear them quarreling in the playroom down the hall.

"Well, I'm glad to hear the horrid thing is worth something," I said. "Why don't we sell it and hire a maid?"

Stephen laughed as if I'd made an incredibly good joke. "A maid? You could hire a thousand maids for what that cat would bring at auction. It's a fascinating piece with an extraordinary history. You know, the value of something like this will increase with time. I think we'll do well to keep it awhile."

My fingers grew suddenly icy on the hot rim of the potato bowl. "I wasn't trying to be funny, Stephen. It's ugly and disgusting. If I could, I would make it disappear from the face of the earth."

He raised his eyebrows. "What's this? Rebellion? Look, if you really want a maid, I'll get you one."

"That's not the point. I won't have the damned thing in my house."

"I'd rather you didn't swear, Amelia. The children might hear."

"I don't care if they do."

The whole thing degenerated from there. I tried to explain the cat's connection with Delia's death. But Stephen had stopped listening by then. He sulked through dinner. Eleanor and Rose argued over who got which spoonful of peas. And I struggled with a steadily growing sense of dread that seemed much too large for the facts of the matter.

When dinner was over, Stephen announced with exaggerated brightness, "Girls. We'd like your help in deciding an important question."

"Oh goody," said Rose.

"What is it?" said Eleanor.

"Please don't," I said. It was all I could do to keep from shouting.

Stephen flashed me the boyish grin with which he had originally won my heart. "Oh, come on. Try to look at it objectively. You're just sensitive about this because of an irrational notion from your childhood. Let the girls be the judge. If they like it, why not keep it?"

I should have ended it there. I should have insisted. Hindsight is always perfect, as they say. But inside me a little seed of doubt had sprouted. Stephen was always so logical and so right, especially about financial matters. Maybe he was right about this, too.

He had brought the thing home from the appraiser without telling me. He was never above a little subterfuge if it got him his own way. Now he carried the carton in from the garage and unwrapped it in the middle of our warm hardwood floor with all the lights blazing. Nothing had changed. I found it as frightening as ever. I could feel cold sweat collecting on my forehead as I stared at it, all aglitter in a rainbow of refracted lamplight.

Eleanor was enthralled with it. She caught our real cat, a calico named Jelly, and held it up to the sculpture. "See, Jelly? You've got a handsome partner now." But Jelly twisted and hissed in Eleanor's arms until she let her go. Eleanor laughed and said Jelly was jealous.

Rose was almost as uncooperative as Jelly. She shrank away from the glass cat, peeking at it from between her father's knees. But Stephen would have none of that.

"Go on, Rose," he said. "It's just a kitty made of glass. Touch it and see." And he took her by the shoulders and pushed her gently toward it. She put out one hand, hesitantly, as she would have with a live cat who did not know her. I saw her finger touch a nodule of glass shards that might have been its nose. She drew back with a little yelp of pain. And that's how it began. So innocently.

"He bit me!" she cried.

"What happened?" said Stephen. "Did you break it?" He ran to the sculpture first, the brute, to make sure she hadn't damaged it.

She held her finger out to me. There was a tiny cut with a single drop of bright red blood oozing from it. "Mommy, it burns, it burns." She was no longer just crying. She was screaming.

We took her into the bathroom. Stephen held her while I washed the cut and pressed a cold cloth to it. The bleeding stopped in a moment, but still she screamed. Stephen grew angry. "What's this nonsense? It's a scratch. Just a scratch."

Rose jerked and kicked and bellowed. In Stephen's defense, I tell you now it was a terrifying sight, and he was never able to deal well with real fear, especially in himself. He always tried to mask it with anger. We had a neighbor who was a physician. "If you don't stop it, Rose, I'll call Dr. Pepperman. Is that what you want?" he said, as if Dr. Pepperman, a jolly septuagenarian, were anything but charming and gentle, as if threats were anything but asinine at such a time.

"For God's sake, get Pepperman! Can't you see something's terribly wrong?" I said.

And for once he listened to me. He grabbed Eleanor by the arm. "Come with me," he said, and stomped across the yard through the snow without so much as a coat. I believe he took Eleanor, also without a coat, only because he was so unnerved that he didn't want to face the darkness alone.

Rose was still screaming when Dr. Pepperman arrived fresh from his dinner, specks of gravy clinging to his mustache. He examined Rose's finger, and looked mildly puzzled when he had finished. "Can't see much wrong here. I'd say it's mostly a case of hysteria." He took a vial and a syringe from his small brown case and gave Rose an injection, ". . . to help settle her down," he said. It seemed to work. In a few minutes, Rose's screams had diminished to whimpers. Pepperman swabbed her finger with disinfectant and wrapped it loosely in gauze. "There, Rosie. Nothing like a bandage to make it feel better." He winked at us. "She should be fine in the morning. Take the gauze off as soon as she'll let you."

We put Rose to bed and sat with her till she fell asleep. Stephen unwrapped the gauze from her finger so the healing air could get to it. The cut was a bit red, but looked all right. Then we retired as well, reassured by the doctor, still mystified at Rose's reaction.

I awakened sometime after midnight. The house was muffled in the kind of silence brought by steady, soft snowfall. I thought I had heard a sound. Something odd. A scream? A groan? A snarl? Stephen still slept on the verge of a snore; whatever it was, it hadn't been loud enough to disturb him.

I crept out of bed and fumbled with my robe. There was a short flight of stairs between our room and the rooms where Rose and Eleanor slept. Eleanor, like her father, often snored at night, and I could hear her from the hallway now, probably deep in dreams. Rose's room was silent.

I went in and switched on the night-light. The bulb was very low wattage. I thought at first that the shadows were playing tricks on me. Rose's hand and arm looked black as a bruised banana. There was a peculiar odor in the air, like the smell of a butcher shop on a summer day. Heart galloping, I turned on the overhead light. Poor Rosie. She was so very still and clammy. And her arm was so very rotten.

They said Rose died from blood poisoning—a rare type most often associated with animal bites. I told them over and over again that it fit, that our child had indeed been bitten, by a cat, a most evil glass cat. Stephen was embarrassed. His own theory was that, far from blaming an apparently inanimate object, we ought to be suing

Pepperman for malpractice. The doctors patted me sympathetically at first. Delusions brought on by grief, they said. It would pass. I would heal in time.

I made Stephen take the cat away. He said he would sell it, though in fact he lied to me. And we buried Rose. But I could not sleep. I paced the house each night, afraid to close my eyes because the cat was always there, glaring his satisfied glare, and waiting for new meat. And in the daytime, everything reminded me of Rosie. Fingerprints on the woodwork, the contents of the kitchen drawers, her favorite foods on the shelves of grocery stores. I could not teach. Every child had Rosie's face and Rosie's voice. Stephen and Eleanor were first kind, then gruff, then angry.

One morning I could find no reason to get dressed or to move from my place on the sofa. Stephen shouted at me, told me I was ridiculous, asked me if I had forgotten that I still had a daughter left who needed me. But, you see, I no longer believed that I or anyone else could make any difference in the world. Stephen and Eleanor would get along with or without me. I didn't matter. These was no God of order and cause. Only chaos, cruelty, and whim.

When it was clear to Stephen that his dear wife Amy had turned from an asset into a liability, he sent me to an institution, far away from everyone, where I could safely be forgotten. In time, I grew to like it there. I had no responsibilities at all. And if there was foulness and bedlam, it was no worse than the outside world.

There came a day, however, when they dressed me in a suit of new clothes and stood me outside the big glass and metal doors to wait; they didn't say for what. The air smelled good. It was springtime, and there were dandelions sprinkled like drops of fresh yellow paint across the lawn.

A car drove up, and a pretty young woman got out and took me by the arm.

"Hello, Mother," she said as we drove off down the road.

It was Eleanor, all grown up. For the first time since Rosie died, I wondered how long I had been away, and knew it must have been a very long while.

We drove a considerable distance, to a large suburban house, white, with a sprawling yard and a garage big enough for two cars. It was a mansion compared to the house in which Stephen and I had raised her. By way of making polite small talk, I asked if she were married, whether she had children. She climbed out of the car looking irritated. "Of course I'm married," she said. "You've met Jason. And you've seen pictures of Sarah and Elizabeth often enough." Of this I had no recollection.

She opened the gate in the picket fence, and we started up the neat stone walkway. The front door opened a few inches and small faces peered out. The door opened wider and two little girls ran onto the porch.

"Hello," I said. "And who are you?"

The older one, giggling behind her hand, said, "Don't you know, Grandma? I'm Sarah."

The younger girl stayed silent, staring at me with frank curiosity.

"That's Elizabeth. She's afraid of you," said Sarah.

I bent and looked into Elizabeth's eyes. They were brown and her hair was shining blonde, like Rosie's. "No need to be afraid of me, my dear. I'm just a harmless old woman."

Elizabeth frowned. "Are you crazy?" she asked.

Sarah giggled behind her hand again, and Eleanor breathed loudly through her nose as if this impertinence were simply overwhelming.

I smiled. I liked Elizabeth. Liked her very much. "They say I am," I said, "and it may very well be true."

A tiny smile crossed her face. She stretched on her tiptoes and kissed my cheek, hardly more than the touch of a warm breeze, then turned and ran away. Sarah followed her, and I watched them go, my heart dancing and shivering. I had loved no one in a very long time. I missed it, but dreaded it, too. For I had loved Delia and Rosie, and they were both dead.

The first thing I saw when I entered the house was Chelichev's *Cat in Glass*, glaring evilly from a place of obvious honor on a low pedestal near the sofa. My stomach felt suddenly shrunken.

"Where did you get that?" I said.

Eleanor looked irritated again. "From Daddy, of course."

"Stephen promised me he would sell it!"

"Well, I guess he didn't, did he?"

Anger heightened my pulse. "Where is he? I want to speak to him immediately."

"Mother, don't be absurd. He's been dead for ten years."

I lowered myself into a chair. I was shaking by then, and I fancied I saw a half-smile on the glass cat's cold jowls.

"Get me out of here," I said. A great weight crushed my lungs. I could barely breathe.

With a look, I must say, of genuine worry, Eleanor escorted me onto the porch and brought me a tumbler of ice water.

"Better?" she asked.

I breathed deeply. "A little. Eleanor, don't you realize that monstrosity killed your sister, and mine as well?"

"That simply isn't true."

"But it is, it is! I'm telling you now, get rid of it if you care for the lives of your children."

Eleanor went pale, whether from rage or fear I could not tell. "It isn't yours. You're legally incompetent, and I'll thank you to stay out of my affairs as much as possible till you have a place of your own. I'll move you to an apartment as soon as I can find one."

"An apartment? But I can't. . . ."

"Yes, you can. You're as well as you're ever going to be, Mother. You liked that hospital only because it was easy. Well, it costs a lot of money to keep you there, and we can't afford it anymore. You're just going to have to straighten up and start behaving like a human being again."

By then I was very close to tears, and very confused as well. Only one thing was clear to me, and that was the true nature of the glass cat. I said, in as steady a voice as I could muster, "Listen to me. That cat was made out of madness. It's evil. If you have s single ounce of brains, you'll put it up for auction this very afternoon."

"So I can get enough money to send you back to the hospital, I suppose? Well, I won't do it. That sculpture is priceless. The longer we keep it, the more it's worth."

She had Stephen's financial mind. I would never sway her, and I knew it. I wept in despair, hiding my face in my hands. I was thinking of Elizabeth. The sweet, soft skin of her little arms, the flame in her cheeks, the power of that small kiss. Human beings are such frail works of art, their lives so precarious, and here I was again, my wayward heart gone out to one of them. But the road back to the safety of isolation lay in ruins. The only way out was through.

Jason came home at dinnertime, and we ate a nice meal, seated around the sleek rosewood table in the dining room. He was kind, actually far kinder than Eleanor. He asked the children about their day and listened carefully while they replied. As did I, enraptured by their pink perfection, distraught at the memory of how imperfect a child's flesh can become. He did not interrupt. He did not demand. When Eleanor refused to give me coffee—she said she was afraid it would get me "hyped up"—he admonished her and poured me a cup himself. We talked about my father, whom he knew by reputation, and about art and the cities of Europe. All the while I felt in my bones the baleful gaze of the *Cat in Glass*, burning like the coldest ice through walls and furniture as if they did not exist.

Eleanor made up a cot for me in the guest room. She didn't want me to sleep in the bed, and she wouldn't tell me why. But I overheard Jason arguing with her about it. "What's wrong with the bed?" he said.

"She's mentally ill," said Eleanor. She was whispering, but loudly. "Heaven only knows what filthy habits she's picked up. I won't risk her soiling a perfectly good mattress. If she does well on the cot for a few nights, then we can consider moving her to the bed."

They thought I was in the bathroom, performing whatever unspeakable acts it is that mentally ill people perform in places like that, I suppose. But they were wrong. I was sneaking past their door, on my way to the garage. Jason must have been quite a handyman in his spare time. I found a large selection of hammers on the wall, including an excellent short-handled sledge. I hid it under my bedding. They never even noticed.

The children came in and kissed me good night in a surreal reversal of roles. I lay in the dark on my cot for a long time, thinking of them, especially Elizabeth, the youngest and weakest, who would naturally be the most likely target of an animal's attack. I dozed, dreaming sometimes of a smiling Elizabeth-Rose-Delia, sifting snow, wading through drifts; sometimes of the glass cat, its fierce eyes smoldering, crystalline tongue brushing crystalline jaws. The night was well along when the dreams crashed down like broken mirrors into silence.

The house was quiet except for those ticks and thumps all houses make as they cool in the darkness. I got up and slid the hammer out from under the bedding, not even sure what I was going to do with it, knowing only that the time had come to act.

I crept out to the front room, where the cat sat waiting, as I knew it must. Moonlight gleamed in the chaos of its glass fur. I could feel its power, almost *see* it, a shimmering red aura the length of its malformed spine. The thing was moving, slowly, slowly, smiling now, oh yes, a real smile. I could smell its rotten breath.

For an instant I was frozen. Then I remembered the hammer,

Jason's lovely short-handled sledge. And I raised it over my head, and brought it down in the first crashing blow.

The sound was wonderful. Better than cymbals, better even than holy trumpets. I was trembling all over, but I went on and on in an agony of satisfaction while glass fell like moonlit rain. There were screams. "Grandma, stop! Stop!" I swung the hammer back in the first part of another arc, heard something like the thunk of a fallen ripe melon, swung it down on the cat again. I couldn't see anymore. It came to me that there was glass in my eyes and blood in my mouth. But none of that mattered, a small price to pay for the long-overdue demise of Chelichev's *Cat in Glass*.

So you see how I have come to this, not without many sacrifices along the way. And now the last of all: the sockets where my eyes used to be are infected. They stink. Blood poisoning, I'm sure.

I wouldn't expect Eleanor to forgive me for ruining her prime investment. But I hoped Jason might bring the children a time or two anyway. No word except for the delivery of a single rose yesterday. The matron said it was white, and held it up for me to sniff, and she read me the card that came with it. "Elizabeth was a great one for forgiving. She would have wanted you to have this. Sleep well, Jason."

Which puzzled me.

"You don't even know what you've done, do you?" said the matron.

"I destroyed a valuable work of art," said I.

But she made no reply.

# BRUCE McALLISTER
## The Girl Who Loved Animals

They had her on the seventeenth floor in their new hi-security unit on Figueroa and weren't going to let me up.

Captain Mendoza, the one who thinks I'm the ugliest woman he's ever laid eyes on and somehow manages to take it personally, was up there with her, and no one else was allowed. Or so this young lieutenant with a fresh academy tattoo on his left thumb tries to tell me. I get up real close so that kid can hear me over the screaming media crowd in the lobby and see this infamous face of mine, and I tell him I don't think Chief Stracher will like getting a call at 0200 hours just because some desk cadet can't tell a privileged soc worker from a media rep, and how good friends really shouldn't bother each other at that time of the day anyway, am I right? It's a lie, sure, but he looks worried, and I remember why I haven't had anything done about the face I was born with. He gives me two escorts—a sleek young swatter with an infrared Ruger, and a lady in fatigues who's almost as tall as I am—and up we go. They're efficient kids. They frisk me in the elevator.

Mendoza wasn't with her. Two P.D. medics with side arms were. The girl was sitting on a sensor cot in the middle of their new glass observation room—closed-air, anti-ballistic Plexi, and the rest—and was a mess. The video footage, which four million people had seen at ten, hadn't been pixeled at all.

Their hi-sec floor cost them thirty-three million dollars, I told myself, took them three years of legislation to get, and had everything you'd ever want to keep your witness or assassin or jihad dignitary alive—CCTV, microwave eyes, pressure mats, blast doors, laser blinds, eight different kinds of gas, and, of course, Vulcan minicannons from the helipad three floors up.

I knew that Mendoza would have preferred someone more exciting than a twenty-year-old girl with a V Rating of nine point six and something strange growing inside her, but he was going to have to settle for this christening.

I asked the medics to let me in. They told me to talk into their wall grid so the new computer could hear me. The computer said something like "Yeah, she's okay," and they opened the door and frisked me again.

I asked them to leave, citing Welfare & Institutions Statute Thirty-eight. They wouldn't, citing hi-sec orders under Penal Code Seven-A. I told them to go find Mendoza and tell him I wanted privacy for the official interview.

Very nicely they said that neither of them could leave and that if I kept asking I could be held for obstruction, despite the same statute's cooperation clause. That sounded right to me. I smiled and got to work.

Her name was Lissy Tomer. She was twenty-one, not twenty. According to Records, she'd been born in the east Valley, been abused as a child by both sets of parents, and, as the old story goes, hooked up with a man who would oblige her the same way. What had kept County out of her life, I knew, was the fact that early on, someone in W&I had set her up with an easy spousal-abuse complaint and felony restraining-order option that needed only a phone call to trigger. But she'd never exercised it, though the older bruises said she should have.

She was pale and underweight and wouldn't have looked very good even without the contusions, the bloody nose and lip, the belly, and the shivering. The bloody clothes didn't help either. Neither did the wires and contact gel they had all over her for their beautiful new cot.

But there was a fragility to her—princess-in-the-fairy-tale kind— that almost made her pretty.

She flinched when I said hello, just as if I'd hit her. I wondered which had been worse—the beating or the media. He'd done it in a park and had been screaming at her when Mendoza's finest arrived, and two uniforms had picked up a couple of C's by calling it in to the networks.

She was going to get hit with a beautiful posttraumatic stress disorder sometime down the road even if things didn't get worse for
her—which they would. The press wanted her badly. She was bloody,
showing, and *very* visual.

"Has the fetus been checked?" I asked the side arms. If they were
going to listen, they could help.

The shorter one said yes, a portable sonogram from County, and
the baby looked okay.

I turned back to the girl. She was looking up at me from the cot,
looking hopeful, and I couldn't for the life of me imagine what she
thought I could do for her.

"I'm your new V.R. advocate, Lissy."

She nodded, keeping her hands in her lap like a good girl.

"I'm going to ask you some questions, if that's all right. The more
I know, the more help I can be, Lissy. But you know that, don't you."
I grinned.

She nodded again and smiled, but the lip hurt.

I identified myself, badge and department and appellation, then
read her her rights under Protective Services provisions, as amended—
what we in the trade call the Nhat Hanh Act. What you get and what
you don't.

"First question, Lissy: Why'd you do it?" I asked it as gently as I
could, flicking the hand recorder on. It was the law.

I wondered if she knew what a law was.

Her I.Q. was eighty-four, congenital, and she was a Collins
psycho-type, class three dependent. She'd had six years of school and
had once worked for five months for a custodial service in Monterey
Park. Her Vulnerability Rating, all factors factored, was a whopping
nine point six. It was the rating that had gotten her a felony restraint
complaint option on the marital bond, and County had assumed that
was enough to protect her . . . from him.

As far as the provisions on low-I.Q. cases went, the husband had
been fixed, she had a second-degree dependency on him, and an abortion in event of rape by another was standard. As far as County was
concerned, she was protected, and society had exercised proper conscience. I really couldn't blame her last V.R. advocate. I'd have
assumed the same.

And missed one thing.

"I like animals a lot," she said, and it made her smile. In the middle of a glass room, two armed medics beside her, the media screaming downstairs to get at her, her husband somewhere wishing he'd killed her, it was the one thing that could make her smile.

She told me about a kitten she'd once had at the housing project on Crenshaw. She'd named it Lissy and had kept it alive "all by herself." It was her job, she said, like her mother and fathers had jobs. Her second stepfather—or was it her mother's brother? I couldn't tell, and it didn't matter—had taken it away one day, but she'd had it for a month or two.

When she started living with the man who'd eventually beat her up in a park for the ten o'clock news, he let her have a little dog. He would have killed it out of jealousy in the end, but it died because she didn't know about shots. He wouldn't have paid for them anyway, and she seemed to know that. He hadn't been like that when they first met. It sounded like neurotransmitter blocks, MPHG metabolism. The new bromaine that was on the streets would do it; all the fentanyl analogs would, too. There were a dozen substances on the street that would. You saw it all the time.

She told me how she'd slept with the kitten and the little dog and, when she didn't have them anymore, with the two or three toys she'd had so long that most of their fur was worn off. How she could smell the kitten for months in her room just as if it were still there. How the dog had died in the shower. How her husband had gotten mad, hit her, and taken the thing away. But you could tell she was glad when the body wasn't there in the shower anymore.

"This man was watching me in the park," she said. "He always watched me."

"Why were you in the park, Lissy?"

She looked at me out of the corner of her eye and gave me a smile, the conspiratorial kind. "There's more than one squirrel in those trees. Maybe a whole family. I like to watch them."

I was surprised there were any animals at all in the park. You don't see them anymore, except for the domesticates.

"Did you talk to this man?"

She seemed to know what I was asking. She said, "I wasn't scared of him. He smiled a lot." She laughed at something, and we all jumped. "I knew he wanted to talk to me, so I pretended there was a squirrel over by him, and I fed it. He said, Did I like animals and how I could make a lot of money and help the animals of the world."

It wasn't important. A dollar. A thousand. But I had to ask.

"How much money did he tell you?"

"Nine thousand dollars. That's how much I'm going to get, and I'll be able to see it when it's born, and visit it."

She told me how they entered her, how they did it gently while she watched, the instrument clean and bright.

The fertilized egg would affix to the wall of her uterus, they'd told her, and together they would make a placenta. What the fetus needed nutritionally would pass through the placental barrier, and her body wouldn't reject it.

Her eyes looked worried now. She was remembering things—a beating, men in uniforms with guns, a man with a microphone pushed against her belly. *Had her husband hit her there? If so, how many times?* I wondered.

"Will the baby be okay?" she asked, and I realized I'd never seen eyes so colorless, a face so trusting.

"That's what the doctors say," I said, looking up at the side arms, putting it on them.

Nine thousand. More than a man like her husband would ever see stacked in his life, but he'd beaten her anyway, furious that she could get it in her own way when he'd failed again and again, furious that she'd managed to get it with the one thing he thought he owned— her body.

Paranoid somatopaths are that way.

I ought to know. I married one.

I'm thinking of the mess we've made of it, Lissy. I'm thinking of the three hundred thousand grown children of the walking wounded of an old war in Asia who walk the same way.

I'm thinking of the four hundred thousand walljackers, our living dead. I'm thinking of the zoos, the ones we don't have anymore, and what they must have been like, what little girls like Lissy Tomer must have done there on summer days.

I'm thinking of a father who went to war, came back, but was never the same again, of a mother who somehow carried us all, of how cars and smog and cement can make a childhood and leave you thinking you can change it all.

I wasn't sure, but I could guess. The man in the park was a body broker for pharmaceuticals and nonprofits, and behind him somewhere was a species resurrection group that somehow had the money. He'd gotten a hefty three hundred percent, which meant the investment was already thirty-six grand. He'd spent some of his twenty-seven paying off a few W&I people in the biggest counties, gotten a couple dozen names on high-V.R. searches, watched the best bets himself, and finally made his selection.

The group behind him didn't know how such things worked or didn't particularly care; they simply wanted consenting women of childbearing age, good health, no substance abuse, no walljackers, no suicidal inclinations; and the broker's reputation was good, and he did his job.

Somehow he'd missed the husband.

As I found out later, she was one of ten. Surrogates for human babies were a dime a dozen, had been for years. This was something else.

In a nation of two hundred eighty million, Lissy Tomer was one of ten—but in her heart of hearts she was the only one. Because a man who said he loved animals had talked to her in a park once. Because he'd said she would get a lot of money—money that ought to make a husband who was never happy, happy. Because she would get to see it when it was born and get to visit it wherever it was kept.

The odd thing was, I could understand how she felt.

I called Antalou at three a.m., got her mad but at least awake, and got her to agree we should try to get the girl out that same night—out of that room, away from the press, and into a County unit for a complete fetal check. Antalou is the kind of boss you only get in heaven. She tried, but Mendoza stonewalled her under P.C. Twenty-two, the Jorgenson clause—he was getting all the publicity he and his new unit needed with the press screaming downstairs—and we gave up at five, and I went home for a couple hours of sleep before the paperwork began.

I knew that sitting there in the middle of all that glass with two armed medics was almost as bad as the press, but what could I do, Lissy, what could I do?

I should have gone to the hotel room that night, but the apartment was closer. I slept on the sofa. I didn't look at the bedroom door, which is always locked from the outside. The nurse has a key. Some days it's easier not to think about what's in there. Some days it's harder.

I thought about daughters.

★　　★　　★

We got her checked again, this time at County Medical, and the word came back okay. Echomytic bruises with some placental bleeding, but the fetal signs were fine. I went ahead and asked whether the fetus was a threat to the mother in any case, and they laughed. No more than any human child would be, they said. All you're doing is borrowing the womb, they said. "Sure," this cocky young resident says to me, "it's low-tech all the way." I had a lot of homework to do, I realized.

Security at the hospital reported a visit by a man who was not her husband, and they didn't let him through. The same man called me an hour later. He was all smiles and wore a suit.

I told him we'd have to abort if County, under the Victims' Rights Act, decided it was best or the girl wanted it. He pointed out with a smile that the thing she was carrying was worth a lot of money to the people he represented, and they could make her life more comfortable, and we ought to protect the girl's interests.

I told him what I thought of him, and he laughed. "You've got it all wrong, Doctor."

I let it pass. He knows I'm an MPS-V.R., no PhD., no M.D. He probably even knows I got the degree under duress, years late, because Antalou said we needed all the paper we could get if the department was going to survive. I know what he's doing, and he knows I know.

"The people I represent are caring people, Doctor. Their cause is a good one. They're not what you're accustomed to working with, and they've retained me simply as a program consultant, a 'resource locator.' It's all aboveboard, Doctor, completely legal, I assure you. But I really don't need to tell you any of this, do I?"

"No, you don't."

I added that, legal or not, if he tried to see her again I would have him for harassment under the D.A.'s cooperation clause.

He laughed, and I knew then he had a law degree from one of the local universities. The suit was right. I could imagine him in it at the park that day.

"You may be able to pull that with the mopes and 5150's you work with on the street, Doctor, but I know the law. I'll make you a deal. I'll stay away for the next three months, as long as you look after the girl's best interests, how's that?"

I knew there was more, so I waited.

"My people will go on paying for weekly visits up to the eighth month, then daily through to term, the clinic to be designated by them.

They want ultrasound, CVS, and amniotic antiabort treatments, and the diet and abstinence programs the girl's already agreed to. All you have to do is get her to her appointments, and we pay for it. Save the county some money."

I waited.

His voice changed as I'd known it would. The way they do in the courtrooms. I'd heard it change like that a hundred times before, years of it, both sides of the aisle.

"If County can't oblige," he said, "we'll just have to try Forty-A, right?"

I told him to take a flying something.

Maybe I didn't know the law, but I knew Forty-A. In certain circles it's known simply as Fucker-Forty. Under it—the state's own legislation—he'd be able to sue the county and this V.R. advocate in particular for loss of livelihood—his and hers—and probably win after appeals.

This was the last thing Antalou or any of us needed.

The guy was still smiling.

"You've kept that face for a reason, Doctor. What do young girls think of it?"

I hung up on him.

With Antalou's help I got her into the Huntington on Normandy, a maternal unit for sedated Ward B types. Some of the other women had seen her on the news two evenings before; some hadn't. *It didn't matter*, I thought. *It was about as good a place for her to hide as possible*, I told myself. I was wrong. Everything's on computer these days, and some information's as cheap as a needle.

I get a call the next morning from the unit saying a man had gotten in and tried to kill her, and she was gone.

I'm thinking of the ones I've lost, Lissy. The tenth-generation maggot casings on the one in Koreatown, the door locked for days. The one named Consejo, the one I went with to the morgue, where they cut up babies, looking for hers. The skinny one I thought I'd saved, the way I was supposed to, but he's lying in a pool of O-positive in a room covered with the beautiful pink dust they used for prints.

Or the ones when I was a kid, East L.A., Fontana, the drugs taking them like some big machine, the snipings that always killed the ones that had nothing to do with it—the chubby ones, the ones who liked to read—the man who took Karenna and wasn't gentle, the uncle who killed his own nephews and blamed it on coyotes, which weren't there anymore, hadn't been for years.

I'm thinking of the ones I've lost, Lissy.

I looked for her all day, glad to be out of the apartment, glad to be away from a phone that might ring with a slick lawyer's face on it.

When I went back to the apartment that night to pick up another change of clothes for the hotel room, she was sitting cross-legged by the door.

"Lissy," I said, wondering how she'd gotten the address.

"I'm sorry," she said.

She had her hand on her belly, holding it not out of pain but as if it were the most comforting thing in the world.

"He wants to kill me. He says that anybody who has an animal growing in her is a devil and's got to die. He fell down the stairs. I didn't push him, I didn't."

She was crying, and the only thing I could think to do was get down and put my arms around her and try not to cry myself.

"I know, I know," I said. The symptoms were like Parkinson's. I remembered. You tripped easily.

I wasn't thinking clearly. I hadn't had more than two or three hours of sleep for three nights running, and all I could think of was getting us both inside, away from the steps, the world.

Maybe it was fatigue. Or maybe something else. I should have gotten her to a hospital. I should have called Mendoza for an escort back to his unit. What I did was get her some clothes from the bedroom, keep my eyes on the rug while I was in there, and lock the door again when I came out. She didn't ask why neither of us were going to sleep in the bedroom. She didn't ask about the lock. She just held her belly, and smiled like some Madonna.

I took two Dalmanes from the medicine cabinet, thinking they might be enough to get the pictures of what was in that room out of my head.

I don't know whether they did or not. Lissy was beside me, her shoulder pressing against me, as I got the futon and the sofa ready.

Her stomach growled, and we laughed. I said, "Who's growling? Who's growling?" and we laughed again. I asked her if she was hungry and if she could eat sandwiches. She laughed again, and I got her a fresh one from the kitchen.

She took the futon, lying on her side to keep the weight off. I took the sofa because of my long legs.

I felt something beside me in the dark. She kissed me, said "Goodnight," and I heard her nightgown whisper back into the darkness. I held it in for a while and then couldn't anymore. It didn't last long. Dalmane's a knockout.

The next day I took her to the designated clinic and waited outside for her. She was happy. The big amnio needle they stuck her with didn't bother her, she said. She liked how much bigger her breasts were, she said, like a mother's should be. She didn't mind being careful about what she ate and drank. She even liked the strange V of hair growing on her abdomen, because—because it was hairy, she said, just like the thing inside her. She liked how she felt, and she wanted to know if I could see it, the glow, the one expectant mothers are supposed to have. I told her I could.

I'm thinking of a ten-year-old, the one that used to tag along with me on the median train every Saturday when I went in for caseloads while most mothers had their faces changed, or played, or mothered. We talked a lot back then, and I miss it. She wasn't going to need a lot of work on that face, I knew—maybe the ears, just a little, if she was picky. She'd gotten her father's genes. But she talked like me—like a kid from East L.A.—tough, with a smile, and I thought she was going to end up a D.A. or a showy defense type or at least an exec. That's how stupid we get. In four years she was into molecular opiates and trillazines, and whose fault was that? The top brokers roll over two billion a year in this city alone; the local *capi* net a twentieth of that, their street dealers a fourth; and God knows what the guys in the labs bring home to their families.

It's six years later, and I hear her letting herself in one morning. She's fumbling and stumbling at the front door. I get up, dreading it. What I see tells me that the drugs are nothing, nothing at all. She's running with a strange group of kids, a lot of them older. *This new thing's a fad,* I tell myself. It's like not having your face fixed—like not getting the nasal ramification modified, the mandibular thrust attended to—when you could do it easily, anytime, and cheaply, just because you want to make a point, and it's fun to goose the ones who need goosing. *That's all she's really doing,* you tell yourself.

You've seen her a couple of times like this, but you still don't recognize her. She's heavy around the chest and shoulders, which makes her breasts seem a lot smaller. Her face is heavy; her eyes are puffy, almost closed. She walks with a limp because something hurts down low. Her shoulders are bare, and they've got tattoos now, the new metallic kind, glittery and painful. She's wearing expensive pants, but they're dirty.

So you have a daughter now who's not a daughter, or she's both, boy and girl. The operation cost four grand, and you don't want to think how she got the money. Everyone's doing it, you tell yourself. But the operation doesn't take. She gets an infection, and the thing stops being fun, and six months later she's got no neurological response to some of the tissues the doctors have slapped on her, and pain in the others. It costs money to reverse. She doesn't have it. She spends it on other things, she says.

She wants money for the operation, she says, standing in front of you. You owe it to her, she says.

You try to find the ten-year-old in those eyes, and you can't.

Did you ever?

The call came through at six, and I knew it was County.

A full jacket—ward status, medical action, all of it—had been put through. The fetus would be aborted—"for the mother's safety . . . to prevent further exploitation by private interests . . . and physical endangerment by spouse."

Had Antalou been there, she'd have told me how County had already gotten flak from the board of supervisors, state W&I, and the attorney general's office over a V.R. like this slipping through and getting this much press. They wanted it over, done with. If the fetus were aborted, County's position would be clear—to state, the feds, and the religious groups that were starting to scream bloody murder.

It would be an abortion no one would ever complain about.

The husband was down at County holding with a pretty fibercast on his left tibia, but they weren't taking any chances. Word on two interstate conspiracies to kill the ten women had reached the D.A., and they were, they said, taking it seriously. I was, I said, glad to hear it.

Mendoza said he liked sassy women as much as the next guy, but he wanted her back in custody, and the new D.A. was screaming jurisdiction, too. Everyone wanted a piece of the ten o'clock news before the cameras lost interest and rolled on.

Society wasn't ready for it. The atavistic fears were there. You could be on trillazines, you could have an operation to be both a boy and a girl for the thrill of it, you could be a walljacker, but a mother like this, no, not yet.

I should have told someone but didn't. I took her to the zoo instead. We stood in front of the cages watching the holograms of the big cats, the tropical birds, the grasseaters of Africa—the ones that are gone. She wasn't interested in the real ones, she said—the pigeons, sparrows, coyotes, the dull hardy ones that will outlast us all. She never came here as a child, she said, and I believe it. A boyfriend at her one and only job took her once, and later, because she asked her to, so did a woman who wanted the same thing from her.

We watched the lions, the ibex, the white bears. We watched the long-legged wolf, the harp seals, the rheas. We watched the tapes stop and repeat, stop and repeat: and then she said, "Let's go," pulled at my hand, and we moved on to the most important cage of all.

There, the hologram walked back and forth looking out at us, looking through us, its red sagittal crest and furrowed brow so convincing. Alive, its name had been Mark Anthony, the plaque said. It had weighed two hundred kilos. It had lived to be ten. It wasn't one of the two whose child was growing inside her, but she seemed to know this, and it didn't matter.

"They all died the same way," she said to me. "That's what counts, Jo." *Inbred depression,* I remembered reading. *Petechial hemorrhages, cirrhosis, renal failure.*

Somewhere in the nation the remaining fertilized ova were sitting frozen in a lab, as they had for thirty years. A few dozen had been removed, thawed, encouraged to divide to sixteen cells, and finally implanted that day seven months ago. Ten had taken. As they should have, naturally, apes that we are. "Sure, it could've been done back then," the cocky young resident with insubordination written all over him had said. "All you'd have needed was an egg and a little plastic tube. And, of course,"—I didn't like the way he smiled—"a woman who was willing. . . ."

I stopped her. I asked her if she knew what The Arks were, and she said no. I started to tell her about the intensive-care zoos where for twenty years the best and brightest of them, ten thousand species in all, had been kept while two hundred thousand others disappeared—the toxics, the new diseases, the land-use policies of a new world taking them one by one—how The Arks hadn't worked, how two thirds of the macrokingdom were gone now, and how the thing she carried inside her was one of them and one of the best.

She wasn't listening. She didn't need to hear it, and I knew the man in the suit had gotten his yes without having to say these things. The idea of having it inside her, hers for a little while, had been enough.

She told me what she was going to buy with the money. She asked me whether I thought the baby would end up at this zoo. I told her I didn't know but could check, and hated the lie. She said she might have to move to another city to be near it. I nodded and didn't say a thing.

I couldn't stand it. I sat her down on a bench and told her what the County was going to do to her.

When I was through she looked at me and said she'd known it would happen, it always happened. She didn't cry. I thought maybe she wanted to leave, but she shook her head.

We went through the zoo one more time. We didn't leave until dark.

"Are you out of your mind, Jo?" Antalou said.

"It's not permanent," I said.

"*Of course* it's not permanent. Everyone's been looking everywhere for her. What the hell do you think you're doing?"

I said it didn't matter, did it? The County homes and units weren't safe, and we didn't want her with Mendoza, and who'd think of a soc worker's house—a P.D. safe house maybe, but not a soc worker's because that's against policy, and everyone knows that soc workers are spineless, right?

"Sure," Antalou said. "But you didn't *tell* anybody, Jo."

"I've had some thinking to do."

Suddenly Antalou got gentle, and I knew what she was thinking. I needed downtime, maybe some psychiatric profiling done. She's a friend of mine, but she's a professional, too. The two of us go back all the way to corrections, Antalou and I, and lying isn't easy.

"Get her over to County holding immediately—that's the best we can do for her," she said finally. "And let's have lunch soon, Jo. I want to know what's going on in that head of yours."

$$\star \quad \star \quad \star$$

It took me the night and the morning. They put her in the nicest hold they had and doubled the security, and when I left she cried for a long time, they told me. I didn't want to leave, but I had to get some thinking done.

When it was done, I called Antalou.

She swore at me when I was through but said she'd give it a try. It was crazy, but what isn't these days?

The County bit, but with stipulations. Postpartum wipe. New I.D. Fine, but also a fund set up out of *our* money. Antalou groaned. I said, Why not.

Someone at County had a heart, but it was our mention of Statute Forty-A, I found out later, that cinched it. They saw the thing dragging on through the courts, cameras rolling forever, and that was worse than any temporary heat from state or the feds.

So they let her have the baby. I slept in the waiting room of the maternity unit, and it took local troops as well as hospital security to keep the press away. We used a teaching hospital down south — approved by the group that was funding her—but even then the media found out and came by the droves.

We promised full access at a medically approved moment if they cooled it, which they did. The four that didn't were taken bodily from the building under one penal code section or another.

*At the beginning of the second stage of labor, the infant abruptly rotates from occiput-posterior to right occiput-anterior position; descent is rapid, and a viable two-thousand-gram female is delivered without episiotomy. Interspecific Apgar scores are nine and ten at one and five minutes, respectively.*

The report would sound like all the others I'd read. The only difference would be how the thing looked, and even that wasn't much.

The little head, hairless face, broad nose, black hair sticking up like some old movie comic's. Human eyes, hairless chest, skinny arms. The feet would look like hands, sure, and the skin would be a little gray, but how much was that? To the girl in the bed it wasn't anything at all.

She said she wanted me to be there, and I said sure but didn't know the real reason.

When her water broke, they told me, and I got scrubbed up, put

on the green throw always like they said, and got back to her room
quickly. The contractions had started up like a hammer.

It didn't go smoothly. The cord got hung up on the baby's neck
inside, and the fetal monitor started screaming. She got scared; I got
scared. They put her up on all fours to shift the baby, but it didn't
work. They wheeled her to the O.R. for a C-section, which they
really didn't want to do; and for two hours it was fetal signs getting
better, then worse, doctors preparing for a section, then the signs
somehow getting better again. Epidural block, episiotomy, some con-
certed forceps work, and the little head finally starts to show.

Lissy was exhausted, making little sounds. More deep breaths, a
few encouraging shouts from the doctors, more pushing from Lissy,
and the head was through, then the body, white as a ghost from the
vernix, and someone was saying something to me in a weak voice.

"Will you cut the cord, please?"

It was Lissy.

I couldn't move. She said it again.

The doctor was waiting, the baby slick in his hands. Lissy was
white as a sheet, her forehead shiny with the sweat, and she couldn't
see it from where she was. "It would be special to me, Jo," she said.

One of the nurses was beside me saying how it's done all the
time—by husbands and lovers, sisters and mothers and friends—but
that if I was going to do it I needed to do it now, please.

I tried to remember who had cut the cord when Meg was born,
and I couldn't. I could remember a doctor, that was all.

I don't remember taking the surgical steel snips, but I did. I
remember not wanting to cut it—flesh and blood, the first of its kind in
a long, long time—and when I finally did, it was tough, the cutting
made a noise, and then it was over, the mother had the baby in her
arms, and everyone was smiling.

A woman could have carried a *Gorilla gorilla beringei* to term
without a care in the world a hundred, a thousand, a million years ago.
The placenta would have known what to do; the blood would never
have mixed. The gestation was the same nine months. The only thing
stopping anyone that winter day in '97 when Cleo, the last of her kind
on the face of this earth, died of renal failure in the National Zoo in
DC, was the thought of carrying it.

It had taken three decades, a well-endowed resurrection group, a slick body broker, and a skinny twenty-one-year-old girl who didn't mind the thought of it.

She wants money for the operation, my daughter says to me that day in the doorway, shoulders heavy, face puffy, slurring it, the throat a throat I don't know, the voice deeper. I tell her again I don't have it, that perhaps her friends—the ones she's helped out so often when she had the money and they didn't—could help her. I say it nicely, with no sarcasm, trying not to look at where she hurts, but she knows exactly what I'm saying.

She goes for my eyes, as if she's had practice, and I don't fight back. She gets my cheek and the corner of my eye, screams something about never loving me and me never loving her—which isn't true.

She knows I know how she'll spend the money, and it makes her mad.

I don't remember the ten-year-old ever wanting to get even with anyone, but this one always does. She hurts. She wants to hurt back. If she knew, if she only knew what I'd carry for her.

I'll find her, I know—tonight, tomorrow morning, the next day or two—sitting at a walljack somewhere in the apartment, her body plugged in, the little unit with its Medusa wires sitting in her lap, her heavy shoulders hunched as if she were praying, and I'll unplug her—to show I care.

But she'll have gotten even with me, and that's what counts, and no matter how much I plead with her, promise her anything she wants, she won't try a program, she won't go with me to County—both of us, together—for help.

Her body doesn't hurt at all when she's on the wall. When you're a walljacker you don't care what kind of tissue's hanging off you, you don't care what you look like—what anyone looks like. The universe is inside. The juice is from the wall, the little unit translates, and the right places in your skull—the medulla all the way to the cerebellum, all the right centers—get played like the keys of the most beautiful synthesizer in the world. You see blue skies that make you cry. You see young men and women who make you come in your pants without your even needing to touch them. You see loving mothers. You see fathers that never leave you.

I'll know what to do. I'll flip the circuit breakers and sit in the darkness with a hand light until she comes out of it, cold-turkeying, screaming mad, and I'll say nothing. I'll tell myself once again that it's the drugs, it's the jacking, it's not her. She's dead and gone and hasn't been the little girl on that train with her hair tucked behind her ears for a long time, that this one's a lie but one I've got to keep playing.

So I walk into the bedroom, and she's there, in the chair, like always. She's got clothes on for a change and doesn't smell, and I find myself thinking how neat she looks—chic even. I don't feel a thing.

As I take a step toward the kitchen and the breaker box, I see what she's done.

I see the wires doubling back to the walljack, and I remember hearing about this from someone. It's getting common, a fad.

There are two ways to do it. You can rig it so that anyone who touches you gets ripped with a treble wall dose in a bypass. Or so that anyone who kills the electricity, even touches the wires, kills you.

Both are tamperproof. The M.E. has twenty bodies to prove it, and the guys stuck with the job downtown don't see a breakthrough for months.

She's opted for the second. Because it hurts the most.

She's starving to death in the chair, cells drying out, unless someone I.V.'s her—carefully. Even then the average expectancy is two months, I remember.

I get out. I go to a cheap hotel downtown. I dream about blackouts in big cities and bodies that move but aren't alive and about daughters. The next morning I get a glucose drip into her arm, and I don't need any help with the needle.

That's what's behind the door, Lissy.

We gave them their press conference. The doctors gave her a mild shot of pergisthan to perk her up, since she wouldn't be nursing, and she did it, held the baby in her arms like a pro, smiled though she was pale as a sheet, and the conference lasted two whole hours. Most of the press went away happy, and two of Mendoza's girls roughed up the three that tried to hide out on the floor that night. "Mendoza says hello," they said, grinning.

The floor returned to normal. I went in.

The mother was asleep. The baby was in the incubator. Three nurses were watching over them.

The body broker came with his team two days later and looked happy. Six of his ten babies had made it.

Her name is Mary McLoughlin. I chose it. Her hair is dark, and she wears it short. She lives in Chula Vista, just south of San Diego, and I get down there as often as I can, and we go out.

She doesn't remember a thing, so I was the one who had to suggest it. We go to the zoo, the San Diego Zoo, one of the biggest once. We go to the primates. We stand in front of the new exhibit, and she tells me how the real thing is so much better than the holograms, which she thinks she's seen before but isn't sure.

The baby is a year old now. They've named her Cleo, and they keep her behind glass—two or three vets in gauze masks with her at all times—safe from the air and diseases. But we get to stand there, watching her like the rest, up close, while she looks at us and clowns.

No one recognizes the dark-haired girl I'm with. The other one, the one who'd have good reason to be here, disappeared long ago, the media says. Sometimes the spotlight is just too great, they said.

"I can almost smell her, Jo," she says, remembering a dream, a vague thing, a kitten slept with. "She's not full-grown, you know."

I tell her, yes, I know.

"She's sure funny looking, isn't she."

I nod.

"Hey, I think she knows me!" She says it with a laugh, doesn't know what she's said. "Look at how she's looking at me!"

The creature is looking at her—it's looking at all of us and with eyes that aren't dumb. Looking at us, not through us.

"Can we come back tomorrow, Jo?" she asks when the crowd gets too heavy to see through.

Of course, I say. We'll come a lot, I say.

I've filed for guardianship under Statute Twenty-seven, the old W&I provisions, and if it goes through, Lissy will be moving back to L.A. with me. *I'm hetero, so it won't get kicked for exploitation, and I'm in the right field,* I think. I can't move myself, but we'll go down to the zoo every weekend. It'll be good to get away. Mendoza has asked me out, and who knows, I may say yes.

But I still have to have that lunch with Antalou, and I have no idea what I'm going to tell her.

# KATHE KOJA AND BARRY N. MALZBERG
## Ursus Triad, Later

Now the door, the knob on the door, the small sliver of light dense, concentrated, aiming from the room behind: where the bears nested. The splinters of the floor, the brutal surfaces upon which she had rolled, scrambled, been pawed and lumbered over, half-suffocated between fur and ragged blanket and fear of the splinters, pointed always but always somehow missing puncture: of her eyes, the worn but tender skin beneath; her suffering lips.

Once her perspective had been larger, once—she thought, or believed she had thought—she had seen the house entire, light everywhere: the gleam of glass and porcelain, the glimpse of cages through transparent walls, but that must have been a long time ago or perhaps some trick of perspective, some dull accident of sensibility, for now she could see only that door, that knob, the light, the floor from the position to which she had sunk: the dainty ordnance of paws, the heavy intake of the bears' breath somehow framing conditions without providing illumination. The cages had come open some time ago, were never closed now; the keeper—if there had been a keeper, a jailer, some master who had schooled them (and if so for what extravagant enjoyment, who under God's sun could train animals to purposes like these?)—now fled, the house the bears' alone, she the intruder, she the peeping, curious, external force crushed now to this sullen, sunken wood and the creaking sound of their inhalations as one by one, solemnly, they played with her: over and over, opening her up like a wound, their paws and fur the ancient sutures drawn by that wound, bleached and stanched and then somehow magnified by their with-drawal as one by one, each by each they left on the floor: to gather her own breath and breathing wounds together before another one returned to rend her now anew.

Somehow through all of this she must have eaten, drunk, found a way to eliminate; slid into coma and emerged; there must have been some kind of passage in which the common tasks of consciousness were conducted but she knew—and it was all that she knew—that she had no knowledge of those times, could remember it as little as her initial swim in the womb: it was literally some other life because now every-thing was the bears, the tumbling conjoinment, the snaffle from their muzzles and the cascading, indifferent light which at odd angles swooped over, swooped through her; the dazed and cavernous surfaces of her sensibility sometimes roused briefly by that light, only to plunge again in the tumble and harsh necessity of their breath. She had become emptiness, and they filled her again and again.

Bach, Beethoven, and Brahms: her names for them, her three assailants, masters and dumb slaves as she herself was a slave. Dumb and sullen, beneath or beyond language, but she had to try to assign some meaning to the situation, had given them names to suit what she took to be their personalities in that time before this time when she must have come here, must have had reasons—what were they?—to enter this strange and damaged cloister, this space beyond redemption, to emerge as if from death or fever into the circling stare of the bears: eyes dull and compliant, slow struggle of limbs as they balanced on hind legs, ready to begin the dance anew; and she their silent partner, pink and breathing on the wood.

There was no real communication amongst them; they seemed to her to work within circumscription, intersecting only to bump as one left, another came to snort and root around her stricken body. She had known from the first that appeals, cries, struggles, resistance of any kind would only have attenuated her situation; the animals were beyond command, beyond whatever powers of humanity she had then been still able to summon and so: the splinters: the fur: the paws and the breathy stink. Her agony. Their arabesques. Submitting to them, over and over, submitting to Bach now, the largest of them and the most regular, the most rhythmic, the most metronomic: Bach because this B seemed to believe in order, in a kind of regulation of movement which rattled and thrust in clearly identifiable rhythms, rhythms as solid and inescapable as Bach, Beethoven, and Brahms, as the distorted perspective of this floor, this light, this distance inside and out.

Now Bach yawed and steamed against her, the smell of the beast in her head, on her lips like some dry unguent, his huge body seeking, seeking, humped and breathing, gigue and largo and then subsiding, guiding himself away from her, the turgid genitals of the metronomic bear refracted in the shadows, those shadows already diminishing as Bach moved slowly from her in an odd, abbreviated limp, humping his way into the darkness. The shadows seemed lifeless even in motion, even as she seemed lifeless there on the wood of the floor.

In this silence, in this momentary partition, she thought she might be spared for a while, that Bach had now had his ceremonial fill and that Beethoven and Brahms were in the upper room, casting circles of darkness, silent beyond bearish grunts and small explosions of fathomless feeling, but even as she turned in this moment's relief, moved to gather the ragged blankets, to press that sleeve of insubstantial protection against herself, she felt them eased from her grasp and then Brahms, a huge, sordid mass was settling himself against her. Brahms: the autumnal bear, the bear of sneezes and sighs and small, absent groans, passion expended, fallen desire and she, too, groaned with the futility, the hopelessness of the bear's attributed despair as on her stomach he cast circles with a paw, then clumsy in wintry desire straddled her at last. Sinking slightly beneath the bear, resigned to assist as much as possible; unlike the others Brahms seemed to her to appreciate some kind of gesture, to have a sense of her presence and collaboration whereas the others, so locked into their own spasms and black rhythms, gave no sense of recognition or response at all. Snorts, sighs, the press of fur against her as she raised her hands, grasped the bear to draw him to a kind of crooning concentration as deep underneath the fur the small shudders, foreshadowed expenditure and then the bear's yelp, a human sound, a high, girlish shriek as he rolled away from her to lie, streaked by light, a wheezing heap: damp fur, sweat, soot, and for her again that dim shudder within her thighs, sensibility risen and draining from her just as she had drained from this house that which she had found before her.

She must have found something before her, must have been outside this house at one time, brought into it by accident of desire or curiosity now denied recollection: there was a past beyond and before this house, that smell, those shudders creeping like insects up and down her helpless legs, thighs, spread and spraddled, and she would have wept, great groaning tears against the wood, wood pressed to her lips, splinters like the wafer of God himself between her teeth, but here there was if not godlessness then the orbit of no salvation, here was the constellation, the great cross of heat, sour stink, black upon black upon fur upon flesh; nothing and everything, here in this room. Reeking, aseptic cavern, drawn and enthralled and diminished like the vessel that drains but is not emptied, there must have been *something* prior to this but it was closed to her now, closed forever like the doors of nascence, slammed like the gates of death on the yearning faces of the living: there is no going forward nor back, there is nothing. This is what is: this floor, these animals, the faint metallic scent of her own fluid, her body pinned in rags and speckled with old blood; and the door; and the light.

Brahms sobbed in a corner, again she reached for the blankets but the great sounds of imminence flooded the room and she knew before the collision that Beethoven, the most jolting and demoniac of the three, had come to seek in her his own fulfillment; Beethoven of the sudden, shuddering strokes, the silences, the storms, the great uneven swings of the body: the one she feared most in those broken unleashings of spine and heat grabbing her, grabbing her, the alternating cycles of some unknowable need seizing the hammer and tongs of the bear's body as it rammed against her and this, now, was the present, the animal against her, great in its need but curiously empty and tentative for all that; at the core the same uncertainty and brokenheartedness of Brahms but the shell was hard, hard, and she felt Beethoven pass through, over, above her like a storm, his hoarse grunts of emission, and she thought, eyes closed, *no more, no more* as she sank beneath fur, paws, breath, spasm, eaves, and darkness of the house collapsing around her and all around the darkening trot of the beasts as at some time or perhaps this was earlier—smashed chronology, chronology smashed—they gathered to confer.

It was the feast she remembered, if memory gave her any gifts at all: some telescoping of circumstance found her seated high in the room, a table of fruits and desserts before her, all of the spices and jellied treats and cakes smeared lascivious with icing spread on a table the size of an altar, a table larger than any she had ever seen and she leaned toward that feast, thinking *I want this*, the food enormous in her hand, her hand spreading to encompass the feast entire: and in the moment before enjoyment, before even its possibility she heard them: there at the far side of the room, their small, luminescent eyes fixed upon her, the shaggy blackness of their fur not harbinger but frankest truth: and the seizure of breath, the cakes toppled, the fruit rolling and smashing as she rolled and smashed, pulped and tore, juices everywhere as in that new posture of dreadful and fixed attention they came, one by one, upon her, for the first of an endlessness of times.

Reaching for Brahms' tail as he rooted and muttered around her, lifting herself to some less strenuous accommodation, she felt that she in some way was sinking toward some kind of new, ursine splendor, had somehow—by pain, by terror, by the pink pity of her ravaged limbs—dissolved the barrier between herself and the beast atop her. Picking and poking at the secret heart of the great animal she found herself served as well as serving, become more than sheer receptacle: it was a kind of way out, perhaps: it was the method of escape that sinks one more fully into the pit, and as the bear commenced its familiar, groaning adumbration of expenditure she shouted something, hoarse and guttural, *caw* like the bark of an animal, something before language which was itself language and gripping that fur tried to come *up* with Brahms even in the bear's descent: and the long, pivoting drop which in its suspension and calamitous nature seemed in some way to mimic her confused ideas of escape, to *be* escape: go farther in: become: belong. Sunk into slivers, vaulted into light, she felt herself as one with Brahms ever as the seizure squirted to the expected silence and the bear shambled away as if she did not exist at all.

*The dream of the feast: their waiting eyes.*
*She waited, too.*
*All feasts are one.*

In the rapid metronomic shudderings of Bach, she now found—earlier or later, but *now*—that some deepened surge of her own entrails, her own wordless wants was smoothed, engaged to rhythmic response by the motions of the bear and so it was no surprise at all when, yielding in sudden spasm, Bach broke from that complex rhythm and, balancing perilously on one paw, began a fragmented, syncopated movement which she first accommodated and then seemed to pass through, as light passes through a window, as semen passes through the tubing flesh and in that passing she ascended, risen as Bach, like Brahms, fell to snuffling and somehow troubled silence beside her, before himself rising to shamble away in unaccustomed ursine muttering.

And now she, beyond language but not gesture, beckoned from the floor to Beethoven, beckoned in the light: *Come on,* she said to the beast, *come on then, you too* and against the clasp, the enclosure, the idea bursting in her mind: becoming one with them, grunting and heaving as Beethoven grunted and heaved, her own fur rising in small shreds and hackles as she rotated her knees, her long scarred open legs against the spiteful silence of the bear against her, the gigantic hammer of the bear against her, and this time she took it without a cry, without sound at all until Beethoven's own grunt of sudden and arrhythmic expenditure from which he fell as the others had fallen, shambled as they had shambled, sat now as they sat: staring at her, clumps of soot and sweat, muzzles uplifted as if to scent on the air the smell of her change and she watched them back, watched those brooding and immobile shapes as if she were in control of this situation, which in no real sense could ever be the case. She had abdicated all control in her greed for the feast: very well. Let greed be her master, then; let escape be entrance; let in be furthest in of all.

She had entered in curiosity and hunger, bedazzled by that unexpected house in the shattered woods, untroubled by the warnings of those with whom she had traveled before she had embarked, alone, on this more rigorous journey; and in what measure had they cared, to allow her the journey at all? And so the door, the house, the feast on the table one soaring poem of satiation: *this: here: take. eat:* and reaching beyond the sweetmeats, reaching toward some gorging fulmination which would have been, she knew, as close to ecstasy as she would ever come in the lonely and desperate life which was all that had been granted her, in that reach and grasp she had heard only the marveling thunder of her heart, that aching engine of greed in the presence of fulfillment: but she had not gone far enough, it seemed, had wanted but not fully, had reached but not taken, grasped, eaten, become: had only raised her eyes to see their eyes, little and bright, empty and full, to hear above the bewildered crooning of her own empty breath their breath murmurous, the sour and tangible entry into the world of the door, the floor, the light, the slivers, the odd varying rhythms of the beasts. You wanted to be filled? their postures asked her as they came upon her. Then *be* filled. To bursting.

But that was the secret, was it not? after all? The floor, yes, the slivers and the pains, yes, but yes, too, her own new knowledge, sieved from degradation, obtained from going all the way in: take the bears, receive them, *be* a bear, the Queen of the Bears, the queen of the magic forest and the empty house, daughter of the night born to gambol in stricken and ecstatic pleasure with those three refracted selves restored to her through pain: the autumn, the pedant, and the hammer, all three dense with need, her own need, her own greed as she raised herself on her elbows, there on the floor, there at the feast, and she bared her stained and filthy teeth to say *Come: come to me now*, and as if in their first true moment of attention came the hawking groans, the motions of the bears: turning, first toward one another, then to form a circle, a unit, one lumbering and dreadful mass as all three, as one, advanced upon her: to receive her benediction: to pour and fill and to become.

"When your mama was the geek, my dreamlets," Papa would say, "she made the nipping off of noggins such a crystal mystery that the hens themselves yearned toward her, waltzing around her, hypnotized with longing. 'Spread your lips, sweet Lil,' they'd cluck, 'and show us your choppers!' "

This same Crystal Lil, our star-haired mama, sitting snug on the built-in sofa that was Arty's bed at night, would chuckle at the sewing in her lap and shake her head. "Don't piffle to the children, Al. Those hens ran like whiteheads."

Nights on the road this would be, between shows and towns in some campground or pull-off, with the other vans and trucks and trailers of Binewski's Carnival Fabulon ranged up around us, safe in our portable village.

After supper, sitting with full bellies in the lamp glow, we Binewskis were supposed to read and study. But if it rained the story mood would sneak up on Papa. The hiss and tick on the metal of our big living van distracted him from his papers. Rain on a show night was catastrophe. Rain on the road meant talk, which, for Papa, was pure pleasure.

"It's a shame and a pity, Lil," he'd say, "that these offspring of yours should only know the slumming summer geeks from Yale."

"Princeton, dear," Mama would correct him mildly. "Randall will be a sophomore this fall. I believe he's our first Princeton boy."

We children would sense our story slipping away to trivia. Arty would nudge me and I'd pipe up with, "Tell about the time when Mama was the geek!" and Arty and Elly and Iphy and Chick would all slide into line with me on the floor between Papa's chair and Mama.

Mama would pretend to be fascinated by her sewing and Papa would tweak his swooping mustache and vibrate his tangled eyebrows, pretending reluctance. "Wellll . . ." he'd begin, "it was a long time ago . . ."

"Before we were born!"

"Before . . ." he'd proclaim, waving an arm in his grandest ringmaster style, "before I even dreamed you, my dreamlets!"

"I was still Lillian Hinchcliff in those days," mused Mama. "And when your father spoke to me, which was seldom and reluctantly, he called me 'Miss.' "

"Miss!" we would giggle. Papa would whisper to us loudly, as though Mama couldn't hear, "Terrified! I was so smitten I'd stutter when I tried to talk to her. 'M-M-M-Miss . . .' I'd say."

We'd giggle helplessly at the idea of Papa, the GREAT TALKER, so flummoxed.

"I, of course, addressed your father as *Mister* Binewski."

"There I was," said Papa, "hosing the old chicken blood and feathers out of the geek pit on the morning of July 3rd and congratulating myself for having good geek posters, telling myself I was going to sell tickets by the bale because the weekend of the Fourth is the hottest time for geeks and I had a fine, brawny geek that year. Enthusiastic about the work, he was. So I'm hosing away, feeling very comfortable and proud of myself, when up trips your mama, looking like angelfood, and tells me my geek has done a flit in the night, folded his rags as you might say, and hailed a taxi for the airport. He leaves a note claiming his pop is very sick and he, the geek, must retire from the pit and take his fangs home to Philadelphia to run the family bank."

"Brokerage, dear," corrects Mama.

"And with your mama, Miss Hinchcliff, standing there like three scoops of vanilla I can't even cuss! What am I gonna do? The geek posters are all over town!"

"It was during a war, darlings," explains Mama. "I forget which one precisely. Your father had difficulty getting help at that time or he never would have hired me, even to make costumes, as inexperienced as I was."

"So I'm standing there fuddled from breathing Miss Hinchcliff's Midnight Marzipan perfume and cross-eyed with figuring. I couldn't climb into the pit myself because I was doing twenty jobs already. I couldn't ask Horst the Cat Man because he was a vegetarian to begin with, and his dentures would disintegrate the first time he hit a chicken neck anyhow. Suddenly your mama pops up for all the world like she was offering me sherry and biscuits. 'I'll do it, Mr. Binewski,' she says, and I just about sent a present to my laundryman."

Mama smiled sweetly into her sewing and nodded. "I was anxious to prove myself useful to the show. I'd been with Binewski's Fabulon only two weeks at the time and I felt very keenly that I was on trial."

"So I says," interrupts Papa, " 'But, miss, what about your teeth?' Meaning she might break 'em or chip 'em, and she smiles wide, just like she's smiling now, and says, 'They're sharp enough, I think!' "

We looked at Mama and her teeth were white and straight, but of course by that time they were all false.

"I looked at her delicate little jaw and I just groaned. 'No,' I says, 'I couldn't ask you to . . .' but it did flash into my mind that a blonde and lovely geek with legs—I mean your mama has what we refer to in the trade as LEGS—would do the business no real harm. I'd never heard of a girl geek before and the poster possibilities were glorious. Then I thought again, No . . . she couldn't . . ."

"What your papa didn't know was that I'd watched the geek several times and of course I'd often helped Minna, our cook at home, when she slaughtered a fowl for the table. I had him. He had no choice but to give me a try."

"Oh, but I was scared spitless when her first show came up that afternoon! Scared she'd be disgusted and go home to Boston. Scared she'd flub the deal and have the crowd screaming for their money back. Scared she'd get hurt . . . A chicken could scratch her or peck an eye out quick as a blink."

"I was quite nervous myself," nodded Mama.

"The crowd was good. A hot Saturday that was, and the Fourth of July was the Sunday. I was running like a geeked bird the whole day myself, and just had time to duck behind the pit for one second before I stood up front to lead in the mugs. There she was like a butterfly . . ."

"I wore tatters really, white because it shows the blood so well even in the dark of the pit."

"But such artful tatters! Such low-necked, slit-to-the-thigh, silky tatters! So I took a deep breath and went out to talk 'em in. And in they went. A lot of soldiers in the crowd. I was still selling tickets when the cheers and whistles started inside and the whooping and stomping on those old wood bleachers drew even more people. I finally grabbed a popcorn kid to sell tickets and went inside to see for myself."

Papa grinned at Mama and twiddled his mustache.

"I'll never forget," he chuckled.

"I couldn't growl, you see, or snarl convincingly. So I sang," explained Mama.

"Happy little German songs! In a high, thin voice!"

"Franz Schubert, my dears."

"She fluttered around like a dainty bird, and when she caught those ugly squawking hens you couldn't believe she'd actually do anything. When she went right ahead and geeked 'em that whole larruping crowd went bonzo wild. There never was such a snap and twist of the wrist, such a vampire flick of the jaws over a neck or such a champagne approach to the blood. She'd shake her star-white hair and the bitten-off chicken head would skew off into the corner while she dug her rosy little fingernails in and lifted the flopping, jittering carcass like a golden goblet, and sipped! Absolutely sipped at the wriggling guts! She was magnificent, a princess, a Cleopatra, an elfin queen! That was your mama in the geek pit.

"People swarmed her act. We built more bleachers, moved her into the biggest top we had, eleven hundred capacity, and it was always jammed."

"It was fun." Lil nodded. "But I felt that it wasn't my true métier."

"Yeah." Papa would half frown, looking down at his hands, quieted suddenly.

Feeling the story mood evaporate, one of us children would coax, "What made you quit, Mama?"

She would sigh and look up from under her spun-glass eyebrows at Papa and then turn to where we were huddled on the floor in a heap and say softly, "I had always dreamed of flying. The Antifermos, the Italian trapeze clan, joined the show in Abilene and I begged them to teach me." Then she wasn't talking to us anymore but to Papa. "And, Al, you know you would never have got up the nerve to ask for my hand if I hadn't fallen and got so bunged up. Where would we be now if I hadn't?"

Papa nodded, "Yes, yes, and I made you walk again just fine, didn't I?" But his face went flat and smileless and his eyes went to the poster on the sliding door to their bedroom. It was old silvered paper, expensive, with the lone lush figure of Mama in spangles and smile, high-stepping with arms thrown up so her fingers, in red elbow-length gloves, touched the starry letters arching "CRYSTAL LIL" above her.

My father's name was Aloysius Binewski. He was raised in a traveling carnival owned by his father and called "Binewski's Fabulon." Papa was twenty-four years old when Grandpa died and the carnival fell into his hands. Al carefully bolted the silver urn containing his father's ashes to the hood of the generator truck that powered the midway. The old man had wandered with the show for so long that his dust would have been miserable left behind in some stationary vault.

Times were hard and, through no fault of young Al's, business began to decline. Five years after Grandpa died, the once flourishing carnival was fading.

The show was burdened with an aging lion that repeatedly broke expensive dentures by gnawing the bars of his cage; demands for cost-of-living increases from the fat lady, whose food supply was written into her contract; and the midnight defection of an entire family of animal eroticists, taking their donkey, goat, and Great Dane with them.

The fat lady eventually jumped ship to become a model for a magazine called *Chubby Chaser*. My father was left with a cut-rate, diesel-fueled fire-eater and the prospect of a very long stretch in a trailer park outside of Fort Lauderdale.

Al was a standard-issue Yankee, set on self-determination and independence, but in that crisis his core of genius revealed itself. He decided to breed his own freak show.

My mother, Lillian Hinchcliff, was a water cool aristocrat from the fastidious side of Boston's Beacon Hill, who had abandoned her heritage and joined the carnival to become an aerialist. Nineteen is late to learn to fly and Lillian fell, smashing her elegant nose and her collarbones. She lost her nerve but not her lust for sawdust and honky-tonk lights. It was this passion that made her an eager partner in Al's scheme. She was willing to chip in on any effort to renew public interest in the show. Then, too, the idea of inherited security was ingrained from her childhood. As she often said, "What greater gift could you offer your children than an inherent ability to earn a living just by being themselves?"

The resourceful pair began experimenting with illicit and prescription drugs, insecticides, and eventually radioisotopes. My mother developed a complex dependency on various drugs during this process, but she didn't mind. Relying on Papa's ingenuity to keep her supplied,

Lily seemed to view her addiction as a minor by-product of their creative collaboration.

Their firstborn was my brother Arturo, usually known as Aqua Boy. His hands and feet were in the form of flippers that sprouted directly from his torso without intervening arms or legs. He was taught to swim in infancy and was displayed nude in a big clear-sided tank like an aquarium. His favorite trick at the ages of three and four was to put his face close to the glass, bulging his eyes out at the audience, opening and closing his mouth like a river bass, and then to turn his back and paddle off, revealing the turd trailing from his muscular little buttocks. Al and Lil laughed about it later, but at the time it caused them great consternation as well as the nuisance of sterilizing the tank more often than usual. As the years passed, Arty donned trunks and became more sophisticated, but it's been said, with some truth, that his attitude never really changed.

My sisters, Electra and Iphigenia, were born when Arturo was two years old and starting to haul in crowds. The girls were Siamese twins with perfect upper bodies joined at the waist and sharing one set of hips and legs. They usually sat and walked and slept with their long arms around each other. They were, however, able to face directly forward by allowing the shoulder of one to overlap the other. They were always beautiful, slim, and huge-eyed. They studied the piano and began performing piano duets at an early age. Their compositions for four hands were thought by some to have revolutionized the twelve-tone scale.

I was born three years after my sisters. My father spared no expense in these experiments. My mother had been liberally dosed with cocaine, amphetamines, and arsenic during her ovulation and throughout her pregnancy with me. It was a disappointment when I emerged with such commonplace deformities. My albinism is the regular pink-eyed variety and my hump, though pronounced, is not remarkable in size or shape as humps go. My situation was far too humdrum to be marketable on the same scale as my brother's and sisters'. Still, my parents noted that I had a strong voice and decided I might be an appropriate shill and talker for the business. A bald albino hunchback seemed the right enticement toward the esoteric talents of the rest of the family. The dwarfism, which was very apparent by my third birthday, came as a pleasant surprise to the patient pair and increased my value. From the beginning I slept in the built-in cupboard beneath the sink in the family living van, and had a collection of exotic sunglasses to shield my sensitive eyes.

Despite the expensive radium treatments incorporated in his design, my younger brother, Fortunato, had a close call in being born to apparent normalcy. That drab state so depressed my enterprising parents that they immediately prepared to abandon him on the doorstep of a closed service station as we passed through Green River, Wyoming, late one night. My father had actually parked the van for a quick getaway and had stepped down to help my mother deposit the baby in the cardboard box on some safe part of the pavement. At that precise moment the two-week-old baby stared vaguely at my mother and in a matter of seconds revealed himself as not a failure at all, but in fact my parents' masterwork. It was lucky, so they named him Fortunato. For one reason and another we always called him Chick.

"Papa," said Iphy. "Yes," said Elly. They were behind his big chair, four arms sliding to tangle his neck, two faces framed in smooth black hair peering at him from either side.

"What are you up to, girlies?" He would laugh and put his magazine down.

"Tell us how you thought of us," they demanded.

I leaned on his knee and looked into his good heavy face. "Please, Papa," I begged, "tell us the Rose Garden."

He would puff and tease and refuse and we would coax. Finally Arty would be sitting in his lap with Papa's arms around him and Chick would be in Lily's lap, and I would lean against Lily's shoulder while Elly and Iphy sat cross-legged on the floor with their four arms behind them like Gothic struts supporting their hunched shoulders, and Al would laugh and tell the story.

"It was in Oregon, up in Portland, which they call the Rose City, though I never got in gear to do anything about it until a year or so later when we were stuck in Fort Lauderdale."

He had been restless one day, troubled by business boondoggles. He drove up into a park on a hillside and got out for a walk. "You could see for miles from up there. And there was a big rose garden with arbors and trellises and fountains. The paths were brick and wound in and out." He sat on a step leading from one terrace to another and stared listlessly at the experimental roses. "It was a test garden, and the colors were . . . designed. Striped and layered. One color inside the petal and another color outside.

"I was mad at Maribelle. She was a pinhead who'd been with your mother and me for a long while. She was trying to hold me up for a raise I couldn't afford."

The roses started him thinking, how the oddity of them was beautiful and how that oddity was contrived to give them value. "It just struck me—clear and complete all at once—no long figuring about it." He realized that children could be designed. "And I thought to myself, now *that* would be a rose garden worthy of a man's interest!"

We children would smile and hug him and he would grin around at us and send the twins for a pot of cocoa from the drink wagon and me for a bag of popcorn because the red-haired girls would just throw it out when they finished closing the concession anyway. And we would all be cozy in the warm booth of the van, eating popcorn and drinking cocoa and feeling like Papa's roses.

# NICHOLSON BAKER
## Subsoil

For his book-length monograph on the early harrow, Nyle T. Milner, the agricultural historian, decided that he had to pay one more visit to the Museum of the Tractor in Harvey, New York, an inconsequential town not far from Geneva. He had already been to the Museum of the Tractor three times; each time, he left feeling that he had learned everything he needed about the rare implements of harrowage and soil pulverization in its collection, sure that his further photos and sketches would suffice. But always there was some tiny question that lured him back.

The manager of the Harvey Motel took an interest in Nyle's research and wanted him to recall his stay with pleasure; whenever he came she used a headier brand of air freshener in his room. Rather than discuss with her his preference for unflavored air, which might make her regret her earlier acts of kindness, Nyle decided that for this visit he would try to stay someplace else and hope she didn't find out.

Bill Fipton, who owned and curated the Museum of the Tractor, was at first cagey about recommending a bed-and-breakfast close by. "There is one that some people go to," he said, thoughtfully eyeing a 1931 Gilroy & Selvo variable-impact sod-pounder. "I don't want to dump on anyone, but I say stick with the motel." Bill, who had been quite friendly to Nyle on earlier visits, seemed cooler toward him today—he had been evasive, for instance, about which local hobbyist had done the superior restoration work on one of the more fascinating transitional Unterbey harrows. Nyle got the sense that Bill, who had a

habit of doing something muscular with his tongue before he said anything, apparently to reseat his dental plate, was perhaps beginning to
resent how closely Nyle was scrutinizing the collection.

"Please," Nyle insisted. "I really need to branch out."

"The Taits," said Bill reluctantly. "They'll give you a room." He
gave Nyle the address. "It won't be cheap. And keep an eye open
there. I've heard some stories. But they're supposed to make an interesting soup."

Mrs. Tait led Nyle up the stairs and down a narrow hall hung with
three tiny black-and-white photographs of sliced mushrooms. A cotton
runner, striped in purple and black, ran down the middle of the hall.
She opened a door.

"This is a surprise," said Nyle, taking it all in. He gestured at a tall
tubular brown vase with a single black branch gnarling artily out of it.
"It's so . . . spare. I expected cutesy curtains and ruffled bed skirts."

"We are not exactly *of* Harvey," Mrs. Tait said. She was nearly
fifty, with an attractive, prematurely ravaged neck and an expensive
haircut. A bit of what seemed to be a tattoo, possibly the tail of something, peeped out past the unbuttoned neck of her silvery linen shirt.
"But we do love the town."

"Oh, me too," said Nyle. "The tractors drew me here, as usual—
where tractors are I must go! But I've grown very fond of Main Street.
That sad little Chamber of Commerce."

"And what about dinner?" said Mrs. Tait.

"Do you offer a dinner package?" Nyle asked.

"We could see what we have on hand."

"I've heard high tidings of soup," Nyle said.

"Ah!" said Mrs. Tait, coming alive. "Is that what you would
like?"

Nyle said he would, very much, being a soup person—if it wasn't
too much trouble. Mrs. Tait left him to settle in. He took off his shoes
and scattered his new farm-machinery sketches on the bed. His monograph was taking far too long to finish. Three years was excessive, even
for a subject as far-reaching as his. Nyle was disorganized, a trait sur-
prising in a man so short, and he was having exciting insights now
about the evolution of rotary-hoe blades and diggers which he later
realized were not new to him, ones that he had written down in a state
of euphoria and lost in his briefcase and forgotten. So much of what he
knew was only in his head, unfortunately, and his head couldn't always

be depended on. Driving to Harvey, he had briefly wondered whether, were he to die suddenly, right then, he would have lived his life—not merely as an agricultural historian but even as a human being—entirely in vain. He'd seen it happen recently with the late Raymond Purty, who had known a great deal about early silos—more than anyone else on earth. When Purty was suffocated that muggy April afternoon under three tons of raw soy, everyone in Nyle's circle had expected at least a partial manuscript to come to light. But, sadly, the history of silage had all been in Ray Purty's head.

"This is the last research trip I'll make," said Nyle sternly to himself. "From now on—synthesis, exclusion, and sequential paragraphs." A faint smell of furniture wax and, underneath it, of something earthy and wholesome cheered him. This bed-and-breakfast—in a Greek Revival house with seven thin columns in front—was much better for morale than the well-intentioned instant headache of the Harvey Motel's air freshener. Maybe the town disparaged the Taits just because the Taits had taste.

The room was furnished with extreme, almost oppressive, care. The bureau was an ornamentally incised, Eastlake-style artifact with a large pair of mother-of-pearl wings inlaid in one side. The bed bore puzzling ovoid knobs, about the size of ostrich eggs, on its headboard and footboard. Five tiny safe-deposit-box keys hung next to a tarnished mirror as decoration. Nyle peered closely at the surface of the wall, fascinated by the stippled effect the Taits had achieved. They appeared to have flung or slapped around lengths of thin rope dipped in cinnamon-colored paint. Risky, Nyle felt, but it worked.

Only one pillow was made into the bed, an arrangement that momentarily concerned him, since he always slept with a second between his legs for comfort, having sensitive knees. But in the closet three spares were neatly shelved. Good—no need to bring up matters of ménage with the somewhat intimidating Mrs. Tait. Above the pillows, on the highest closet shelf, Nyle noticed a ziggurat of old children's games. There was a game called Mr. Ree and period Monopoly and Parcheesi boxes. And there was also—the obvious treasure of the collection—an old Mr. Potato Head kit. "Ho!" he cried, gingerly sliding it from its place on the shelf and carrying it to the bed. He had played Mr. Potato Head a few times as a child—back in the days before child safety, when you used a real baking potato and you stabbed the facial features, fitted with sharp points, into it. The joy of the old game came in imposing the stock nose- and ear- and eyepieces on the unique

Gothic shape of a real potato. Man and nature in concert; "the encrustation of the mechanical upon the organic," or however it was that Bergson defined laughter. The modern Mr. Potato Head, which included an artificial base potato with holes, was, Nyle felt, a mistake—now you merely joined bought plastic to bought plastic in various fixed permutations. Why continue the affectation of a potato at all?

He pulled the lid slowly off the box, feeling the air slip in to fill the increasing volume. And then he had a nasty shock. Fully prepared for a quick, happy *poof* of nostalgia—needing it, in fact, since he was more than a little discouraged by the progress of his research—he was instead confronted by something unpleasant and even, for a moment at least, outright frightening. A real potato, or a former potato, a now dead potato, still rested within the box. The last person who had played with the set had carelessly left the face he had created inside, with its proptotic yellow eyes and enormous, red-lipped, toothy, Milton Berlesque smile still stabbed in place, and over time—how long Nyle didn't want to guess—the potato's flesh had shrunk to a wizened leer of agonized supplication or self-mockery while it had grown seven long unhealthy sprouts that had curved and wandered around their paper chamber, feeling softly for the earth hold they never found. They resembled sparse hair and gastrointestinal parasites and certain weedy, wormy, albino things that live underwater; Nyle looked on them with disgust. Hurriedly he replaced the top and stuffed the box away in the closet again.

He rested for a moment on the bed, blinking regularly. The expression on the Mr. Potato Head intruded itself several times into his imagination—mummified, it had seemed, but conscious, in a state of sentient misery. The really disturbing thing was that, despite its appliqué grin and hefty comic nose, it had, Nyle felt, looked at him with a fixed intent to do him harm. The apparent animosity, though he could discount it as a trick of decomposition, bothered Nyle; he had never been hated by a potato before.

From downstairs came the cheerful eruption of a blender.

Mrs. Tait held a low green bowl over the table, waiting for Nyle to remove his politely clasped hands from the placemat. "There!" she said, giving the bowl a half turn as she positioned it in front of him. She sat down across from her husband. Mr. Tait had a carefully sculpted silver beard and wore a soft formless jacket over a black sweater with three brown buttons. The two of them were the least likely bed-and-breakfast owners Nyle had run into a long time.

He turned his attention to his dinner. The soup had a grainy pallor, with parsley shrapnel distributed equitably throughout. "Mm, boy," he said, sniffing deeply. "Leek?"

Mrs. Tait gave him an eighteenth-century smile. "And potato."

Potato! Nyle flinched. On each of his hosts' plates were three dried apricots. "Aren't you having any?" he asked them. Mr. Tait discreetly slipped an apricot in his mouth, as if he were taking a pill, and began dismantling it with toothy care.

"We seldom eat the soup ourselves," Mrs. Tait explained. She put a light finger on her abdomen. "I would like to, but I can't. Potatoes upset me now."

"Juliette makes the soup for our guests only," said Mr. Tait. "It's labor-intensive. Please start."

"Oh, potatoes are not for everyone, that's for sure," said Nyle, his mind racing. "Especially sweet potatoes. I know five, no, more—six—people who hate sweet potatoes."

Mrs. Tait slipped a disk of apricot in her mouth and sucked on it like a cough drop. "Please start," she quietly hissed.

"Pumpkin pie's stock has plunged, don't ask me why," Nyle nattered. "I do enjoy a good boiled potato, though, especially mashed up nicely."

"Oh—you like them mashed?" said Mrs. Tait, with a distant look, as if recalling early felonies. "*Please*, won't you?"

Why was he hesitating? What reason could he possibly have for his sense of vague unease? Suppressing his doubts, the agricultural historian took a big noisy spoonful, feeling immediately juvenile, as he always did when he ate soup as a guest. "Very nice," he said.

Mrs. Tait was pleased. "We're known for it, at least within Harvey."

"I'll tell my colleagues," said Nyle.

By the time he had accepted his second bowl, Nyle's doubts and suspicions were altogether gone. And the Taits, who had been keyed up at first, seemed to relax completely as well. They drank wine and ate their dried fruits and asked Nyle informed questions about his field. When he determined that the term "rear-power takeoff," as applied to the tractor, was not entirely new to them, he grew animated and confessional. As he described his work, he began to think that it was—though obviously influenced (as whose could not be?) by the insights of

Chatternan Gough, Paul Uselding, and M. J. French—something well worth finishing. He found himself describing to the Taits his recent fears: he sketched the story of Purty and the terrible soy suffocation, from which the history of "spouted beds" and other fermentational mechanisms might never fully recover.

"I'm feeling unusually mortal at the moment," Nyle was finally drawn to say, wiping his mouth and sitting back. His hosts were arranged in casual poses. Slightly more of Mrs. Tait's tattoo was visible: it now looked like part of a vine, perhaps, rather than like a lizard's tail. "If I were Keats," Nyle went on, "and thankfully I'm not, cough cough, I would be making every attempt to use the word 'glean' in a sonnet."

"I hope your stay here will help," said Mrs. Tait carefully.

"Oh, yes. Although . . ." Hesitating briefly, Nyle decided that he would probably trust the Taits more if he just went ahead and told them. "An oddly upsetting thing happened in my room just before you called me down. I probably shouldn't have, but I took a quick peek inside the Mr. Potato Head box in the closet."

"You opened the box," said Mr. Tait, leaning forward.

"I'm a Curious George sort of person," Nyle explained. "It's the historian in me. Well—there was a highly unattractive dead potato in there. Ugh! Not good."

Mrs. Tait looked thoughtful. "Douglas Grieb was the one who saw that set last, if I remember right," she said. "He was here visiting the Museum of the Tractor, too, from the University of Somewhere—Illinois, was it, Carl?"

"Oh, Grieb," said Nyle, waving dismissively. "A controversial figure, not universally liked. Well, his potato head has not aged well. It scared the starch out of me, quite frankly."

Mrs. Tait rose and removed the plates. "Come with me," she said, and led Nyle into the green-trimmed kitchen. Two Yixing teapots in the shape of cabbages were arranged to the right of a vintage porcelain sink. Mrs. Tait bent and opened all the beautifully mitred doors to the cabinets under the counter. In the shadows were three rotating storage carrousels. Crowded on their round shelves were dozens of silent potatoes. Some were dark-brown; some were deep-red. Some had eyes that looked like bicuspids; some had sprouted and evidently had their sprouts clipped off. A few were extraordinarily large. A smell of earth and rhizomes and of things below consciousness pervaded the room.

Nyle made a whistle of amazement. Then he said, "One or two of those larger gentlemen do not look particularly . . . recent."

"The secret to a good earth-apple soup," explained Mr. Tait, squeezing his wife's arm, "is to age the ingredients."

Nyle sent his sensibility on a little stomach check and then quickly recalled it. All seemed well. "I had no idea," he said.

Mrs. Tait bent and gave one of the carrousels a turn. She leaned forward and lightly caressed a huge russet. "We eat only the fruit of a plant," she said, "and never its tuber, since its tuber is not something it intended to offer the world."

"But—" Nyle began, indicating the gleaming components of the blender which were upended in the black dish drainer. The blender blade sat drying like a blown rose. "You made the soup."

"It was our pleasure," said Mrs. Tait. "It was for you." She closed all but one of the doors to the potato cabinets and turned off the light. The only illumination in the room now came from a small bulb within the oven.

"At this time of evening, we generally watch 'Nick at Nite,'" said Mr. Tait, escorting Nyle into the front hall.

"Oh, thanks—I think I'll head on up," said Nyle. "I've got some more notes that I should expand."

"While the tractor museum is still fresh in your mind?" said Mrs. Tait.

"Exactly," said Nyle. He waved a cheerful good night to his hosts and ascended the stairs, humming. But as he walked down the narrow hallway, paying no notice to the riven mushrooms, he suddenly thought, Why did Mrs. Tait use that particular word; that "fresh"? And were those—could those be—*potato prints* of some kind on the walls of his room?

Nyle had difficulty getting to sleep that night. The Taits had kindly provided some light reading on a shelf by the bed; Nyle got through a short Wilkie Collins story and half of a longer Sheridan Le Fanu. He liked being mildly frightened by fiction when he was uneasy in fact. When he turned out the light, waiting for sleep to come, he was visited by the memory of the now sinister-seeming black rectangle of the half-open kitchen cabinet downstairs. Why hadn't Mrs. Tait closed the last cabinet door? This was like trying to fall asleep after you remembered that you'd left a radio on in the basement, he thought. And the sheer size of some of the potatoes she had shown him! They were phenomenal, unnatural. *Boulders* of carbohydrate. Finally, he was able to worm his way into a fairly satisfactory half sleep by imagining himself tearing up large damp pieces of corrugated cardboard.

He woke some hours later feeling sorry for a minor engineer named Shelby Hemper Fairchild, whose career had been cut short in the early thirties by the unfortunate inhalation of a cotton ball. (Fairchild—and not Edward Lyrielle, as some wrongly asserted—developed Bleidman & Co.'s famous Guttersnipe, an erratic but groundbreaking turf flail and trencher.) Without moving, Nyle worked his unpillowed eyeball so as to take in as much of his room as he could. Moonlight furbished the brown cylindrical floor vase and its gnarled branch, as well as an aquarium bibelot in the shape of a ruined arch on his bedside table. He felt strange suspicions and recalled the kitchen cabinet. Big hostile pocked things were waiting in there. That cabinet door was open. Wouldn't it be a good idea to nip quickly downstairs and close it himself? Clearly he wasn't going to sleep properly until this state of affairs was resolved.

Pulling the pillow from between his legs, he put on his paper slippers (hospital wear, salvaged from an appendectomy performed several years earlier) and made his way in the half-light toward the door—where he discovered something. A long, glimmering white sprout, with violet accents—a lengthy potato sprout, by all indications—had grown through the keyhole. It curved motionlessly to the floor. Perplexed, on the verge of being horrified, he glanced at his watch, more to steady himself than to check the time. The notion that this sprout had grown its way out of the kitchen cabinet, originating in one of those prodigies of mass storage downstairs, and that it had then worked its way slowly up to him, all while he slept, disturbed Nyle exceedingly. His watch claimed that it was almost three.

"Hello?" he called softly, in case someone or something was on the other side of the door. There was no answer.

Closer up, the feeler appeared harmless. He touched it quickly, testingly. It was cold and didn't move. He grasped it; he wound it around his trembling finger. He pulled.

The soft, unchlorophylled plant flesh gave way against the metal edge of the keyhole, making a tiny rending sound. Carefully Nyle fed the broken mystery frond back out under the doorway. "Out you go," he whispered. He waited for some time, listening. We have scotched the snake, not killed it, he thought to himself, drawing comfort from the scrap of pentameter—and then, reminded that he had some Scotch

Tape in his briefcase, he carefully sealed the keyhole. The sensation of the sticky tape on his fingers left him feeling almost brave. It was time to confront the hall.

He turned the knob and peered tentatively out. The long, pale petitioner with the torn end receded kinklessly from his doorway into the shadows along the black-and-purple runner. Nyle tiptoed along it to the head of the stairway and looked down, craning his neck to determine the shoot's route up the stairs. What he then saw, as his gaze penetrated the grainy obscurity of the front hall, made a terror gong go off in his mind.

A dozen or more sinuous emissaries from the kitchen, similar to the first, were just turning the corner from the dining room and beginning the climb toward him.

"Good gravy!" he gasped, hotfooting it back to his room. "They're out to get me!" He slid the bolt and tried to think. The proliferating sprouts, though he suspected that they were up to no good, were none too strong, judging by the one that he had held. They couldn't push their way past the taped-up keyhole. But he had to take reasonable measures to protect himself. If he stuffed something *under* the door, he theorized, these hellish hawsers would never find him.

He took off his pajama bottoms and wedged them into the space between the door and the floor. Immediately he felt much better. No, they were not strong sprouts. They were not robust. They were attenuated and colorless and slow and soft. That was what he didn't like about them, in fact. That and that they seemed, in their blind, tentative way, to want to find him.

Ten minutes went by. Twelve. Nyle craved to know how fast they were growing, if they were growing at all. Maybe they had withdrawn. Were they already at the top of the stairs? Did they grow only while he slept? In that case, he had but to stay awake all night. A watched pot never boils. Or were they already nudging gently against the pajama-bottom buffer—and, if so, would such insistent pushings finally dislodge it entirely? He wheeled around, looking for some backup. A *drawer*. One of the heavy lower drawers from the big ornamental bureau. He seized its two handles and pulled.

Again he heard a soft rending sound, louder this time. The drawer was not empty. Inside was a plastic sack of enormous aging Valley Star potatoes, the biggest Nyle had ever seen. Through the ventilation holes of the plastic had grown a horror whorl of intertwining white shoots and root hairs. Some of the shoots bore new radish-size dark tubers.

The upper surface of the conjoined growth was flat, like a Jackson Pol-
lock, having encountered the plane of the drawer above. Freed and
slightly injured, the bureau's brood now began to awaken. Nyle stared
for an instant at their sullen stirrings. Then he reverse-salaamed,
barking once with shock and revulsion. When he moved, his ankle
bone made contact with something more yielding than an electrical
cord. He glanced down. A gap in the baseboard molding had allowed
entrance to more questing feelers from downstairs. There seemed to be
some wispy activity at the window. Something was floating up through
a loose floorboard. Nyle stamped on the board, severing the fiendish
sucker. Grabbing his briefcase, he backed slowly across the room. "Mr.
and Mrs. Tait?" he quavered. But there was no answer.

Sensing his movements and his noise, the sallow stolons began a
languorous, low creep toward him. He could see them move
now. "No! You're disgusting!" he cried, flicking at them with his fingers. His back bumped against the closet door. I'm doomed, he
thought. And yet maybe they feared light. If he could get in the closet
and turn on the closet light, maybe they would rethink and withdraw.

He bumbled inside and shut the door. He yanked on the light
cord, which sprang away from his hand. A coruscation of bulb yellow
filled the space. He waited, squinting, wishing he were wearing his
pajama bottoms. A minute or two passed, and he began to think he was
safe. And then he heard sounds from the room: his overnight bag
seemed to be on the move; softnesses were sweeping the walls. He
spotted the tips of three or four lissome elongations peeping under the
door. With a terrified, saliva-rich curse, he grabbed a dark-green
rubber boot and began pounding their growth tips as they emerged.
But the light seemed to stimulate them, and many now vied for
entrance. Was there no escape? He looked up. Past the light bulb,
which was mounted on the wall, he saw a trapdoor. It must lead to an
attic space. He could climb up there, kick out an attic window, climb
out onto the porch roof, shimmy down one of the front columns,
and run.

He grabbed two clothes hooks and started to hoist himself up
toward the closet ceiling. His eyes drew even with the top shelf. From
inside the Mr. Potato Head box came a leisurely scrabbling. Its top
began to lift. The Parcheesi game slid to one side. The Monopoly game
tumbled. The fixed orange eyes of the dead and shrunken Mr. Potato
Head appeared from under the rising top, and then one or two—four,

*seven*—limply questing spud spawn veered into the air toward Nyle's face, root hairs aquiver.

"Help!" Nyle wailed, and he fell. The floor of the closet was asquirm. Whitish-purple growth enveloped him. He waved his arms and plucked at himself hectically, but the soil-starved delvers were persistent. When they touched his face, he began to feel sad that he would never finish his history of the harrow. A sprout grew smoothly into his right knee, seeking his synovial fluid. Several more penetrated his elbows. These hurt quite a lot, though not nearly as much as the one that found its way into his urethra. One wan ganglion discovered his ear canal, and another a tear duct, and Nyle began to hear only the dim, low pulsation of plant hormones and potato ideology. Let it go, he thought. Let it all go. They found the routes his blood took, and they followed these deeper; by dawn they had grown the fresh, lumpy tuber that burst his heart.

What once was Nyle woke in a very dark place. Many Krebs cycles had passed; many more would pass. He felt himself being slowly turned. His fellows were dozing by the dozen near him. A child's voice was saying, "That one! That big one!" He was lifted and cradled in the child's gentle hand. His vision wasn't working properly—he saw several different views of the world. The child with a cry of happiness, plunged the fake nose into Nyle's crisp body flesh. Nyle screamed, but it was a potato scream, below the hearing of all but tree stumps and extinct volcanoes. The child stabbed in the orange pop eyes, and then the big red smiley mouth, and the little black pipe. Each face piece had points. The child wasn't quite sure what it wanted; it rearranged the Potato Head features several times. Nyle leaked a little from his puncture wounds. The child grew bored and put Nyle back in the box, tossing the unused face parts in after. Then there was a long, dark time.

He felt himself shrinking, and the shrinking was agony. He forgot what he had known, he began to know only what potatoes know. He sensed the changes of geothermic pressure; he heard the earth's slow resentments. He exhausted himself doing the only thing he could do, which was trying to send out underground shoots to form more potatoes like himself—but the shoots were hindered by a dry, smooth plant product that Nyle dimly remembered as cardboard. Nyle's face collapsed and partially liquefied—an uncomfortable process he did not soon wish to repeat. As moon followed moon he felt long-suffering, and then he forgot how to feel long-suffering and began to feel a crude, incurious misanthropy. When his dark chamber moved, and when suddenly, tumbling, he was swarmed with light prickles that reached down to the few places in his starchy interior that still lived, he made out a looming human face and saw it recoil. There was an exclamation of fear which pleased him. "It's vile!" he heard the face say. *Ah,* soundlessly chuckled the thing that was once Nyle, *it's another historian of agricultural technology.* Emboldened by the fresher air, he readied his pale tentacles for the final gleaning, waiting for nightfall.